LVIS
BOOK AWARD

Presented to _Sadie Ward_

In Recognition of _Individual Progress_

Date _May 2011_ _grade 4_

THE COLOR PURPLE

THE TEMPLE OF MY FAMILIAR

BOOKS BY ALICE WALKER

The Color Purple

The Temple of My Familiar

ALICE WALKER

Houghton Mifflin Harcourt

BOSTON · NEW YORK

2011

Library of Congress Cataloging-in-Publication Data
Walker, Alice, date.
The color purple ; The temple of my familiar / Alice Walker.
p. cm.
ISBN 978-0-547-55563-8
1. African Americans—Fiction. 2. African American women—Fiction.
3. Adult child sexual abuse victims—Fiction. 4. Southern States—Fiction.
I. Walker, Alice, date. Temple of my familiar II. Title.
III. Title: Temple of my familiar.
PS3573.A425C6 2011
813'.54—dc22   2010052593

Book design by Melissa Lotfy
Illustrations in *The Temple of My Familiar* by Jennifer Hewitson.

Printed in the United States of America

DOC 10 9 8 7 6 5 4 3 2 1

The Color Purple

To the Spirit:

Without whose assistance
Neither this book
Nor I
Would have been
Written.

Show me how to do like you
Show me how to do it.

—STEVIE WONDER

Preface

WHATEVER else *The Color Purple* has been taken for during the years since its publication, it remains for me the theological work examining the journey from the religious back to the spiritual that I spent much of my adult life, prior to writing it, seeking to avoid. Having recognized myself as a worshiper of Nature by age eleven, because my spirit resolutely wandered out the window to find trees and wind during Sunday sermons, I saw no reason why, once free, I should bother with religious matters at all.

I would have thought that a book that begins "Dear God" would immediately have been identified as a book about the desire to encounter, to hear from, the Ultimate Ancestor. Perhaps it is a sign of our times that this was infrequently the case. Or perhaps it is the pagan transformation of God from patriarchal male supremacist into trees, stars, wind, and everything else, that camouflaged for many readers the book's intent: to explore the difficult path of someone who starts out in life already a spiritual captive, but who, through her own courage and the help of others, breaks free into the realization that she, like Nature itself, is a radiant expression of the heretofore perceived as quite distant Divine.

If it is true that it is what we run from that chases us, the *The Color Purple* (this color that is always a surprise but is everywhere in nature) is the book that ran me down while I sat with my back to it in a field. Without the Great Mystery's word coming from any Sunday sermon or through any human mouth, there I heard and saw it moving in beauty across the grassy hills.

No one is exempt from the possibility of a conscious connection to All That Is. Not the poor. Not the suffering. Not the writer sitting in an open field. This is the book in which I was able to express a new spiritual awareness, a rebirth into strong feelings of Oneness I realized I had experienced and taken for granted as a child; a chance for me as well as the main character, Celie, to encounter That Which Is Beyond Understanding But Not Beyond Loving and to say: I see and hear you clearly, Great Mystery, now that I expect to see and hear you everywhere I am, which is the right place.

You better not never tell nobody but God. It'd kill your mammy.

Dear God,

I am fourteen years old. ~~I am~~ I have always been a good girl. Maybe you can give me a sign letting me know what is happening to me.

Last spring after little Lucious come I heard them fussing. He was pulling on her arm. She say It too soon, Fonso, I ain't well. Finally he leave her alone. A week go by, he pulling on her arm again. She say Naw, I ain't gonna. Can't you see I'm already half dead, an all of these chilren.

She went to visit her sister doctor over Macon. Left me to see after the others. He never had a kine word to say to me. Just say You gonna do what your mammy wouldn't. First he put his thing up gainst my hip and sort of wiggle it around. Then he grab hold my titties. Then he push his thing inside my pussy. When that hurt, I cry. He start to choke me, saying You better shut up and git used to it.

But I don't never git used to it. And now I feels sick every time I be the one to cook. My mama she fuss at me an look at me. She happy, cause he good to her now. But too sick to last long.

9

Dear God,

My mama dead. She die screaming and cussing. She scream at me. She cuss at me. I'm big. I can't move fast enough. By time I git back from the well, the water be warm. By time I git the tray ready the food be cold. By time I git all the children ready for school it be dinner time. He don't say nothing. He set there by the bed holding her hand an cryin, talking bout don't leave me, don't go.

She ast me bout the first one Whose it is? I say God's. I don't know no other man or what else to say. When I start to hurt and then my stomach start moving and then that little baby come out my pussy chewing on it fist you could have knock me over with a feather.

Don't nobody come see us.

She got sicker an sicker.

Finally she ast Where it is?

I say God took it.

He took it. He took it while I was sleeping. Kilt it out there in the woods. Kill this one too, if he can.

Dear God,
   He act like he can't stand me no more. Say I'm evil an
always up to no good. He took my other little baby, a boy this
time. But I don't think he kilt it. I think he sold it to a man
an his wife over Monticello. I got breasts full of milk running
down myself. He say Why don't you look decent? Put on
something. But what I'm sposed to put on? I don't have
nothing.
   I keep hoping he fine somebody to marry. I see him
looking at my little sister. She scared. But I say I'll take care of
you. With God help.

Dear God,

He come home with a girl from round Gray. She be my age but they married. He be on her all the time. She walk round like she don't know what hit her. I think she thought she love him. But he got so many of us. All needing somethin.

My little sister Nettie is got a boyfriend in the same shape almost as Pa. His wife died. She was kilt by her boyfriend coming home from church. He got only three children though. He seen Nettie in church and now every Sunday evening here come Mr. ___. I tell Nettie to keep at her books. It be more then a notion taking care of children ain't even yourn. And look what happen to Ma.

Dear God,

   He beat me today cause he say I winked at a boy in church. I may have got somethin in my eye but I didn't wink. I don't even look at mens. That's the truth. I look at women, tho, cause I'm not scared of them. Maybe cause my mama cuss me you think I kept mad at her. But I ain't. I felt sorry for mama. Trying to believe his story kilt her.

   Sometime he still be looking at Nettie, but I always git in his light. Now I tell her to marry Mr. ____. I don't tell her why.

   I say Marry him, Nettie, an try to have one good year out your life. After that, I know she be big.

   But me, never again. A girl at church say you git big if you bleed every month. I don't bleed no more.

Dear God,

Mr. _____ finally come right out an ast for Nettie hand in marriage. But He won't let her go. He say she too young, no experience. Say Mr. _____ got too many children already. Plus What about the scandal his wife cause when somebody kill her? And what about all this stuff he hear bout Shug Avery? What bout that?

I ast our new mammy bout Shug Avery. What it is? I ast. She don't know but she say she gon fine out.

She do more then that. She git a picture. The first one of a real person I ever seen. She say Mr. _____ was taking somethin out his billfold to show Pa an it fell out an slid under the table. Shug Avery was a woman. The most beautiful woman I ever saw. She more pretty then my mama. She bout ten thousand times more prettier then me. I see her there in furs. Her face rouge. Her hair like somethin tail. She grinning with her foot up on somebody motocar. Her eyes serious tho. Sad some.

I ast her to give me the picture. An all night long I stare at it. An now when I dream, I dream of Shug Avery. She be dress to kill, whirling and laughing.

Dear God,

I ast him to take me instead of Nettie while our new mammy sick. But he just ast me what I'm talking bout. I tell him I can fix myself up for him. I duck into my room and come out wearing horsehair, feathers, and a pair of our new mammy high heel shoes. He beat me for dressing trampy but he do it to me anyway.

Mr. ____ come that evening. I'm in the bed crying. Nettie she finally see the light of day, clear. Our new mammy she see it too. She in her room crying. Nettie tend to first one, then the other. She so scared she go out doors and vomit. But not out front where the two mens is.

Mr. ____ say, Well Sir, I sure hope you done change your mind.

He say, Naw, Can't say I is.

Mr. ____ say, Well, you know, my poor little ones sure could use a mother.

Well, He say, real slow, I can't let you have Nettie. She too young. Don't know nothing but what you tell her. Sides, I want her to git some more schooling. Make a schoolteacher out of her. But I can let you have Celie. She the oldest anyway.

She ought to marry first. She ain't fresh tho, but I spect you know that. She spoiled. Twice. But you don't need a fresh woman no how. I got a fresh one in there myself and she sick all the time. He spit, over the railing. The children git on her nerve, she not much of a cook. And she big already.

Mr. ____ he don't say nothing. I stop crying I'm so surprise.

She ugly. He say. But she ain't no stranger to hard work. And she clean. And God done fixed her. You can do everything just like you want to and she ain't gonna make you feed it or clothe it.

Mr. ____ still don't say nothing. I take out the picture of Shug Avery. I look into her eyes. Her eyes say Yeah, it bees that way sometime.

Fact is, he say, I got to git rid of her. She too old to be living here at home. And she a bad influence on my other girls. She'd come with her own linen. She can take that cow she raise down there back of the crib. But Nettie you flat out can't have. Not now. Not never.

Mr. ____ finally speak. Clearing his throat. I ain't never really look at that one, he say.

Well, next time you come you can look at her. She ugly. Don't even look like she kin to Nettie. But she'll make the better wife. She ain't smart either, and I'll just be fair, you have to watch her or she'll give away everything you own. But she can work like a man.

Mr. ____ say How old she is?

He say, She near twenty. And another thing—She tell lies.

Dear God,

It took him the whole spring, from March to June, to make up his mind to take me. All I thought about was Nettie. How she could come to me if I marry him and he be so love struck with her I could figure out a way for us to run away. Us both be hitting Nettie's schoolbooks pretty hard, cause us know we got to be smart to git away. I know I'm not as pretty or as smart as Nettie, but she say I ain't dumb.

The way you know who discover America, Nettie say, is think bout cucumbers. That what Columbus sound like. I learned all about Columbus in first grade, but look like he the first thing I forgot. She say Columbus come here in boats call the Neater, the Peter, and the Santomareater. Indians so nice to him he force a bunch of 'em back home with him to wait on the queen.

But it hard to think with gitting married to Mr. _____ hanging over my head.

The first time I got big Pa took me out of school. He never care that I love it. Nettie stood there at the gate holding tight to my hand. I was all dress for first day. You too dumb to keep going to school, Pa say. Nettie the clever one in this bunch.

But Pa, Nettie say, crying, Celie smart too. Even Miss Beasley say so. Nettie dote on Miss Beasley. Think nobody like her in the world.

Pa say, Whoever listen to anything Addie Beasley have to say. She run off at the mouth so much no man would have her. That how come she have to teach school. He never look up from cleaning his gun. Pretty soon a bunch of white mens come walking cross the yard. They have guns too.

Pa git up and follow 'em. The rest of the week I vomit and dress wild game.

But Nettie never give up. Next thing I know Miss Beasley at our house trying to talk to Pa. She say long as she been a teacher she never know nobody want to learn bad as Nettie and me. But when Pa call me out and she see how tight my dress is, she stop talking and go.

Nettie still don't understand. I don't neither. All us notice is I'm all the time sick and fat.

I feel bad sometime Nettie done pass me in learnin. But look like nothing she say can git in my brain and stay. She try to tell me something bout the ground not being flat. I just say, Yeah, like I know it. I never tell her how flat it look to me.

Mr. ____ come finally one day looking all drug out. The woman he had helping him done quit. His mammy done said No More.

He say, Let me see her again.

Pa call me. *Celie*, he say. Like it wasn't nothing. Mr. ____ want another look at you.

I go stand in the door. The sun shine in my eyes. He's still up on his horse. He look me up and down.

Pa rattle his newspaper. Move up, he won't bite, he say.

I go closer to the steps, but not too close cause I'm a little scared of his horse.

Turn round, Pa say.

I turn round. One of my little brothers come up. I think it was Lucious. He fat and playful, all the time munching on something.

He say, What you doing that for?

Pa say, Your sister thinking bout marriage.

Didn't mean nothing to him. He pull my dresstail and ast can he have some blackberry jam out the safe.

I say, Yeah.

She good with children, Pa say, rattling his paper open more. Never heard her say a hard word to nary one of them. Just give 'em everything they ast for, is the only problem.

Mr. _____ say, That cow still coming?

He say, Her cow.

Dear God,

I spend my wedding day running from the oldest boy. He twelve. His mama died in his arms and he don't want to hear nothing bout no new one. He pick up a rock and laid my head open. The blood run all down tween my breasts. His daddy say Don't *do* that! But that's all he say. He got four children, instead of three, two boys and two girls. The girls hair ain't been comb since their mammy died. I tell him I'll just have to shave it off. Start fresh. He say bad luck to cut a woman hair. So after I bandage my head best I can and cook dinner—they have a spring, not a well, and a wood stove look like a truck—I start trying to untangle hair. They only six and eight and they cry. They scream. They cuse me of murder. By ten o'clock I'm done. They cry theirselves to sleep. But I don't cry. I lay there thinking bout Nettie while he on top of me, wonder if she safe. And then I think bout Shug Avery. I know what he doing to me he done to Shug Avery and maybe she like it. I put my arm around him.

Dear God,
 I was in town sitting on the wagon while Mr. ____ was in
the dry good store. I seen my baby girl. I knowed it was her.
She look just like me and my daddy. Like more us then us
is ourself. She be tagging long hind a lady and they be dress
just alike. They pass the wagon and I speak. The lady speak
pleasant. My little girl she look up and sort of frown. She
fretting over something. She got my eyes just like they is
today. Like everything I seen, she seen, and she pondering it.
 I think she mine. My heart say she mine. But I don't know
she mine. If she mine, her name Olivia. I embroder Olivia
in the seat of all her daidies. I embrody lot of little stars and
flowers too. He took the daidies when he took her. She was
bout two month old. Now she bout six.
 I clam down from the wagon and I follow Olivia and her
new mammy into a store. I watch her run her hand long side
the counter, like she ain't interested in nothing. Her ma is
buying cloth. She say Don't touch nothing. Olivia yawn.
 That real pretty, I say, and help her mama drape a piece of
cloth close to her face.
 She smile. Gonna make me an my girl some new dresses,
she say. Her daddy be so proud.

Who her daddy, I blurt out. It like *at last* somebody know.

She say Mr. ____. But that ain't my daddy name.

Mr. ____? I say. Who he?

She look like I ast something none of my bidniss.

The *Reverend* Mr. ____, she say, then turn her face to the clerk. He say, Girl you want that cloth or not? We got other customers sides you.

She say, Yes sir. I want five yards, please sir.

He snatch the cloth and thump down the bolt. He don't measure. When he think he got five yard he tare it off. That be a dollar and thirty cent, he say. You need thread?

She say, Naw suh.

He say, You can't sew thout thread. He pick up a spool and hold it gainst the cloth. That look like it bout the right color. Don't you think.

She say, Yessuh.

He start to whistle. Take two dollars. Give her a quarter back. He look at me. You want something gal? I say, Naw Suh.

I trail long behind them on the street.

I don't have nothing to offer and I feels poor.

She look up and down the street. He ain't here. He ain't here. She say like she gon cry.

Who ain't? I ast.

The Reverend Mr. ____, she say. He took the wagon.

My husband wagon right here, I say.

She clam up. I thank you kindly, she say. Us sit looking at all the folks that's come to town. I never seen so many even at church. Some be dress too. Some don't hit on much. Dust git all up the ladies dress.

She ast me Who is my husband, now I know all bout hers. She laugh a little. I say Mr. ____. She say, Sure nuff? Like she know all about him. Just didn't know he was married. He a fine looking man, she say. Not a finer looking one in the county. White or black, she say.

He do look all right, I say. But I don't think about it while I say it. Most times mens look pretty much alike to me.

How long you had your little girl? I ast.

Oh, she be seven her next birthday.

When that? I ast.

She think back. Then she say, December.

I think, November.

I say, real easy, What you call her?

She say, oh, we calls her Pauline.

My heart knock.

Then she frown. But I calls her Olivia.

Why you call her Olivia if it ain't her name? I ast.

Well, just look at her, she say sort of impish, turning to look at the child, don't she look like a Olivia to you? Look at her eyes, for god's sake. Somebody ole would have eyes like that. So I call her *ole* Livia. She chuckle. Naw. Olivia, she say, patting the child hair. Well, here come the Reverend Mr. _____, she say. I see a wagon and a great big man in black holding a whip. We sure do thank you for your hospitality. She laugh again, look at the horses flicking flies off they rump. *Horse*pitality, she say. And I git it and laugh. It feel like to split my face.

Mr. _____, come out the store. Clam up in the wagon. Set down. Say real slow. What you setting here laughing like a fool fer?

Dear God,

Nettie here with us. She run way from home. She say she hate to leave our stepma, but she had to git out, maybe fine help for the other little ones. The boys be alright, she say. They can stay out his way. When they git big they gon fight him.

Maybe kill, I say.

How is it with you and Mr. _____? she ast. But she got eyes. He still like her. In the evening he come out on the porch in his Sunday best. She be sitting there with me shelling peas or helping the children with they spelling. Helping me with spelling and everything else she think I need to know. No matter what happen, Nettie steady try to teach me what go on in the world. And she a good teacher too. It nearly kill me to think she might marry somebody like Mr. _____ or wind up in some white lady kitchen. All day she read, she study, she practice her handwriting, and try to git us to think. Most days I feel too tired to think. But Patient her middle name.

Mr. _____ children all bright but they mean. They say Celie, I want dis. Celie, I want dat. Our Mama let us have it. He don't say nothing. They try to get his tention, he hide hind a puff of smoke.

Don't let them run over you, Nettie say. You got to let them know who got the upper hand.

They got it, I say.

But she keep on, You got to fight. You got to fight.

But I don't know how to fight. All I know how to do is stay alive.

That's a real pretty dress you got on, he say to Nettie.

She say, Thank you.

Them shoes look just right.

She say, Thank you.

Your skin. Your hair. Your teefs. Everyday it something else to make miration over.

First she smile a little. Then she frown. Then she don't look no special way at all. She just stick close to me. She tell me, Your skin. Your hair. Your teefs. He try to give her a compliment, she pass it on to me. After while I git to feeling pretty cute.

Soon he stop. He say one night in bed, Well, us done help Nettie all we can. Now she got to go.

Where she gon go? I ast.

I don't care, he say.

I tell Nettie the next morning. Stead of being mad, she glad to go. Say she hate to leave me is all. Us fall on each other neck when she say that.

I sure hate to leave you here with these rotten children, she say. Not to mention with Mr. ____. It's like seeing you buried, she say.

It's worse than that, I think. If I was buried, I wouldn't have to work. But I just say, Never mine, never mine, long as I can spell G-o-d I got somebody along.

But I only got one thing to give her, the name of Reverend
Mr. _____. I tell her to ast for his wife. That maybe she would
help. She the only woman I even seen with money.

I say, Write.

She say, What?

I say, Write.

She say, Nothing but death can keep me from it.

She never write.

G-o-d,

Two of his sister come to visit. They dress all up. Celie, they say. One thing is for sure. You keep a clean house. It not nice to speak ill of the dead, one say, but the truth never can be ill. Annie Julia was a nasty 'oman bout the house.

She never want to be here in the first place, say the other.

Where she want to be? I ast.

At home. She say.

Well that's no excuse, say the first one, Her name Carrie, other one name Kate. When a woman marry she spose to keep a decent house and a clean family. Why, wasn't nothing to come here in the winter time and all these children have colds, they have flue, they have direar, they have newmonya, they have worms, they have the chill and fever. They hungry. They hair ain't comb. They too nasty to touch.

I touch 'em. Say Kate.

And cook. She wouldn't cook. She act like she never seen a kitchen.

She hadn't never seen his.

Was a scandal, say Carrie.

He sure was, say Kate.

What you mean? say Carrie.

I mean he just brought her here, dropped her, and kept right on running after Shug Avery. That what I mean. Nobody to talk to, nobody to visit. He be gone for days. Then she start having babies. And she young and pretty.

Not so pretty, say Carrie, looking in the looking glass. Just that head of hair. She too black.

Well, brother must like black. Shug Avery black as my shoe.

Shug Avery, Shug Avery, Carrie say. I'm sick of her. Somebody say she going round trying to sing. Umph, what she got to sing about. Say she wearing dresses all up her leg and headpieces with little balls and tassles hanging down, look like window dressing.

My ears perk up when they mention Shug Avery. I feel like I want to talk about her my own self. They hush.

I'm sick of her too, say Kate, letting out her breath. And you right about Celie, here. Good housekeeper, good with children, good cook. Brother couldn't have done better if he tried.

I think about how he tried.

This time Kate come by herself. She maybe twenty-five. Old maid. She look younger than me. Healthy. Eyes bright. Tongue sharp.

Buy Celie some clothes. She say to Mr. ＿＿.

She need clothes? he ast.

Well look at her.

He look at me. It like he looking at the earth. It need somethin? his eyes say.

She go with me in the store. I think what color Shug Avery would wear. She like a queen to me so I say to Kate, Somethin purple, maybe little red in it too. But us look an look and no purple. Plenty red but she say, Naw, he won't want to pay for red. Too happy lookin. We got choice of brown, maroon or navy blue. I say blue.

I can't remember being the first one in my own dress. Now to have one made just for me. I try to tell Kate what it mean. I git hot in the face and stutter.

She say. It's all right, Celie. You deserve more than this.

Maybe so. I think.

Harpo, she say. Harpo the oldest boy. Harpo, don't let Celie be the one bring in all the water. You a big boy now. Time for you to help out some.

Women work, he say.

What? she say.

Women work. I'm a man.

You're a trifling nigger, she say. You git that bucket and bring it back full.

He cut his eye at me. Stumble out. I hear him mutter somethin to Mr. ____ sitting on the porch. Mr. ____ call his sister. She stay out on the porch talking a little while, then she come back in, shaking.

Got to go, Celie, she say.

She so mad tears be flying every which way while she pack.

You got to fight them, Celie, she say. I can't do it for you. You got to fight them for yourself.

I don't say nothing. I think bout Nettie, dead. She fight, she run away. What good it do? I don't fight, I stay where I'm told. But I'm alive.

Dear God,

Harpo ast his daddy why he beat me. Mr. _____ say, Cause she my wife. Plus, she stubborn. All women good for—he don't finish. He just tuck his chin over the paper like he do. Remind me of Pa.

Harpo ast me, How come you stubborn? He don't ast How come you his wife? Nobody ast that.

I say, Just born that way, I reckon.

He beat me like he beat the children. Cept he don't never hardly beat them. He say, Celie, git the belt. The children be outside the room peeking through the cracks. It all I can do not to cry. I make myself wood. I say to myself, Celie, you a tree. That's how come I know trees fear man.

Harpo say, I love Somebody.

I say, Huh?

He say, A Girl.

I say, You do?

He say, Yeah. Us plan to marry.

Marry, I say. You not old enough to marry.

I is, he say. I'm seventeen. She fifteen. Old enough.

What her mama say, I ast.

Ain't talk to her mama.

What her daddy say?

Ain't talk to him neither.

Well, what *she* say?

Us ain't never spoke. He duck his head. He ain't so bad looking. Tall and skinny, black like his mama, with great big bug eyes.

Where yall see each other? I ast. I see her in church, he say. She see me outdoors.

She like you?

I don't know. I wink at her. She act like she scared to look.

Where her daddy at while all this going on?

Amen corner, he say.

Dear God,

Shug Avery is coming to town! She coming with her orkestra. She going to sing in the Lucky Star out on Coalman road. Mr. ____ going to hear her. He dress all up in front the glass, look at himself, then undress and dress all over again. He slick back his hair with pomade, then wash it out again. He been spitting on his shoes and hitting it with a quick rag.

He tell me, Wash this. Iron that. Look for this. Look for that. Find this. Find that. He groan over holes in his sock.

I move round darning and ironing, finding hanskers. Anything happening? I ast.

What you mean? he say, like he mad. Just trying to git some of the hick farmer off myself. Any other woman be glad.

I'm is glad, I say.

What you mean? he ast.

You looks nice, I say. Any woman be proud.

You think so? he say.

First time he ast me. I'm so surprise, by time I say Yeah, he out on the porch, trying to shave where the light better.

I walk round all day with the announcement burning a hole in my pocket. It pink. The trees tween the turn off to our road

and the store is lit up with them. He got bout five dozen in his
trunk.

Shug Avery standing upside a piano, elbow crook, hand
on her hip. She wearing a hat like Indian Chiefs. Her mouth
open showing all her teef and don't nothing seem to be
troubling her mind. Come one, come all, it say. The Queen
Honeybee is back in town.

Lord, I wants to go so bad. Not to dance. Not to drink.
Not to play card. Not even to hear Shug Avery sing. I just be
thankful to lay eyes on her.

Dear God,

Mr. ____ be gone all night Saturday, all night Sunday and most all day Monday. Shug Avery in town for the weekend. He stagger in, throw himself on the bed. He tired. He sad. He weak. He cry. Then he sleep the rest of the day and all night.

He wake up while I'm in the field. I been chopping cotton three hours by time he come. Us don't say nothing to each other.

But I got a million question to ast. What she wear? Is she still the same old Shug, like in my picture? How her hair is? What kind lipstick? Wig? She stout? She skinny? She sound well? Tired? Sick? Where you all children at while she singing all over the place? Do she miss 'em? Questions be running back and forth through my mind. Feel like snakes. I pray for strength, bite the insides of my jaws.

Mr. ____ pick up a hoe and start to chop. He chop bout three chops then he don't chop again. He drop the hoe in the furrow, turn right back on his heel, walk back to the house, go git him a cool drink of water, git his pipe, sit on the porch and stare. I follow cause I think he sick. Then he say, You better git on back to the field. Don't wait for me.

Dear God,

Harpo no better at fighting his daddy back than me. Every day his daddy git up, sit on the porch, look out at nothing. Sometime look at the trees out front the house. Look at a butterfly if it light on the rail. Drink a little water in the day. A little wine in the evening. But mostly never move.

Harpo complain bout all the plowing he have to do.

His daddy say, You gonna do it.

Harpo nearly big as his daddy. He strong in body but weak in will. He scared.

Me and him out in the field all day. Us sweat, chopping and plowing. I'm roasted coffee bean color now. He black as the inside of a chimney. His eyes be sad and thoughtful. His face begin to look like a woman face.

Why you don't work no more? he ast his daddy.

No reason for me to. His daddy say. You here, aint you? He say this nasty. Harpos feeling be hurt.

Plus, he still in love.

Dear God,

Harpo girl daddy say Harpo not good enough for her. Harpo been courting the girl a while. He say he sit in the parlor with her, the daddy sit right there in the corner till everybody feel terrible. Then he go sit on the porch in front the open door where he can hear everything. Nine o'clock come, he bring Harpo his hat.

Why I'm not good enough? Harpo ast Mr. ____. Mr. ____ say, Your mammy.

Harpo say, What wrong with my mammy?

Mr. ____ say, Somebody kill her.

Harpo be trouble with nightmares. He see his mama running cross the pasture trying to git home. Mr. ____, the man they say her boyfriend, catch up with her. She got Harpo by the hand. They both running and running. He grab hold of her shoulder, say, You can't quit me now. You mine. She say, No I ain't. My place is with my children. He say, Whore, you ain't got no place. He shoot her in the stomach. She fall down. The man run. Harpo grab her in his arms, put her head in his lap.

He start to call, Mama, Mama. It wake me up. The other

children, too. They cry like they mama just die. Harpo come
to, shaking.

I light the lamp and stand over him, patting his back.

It not her fault somebody kill her, he say. It not! It not!

Naw, I say. It not.

Everybody say how good I is to Mr. _____ children. I be good
to them. But I don't feel nothing for them. Patting Harpo
back not even like patting a dog. It more like patting another
piece of wood. Not a living tree, but a table, a chifferobe.
Anyhow, they don't love me neither, no matter how good I is.

They don't mind. Cept for Harpo they won't work. The
girls face always to the road. Bub be out all times of night
drinking with boys twice his age. They daddy puff on his pipe.

Harpo tell me all his love business now. His mind on Sofia
Butler day and night.

She pretty, he tell me. Bright.

Smart?

Naw. Bright skin. She smart too though, I think. Sometime
us can git her away from her daddy.

I know right then the next thing I hear, she be big.

If she so smart how come she big? I ast.

Harpo shrug. She can't git out the house no other way, he
say. Mr. _____ won't let us marry. Say I'm not good enough to
come in his parlor. But if she big I got a right to be with her,
good enough or no.

Where yall gon stay?

They got a big place, he say. When us marry I'll be just like
one of the family.

Humph, I say. Mr. _____ didn't like you before she big, he
ain't gonna like you cause she big.

Harpo look trouble.

Talk to Mr. ____, I say. He your daddy. Maybe he got some good advice.

Maybe not. I think.

Harpo bring her over to meet his daddy. Mr. ____ say he want to have a look at her. I see 'em coming way off up the road. They be just marching, hand in hand, like going to war. She in front a little. They come up on the porch, I speak and move some chairs closer to the railing. She sit down and start to fan herself with a hansker. It sure is hot, she say. Mr. ____ don't say nothing. He just look her up and down. She bout seven or eight months pregnant, bout to bust out her dress. Harpo so black he think she bright, but she ain't that bright. Clear medium brown skin, gleam on it like on good furniture. Hair notty but a lot of it, tied up on her head in a mass of plaits. She not quite as tall as Harpo but much bigger, and strong and ruddy looking, like her mama brought her up on pork.

She say, How you, Mr. ____?

He don't answer the question. He say, Look like you done got yourself in trouble.

Naw suh, she say. I ain't in no trouble. Big, though.

She smooth the wrinkles over her stomach with the flats of her hands.

Who the father? he ast.

She look surprise. Harpo, she say.

How he know that?

He know. She say.

Young womens no good these days, he say. Got they legs open to every Tom, Dick and Harry.

Harpo look at his daddy like he never seen him before. But he don't say nothing.

Mr. ____ say, No need to think I'm gon let my boy marry you just cause you in the family way. He young and limited. Pretty gal like you could put anything over on him.

Harpo still don't say nothing.

Sofia face git more ruddy. The skin move back on her forehead. Her ears raise.

But she laugh. She glance at Harpo sitting there with his head down and his hands tween his knees.

She say, What I need to marry Harpo for? He still living here with you. What food and clothes he git, you buy.

He say, Your daddy done throwed you out. Ready to live in the street I guess.

She say, Naw. I ain't living in the street. I'm living with my sister and her husband. They say I can live with them for the rest of my life. She stand up, big, strong, healthy girl, and she say, Well, nice visiting. I'm going home.

Harpo get up to come too. She say, Naw, Harpo, you stay here. When you free, me and the baby be waiting.

He sort of hang there between them a while, then he sit down again. I look at her face real quick then, and seem like a shadow go cross it. Then she say to me, Mrs. _____, I'd thank you for a glass of water before I go, if you don't mind.

The bucket on the shelf right there on the porch. I git a clean glass out the safe and dip her up some water. She drink it down, almost in one swallow. Then she run her hands over her belly again and she take off. Look like the army change direction, and she heading off to catch up.

Harpo never git up from his chair. Him and his daddy sit there and sit there and sit there. They never talk. They never move. Finally I have supper and go to bed. I git up in the morning it feel like they still sitting there. But Harpo be in the outhouse, Mr. _____ be shaving.

Dear God,

Harpo went and brought Sofia and the baby home. They got married in Sofia sister house. Sister's husband stand up with Harpo. Other sister sneak way from home to stand up with Sofia. Another sister come to hold the baby. Say he cry right through the service, his mama stop everything to nurse him. Finish saying I do with a big ole nursing boy in her arms.

Harpo fix up the little creek house for him and his family. Mr. _____ daddy used it for a shed. But it sound. Got windows now, a porch, back door. Plus it cool and green down by the creek.

He ast me to make some curtains and I make some out of flower sack. It not big, but it homey. Got a bed, a dresser, a looking glass, and some chairs. Cookstove for cooking and heating, too. Harpo daddy give him wages for working now. He say Harpo wasn't working hard like he should. Maybe little money goose his interest.

Harpo told me, Miss Celie, I'm going on strike.

On what?

I ain't going to work.

And he don't. He come to the field, pull two ears of corn,

let the birds and weevil eat two hundred. Us don't make
nothing much this year.

But now Sofia coming, he always busy. He chop, he
hammer, he plow. He sing and whistle.

Sofia look half her size. But she still a big strong girl.
Arms got muscle. Legs, too. She swing that baby about like
it nothing. She got a little pot on her now and give you the
feeling she all there. Solid. Like if she sit down on something,
it be mash.

She tell Harpo, Hold the baby, while she come back in the
house with me to git some thread. She making some sheets.
He take the baby, give it a kiss, chuck it under the chin. Grin,
look up on the porch at his daddy.

Mr. _____ blow smoke, look down at him, and say, Yeah, I
see now she going to switch the traces on you.

Dear God,

Harpo want to know what to do to make Sofia mind. He sit out on the porch with Mr. ____. He say, I tell her one thing, she do another. Never do what I say. Always backtalk.

To tell the truth, he sound a little proud of this to me.

Mr. ____ don't say nothing. Blow smoke.

I tell her she can't be all the time going to visit her sister. Us married now, I tell her. Your place is here with the children. She say, I'll take the children with me. I say, Your place is with me. She say, You want to come? She keep primping in front of the glass, getting the children ready at the same time.

You ever hit her? Mr. ____ ast.

Harpo look down at his hands. Naw suh, he say low, embarrass.

Well how you spect to make her mind? Wives is like children. You have to let 'em know who got the upper hand. Nothing can do that better than a good sound beating.

He puff on his pipe.

Sofia think too much of herself anyway, he say. She need to be taken down a peg.

I like Sofia, but she don't act like me at all. If she talking when Harpo and Mr. _____ come in the room, she keep right on. If they ast her where something at, she say she don't know. Keep talking.

I think bout this when Harpo ast me what he ought to do to her to make her mind. I don't mention how happy he is now. How three years pass and he still whistle and sing. I think bout how every time I jump when Mr. _____ call me, she look surprise. And like she pity me.

Beat her. I say.

Next time us see Harpo his face a mess of bruises. His lip cut. One of his eyes shut like a fist. He walk stiff and say his teef ache.

I say, What happen to you, Harpo?

He say, Oh, me and that mule. She fractious, you know. She went crazy in the field the other day. By time I got her to head for home I was all banged up. Then when I got home, I walked smack dab into the crib door. Hit my eye and scratch my chin. Then when that storm come up last night I shet the window down on my hand.

Well, I say, After all that, I don't spect you had a chance to see if you could make Sofia mind.

Nome, he say.

But he keep trying.

Dear God,

Just when I was bout to call out that I was coming in the yard, I hear something crash. It come from inside the house, so I run up on the porch. The two children be making mud pies on the edge of the creek, they don't even look up.

I open the door cautious, thinking bout robbers and murderers. Horsethieves and hants. But it Harpo and Sofia. They fighting like two mens. Every piece of furniture they got is turned over. Every plate look like it broke. The looking glass hang crooked, the curtains torn. The bed look like the stuffing pulled out. They don't notice. They fight. He try to slap her. What he do that for? She reach down and grab a piece of stove wood and whack him cross the eyes. He punch her in the stomach, she double over groaning but come up with both hands lock right under his privates. He roll on the floor. He grab her dress tail and pull. She stand there in her slip. She never blink a eye. He jump up to put a hammer lock under her chin, she throw him over her back. He fall *bam* up gainst the stove.

I don't know how long this been going on. I don't know

when they spect to conclude. I ease on back out, wave to the children by the creek, walk back on up home.

Saturday morning early, us hear the wagon. Harpo, Sofia, the two babies be going off for the week-end, to visit Sofia sister.

Dear God,

For over a month I have trouble sleeping. I stay up late as I can before Mr. _____ start complaining bout the price of kerosene, then I soak myself in a warm bath with milk and epsom salts, then sprinkle little witch hazel on my pillow and curtain out all the moonlight. Sometimes I git a few hours sleep. Then just when it look like it ought to be gitting good, I wakes up.

At first I'd git up quick and drink some milk. Then I'd think bout counting fence post. Then I'd think bout reading the Bible.

What it is? I ast myself.

A little voice say, Something you done wrong. Somebody spirit you sin against. Maybe.

Way late one night it come to me. Sofia. I sin against Sofia spirit.

I pray she don't find out, but she do.

Harpo told.

The minute she hear it she come marching up the path, toting a sack. Little cut all blue and red under her eye.

She say, Just want you to know I looked to you for help.

Ain't I been helpful? I ast.

She open up her sack. Here your curtains, she say. Here your thread. Here a dollar for letting me use 'em.

They yourn, I say, trying to push them back. I'm glad to help out. Do what I can.

You told Harpo to beat me, she said.

No I didn't, I said.

Don't lie, she said.

I didn't mean it, I said.

Then what you say it for? she ast.

She standing there looking me straight in the eye. She look tired and her jaws full of air.

I say it cause I'm a fool, I say. I say it cause I'm jealous of you. I say it cause you do what I can't.

What that? she say.

Fight. I say.

She stand there a long time, like what I said took the wind out her jaws. She mad before, sad now.

She say, All my life I had to fight. I had to fight my daddy. I had to fight my brothers. I had to fight my cousins and my uncles. A girl child ain't safe in a family of men. But I never thought I'd have to fight in my own house. She let out her breath. I loves Harpo, she say. God knows I do. But I'll kill him dead before I let him beat me. Now if you want a dead son-in-law you just keep on advising him like you doing. She put her hand on her hip. I used to hunt game with a bow and arrow, she say.

I stop the little trembling that started when I saw her coming. I'm so shame of myself, I say. And the Lord he done whip me little bit too.

The Lord don't like ugly, she say.

And he ain't stuck on pretty.

This open the way for our talk to turn another way.

I say, You feels sorry for me, don't you?

She think a minute. Yes ma'am, she say slow, I do.

I think I know how come, but I ast her anyhow.

She say, To tell the truth, you remind me of my mama.
She under my daddy thumb. Naw, she under my daddy foot.
Anything he say, goes. She never say nothing back. She never
stand up for herself. Try to make a little half stand sometime
for the children but that always backfire. More she stand up
for us, the harder time he give her. He hate children and he
hate where they come from. Tho from all the children he got,
you'd never know it.

I never know nothing bout her family. I thought, looking at
her, nobody in her family could be scared.

How many he got? I ast.

Twelve. She say.

Whew, I say. My daddy got six by my mama before she
die, I say. He got four more by the wife he got now. I don't
mention the two he got by me.

How many girls? she ast.

Five, I say. How bout in your family?

Six boys, six girls. All the girls big and strong like me.
Boys big and strong too, but all the girls stick together. Two
brothers stick with us too, sometime. Us git in a fight, it's a
sight to see.

I ain't never struck a living thing, I say. Oh, when I was at
home I tap the little ones on the behind to make 'em behave,
but not hard enough to hurt.

What you do when you git mad? she ast.

I think. I can't even remember the last time I felt mad, I say.
I used to git mad at my mammy cause she put a lot of work
on me. Then I see how sick she is. Couldn't stay mad at her.
Couldn't be mad at my daddy cause he my daddy. Bible say,
Honor father and mother no matter what. Then after while

every time I got mad, or start to feel mad, I got sick. Felt like throwing up. Terrible feeling. Then I start to feel nothing at all.

Sofia frown. Nothing at all?

Well, sometime Mr. _____ git on me pretty hard. I have to talk to Old Maker. But he my husband. I shrug my shoulders. This life soon be over, I say. Heaven last all ways.

You ought to bash Mr. _____ head open, she say. Think bout heaven later.

Not much funny to me. That funny. I laugh. She laugh. Then us both laugh so hard us flop down on the step.

Let's make quilt pieces out of these messed up curtains, she say. And I run git my pattern book.

I sleeps like a baby now.

Dear God,

Shug Avery sick and nobody in this town want to take the Queen Honeybee in. Her mammy say She told her so. Her pappy say, Tramp. A woman at church say she dying—maybe two berkulosis or some kind of nasty woman disease. What? I want to ast, but don't. The women at church sometime nice to me. Sometime not. They look at me there struggling with Mr. ____ children. Trying to drag 'em to the church, trying to keep 'em quiet after us get there. They some of the same ones used to be here both times I was big. Sometimes they think I don't notice, they stare at me. Puzzle.

I keep my head up, best I can. I do a right smart for the preacher. Clean the floor and windows, make the wine, wash the altar linen. Make sure there's wood for the stove in wintertime. He call me Sister Celie. Sister Celie, he say, You faithful as the day is long. Then he talk to the other ladies and they mens. I scurry bout, doing this, doing that. Mr. ____ sit back by the door gazing here and there. The womens smile in his direction every chance they git. He never look at me or even notice.

Even the preacher got his mouth on Shug Avery, now she

down. He take her condition for his text. He don't call no name, but he don't have to. Everybody know who he mean. He talk bout a strumpet in short skirts, smoking cigarettes, drinking gin. Singing for money and taking other women mens. Talk bout slut, hussy, heifer and streetcleaner.

I cut my eyes back at Mr. ____ when he say that. Streetcleaner. Somebody got to stand up for Shug, I think. But he don't say nothing. He cross his legs first to one side, then to the other. He gaze out the window. The same women smile at him, say amen gainst Shug.

But once us home he never stop to take off his clothes. He call down to Harpo and Sofia house. Harpo come running.

Hitch up the wagon, he say.

Where us going? say Harpo.

Hitch up the wagon, he say again.

Harpo hitch up the wagon. They stand there and talk a few minutes out by the barn. Then Mr. ____ drive off.

One good thing bout the way he never do any work round the place, us never miss him when he gone.

Five days later I look way off up the road and see the wagon coming back. It got sort of a canopy over it now, made out of old blankets or something. My heart begin to beat like furry, and the first thing I try to do is change my dress.

But too late for that. By time I git my head and arm out the old dress, I see the wagon pull up in the yard. Plus a new dress won't help none with my notty head and dusty headrag, my old everyday shoes and the way I smell.

I don't know what to do, I'm so beside myself. I stand there in the middle of the kitchen. Mind whirling. I feels like Who Would Have Thought.

Celie, I hear Mr. ____ call. *Harpo.*

I stick my head and my arm back in my old dress and wipe the sweat and dirt off my face as best I can. I come to the door. Yessir? I ast, and trip over the broom I was sweeping with when I first notice the wagon.

Harpo and Sofia in the yard now, looking inside the wagon. They faces grim.

Who this? Harpo ast.

The woman should have been your mammy, he say.

Shug Avery? Harpo ast. He look up at me.

Help me git her in the house, Mr. _____ say.

I think my heart gon fly out my mouth when I see one of her foots come poking out.

She not lying down. She climbing down tween Harpo and Mr. _____. And she dress to kill. She got on a red wool dress and chestful of black beads. A shiny black hat with what look like chickinhawk feathers curve down side one cheek, and she carrying a little snakeskin bag, match her shoes.

She look so stylish it like the trees all round the house draw themself up tall for a better look. Now I see she stumble, tween the two men. She don't seem that well acquainted with her feets.

Close up I see all this yellow powder caked up on her face. Red rouge. She look like she ain't long for this world but dressed well for the next. But I know better.

Come on in, I want to cry. To shout. Come on in. With God help, Celie going to make you well. But I don't say nothing. It not my house. Also I ain't been told nothing.

They git halfway up the step, Mr. _____ look up at me. Celie, he say. This here Shug Avery. Old friend of the family. Fix up the spare room. Then he look down at her, hold her in one arm, hold on to the rail with the other. Harpo on the other side, looking sad. Sofia and the children in the yard, watching.

I don't move at once, cause I can't. I need to see her eyes. I feel like once I see her eyes my feets can let go the spot where they stuck.

Git moving, he say, sharp.

And then she look up.

Under all that powder her face black as Harpo. She got a long pointed nose and big fleshy mouth. Lips look like black plum. Eyes big, glossy. Feverish. And mean. Like, sick as she is, if a snake cross her path, she kill it.

She look me over from head to foot. Then she cackle. Sound like a death rattle. You sure *is* ugly, she say, like she ain't believed it.

Dear God,

Ain't nothing wrong with Shug Avery. She just sick. Sicker than anybody I ever seen. She sicker than my mama was when she die. But she more evil than my mama and that keep her alive.

Mr. _____ be in the room with her all time of the night or day. He don't hold her hand though. She too evil for that. Turn loose my goddam hand, she say to Mr. _____. What the matter with you, you crazy? I don't need no weak little boy can't say no to his daddy hanging on me. I need me a man, she say. A man. She look at him and roll her eyes and laugh. It not much of a laugh but it keep him away from the bed. He sit over in the corner away from the lamp. Sometime she wake up in the night and don't even see. But he there. Sitting in the shadows chewing on his pipe. No tobacco in it. First thing she said, I don't want to smell no stinking blankety-blank pipe, you hear me, Albert?

Who Albert, I wonder. Then I remember Albert Mr. _____ first name.

Mr. _____ don't smoke. Don't drink. Don't even hardly eat. He just got her in that little room, watching every breath.

What happen to her I ast?

You don't want her here, just say so, he say. Won't do no good. But if that the way you feel . . . He don't finish.

I want her here, I say, too quick. He look at me like maybe I'm planning something bad.

I just want to know what happen, I say.

I look at his face. It tired and sad and I notice his chin weak. Not much chin there at all. I have more chin, I think. And his clothes dirty, dirty. When he pull them off, dust rise.

Nobody fight for Shug, he say. And a little water come to his eyes.

Dear God,

They have made three babies together but he squeamish bout giving her a bath. Maybe he figure he start thinking bout things he shouldn't. But what bout me? First time I got the full sight of Shug Avery long black body with it black plum nipples, look like her mouth, I thought I had turned into a man.

What you staring at? she ast. Hateful. She weak as a kitten. But her mouth just pack with claws. You never seen a naked woman before?

No ma'am, I said. I never did. Cept for Sofia, and she so plump and ruddy and crazy she feel like my sister.

She say, Well take a good look. Even if I is just a bag of bones now. She have the nerve to put one hand on her naked hip and bat her eyes at me. Then she suck her teef and roll her eyes at the ceiling while I wash her.

I wash her body, it feel like I'm praying. My hands tremble and my breath short.

She say, You ever have any kids?

I say, Yes ma'am.

She say, How many and don't you yes ma'am me, I ain't that old.

I say, two.

She ast me Where they is?

I say, I don't know.

She look at me funny.

My kids with they grandma, she say. She could stand the kids, I had to go.

You miss 'em? I ast.

Naw, she say. I don't miss nothing.

Dear God,

I ast Shug Avery what she want for breakfast. She say, What yall got? I say ham, grits, eggs, biscuits, coffee, sweet milk or butter milk, flapjacks. Jelly and jam.

She say, Is that all? What about orange juice, grapefruit, strawberries and cream. Tea. Then she laugh.

I don't want none of your damn food, she say. Just gimme a cup of coffee and hand me my cigarettes.

I don't argue. I git the coffee and light her cigarette. She wearing a long white gown and her thin black hand stretching out of it to hold the white cigarette looks just right. Something bout it, maybe the little tender veins I see and the big ones I try not to, make me scared. I feel like something pushing me forward. If I don't watch out I'll have hold of her hand, tasting her fingers in my mouth.

Can I sit in here and eat with you? I ast.

She shrug. She busy looking at a magazine. White women in it laughing, holding they beads out on one finger, dancing on top of motocars. Jumping into fountains. She flip the pages. Look dissatisfied. Remind me of a child trying to git something out a toy it can't work yet.

She drink her coffee, puff on her cigarette. I bite into a big juicy piece of home cured ham. You can smell this ham for a mile when you cooking it, it perfume up her little room with no trouble at all.

I lavish butter on a hot biscuit, sort of wave it about. I sop up ham gravey and splosh my eggs in with my grits.

She blow more and more smoke. Look down in her coffee like maybe its something solid at the bottom.

Finally she say, Celie, I believe I could drink a glass of water. And this here by the bed ain't fresh.

She hold out her glass.

I put my plate down on the card table by the bed. I go dip her up some water. I come back, pick up my plate. Look like a little mouse been nibbling the biscuit, a rat run off with the ham.

She act like nothing happen. Begin to complain bout being tired. Doze on off to sleep.

Mr. _____ ast me how I git her to eat.

I say, Nobody living can stand to smell home cured ham without tasting it. If they dead they got a chance. Maybe.

Mr. _____ laugh.

I notice something crazy in his eyes.

I been scared, he say. Scared. And he cover up his eyes with his hands.

Dear God,

Shug Avery sit up in bed a little today. I wash and comb out her hair. She got the nottiest, shortest, kinkiest hair I ever saw, and I loves every strand of it. The hair that come out in my comb I kept. Maybe one day I'll get a net, make me a rat to pomp up my own hair.

I work on her like she a doll or like she Olivia—or like she mama. I comb and pat, comb and pat. First she say, hurry up and git finish. Then she melt down a little and lean back gainst my knees. That feel just right, she say. That feel like mama used to do. Or maybe not mama. Maybe grandma. She reach for another cigarette. Start hum a little tune.

What that song? I ast. Sound low down dirty to me. Like what the preacher tell you its sin to hear. Not to mention sing.

She hum a little more. Something come to me, she say. Something I made up. Something you help scratch out my head.

Dear God,

Mr. ____ daddy show up this evening. He a little short shrunk up man with a bald head and gold spectacles. He clear his throat a lot, like everything he say need announcement. Talk with his head leant to the side.

He come right to the point.

Just couldn't rest till you got her in your house, could you? he say, coming up the step.

Mr. ____ don't say nothing. Look out cross the railing at the trees, over the top of the well. Eyes rest on the top of Harpo and Sofia house.

Won't you have a seat? I ast, pushing him up a chair. How bout a cool drink of water?

Through the window I hear Shug humming and humming, practicing her little song. I sneak back to her room and shet the window.

Old Mr. ____ say to Mr. ____, Just what is it bout this Shug Avery anyway, he say. She black as tar, she nappy headed. She got legs like baseball bats.

Mr. ____ don't say nothing. I drop little spit in Old Mr. ____ water.

61

Why, say Old Mr. ____, she ain't even clean. I hear she got
the nasty woman disease.

I twirl the spit round with my finger. I think bout ground
glass, wonder how you grind it. But I don't feel mad at all. Just
interest.

Mr. ____ turn his head slow, watch his daddy drink. Then
say, real sad, You ain't got it in you to understand, he say.
I love Shug Avery. Always have, always will. I should have
married her when I had the chance.

Yeah, say Old Mr. ____. And throwed your life away. (Mr.
____ grunt right there.) And a right smart of my money with
it. Old Mr. ____ clear his throat. Nobody even sure exactly
who her daddy is.

I never care who her daddy is, say Mr. ____.

And her mammy take in white people dirty clothes to this
day. Plus all her children got different daddys. It all just too
trifling and confuse.

Well, say Mr. ____ and turn full face on his daddy, All Shug
Avery children got the same daddy. I vouch for that.

Old Mr. ____ clear his throat. Well, this my house. This
my land. Your boy Harpo in one of my houses, on my land.
Weeds come up on my land, I chop 'em up. Trash blow over it
I burn it. He rise to go. Hand me his glass. Next time he come
I put a little Shug Avery pee in his glass. See how he like that.

Celie, he say, you have my sympathy. Not many women let
they husband whore lay up in they house.

But he not saying to me, he saying it to Mr. ____.

Mr. ____ look up at me, our eyes meet. This the closest us
ever felt.

He say, Hand Pa his hat, Celie.

And I do. Mr. ____ don't move from his chair by the
railing. I stand in the door. Us watch Old Mr. ____ begin
harrumping and harrumping down the road home.

• • •

Next one come visit, his brother Tobias. He real fat and tall, look like a big yellow bear. Mr. _____ small like his daddy, his brother stand way taller.

Where she at? he ast, grinning. Where the Queen Honeybee? Got something for her, he say. He put little box of chocolate on the railing.

She sleeping, I say. Didn't sleep much last night.

How you doing there, Albert, he say, dragging up a chair. He run his hand over his slicked back hair and try to feel if there's a bugga in his nose. Wipe his hand on his pants. Shake out the crease.

I just heard Shug Avery was here, he say. How long you had her?

Oh, say Mr. _____, couple of months.

Hell, say Tobias, I heard she was dying. That goes to show, don't it, that you can't believe everything you hear. He smooth down his mustache, run his tongue out the corners of his lips.

What you know good, Miss Celie? he say.

Not much, I say.

Me and Sofia piecing another quilt together. I got bout five squares pieced, spread out on the table by my knee. My basket full of scraps on the floor.

Always busy, always busy, he say. I wish Margaret was more like you. Save me a bundle of money.

Tobias and his daddy always talk bout money like they still got a lot. Old Mr. _____ been selling off the place so that nothing much left but the houses and the fields. My and Harpo fields bring in more than anybody.

I piece on my square. Look at the colors of the cloth.

Then I hear Tobias chair fall back and he say, Shug.

Shug halfway tween sick and well. Halfway tween good and evil, too. Most days now she show me and Mr. _____ her good side. But evil all over her today. She smile, like a razor opening. Say, Well, well, look who's here today.

She wearing a little flowery shift I made for her and
nothing else. She look bout ten with her hair all cornrowed.
She skinny as a bean, and her face full of eyes.

Me and Mr. _____ both look up at her. Both move to help
her sit down. She don't look at him. She pull up a chair next
to me.

She pick up a random piece of cloth out the basket. Hold it
up to the light. Frown. How you sew this damn thing? she say.

I hand her the square I'm working on, start another
one. She sew long crooked stiches, remind me of that little
crooked tune she sing.

That real good, for first try, I say. That just fine and dandy.
She look at me and snort. Everything I do is fine and dandy
to you, Miss Celie, she say. But that's cause you ain't got good
sense. She laugh. I duck my head.

She got a heap more than Margaret, say Tobias. Margaret
take that needle and sew your nostrils together.

All womens not alike, Tobias, she say. Believe it or not.

Oh, I believe it, he say. Just can't prove it to the world.

First time I think about the world.

What the world got to do with anything, I think. Then I
see myself sitting there quilting tween Shug Avery and Mr.
_____. Us three set together gainst Tobias and his fly speck box
of chocolate. For the first time in my life, I feel just right.

Dear God,

Me and Sofia work on the quilt. Got it frame up on the porch. Shug Avery donate her old yellow dress for scrap, and I work in a piece every chance I get. It a nice pattern call Sister's Choice. If the quilt turn out perfect, maybe I give it to her, if it not perfect, maybe I keep. I want it for myself, just for the little yellow pieces, look like stars, but not. Mr. _____ and Shug walk up the road to the mailbox. The house quiet, cept for the flies. They swing through every now and then, drunk from eating and enjoying the heat, buzz enough to make me drowsy.

Sofia look like something on her mind, she just not sure what. She bend over the frame, sew a little while, then rear back in her chair and look out cross the yard. Finally she rest her needle, say, Why do people eat, Miss Celie, tell me that.

To stay alive, I say. What else? Course some folks eat cause food taste good to 'em. Then some is gluttons. They love to feel they mouth work.

Them the only reasons you can think of? she ast.

Well, sometime it might be a case of being undernourish, I say.

She muse. He not undernourish, she say.

Who ain't? I ast.

Harpo. She say.

Harpo?

He eating more and more every day.

Maybe he got a tape worm?

She frown. Naw, she say. I don't think it a tape worm. Tape worm make you hungry. Harpo eat when he ain't even hungry.

What, force it down? This hard to believe, but sometime you hear new things everyday. Not me, you understand, but some folk do say that.

Last night for supper he ate a whole pan of biscuits by himself.

Naw. I say.

He sure did. And had two big glasses of butter milk along with it. This was after supper was over, too. I was giving the children they baths, getting 'em ready for bed. He sposed to be washing the dishes. Stead of washing plates, he cleaning 'em with his mouth.

Well maybe he was extra hungry. Yall is been working hard.

Not that hard, she say. And this morning, for breakfast, darn if he didn't have six eggs. After all that food he look too sick to walk. When us got to the field I thought he was going to faint.

If Sofia say DARN something wrong. Maybe he don't want to wash dishes, I say. His daddy never wash a dish in his life.

You reckon? she say. He seem so much to love it. To tell the truth, he love that part of housekeeping a heap more 'en me. I rather be out in the fields or fooling with the animals. Even chopping wood. But he love cooking and cleaning and doing little things round the house.

He sure is a good cook, I say. Big surprise to me that he knew anything about it. He never cooked so much as a egg when he lived at home.

I bet he wanted to, she said. It seem so natural to him. But Mr. _____. You know how he is.

Oh, he all right, I say.

You feeling yourself, Miss Celie? Sofia ast.

I mean, he all right in some things, not in others.

Oh, she say. Anyway, next time he come here, notice if he eat anything.

I notice what he eat all right. First thing, coming up the steps, I give him a close look. He still skinny, bout half Sofia size, but I see a little pot beginning under his overalls.

What you got to eat, Miss Celie? he say, going straight to the warmer and a piece of fried chicken, then on to the safe for a slice of blackberry pie. He stand by the table and munch, munch. You got any sweet milk? he ast.

Got clabber, I say.

He say, Well, I love clabber. And dip him out some.

Sofia must not be feeding you, I say.

Why you say that? he ast with his mouth full.

Well, it not that long after dinner and here you is hungry again.

He don't say nothing. Eat.

Course, I say, suppertime not too far off either. Bout three four hours.

He rummage through the drawer for a spoon to eat the clabber with. He see a slice of cornbread on the shelf back of the stove, he grab it and crumble it into the glass.

Us go back out on the porch and he put his foots up on the railing. Eat his clabber and cornbread with the glass near bout to his nose. Remind me of a hog at the troth.

Food tasting like food to you these days huh, I say, listening to him chew.

He don't say nothing. Eat.

I look out cross the yard. I see Sofia dragging a ladder and then lean it up gainst the house. She wearing a old pair of Harpo pants. Got her head tied up in a headrag. She clam up the ladder to the roof, begin to hammer in nails. Sound echo cross the yard like shots.

Harpo eat, watch her.

Then he belch. Say, Scuse me, Miss Celie. Take the glass and spoon back in the kitchen. Come out and say Bye.

No matter what happening now. No matter who come. No matter what they say or do, Harpo eat through it. Food on his mind morning, noon and night. His belly grow and grow, but the rest of him don't. He begin to look like he big.

When it due? us ast.

Harpo don't say nothing. Reach for another piece of pie.

Dear God,

Harpo staying with us this week-end. Friday night after Mr. ____ and Shug and me done gone to bed, I heard this somebody crying. Harpo sitting out on the steps, crying like his heart gon break. Oh, boo-hoo, and boo-hoo. He got his head in his hands, tears and snot running down his chin. I give him a hansker. He blow his nose, look up at me out of two eyes close like fists.

What happen to your eyes? I ast.

He clam round in his mind for a story to tell, then fall back on the truth.

Sofia, he say.

You still bothering Sofia? I ast.

She my wife, he say.

That don't mean you got to keep on bothering her, I say. Sofia love you, she a good wife. Good to the children and good looking. Hardworking. Godfearing and *clean*. I don't know what more you want.

Harpo sniffle.

I want her to do what I say, like you do for Pa.

Oh, Lord, I say.

When Pa tell you to do something, you do it, he say. When he say not to, you don't. You don't do what he say, he beat you.

Sometime beat me anyhow, I say, whether I do what he say or not.

That's right, say Harpo. But not Sofia. She do what she want, don't pay me no mind at all. I try to beat her, she black my eyes. Oh, boo-hoo, he cry. Boo-hoo-hoo.

I start to take back my hansker. Maybe push him and his black eyes off the step. I think bout Sofia. She tickle me. I used to hunt game with a bow and arrow, she say.

Some womens can't be beat, I say. Sofia one of them. Besides, Sofia love you. She probably be happy to do most of what you say if you ast her right. She not mean, she not spiteful. She don't hold a grudge.

He sit there hanging his head, looking retard.

Harpo, I say, giving him a shake, Sofia *love* you. You *love* Sofia.

He look up at me best he can out his fat little eyes. Yes ma'am? he say.

Mr. _____ marry me to take care of his children. I marry him cause my daddy made me. I don't love Mr. _____ and he don't love me.

But you his wife, he say, just like Sofia mine. The wife spose to mind.

Do Shug Avery mind Mr. _____? I ast. She the woman he wanted to marry. She call him Albert, tell him his drawers stink in a minute. Little as he is, when she git her weight back she can sit on him if he try to bother her.

Why I mention weight. Harpo start to cry again. Then he start to be sick. He lean over the edge of the step and vomit and vomit. Look like every piece of pie for the last year come up. When he empty I put him in the bed next to Shug's little room. He fall right off to sleep.

Dear God,

I go visit Sofia, she still working on the roof.

The darn thing leak, she say.

She out to the woodpile making shingles. She put a big square piece of wood on the chopping block and chop, chop, she make big flat shingles. She put the ax down and ast me do I want some lemonade.

I look at her good. Except for a bruise on her wrist, she don't look like she got a scratch on her.

How it going with you and Harpo? I ast.

Well, she say, he stop eating so much. But maybe this just a spell.

He trying to git as big as you, I say.

She suck in her breath. I kinda thought so, she say, and let out her breath real slow.

All the children come running up, Mama, Mama, us want lemonade. She pour out five glasses for them, two for us. Us sit in a wooden swing she made last summer and hung on the shady end of the porch.

I'm gitting tired of Harpo, she say. All he think about since us married is how to make me mind. He don't want a wife, he want a dog.

He your husband, I say. Got to stay with him. Else, what you gon do?

My sister husband caught in the draft, she say. They don't have no children, Odessa love children. He left her on a little farm. Maybe I go stay with them a while. Me and my children.

I think bout my sister Nettie. Thought so sharp it go through me like a pain. Somebody to run to. It seem too sweet to bear.

Sofia go on, frowning at her glass.

I don't like to go to bed with him no more, she say. Used to be when he touch me I'd go all out my head. Now when he touch me I just don't want to be bothered. Once he git on top of me I think bout how that's where he always want to be. She sip her lemonade. I use to love that part of it, she say. I use to chase him home from the field. Git all hot just watching him put the children to bed. But no more. Now I feels tired all the time. No interest.

Now, now, I say. Sleep on it some, maybe it come back. But I say this just to be saying something. I don't know nothing bout it. Mr. _____ clam on top of me, do his business, in ten minutes us both sleep. Only time I feel something stirring down there is when I think bout Shug. And that like running to the end of the road and it turn back on itself.

You know the worst part? she say. The worst part is I don't think he notice. He git up there and enjoy himself just the same. No matter what I'm thinking. No matter what I feel. It just him. Heartfeeling don't even seem to enter into it. She snort. The fact he can do it like that make me want to kill him.

Us look up the path to the house, see Shug and Mr. _____ sitting on the steps. He reach over and pick something out her hair.

I don't know, say Sofia. Maybe I won't go. Deep down I still love Harpo, but—he just makes me *real* tired. She yawn. Laugh. I need a vacation, she say. Then she go back to the woodpile, start making some more shingles for the roof.

Dear God,

Sofia right about her sisters. They all big strong healthy girls, look like amazons. They come early one morning in two wagons to pick Sofia up. She don't have much to take, her and the children clothes, a mattress she made last winter, a looking glass and a rocking chair. The children.

Harpo sit on the steps acting like he don't care. He making a net for seining fish. He look out toward the creek every once in a while and whistle a little tune. But it nothing compared to the way he usually whistle. His little whistle sound like it lost way down in a jar, and the jar in the bottom of the creek.

At the last minute I decide to give Sofia the quilt. I don't know what her sister place be like, but we been having right smart cold weather long in now. For all I know, she and the children have to sleep on the floor.

You gon let her go? I ast Harpo.

He look like only a fool could ast the question. He puff back, She made up her mind to go, he say. How I'm gon stop her? Let her go on, he say, cutting his eyes at her sister wagons.

Us sit on the steps together. All us hear from inside is the thump, thump, thump of plump and stout feet. All Sofia sisters moving round together at one time make the house shake.

Where us going? ast the oldest girl.

Going to visit Aunt Odessa, say Sofia.

Daddy coming? she ast.

Naw, say Sofia.

How come daddy ain't coming? another one ast.

Daddy need to stay here and take care of the house. Look after Dilsey, Coco and Boo.

The child come stand in front of his daddy and just look at him real good.

You not coming? he say.

Harpo say, Naw.

Child go whisper to the baby crawling round on the floor, Daddy not coming with us, what you think of that.

Baby sit real still, strain real hard, fart.

Us all laugh, but it sad too. Harpo pick it up, finger the daidie, and get her ready for a change.

I don't think she wet, say Sofia. Just gas.

But he change her anyway. Him and the baby over in a corner of the little porch out of the way of traffic. He use the old dry daidie to wipe his eyes.

At the last, he hand Sofia the baby and she sling it up side her hip, sling a sack of daidies and food over her shoulder, corral all the little ones together, tell 'em to Say Good-bye to Daddy. Then she hug me best she can what with the baby and all, and she clam up on the wagon. Every sister just about got a child tween her knees, cept the two driving the mules, and they all quiet as they leave Sofia and Harpo yard and drive on up past the house.

Dear God,

Sofia gone six months, Harpo act like a different man. Used to be a homebody, now all the time in the road.

I ast him what going on. He say, Miss Celie, I done learned a few things.

One thing he learned is that he cute. Another that he smart. Plus, he can make money. He don't say who the teacher is.

I hadn't heard so much hammering since before Sofia left, but every evening after he leave the field, he knocking down and nailing up. Sometime his friend Swain come by to help. The two of them work all into the night. Mr. _____ have to call down to tell them to shut up the racket.

What you building? I ast.

Jukejoint, he say.

Way back here?

No further back than any of the others.

I don't know nothing bout no others, only bout the Lucky Star.

Jukejoint sposed to be back in the woods, say Harpo. Nobody be bothered by the loud music. The dancing. The fights.

Swain say, the killings.

Harpo say, and the polices don't know where to look.

What Sofia gon say bout what you doing to her house? I ast. Spose she and the children come back. Where they gon sleep.

They ain't coming back, say Harpo, nailing together planks for a counter.

How you know? I ast.

He don't answer. He keep working, doing every thing with Swain.

Dear God,

The first week, nobody come. Second week, three or four. Third week, one. Harpo sit behind his little counter listening to Swain pick his box.

He got cold drinks, he got barbecue, he got chitlins, got store bought bread. He got a sign saying Harpo's tacked up on the side of the house and another one out on the road. But he ain't got no customers.

I go down the path to the yard, stand outside, look in. Harpo look out and wave.

Come on in, Miss Celie, he say.

I say, Naw thank you.

Mr. _____ sometime walk down, have a cold drink, listen to Swain. Miss Shug walk down too, every once in a while. She still wearing her little shifts, and I still cornrow her hair, but it getting long now and she say soon she want it press.

Harpo puzzle by Shug. One reason is she say whatever come to mind, forgit about polite. Sometime I see him staring at her real hard when he don't think I'm looking.

One day he say, Nobody coming way out here just to hear Swain. Wonder could I get the Queen Honeybee?

I don't know, I said. She a lot better now, always humming or singing something. She probably be glad to git back to work. Why don't you ask her?

Shug say his place not much compared to what she used to, but she think maybe she might grace it with a song.

Harpo and Swain got Mr. ____ to give 'em some of Shug old announcements from out the trunk. Crossed out The Lucky Star of Coalman Road, put in Harpo's of ____ plantation. Stuck 'em on trees tween the turn off to our road and town. The first Saturday night so many folks come they couldn't git in.

Shug, Shug baby, us thought you was dead.

Five out of a dozen say hello to Shug like that.

And come to find out it was you, Shug say with a big grin.

At last I git to see Shug Avery work. I git to watch her. I git to hear her.

Mr. ____ didn't want me to come. Wives don't go to places like that, he say.

Yeah, but Celie going, say Shug, while I press her hair. Spose I git sick while I'm singing, she say. Spose my dress come undone? She wearing a skintight red dress look like the straps made out of two pieces of thread.

Mr. ____ mutter, putting on his clothes. My wife can't do this. My wife can't do that. No wife of mines . . . He go on and on.

Shug Avery finally say, Good thing I ain't your damn wife.

He hush then. All three of us go down to Harpo's. Mr. ____ and me sit at the same table. Mr. ____ drink whiskey. I have a cold drink.

First Shug sing a song by somebody name Bessie Smith. She say Bessie somebody she know. Old friend. It call A Good Man Is Hard to Find. She look over at Mr. ____ a little when she sing that. I look over at him too. For such a little man, he all puff up. Look like all he can do to stay in his chair. I look at Shug and I feel my heart begin to cramp. It hurt me so, I cover it with my hand. I think I might as well be under the table, for all they care. I hate the way I look, I hate the way I'm dress. Nothing but churchgoing clothes in my chifferobe. And Mr. _____ looking at Shug's bright black skin in her tight red dress, her feet in little sassy red shoes. Her hair shining in waves.

Before I know it, tears meet under my chin.

And I'm confuse.

He love looking at Shug. I love looking at Shug.

But Shug don't love looking at but one of us. Him.

But that the way it spose to be. I know that. But if that so, why my heart hurt me so?

My head droop so it near bout in my glass.

Then I hear my name.

Shug saying Celie. Miss Celie. And I look up where she at.

She say my name again. She say this song I'm bout to sing is call Miss Celie's song. Cause she scratched it out of my head when I was sick.

First she hum it a little, like she do at home. Then she sing the words.

It all about some no count man doing her wrong, again. But I don't listen to that part. I look at her and I hum along a little with the tune.

First time somebody made something and name it after me.

Dear God,

Pretty soon it be time for Shug to go. She sing every week-end now at Harpo's. He make right smart money off of her, and she make some too. Plus she gitting strong again and stout. First night or two her songs come out good but a little weak, now she belt them out. Folks out in the yard hear her with no trouble. She and Swain sound real good together. She sing, he pick his box. It nice at Harpo's. Little tables all round the room with candles on them that I made, lot of little tables outside too, by the creek. Sometime I look down the path from our house and it look like a swarm of lightening bugs all in and through Sofia house. In the evening Shug can't wait to go down there.

One day she say to me, Well, Miss Celie, I believe it time for me to go.

When? I ast.

Early next month, she say. June. June a good time to go off into the world.

I don't say nothing. Feel like I felt when Nettie left.

She come over and put her hand on my shoulder.

He beat me when you not here, I say.

Who do, she say, Albert?

Mr. ＿＿, I say.

I can't believe it, she say. She sit down on the bench next to me real hard, like she drop.

What he beat you for? she ast.

For being me and not you.

Oh, Miss Celie, she say, and put her arms around me.

Us sit like that for maybe half a hour. Then she kiss me on the fleshy part of my shoulder and stand up.

I won't leave, she say, until I know Albert won't even think about beating you.

Dear God,

Now we all know she going sometime soon, they sleep together at night. Not every night, but almost every night, from Friday to Monday.

He go down to Harpo's to watch her sing. And just to look at her. Then way late they come home. They giggle and they talk and they rassle until morning. Then they go to bed until it time for her to get ready to go back to work.

First time it happen, it was a accident. Feeling just carried them away. That what Shug say. He don't say nothing.

She ast me, Tell me the truth, she say, do you mind if Albert sleep with me?

I think, I don't care who Albert sleep with. But I don't say that.

I say, You might git big again.

She say, Naw, not with my sponge and all.

You still love him, I ast.

She say, I got what you call a passion for him. If I was ever going to have a husband he'd a been it. But he weak, she say. Can't make up his mind what he want. And from what you tell me he a bully. Some things I love about him though, she say. He smell right to me. He so little. He make me laugh.

You like to sleep with him? I ast.

Yeah, Celie she say, I have to confess, I just love it. Don't you?

Naw, I say. Mr. _____ can tell you, I don't like it at all. What is it like? He git up on you, heist your nightgown round your waist, plunge in. Most times I pretend I ain't there. He never know the difference. Never ast me how I feel, nothing. Just do his business, get off, go to sleep.

She start to laugh. Do his business, she say. Do his business. Why, Miss Celie. You make it sound like he going to the toilet on you.

That what it feel like, I say.

She stop laughing.

You never enjoy it at all? she ast, puzzle. Not even with your children daddy?

Never, I say.

Why Miss Celie, she say, you still a virgin.

What? I ast.

Listen, she say, right down there in your pussy is a little button that gits real hot when you do you know what with somebody. It git hotter and hotter and then it melt. That the good part. But other parts good too, she say. Lot of sucking go on, here and there, she say. Lot of finger and tongue work.

Button? Finger and *tongue*? My face hot enough to melt itself.

She say, Here, take this mirror and go look at yourself down there, I bet you never seen it, have you?

Naw.

And I bet you never seen Albert down there either.

I felt him, I say.

I stand there with the mirror.

She say, What, too shame even to go off and look at yourself? And you look so cute too, she say, laughing. All

dressed up for Harpo's, smelling good and everything, but
scared to look at your own pussy.

You come with me while I look, I say.

And us run off to my room like two little prankish girls.

You guard the door, I say.

She giggle. Okay, she say. Nobody coming. Coast clear.

I lie back on the bed and haul up my dress. Yank down my
bloomers. Stick the looking glass tween my legs. Ugh. All that
hair. Then my pussy lips be black. Then inside look like a wet
rose.

It a lot prettier than you thought, ain't it? she say from the
door.

It mine, I say. Where the button?

Right up near the top, she say. The part that stick out a
little.

I look at her and touch it with my finger. A little shiver go
through me. Nothing much. But just enough to tell me this
the right button to mash. Maybe.

She say, While you looking, look at your titties too. I haul
up my dress and look at my titties. Think bout my babies
sucking them. Remember the little shiver I felt then too.
Sometimes a big shiver. Best part about having the babies was
feeding 'em.

Albert and Harpo coming, she say. And I yank up my
drawers and yank down my dress. I feel like us been doing
something wrong.

I don't care if you sleep with him, I say.

And she take me at my word.

I take me at my word too.

But when I hear them together all I can do is pull the quilt
over my head and finger my little button and titties and cry.

Dear God,

One night while Shug singing a hot one, who should come, prancing through the door of Harpo's but Sofia.

She with a big tall hefty man look like a prizefighter.

She her usual stout and bouncy self.

Oh, Miss Celie, she cry. It so good to see you again. It even good to see Mr. ____, she say. She take one of his hands. Even if his handshake is a little weak, she say.

He act real glad to see her.

Here, pull up a chair, he say. Have a cold drink.

Gimme a shot of white lightening, she say.

Prizefighter pull up a chair, straddle it backwards, hug on Sofia like they at home.

I see Harpo cross the room with his little yellowskin girlfriend. He look at Sofia like she a hant.

This Henry Broadnax, Sofia say. Everybody call him Buster. Good friend of the family.

How you all? he say. He smile pleasant and us keep listening to the music. Shug wearing a gold dress that show her titties near bout to the nipple. Everybody sorta hoping something break. But that dress strong.

Man oh man, say Buster. Fire department won't do. Somebody call the Law.

Mr. ____ whisper to Sofia. Where your children at?

She whisper back, My children at home, where yours?

He don't say nothing.

Both the girls bigged and gone. Bub in and out of jail. If his grandaddy wasn't the colored uncle of the sheriff who look just like Bub, Bub be lynch by now.

I can't git over how good Sofia look.

Most women with five children look a little peaked, I say to her cross the table when Shug finish her song. You look like you ready for five more.

Oh, she say, I got six children now, Miss Celie.

Six. I am shock.

She toss her head, look over at Harpo. Life don't stop just cause you leave home, Miss Celie. You know that.

My life stop when I left home, I think. But then I think again. It stop with Mr. ____ maybe, but start up again with Shug.

Shug come over and she and Sofia hug.

Shug say, Girl, you look like a good time, you do.

That when I notice how Shug talk and act sometimes like a man. Men say stuff like that to women, Girl, you look like a good time. Women always talk bout hair and health. How many babies living or dead, or got teef. Not bout how some woman they hugging on look like a good time.

All the men got they eyes glued to Shug's bosom. I got my eyes glued there too. I feel my nipples harden under my dress. My little button sort of perk up too. Shug, I say to her in my mind, Girl, you looks like a real good time, the Good Lord knows you do.

What you doing here? ast Harpo.

Sofia say, Come to hear Miss Shug. You got a nice place

here Harpo. She look around. This and that her eyes
admire.

Harpo say, It just a scandless, a woman with five children
hanging out in a jukejoint at night.

Sofia eye go cool. She look him up and down.

Since he quit stuffing himself, he gained a bunch of weight,
face, head and all, mostly from drinking home brew and
eating left-over barbecue. By now he just about her size.

A woman need a little fun, once in a while, she say.

A woman need to be at home, he say.

She say, This is my home. Though I do think it go better as
a jukejoint.

Harpo look at the prizefighter. Prizefighter push back his
chair a little, pick up his drink.

I don't fight Sofia battle, he say. My job to love her and take
her where she want to go.

Harpo breathe some relief.

Let's dance, he say.

Sofia laugh, git up. Put both arms round his neck. They
slow drag out cross the floor.

Harpo little yellowish girlfriend sulk, hanging over the bar.
She a nice girl, friendly and everything, but she like me. She
do anything Harpo say.

He give her a little nickname, too, call her Squeak.

Pretty soon Squeak git up her nerve to try to cut in.

Harpo try to turn Sofia so she can't see. But Squeak keep
on tapping and tapping on his shoulder.

Finally he and Sofia stop dancing. They bout two feet from
our table.

Shug say, uh-oh, and point with her chin, something bout
to blow right there.

Who dis woman, say Squeak, in this little teenouncy voice.

You know who she is, say Harpo.

Squeak turn to Sofia. Say, You better leave him alone.

Sofia say, Fine with me. She turn round to leave.

Harpo grab her by the arm. Say, You don't have to go no where. Hell, this your house.

Squeak say, What you mean, Dis her house? She walk out on you. Walk away from the house. It over now, she say to Sofia.

Sofia say, Fine with me. Try to pull away from Harpo grip. He hold her tight.

Listen Squeak, say Harpo, Can't a man dance with his own wife?

Squeak say, Not if he my man he can't. You hear that, bitch, she say to Sofia.

Sofia gitting a little tired of Squeak, I can tell by her ears. They sort of push back. But she say again, sorta end of argument like, Hey, fine with me.

Squeak slap her up cross the head.

What she do that for. Sofia don't even deal in little ladyish things such as slaps. She ball up her fist, draw back, and knock two of Squeak's side teef out. Squeak hit the floor. One toof hanging on her lip, the other one upside my cold drink glass.

Then Squeak start banging on Harpo leg with her shoe.

You git that bitch out a here, she cry, blood and slobber running down her chin.

Harpo and Sofia stand side by side looking down at Squeak, but I don't think they hear her. Harpo still holding Sofia arm. Maybe half a minute go by. Finally he turn loose her arm, reach down and cradle poor little Squeak in his arms. He coo and coo at her like she a baby.

Sofia come over and git the prizefighter. They go out the door and don't look back. Then us hear a car motor start.

Dear God,

Harpo mope. Wipe the counter, light a cigarette, look outdoors, walk up and down. Little Squeak run long all up under him trying to git his tension. Baby this, she say, Baby that. Harpo look through her head, blow smoke.

Squeak come over to the corner where me and Mr. _____ at. She got two bright gold teef in the side of her mouth, generally grin all the time. Now she cry. Miss Celie, she say, What the matter with Harpo?

Sofia in jail, I say.

In jail? She look like I say Sofia on the moon.

What she in jail for? she ast.

Sassing the mayor's wife, I say.

Squeak pull up a chair. Look down my throat.

What your real name? I ast her. She say, Mary Agnes.

Make Harpo call you by your real name, I say. Then maybe he see you even when he trouble.

She look at me puzzle. I let it go. I tell her what one of Sofia sister tell me and Mr. _____.

Sofia and the prizefighter and all the children got in the prizefighter car and went to town. Clam out on the street looking like somebody. Just then the mayor and his wife come by.

All these children, say the mayor's wife, digging in her pocketbook. Cute as little buttons though, she say. She stop, put her hand on one of the children head. Say, and such strong white teef.

Sofia and the prizefighter don't say nothing. Wait for her to pass. Mayor wait too, stand back and tap his foot, watch her with a little smile. Now Millie, he say. Always going on over colored. Miss Millie finger the children some more, finally look at Sofia and the prizefighter. She look at the prizefighter car. She eye Sofia wristwatch. She say to Sofia, All your children so clean, she say, would you like to work for me, be my maid?

Sofia say, Hell no.

She say, What you say?

Sofia say, Hell no.

Mayor look at Sofia, push his wife out the way. Stick out his chest. Girl, what you say to Miss Millie?

Sofia say, I say, Hell no.

He slap her.

I stop telling it right there.

Squeak on the edge of her seat. She wait. Look down my throat some more.

No need to say no more, Mr. _____ say. You know what happen if somebody slap Sofia.

Squeak go white as a sheet. Naw, she say.

Naw nothing, I say. Sofia knock the man down.

The polices come, start slinging the children off the mayor, bang they heads together. Sofia really start to fight. They drag her to the ground.

This far as I can go with it, look like. My eyes git full of water and my throat close.

Poor Squeak all scrunch down in her chair, trembling.

They beat Sofia, Mr. ____ say.

Squeak fly up like she sprung, run over hind the counter to Harpo, put her arms round him. They hang together a long time, cry.

What the prizefighter do in all this? I ast Sofia sister, Odessa.

He want to jump in, she say. Sofia say No, take the children home.

Polices have they guns on him anyway. One move, he dead. Six of them, you know.

Mr. ____ go plead with the sheriff to let us see Sofia. Bub be in so much trouble, look so much like the sheriff, he and Mr. ____ almost on family terms. Just long as Mr. ____ know he colored.

Sheriff say, She a crazy woman, your boy's wife. You know that?

Mr. ____ say, Yassur, us do know it. Been trying to tell Harpo she crazy for twelve years. Since way before they marry. Sofia come from crazy peoples, Mr. ____ say, it not all her fault. And then again, the sheriff know how womens is, anyhow.

Sheriff think bout the women he know, say, Yep, you right there.

Mr. ____ say, We gon tell her she crazy too, if us ever do git in to see her.

Sheriff say, Well make sure you do. And tell her she lucky she alive.

When I see Sofia I don't know why she still alive. They crack her skull, they crack her ribs. They tear her nose loose on one side. They blind her in one eye. She swole from head to foot. Her tongue the size of my arm, it stick out tween her teef like a piece of rubber. She can't talk. And she just about the color of a eggplant.

Scare me so bad I near bout drop my grip. But I don't.
I put it on the floor of the cell, take out comb and brush,
nightgown, witch hazel and alcohol and I start to work on her.
The colored tendant bring me water to wash her with, and I
start at her two little slits for eyes.

Dear God,

They put Sofia to work in the prison laundry. All day long from five to eight she washing clothes. Dirty convict uniforms, nasty sheets and blankets piled way over her head. Us see her twice a month for half a hour. Her face yellow and sickly, her fingers look like fatty sausage.

Everything nasty here, she say, even the air. Food bad enough to kill you with it. Roaches here, mice, flies, lice and even a snake or two. If you say anything they strip you, make you sleep on a cement floor without a light.

How you manage? us ast.

Every time they ast me to do something, Miss Celie, I act like I'm you. I jump right up and do just what they say.

She look wild when she say that, and her bad eye wander round the room.

Mr. ____ suck in his breath. Harpo groan. Miss Shug cuss. She come from Memphis special to see Sofia.

I can't fix my mouth to say how I feel.

I'm a good prisoner, she say. Best convict they ever see. They can't believe I'm the one sass the mayor's wife, knock the mayor down. She laugh. It sound like something from a song. The part where everybody done gone home but you.

Twelve years a long time to be good though, she say.

Maybe you git out on good behavior, say Harpo.

Good behavior ain't good enough for them, say Sofia. Nothing less than sliding on your belly with your tongue on they boots can even git they attention. I dream of murder, she say, I dream of murder sleep or wake.

Us don't say nothing.

How the children? she ast.

They all fine, say Harpo. Tween Odessa and Squeak, they git by.

Say thank you to Squeak, she say. Tell Odessa I think about her.

Dear God,

Us all sit round the table after supper. Me, Shug, Mr. _____, Squeak, the prizefighter, Odessa and two more of Sofia sisters.

Sofia not gon last, say Mr. _____.

Yeah, say Harpo, she look little crazy to me.

And what she had to say, say Shug. My God.

Us got to do something, say Mr. _____ and be right quick about it.

What can us do? ast Squeak. She look a little haggard with all Sofia and Harpo children sprung on her at once, but she carry on. Hair a little stringy, slip show, but she carry on.

Bust her out, say Harpo. Git some dynamite off the gang that's building that big bridge down the road, blow the whole prison to kingdom come.

Shut up, Harpo, say Mr. _____, us trying to think.

I got it, say the prizefighter, smuggle in a gun. Well, he rub his chin, maybe smuggle in a file.

Naw, say Odessa. They just come after her if she leave that way.

Me and Squeak don't say nothing. I don't know what she

think, but I think bout angels, God coming down by chariot, swinging down real low and carrying ole Sofia home. I see 'em all as clear as day. Angels all in white, white hair and white eyes, look like albinos. God all white too, looking like some stout white man work at the bank. Angels strike they cymbals, one of them blow his horn, God blow out a big breath of fire and suddenly Sofia free.

Who the warden's black kinfolks? say Mr. ____.

Nobody say nothing.

Finally the prizefighter speak. What his name? he ast.

Hodges, say Harpo. Bubber Hodges.

Old man Henry Hodges' boy, say Mr. ____. Used to live out on the old Hodges' place.

Got a brother name Jimmy? ast Squeak.

Yeah, say Mr. ____. Brother name Jimmy. Married to that Quitman girl. Daddy own the hardware. You know them?

Squeak duck her head. Mumble something.

Say what? ast Mr. ____.

Squeak cheek turn red. She mumble again.

He your what? Mr. ____ ast.

Cousin, she say.

Mr. ____ look at her.

Daddy, she say. She cut her eye at Harpo. Look at the floor.

He know anything bout it? ast Mr. ____.

Yeah, she say. He got three children by my mama. Two younger than me.

His brother know anything bout it? ast Mr. ____.

One time he come by the house with Mr. Jimmy, he give us all quarters, say we sure do look like Hodges.

Mr. ____ rear back in his chair, give Squeak a good look from head to foot. Squeak push her greasy brown hair back from her face.

Yeah, say Mr. ____. I see the resemblance. He bring his chair down on the floor.

Well, look like you the one to go.

Go where, ast Squeak.

Go see the warden. He your uncle.

Dear God,

Us dress Squeak like she a white woman, only her clothes patch. She got on a starch and iron dress, high heel shoes with scuffs, and a old hat somebody give Shug. Us give her a old pocketbook look like a quilt and a little black bible. Us wash her hair and git all the grease out, then I put it up in two plaits that cross over her head. Us bathe her so clean she smell like a good clean floor.

What I'm gon say? she ast.

Say you living with Sofia husband and her husband say Sofia not being punish enough. Say she laugh at the fool she make of the guards. Say she gitting along just fine where she at. Happy even, long as she don't have to be no white woman maid.

Gracious God, say Squeak, how I'm gonna tune up my mouth to say all that?

He ast you who you is, make him remember. Tell him how much that quarter he give you meant to you.

That was fifteen years ago, say Squeak, he ain't gonna remember that.

Make him see the Hodges in you, say Odessa. He'll remember.

Tell him you just think justice ought to be done, yourself. But make sure he know you living with Sofia husband, say Shug. Make sure you git in the part bout being happy where she at, worse thing could happen to her is to be some white lady maid.

I don't know, say the prizefighter. This sound mighty much like some ole uncle Tomming to me.

Shug snort, Well, she say, Uncle Tom wasn't call Uncle for nothing.

Dear God,

Poor little Squeak come home with a limp. Her dress rip. Her hat missing and one of the heels come off her shoe.

What happen? us ast.

He saw the Hodges in me, she say. And he didn't like it one bit.

Harpo come up the steps from the car. My wife beat up, my woman rape, he say. I ought to go back out there with guns, maybe set fire to the place, burn the crackers up.

Shut up, Harpo, say Squeak. I'm telling it.

And she do.

Say, the minute I walk through the door, he remembered me.

What he say? us ast.

Say, What you want? I say, I come out of the interest I haves in seeing justice is done. What you say you want? he ast again.

I say what yall told me to say. Bout Sofia not being punish enough. Say she happy in prison, strong girl like her. Her main worry is just the thought of ever being some white woman maid. That what start the fight, you know, I say.

Mayor's wife ask Sofia to be her maid. Sofia say she never going to be no white woman's nothing, let alone maid.

That so? he ast, all the time looking me over real good.

Yessir, I say. Say, prison suit her just fine. Shoot, washing and ironing all day is all she do at home. She got six children, you know.

That a fact? he say.

He come from behind his desk, lean over my chair.

Who your folks? he ast.

I tell him my mama's name, grandmama's name. Grandpa's name.

Who your daddy? he ast. Where you git them eyes?

Ain't got no daddy, I say.

Come on now, he say. Ain't I seen you before?

I say, Yessir. And one time bout ten years ago, when I was a little girl, you give me a quarter. I sure did preshate it, I say.

I don't remember that, he say.

You come by the house with my mama friend, Mr. Jimmy, I say.

Squeak look round at all of us. Then take a deep breath. Mumble.

Say what? ast Odessa.

Yeah, say Shug, if you can't tell us, who you gon tell, God?

He took my hat off, say Squeak. Told me to undo my dress. She drop her head, put her face in her hands.

My God, say Odessa, and he your uncle.

He say if he was my uncle he wouldn't do it to me. That be a sin. But this just little fornication. Everybody guilty of that.

She turn her face up to Harpo. Harpo, she say, do you really love me, or just my color?

Harpo say, I love you, Squeak. He kneel down and try to put his arms round her waist.

She stand up. My name Mary Agnes, she say.

Dear God,

Six months after Mary Agnes went to git Sofia out of prison, she begin to sing. First she sing Shug's songs, then she begin to make up songs her own self.

She got the kind of voice you never think of trying to sing a song. It little, it high, it sort of meowing. But Mary Agnes don't care.

Pretty soon, us git used to it. Then us like it a whole lot.

Harpo don't know what to make of it.

It seem funny to me, he say to me and Mr. ____. So sudden. It put me in the mind of a gramaphone. Sit in the corner a year silent as the grave. Then you put a record on, it come to life.

Wonder if she still mad Sofia knock her teef out? I ast.

Yeah, she mad. But what good being mad gon do? She not evil, she know Sofia life hard to bear right now.

How she git long with the children? ast Mr. ____.

They love her, say Harpo. She let 'em do anything they want.

Oh-oh, I say.

Besides, he say, Odessa and Sofia other sisters always

on hand to take up the slack. They bring up children like
military.

Squeak sing,

> *They calls me yellow*
> *like yellow be my name*
>
> *They calls me yellow*
> *like yellow be my name*
>
> *But if yellow is a name*
> *Why ain't black the same*
>
> *Well, if I say Hey black girl*
> *Lord, she try to ruin my game*

Dear God,

Sofia say to me today, I just can't understand it.

What that? I ast.

Why we ain't already kill them off.

Three years after she beat she out of the wash house, got her color and her weight back, look like her old self, just all time think bout killing somebody.

Too many to kill off, I say. Us outnumbered from the start. I speck we knock over one or two, though, here and there, through the years, I say.

We sit on a piece of old crate out near the edge of Miss Millie's yard. Rusty nails stick out long the bottom and when us move they creak gainst the wood.

Sofia job to watch the children play ball. The little boy throw the ball to the little girl, she try to catch it with her eyes shut. It roll up under Sofia foot.

Throw me the ball, say the little boy, with his hands on his hip. Throw me the ball.

Sofia mutter to herself, half to me. I'm here to watch, not to throw, she say. She don't make a move toward the ball.

Don't you hear me talking to you, he shout. He maybe six

years old, brown hair, ice blue eyes. He come steaming up to where us sit, haul off and kick Sofia leg. She swing her foot to one side and he scream.

What the trouble? I ast.

Done stab his foot with a rusty nail, Sofia say.

Sure enough, blood come leaking through his shoe.

His little sister come watch him cry. He turn redder and redder. Call his mama.

Miss Millie come running. She scared of Sofia. Everytime she talk to her it like she expect the worst. She don't stand close to her either. When she git a few yards from where us sit, she motion for Billy to come there.

My foot, he say to her.

Sofia do it? she ast.

Little girl pipe up. Billy do it his own self, she say. Trying to kick Sofia leg. The little girl dote on Sofia, always stick up for her. Sofia never notice, she as deef to the little girl as she is to her brother.

Miss Millie cut her eyes at her, put one arm round Billy shoulder and they limp into the back of the house. Little girl follow, wave bye-bye to us.

She seem like a right sweet little thing, I say to Sofia.

Who is? She frown.

The little girl, I say. What they call her, Eleanor Jane?

Yeah, say Sofia, with a real puzzle look on her face, I wonder why she was ever born.

Well, I say, us don't have to wonder that bout darkies.

She giggle. Miss Celie, she say, you just as crazy as you can be.

This the first giggle I heard in three years.

Dear God,

Sofia would make a dog laugh, talking about those people she work for. They have the nerve to try to make us think slavery fell through because of us, say Sofia. Like us didn't have sense enough to handle it. All the time breaking hoe handles and letting the mules loose in the wheat. But how anything they build can last a day is a wonder to me. They backward, she say. Clumsy, and unlucky.

Mayor _____ bought Miz Millie a new car, cause she said if colored could have cars then one for her was past due. So he bought her a car, only he refuse to show her how to drive it. Every day he come home from town he look at her, look out the window at her car, say, How you enjoying 'er Miz Millie. She fly off the sofa in a huff, slam the door going in the bathroom.

She ain't got no friends.

So one day she say to me, car been sitting out in the yard two months, Sofia, do you know how to drive? I guess she remembered first seeing me up gainst Buster Broadnax car.

Yes ma'am, I say. I'm slaving away cleaning that big post they got down at the bottom of the stair. They act real funny bout that post. No finger prints is sposed to be on it, ever.

Do you think you could teach me? she says.

One of Sofia children break in, the oldest boy. He tall and handsome, all the time serious. And mad a lot.

He say, Don't say slaving, Mama.

Sofia say, Why not? They got me in a little storeroom up under the house, hardly bigger than Odessa's porch, and just about as warm in the winter time. I'm at they beck and call all night and all day. They won't let me see my children. They won't let me see no mens. Well, after five years they let me see you once a year. I'm a slave, she say. What would you call it?

A captive, he say.

Sofia go on with her story, only look at him like she glad he hers.

So I say, Yes ma'am. I can teach you, if it the same kind of car I learned on.

Next thing you know there go me and Miz Millie all up and down the road. First I drive and she watch, then she start to try to drive and I watch her. Up and down the road. Soon as I finish cooking breakfast, putting it on the table, washing dishes and sweeping the floor—and just before I go git the mail out of the box down by the road—we go give Miz Millie her driving lesson.

Well, after while she got the hang of it, more or less. Then she really git it. Then one day when we come home from riding, she say to me, I'm gonna drive you home. Just like that.

Home? I ast.

Yes, she say. Home. You ain't been home or seen your children in a while, she say. Ain't that right?

I say, Yes ma'am. It been five years.

She say, That's a shame. You just go git your things right now. Here it is, Christmas. Go get your things. You can stay all day.

For all day I don't need nothing but what I got on, I say.

Fine, she say. Fine. Well git in.

Well, say Sofia, I was so use to sitting up there next to her teaching her how to drive, that I just naturally clammed into the front seat.

She stood outside on her side the car clearing her throat.

Finally she say, Sofia, with a little laugh, This is the South.

Yes ma'am, I say.

She clear her throat, laugh some more. Look where you sitting, she say.

I'm sitting where I always sit, I say.

That's the problem, she say. Have you ever seen a white person and a colored sitting side by side in a car, when one of 'em wasn't showing the other one how to drive it or clean it?

I got out the car, opened the back door and clammed in. She sat down up front. Off us traveled down the road, Miz Millie hair blowing all out the window.

It's real pretty country out this way, she say, when we hit the Marshall county road, coming toward Odessa's house.

Yes ma'am, I say.

Then us pull into the yard and all the children come crowding round the car. Nobody told them I was coming, so they don't know who I is. Except the oldest two. They fall on me, and hug me. And then all the little ones start to hug me too. I don't think they even notice I was sitting in the back of the car. Odessa and Jack come out after I was out, so they didn't see it.

Us all stand round kissing and hugging each other, Miz Millie just watching. Finally, she lean out the window and say, Sofia, you only got the rest of the day. I'll be back to pick you up at five o'clock. The children was all pulling me into the house, so sort of over my shoulder I say, Yes ma'am, and I thought I heard her drive off.

• • •

But fifteen minutes later, Marion says, That white lady still out there.

Maybe she going to wait to take you back, say Jack.

Maybe she sick, say Odessa. You always say how sickly they is.

I go out to the car, say Sofia, and guess what the matter is? The matter is, she don't know how to do nothing but go forward, and Jack and Odessa's yard too full of trees for that.

Sofia, she say, How you back this thing up?

I lean over the car window and try to show her which way to move the gears. But she flustered and all the children and Odessa and Jack all standing round the porch watching her.

I go round on the other side. Try to explain with my head poked through that window. She stripping gears aplenty by now. Plus her nose red and she look mad and frustrate both.

I clam in the back seat, lean over the back of the front, steady trying to show her how to operate the gears. Nothing happen. Finally the car stop making any sound. Engine dead.

Don't worry, I say, Odessa's husband Jack will drive you home. That's his pick-up right there.

Oh, she say, I couldn't ride in a pick-up with a strange colored man.

I'll ask Odessa to squeeze in too, I say. That would give me a chance to spend a little time with the children, I thought. But she say, No, I don't know her neither.

So it end up with me and Jack driving her back home in the pick-up, then Jack driving me to town to git a mechanic, and at five o'clock I was driving Miz Millie's car back to her house.

I spent fifteen minutes with my children.

And she been going on for months bout how ungrateful I is.

White folks is a miracle of affliction, say Sofia.

Dear God,

Shug write she got a big surprise, and she intend to bring it home for Christmas.

What it is? us wonder.

Mr. _____ think it a car for him. Shug making big money now, dress in furs all the time. Silk and satin too, and hats made out of gold.

Christmas morning us hear this motor outside the door. Us look out.

Hot diggidy dog, say Mr. _____ throwing on his pants. He rush to the door. I stand in front the glass trying to make something out my hair. It too short to be long, too long to be short. Too nappy to be kinky, too kinky to be nappy. No set color to it either. I give up, tie on a headrag.

I hear Shug cry, Oh, Albert. He say, *Shug*. I know they hugging. Then I don't hear nothing.

I run out the door. *Shug*, I say, and put out my arms. But before I know anything a skinny big toof man wearing red suspenders is all up in my face. Fore I can wonder whose dog he is, he hugging me.

Miss Celie, he say. Aw, Miss Celie. I heard so much about you. Feel like we old friends.

Shug standing back with a big grin.

This Grady, she say. This my husband.

The minute she say it I know I don't like Grady. I don't like his shape, I don't like his teef, I don't like his clothes. Seem like to me he smell.

Us been driving all night, she say. Nowhere to stop, you know. But here us is. She come over to Grady and put her arms round him, look up at him like he cute and he lean down and give her a kiss.

I glance round at Mr. ____. He look like the end of the world. I know I don't look no better.

And this my wedding present to us, say Shug. The car big and dark blue and say Packard on the front. Brand new, she say. She look at Mr. ____, take his arm, give it a little squeeze. While we here, Albert, she say, I want you to learn how to drive. She laugh. Grady drive like a fool, she say. I thought the polices was gonna catch us for sure.

Finally Shug really seem to notice me. She come over and hug me a long time. Us two married ladies now, she say. Two married ladies. And hungry, she say. What us got to eat?

Dear God,

Mr. ____ drink all through Christmas. Him and Grady. Me
and Shug cook, talk, clean the house, talk, fix up the tree, talk,
wake up in the morning, talk.

She singing all over the country these days. Everybody
know her name. She know everybody, too. Know Sophie
Tucker, know Duke Ellington, know folks I ain't never heard
of. And money. She make so much money she don't know
what to do with it. She got a fine house in Memphis, another
car. She got one hundred pretty dresses. A room full of shoes.
She buy Grady anything he think he want.

Where you find him at? I ast.

Up under my car, she say. The one at home. I drove it after
the oil gave out, kilt the engine. He the man fixed it. Us took
one look at one nother, that was it.

Mr. ____ feelings hurt, I say. I don't mention mine.

Aw, she say. That old stuff finally over with. You and Albert
feel just like family now. Anyhow, once you told me he beat
you, and won't work, I felt different about him. If you was my
wife, she say, I'd cover you up with kisses stead of licks, and
work hard for you too.

He ain't beat me much since you made him quit, I say. Just a slap now and then when he ain't got nothing else to do.

Yall make love any better? she ast.

Us try, I say. He try to play with the button but feel like his fingers dry. Us don't git nowhere much.

You still a virgin? she ast.

I reckon, I say.

Dear God,

Mr. ____ and Grady gone off in the car together. Shug ast me could she sleep with me. She cold in her and Grady bed all alone. Us talk bout this and that. Soon talk about making love. Shug don't actually say making love. She say something nasty. She say fuck.

She ast me, How was it with your children daddy?

The girls had a little separate room, I say, off to itself, connected to the house by a little plank walk. Nobody ever come in there but Mama. But one time when mama not at home, he come. Told me he want me to trim his hair. He bring the scissors and comb and brush and a stool. While I trim his hair he look at me funny. He a little nervous too, but I don't know why, till he grab hold of me and cram me up tween his legs.

I lay there quiet, listening to Shug breathe.

It hurt me, you know, I say. I was just going on fourteen. I never even thought bout men having nothing down there so big. It scare me just to see it. And the way it poke itself and grow.

Shug so quiet I think she sleep.

After he through, I say, he make me finish trimming his hair.

I sneak a look at Shug.

Oh, Miss Celie, she say. And put her arms round me They black and smooth and kind of glowy from the lamplight.

I start to cry too. I cry and cry and cry. Seem like it all come back to me, laying there in Shug arms. How it hurt and how much I was surprise. How it stung while I finish trimming his hair. How the blood drip down my leg and mess up my stocking. How he don't never look at me straight after that. And Nettie.

Don't cry, Celie, Shug say. Don't cry. She start kissing the water as it come down side my face.

After while I say, Mama finally ast how come she find his hair in the girls room if he don't never go in there like he say. That when he told her I had a boyfriend. Some boy he say he seen sneaking out the back door. It the boy's hair, he say, not his. You know how she love to cut anybody hair, he say.

I did love to cut hair, I say to Shug, since I was a little bitty thing. I'd run go git the scissors if I saw hair coming, and I'd cut and cut, long as I could. That how come I was the one cut his hair. But always before I cut it on the front porch. It got to the place where everytime I saw him coming with the scissors and the comb and the stool, I start to cry.

Shug say, Wellsah, and I thought it was only whitefolks do freakish things like that.

My mama die, I tell Shug. My sister Nettie run away. Mr. _____ come git me to take care his rotten children. He never ast me nothing bout myself. He clam on top of me and fuck and fuck, even when my head bandaged. Nobody ever love me, I say.

She say, I love you, Miss Celie. And then she haul off and kiss me on the mouth.

Um, she say, like she surprise. I kiss her back, say, *um*, too. Us kiss and kiss till us can't hardly kiss no more. Then us touch each other.

I don't know nothing bout it, I say to Shug.

I don't know much, she say.

Then I feels something real soft and wet on my breast, feel like one of my little lost babies mouth.

Way after while, I act like a little lost baby too.

Dear God,

Grady and Mr. ____ come staggering in round daybreak. Me and Shug sound asleep. Her back to me, my arms round her waist. What it like? Little like sleeping with mama, only I can't hardly remember ever sleeping with her. Little like sleeping with Nettie, only sleeping with Nettie never feel this good. It warm and cushiony, and I feel Shug's big tits sorta flop over my arms like suds. It feel like heaven is what it feel like, not like sleeping with Mr. ____ at all.

Wake up Sugar, I say. They back. And Shug roll over, hug me, and git out of the bed. She stagger into the other room and fall on the bed with Grady. Mr. ____ fall into bed next to me, drunk, and snoring before he hit the quilts.

I try my best to like Grady, even if he do wear red suspenders and bow ties. Even if he do spend Shug's money like he made it himself. Even if he do try to talk like somebody from the North. Memphis, Tennessee ain't North, even I know that. But one thing I sure nuff can't stand, the way he call Shug Mama.

I ain't your fucking mama, Shug say. But he don't pay her no mind.

Like when he be making goo-goo eyes at Squeak and Shug
sorta tease him about it, he say, Aw, Mama, you know I don't
mean no harm.

Shug like Squeak too, try to help her sing. They sit in
Odessa's front room with all the children crowded round
them singing and singing. Sometime Swain come with
his box, Harpo cook dinner, and me and Mr. ____ and the
prizefighter bring our preshation.

It nice.

Shug say to Squeak, I mean, Mary Agnes, You ought to sing
in public.

Mary Agnes say, *Naw.* She think cause she don't sing big
and broad like Shug nobody want to hear her. But Shug say
she wrong.

What about all them funny voices you hear singing in
church? Shug say. What about all them sounds that sound
good but they not the sounds you thought folks could make?
What bout that? Then she start moaning. Sound like death
approaching, angels can't prevent it. It raise the hair on the
back of your neck. But it really sound sort of like panthers
would sound if they could sing.

I tell you something else, Shug say to Mary Agnes, listening
to you sing, folks git to thinking bout a good screw.

Aw, *Miss Shug,* say Mary Agnes, changing color.

Shug say, What, too shamefaced to put singing and dancing
and fucking together? She laugh. That's the reason they call
what us sing the devil's music. Devils love to fuck. Listen, she
say, Let's go sing one night at Harpo place. Be like old times
for me. And if I bring you before the crowd, they better listen
with respect. Niggers don't know how to act, but if you git
through the first half of one song, you got 'em.

You reckon that's the truth? say Mary Agnes. She all big
eyed and delight.

I don't know if I want her to sing, say Harpo.

How come? ast Shug. That woman you got singing now can't git her ass *out* the church. Folks don't know whether to dance or creep to the mourner's bench. Plus, you dress Mary Agnes up the right way and you'll make piss pots of money. Yellow like she is, stringy hair and cloudy eyes, the men'll be crazy bout her. Ain't that right, Grady, she say.

Grady look little sheepish. Grin. Mama you don't miss a thing, he say.

And don't you forgit it, say Shug.

Dear God,
This the letter I been holding in my hand.

Dear Celie,
I know you think I am dead. But I am not. I been writing to you too, over the years, but Albert said you'd never hear from me again and since I never heard from you all this time, I guess he was right. Now I only write at Christmas and Easter hoping my letter get lost among the Christmas and Easter greetings, or that Albert get the holiday spirit and have pity on us.

There is so much to tell you that I don't know, hardly, where to begin—and anyway, you probably won't get this letter, either. I'm sure Albert is still the only one to take mail out of the box.

But if this do get through, one thing I want you to know, I love you, and I am not dead. And Olivia is fine and so is your son.

We are all coming home before the end of another year.
                                        Your loving sister, Nettie

• • •

One night in bed Shug ast me to tell her bout Nettie. What she like? Where she at?

I tell her how Mr. ____ try to turn her head. How Nettie refuse him, and how he say Nettie have to go.

Where she go? she ast.

I don't know, I say. She leave here.

And no word from her yet? she ast.

Naw, I say. Every day when Mr. ____ come from the mailbox I hope for news. But nothing come. She dead, I say.

Shug say, She wouldn't be someplace with funny stamps, you don't reckon? She look like she studying. Say, Sometimes when Albert and me walk up to the mailbox there be a letter with a lot of funny looking stamps. He never say nothing bout it, just put it in his inside pocket. One time I ast him could I look at the stamps but he said he'd take it out later. But he never did.

She was just on her way to town, I say. Stamps look like stamps round here. White men with long hair.

Hm, she say, look like a little fat white woman was on one. What your sister Nettie like? she ast. Smart?

Yes, Lord, I say. Smart as anything. Read the newspapers when she was little more than talking. Did figures like they was nothing. Talked real well too. And sweet. There never was a sweeter girl, I say. Eyes just brimming over with it. She love me too, I say to Shug.

She tall or short? Shug ast. What kind of dress she like to wear? What her birthday? What her favorite color? Can she cook? Sew? What about hair?

Everything bout Nettie she want to know.

I talk so much my voice start to go. Why you want to know so much bout Nettie? I ast.

Cause she the only one you ever love, she say, sides me.

Dear God,

All of a sudden Shug buddy-buddy again with Mr. ____.
They sit on the steps, go down Harpo's. Walk to the mailbox.

Shug laugh and laugh when he got anything to say. Show
teef and tits aplenty.

Me and Grady try to carry on like us civilize. But it hard.
When I hear Shug laugh I want to choke her, slap Mr. ____
face.

All this week I suffer. Grady and me feel so down he turn
to reefer, I turn to prayer.

Saturday morning Shug put Nettie letter in my lap. Little
fat queen of England stamps on it, plus stamps that got
peanuts, coconuts, rubber trees and say Africa. I don't know
where England at. Don't know where Africa at either. So I still
don't know where Nettie at.

He been keeping your letters, say Shug.

Naw, I say. Mr. ____ mean sometimes, but he not that
mean.

She say, Humpf, he that mean.

But how come he do it? I ast. He know Nettie mean
everything in the world to me.

Shug say she don't know, but us gon find out.

Us seal the letter up again and put it back in Mr. _____ pocket.

He walk round with it in his coat all day. He never mention it. Just talk and laugh with Grady, Harpo and Swain, and try to learn how to drive Shug car.

I watch him so close, I begin to feel a lightening in the head. Fore I know anything I'm standing hind his chair with his razor open.

Then I hear Shug laugh, like something just too funny. She say to me, I know I told you I need something to cut this hangnail with, but Albert git real niggerish bout his razor.

Mr. _____ look behind him. Put that down, he say. Women, always needing to cut this and shave that, and always gumming up the razor.

Shug got her hand on the razor now. She say, Oh it look dull anyway. She take and sling it back in the shaving box.

All day long I act just like Sofia. I stutter. I mutter to myself. I stumble bout the house crazy for Mr. _____ blood. In my mind, he falling dead every which a way. By time night come, I can't speak. Every time I open my mouth nothing come out but a little burp.

Shug tell everybody I got a fever and she put me to bed. It probably catching, she say to Mr. _____. Maybe you better sleep somewhere else. But she stay with me all night long. I don't sleep. I don't cry. I don't do nothing. I'm cold too. Pretty soon I think maybe I'm dead.

Shug hold me close to her and sometimes talk.

One thing my mama hated me for was how much I love to fuck, she say. She never love to do nothing had anything to do with touching nobody, she say. I try to kiss her, she turn her mouth away. Say, Cut that out Lillie, she say. Lillie Shug's real name. She just so sweet they call her Shug.

My daddy love me to kiss and hug him, but she didn't like
the looks of that. So when I met Albert, and once I got in his
arms, nothing could git me out. It was good, too, she say. You
know for me to have three babies by Albert and Albert weak
as he is, it had to be good.

I had every one of my babies at home, too. Midwife come,
preacher come, a bunch of the good ladies from the church.
Just when I hurt so much I don't know my own name, they
think a good time to talk bout repent.

She laugh. I was too big a fool to repent. Then she say, I
loved me some Albert _____.

I don't even want to say nothing. Where I'm at it peaceful.
It calm. No Albert there. No Shug. Nothing.

Shug say, the last baby did it. They turned me out. I went
to stay with my mama wild sister in Memphis. She just like
me, Mama say. She drink, she fight, she love mens to death.
She work in a roadhouse. Cook. Feed fifty men, screw
fifty-five.

Shug talk and talk.

And dance, she say. Nobody dance like Albert when he was
young. Sometime us did the moochie for a hour. After that,
nothing to do but go somewhere and lay down. And funny.
Albert was *so funny*. He kept me laughing. How come he ain't
funny no more? she ast. How come he never hardly laugh?
How come he don't dance? she say. Good God, Celie, she say,
What happen to the man I love?

She quiet a little while. Then she say, I was so surprise
when I heard he was going to marry Annie Julia, she say. Too
surprise to be hurt. I didn't believe it. After all, Albert knew as
well as me that love would have to go some to be better than
ours. Us had the kind of love couldn't be improve. That's what
I thought.

But, he weak, she say. His daddy told him I'm trash, my

mama trash before me. His brother say the same. Albert try to
stand up for us, git knock down. One reason they give him for
not marrying me is cause I have children.

But they *his*, I told old Mr. _____.

How us know? He ast.

Poor Annie Julia, Shug say. She never had a chance. I was
so mean, and so wild, Lord. I used to go round saying, I don't
care who he married to, I'm gonna fuck him. She stop talking
a minute. Then she say, And I did, too. Us fuck so much in the
open us give fucking a bad name.

But he fuck Annie Julia too, she say, and she didn't have
nothing, not even a liking for him. Her family forgot about
her once she married. And then Harpo and all the children
start to come. Finally she start to sleep with that man that
shot her down. Albert beat her. The children dragged on
her. Sometimes I wonder what she thought about while she
died.

I know what I'm thinking bout, I think. Nothing. And as
much of it as I can.

I went to school with Annie Julia, Shug say. She was pretty,
man. Black as anything, and skin just as smooth. Big black
eyes look like moons. And sweet too. Hell, say Shug, I liked
her myself. Why I hurt her so? I used to keep Albert away
from home for a week at the time. She'd come and beg him
for money to buy groceries for the children.

I feel a few drops of water on my hand.

And when I come here, say Shug, I treated you so mean.
Like you was a servant. And all because Albert married you.
And I didn't even want him for a husband, she say. I never
really wanted Albert for a husband. But just to choose me, you
know, cause nature had already done it. Nature said, You two
folks, hook up, cause you a good example of how it sposed to
go. I didn't want nothing to be able to go against that. But

what was good tween us must have been nothing but bodies, she say. Cause I don't know the Albert that don't dance, can't hardly laugh, never talk bout nothing, beat you and hid your sister Nettie's letters. Who he?

I don't know nothing, I think. And glad of it.

Dear God,

Now that I know Albert hiding Nettie's letters, I know exactly where they is. They in his trunk. Everything that mean something to Albert go in his trunk. He keep it locked up tight, but Shug can git the key.

One night when Mr. ____ and Grady gone, us open the trunk. Us find a lot of Shug's underclothes, some nasty picture postcards, and way down under his tobacco, Nettie's letters. Bunches and bunches of them. Some fat, some thin. Some open, some not.

How us gon do this? I ast Shug.

She say, Simple. We take the letters out of the envelopes, leave the envelopes just like they is. I don't think he look in this corner of the trunk much, she say.

I heated the stove, put on the kettle. Us steam and steam the envelopes until we had all the letters laying on the table. Then us put the envelopes back inside the trunk.

I'm gonna put them in some kind of order for you, say Shug.

Yeah, I say, but don't let's do it in here, let's go in you and Grady room.

So she got up and us went into they little room. Shug sat in a chair by the bed with all Nettie letters spread round her, I got on the bed with the pillows behind my back.

These the first ones, say Shug. They postmark right here.

Dear Celie, *the first letter say,*

You've got to fight and get away from Albert. He ain't no good.

When I left you all's house, walking, he followed me on his horse. When we was well out of sight of the house he caught up with me and started trying to talk. You know how he do, You sure is looking fine, Miss Nettie, and stuff like that. I tried to ignore him and walk faster, but my bundles was heavy and the sun was hot. After while I had to rest, and that's when he got down from his horse and started to try to kiss me, and drag me back in the woods.

Well, I started to fight him, and with God's help, I hurt him bad enough to make him let me alone. But he was some mad. He said because of what I'd done I'd never hear from you again, and you would never hear from me.

I was so mad myself I was shaking.

Anyhow, I got a ride into town on somebody's wagon. And that same somebody pointed me in the direction of the Reverend Mr. ____'s place. And what was my surprise when a little girl opened the door and she had your eyes set in your face.

love, Nettie

Next one said,

Dear Celie,

I keep thinking it's too soon to look for a letter from you. And I know how busy you is with all Mr. ___'s children. But I miss you so much. Please write to me, soon as you have a chance. Every day I think about you. Every minute.

The lady you met in town is name Corrine. The little girl's name is Olivia. The husband's name is Samuel. The little boy's name is Adam. They are sanctified religious and very good to me. They live in a nice house next to the church where Samuel preaches, and we spend a lot of time on church business. I say "we" because they always try to include me in everything they do, so I don't feel so left out and alone.

But God, I miss you, Celie. I think about the time you laid yourself down for me. I love you with all my heart,

Your sister, Nettie

Next one say,

Dearest Celie,

By now I am almost crazy. I think Albert told me the truth, and that he is not giving you my letters. The only person I can think of who could help us out is Pa, but I don't want him to know where I am.

I asked Samuel if he would visit you and Mr. ____, just to see how you are. But he says he can't risk putting himself between man and wife, especially when he don't know them. And I felt bad for having to ask him, he and Corrine have been so nice to me. But my heart is breaking. It is breaking because I can not find any work in this town, and I will have to leave. After I leave, what will happen to us? How will we ever know what is going on?

Corrine and Samuel and the children are part of a group of people called Missionaries, of the American and African Missionary Society. They have ministered to the Indians out west and are ministering to the poor of this town. All in preparation for the work they feel they were born for, missionary work in Africa.

I dread parting from them because in the short time we've been together they've been like family to me. Like family might have been, I mean.

Write if you can. Here are some stamps.

love, Nettie

Next one, fat, dated two months later, say,

Dear Celie,

I wrote a letter to you almost every day on the ship coming to Africa. But by the time we docked I was so down, I tore them into little pieces and dropped them into the water. Albert is not going to let you have my letters and so what use is there in writing them. That's the way I felt when I tore them up and sent them to you on the waves. But now I feel different.

I remember one time you said your life made you feel so ashamed you couldn't even talk about it to God, you had to write it, bad as you thought your writing was. Well, now I know what you meant. And whether God will read letters or no, I know you will go on writing them; which is guidance enough for me. Anyway, when I don't write to you I feel as bad as I do when I don't pray, locked up in myself and choking on my own heart. I am so *lonely*, Celie.

The reason I am in Africa is because one of the missionaries that was supposed to go with Corrine and Samuel to help with the children and with setting up a school suddenly married a man who was afraid to let her go, and refused to come to Africa with her. So there they were, all set to go, with a ticket suddenly available and no missionary to give it to. At the same time, I wasn't able to find a job anywhere around town. But I never dreamed of going to Africa! I never even thought about it as a real place, though Samuel and Corrine and even the children talked about it all the time.

Miss Beasley used to say it was a place overrun with savages who didn't wear clothes. Even Corrine and Samuel thought like this at times. But they know a lot more about it than Miss Beasley or any of our other teachers, and besides, they spoke of all the good things they could do for the downtrodden people from whom they sprang. People who need Christ and good medical advice.

One day I was in town with Corrine and we saw the mayor's wife and her maid. The mayor's wife was shopping—going in and out of stores—and her maid was waiting for her on the street and taking the packages. I don't know if you have ever seen the mayor's wife. She looks like a wet cat. And there was her maid looking like the very last person in the world you'd expect to see waiting on anybody, and in particular not on anybody that looked like that.

I spoke. But just speaking to me seemed to make her embarrassed and she suddenly sort of erased herself. It was the strangest thing, Celie! One minute I was saying howdy to a living woman. The next minute nothing living was there. Only its shape.

All that night I thought about it. Then Samuel and Corrine told me what they'd heard about how she got to be the mayor's maid. That she attacked the mayor, and then the mayor and his wife took her from the prison to work in their home.

In the morning I started asking questions about Africa and started reading all the books Samuel and Corrine have on the subject.

Did you know there were great cities in Africa, greater than Milledgeville or even Atlanta, thousands of years ago? That the Egyptians who built the pyramids and enslaved the Israelites were colored? That Egypt is in Africa? That the Ethiopia we read about in the Bible meant all of Africa?

Well, I read and I read until I thought my eyes would fall out. I read where the Africans sold us because they loved money more than their own sisters and brothers. How we came to America in ships. How we were made to work.

I hadn't realized I was so *ignorant*, Celie. The little I knew about my own self wouldn't have filled a thimble! And to think Miss Beasley always said I was the smartest child she ever taught! But one thing I do thank her for, for teaching me to learn for myself, by reading and studying and writing a clear hand. And for keeping alive in me somehow the desire to *know*. So when Corrine and Samuel asked me if I would come with them and help them build a school in the middle of Africa, I said yes. But only if they would teach me everything they knew to make me useful as a missionary and someone they would not be ashamed to call a friend. They agreed to this condition, and my real education began at that time.

They have been as good as their word. And I study everything night and day.

Oh, Celie, there are colored people in the world who want us to know! Want us to grow and see the light! They are not all mean like Pa and Albert, or beaten down like Ma was. Corrine and Samuel have a wonderful marriage. Their only sorrow in the beginning was that they could not have children. And then, they say, "God" sent them Olivia and Adam.

I wanted to say, "God" has sent you their sister and aunt, but I didn't. Yes, their children, sent by "God" are your children, Celie. And they are being brought up in love, Christian charity and awareness of God. And now "God" has sent me to watch over them, to protect and cherish them. To lavish all the love I feel for you on them. It is a miracle, isn't it? And no doubt impossible for you to believe.

But on the other hand, if you can believe I am in Africa, and I am, you can believe anything.

Your sister, Nettie

The next letter after that one say,

Dear Celie,

While we were in town Corrine bought cloth to make me
two sets of traveling outfits. One olive green and the other
gray. Long gored skirts and suit jackets to be worn with
white cotton blouses and lace-up boots. She also bought me a
woman's boater with a checkered band.

Although I work for Corrine and Samuel and look after the
children, I don't feel like a maid. I guess this is because they
teach me, and I teach the children and there's no beginning
or end to teaching and learning and working—it all runs
together.

Saying good-bye to our church group was hard. But happy,
too. Everyone has such high hopes for what can be done in
Africa. Over the pulpit there is a saying: *Ethiopia Shall Stretch
Forth Her Hands to God.* Think what it means that Ethiopia
is Africa! All the Ethiopians in the bible were colored. It had
never occurred to me, though when you read the bible it is
perfectly plain if you pay attention only to the words. It is the
pictures in the bible that fool you. The pictures that illustrate

the words. All of the people are white and so you just think
all the people from the bible were white too. But really *white*
white people lived somewhere else during those times. That's
why the bible says that Jesus Christ had hair like lamb's wool.
Lamb's wool is not straight, Celie. It isn't even curly.

What can I tell you about New York—or even about
the train that took us there! We had to ride in the sit-down
section of the train, but Celie, there are beds on trains! And a
restaurant! And toilets! The beds come down out of the walls,
over the tops of the seats, and are called berths. Only white
people can ride in the beds and use the restaurant. And they
have different toilets from colored.

One white man on the platform in South Carolina asked
us where we were going—we had got off the train to get
some fresh air and to dust the grit and dust out of our clothes.
When we said Africa he looked offended and tickled too.
Niggers going to Africa, he said to his wife. Now I have seen
everything.

When we got to New York we were tired and dirty. But
so excited! Listen, Celie, New York is a *beautiful* city. And
colored own a whole section of it, called Harlem. There are
colored people in more fancy motor cars than I thought
existed, and living in houses that are finer than any white
person's house down home. There are more than a hundred
churches! And we went to every one of them. And I stood
before each congregation with Samuel and Corrine and the
children and sometimes our mouths just dropped open from
the generosity and goodness of those Harlem people's hearts.
They live in such beauty and dignity, Celie. And they give
and give and then reach down and give some more, when the
name "Africa" is mentioned.

They *love* Africa. They defend it at the drop of a hat.
And speaking of hats, if we had passed our hats alone they

would not have been enough to hold all the donations to our enterprise. Even the children dredged up their pennies. Please give these to the children of Africa, they said. They were all dressed so beautifully, too, Celie. I wish you could have seen them. There is a fashion in Harlem now for boys to wear something called knickers—sort of baggy pants, fitted tight just below the knee, and for girls to wear garlands of flowers in their hair. They must be the most beautiful children alive, and Adam and Olivia couldn't take their eyes off them.

Then there were the dinners we were invited to, the breakfasts, lunches, and suppers. I gained five pounds just from tasting. I was too excited to really eat.

And all the people have indoor toilets, Celie. And gas or electric lights!

Well, we had two weeks of study in the Olinka dialect, which the people in this region speak. Then we were examined by a doctor (colored!) and given medical supplies for ourselves and for our host village by the Missionary Society of New York. It is run by white people and they didn't say anything about caring about Africa, but only about duty. There is already a white woman missionary not far from our village who has lived in Africa for the past twenty years. She is said to be much loved by the natives even though she thinks they are an entirely different species from what she calls Europeans. Europeans are white people who live in a place called Europe. That is where the white people down home came from. She says an African daisy and an English daisy are both flowers, but totally different kinds. The man at the Society says she is successful because she doesn't "coddle" her charges. She also speaks their language. He is a white man who looks at us as if we cannot possibly be as good with the Africans as this woman is.

My spirits sort of drooped after being at the Society. On

every wall there was a picture of a white man. Somebody
called Speke, somebody called Livingstone. Somebody called
Daly. Or was it Stanley? I looked for a picture of the white
woman but didn't see one. Samuel looked a little sad too,
but then he perked up and reminded us that there is one big
advantage we have. We are not white. We are not Europeans.
We are black like the Africans themselves. And that we and
the Africans will be working for a common goal: the uplift of
black people everywhere.

Your sister, Nettie

Dear Celie,

Samuel is a big man. He dresses in black almost all the time, except for his white clerical collar. And *he* is black. Until you see his eyes you think he's somber, even mean, but he has the most thoughtful and gentle brown eyes. When he says something it settles you, because he never says anything off the top of his head and he's never out to dampen your spirit or to hurt. Corrine is a lucky woman to have him as her husband.

But let me tell you about the ship! The ship, called The Malaga, was three stories high! And we had rooms (called cabins) with beds. Oh, Celie, to lie in a bed in the middle of the ocean! And the ocean! Celie, more water than you can imagine in one place. It took us two weeks to cross it! And then we were in England, which is a country full of white people and some of them very nice and with their own Anti-Slavery & Missionary Society. The churches in England were also very eager to help us and white men and women, who looked just like the ones at home, invited us to their gatherings and into their homes for tea, and to talk about our work. "Tea" to the English is really a picnic indoors. Plenty of sandwiches and cookies and of course hot tea. We all used the same cups and plates.

Everyone said I seemed very young to be a missionary, but Samuel said that I was very willing, and that, anyway, my primary duties would be helping with the children and teaching a kindergarten class or two.

Our work began to seem somewhat clearer in England because the English have been sending missionaries to Africa and India and China and God knows where all, for over a hundred years. And the things they have brought back! We spent a morning in one of their museums and it was packed with jewels, furniture, fur carpets, swords, clothing, even *tombs* from all the countries they have been. From Africa they have *thousands* of vases, jars, masks, bowls, baskets, statues—and they are all so beautiful it is hard to imagine that the people who made them don't still exist. And yet the English assure us they do not. Although Africans once had a better civilization than the European (though of course even the English do not say this: I get this from reading a man named J. A. Rogers) for several centuries they have fallen on hard times. "Hard times" is a phrase the English love to use, when speaking of Africa. And it is easy to forget that Africa's "hard times" were made harder by them. Millions and millions of Africans were captured and sold into slavery—you and me, Celie! And whole cities were destroyed by slave catching wars. Today the people of Africa—having murdered or sold into slavery their strongest folks—are riddled by disease and sunk in spiritual and physical confusion. They believe in the devil and worship the dead. Nor can they read or write.

Why did they sell us? How could they have done it? And why do we still love them? These were the thoughts I had as we tramped through the chilly streets of London. I studied England on a map, so neat and serene, and I became hopeful in spite of myself that much good for Africa is possible, given hard work and the right frame of mind. And then we sailed for Africa. Leaving Southampton, England on the 24th of July and arriving in Monrovia, Liberia on the 12th of September. On the way we stopped in Lisbon, Portugal and Dakar, Senegal.

Monrovia was the last place we were among people we were somewhat used to, since it is an African country that was "founded" by ex-slaves from America who came back to Africa to live. Had any of their parents or grandparents been sold *from* Monrovia, I wondered, and what was their feeling, once sold as slaves, now coming back, with close ties to the country that bought them, to rule.

Celie, I must stop now. The sun is not so hot now and I must prepare for the afternoon classes and vesper service.

I wish you were with me, or I with you.

My love,
Your sister, Nettie

Dearest Celie,

It was the funniest thing to stop over in Monrovia after my first glimpse of Africa, which was Senegal. The capital of Senegal is Dakar and the people speak their own language, Senegalese I guess they would call it, and French. They are the blackest people I have ever seen, Celie. They are black like the people we are talking about when we say, "So and so is blacker than black, he's *blue*black." They are so black, Celie, they shine. Which is something else folks down home like to say about real black folks. But Celie, try to imagine a city full of these shining, blueblack people wearing brilliant blue robes with designs like fancy quilt patterns. Tall, thin, with long necks and straight backs. Can you picture it at all, Celie? Because I felt like I was seeing black for the first time. And Celie, there is something magical about it. Because the black is so black the eye is simply dazzled, and then there is the shining that seems to come, really, from moonlight, it is so luminous, but their skin glows even in the sun.

But I did not really like the Senegalese I met in the market. They were concerned only with their sale of produce. If we did not buy, they looked through us as quickly as they looked through the white French people who live there. Somehow I had not expected to see any white people in Africa, but they are here in droves. And not all are missionaries.

There are bunches of them in Monrovia, too. And the president, whose last name is Tubman, has some in his cabinet. He also has a lot of white-looking colored men in his cabinet. On our second evening in Monrovia we had tea at the presidential palace. It looks very much like the American white house (where our president lives) Samuel says. The president talked a good bit about his efforts trying to develop the country and about his problems with the natives, who don't want to work to help build the country up. It was the first time I'd heard a black man use that word. I knew that to white people all colored people are natives. But he cleared his throat and said he only meant "native" to Liberia. I did not see any of these "natives" in his cabinet. And none of the cabinet members' wives could pass for natives. Compared to them in their silks and pearls, Corrine and I were barely dressed, let alone dressed for the occasion. But I think the women we saw at the palace spend a lot of their time dressing. Still, they look dissatisfied. Not like the cheery schoolteachers we saw only by chance, as they herded their classes down to the beach for a swim.

Before we left we visited one of the large cacoa plantations they have. Nothing but cacoa trees as far as the eye can see. And whole villages built right in the middle of the fields. We watched the weary families come home from work, still carrying their cacoa seed buckets in their hands (these double as lunch buckets next day), and sometimes—if they are women—their children on their backs. As tired as they are, they sing! Celie. Just like we do at home. Why do tired people sing? I asked Corrine. Too tired to do anything else, she said. Besides, they don't own the cacoa fields, Celie, even president

Tubman doesn't own them. People in a place called Holland do. The people who make Dutch chocolate. And there are overseers who make sure the people work hard, who live in stone houses in the corners of the fields.

Again I must go. Everyone is in bed and I am writing by lamplight. But the light is attracting so many bugs I am being eaten alive. I have bites everywhere, including my scalp and the bottoms of my feet.

But—

Did I mention my first sight of the African coast? Something struck in me, in my soul, Celie, like a large bell, and I just vibrated. Corrine and Samuel felt the same. And we kneeled down right on deck and gave thanks to God for letting us see the land for which our mothers and fathers cried—and lived and died—to see again.

Oh, Celie! Will I ever be able to tell you all?

I dare not ask, I know. But leave it all to God.

Your everloving sister, Nettie

Dear God,

What with being shock, crying and blowing my nose, and trying to puzzle out words us don't know, it took a long time to read just the first two or three letters. By the time us got up to where she good and settled in Africa, Mr. _____ and Grady come home.

Can you handle it? ast Shug.

How I'm gon keep from killing him, I say.

Don't kill, she say. Nettie be coming home before long. Don't make her have to look at you like us look at Sofia.

But it so hard, I say, while Shug empty her suitcase and put the letters inside.

Hard to be Christ too, say Shug. But he manage. Remember that. Thou Shalt Not Kill, He said. And probably wanted to add on to that, Starting with me. He knowed the fools he was dealing with.

But Mr. _____ not Christ. I'm not Christ, I say.

You somebody to Nettie, she say. And she be pissed if you change on her while she on her way home.

Us hear Grady and Mr. _____ in the kitchen. Dishes rattling, safe door open and shut.

Naw, I think I feel better if I kill him, I say. I feels sickish. Numb, now.

Naw you won't. Nobody feel better for killing nothing. They feel *something* is all.

That better than nothing.

Celie, she say, Nettie not the only one you got to worry bout.

Say what, I ast.

Me, Celie, think about me a little bit. Miss Celie, if you kill Albert, Grady be all I got left. I can't even stand the thought of that.

I laugh, thinking bout Grady's big toofs.

Make Albert let me sleep with you from now on, while you here, I say.

And somehow or other, she do.

Dear God,

Us sleep like sisters, me and Shug. Much as I still want to be with her, much as I love to look, my titties stay soft, my little button never rise. Now I know I'm dead. But she say, Naw, just being mad, grief, wanting to kill somebody will make you feel this way. Nothing to worry about. Titties gonna perk up, button gonna rise again.

I loves to hug up, period, she say. Snuggle. Don't need nothing else right now.

Yeah, I say. Hugging is good. Snuggle. All of it's good.

She say, Times like this, lulls, us ought to do something different.

Like what? I ast.

Well, she say, looking me up and down, let's make you some pants.

What I need pants for? I say. I ain't no man.

Don't git uppity, she say. But you don't have a dress do nothing for you. You not made like no dress pattern, neither.

I don't know, I say. Mr. _____ not going to let his wife wear pants.

Why not? say Shug. You do all the work around here. It's a

scandless, the way you look out there plowing in a dress. How you keep from falling over it or getting the plow caught in it is beyond me.

Yeah? I say.

Yeah. And another thing, I used to put on Albert's pants when we was courting. And he one time put on my dress.

No he didn't.

Yes he did. He use to be a lot of fun. Not like now. But he loved to see me in pants. It was like a red flag to a bull.

Ugh, I say. I could just picture it, and I didn't like it one bit.

Well, you know how they is, say Shug.

What us gon make 'em out of, I say.

We have to git our hands on somebody's army uniform, say Shug. For practice. That good strong material and free.

Jack, I say. Odessa's husband.

Okay, she say. And everyday we going to read Nettie's letters and sew.

A needle and not a razor in my hand, I think.

She don't say nothing else, just come over to me and hug.

Dear God,

Now I know Nettie alive I begin to strut a little bit. Think, When she come home us leave here. Her and me and our two children. What they look like, I wonder. But it hard to think bout them. I feels shame. More than love, to tell the truth. Anyway, is they all right here? Got good sense and all? Shug say children got by incest turn into dunces. Incest part of the devil's plan.

But I think bout Nettie.

It's hot, here, Celie, she write. Hotter than July. Hotter than August and July. Hot like cooking dinner on a big stove in a little kitchen in August and July. Hot.

Dear Celie,

We were met at the ship by an African from the village we are settling in. His Christian name is Joseph. He is short and fat, with hands that seem not to have any bones in them. When he shook my hand it felt like something soft and damp was falling and I almost caught it. He speaks a little English, what they call pidgin English. It is very different from the way we speak English, but somehow familiar. He helped us unload our things from the ship into the boats that came out to get us. These boats are really dugout canoes, like the Indians had, the ones you see in pictures. With all our belongings we filled three of them, and a fourth one carried our medical and teaching supplies.

Once in the boat we were entertained by the songs of our boatmen as they tried to outpaddle each other to the shore. They paid very little attention to us or our cargo. When we reached the shore they didn't bother to help us alight from the boat and actually set some of our supplies right down in the water. As soon as they had browbeat poor Samuel out of a tip that Joseph said was too big, they were off hallooing another group of people who were waiting at the edge of the water to be taken to the ship.

The port is pretty, but too shallow for large ships to use. So there is a good business for the boatmen, during the season the ships come by. These boatmen were all considerably larger and more muscular than Joseph, though all of them, including Joseph, are a deep chocolate brown. Not black, like the Senegalese. And Celie, they all have the strongest, cleanest, whitest teeth! I was thinking about teeth a lot on the voyage over, because I had toothache nearly the entire time. You know how rotten my back teeth are. And in England I was struck by the English people's teeth. So crooked, usually, and blackish with decay. I wondered if it was the English water. But the Africans' teeth remind me of horses' teeth, they are so fully formed, straight and strong.

The port's "town" is the size of the hardware store in town. Inside there are stalls filled with cloth, hurricane lamps and oil, mosquito netting, camp bedding, hammocks, axes and hoes and machetes and other tools. The whole place is run by a white man, but some of the stalls that sell produce are rented out to Africans. Joseph showed us things we needed to buy. A large iron pot for boiling water and our clothes, a zinc basin. Mosquito netting. Nails. Hammer and saw and pick-ax. Oil and lamps.

Since there was nowhere to sleep in the port, Joseph hired some porters from among the young men loafing around the trading post and we left right away for Olinka, some four days march through the bush. Jungle, to you. Or maybe not. Do you know what a jungle is? Well. Trees and trees and then more trees on top of that. And big. They are so big they look like they were built. And vines. And ferns. And little animals. Frogs. Snakes too, according to Joseph. But thank God we did not see any of these, only humpbacked lizards as big as your arm which the people here catch and eat.

They love meat. All the people in this village. Sometimes if you can't get them to do anything any other way, you start to mention meat, either a little piece extra you just happen to have or maybe, if you want them to do something big, you talk about a barbecue. Yes, a barbecue. They remind me of folks at home!

Well, we got here. And I thought I would never get the kinks out of my hips from being carried in a hammock the whole way. Everybody in the village crowded round us. Coming out of little round huts with something that I thought was straw on top of them but is really a kind of leaf that grows everywhere. They pick it and dry it and lay it so it overlaps to make the roof rainproof. This part is women's work. Menfolks drive the stakes for the hut and sometimes help build the walls with mud and rock from the streams.

You never saw such curious faces as the village folks surrounded us with. At first they just looked. Then one or two of the women touched my and Corrine's dresses. My dress was so dirty round the hem from dragging on the ground for three nights of cooking round a campfire that I was ashamed

of myself. But then I took a look at the dresses they were
wearing. Most looked like they'd been drug across the yard
by the pigs. And they don't fit. So then they moved up a little
bit—nobody saying a word yet—and touched our hair. Then
looked down at our shoes. We looked at Joseph. Then he told
us they were acting this way because the missionaries before
us were white people, and vice versa. The men had been to
the port, some of them, and had seen the white merchant, so
they knew white men could be something else too. But the
women had never been to the port and the only white person
they'd seen was the missionary they had buried a year ago.

Samuel asked if they'd ever seen the white woman
missionary twenty miles farther on, and he said no. Twenty
miles through the jungle is a very long trip. The men might
hunt up to ten miles around the village, but the women stayed
close to their huts and fields.

Then one of the women asked a question. We looked at
Joseph. He said the woman wanted to know if the children
belonged to me or to Corrine or to both of us. Joseph said
they belonged to Corrine. The woman looked us both over,
and said something else. We looked at Joseph. He said the
woman said they both looked like me. We all laughed politely.

Then another woman had a question. She wanted to know
if I was also Samuel's wife.

Joseph said no, that I was a missionary just like Samuel
and Corrine. Then someone said they never suspected
missionaries could have children. Then another said he never
dreamed missionaries could be black.

Then someone said, That the new missionaries would
be black and two of them women was exactly what he had
dreamed, and just last night, too.

By now there was a lot of commotion. Little heads began
to pop from behind mothers' skirts and over big sisters'

shoulders. And we were sort of swept along among the villagers, about three hundred of them, to a place without walls but with a leaf roof, where we all sat down on the ground, men in front, women and children behind. Then there was loud whispering among some very old men who looked like the church elders back home—with their baggy trousers and shiny, ill-fitting coats—Did black missionaries drink palm wine?

Corrine looked at Samuel and Samuel looked at Corrine. But me and the children were already drinking it, because someone had already put the little brown clay glasses in our hands and we were too nervous not to start sipping.

We got there around four o'clock, and sat under the leaf canopy until nine. We had our first meal there, a chicken and groundnut (peanut) stew which we ate with our fingers. But mostly we listened to songs and watched dances that raised lots of dust.

The biggest part of the welcoming ceremony was about the roofleaf, which Joseph interpreted for us as one of the villagers recited the story that it is based upon. The people of this village think they have always lived on the exact spot where their village now stands. And this spot has been good to them. They plant cassava fields that yield huge crops. They plant groundnuts that do the same. They plant yam and cotton and millet. All kinds of things. But once, a long time ago, one man in the village wanted more than his share of land to plant. He wanted to make more crops so as to use his surplus for trade with the white men on the coast. Because he was chief at the time, he gradually took more and more of the common land, and took more and more wives to work it. As his greed increased he also began to cultivate the land on which the roofleaf grew. Even his wives were upset by this and tried to complain, but they were lazy women and no one paid any attention to them. Nobody could remember a time when roofleaf did not exist in overabundant amounts. But eventually, the greedy chief took so much of this land that even the elders were disturbed. So he simply bought them off—with axes and cloth and cooking pots that he got from the coast traders.

But then there came a great storm during the rainy season that destroyed all the roofs on all the huts in the village, and the people discovered to their dismay that there was no longer any roofleaf to be found. Where roofleaf had flourished from time's beginning, there was cassava. Millet. Groundnuts.

For six months the heavens and the winds abused the people of Olinka. Rain came down in spears, stabbing away the mud of their walls. The wind was so fierce it blew the rocks out of the walls and into the people's cooking pots. Then cold rocks, shaped like millet balls, fell from the sky, striking everyone, men and women and children alike, and giving them fevers. The children fell ill first, then their parents. Soon the village began to die. By the end of the rainy season, half the village was gone.

The people prayed to their gods and waited impatiently for the seasons to change. As soon as the rain stopped they rushed to the old roofleaf beds and tried to find the old roots. But of the endless numbers that had always grown there, only a few dozen remained. It was five years before the roofleaf became plentiful again. During those five years many more in the village died. Many left, never to return. Many were eaten by animals. Many, many were sick. The chief was given all his storebought utensils and forced to walk away from the village forever. His wives were given to other men.

On the day when all the huts had roofs again from the roofleaf, the villagers celebrated by singing and dancing and telling the story of the roofleaf. The roofleaf became the thing they worship.

Looking over the heads of the children at the end of this tale, I saw coming slowly towards us, a large brown spiky thing as big as a room, with a dozen legs walking slowly and carefully under it. When it reached our canopy, it was presented to us. It was our roof.

As it approached, the people bowed down.

The white missionary before you would not let us have this ceremony, said Joseph. But the Olinka like it very much. We know a roofleaf is not Jesus Christ, but in its own humble way, is it not God?

So there we sat, Celie, face to face with the Olinka God. And Celie, I was so tired and sleepy and full of chicken and groundnut stew, my ears ringing with song, that all that Joseph said made perfect sense to me.

I wonder what you will make of all this?

I send my love,

Your sister, Nettie

Dear Celie,

It has been a long time since I had time to write. But always, no matter what I'm doing, I am writing to you. Dear Celie, I say in my head in the middle of Vespers, the middle of the night, while cooking, Dear, dear Celie. And I imagine that you really do get my letters and that you are writing me back: Dear Nettie, this is what life is like for me.

We are up at five o'clock for a light breakfast of millet porridge and fruit, and the morning classes. We teach the children English, reading, writing, history, geography, arithmetic and the stories of the bible. At eleven o'clock we break for lunch and household duties. From one until four it is too hot to move, though some of the mothers sit behind their huts and sew. At four o'clock we teach the older children and at night we are available for adults. Some of the older children are used to coming to the mission school, but the smaller ones are not. Their mothers sometimes drag them here, screaming and kicking. They are all boys. Olivia is the only girl.

The Olinka do not believe girls should be educated. When I asked a mother why she thought this, she said: A girl

is nothing to herself; only to her husband can she become
something.

What can she become? I asked.

Why, she said, the mother of his children.

But I am not the mother of anybody's children, I said, and I
am something.

You are not much, she said. The missionary's drudge.

It is true that I work harder here than I ever dreamed I
could work, and that I sweep out the school and tidy up after
service, but I don't feel like a drudge. I was surprised that this
woman, whose Christian name is Catherine, saw me in this
light.

She has a little girl, Tashi, who plays with Olivia after
school. Adam is the only boy who will speak to Olivia at
school. They are not mean to her, it is just—what is it?
Because she is where they are doing "boys' things" they
do not see her. But never fear, Celie, Olivia has your
stubbornness and clearsightedness, and she is smarter
than all of them, including Adam, put together.

Why can't Tashi come to school? she asked me. When I
told her the Olinka don't believe in educating girls she said,
quick as a flash, They're like white people at home who don't
want colored people to learn.

Oh, she's sharp, Celie. At the end of the day, when Tashi
can get away from all the chores her mother assigns her, she
and Olivia secret themselves in my hut and everything Olivia
has learned she shares with Tashi. To Olivia right now Tashi
alone is Africa. The Africa she came beaming across the ocean
hoping to find. Everything else is difficult for her.

The insects, for instance. For some reason, all of her bites
turn into deep, runny sores, and she has a lot of trouble
sleeping at night because the noises from the forest frighten
her. It is taking a long time for her to become used to the
food, which is nourishing but, for the most part, indifferently

prepared. The women of the village take turns cooking for us, and some are cleaner and more conscientious than others. Olivia gets sick from the food prepared by any of the chief's wives. Samuel thinks it may be the water they use, which comes from a separate spring that runs clear even in the dry season. But the rest of us have no ill effects. It is as if Olivia fears the food from these wives because they all look so unhappy and work so hard. Whenever they see her they talk about the day when she will become their littlest sister/wife. It is just a joke, and they like her, but I wish they wouldn't say it. Even though they are unhappy and work like donkeys they still think it is an honor to be the chief's wife. He walks around all day holding his belly up and talking and drinking palm wine with the healer.

Why do they say I will be a wife of the chief? asks Olivia.

That is as high as they can think, I tell her.

He is fat and shiny with huge perfect teeth. She thinks she has nightmares about him.

You will grow up to be a strong Christian woman, I tell her. Someone who helps her people to advance. You will be a teacher or a nurse. You will travel. You will know many people greater than the chief.

Will Tashi? she wants to know.

Yes, I tell her, Tashi too.

Corrine said to me this morning, Nettie, to stop any kind of confusion in the minds of these people, I think we should call one another brother and sister, all the time. Some of them can't seem to get it through their thick skulls that you are not Samuel's other wife. I don't like it, she said.

Almost since the day we arrived I've noticed a change in Corrine. She isn't sick. She works as hard as ever. She is still sweet and good-natured. But sometimes I sense her spirit is being tested and that something in her is not at rest.

That's fine, I said. I'm glad you brought it up.

And don't let the children call you Mama Nettie, she said, even in play.

This bothered me a little, but I didn't say anything. The children do call me Mama Nettie sometimes because I do a good bit of fussing over them. But I never try to take Corrine's place.

And another thing, she said. I think we ought to try not to borrow each other's clothes.

Well, she never borrowed anything of mine because I don't have much. But I'm all the time borrowing something of hers.

You feeling yourself? I asked her.

She said yes.

I wish you could see my hut, Celie. I *love* it. Unlike our school, which is square, and unlike our church, which doesn't have walls—at least during the dry season—my hut is round, walled, with a round roofleaf roof. It is twenty steps across the middle and fits me to a T. Over the mud walls I have hung Olinka platters and mats and pieces of tribal cloth. The Olinka are known for their beautiful cotton fabric which they handweave and dye with berries, clay, indigo and tree bark. Then there is my paraffin camp stove in the center, and my camp bed to one side, covered with mosquito netting so that it almost looks like the bed of a bride. Then I have a small writing table where I write to you, a lamp, and a stool. Some wonderful rush mats on the floor. It is all colorful and warm and homey. My only desire for it now is a window! None of the village huts have windows, and when I spoke of a window to the women they laughed heartily. The rainy season makes the thought of a window ridiculous, apparently. But I am determined to have one, even if a flood collects daily on my floor.

I would give anything for a picture of you, Celie. In my trunk I have pictures donated to us by the missionary societies in England and America. Pictures of Christ, the Apostles, Mary, the Crucifixion. Speke, Livingstone, Stanley, Schweitzer. Maybe one day I'll put them up, but once, when I held them up to my fabric and mat covered walls they made me feel very small and unhappy, so I took them down. Even the picture of Christ which generally looks good anywhere looks peculiar here. We of course have all of these pictures hung in the school and many of Christ behind the altar at the church. That is enough, I think, though Samuel and Corrine have pictures and relics (crosses) in their hut as well.

Your sister, Nettie

Dear Celie,

Tashi's mother and father were just here. They are upset because she spends so much time with Olivia. She is changing, becoming quiet and too thoughtful, they say. She is becoming someone else; her face is beginning to show the spirit of one of her aunts who was sold to the trader because she no longer fit into village life. This aunt refused to marry the man chosen for her. Refused to bow to the chief. Did nothing but lay up, crack cola nuts between her teeth and giggle.

They want to know what Olivia and Tashi do in my hut when all the other little girls are busy helping their mothers.

Is Tashi lazy at home? I asked.

The father looked at the mother. She said, No, on the contrary, Tashi works harder than most girls her age. And is quicker to finish her work. But it is only because she wishes to spend her afternoons with Olivia. She learns everything I teach her as if she already knows it, said the mother, but this knowledge does not really enter her soul.

The mother seemed puzzled and afraid.

The father, angry,

I thought: Aha. Tashi knows she is learning a way of life she will never live. But I did not say this.

The world is changing, I said. It is no longer a world just for boys and men.

Our women are respected here, said the father. We would never let them tramp the world as American women do. There is always someone to look after the Olinka woman. A father. An uncle. A brother or nephew. Do not be offended, Sister Nettie, but our people pity women such as you who are cast out, we know not from where, into a world unknown to you, where you must struggle all alone, for yourself.

So I am an object of pity and contempt, I thought, to men and women alike.

Furthermore, said Tashi's father, we are not simpletons. We understand that there are places in the world where women live differently from the way our women do, but we do not approve of this different way for our children.

But life is changing, even in Olinka, I said. We are here.

He spat on the ground. What are you? Three grownups and two children. In the rainy season some of you will probably die. You people do not last long in our climate. If you do not die, you will be weakened by illness. Oh, yes. We have seen it all before. You Christians come here, try hard to change us, get sick and go back to England, or wherever you come from. Only the trader on the coast remains, and even he is not the same white man, year in and year out. We know because we send him women.

Tashi is very intelligent, I said. She could be a teacher. A nurse. She could help the people in the village.

There is no place here for a woman to do those things, he said.

Then we should leave, I said. Sister Corrine and I.

No, no, he said.

Teach only the boys? I asked.

Yes, he said, as if my question was agreement.

There is a way that the men speak to women that reminds

me too much of Pa. They listen just long enough to issue instructions. They don't even look at women when women are speaking. They look at the ground and bend their heads toward the ground. The women also do not "look in a man's face" as they say. To "look in a man's face" is a brazen thing to do. They look instead at his feet or his knees. And what can I say to this? Again, it is our own behavior around Pa.

Next time Tashi appears at your gate, you will send her straight home, her father said. Then he smiled. Your Olivia can visit her, and learn what women are for.

I smiled also. Olivia must learn to take her education about life where she can find it, I thought. His offer will make a splendid opportunity.

Good-bye until the next time, dear Celie, from a pitiful, castout woman who may perish during the rainy season.

Your loving sister, Nettie

Dear Celie,

At first there was the faintest sound of movement in the forest. A kind of low humming. Then there was chopping and the sound of dragging. Then a scent, some days, of smoke. But now, after two months, during which I or the children or Corrine has been sick, all we hear is chopping and scraping and dragging. And every day we smell smoke.

Today one of the boys in my afternoon class burst out, as he entered, The road approaches! The road approaches! He had been hunting in the forest with his father and seen it.

Every day now the villagers gather at the edge of the village near the cassava fields, and watch the building of the road. And watching them, some on their stools and some squatted down on their haunches, all chewing cola nuts and making patterns in the dirt, I feel a great surge of love for them. For they do not approach the roadbuilders empty-handedly. Oh, no. Each day since they saw the road's approach they have been stuffing the roadbuilders with goat meat, millet mush, baked yam and cassava, cola nuts and palm wine. Each day is like a picnic, and I believe many friendships have been made, although the roadbuilders are

from a different tribe some distance to the North and nearer
the coast, and their language is somewhat different. I don't
understand it, anyway, though the people of Olinka seem to.
But they are clever people about most things, and understand
new things very quickly.

It is hard to believe we've been here five years. Time moves
slowly, but passes quickly. Adam and Olivia are nearly as tall as
me and doing very well in all their studies. Adam has a special
aptitude for figures and it worries Samuel that soon he will
have nothing more to teach him in this field, having exhausted
his own knowledge.

When we were in England we met missionaries who sent
their children back home when it was no longer possible
to teach them in the bush. But it is hard to imagine life
here without the children. They love the open feeling of
the village, and love living in huts. They are excited by the
hunting expertise of the men and the self-sufficiency of the
women in raising their crops. No matter how down I may be,
and sometimes I get very down indeed, a hug from Olivia or
Adam completely restores me to the level of functioning, if
nothing else. Their mother and I are not as close as we once
were, but I feel more like their aunt than ever. And the three
of us look more and more alike every day.

About a month ago, Corrine asked me not to invite Samuel
to my hut unless she were present. She said it gave the
villagers the wrong idea. This was a real blow to me because
I treasure his company. Since Corrine almost never visits me
herself I will have hardly anybody to talk to, just in friendship.
But the children still come and sometimes spend the night
when their parents want to be alone. I love those times. We
roast groundnuts on my stove, sit on the floor and study maps
of all the countries in the world. Sometimes Tashi comes over
and tells stories that are popular among the Olinka children. I
am encouraging her and Olivia to write them down in Olinka

and English. It will be good practice for them. Olivia feels
that, compared to Tashi, she has no good stories to tell. One
day she started in on an "Uncle Remus" tale only to discover
Tashi had the original version of it! Her little face just fell.
But then we got into a discussion of how Tashi's people's
stories got to America, which fascinated Tashi. She cried when
Olivia told how her grandmother had been treated as a slave.

No one else in this village wants to hear about slavery,
however. They acknowledge no responsibility whatsoever.
This is one thing about them that I definitely do not like.

We lost Tashi's father during the last rainy season. He fell
ill with malaria and nothing the healer concocted saved him.
He refused to take the medicine we use for it, or to let Samuel
visit him at all. It was my first Olinka funeral. The women
paint their faces white and wear white shroudlike garments
and cry in a high keening voice. They wrapped the body in
barkcloth and buried it under a big tree in the forest. Tashi
was heartbroken. All her young life she has tried to please her
father, never quite realizing that, as a girl, she never could.
But the death brought her and her mother closer together,
and now Catherine feels like one of us. By one of us I mean
me and the children and sometimes Samuel. She is still in
mourning and sticking close to her hut, but she says she will
not marry again (since she already has five boy children she
can now do whatever she wants. She has become an honorary
man) and when I went to visit her she made it very clear that
Tashi must continue to learn. She is the most industrious of
all Tashi's father's widows, and her fields are praised for their
cleanliness, productivity and general attractiveness. Perhaps I
can help her with her work. It is in work that the women get
to know and care about each other. It was through work that
Catherine became friends with her husband's other wives.

This friendship among women is something Samuel often
talks about. Because the women share a husband but the

husband does not share their friendships, it makes Samuel
uneasy. It is confusing, I suppose. And it is Samuel's duty as
a Christian minister to preach the bible's directive of one
husband and one wife. Samuel is confused because to him,
since the women are friends and will do anything for one
another—not always, but more often than anyone from
America would expect—and since they giggle and gossip and
nurse each other's children, then they must be happy with
things as they are. But many of the women rarely spend time
with their husbands. Some of them were promised to old or
middle-aged men at birth. Their lives always center around
work and their children and other women (since a woman
cannot really have a man for a friend without the worst kind
of ostracism and gossip). They indulge their husbands, if
anything. You should just see how they make admiration over
them. Praise their smallest accomplishments. Stuff them with
palm wine and sweets. No wonder the men are often childish.
And a grown child is a dangerous thing, especially since,
among the Olinka, the husband has life and death power
over the wife. If he accuses one of his wives of witchcraft or
infidelity, she can be killed.

Thank God (and sometimes Samuel's intervention) this has
not happened since we've been here. But the stories Tashi tells
are often about such gruesome events that happened in the
recent past. And God forbid that the child of a favorite wife
should fall ill! That is the point at which even the women's
friendships break down, as each woman fears the accusation of
sorcery from the other, or from the husband.

Merry Christmas to you and yours, dear Celie. We
celebrate it here on the "dark" continent with prayer and
song and a large picnic complete with watermelon, fresh fruit
punch, and barbecue!

                              God bless you,
                              Nettie

Dearest Celie,

I meant to write you in time for Easter, but it was not a good time for me and I did not want to burden you with any distressing news. So a whole year has gone by. The first thing I should tell you about is the road. The road finally reached the cassava fields about nine months ago and the Olinka, who love nothing better than a celebration, outdid themselves preparing a feast for the roadbuilders who talked and laughed and cut their eyes at the Olinka women the whole day. In the evening many were invited into the village itself and there was merrymaking far into the night.

I think Africans are very much like white people back home, in that they think they are the center of the universe and that everything that is done is done for them. The Olinka definitely hold this view. And so they naturally thought the road being built was for them. And, in fact, the roadbuilders talked much of how quickly the Olinka will now be able to get to the coast. With a tarmac road it is only a three-day journey. By bicycle it will be even less. Of course no one in Olinka owns a bicycle, but one of the roadbuilders has one, and all the Olinka men covet it and talk of someday soon purchasing their own.

Well, the morning after the road was "finished" as far as the Olinka were concerned (after all, it had reached their village), what should we discover but that the roadbuilders were back at work. They have instructions to continue the road for another thirty miles! And to continue it on its present course right through the village of Olinka. By the time we were out of bed, the road was already being dug through Catherine's newly planted yam field. Of course the Olinka were up in arms. But the roadbuilders were literally up in arms. They had guns, Celie, with orders to shoot!

It was pitiful, Celie. The people felt so betrayed! They stood by helplessly—they really don't know how to fight, and rarely think of it since the old days of tribal wars—as their crops and then their very homes were destroyed. Yes. The roadbuilders didn't deviate an inch from the plan the headman was following. Every hut that lay in the proposed roadpath was leveled. And, Celie, our church, our school, my hut, all went down in a matter of hours. Fortunately, we were able to save all of our things, but with a tarmac road running straight through the middle of it, the village itself seems gutted.

Immediately after understanding the roadbuilders' intentions, the chief set off toward the coast, seeking explanations and reparations. Two weeks later he returned with even more disturbing news. The whole territory, including the Olinka's village, now belongs to a rubber manufacturer in England. As he neared the coast, he was stunned to see hundreds and hundreds of villagers much like the Olinka clearing the forests on each side of the road, and planting rubber trees. The ancient, giant mahogany trees, all the trees, the game, everything of the forest was being destroyed, and the land was forced to lie flat, he said, and bare as the palm of his hand.

At first he thought the people who told him about the English rubber company were mistaken, if only about its territory including the Olinka village. But eventually he was directed to the governor's mansion, a huge white building, with flags flying in its yard, and there had an audience with the white man in charge. It was this man who gave the roadbuilders their orders, this man who knew about the Olinka only from a map. He spoke in English, which our chief tried to speak also.

It must have been a pathetic exchange. Our chief never learned English beyond an occasional odd phrase he picked up from Joseph, who pronounces "English" "Yanglush."

But the worst was yet to be told. Since the Olinka no longer own their village, they must pay rent for it, and in order to use the water, which also no longer belongs to them, they must pay a water tax.

At first the people laughed. It really did seem crazy. They've been here forever. But the chief did not laugh.

We will fight the white man, they said.

But the white man is not alone, said the chief. He has brought his army.

That was several months ago, and so far nothing has happened. The people live like ostriches, never setting foot on the new road if they can help it, and never, ever, looking towards the coast. We have built another church and school. I have another hut. And so we wait.

Meanwhile, Corrine has been very ill with African fever. Many missionaries in the past have died from it.

But the children are fine. The boys now accept Olivia and Tashi in class and more mothers are sending their daughters to school. The men do not like it: who wants a wife who knows everything her husband knows? they fume. But the women have their ways, and they love their children, even their girls.

I will write more when things start looking up. I trust God they will.

Your sister, Nettie

Dearest Celie,

This whole year, after Easter, has been difficult. Since Corrine's illness, all her work has fallen on me, and I must nurse her as well, which she resents.

One day when I was changing her as she lay in bed, she gave me a long, mean, but somehow pitiful look. Why do my children look like you? she asked.

Do you really think they look so much like me? I said.

You could have spit them out, she said.

Maybe just living together, loving people makes them look like you, I said. You know how much some old married people look alike.

Even these women saw the resemblance the first day we came, she said.

And that's worried you all this time? I tried to laugh it off. But she just looked at me.

When did you first meet my husband? she wanted to know.

And that was when I knew what she thought. She thinks Adam and Olivia are my children, and that Samuel is their father!

Oh, Celie, this thing has been gnawing away at her all these years!

I met Samuel the same day I met you, Corrine, I said. (I still haven't got the hang of saying "Sister" all the time.) As God is my witness, that's the truth.

Bring the bible, she said.

I brought the bible, and placed my hand on it, and swore.

You've never known me to lie, Corrine, I said. Please believe I am not lying now.

Then she called Samuel, and made him swear that the day she met me was the day he met me also.

He said: I apologize for this, Sister Nettie, please forgive us.

As soon as Samuel left the room she made me raise my dress and she sat up in her sickbed to examine my stomach.

I felt so sorry for her, and so humiliated, Celie. And the way she treats the children is the hardest part. She doesn't want them near her, which they don't understand. How could they? They don't even know they were adopted.

The village is due to be planted in rubber trees this coming season. The Olinka hunting territory has already been destroyed, and the men must go farther and farther away to find game. The women spend all their time in the fields, tending their crops and praying. They sing to the earth and to the sky and to their cassava and groundnuts. Songs of love and farewell.

We are all sad, here, Celie. I hope life is happier for you.

Your sister, Nettie

Dear Celie,

Guess what? Samuel thought the children were mine too! That is why he urged me to come to Africa with them. When I showed up at their house he thought I was following my children, and, soft-hearted as he is, didn't have the heart to turn me away.

If they are not yours, he said, whose are they?

But I had some questions for him, first.

Where did you get them? I asked. And Celie, he told me a story that made my hair stand on end. I hope you, poor thing, are ready for it.

Once upon a time, there was a well-to-do farmer who owned his own property near town. Our town, Celie. And as he did so well farming and everything he turned his hand to prospered, he decided to open a store, and try his luck selling dry goods as well. Well, his store did so well that he talked two of his brothers into helping him run it, and, as the months went by, they were doing better and better. Then the white merchants began to get together and complain that this store was taking all the black business away from them, and the man's blacksmith shop that he set up behind the store, was taking some of the white. This would not do. And so, one night, the man's store was burned down, his smithy destroyed, and the man and his two brothers dragged out of their homes in the middle of the night and hanged.

The man had a wife whom he adored, and they had a little girl, barely two years old. She was also pregnant with another child. When the neighbors brought her husband's body home, it had been mutilated and burnt. The sight of it nearly killed her, and her second baby, also a girl, was born at this time. Although the widow's body recovered, her mind was never the same. She continued to fix her husband's plate at mealtimes just as she'd always done and was always full of talk about the plans she and her husband had made. The neighbors, though not always intending to, shunned her more and more, partly because the plans she talked about were grander than anything they could even conceive of for colored people, and partly because her attachment to the past was so pitiful. She was a good-looking woman, though, and still owned land, but there was no one to work it for her, and she didn't know how herself; besides she kept waiting for her husband to finish the meal she'd cooked for him and go to the fields himself. Soon there was nothing to eat that the neighbors did not bring, and she and her small children grubbed around in the yard as best they could.

While the second child was still a baby, a stranger appeared in the community, and lavished all his attention on the widow and her children; in a short while, they were married. Almost at once she was pregnant a third time, though her mental health was no better. Every year thereafter, she was pregnant, every year she became weaker and more mentally unstable, until, many years after she married the stranger, she died.

Two years before she died she had a baby girl that she was too sick to keep. Then a baby boy. These children were named Olivia and Adam.

This is Samuel's story, almost word for word.

The stranger who married the widow was someone Samuel had run with long before he found Christ. When the man showed up at Samuel's house with first Olivia and then Adam, Samuel felt not only unable to refuse the children, but as if God had answered his and Corrine's prayers.

He never told Corrine about the man or about the children's "mother" because he hadn't wanted any sadness to cloud her happiness.

But then, out of nowhere, I appeared. He put two and two together, remembered that his old running buddy had always been a scamp, and took me in without any questions. Which, to tell the truth, had always puzzled me, but I put it down to Christian charity. Corrine had asked me once whether I was running away from home. But I explained I was a big girl now, my family back home very large and poor, and it was time for me to get out and earn my own living.

Tears had soaked my blouse when Samuel finished telling me all this. I couldn't begin, then, to tell him the truth. But Celie, I can tell you. And I pray with all my heart that you will get this letter, if none of the others.

Pa is not our pa!

Your devoted Sister, Nettie

Dear God,

That's it, say Shug. Pack your stuff. You coming back to Tennessee with me.

But I feels daze.

My daddy lynch. My mama crazy. All my little half-brothers and sisters no kin to me. My children not my sister and brother. Pa not pa.

You must be sleep.

Dear Nettie,

For the first time in my life I wanted to see Pa. So me and Shug dress up in our new blue flower pants that match and big floppy Easter hats that match too, cept her roses red, mine yellow, and us clam in the Packard and glide over there. They put in paved roads all up and down the county now and twenty miles go like nothing.

I saw Pa once since I left home. One day me and Mr. _____ was loading up the wagon at the feed store. Pa was with May Ellen and she was trying to fix her stocking. She was bent down over her leg and twisting the stocking into a knot above her knee, and he was standing over her tap-tap-tapping on the gravel with his cane. Look like he was thinking bout hitting her with it.

Mr. _____ went up to them all friendly, with his hand stuck out, but I kept loading the wagon and looking at the patterns on the sacks. I never thought I'd ever want to see him again.

Well, it was a bright Spring day, sort of chill at first, like it be round Easter, and the first thing us notice soon as we turn into the lane is how green everything is, like even though the ground everywhere else not warmed up good, Pa's land

is warm and ready to go. Then all along the road there's
Easter lilies and jonquils and daffodils and all kinds of little
early wildflowers. Then us notice all the birds singing they
little cans off, all up and down the hedge, that itself is putting
out little yellow flowers smell like Virginia creeper. It all so
different from the rest of the country us drive through, it
make us real quiet. I know this sound funny, Nettie, but even
the sun seemed to stand a little longer over our heads.

Well, say Shug, all this is pretty enough. You never said
how pretty it was.

It wasn't this pretty, I say. Every Easter time it used to
flood, and all us children had colds. Anyhow, I say, us stuck
close to the house, and it sure ain't so hot.

That ain't so hot? she ast, as we swung up a long curving
hill I didn't remember, right up to a big yellow two story
house with green shutters and a steep green shingle roof.

I laughed. Us must have took the wrong turn, I say. This
some white person's house.

It was so pretty though that us stop the car and just set
looking at it.

What kind of trees all them flowering? ast Shug.

I don't know, I say. Look like peach, plum, apple, maybe
cherry. But whatever they is, they sure pretty.

All round the house, all in back of it, nothing but blooming
trees. Then more lilies and jonquils and roses clamming over
everything. And all the time the little birds from all over the
rest of the county sit up in these trees just going to town.

Finally, after us look at it awhile, I say, it so quiet, nobody
home, I guess.

Naw, say Shug, probably in church. A nice bright Sunday
like this.

Us better leave then, I say, before whoever it is lives here
gits back. But just as I say that I notice my eye is staying on

a fig tree it recognize, and us hear a car turning up the drive.
Who should be in the car but Pa and some young girl look
like his child.

He git out on his side, then go round to open the door
for her. She dress to kill in a pink suit, big pink hat and pink
shoes, a little pink purse hanging on her arm. They look at
our license tag and then come up to the car. She put her hand
through his arm.

Morning, he says, when he gits up to Shug's window.

Morning, she says slow, and I can tell he not what she
expect.

Anything I can do for you? He ain't notice me and
probably wouldn't even if he looked at me.

Shug say, under her breath, Is this him?

I say, Yeah.

What shock Shug and shock me too is how young he look.
He look older than the child he with, even if she is dress up
like a woman, but he look young for somebody to be anybody
that got grown children and nearly grown grandchildren. But
then I remember, he not my daddy, just my children daddy.

What your mama do, ast Shug, rob the cradle?

But he not so young.

I brought Celie, say Shug. Your daughter Celie. She wanted
to visit you. Got some questions to ast.

He seem to think back a second. *Celie?* he say. Like, Who
Celie? Then he say, Yall git out and come up on the porch.
Daisy, he say to the little woman with him, go tell Hetty to
hold dinner. She squeeze his arm, reach up and kiss him on
the jaw. He turn his head and watch her go up the walk, up
the steps, and through the front door. He follow us up the
steps, up on the porch, help us pull out rocking chairs, then
say, Now, what yall want?

The children here? I ast.

What children? he say. Then he laugh. Oh, they gone with
they mama. She up and left me, you know. Went back to her
folks. Yeah, he say, you would remember May Ellen.

Why she leave? I ast.

He laugh some more. Got too old for me, I reckon.

Then the little woman come back out and sit on the
armrest of his chair. He talk to us and fondle her arm.

This Daisy, he say. My new wife.

Why, say Shug, you don't look more than fifteen.

I ain't, say Daisy.

I'm surprise your people let you marry.

She shrug, look at Pa. They work for him, she say. Live on
his land.

I'm her people now, he say.

I feels so sick I almost gag. Nettie in Africa, I say. A
missionary. She wrote me that you ain't our real Pa.

Well, he say. So now you know.

Daisy look at me with pity all over her face. It just like him
to keep that from you, she say. He told me how he brought
up two little girls that wasn't even his, she say. I don't think I
really believed it, till now.

Naw, he never told them, say Shug.

What a old sweetie pie, say Daisy, kissing him on top the
head. He fondle and fondle her arm. Look at me and grin.

Your daddy didn't know how to git along, he say.
Whitefolks lynch him. Too sad a story to tell pitiful little
growing girls, he say. Any man would have done what I done.

Maybe not, say Shug.

He look at her, then look at me. He can tell she know. But
what do he care?

Take me, he say, I know how they is. The key to all of 'em
is money. The trouble with our people is as soon as they
got out of slavery they didn't want to give the white man

nothing else. But the fact is, you got to give 'em something. Either your money, your land, your woman or your ass. So what I did was just right off offer to give 'em money. Before I planted a seed, I made sure this one and that one knowed one seed out of three was planted for *him*. Before I ground a grain of wheat, the same thing. And when I opened up your daddy's old store in town, I bought me my own white boy to run it. And what make it so good, he say, I bought him with whitefolks' money.

Ask the busy man your questions, Celie, say Shug. I think his dinner getting cold.

Where my daddy buried, I ast. That all I really want to know.

Next to your mammy, he say.

Any marker, I ast.

He look at me like I'm crazy. Lynched people don't git no marker, he say. Like this something everybody know.

Mama got one? I ast.

He say, Naw.

The birds sing just as sweet when us leave as when us come. Then, look like as soon as us turn back on the main road, they stop. By the time us got to the cemetery, the sky gray.

Us look for Ma and Pa. Hope for some scrap of wood that say something. But us don't find nothing but weeds and cockleburrs and paper flowers fading on some of the graves. Shug pick up a old horseshoe somebody horse lose. Us took that old horseshoe and us turned round and round together until we were dizzy enough to fall out, and where us would have fell us stuck the horseshoe in the ground.

Shug say, Us each other's peoples now, and kiss me.

Dear Celie,

I woke up this morning bound to tell Corrine and Samuel everything. I went over to their hut and pulled up a stool next to Corrine's bed. She's so weak by now that all she can do is look unfriendly—and I could tell I wasn't welcome.

I said, Corrine, I'm here to tell you and Samuel the truth.

She said, Samuel already told me. If the children yours, why didn't you just say so?

Samuel said, Now, honey.

She said, Don't Now Honey me. Nettie swore on the bible to tell me the truth. To tell God the truth, and she lied.

Corrine, I said, I didn't lie. I sort of turned my back more on Samuel and whispered: You saw my stomach, I said.

What do I know about pregnancy, she said. I never experienced it myself. For all I know, women may be able to rub out all the signs.

They can't rub out stretch marks, I said. Stretch marks go right into the skin, and a woman's stomach stretches enough so that it keeps a little pot, like all the women have here.

She turned her face to the wall.

Corrine, I said, I'm the children's aunt. Their mother is my older sister, Celie.

Then I told them the whole story. Only Corrine was still not convinced.

You and Samuel telling so many lies, who can believe anything you say? she asked.

You've got to believe Nettie, said Samuel. Though the part about you and Pa was a real shock to him.

Then I remembered what you told me about seeing Corrine and Samuel and Olivia in town, when she was buying cloth to make her and Olivia dresses, and how you sent me to her because she was the only woman you'd ever seen with money. I tried to make Corrine remember that day, but she couldn't.

She gets weaker and weaker, and unless she can believe us and start to feel something for her children, I fear we will lose her.

Oh, Celie, unbelief is a terrible thing. And so is the hurt we cause others unknowingly.

Pray for us,
Nettie

Dearest Celie,

Every day for the past week I've been trying to get Corrine to remember meeting you in town. I know if she can just recall your face, she will believe Olivia (if not Adam) is your child. They think Olivia looks like me, but that is only because I look like you. Olivia has your face and eyes, exactly. It amazes me that Corrine didn't see the resemblance.

Remember the main street of town? I asked. Remember the hitching post in front of Finley's dry goods store? Remember how the store smelled like peanut shells?

She says she remembers all this, but no men speaking to her.

Then I remember her quilts. The Olinka men make beautiful quilts which are full of animals and birds and people. And as soon as Corrine saw them, she began to make a quilt that alternated one square of appliquéd figures with one nine-patch block, using the clothes the children had outgrown, and some of her old dresses.

I went to her trunk and started hauling out quilts.

Don't touch my things, said Corrine. I'm not gone yet.

I held up first one and then another to the light, trying to find the first one I remembered her making. And trying to remember, at the same time, the dresses she and Olivia were wearing the first months I lived with them.

Aha, I said, when I found what I was looking for, and laid the quilt across the bed.

Do you remember buying this cloth? I asked, pointing to a flowered square. And what about this checkered bird?

She traced the patterns with her finger, and slowly her eyes filled with tears.

She was so much like Olivia! she said. I was afraid she'd want her back. So I forgot her as soon as I could. All I let myself think about was how the clerk treated me! I was acting like somebody because I was Samuel's wife, and a Spelman Seminary graduate, and he treated me like any ordinary nigger. Oh, my feelings were hurt! And I was mad! And that's what I thought about, even told Samuel about, on the way home. Not about your sister—what was her name?—Celie? Nothing about her.

She began to cry in earnest. Me and Samuel holding her hands.

Don't cry. Don't cry, I said. My sister was glad to see Olivia with you. Glad to see her alive. She thought both her children were dead.

Poor thing! said Samuel. And we sat there talking a little and holding on to each other until Corrine fell off to sleep.

But, Celie, in the middle of the night she woke up, turned to Samuel and said: I believe. And died anyway.

Your Sister in Sorrow, Nettie

Dearest Celie,

Just when I think I've learned to live with the heat, the constant dampness, even steaminess of my clothes, the swampiness under my arms and between my legs, my friend comes. And cramps and aches and pains—but I must still keep going as if nothing is happening, or be an embarrassment to Samuel, the children and myself. Not to mention the villagers, who think women who have their friends should not even be seen.

Right after her mother's death, Olivia got *her* friend; she and Tashi tend to each other is my guess. Nothing is said to me, in any event, and I don't know how to bring the subject up. Which feels wrong to me; but if you talk to an Olinka girl about her private parts, her mother and father will be annoyed, and it is very important to Olivia not to be looked upon as an outsider. Although the one ritual they do have to celebrate womanhood is so bloody and painful, I forbid Olivia to even think about it.

Do you remember how scared I was when it first happened to me? I thought I had cut myself. But thank God you were there to tell me I was all right.

We buried Corrine in the Olinka way, wrapped in barkcloth under a large tree. All of her sweet ways went with her. All of her education and a heart intent on doing good. She taught me so much! I know I will miss her always. The children were stunned by their mother's death. They knew she was very sick, but death is not something they think about in relation to their parents or themselves. It was a strange little procession. All of us in our white robes and with our faces painted white. Samuel is like someone lost. I don't believe they've spent a night apart since their marriage.

And how are you, dear Sister? The years have come and gone without a single word from you. Only the sky above us do we hold in common. I look at it often as if, somehow, reflected from its immensities, I will one day find myself gazing into your eyes. Your dear, large, clean and beautiful eyes. Oh, Celie! My life here is nothing but work, work, work, and worry. What girlhood I might have had passed me by. And I have nothing of my own. No man, no children, no close friend, except for Samuel. But I *do* have children, Adam and Olivia. And I *do* have friends, Tashi and Catherine. I even have a family—this village, which has fallen on such hard times.

Now the engineers have come to inspect the territory. Two white men came yesterday and spent a couple of hours strolling about the village, mainly looking at the wells. Such is the innate politeness of the Olinka that they rushed about preparing food for them, though precious little is left, since many of the gardens that flourish at this time of the year have been destroyed. And the white men sat eating as if the food was beneath notice.

It is understood by the Olinka that nothing good is likely to come from the same persons who destroyed their houses, but custom dies hard. I did not speak to the men myself, but Samuel did. He said their talk was all of workers, kilometers of land, rainfall, seedlings, machinery, and whatnot. One seemed totally indifferent to the people around him—simply eating and then smoking and staring off into the distance—and the other, somewhat younger, appeared to be enthusiastic about learning the language. Before, he says, it dies out.

I did not enjoy watching Samuel speaking to either of them. The one who hung on every word, or the one who looked through Samuel's head.

Samuel gave me all of Corrine's clothes, and I need them, though none of our clothing is suitable in this climate. This is true even of the clothing the Africans wear. They used to wear very little, but the ladies of England introduced the Mother Hubbard, a long, cumbersome, ill-fitting dress, completely shapeless, that inevitably gets dragged in the fire, causing burns aplenty. I have never been able to bring myself to wear one of these dresses, which all seem to have been made with giants in mind, so I was glad to have Corrine's things. At the same time, I dreaded putting them on. I remembered her saying we should stop wearing each other's clothes. And the memory pained me.

Are you sure Sister Corrine would want this? I asked Samuel.

Yes, Sister Nettie, he said. Try not to hold her fears against her. At the end she understood, and believed. And forgave—whatever there was to forgive.

I should have said something sooner, I said.

He asked me to tell him about you, and the words poured out like water. I was dying to tell someone about us. I told him about my letters to you every Christmas and Easter, and about how much it would have meant to us if he had gone to see you after I left. He was sorry he hesitated to become involved.

If only I'd understood then what I know now! he said.

But how could he? There is so much we don't understand. And so much unhappiness comes because of that.

> love and Merry Christmas
> to you,
> Your sister, Nettie

Dear Nettie,

I don't write to God no more. I write to you.

What happen to God? ast Shug.

Who that? I say.

She look at me serious.

Big a devil as you is, I say, you not worried bout no God, surely.

She say, Wait a minute. Hold on just a minute here. Just because I don't harass it like some peoples us know don't mean I ain't got religion.

What God do for me? I ast.

She say, Celie! Like she shock. He gave you life, good health, and a good woman that love you to death.

Yeah, I say, and he give me a lynched daddy, a crazy mama, a lowdown dog of a step pa and a sister I probably won't ever see again. Anyhow, I say, the God I been praying and writing to is a man. And act just like all the other mens I know. Trifling, forgitful and lowdown.

She say, Miss Celie, You better hush. God might hear you.

Let 'im hear me, I say. If he ever listened to poor colored women the world would be a different place, I can tell you.

She talk and she talk, trying to budge me way from blasphemy. But I blaspheme much as I want to.

All my life I never care what people thought bout nothing I did, I say. But deep in my heart I care about God. What he going to think. And come to find out, he don't think. Just sit up there glorying in being deef, I reckon. But it ain't easy, trying to do without God. Even if you know he ain't there, trying to do without him is a strain.

I is a sinner, say Shug. Cause I was born. I don't deny it. But once you find out what's out there waiting for us, what else can you be?

Sinners have more good times, I say.

You know why? she ast.

Cause you ain't all the time worrying bout God, I say.

Naw, that ain't it, she say. Us worry bout God a lot. But once us feel loved by God, us do the best us can to please him with what us like.

You telling me God love you, and you ain't never done nothing for him? I mean, not go to church, sing in the choir, feed the preacher and all like that?

But if God love me, Celie, I don't have to do all that. Unless I want to. There's a lot of other things I can do that I speck God likes.

Like what? I ast.

Oh, she say. I can lay back and just admire stuff. Be happy. Have a good time.

Well, this sound like blasphemy sure nuff.

She say, Celie, tell the truth, have you ever found God in church? I never did. I just found a bunch of folks hoping for him to show. Any God I ever felt in church I brought in with me. And I think all the other folks did too. They come to church to share God, not find God.

Some folks didn't have him to share, I said. They the ones

didn't speak to me while I was there struggling with my big belly and Mr. ____ children.

Right, she say.

Then she say: Tell me what your God look like, Celie.

Aw naw, I say. I'm too shame. Nobody ever ast me this before, so I'm sort of took by surprise. Besides, when I think about it, it don't seem quite right. But it all I got. I decide to stick up for him, just to see what Shug say.

Okay, I say. He big and old and tall and graybearded and white. He wear white robes and go barefooted.

Blue eyes? she ast.

Sort of bluish-gray. Cool. Big though. White lashes. I say.

She laugh.

Why you laugh? I ast. I don't think it so funny. What you expect him to look like, Mr. ____?

That wouldn't be no improvement, she say. Then she tell me this old white man is the same God she used to see when she prayed. If you wait to find God in church, Celie, she say, that's who is bound to show up, cause that's where he live.

How come? I ast.

Cause that's the one that's in the white folks' white bible.

Shug! I say. God wrote the bible, white folks had nothing to do with it.

How come he look just like them, then? she say. Only bigger? And a heap more hair. How come the bible just like everything else they make, all about them doing one thing and another, and all the colored folks doing is gitting cursed?

I never thought bout that.

Nettie say somewhere in the bible it say Jesus' hair was Like lamb's wool, I say.

Well, say Shug, if he came to any of these churches we talking bout he'd have to have it conked before anybody paid him any attention. The last thing niggers want to think about they God is that his hair kinky.

That's the truth, I say.

Ain't no way to read the bible and not think God white, she say. Then she sigh. When I found out I thought God was white, and a man, I lost interest. You mad cause he don't seem to listen to your prayers. Humph! Do the mayor listen to anything colored say? Ask Sofia, she say.

But I don't have to ast Sofia. I know white people never listen to colored, period. If they do, they only listen long enough to be able to tell you what to do.

Here's the thing, say Shug. The thing I believe. God is inside you and inside everybody else. You come into the world with God. But only them that search for it inside find it. And sometimes it just manifest itself even if you not looking, or don't know what you looking for. Trouble do it for most folks, I think. Sorrow, lord. Feeling like shit.

It? I ast.

Yeah, It. God ain't a he or a she, but a It.

But what do it look like? I ast.

Don't look like nothing, she say. It ain't a picture show. It ain't something you can look at apart from anything else, including yourself. I believe God is everything, say Shug. Everything that is or ever was or ever will be. And when you can feel that, and be happy to feel that, you've found It.

Shug a beautiful something, let me tell you. She frown a little, look out cross the yard, lean back in her chair, look like a big rose.

She say, My first step from the old white man was trees. Then air. Then birds. Then other people. But one day when I was sitting quiet and feeling like a motherless child, which I was, it come to me: that feeling of being part of everything, not separate at all. I knew that if I cut a tree, my arm would bleed. And I laughed and I cried and I run all around the house. I knew just what it was. In fact, when it happen, you can't miss it. It sort of like you know what, she say, grinning and rubbing high up on my thigh.

Shug! I say.

Oh, she say. God love all them feelings. That's some of the best stuff God did. And when you know God loves 'em you enjoys 'em a lot more. You can just relax, go with everything that's going, and praise God by liking what you like.

God don't think it dirty? I ast.

Naw, she say. God made it. Listen, God love everything you love—and a mess of stuff you don't. But more than anything else, God love admiration.

You saying God vain? I ast.

Naw, she say. Not vain, just wanting to share a good thing. I think it pisses God off if you walk by the color purple in a field somewhere and don't notice it.

What it do when it pissed off? I ast.

Oh, it make something else. People think pleasing God is all God care about. But any fool living in the world can see it always trying to please us back.

Yeah? I say.

Yeah, she say. It always making little surprises and springing them on us when us least expect.

You mean it want to be loved, just like the bible say.

Yes, Celie, she say. Everything want to be loved. Us sing and dance, make faces and give flower bouquets, trying to be loved. You ever notice that trees do everything to git attention we do, except walk?

Well, us talk and talk bout God, but I'm still adrift. Trying to chase that old white man out of my head. I been so busy thinking bout him I never truly notice nothing God make. Not a blade of corn (how it do that?) not the color purple (where it come from?). Not the little wildflowers. Nothing.

Now that my eyes opening, I feels like a fool. Next to any little scrub of a bush in my yard, Mr. ___'s evil sort of shrink. But not altogether. Still, it is like Shug say, You have to git man off your eyeball, before you can see anything a'tall.

Man corrupt everything, say Shug. He on your box of grits, in your head, and all over the radio. He try to make you think he everywhere. Soon as you think he everywhere, you think he God. But he ain't. Whenever you trying to pray, and man plop himself on the other end of it, tell him to git lost, say Shug. Conjure up flowers, wind, water, a big rock.

But this hard work, let me tell you. He been there so long, he don't want to budge. He threaten lightening, floods and earthquakes. Us fight. I hardly pray at all. Every time I conjure up a rock, I throw it.

Amen

Dear Nettie,

When I told Shug I'm writing to you instead of to God, she laugh. Nettie don't know these people, she say. Considering who I been writing to, this strike me funny.

It was Sofia you saw working as the mayor's maid. The woman you saw carrying the white woman's packages that day in town. Sofia Mr. ____'s son Harpo's wife. Polices lock her up for sassing the mayor's wife and hitting the mayor back. First she was in prison working in the laundry and dying fast. Then us got her move to the mayor's house. She had to sleep in a little room up under the house, but it was better than prison. Flies, maybe, but no rats.

Anyhow, they kept her eleven and a half years, give her six months off for good behavior so she could come home early to her family. Her bigger children married and gone, and her littlest children mad at her, don't know who she is. Think she act funny, look old and dote on that little white gal she raise.

Yesterday us all had dinner at Odessa's house. Odessa Sofia's sister. She raise the kids. Her and her husband Jack. Harpo's woman Squeak, and Harpo himself.

Sofia sit down at the big table like there's no room for

her. Children reach cross her like she not there. Harpo and Squeak act like a old married couple. Children call Odessa mama. Call Squeak little mama. Call Sofia "Miss." The only one seem to pay her any tention at all is Harpo and Squeak's little girl, Suzie Q. She sit cross from Sofia and squinch up her eyes at her.

As soon as dinner over, Shug push back her chair and light a cigarette. Now is come the time to tell yall, she say.

Tell us what? Harpo ast.

Us leaving, she say.

Yeah? say Harpo, looking round for the coffee. And then looking over at Grady.

Us leaving, Shug say again. Mr. _____ look struck, like he always look when Shug say she going anywhere. He reach down and rub his stomach, look off side her head like nothing been said.

Grady say, Such good peoples, that's the truth. The salt of the earth. But—time to move on.

Squeak not saying nothing. She got her chin glued to her plate. I'm not saying nothing either. I'm waiting for the feathers to fly.

Celie is coming with us, say Shug.

Mr. _____'s head swivel back straight. Say what? he ast.

Celie is coming to Memphis with me.

Over my dead body, Mr. _____ say.

You satisfied that what you want, Shug say, cool as clabber.

Mr. _____ start up from his seat, look at Shug, plop back down again. He look over at me. I thought you was finally happy, he say. What wrong now?

You a lowdown dog is what's wrong, I say. It's time to leave you and enter into the Creation. And your dead body just the welcome mat I need.

Say what? he ast. Shock.

All round the table folkses mouths be dropping open.

You took my sister Nettie away from me, I say. And she was the only person love me in the world.

Mr. ____ start to sputter. ButButButButBut. Sound like some kind of motor.

But Nettie and my children coming home soon, I say. And when she do, all us together gon whup your ass.

Nettie and your children! say Mr. ____. You talking crazy.

I got children, I say. Being brought up in Africa. Good schools, lots of fresh air and exercise. Turning out a heap better than the fools you didn't even try to raise.

Hold on, say Harpo.

Oh, hold on hell, I say. If you hadn't tried to rule over Sofia the white folks never would have caught her.

Sofia so surprise to hear me speak up she ain't chewed for ten minutes.

That's a lie, say Harpo.

A little truth in it, say Sofia.

Everybody look at her like they surprise she there. It like a voice speaking from the grave.

You was all rotten children, I say. You made my life a hell on earth. And your daddy here ain't dead horse's shit.

Mr. ____ reach over to slap me. I jab my case knife in his hand.

You bitch, he say. What will people say, you running off to Memphis like you don't have a house to look after?

Shug say, Albert. Try to think like you got some sense. Why any woman give a shit what people think is a mystery to me.

Well, say Grady, trying to bring light. A woman can't git a man if peoples talk.

Shug look at me and us giggle. Then us laugh sure nuff. Then Squeak start to laugh. Then Sofia. All us laugh and laugh.

Shug say, Ain't they something? Us say um *hum*, and slap the table, wipe the water from our eyes.

Harpo look at Squeak. Shut up Squeak, he say. It bad luck for women to laugh at men.

She say, Okay. She sit up straight, suck in her breath, try to press her face together.

He look at Sofia. She look at him and laugh in his face. I already had my bad luck, she say. I had enough to keep me laughing the rest of my life.

Harpo look at her like he did the night she knock Mary Agnes down. A little spark fly cross the table.

I got six children by this crazy woman, he mutter.

Five, she say.

He so outdone he can't even say, Say what?

He look over at the youngest child. She sullen, mean, mischeevous and too stubborn to live in this world. But he love her best of all. Her name Henrietta.

Henrietta, he say.

She say, Yesssss . . . like they say it on the radio.

Everything she say confuse him. Nothing, he say. Then he say, Go git me a cool glass of water.

She don't move.

Please, he say.

She go git the water, put it by his plate, give him a peck on the cheek. Say, Poor Daddy. Sit back down.

You not gitting a penny of my money, Mr. ____ say to me. Not one thin dime.

Did I ever ast you for money? I say. I never ast you for nothing. Not even for your sorry hand in marriage.

Shug break in right there. Wait, she say. Hold it. Somebody else going with us too. No use in Celie being the only one taking the weight.

Everybody sort of cut they eyes at Sofia. She the one they can't quite find a place for. She the stranger.

It ain't me, she say, and her look say, Fuck you for entertaining the thought. She reach for a biscuit and sort of root her behind deeper into her seat. One look at this big stout graying, wildeyed woman and you know not even to ast. Nothing.

But just to clear this up neat and quick, she say, I'm home. Period.

Her sister Odessa come and put her arms round her. Jack move up close.

Course you is, Jack say.

Mama crying? ast one of Sofia children.

Miss Sofia too, another one say.

But Sofia cry quick, like she do most things.

Who going? she ast.

Nobody say nothing. It so quiet you can hear the embers dying back in the stove. Sound like they falling in on each other.

Finally, Squeak look at everybody from under her bangs. Me, she say. I'm going North.

You going What? say Harpo. He so surprise. He begin to sputter, sputter, just like his daddy. Sound like I don't know what.

I want to sing, say Squeak.

Sing! say Harpo.

Yeah, say Squeak. Sing. I ain't sung in public since Jolentha was born. Her name Jolentha. They call her Suzie Q.

You ain't had to sing in public since Jolentha was born. Everything you need I done provided for.

I need to sing, say Squeak.

Listen Squeak, say Harpo. You can't go to Memphis. That's all there is to it.

Mary Agnes, say Squeak.

Squeak, Mary Agnes, what difference do it make?

It make a lot, say Squeak. When I was Mary Agnes I could sing in public.

Just then a little knock come on the door.

Odessa and Jack look at each other. Come in, say Jack.

A skinny little white woman stick most of herself through the door.

Oh, you all are eating dinner, she say. Excuse me.

That's all right, say Odessa. Us just finishing up. But there's plenty left. Why don't you sit down and join us. Or I could fix you something to eat on the porch.

Oh lord, say Shug.

It Eleanor Jane, the white girl Sofia used to work for.

She look round till she spot Sofia, then she seem to let her breath out. No thank you, Odessa, she say. I ain't hungry. I just come to see Sofia.

Sofia, she say. Can I see you on the porch for a minute.

All right, Miss Eleanor, she say. Sofia push back from the table and they go out on the porch. A few minutes later us hear Miss Eleanor sniffling. Then she really boo-hoo.

What the matter with her? Mr. ____ ast.

Henrietta say, Prob-limbszzzz . . . like somebody on the radio.

Odessa shrug. She always underfoot, she say.

A lot of drinking in that family, say Jack. Plus, they can't keep that boy of theirs in college. He get drunk, aggravate his sister, chase women, hunt niggers, and that ain't all.

That enough, say Shug. Poor Sofia.

Pretty soon Sofia come back in and sit down.

What the matter? ast Odessa.

A lot of mess back at the house, say Sofia.

You got to go back up there? Odessa ast.

Yeah, say Sofia. In a few minutes. But I'll try to be back before the children go to bed.

Henrietta ast to be excuse, say she got a stomach ache.

Squeak and Harpo's little girl come over, look up at Sofia, say, You gotta go Misofia?

Sofia say, Yeah, pull her up on her lap. Sofia on parole, she say. Got to act nice.

Suzie Q lay her head on Sofia chest. Poor Sofia, she say, just like she heard Shug. Poor Sofia.

Mary Agnes, darling, say Harpo, look how Suzie Q take to Sofia.

Yeah, say Squeak, children know good when they see it. She and Sofia smile at one nother.

Go on sing, say Sofia, I'll look after this one till you come back.

You will? say Squeak.

Yeah, say Sofia.

And look after Harpo, too, say Squeak. Please ma'am.

Amen

Dear Nettie,

Well, you know wherever there's a man, there's trouble. And it seem like, going to Memphis, Grady was all over the car. No matter which way us change up, he want to sit next to Squeak.

While me and Shug sleeping and he driving, he tell Squeak all about life in North Memphis, Tennessee. I can't half sleep for him raving bout clubs and clothes and forty-nine brands of beer. Talking so much bout stuff to drink make me have to pee. Then us have to find a road going off into the bushes to relieve ourselves.

Mr. _____ try to act like he don't care I'm going.

You'll be back, he say. Nothing up North for nobody like you. Shug got talent, he say. She can sing. She got spunk, he say. She can talk to anybody. Shug got looks, he say. She can stand up and be notice. But what you got? You ugly. You skinny. You shape funny. You too scared to open your mouth to people. All you fit to do in Memphis is be Shug's maid. Take out her slop-jar and maybe cook her food. You not that good a cook either. And this house ain't been clean good since my first wife died. And nobody crazy or backward enough to

want to marry you, neither. What you gon do? Hire yourself
out to farm? He laugh. Maybe somebody let you work on
they railroad.

Any more letters come? I ast.

He say, What?

You heard me, I say. Any more letters from Nettie come?

If they did, he say, I wouldn't give 'em to you. You two of a
kind, he say. A man try to be nice to you, you fly in his face.

I curse you, I say.

What that mean? he say.

I say, Until you do right by me, everything you touch will
crumble.

He laugh. Who you think you is? he say. You can't curse
nobody. Look at you. You black, you pore, you ugly, you a
woman. Goddam, he say, you nothing at all.

Until you do right by me, I say, everything you even dream
about will fail. I give it to him straight, just like it come to me.
And it seem to come to me from the trees.

Whoever heard of such a thing, say Mr. ____. I probably
didn't whup your ass enough.

Every lick you hit me you will suffer twice, I say. Then I
say, You better stop talking because all I'm telling you ain't
coming just from me. Look like when I open my mouth the
air rush in and shape words.

Shit, he say. I should have lock you up. Just let you out to
work.

The jail you plan for me is the one in which you will rot, I
say.

Shug come over to where us talking. She take one look
at my face and say Celie! Then she turn to Mr. ____. Stop
Albert, she say. Don't say no more. You just going to make it
harder on yourself.

I'll fix her wagon! say Mr. ____, and spring toward me.

A dust devil flew up on the porch between us, fill my mouth with dirt. The dirt say, Anything you do to me, already done to you.

Then I feel Shug shake me. Celie, she say. And I come to myself.

I'm pore, I'm black, I may be ugly and can't cook, a voice say to everything listening. But I'm here.

Amen, say Shug. Amen, amen.

Dear Nettie,

So what is it like in Memphis? Shug's house is big and pink and look sort of like a barn. Cept where you would put hay, she got bedrooms and toilets and a big ballroom where she and her band sometime work. She got plenty grounds round the house and a bunch of monuments and a fountain out front. She got statues of folks I never heard of and never hope to see. She got a whole bunch of elephants and turtles everywhere. Some big, some little, some in the fountain, some up under the trees. Turtles and elephants. And all over her house. Curtains got elephants, bedspreads got turtles.

Shug give me a big back bedroom overlook the backyard and the bushes down by the creek.

I know you use to morning sun, she say.

Her room right cross from mine, in the shade. She work late, sleep late, git up late. No turtles or elephants on her bedroom furniture, but a few statues spread out round the room. She sleep in silks and satins, even her sheets. And her bed round!

I wanted to build me a round house, say Shug, but everybody act like that's backward. You can't put windows in a round house, they say. But I made me up some plans, anyway. One of these days . . . she say, showing me the papers.

It a big round pink house, look sort of like some kind of fruit. It got windows and doors and a lot of trees round it.

What it made of? I ast.

Mud, she say. But I wouldn't mind concrete. I figure you could make the molds for each section, pour the concrete in, let it get hard, knock off the mold, glue the parts together somehow and you'd have your house.

Well, I like this one you got, I say. That one look a little small.

It ain't bad, say Shug. But I just feel funny living in a square. If I was square, then I could take it better, she say.

Us talk bout houses a lot. How they built, what kind of wood people use. Talk about how to make the outside around your house something you can use. I sit down on the bed and start to draw a kind of wood skirt around her concrete house. You can sit on this, I say, when you get tired of being in the house.

Yeah, she say, and let's put awning over it. She took the pencil and put the wood skirt in the shade.

Flower boxes go here, she say, drawing some.

And geraniums in them, I say, drawing some.

And a few stone elephants right here, she say.

And a turtle or two right here.

And how us know you live here too? she ast.

Ducks! I say.

By the time us finish our house look like it can swim or fly.

Nobody cook like Shug when she cook.

She get up early in the morning and go to market. Buy only stuff that's fresh. Then she come home and sit on the back step humming and shelling peas or cleaning collards or fish or whatever she bought. Then she git all her pots going at once and turn on the radio. By one o'clock everything ready and she call us to the table. Ham and greens and chicken and cornbread. Chitlins and blackeyed peas and souse. Pickled okra and watermelon rind. Caramel cake and blackberry pie.

Us eat and eat, and drink a little sweet wine and beer too.

Then Shug and me go fall out in her room to listen to music till all that food have a chance to settle. It cool and dark in her room. Her bed soft and nice. Us lay with our arms round each other. Sometimes Shug read the paper out loud. The news always sound crazy. People fussing and fighting and pointing fingers at other people, and never even looking for no peace.

People insane, say Shug. Crazy as betsy bugs. Nothing built this crazy can last. Listen, she say. Here they building a dam so they can flood out a Indian tribe that been there since time. And look at this, they making a picture bout that man that kilt all them women. The same man that play the killer is playing the priest. And look at these shoes they making now, she say. Try to walk a mile in a pair of them, she say. You be limping all the way home. And you see what they trying to do with that man that beat the Chinese couple to death. Nothing whatsoever.

Yeah, I say, but some things pleasant.

Right, say Shug, turning the page. Mr. and Mrs. Hamilton Hufflemeyer are pleased to announce the wedding of their daughter June Sue. The Morrises of Endover Road are spearheading a social for the Episcopal church. Mrs. Herbert Edenfail was on a visit last week to the Adirondacks to see her ailing mother, the former Mrs. Geoffrey Hood.

All these faces look happy enough, say Shug. Big and beefy. Eyes clear and innocent, like they don't know them other crooks on the front page. But they the same folks, she say.

But pretty soon, after cooking a big dinner and making a
to-do about cleaning the house, Shug go back to work. That
mean she never give a thought to what she eat. Never give a
thought to where she sleep. She on the road somewhere for
weeks at a time, come home with bleary eyes, rotten breath,
overweight and sort of greasy. No place hardly to stop and
really wash herself, especially her hair, on the road.

Let me go with you, I say. I can press your clothes, do
your hair. It would be like old times, when you was singing at
Harpo's.

She say, Naw. She can act like she not bored in front of a
audience of strangers, a lot of them white, but she wouldn't
have the nerve to try to act in front of me.

Besides, she say. You not my maid. I didn't bring you to
Memphis to be that. I brought you here to love you and help
you get on your feet.

And now she off on the road for two weeks, and me and
Grady and Squeak rattle round the house trying to get our
stuff together. Squeak been going round to a lot of clubs
and Grady been taking her. Plus he seem to be doing a little
farming out back the house.

I sit in the dining room making pants after pants. I got
pants now in every color and size under the sun. Since us
started making pants down home, I ain't been able to stop.
I change the cloth, I change the print, I change the waist, I
change the pocket. I change the hem, I change the fullness of
the leg. I make so many pants Shug tease me. I didn't know
what I was starting, she say, laughing. Pants all over her chairs,
hanging all in front of the china closet. Newspaper patterns
and cloth all over the table and the floor. She come home, kiss
me, step over all the mess. Say, before she leave again, How
much money you think you need *this* week?

Then finally one day I made the perfect pair of pants. For

my sugar, naturally. They soft dark blue jersey with teeny
patches of red. But what make them so good is, they totally
comfortable. Cause Shug eat a lot of junk on the road, and
drink, her stomach bloat. So the pants can be let out without
messing up the shape. Because she have to pack her stuff and
fight wrinkles, these pants are soft, hardly wrinkle at all, and
the little figures in the cloth always look perky and bright.
And they full round the ankle so if she want to sing in 'em and
wear 'em sort of like a long dress, she can. Plus, once Shug
put them on, she knock your eyes out.

Miss Celie, she say. You is a wonder to behold.

I duck my head. She run round the house looking at herself
in mirrors. No matter how she look, she look good.

You know how it is when you don't have nothing to do, I
say, when she brag to Grady and Squeak bout her pants. I sit
here thinking bout how to make a living and before I know it
I'm off on another pair pants.

By now Squeak see a pair she like. Oh, Miss Celie, she say.
Can I try on those?

She put on a pair the color of sunset. Orangish with a little
grayish fleck. She come back out looking just fine. Grady look
at her like he could eat her up.

Shug finger the pieces of cloth I got hanging on everything.
It all soft, flowing, rich and catch the light. This a far cry from
that stiff army shit us started with, she say. You ought to make
up a special pair to thank and show Jack.

What she say that for. The next week I'm in and out of
stores spending more of Shug's money. I sit looking out cross
the yard trying to see in my mind what a pair of pants for
Jack would look like. Jack is tall and kind and don't hardly
say anything. Love children. Respect his wife, Odessa, and all
Odessa amazon sisters. Anything she want to take on, he right
there. Never talking much, though. That's the main thing.
And then I remember one time he touch me. And it felt like

his fingers had eyes. Felt like he knew me all over, but he just touch my arm up near the shoulder.

I start to make pants for Jack. They have to be camel. And soft and strong. And they have to have big pockets so he can keep a lot of children's things. Marbles and string and pennies and rocks. And they have to be washable and they have to fit closer round the leg than Shug's so he can run if he need to snatch a child out the way of something. And they have to be something he can lay back in when he hold Odessa in front of the fire. And . . .

I dream and dream and dream over Jack's pants. And cut and sew. And finish them. And send them off.

Next thing I hear, Odessa want a pair.

Then Shug want two more pair just like the first. Then everybody in her band want some. Then orders start to come in from everywhere Shug sing. Pretty soon I'm swamp.

One day when Shug come home, I say, You know, I love doing this, but I got to git out and make a living pretty soon. Look like this just holding me back.

She laugh. Let's us put a few advertisements in the paper, she say. And let's us raise your prices a hefty notch. And let's us just go ahead and give you this diningroom for your factory and git you some more women in here to cut and sew, while you sit back and design. You making your living, Celie, she say. Girl, you on your way.

Nettie, I am making some pants for you to beat the heat in Africa. Soft, white, thin. Drawstring waist. You won't ever have to feel too hot and overdress again. I plan to make them by hand. Every stitch I sew will be a kiss.

> Amen,
> Your Sister, Celie
> Folkspants, Unlimited.
> Sugar Avery Drive
> Memphis, Tennessee

Dear Nettie,

I am so happy. I got love, I got work, I got money, friends and time. And you alive and be home soon. With our children.

Jerene and Darlene come help me with the business. They twins. Never married. Love to sew. Plus, Darlene trying to teach me how to talk. She say US not so hot. A dead country give-away. You say US where most folks say WE, she say, and peoples think you dumb. Colored peoples think you a hick and white folks be amuse.

What I care? I ast. I'm happy.

But she say I feel more happier talking like she talk. Can't nothing make me happier than seeing you again, I think, but I don't say nothing. Every time I say something the way I say it, she correct me until I say it some other way. Pretty soon it feel like I can't think. My mind run up on a thought, git confuse, run back and sort of lay down.

You sure this worth it? I ast.

She say Yeah. Bring me a bunch of books. Whitefolks all over them, talking bout apples and dogs.

What I care bout dogs? I think.

Darlene keep trying. Think how much better Shug feel

with you educated, she say. She won't be shame to take you anywhere.

Shug not shame no how, I say. But she don't believe this the truth. Sugar, she say one day when Shug home, don't you think it be nice if Celie could talk proper?

Shug say, She can talk in sign language for all I care. She make herself a nice cup of herb tea and start talking bout hot oiling her hair.

But I let Darlene worry on. Sometimes I think bout the apples and the dogs, sometimes I don't. Look like to me only a fool would want you to talk in a way that feel peculiar to your mind. But she sweet and she sew good and us need something to haggle over while us work.

I'm busy making pants for Sofia now. One leg be purple, one leg be red. I dream Sofia wearing these pants, one day she was jumping over the moon.

Amen,
Your sister, Celie

Dear Nettie,

Walking down to Harpo and Sofia house it feel just like old times. Cept the house new, down below the juke-joint, and it a lot bigger than it was before. Then too I feels different. Look different. Got on some dark blue pants and a white silk shirt that look righteous. Little red flat-heel slippers, and a flower in my hair. I pass Mr. ____ house and him sitting up on the porch and he didn't even know who I was.

Just when I raise my hand to knock, I hear a crash. Sound like a chair falling over. Then I hear arguing.

Harpo say, Whoever heard of women pallbearers. That all I'm trying to say.

Well, say Sofia, you said it. Now you can hush.

I know she your mother, say Harpo. But still.

You gon help us or not? say Sofia.

What it gon look like? say Harpo. Three big stout women pallbearers look like they ought to be home frying chicken.

Three of our brothers be with us, on the other side, say Sofia. I guess they look like field hands.

But peoples use to men doing this sort of thing. Women weaker, he say. People think they weaker, say they weaker, anyhow. Women spose to take it easy. Cry if you want to. Not try to take over.

Try to take over, say Sofia. The woman dead. I can cry and take it easy and lift the coffin too. And whether you help us or not with the food and the chairs and the get-together afterward, that's exactly what I plan to do.

It git real quiet. After while Harpo say, real soft to Sofia, Why you like this, huh? Why you always think you have to do things your own way? I ast your mama bout it one time, while you was in jail.

What she say? ast Sofia.

She say you think your way as good as anybody else's. Plus, it yours.

Sofia laugh.

I know my timing bad, but I knock anyhow.

Oh, Miss Celie, say Sofia, flinging open the screen. How good you look. Don't she look good, Harpo? Harpo stare at me like he never seen me before.

Sofia give me a big hug and kiss me on the jaw. Where Miss Shug? she ast.

She on the road, I say. But she was real sorry to hear your mama pass.

Well, say Sofia, Mama fight the good fight. If there's a glory anywhere she right in the middle of it.

How you, Harpo? I ast. Still eating?

He and Sofia laugh.

I don't reckon Mary Agnes could come back this time, say Sofia. She was just here bout a month ago. You just ought to see her and Suzie Q.

Naw, I say. She finally working steady, singing at two or three clubs round town. Folks love her a lot.

Suzie Q so proud of her, she say. Love her singing. Love her perfume. Love her dresses. Love to wear her hats and shoes.

How she doing in school? I ast.

Oh, she fine, say Sofia. Smart as a little whip. Once she got over being mad her mama left her and found out I was Henrietta's real mama, she was all right. She dote on Henrietta.

How Henrietta?

Evil, say Sofia. Little face always look like stormy weather. But maybe she'll grow out of it. It took her daddy forty years to learn to be pleasant. He used to be nasty to his own ma.

Yall see much of him? I ast.

Bout as much as us see of Mary Agnes, say Sofia.

Mary Agnes not the same, say Harpo.

What you mean? I ast.

I don't know, he say. Her mind wander. She talk like she drunk. And every time she turn round look like she want to see Grady.

They both smoke a lot of reefer, I say.

Reefer, say Harpo. What kind of a thing is that?

Something make you feel good, I say. Something make you see visions. Something make your love come down. But if you smoke it too much it make you feebleminded. Confuse. Always need to clutch hold of somebody. Grady grow it in the backyard, I say.

I never heard of such a thing, say Sofia. It grow in the ground?

Like a weed, I say. Grady got half a acre if he got a row.

How big it git? ast Harpo.

Big, I say. Way up over my head. And bushy.

And what part they smoke?

The leaf, I say.

And they smoke up all that? he ast.

I laugh. Naw, he sell most of it.

You ever taste it? he ast.

Yeah, I say. He make it up in cigarettes, sell 'em for a dime. It rot your breath, I say, but yall want to try one?

Not if it make us crazy, say Sofia. It hard enough to get by without being a fool.

It just like whiskey, I say. You got to stay ahead of it. You know a little drink now and then never hurt nobody, but when you can't git started without asking the bottle, you in trouble.

You smoke it much, Miss Celie? Harpo ast.

Do I look like a fool? I ast. I smoke when I want to talk to God. I smoke when I want to make love. Lately I feel like me and God make love just fine anyhow. Whether I smoke reefer or not.

Miss Celie! say Sofia. Shock.

Girl, I'm bless, I say to Sofia. God know what I mean.

Us sit round the kitchen table and light up. I show 'em how to suck in they wind. Harpo git strangle. Sofia choke.

Pretty soon Sofia say, That funny, I never heard that humming before.

What humming? Harpo ast.

Listen, she say.

Us git real quiet and listen. Sure enough, us hear ummmmmmmm.

What it coming from? ast Sofia. She git up and go look out the door. Nothing there. Sound git louder. Ummmmmmmm.

Harpo go look out the window. Nothing out there, he say. Humming say UMMMMMMM.

I think I know what it is, I say.

They say, What?

I say, Everything.

Yeah, they say. That make a lots of sense.

Well, say Harpo at the funeral, here come the amazons.

Her brothers there too, I whisper back. What you call them?

I don't know, he say. Them three always stood by they crazy sisters. Nothing yet could get 'em to budge. I wonder what they wives have to put up with.

They all march stoutly in, shaking the church, and place Sofia mother in front the pulpit.

Folks crying and fanning and trying to keep a stray eye on they children, but they don't stare at Sofia and her sisters. They act like this the way it always done. I love folks.

Amen

Dear Nettie,

The first thing I notice bout Mr. _____ is how clean he is. His skin shine. His hair brush back.

When he walk by the casket to review Sofia mother's body he stop, whisper something to her. Pat her shoulder. On his way back to his seat he look over at me. I raise my fan and look off the other way.

Us went back to Harpo's after the funeral.

I know you won't believe this, Miss Celie, say Sofia, but Mr. _____ act like he trying to git religion.

Big a devil as he is, I say, trying is bout all he can do.

He don't go to church or nothing, but he not so quick to judge. He work real hard too.

What? I say. Mr. _____ work!

He sure do. He out there in the field from sunup to sundown. And clean that house just like a woman.

Even cook, say Harpo. And what more, wash the dishes when he finish.

Naw, I say. Yall must still be dope.

But he don't talk much or be round people, Sofia say.

Sound like craziness closing in to me, I say.

Just then, Mr. ___ walk up.

How you Celie, he say.

Fine, I say. I look in his eyes and I see he feeling scared of me. Well, good, I think. Let him feel what I felt.

Shug didn't come with you this time? he say.

Naw, I say. She have to work. Sorry bout Sofia mama though.

Anybody be sorry, he say. The woman that brought Sofia in the world brought something.

I don't say nothing.

They put her away nice, he say.

They sure did, I say.

And so many grandchildren, he say. Well. Twelve children, all busy multiplying. Just the family enough to fill the church.

Yeah, I say. That's the truth.

How long you here for? he say.

Maybe a week, I say.

You know Harpo and Sofia baby girl real sick? he say.

Naw, I didn't, I say. I point to Henrietta in the crowd. There she is over there, I say. She look just fine.

Yeah, she look fine, he say, but she got some kind of blood disease. Blood sort of clot up in her veins every once in a while, make her sick as a dog. I don't think she gon make it, he say.

Great goodness of life, I say.

Yeah, he say. It hard for Sofia. She still have to try to prop up that white gal she raise. Now her mama dead. Her health not that good either. Plus, Henrietta a hard row to hoe whether she sick or well.

Oh, she a little mess, I say. Then I think back to one of Nettie's letters bout the sicknesses children have where she at in Africa. Seem like to me she mention something bout blood clots. I try to remember what she say African peoples do, but

I can't. Talking to Mr. ____ such a surprise I can't think of
nothing. Not even nothing else to say.

Mr. ____ stand waiting for me to say something, looking
off up to his house. Finally he say, Good evening, and walk
away.

Sofia say after I left, Mr. ____ live like a pig. Shut up in the
house so much it stunk. Wouldn't let nobody in until finally
Harpo force his way in. Clean the house, got food. Give his
daddy a bath. Mr. ____ too weak to fight back. Plus, too far
gone to care.

He couldn't sleep, she say. At night he thought he heard
bats outside the door. Other things rattling in the chimney.
But the worse part was having to listen to his own heart. It
did pretty well as long as there was daylight, but soon as night
come, it went crazy. Beating so loud it shook the room. Sound
like drums.

Harpo went up there plenty nights to sleep with him, say
Sofia. Mr. ____ would be all cram up in a corner of the bed.
Eyes clamp on different pieces of furniture, see if they move
in his direction. You know how little he is, say Sofia. And how
big and stout Harpo is. Well, one night I walked up to tell
Harpo something—and the two of them was just laying there
on the bed fast asleep. Harpo holding his daddy in his arms.

After that, I start to feel again for Harpo, Sofia say. And
pretty soon us start work on our new house. She laugh. But
did I say it been easy? If I did, God would make me cut my
own switch.

What make him pull through? I ast.

Oh, she say, Harpo made him send you the rest of your
sister's letters. Right after that he start to improve. You know
meanness kill, she say.

Amen

Dearest Celie,

By now I expected to be home. Looking into your face and saying Celie, is it really you? I try to picture what the years have brought you in the way of weight and wrinkles — or how you fix your hair. From a skinny, hard little something I've become quite plump. And some of my hair is gray!

But Samuel tells me he loves me plump and graying.

Does this surprise you?

We were married last Fall in England where we tried to get relief for the Olinka from the churches and the Missionary Society.

As long as they could, the Olinka ignored the road and the white builders who came. But eventually they had to notice them because one of the first things the builders did was tell the people they must be moved elsewhere. The builders wanted the village site as headquarters for the rubber plantation. It is the only spot for miles that has a steady supply of fresh water.

Protesting and driven, the Olinka, along with their missionaries, were placed on a barren stretch of land that has no water at all for six months of the year. During that time,

they must buy water from the planters. During the rainy
season there is a river and they are trying to dig holes in the
nearby rocks to make cisterns. So far they collect water in
discarded oil drums, which the builders brought.

But the most horrible thing to happen had to do with
the roofleaf, which, as I must have written you, the people
worship as a God and which they use to cover their huts.
Well, on this barren strip of ground the planters erected
workers' barracks. One for men and one for women and
children. But, because the Olinka swore they would never live
in a dwelling not covered by their God, Roofleaf, the builders
left these barracks uncovered. Then they proceeded to plow
under the Olinka village and everything else for miles around.
Including every last stalk of roofleaf.

After nearly unbearable weeks in the hot sun, we were
awakened one morning by the sound of a large truck pulling
into the compound. It was loaded with sheets of corrugated
tin.

Celie, we had to *pay* for the tin. Which exhausted what
meager savings the Olinka had, and nearly wiped out the
money Samuel and I had managed to put by for the education
of the children once we return home. Which we have planned
to do each year since Corrine died, only to find ourselves
more and more involved in the Olinka's problems. Nothing
could be uglier than corrugated tin, Celie. And as they
struggled to put up roofs of this cold, hard, glittery, ugly metal
the women raised a deafening ululation of sorrow that echoed
off the cavern walls for miles around. It was on this day that
the Olinka acknowledged at least temporary defeat.

Though the Olinka no longer ask anything of us, beyond
teaching their children—because they can see how powerless
we and our God are—Samuel and I decided we must do
something about this latest outrage, even as many of the

people to whom we felt close ran away to join the *mbeles* or forest people, who live deep in the jungle, refusing to work for whites or be ruled by them.

So off we went, with the children, to England.

It was an incredible voyage, Celie, not only because we had almost forgot about the rest of the world, and such things as ships and coal fires and streetlights and oatmeal, but because on the ship with us was the white woman missionary whom we'd heard about years ago. She was now retired from missionary work and going back to England to live. She was traveling with a little African boy whom she introduced as her grandchild!

Of course it was impossible to ignore the presence of an aging white woman accompanied by a small black child. The ship was in a tither. Each day she and the child walked about the deck alone, groups of white people falling into silence as they passed.

She is a jaunty, stringy, blue-eyed woman, with hair the color of silver and dry grass. A short chin, and when she speaks she seems to be gargling.

I'm pushing on for sixty-five, she told us, when we found ourselves sharing a table for dinner one night. Been in the tropics most of my life. But, she said, a big war is coming. Bigger than the one they were starting when I left. It'll go hard on England, but I expect we'll survive. I missed the other war, she said. I mean to be present for this one.

Samuel and I had never really thought about war.

Why, she said, the signs are all over Africa. India too, I expect. First there's a road built to where you keep your goods. Then your trees are hauled off to make ships and captain's furniture. Then your land is planted with something you can't eat. Then you're forced to work it. That's happening all over Africa, she said. Burma too, I expect.

But Harold here and I decided to get out. Didn't we

Harry? she said, giving the little boy a biscuit. The child said nothing, just chewed his biscuit thoughtfully. Adam and Olivia soon took him off to explore the lifeboats.

Doris' story—the woman's name is Doris Baines—is an interesting one. But I won't bore you with it as we eventually became bored.

She was born to great wealth in England. Her father was Lord Somebody or Other. They were forever giving or attending parties that were no fun. Besides, she wanted to write books. Her family was against it. Totally. They hoped she'd marry.

Me *marry*! she hooted. (Really, she has the oddest ideas.)

They did everything to convince me, she said. You can't imagine. I never saw so many milkfed young men in all my life as when I was nineteen and twenty. Each one more boring than the last. Can anything be more boring than an upper-class Englishman? she said. They remind one of bloody mushrooms.

Well, she rattled on, through endless dinners, because the captain assigned us permanently to the same table. It seems the notion of becoming a missionary struck her one evening she was getting ready for yet another tedious date, and lay in the tub thinking a convent would be better than the castle in which she lived. She could think, she could write. She could be her own boss. But wait. As a nun she would not be her own boss. God would be boss. The virgin mother. The mother superior. Etc. Etc. Ah, but a missionary! Far off in the wilds of India, alone! It seemed like bliss.

And so she cultivated a pious interest in heathens. Fooled her parents. Fooled the Missionary Society, who were so taken with her quick command of languages they sent her to Africa (worst luck!) where she began writing novels about everything under the sun.

My pen name is Jared Hunt, she said. In England and

even in America, I'm a run-away success. Rich, famous. An eccentric recluse who spends most of his time shooting wild game.

Well now, she continued, several evenings later, you don't think I paid much attention to the heathen? I saw nothing wrong with them as they were. And they seemed to like *me* well enough. I was actually able to help them a good deal. I was a writer, after all, and I wrote reams of paper on their behalf: about their culture, their behavior, their needs, that sort of thing. You'd be surprised how good writing matters when you're going after money. I learned to speak their language faultlessly, and to throw off the missionary snoopers back at headquarters I wrote entire reports in it. I tapped the family vaults for close on to a million pounds before I got anything from the missionary societies or rich old family friends. I built a hospital, a grammar school. A college. A swimming pool—the one luxury I permitted myself, since swimming in the river one is subject to attack by leeches.

You wouldn't believe the peace! she said, at breakfast, halfway to England. Within a year everything as far as me and the heathen were concerned ran like clockwork. I told them right off that their souls were no concern of mine, that I wanted to write books and not be disturbed. For this pleasure I was prepared to pay. Rather handsomely.

In a burst of appreciation one day, I'm afraid the chief—not knowing what else to do, no doubt—presented me with a couple of wives. I don't think it was commonly believed I was a woman. There seemed some question in their minds just what I was. Anyhow. I educated the two young girls as best I could. Sent them to England, of course, to learn medicine and agriculture. Welcomed them home when they returned, gave them away in marriage to two young chaps who were always about the place, and began the happiest period of my life as the grandmother of their children. I must say, she beamed, I've turned out to be fab-o as a grand*mama*. I learned it from the Akweans. They never spank their children. Never lock them away in another part of the hut. They do a bit of bloody cutting around puberty. But Harry's mother the doctor is going to change all that. Isn't she Harold?

Anyway, she said. When I get to England I'll put a stop to their bloody encroachments. I'll tell them what to do with their bloody road and their bloody rubber plantations and their bloody sunburned but still bloody boring English planters and engineers. I am a very wealthy woman, and I *own* the village of Akwee.

We listened to most of this in more or less respectful silence. The children were very taken with young Harold, though he never said a word in our presence. He seemed fond of his grandmother and used to her, but her verbosity produced in him a kind of soberly observant speechlessness.

He's quite different with us though, said Adam, who is really a great lover of children, and could get through to any child given half an hour. Adam makes jokes, he sings, he clowns and knows games. And he has the sunniest smile, most of the time—and great healthy African teeth.

As I write about his sunny smile I realize he's been unusually glum during this trip. Interested and excited, but not really *sunny*, except when he's with young Harold.

I will have to ask Olivia what's wrong. She is thrilled at the thought of going back to England. Her mother used to tell her about the thatched cottages of the English and how they reminded her of the roofleaf huts of the Olinka. They are square, though, she'd say. More like our church and school than like our homes, which Olivia thought very strange.

When we reached England, Samuel and I presented the Olinka's grievances to the bishop of the English branch of our

church, a youngish man wearing spectacles who sat thumbing
through a stack of Samuel's yearly reports. Instead of even
mentioning the Olinka the bishop wanted to know how long
it had been since Corrine's death, and why, as soon as she
died, I had not returned to America.

I really did not understand what he was driving at.

Appearances, Miss ____, he said. Appearances. What must
the natives think?

About what? I asked.

Come, come, he said.

We behave as brother and sister to each other, said Samuel.

The bishop smirked. Yes, he did.

I felt my face go hot.

Well, there was more of this, but why burden you with
it? You know what some people are, and the bishop was one
of them. Samuel and I left without even a word about the
Olinka's problems.

Samuel was so angry, I was frightened. He said the only
thing for us to do, if we wanted to remain in Africa, was join
the *mbeles* and encourage all the Olinka to do the same.

But suppose they do not want to go? I asked. Many of them
are too old to move back into the forest. Many are sick. The
women have small babies. And then there are the youngsters
who want bicycles and British clothes. Mirrors and shiny
cooking pots. They want to work for the white people in
order to have these things.

Things! he said, in disgust. Bloody *things*!

Well, we have a month here anyway, I said, let's make the
most of it.

Because we had spent so much of our money on tin roofs
and the voyage over, it had to be a poor man's month in
England. But it was a very good time for us. We began to feel
ourselves a family, without Corrine. And people meeting us

on the street never failed (if they spoke to us at all) to express
the sentiment that the children looked just like the two of us.
The children began to accept this as natural, and began going
out to view the sights that interested them, alone. Leaving
their father and me to our quieter, more sedate pleasures, one
of which was simple conversation.

Samuel, of course, was born in the North, in New York,
and grew up and was educated there. He met Corrine through
his aunt who had been a missionary, along with Corrine's
aunt, in the Belgian Congo. Samuel frequently accompanied
his aunt Althea to Atlanta, where Corrine's aunt Theodosia
lived.

These two ladies had been through marvelous things
together, said Samuel, laughing. They'd been attacked by
lions, stampeded by elephants, flooded out by rains, made war
on by "natives." The tales they told were simply incredible.
There they sat on a heavily antimacassared horsehair sofa,
two prim and proper ladies in ruffles and lace, telling these
stupendous stories over tea.

Corrine and I as teenagers used to attempt to stylize these
tales into comics. We called them such things as THREE
MONTHS IN A HAMMOCK, or SORE HIPS OF THE DARK
CONTINENT. Or, A MAP OF AFRICA: A GUIDE TO NATIVE
INDIFFERENCE TO THE HOLY WORD.

We made fun of them, but we were riveted on their
adventures, and on the ladies' telling of them. They were so
staid looking. So proper. You really couldn't imagine them
actually building—with their own hands—a school in
the bush. Or battling reptiles. Or unfriendly Africans who
thought, since they were wearing dresses with things that
looked like wings behind, they should be able to fly.

Bush? Corrine would snicker to me or me to her. And just
the sound of the word would send us off into quiet hysteria,

while we calmly sipped our tea. Because of course they didn't
realize they were being funny, and to us they were, very. And
of course the prevailing popular view of Africans at that time
contributed to our feeling of amusement. Not only were
Africans savages, they were bumbling, inept savages, rather
like their bumbling, inept brethren at home. But we carefully,
not to say studiously, avoided this very apparent connection.

Corrine's mother was a dedicated housewife and mother
who disliked her more adventurous sister. But she never
prevented Corrine from visiting. And when Corrine was
old enough, she sent her to Spelman Seminary where Aunt
Theodosia had gone. This was a very interesting place. It was
started by two white missionaries from New England who
used to wear identical dresses. Started in a church basement, it
soon moved up to Army barracks. Eventually these two ladies
were able to get large sums of money from some of the richest
men in America, and so the place grew. Buildings, trees.
Girls were taught everything: Reading, Writing, Arithmetic,
sewing, cleaning, cooking. But more than anything else, they
were taught to serve God and the colored community. Their
official motto was OUR WHOLE SCHOOL FOR CHRIST. But I
always thought their unofficial motto should have been OUR
COMMUNITY COVERS THE WORLD, because no sooner had
a young woman got through Spelman Seminary than she
began to put her hand to whatever work she could do for her
people, anywhere in the world. It was truly astonishing. These
very polite and proper young women, some of them never
having set foot outside their own small country towns, except
to come to the Seminary, thought nothing of packing up for
India, Africa, the Orient. Or for Philadelphia or New York.

Sixty years or so before the founding of the school, the
Cherokee Indians who lived in Georgia were forced to leave
their homes and walk, through the snow, to resettlement

camps in Oklahoma. A third of them died on the way. But
many of them refused to leave Georgia. They hid out as
colored people and eventually blended with us. Many of these
mixed-race people were at Spelman. Some remembered who
they actually were, but most did not. If they thought about
it at all (and it became harder to think about Indians because
there were none around) they thought they were yellow or
reddish brown and wavy haired because of white ancestors,
not Indian.

Even Corrine thought this, he said. And yet, I always felt
her Indianness. She was so quiet. So reflective. And she could
erase herself, her spirit, with a swiftness that truly startled,
when she knew the people around her could not respect it.

It did not seem hard for Samuel to talk about Corrine
while we were in England. It wasn't hard for me to listen.

It all seems so improbable, he said. Here I am, an aging
man whose dreams of helping people have been just that,
dreams. How Corrine and I as children would have laughed
at ourselves. TWENTY YEARS A FOOL OF THE WEST,
OR MOUTH AND ROOFLEAF DISEASE: A TREATISE ON
FUTILITY IN THE TROPICS. Etc. Etc. We failed so utterly, he
said. We became as comical as Althea and Theodosia. I think
her awareness of this fueled Corrine's sickness. She was far
more intuitive than I. Her gift for understanding people much
greater. She used to say the Olinka resented us, but I wouldn't
see it. But they do, you know.

No, I said, it isn't resentment, exactly. It really is
indifference. Sometimes I feel our position is like that of
flies on an elephant's hide.

I remember once, before Corrine and I were married,
Samuel continued, Aunt Theodosia had one of her at-homes.
She had them every Thursday. She'd invited a lot of "serious
young people" as she called them, and one of them was a

young Harvard scholar named Edward. DuBoyce was his last
name, I think. Anyhow, Aunt Theodosia was going on about
her African adventures, leading up to the time King Leopold
of Belgium presented her with a medal. Well Edward, or
perhaps his name was Bill, was a very impatient sort. You saw
it in his eyes, you could see it in the way he moved his body.
He was never still. As Aunt Theodosia got closer to the part
about her surprise and joy over receiving this medal—which
validated her service as an exemplary missionary in the King's
colony—DuBoyce's foot began to pat the floor rapidly and
uncontrollably. Corrine and I looked at each other in alarm.
Clearly this man had heard this tale before and was not
prepared to endure it a second time.

Madame, he said, when Aunt Theodosia finished her story
and flashed her famous medal around the room, do you
realize King Leopold cut the hands off workers who, in the
opinion of his plantation overseers, did not fulfill their rubber
quota? Rather than cherish that medal, Madame, you should
regard it as a symbol of your unwitting complicity with this
despot who worked to death and brutalized and eventually
exterminated thousands and thousands of African peoples.

Well, said Samuel, silence struck the gathering like a
blight. Poor Aunt Theodosia! There's something in all of us
that wants a medal for what we have done. That wants to be
appreciated. And Africans certainly don't deal in medals. They
hardly seem to care whether missionaries exist.

Don't be bitter, I said.

How can I not? he said.

The Africans never asked us to come, you know. There's no
use blaming them if we feel unwelcome.

It's worse than unwelcome, said Samuel. The Africans don't
even see us. They don't even recognize us as the brothers and
sisters they sold.

Oh, Samuel, I said. Don't.

But you know, he had started to cry. Oh Nettie, he said. That's the heart of it, don't you see. We love them. We try every way we can to show that love. But they reject us. They never even listen to how we've suffered. And if they listen they say stupid things. Why don't you speak our language? they ask. Why can't you remember the old ways? Why aren't you happy in America, if everyone there drives motorcars?

Celie, it seemed as good a time as any to put my arms around him. Which I did. And words long buried in my heart crept to my lips. I stroked his dear head and face and I called him darling and dear. And I'm afraid, dear, dear Celie, that concern and passion soon ran away with us.

I hope when you receive this news of your sister's forward behavior you will not be shocked or inclined to judge me harshly. Especially when I tell you what a total joy it was. I was transported by ecstasy in Samuel's arms.

You may have guessed that I loved him all along; but I did not know it. Oh, I loved him as a brother and respected him as a friend, but Celie, I love him bodily, *as a man!* I love his walk, his size, his shape, his smell, the kinkiness of his hair. I love the very texture of his palms. The pink of his inner lip. I love his big nose. I love his brows. I love his feet. And I love his dear eyes in which the vulnerability and beauty of his soul can be plainly read.

The children saw the change in us immediately. I'm afraid, my dear, we were radiant.

We love each other dearly, Samuel told them, with his arm around me. We intend to marry.

But before we do, I said, I must tell you something about my life and about Corrine and about someone else. And it was then I told them about you, Celie. And about their mother Corrine's love of them. And about being their aunt.

But where is this other woman, your sister? asked Olivia.

I explained your marriage to Mr. _____ as best I could.

Adam was instantly alarmed. He is a very sensitive soul who hears what isn't said as clearly as what is.

We will go back to America soon, said Samuel to reassure him, and see about her.

The children stood up with us in a simple church ceremony in London. And it was that night, after the wedding dinner, when we were all getting ready for bed, that Olivia told me what has been troubling her brother. He is missing Tashi.

But he's also very angry with her, she said, because when we left, she was planning to scar her face.

I didn't know this. One of the things we thought we'd helped stop was the scarring or cutting of tribal marks on the faces of young women.

It is a way the Olinka can show they still have their own ways, said Olivia, even though the white man has taken everything else. Tashi didn't want to do it, but to make her people feel better, she's resigned. She's going to have the female initiation ceremony too, she said.

Oh, no, I said. That's so dangerous. Suppose she becomes infected?

I know, said Olivia. I told her nobody in America or Europe cuts off pieces of themselves. And anyway, she would have had it when she was eleven, if she was going to have it. She's too old for it now.

Well, some men are circumcized, I said, but that's just the removal of a bit of skin.

Tashi was happy that the initiation ceremony isn't done in Europe or America, said Olivia. That makes it even more valuable to her.

I see, I said.

She and Adam had an awful fight. Not like any they've had before. He wasn't teasing her or chasing her around the village or trying to tie roofleaf twigs in her hair. He was mad enough to strike her.

Well, it's a good thing he didn't, I said. Tashi would have jammed his head through her rug loom.

I'll be glad when we get back home, said Olivia. Adam isn't the only one who misses Tashi.

She kissed me and her father good night. Adam soon came in to do the same.

Mama Nettie, he said, sitting on the bed next to me, how do you know when you really love someone?

Sometimes you don't know, I said.

He is a beautiful young man, Celie. Tall and broad-shouldered, with a deep, thoughtful voice. Did I tell you he writes verses? And loves to sing? He's a son to make you proud.

Your loving sister, Nettie

P.S. Your brother Samuel sends his love as well.

Dearest Celie,

When we returned home everyone seemed happy to see us. When we told them our appeal to the church and the Missionary Society failed, they were disappointed. They literally wiped the smiles off their faces along with the sweat, and returned, dejected, to their barracks. We went on to our building, a combination church, house and school, and began to unpack our things.

The children . . . I realize I shouldn't call them children, they're grown, went in search of Tashi; an hour later they returned dumbfounded. They discovered no sign of her. Catherine, her mother, is planting rubber trees some distance from the compound, they were told. But no one had seen Tashi all day.

Olivia was very disappointed. Adam was trying to appear unconcerned, but I noticed he was absentmindedly biting the skin around his nails.

After two days it became clear that Tashi was deliberately hiding. Her friends said while we were away she'd undergone both the facial scarification ceremony and the rite of female initiation. Adam went quite gray at this news.

Olivia merely stricken and more concerned than ever to find her.

It was not until Sunday that we saw Tashi. She'd lost a considerable amount of weight, and seemed listless, dull-eyed and tired. Her face was still swollen from half a dozen small, neat incisions high on each cheek. When she put out her hand to Adam he refused to take it. He just looked at her scars, turned on his heel and left.

She and Olivia hugged. But it was a quiet, heavy embrace. Nothing like the boisterous, giggling behavior I expect from them.

Tashi is, unfortunately, ashamed of these scars on her face, and now hardly ever raises her head. They must be painful too because they look irritated and red.

But this is what the villagers are doing to the young women and even the men. Carving their identification as a people into their children's faces. But the children think of scarification as backward, something from their grandparents' generation, and often resist. So the carving is done by force, under the most appalling conditions. We provide antiseptics and cotton and a place for the children to cry and nurse their wounds.

Each day Adam presses us to leave for home. He can no longer bear living as we do. There aren't even any trees near us, just giant boulders and smaller rocks. And more and more of his companions are running away. The real reason, of course, is he can no longer bear his conflicting feelings about Tashi, who is beginning, I think, to appreciate the magnitude of her mistake.

Samuel and I are truly happy, Celie. And so grateful to God that we are! We still keep a school for the littlest children; those eight and over are already workers in the fields. In order to pay rent for the barracks, taxes on the land, and to buy

water and wood and food, everyone must work. So, we teach
the young ones, babysit the babies, look after the old and sick,
and attend birthing mothers. Our days are fuller than ever,
our sojourn in England already a dream. But all things look
brighter because I have a loving soul to share them with.

Your sister, Nettie

Dearest Nettie,

The man us knowed as Pa is dead.

How come you still call him Pa? Shug ast me the other day.

But, too late to call him Alphonso. I never even remember Ma calling him by his name. She always said, Your Pa. I reckon to make us believe it better. Anyhow, his little wife, Daisy, call me up on the telephone in the middle of the night.

Miss Celie, she say, I got bad news. Alphonso dead.

Who? I ast.

Alphonso, she say. Your stepdaddy.

How he die? I ast. I think of killing, being hit by a truck, struck by lightening, lingering disease. But she say, Naw, he died in his sleep. Well, not quite in his sleep, she say. Us was spending a little time in bed together, you know, before us drop off.

Well, I say, you have my sympathy.

Yes ma'am, she say, and I thought I had this house too, but look like it belong to your sister Nettie and you.

Say what? I ast.

Your stepdaddy been dead over a week, she say. When us went to town to hear the will read yesterday, you could have

knock me over with a feather. Your real daddy owned the land
and the house and the store. He left it to your mama. When
your mama died, it passed on to you and your sister Nettie. I
don't know why Alphonso never told you that.

Well, I say, anything coming from him, I don't want it.

I hear Daisy suck in her breath. How about your sister
Nettie, she say. You think she feel the same way?

I wake up a little bit then. By the time Shug roll over and
ast me who it is, I'm beginning to see the light.

Don't be a fool, Shug say, nudging me with her foot. You
got your own house now. Your daddy and mama left it for you.
That dog of a stepdaddy just a bad odor passing through.

But I never had no house, I say. Just to think about having
my own house enough to scare me. Plus, this house I'm
gitting is bigger than Shug's, got more land around it. And, it
come with a store.

My God, I say to Shug. Me and Nettie own a drygood
store. What us gon sell?

How bout pants? she say.

So us hung up the phone and rush down home again to
look at the property.

About a mile before us got to town us come up on the
entrance to the colored cemetery. Shug was sound asleep,
but something told me I ought to drive in. Pretty soon I see
something look like a short skyscraper and I stop the car and
go up to it. Sure enough it's got Alphonso's name on it. Got a
lot of other stuff on it too. Member of this and that. Leading
businessman and farmer. Upright husband and father. Kind
to the poor and helpless. He been dead two weeks but fresh
flowers still blooming on his grave.

Shug git out the car and come stand by me.

Finally she yawn loud and stretch herself. The son of a
bitch still dead, she say.

Daisy try to act like she glad to see us, but she not. She got two children and look pregnant with one more. But she got nice clothes, a car, and Alphonso left her all his money. Plus, I think she manage to set her folks up while she live with him.

She say, Celie, the old house you remember was torn down so Alphonso could build this one. He got an Atlanta architect to design it, and these tiles come all the way from New York. We was standing in the kitchen at the time. But he put tiles everywhere. Kitchen, toilet, back porch. All around the fireplaces in back and front parlour. But this the house go with the place, right on, she say. Of course I did take the furniture, because Alphonso bought it special for me.

Fine with me, I say. I can't get over having a house. Soon as Daisy leave me with the keys I run from one room to another like I'm crazy. Look at this, I say to Shug. Look at that! She look, she grin. She hug me whenever she git the chance and I stand still.

You doin' all right, Miss Celie, she say. God know where you live.

Then she took some cedar sticks out of her bag and lit them and gave one of them to me. Us started at the very top of the house in the attic, and us smoked it all the way down to the basement, chasing out all the evil and making a place for good.

Oh, Nettie, us have a house! A house big enough for us and our children, for your husband and Shug. Now you can come home cause you have a home to come to!

Your loving sister, Celie

Dear Nettie,

My heart broke.

Shug love somebody else.

Maybe if I had stayed in Memphis last summer it never would have happen. But I spent the summer fixing up the house. I thought if you come anytime soon, I want it to be ready. And it is real pretty, now, and comfortable. And I found me a nice lady to live in it and look after it. Then I come home to Shug.

Miss Celie, she say, how would you like some Chinese food to celebrate your coming home?

I loves Chinese food. So off us go to the restaurant. I'm so excited about being home again I don't even notice how nervous Shug is. She a big graceful woman most of the time, even when she mad. But I notice she can't git her chopsticks to work right. She knock over her glass of water. Somehow or nother her eggroll come unravel.

But I think she just so glad to see me. So I preen and pose for her and stuff myself with wonton soup and fried rice.

Finally the fortune cookies come. I love fortune cookies. They so cute. And I read my fortune right away. It say, because you are who you are, the future look happy and bright.

I laugh. Pass it on to Shug. She look at it and smile. I feel at peace with the world.

Shug pull her slip of paper out real slow, like she scared of what might be on it.

Well? I say, watching her read it. What it say?

She look down at it, look up at me. Say, It say I got the hots for a boy of nineteen.

Let me see, I say, laughing. And I read it out loud. A burnt finger remember the fire, it say.

I'm trying to tell you, Shug say.

Trying to tell me what? I'm so dense it still don't penetrate. For one thing, it been a long time since I thought about boys and I ain't never thought about men.

Last year, say Shug, I hired a new man to work in the band. I almost didn't because he can't play nothing but flute. And who ever heard of blues flute? I hadn't. The very notion sound crazy. But it was just my luck that blues flute is the one thing blues music been lacking and the minute I heard Germaine play I knew this for a fact.

Germaine? I ast.

Yeah, she say, Germaine. I don't know who gave him that flittish name, but it suit him.

Then she start right in to rave about this boy. Like all his good points have to be stuff I'm dying to hear.

Oh, she say. He little. He cute. Got nice buns. You know, real bantu. She so used to telling me everything she rattle on and on, gitting more excited and in-love looking by the minute. By the time she finish talking about his neat little dancing feet and git back up to his honey brown curly hair, I feel like shit.

Hold it, I say. Shug, you killing me.

She halt in mid-praise. Her eyes fill with tears and her face crumple. Oh God, Celie, she say. I'm sorry. I just been dying to tell somebody, and you the somebody I usually tell.

Well, I say, if words could kill, I'd be in the ambulance.

She put her face in her hands and start to cry. Celie, she say, through her fingers, I still love you.

But I just sit there and watch her. Seem like all my wonton soup turn to ice.

Why you so upset? she ast, when us got back home. You never seem to git upset bout Grady. And he was my husband.

Grady never bring no sparkle to your eye, I think. But I don't say nothing, I'm too far away.

Course, she say, Grady so dull, Jesus. And when you finish talking bout women and reefer you finish Grady. But still, she say.

I don't say nothing.

She try to laugh. I was so glad he lit out after Mary Agnes I didn't know what to do, she say. I don't know who tried to teach him what to do in the bedroom, but it must have been a furniture salesman.

I don't say nothing. Stillness, coolness. Nothingness. Coming fast.

You notice when they left here together going to Panama I didn't shed a tear? But now really, she say, what they gon look like in Panama?

Poor Mary Agnes, I think. How could anybody guess old dull Grady would end up running a reefer plantation in Panama?

Course they making boocoos of money, say Shug. And Mary Agnes outdress everybody down there, the way she tell it in her letters. And at least Grady let her sing. What little snatches of her songs she can still remember. But really, she say, Panama? Where is it at, anyhow? Is it down there round

Cuba? Us ought to go to Cuba, Miss Celie, you know? Lots
of gambling there and good times. A lots of colored folks
look like Mary Agnes. Some real black, like us. All in the same
family though. Try to pass for white, somebody mention your
grandma.

I don't say nothing. I pray to die, just so I don't never have
to speak.

All right, say Shug. It started when you was down home. I
missed you, Celie. And you know I'm a high natured woman.

I went and got a piece of paper that I was using for cutting
patterns. I wrote her a note. It said, Shut up.

But Celie, she say. I have to make you understand. Look,
she say. I'm gitting old. I'm fat. Nobody think I'm good
looking no more, but you. Or so I thought. He's nineteen. A
baby. How long can it last?

He's a man. I write on the paper.

Yeah, she say. He is. And I know how you feel about men.
But I don't feel that way. I would never be fool enough to take
any of them seriously, she say, but some mens can be a lots of
fun.

Spare me, I write.

Celie, she say. All I ast is six months. Just six months to
have my last fling. I got to have it Celie. I'm too weak a
woman not to. But if you just give me six months, Celie, I will
try to make our life together like it was.

Not hardly. I write.

Celie, she say, Do you love me? She down on her knees by
now, tears falling all over the place. My heart hurt so much I
can't believe it. How can it keep beating, feeling like this? But
I'm a woman. I love you, I say. Whatever happen, whatever
you do, I love you.

She whimper a little, lean her head against my chair. Thank
you, she say.

But I can't stay here, I say.

But Celie, she say, how can you leave me? You're my friend. I love this child and I'm scared to death. He's a third of my age. A third of my size. Even a third of my color. She try to laugh again. You know he gon hurt me worse than I'm hurting you. Don't leave me, please.

Just then the door bell ring. Shug wiped her face and went to answer it, saw who it was and kept on out the door. Soon I heard a car drive off. I went on up to bed. But sleep remain a stranger to this night.

> Pray for me,
> Your sister, Celie

Dear Nettie,

The only thing keep me alive is watching Henrietta fight for her life. And boy can she fight. Every time she have an attack she scream enough to wake the dead. Us do what you say the peoples do in Africa. Us feed her yams every single day. Just our luck she hate yams and she not too polite to let us know. Everybody for miles around try to come up with yam dishes that don't taste like yams. Us git plates of yam eggs, yam chitlins, yam goat. And soup. My God, folks be making soup out of everything but shoe leather trying to kill off the yam taste. But Henrietta claim she still taste it, and is likely to throw whatever it is out the window. Us tell her in a little while she'll have three months not to eat yams, but she say that day don't seem like it ever want to come. Meanwhile, her joints all swole, she hot enough to burn, she say her head feel like its full of little white men with hammers.

Sometime I meet up with Mr. ____ visiting Henrietta. He dream up his own little sneaky recipes. For instance, one time he hid the yams in peanut butter. Us sit by the fire with Harpo and Sofia and play a hand or two of bid whist, while Suzie Q and Henrietta listen to the radio. Sometime he drive me home in his car. He still live in the same little house. He been there so long, it look just like him. Two straight chairs always on the porch, turned against the wall. Porch railings with flower cans on them. He keep it painted now though. Fresh and white. And guess what he collect just cause he like them? He collect shells. All kinds of shells. Tarrapin, snail and all kinds of shells from the sea.

Matter of fact, that's how he got me up to the house again. He was telling Sofia bout some new shell he had that made a loud sea sound when you put it to your ear. Us went up to see it. It was big and heavy and speckled like a chicken and sure enough, seem like you could hear the waves or something crashing against your ear. None of us ever seen the ocean, but Mr. ____ learn about it from books. He order shells from books too, and they all over the place.

He don't say that much about them while you looking, but he hold each one like it just arrive.

Shug one time had a seashell, he say. Long time ago, when us first met. Big white thing look like a fan. She still love shells? he ast.

Naw, I say. She love elephants now.

He wait a little while, put all the shells back in place. Then he ast me, You like any special thing?

I love birds, I say.

You know, he say, you use to remind me of a bird. Way back when you first come to live with me. You was so skinny, Lord, he say. And the least little thing happen, you looked about to fly away.

You saw that, I say.

I saw it, he said, just too big a fool to let myself care.

Well, I say, us lived through it.

We still man and wife, you know, he say.

Naw, I say, we never was.

You know, he say, you look real good since you been up in Memphis.

Yeah, I say, Shug take good care of me.

How you make your living up there? he say.

Making pants, I say.

He say, I notice everybody in the family just about wearing pants you made. But you mean you turned it into a business?

That's right, I say. But I really started it right here in your house to keep from killing you.

· He look down at the floor.

Shug help me make the first pair I ever did, I say. And then, like a fool, I start to cry.

He say, Celie, tell me the truth. You don't like me cause I'm a man?

I blow my nose. Take off they pants, I say, and men look like frogs to me. No matter how you kiss 'em, as far as I'm concern, frogs is what they stay.

I see, he say.

By the time I got back home I was feeling so bad I couldn't do nothing but sleep. I tried to work on some new pants I'm trying to make for pregnant women, but just the thought of anybody gitting pregnant make me want to cry.

Your sister, Celie

Dear Nettie,

The only piece of mail Mr. _____ ever put directly in my hand is a telegram that come from the United States Department of Defense. It say the ship you and the children and your husband left Africa in was sunk by German mines off the coast of someplace call Gibralta. They think you all drowned. Plus, the same day, all the letters I wrote to you over the years come back unopen.

I sit here in this big house by myself trying to sew, but what good is sewing gon do? What good is anything? Being alive begin to seem like a awful strain.

Your sister, Celie

Dearest Celie,

Tashi and her mother have run away. They have gone to
join the *mbeles*. Samuel and the children and I were discussing
it just yesterday, and we realized we do not even know for
sure the *mbeles* exist. All we know is that they are said to
live deep in the forest, that they welcome runaways, and
that they harass the white man's plantations and plan his
destruction—or at least for his removal from their continent.

Adam and Olivia are heartbroken because they love Tashi
and miss her, and because no one who has gone to join the
mbeles ever returned. We try to keep them busy around
the compound and because there is so much sickness from
malaria this season there is plenty for them to do. In plowing
under the Olinka's yam crop and substituting canned and
powdered goods, the planters destroyed what makes them
resistant to malaria. Of course they did not know this, they
only wanted to take the land for rubber, but the Olinka have
been eating yams to prevent malaria and to control chronic
blood disease for thousands and thousands of years. Left
without a sufficient supply of yams, the people—what's left of
them—are sickening and dying at an alarming rate.

To tell you the truth, I fear for our own health, and especially for the children. But Samuel feels we will probably be all right, having had bouts with malaria during the first years we were here.

And how are you, dearest sister? Nearly thirty years have passed without a word between us. For all I know you may be dead. As the time nears for us to come home, Adam and Olivia ask endless questions about you, few of which I can answer. Sometimes I tell them Tashi reminds me of you. And, because there is no one finer to them than Tashi, they glow with delight. But will you still have Tashi's honest and open spirit, I wonder, when we see you again? Or will years of childbearing and abuse from Mr. _____ have destroyed it? These are thoughts I don't pursue with the children, only with my beloved companion, Samuel, who advises me not to worry, to trust in God, and to have faith in the sturdiness of my sister's soul.

God is different to us now, after all these years in Africa. More spirit than ever before, and more internal. Most people think he has to look like something or someone—a roofleaf or Christ—but we don't. And not being tied to what God looks like, frees us.

When we return to America we must have long talks about this, Celie. And perhaps Samuel and I will found a new church in our community that has no idols in it whatsoever, in which each person's spirit is encouraged to seek God directly, his belief that this is possible strengthened by us as people who also believe.

There is little to do here for entertainment, as you can imagine. We read the papers and magazines from home, play any number of African games with the children. Rehearse the African children in parts of Shakespeare's plays—Adam was always very good as Hamlet giving his To Be or Not to Be soliloquy. Corrine had firm notions of what the children should be taught and saw to it that every good work advertised in the papers became part of their library. They know many things, and I think will not find American society such a shock, except for the hatred of black people, which is also very clear in all the news. But I worry about their very African independence of opinion and outspokenness, also extreme self-centeredness. And we will be poor, Celie, and it will be years no doubt before we even own a home. How will they manage the hostility towards them, having grown up here? When I think of them in America I see them as much younger than they appear here. Much more naive. The worst we have had to endure here is indifference and a certain understandable shallowness in our personal relationships—excluding our relationship with Catherine and Tashi. After all, the Olinka know we can leave, they must stay. And, of course, none of this has to do with color. And—

Dearest Celie,

Last night I stopped writing because Olivia came in to tell me Adam is missing. He can only have gone after Tashi.

Pray for his safety,
Your sister, Nettie

Dearest Nettie,

Sometimes I think Shug never love me. I stand looking
at my naked self in the looking glass. What would she love?
I ast myself. My hair is short and kinky because I don't
straighten it anymore. Once Shug say she love it no need to.
My skin dark. My nose just a nose. My lips just lips. My body
just any woman's body going through the changes of age.
Nothing special here for nobody to love. No honey colored
curly hair, no cuteness. Nothing young and fresh. My heart
must be young and fresh though, it feel like it blooming
blood.

I talk to myself a lot, standing in front the mirror. Celie,
I say, happiness was just a trick in your case. Just cause you
never had any before Shug, you thought it was time to have
some, and that it was gon last. Even thought you had the trees
with you. The whole earth. The stars. But look at you. When
Shug left, happiness desert.

Every once in a while I git a postcard from Shug. Her and
Germaine in New York, in California. Gone to see Mary
Agnes and Grady in Panama.

Mr. ____ seem to be the only one understand my feeling.

I know you hate me for keeping you from Nettie, he say.
And now she dead.

But I don't hate him, Nettie. And I don't believe you dead.
How can you be dead if I still feel you? Maybe, like God, you
changed into something different that I'll have to speak to in
a different way, but you not dead to me Nettie. And never will
be. Sometime when I git tired of talking to myself I talk to
you. I even try to reach our children.

Mr. ____ still can't believe I have children. Where you git
children from? he ast.

My stepdaddy, I say.

You mean he knowed he was the one damage you all along?
he ast.

I say, Yeah.

Mr. ____ shake his head.

After all the evil he done I know you wonder why I don't
hate him. I don't hate him for two reasons. One, he love Shug.
And two, Shug use to love him. Plus, look like he trying to
make something out of himself. I don't mean just that he
work and he clean up after himself and he appreciate some of
the things God was playful enough to make. I mean when you
talk to him now he really listen, and one time, out of nowhere
in the conversation us was having, he said Celie, I'm satisfied
this the first time I ever lived on Earth as a natural man. It
feel like a new experience.

Sofia and Harpo always try to set me up with some man.
They know I love Shug but they think womens love just
by accident, anybody handy likely to do. Everytime I go to
Harpo's some little policy salesman git all up in my face.
Mr. ____ have to come to the rescue. He tell the man, This
lady my wife. The man vanish out the door.

Us sit, have a cold drink. Talk about our days together with
Shug. Talk about the time she come home sick. The little

crooked song she use to sing. All our fine evenings down at
Harpo's.

You was even sewing good way back then, he say. I
remember the nice little dresses Shug always wear.

Yeah, I say. Shug could wear a dress.

Remember the night Sofia knock Mary Agnes toofs out?
he ast.

Who could forget it? I say.

Us don't say nothing bout Sofia's troubles. Us still cant
laugh at that. Plus, Sofia still have trouble with that family.
Well, trouble with Miss Eleanor Jane.

You just don't know, say Sofia, what that girl done put
me through. You know how she use to bother me all the
time when she had problems at home? Well finally she start
bothering me when anything good happen. Soon as she snag
that man she married she come running to me. Oh, Sofia,
she say, you just have to meet Stanley Earl. And before I
can say anything, Stanley Earl is in the middle of my front
room.

How you, Sofia, he say, grinning and sticking out his hand.
Miss Eleanor Jane done told me so much about you.

I wonder if she told him they made me sleep up under their
house, say Sofia. But I don't ask. I try to be polite, act pleasant.
Henrietta turn the radio up loud in the back room. I have to
almost holler to make myself understood. They stand round
looking at the children's pictures on the wall and saying how
good my boys look in they army uniforms.

Where they fighting? Stanley Earl want to know.

They in the service right here in Georgia, I say. But pretty
soon they be bound for overseas.

He ast me do I know which part they be station in? France,
Germany or the Pacific.

I don't know where none of that is so I say, Naw. He say he

want to fight but got to stay home and run his daddy's cotton gin.

Army got to wear clothes, he say, if they fighting in Europe. Too bad they not fighting in Africa. He laugh. Miss Eleanor Jane smile. Henrietta turn the dial as high as it can go. Got on some real sorry whitefolks music sound like I don't know what. Stanley Earl snap his fingers and try to tap one of his good size foots. He got a long head go straight up and hair cut so short it look fuzzy. His eyes real bright blue and never hardly blink. Good God, I think.

Sofia raise me, practically, say Miss Eleanor Jane. Don't know what we would have done without her.

Well, say Stanley Earl, everybody round here raise by colored. That's how come we turn out so well. He wink at me, say, Well Sugar Pie, to Miss Eleanor Jane, time for us to mosey along.

She leap up like somebody stuck her with a pin. How Henrietta doing? she ast. Then she whisper, I brought her something with yams so well hid she won't never suspect. She run out to the car and come back with a tuna casserole.

Well, say Sofia, one thing you have to say for Miss Eleanor Jane, her dishes almost always fool Henrietta. And that mean a lots to me. Of course I never tell Henrietta where they come from. If I did, out the window they would go. Else she'd vomit, like it made her sick.

But finally, the end come to Sofia and Miss Eleanor Jane, I think. And it wasn't nothing to do with Henrietta, who hate Miss Eleanor Jane's guts. It was Miss Eleanor Jane herself and that baby she went and had. Every time Sofia turned round Miss Eleanor Jane was shoving Reynolds Stanley Earl in her face. He a little fat white something without much hair, look like he headed for the Navy.

Ain't little Reynolds sweet? say Miss Eleanor Jane, to Sofia.

Daddy just love him, she say. Love having a grandchild name for him and look so much like him, too.

Sofia don't say nothing, stand there ironing some of Susie Q and Henrietta's clothes.

And so smart, say Eleanor Jane. Daddy say he never saw a smarter baby. Stanley Earl's mama say he smarter than Stanley Earl was when he was this age.

Sofia still don't say nothing.

Finally Eleanor Jane notice. And you know how some whitefolks is, won't let well enough alone. If they want to bad enough, they gon harass a blessing from you if it kill.

Sofia mighty quiet this morning, Miss Eleanor Jane say, like she just talking to Reynolds Stanley. He stare back at her out of his big stuck open eyes.

Don't you think he sweet? she ast again.

He sure fat, say Sofia, turning over the dress she ironing.

And he sweet, too, say Miss Eleanor Jane.

Just as plump as he can be, say Sofia. And tall.

But he sweet, too, say Eleanor Jane. And he smart. She haul off and kiss him up side the head. He rub his head, say Yee.

Ain't he the smartest baby you ever saw? she ast Sofia.

He got a nice size head on him, say Sofia. You know some peoples place a lot of weight on head size. Not a whole lot of hair on it either. He gon be cool this summer, for sure. She fold the piece she iron and put it on a chair.

Just a sweet, smart, cute, *innocent* little baby boy, say Miss Eleanor Jane. Don't you just love him? she ast Sofia point blank.

Sofia sigh. Put down her iron. Stare at Miss Eleanor Jane and Reynolds Stanley. All the time me and Henrietta over in the corner playing pitty pat. Henrietta act like Miss Eleanor Jane ain't alive, but both of us hear the way the iron sound when Sofia put it down. The sound have a lot of old and new stuff in it.

No ma'am, say Sofia. I do not love Reynolds Stanley Earl. Now. That's what you been trying to find out ever since he was born. And now you know.

Me and Henrietta look up. Miss Eleanor Jane just that quick done put Reynolds Stanley on the floor where he crawling round knocking stuff over. Head straight for Sofia's stack of ironed clothes and pull it down on his head. Sofia take up the clothes, straighten them out, stand by the ironing board with her hand on the iron. Sofia the kind of woman no matter what she have in her hand it look like a weapon.

Eleanor Jane start to cry. She always have felt something for Sofia. If not for her, Sofia never would have survive living in her daddy's house. But so what? Sofia never wanted to be there in the first place. Never wanted to leave her own children.

Too late to cry, Miss Eleanor Jane, say Sofia. All us can do now is laugh. Look at him, she say. And she do laugh. He can't even walk and already he in my house messing it up. Did I ast him to come? Do I care whether he sweet or not? Will it make any difference in the way he grow up to treat me what I think?

You just don't like him cause he look like daddy, say Miss Eleanor Jane.

You don't like him cause he look like daddy, say Sofia. I don't feel nothing about him at all. I don't love him, I don't hate him. I just wish he couldn't run loose all the time messing up folks stuff.

All the time! All the time! say Miss Eleanor Jane. Sofia, he just a baby. Not even a year old. He only been here five or six times.

I feel like he been here forever, say Sofia.

I just don't understand, say Miss Eleanor Jane. All the other colored women I know love children. The way you feel is something unnatural.

I love children, say Sofia. But all the colored women that say they love yours is lying. They don't love Reynolds Stanley any more than I do. But if you so badly raise as to ast 'em, what you expect them to say? Some colored people so scared of whitefolks they claim to love the cotton gin.

But he just a little baby! say Miss Eleanor Jane, like saying this is spose to clear up everything.

What you want from me? say Sofia. I feel something for you because out of all the people in your daddy's house you showed me some human kindness. But on the other hand, out of all the people in your daddy's house, I showed you some. Kind feeling is all I have to offer you. I don't have nothing to offer your relatives but just what they offer me. I don't have nothing to offer him.

Reynolds Stanley by this time is over on Henrietta pallet look like trying to rape her foot. Finally he start to chew her leg and Henrietta reach up on the windowsill and hand him a cracker.

I feel like you the only person love me, say Miss Eleanor Jane. Mama only love Junior, she say. Cause that's who daddy really love.

Well, say Sofia. You got your own husband to love you now.

Look like he don't love nothing but that cotton gin, she say. Ten o'clock at night and he still down there working. When he not working, he playing poker with the boys. My brother see a lot more of Stanley Earl than I do.

Maybe you ought to leave him, say Sofia. You got kin in Atlanta, go stay with some of them. Git a job.

Miss Eleanor Jane toss her hair back, act like she don't even hear this, it such a wild notion.

I got my own troubles, say Sofia, and when Reynolds Stanley grow up, he's gon be one of them.

But he won't, say Miss Eleanor Jane. I'm his mama and I won't let him be mean to colored.

You and whose army? say Sofia. The first word he likely to speak won't be nothing he learn from you.

You telling me I won't even be able to love my own son, say Miss Eleanor Jane.

No, say Sofia. That's not what I'm telling you. I'm telling you I won't be able to love your own son. You can love him just as much as you want to. But be ready to suffer the consequences. That's how the colored live.

Little Reynolds Stanley all up on top Henrietta's face by now, just slobbering and sucking. Trying to kiss. Any second I think she gon knock him silly. But she lay real still while he zamine her. Every once in a while he act like he peeking into her eyeball. Then he sit down with a bounce on top her chest and grin. He take one of her playing cards and try to give her a bite of it.

Sofia come over and lift him off.

He not bothering me, say Henrietta. He make me tickle.

He bother me, say Sofia.

Well, Miss Eleanor Jane say to the baby, picking him up, we not wanted here. She say it real sad, like she done run out of places to go.

Thank you for all you done for us, say Sofia. She don't look so good herself, and a little water stand in her eyes. After Miss Eleanor Jane and Reynolds Stanley leave, she say, It's times like this make me know us didn't make this world. And all the colored folks talking bout loving everybody just ain't looked hard at what they thought they said.

So what else new?

Well, your sister too crazy to kill herself. Most times I feels like shit but I felt like shit before in my life and what happen? I had me a fine sister name Nettie. I had me another fine woman friend name Shug. I had me some fine children growing up in Africa, singing and writing verses. The first two months was hell though, I tell the world. But now Shug's six

months is come and gone and she ain't come back. And I try
to teach my heart not to want nothing it can't have.

Besides, she give me so many good years. Plus, she learning
new things in her new life. Now she and Germaine staying
with one of her children.

Dear Celie, she wrote me, Me and Germaine ended up in
Tucson, Arizona where one of my children live. The other
two alive and turned out well but they didn't want to see me.
Somebody told them I lives a evil life. This one say he want to
see his mama no matter what. He live in a little mud looking
house like they have out here, call adobe, so you know I feels
right at home (smile). He a schoolteacher too and work on
the Indian reservation. They call him the black white man.
They have a word that mean that, too, and it really bother
him. But even if he try to tell them how he feel, they don't
seem to care. They so far gone nothing strangers say mean
nothing. Everybody not a Indian they got no use for. I hate to
see his feelings hurt, but that's life.

It was Germaine who had the idea to look up my children.
He notice how I always love dressing him up and playing with
his hair. He didn't make it like a mean suggestion. He just said
if I knowed how my children was doing I would probably feel
better in my life.

This son we staying with is name James. His wife is name
Cora Mae. They have two kids name Davis and Cantrell.
He say he thought something was funny bout his mama (my
mama) cause she and big daddy was so old and strict and set
in they ways. But still, he felt a lot of love from them, he say.

Yeah son, I tell him. They had a lot of love to give. But I
needed love plus understanding. They run a little short of
that.

They *been* dead now, he say. Nine or ten years. Sent us all
to school as far as they could.

You know I never think bout mama and daddy. You know how tough I think I is. But now that they dead and I see my children doing well, I like to think about them. Maybe when I come back I can put some flowers on they graves.

Oh, she write me now near bout every week. Long newsy letters full of stuff she thought she had forgot. Plus stuff bout the desert and the Indians and the rocky mountains. I wish I could be traveling with her, but thank God she able to do it. Sometimes I feel mad at her. Feel like I could scratch her hair right off her head. But then I think, Shug got a right to live too. She got a right to look over the world in whatever company she choose. Just cause I love her don't take away none of her rights.

The only thing bother me is she don't never say nothing bout coming back. And I miss her. I miss her friendship so much that if she want to come back here dragging Germaine I'd make them both welcome, or die trying. Who am I to tell her who to love? My job just to love her good and true myself.

Mr. _____ ast me the other day what it is I love so much bout Shug. He say he love her style. He say to tell the truth, Shug act more manly than most men. I mean she upright, honest. Speak her mind and the devil take the hindmost, he say. You know Shug will fight, he say. Just like Sofia. She bound to live her life and be herself no matter what.

Mr. _____ think all this is stuff men do. But Harpo not like this, I tell him. You not like this. What Shug got is womanly it seem like to me. Specially since she and Sofia the ones got it.

Sofia and Shug not like men, he say, but they not like women either.

You mean they not like you or me.

They hold they own, he say. And it's different.

What I love best bout Shug is what she been through, I say. When you look in Shug's eyes you know she been where

she been, seen what she seen, did what she did. And now she
know.

That's the truth, say Mr. _____.

And if you don't git out the way, she'll tell you about it.

Amen, he say. Then he say something that really surprise
me cause it so thoughtful and common sense. When it come
to what folks do together with they bodies, he say, anybody's
guess is as good as mine. But when you talk bout love I don't
have to guess. I have love and I have been love. And I thank
God he let me gain understanding enough to know love can't
be halted just cause some peoples moan and groan. It don't
surprise me you love Shug Avery, he say. I have love Shug
Avery all my life.

What load of bricks fell on you? I ast.

No bricks, he say. Just experience. You know, everybody
bound to git some of that sooner or later. All they have to do
is stay alive. And I start to git mine real heavy long about the
time I told Shug it was true that I beat you cause you was you
and not her.

I told her, I say.

I know it, he say, and I don't blame you. If a mule could tell
folks how it's treated, it would. But you know some womens
would have just love to hear they man say he beat his wife
cause she wasn't them. Shug one time was like that bout
Annie Julia. Both of us messed over my first wife a scanless.
And she never told nobody. Plus, she didn't have nobody to
tell. After they married her off to me her folks behave like
they'd throwed her down a well. Or off the face of the earth.
I didn't want her. I wanted Shug. But my daddy was the boss.
He give me the wife he wanted me to have.

But Shug spoke right up for you, Celie, he say. She say
Albert, you been mistreating somebody I love. So as far as you
concern, I'm gone. I couldn't believe it, he say. All along in

there we was as hot for each other as two pistols. Excuse me, he say. But we was. I tried to laugh it off. But she meant what she said.

I tried to tease her. You don't love old dumb Celie, I said. She ugly and skinny and can't hold a candle to you. She can't even screw.

What I want to say that for. From what she tell me, Shug said, she don't have no reason to screw. You on and off like a jackrabbit. Plus, she say, Celie say you not always clean. And she turn up her nose.

I wanted to kill you, said Mr. ____ and I did slap you around a couple of times. I never understood how you and Shug got along so well together and it bothered the hell out of me. When she was mean and nasty to you, I understood. But when I looked around and the two of you was always doing each other's hair, I start to worry.

She still feel for you, I say.

Yeah, he say. She feel like I'm her brother.

What so bad about that, I ast. Don't her brothers love her?

Them clowns, he say. They still act the fool I use to be.

Well, I say, we all have to start somewhere if us want to do better, and our own self is what us have to hand.

I'm real sorry she left you, Celie. I remember how I felt when she left me.

Then the old devil put his arms around me and just stood there on the porch with me real quiet. Way after while I bent my stiff neck onto his shoulder. Here us is, I thought, two old fools left over from love, keeping each other company under the stars.

Other times he want to know bout my children.

I told him you say they both wear long robes, sort of like dresses. That was the day he come to visit me while I was sewing and ast me what was so special bout my pants.

Anybody can wear them, I said.

Men and women not suppose to wear the same thing, he said. Men spose to wear the pants.

So I said, You ought to tell that to the mens in Africa.

Say what? he ast. First time he ever thought bout what Africans do.

People in Africa try to wear what feel comfortable in the heat, I say. Of course, missionaries have they own ideas bout dress. But left to themself, Africans wear a little sometimes, or a lot, according to Nettie. But men and women both preshate a nice dress.

Robe you said before, he say.

Robe, dress. Not pants, anyhow.

Well, he say. I'll be dog.

And men sew in Africa, too, I say.

They do? he ast.

Yeah, I say. They not so backward as mens here.

When I was growing up, he said, I use to try to sew along with mama cause that's what she was always doing. But everybody laughed at me. But you know, I liked it.

Well, nobody gon laugh at you now, I said. Here, help me stitch in these pockets.

But I don't know how, he say.

I'll show you, I said. And I did.

Now us sit sewing and talking and smoking our pipes.

Guess what, I say to him, folks in Africa where Nettie and the children is believe white people is black peoples children.

Naw, he say, like this interesting but his mind really on the slant of his next stitch.

They named Adam some other name soon as he arrive. They say the white missionaries before Nettie and them come told them all about Adam from the white folks point of view and what the white folks know. But they know who Adam is from they own point of view. And for a whole lot longer time ago.

And who that? Mr. _____ ast.

The first man that was white. Not the first man. They say nobody so crazy they think they can say who was the first man. But everybody notice the first white man cause he was white.

Mr. _____ frown, look at the different color thread us got. Thread his needle, lick his finger, tie a knot.

They say everybody before Adam was black. Then one day some woman they just right away kill, come out with this colorless baby. They thought at first it was something she ate. But then another one had one and also the women start to have twins. So the people start to put the white babies and the twins to death. So really Adam wasn't even the first white man. He was just the first one the people didn't kill.

Mr. _____ look at me real thoughtful. He not such a bad looking man, you know, when you come right down to it. And now it do begin to look like he got a lot of feeling hind his face.

Well, I say, you know black folks have what you call albinos to this day. But you never hear of white folks having nothing black unless some black man been messing with 'em. And no white folks been in Africa back yonder when all this happen.

So these Olinka people heard about Adam and Eve from the white missionaries and they heard about how the serpent tricked Eve and how God chased them out of the garden of Eden. And they was real curious to hear this, cause after they had chased the white Olinka children out of the village they hadn't hardly thought no more about it. Nettie say one thing about Africans. Out of sight, out of mind. And another thing, they don't like nothing around them that look or act different. They want everybody to be just alike. So you know somebody white wouldn't last long. She say seem like to her the Africans throwed out the white Olinka-peoples for how they look. They throwed out the rest of us, all us who become slaves, for how us act. Seem like us just wouldn't do right no matter how us try. Well, you know how niggers is. Can't nobody tell 'em nothing even today. Can't be rule. Every nigger you see got a kingdom in his head.

But guess what else, I say to Mr. ____. When the missionaries got to the part bout Adam and Eve being naked, the Olinka peoples nearly bust out laughing. Especially when the missionaries tried to make them put on clothes because of this. They tried to explain to the missionaries that it was they who put Adam and Eve out of the village because they was naked. Their word for naked is white. But since they are covered by color they are not naked. They said anybody looking at a white person can tell they naked, but black people can not be naked because they can not be white.

Yeah, say Mr. ____. But they was wrong.

Right, I said. Adam and Eve prove it. What they did, these Olinka peoples, was throw out they own children, just cause they was a little different.

I bet they do that same kind of stuff today, Mr. ____ say.

Oh, from what Nettie say, them Africans is a mess. And you know what the bible say, the fruit don't fall too far from the tree. And something else, I say. Guess who they say the snake is?

Us, no doubt, say Mr. ____.

Right, I say. Whitefolks sign for they parents. They was so mad to git throwed out and told they was naked they made up they minds to crush us wherever they find us, same as they would a snake.

You reckon? Mr. ____ ast.

That's what these Olinka peoples say. But they say just

like they know history before the white children start to
come, they know the future after the biggest of 'em leave.
They say they know these particular children and they gon
kill each other off, they still so mad bout being unwanted.
Gon kill off a lot of other folk too who got some color. In
fact, they gon kill off so much of the earth and the colored
that everybody gon hate them just like they hate us today.
Then they will become the new serpent. And wherever a
white person is found he'll be crush by somebody not white,
just like they do us today. And some of the Olinka peoples
believe life will just go on and on like this forever. And every
million years or so something will happen to the earth and
folks will change the way they look. Folks might start growing
two heads one of these days, for all we know, and then the
folks with one head will send 'em all someplace else. But some
of 'em don't think like this. They think, after the biggest of
the white folks no longer on the earth, the only way to stop
making somebody the serpent is for everybody to accept
everybody else as a child of God, or one mother's children, no
matter what they look like or how they act. And guess what
else about the snake?

What? he ast.

These Olinka people worship it. They say who knows,
maybe it is kinfolks, but for sure it's the smartest, cleanest,
slickest thing they ever seen.

These folks sure must have a heap of time just to sit and
think, say Mr. ____.

Nettie say they real good at thinking, I say. But they think
so much in terms of thousands of years they have a hard time
gitting themself through one.

So what they name Adam?

Something sound like Omatangu, I say. It mean a un-naked
man somewhere near the first one God made that knowed

what he was. A whole lot of the men that come before the first man was men, but none of 'em didn't know it. You know how long it take some mens to notice anything, I say.

Took me long enough to notice you such good company, he say. And he laugh.

He ain't Shug, but he begin to be somebody I can talk to.

And no matter how much the telegram said you must be drown, I still git letters from you.

Your sister, Celie

Dear Celie,

After two and a half months Adam and Tashi returned! Adam overtook Tashi and her mother and some other members of our compound as they were nearing the village where the white woman missionary had lived, but Tashi would not hear of turning back, nor would Catherine, and so Adam accompanied them to the *mbeles* encampment.

Oh, he says, it is the most extraordinary place!

You know, Celie, in Africa there is a huge depression in the earth called the great rift valley, but it is on the other side of the continent from where we are. However, according to Adam, there is a "small" rift on our side, several thousand acres large and even deeper than the great rift, which covers millions of acres. It is a place set so deep into the earth that it can only really be seen, Adam thinks, from the air, and then it would seem just an overgrown canyon. Well, in this overgrown canyon are a thousand people from dozens of African tribes, and even one colored man—Adam swears—from Alabama! There are farms. There is a school. An infirmary. A temple. And there are male and female warriors who do indeed go on missions of sabotage against the white plantations.

But all this seemed more a marvel in the recounting than in the actual experiencing of it, if I am any judge of Adam and Tashi. Their minds seem to have been completely riveted on each other.

I wish you could have seen them as they staggered into the compound. Filthy as hogs, hair as wild as could be. Sleepy. Exhausted. Smelly. God knows. But still arguing.

Just because I came back with you, don't think I am saying yes to marriage, says Tashi.

Oh yes you are, says Adam, heatedly, but through a yawn. You promised your mother. *I* promised your mother.

Nobody in America will like me, says Tashi.

I will like you, says Adam.

Olivia ran and enfolded Tashi in her arms. Ran about preparing food and a bath.

Last night, after Tashi and Adam had slept most of the day, we had a family conference. We informed them that because so many of our people had gone to join the *mbeles* and the planters were beginning to bring in Moslem workers from the North, and because it was time for us to do so, we would be leaving for home in a matter of weeks.

Adam announced his desire to marry Tashi.

Tashi announced her refusal to be married.

And then, in that honest, forthright way of hers, she gave her reasons. Paramount among them that, because of the scarification marks on her cheeks Americans would look down on her as a savage and shun her, and whatever children she and Adam might have. That she had seen the magazines we receive from home and that it was very clear to her that black people did not truly admire blackskinned black people like herself, and especially did not admire blackskinned black women. They bleach their faces, she said. They fry their hair. They try to look naked.

Also, she continued, I fear Adam will be distracted by one of these naked looking women and desert me. Then I would have no country, no people, no mother and no husband and brother.

You'd have a sister, said Olivia,

Then Adam spoke. He asked Tashi to forgive his initial stupid response to the scarification. And to forgive the repugnance he'd felt about the female initiation ceremony. He assured Tashi that it was she he loved and that in America she would have country, people, parents, sister, husband, brother and lover, and that whatever befell her in America would also be his own choice and his own lot.

Oh, Celie.

So, the next day, our boy came to us with scars identical to Tashi's on his cheeks.

And they are so happy. So happy, Celie. Tashi and Adam Omatangu.

Samuel married them, of course, and all the people left in the compound came to wish them happiness and an abundance of roofleaf forever. Olivia stood up with the bride and a friend of Adam's—a man too old to have joined the *mbeles*—stood up with him. Immediately after the wedding we left the compound, riding in a lorry that took us to a boat at the coast inlet that flows out to sea.

In a few weeks, we will all be home.

Your loving sister, Nettie

Dear Nettie,

Mr. _____ talk to Shug a lot lately by telephone. He say as soon as he told her my sister and her family was missing, she and Germaine made a beeline for the State department trying to find out what happen. He say Shug say it just kill her to think I'm down here suffering from not knowing. But nothing happen at the State department. Nothing at the department of defense. It's a big war. So much going on. One ship lost feel like nothing, I guess. Plus, colored don't count to those people.

Well, they just don't know, and never did. Never will. And so what? I know you on your way home and you may not git here till I'm ninety, but one of these days I do expect to see your face.

Meanwhile, I hired Sofia to clerk in our store. Kept the white man Alphonso got to run it, but put Sofia in there to wait on colored cause they never had nobody in a store to wait on 'em before and nobody in a store to treat 'em nice. Sofia real good at selling stuff too cause she act like she don't care if you buy or not. No skin off her nose. And then if you decide to buy anyhow, well, she might exchange a few pleasant

words with you. Plus, she scare that white man. Anybody else
colored he try to call 'em auntie or something. First time he
try that with Sofia she ast him which colored man his mama
sister marry.

I ast Harpo do he mind if Sofia work.

What I'm gon mind for? he say. It seem to make her happy.
And I can take care of anything come up at home. Anyhow,
he say, Sofia got me a little help for when Henrietta need
anything special to eat or git sick.

Yeah, say Sofia. Miss Eleanor Jane gon look in on Henrietta
and every other day promise to cook her something she'll
eat. You know white people have a look of machinery in they
kitchen. She whip up stuff with yams you'd never believe. Last
week she went and made yam ice cream.

How this happen? I ast. I thought the two of you was
through.

Oh, say Sofia. It finally dawn on her to ast her mama why I
come to work for them.

I don't expect it to last, though, say Harpo. You know how
they is.

Do her peoples know? I ast.

They know, say Sofia. They carrying on just like you know
they would. Whoever heard of a white woman working for
niggers, they rave. She tell them, Whoever heard of somebody
like Sofia working for trash.

She bring Reynolds Stanley with her? I ast.

Henrietta say she don't mind him.

Well, say Harpo, I'm satisfied if her menfolks against her
helping you, she gon quit.

Let her quit, say Sofia. It not my salvation she working for.
And if she don't learn she got to face judgment for herself, she
won't even have live.

Well, you got me behind you, anyway, say Harpo. And I

loves every judgment you ever made. He move up and kiss her where her nose was stitch.

Sofia toss her head. Everybody learn something in life, she say. And they laugh.

Speaking of learning, Mr. _____ say one day us was sewing out on the porch, I first start to learn all them days ago I use to sit up there on my porch, staring out cross the railing.

Just miserable. That's what I was. And I couldn't understand why us have life at all if all it can do most times is make us feel bad. All I ever wanted in life was Shug Avery, he say. And one while, all she wanted in life was me. Well, us couldn't have each other, he say. I got Annie Julia. Then you. All them rotten children. She got Grady and who know who all. But still, look like she come out better than me. A lot of people love Shug, but nobody but Shug love me.

Hard not to love Shug, I say. She know how to love somebody back.

I tried to do something bout my children after you left me. But by that time it was too late. Bub come with me for two weeks, stole all my money, laid up on the porch drunk. My girls so far off into mens and religion they can't hardly talk. Everytime they open they mouth some kind of plea come out. Near bout to broke my sorry heart.

If you know your heart sorry, I say, that mean it not quite as spoilt as you think.

Anyhow, he say, you know how it is. You ast yourself one question, it lead to fifteen. I start to wonder why us need love. Why us suffer. Why us black. Why us men and women. Where do children really come from. It didn't take long to realize I didn't hardly know nothing. And that if you ast yourself why you black or a man or a woman or a bush it don't mean nothing if you don't ast why you here, period.

So what you think? I ast.

I think us here to wonder, myself. To wonder. To ast. And that in wondering bout the big things and asting bout the big things, you learn about the little ones, almost by accident. But you never know nothing more about the big things than you start out with. The more I wonder, he say, the more I love.

And people start to love you back, I bet, I say.

They do, he say, surprise. Harpo seem to love me. Sofia and the children. I think even ole evil Henrietta love me a little bit, but that's cause she know she just as big a mystery to me as the man in the moon.

Mr. ____ is busy patterning a shirt for folks to wear with my pants.

Got to have pockets, he say. Got to have loose sleeves. And definitely you not spose to wear it with no tie. Folks wearing ties look like they being lynch.

And then, just when I know I can live content without Shug, just when Mr. ____ done ast me to marry him again, this time in the spirit as well as in the flesh, and just after I say Naw, I still don't like frogs, but let's us be friends, Shug write me she coming home.

Now. Is this life or not?

I be so calm.

If she come, I be happy. If she don't, I be content.

And then I figure this the lesson I was suppose to learn.

Oh Celie, she say, stepping out of the car, dress like a moving star, I missed you more than I missed my own mama.

Us hug.

Come on in, I say.

Oh, the house look so nice, she say, when us git to her room. You know I love pink.

Got you some elephants and turtles coming, too, I say.

Where your room? she ast.

Down the hall, I say.

Let's go see it, she say.

Well, here it is, I say, standing in the door. Everything in my room purple and red cept the floor, that painted bright yellow. She go right to the little purple frog perch on my mantlepiece.

What this? she ast.

Oh, I say, a little something Albert carve for me.

She look at me funny for a minute, I look at her. Then us laugh.

Where Germaine at? I ast.

In college, she say. Wilberforce. Can't let all that talent go to waste. Us through, though, she say. He feel just like family now. Like a son. Maybe a grandson. What you and Albert been up to? she ast.

Nothing much, I say.

She say, I know Albert and I bet he been up to *some*thing, with you looking as fine as you look.

Us sew, I say. Make idle conversation.

How idle? she ast.

What do you know, I think. Shug jealous. I have a good mind to make up a story just to make her feel bad. But I don't.

Us talk bout you, I say. How much us love you.

She smile, come put her head on my breast. Let out a long breath.

Your sister, Celie

Dear God. Dear stars, dear trees, dear sky, dear peoples. Dear Everything. Dear God.

Thank you for bringing my sister Nettie and our children home. Wonder who that coming yonder? ast Albert, looking up the road. Us can see the dust just aflying.

Me and him and Shug sitting out on the porch after dinner. Talking. Not talking. Rocking and fanning flies. Shug mention she don't want to sing in public no more—well, maybe a night or two at Harpo's. Think maybe she retire. Albert say he want her to try on his new shirt. I talk bout Henrietta. Sofia. My garden and the store. How things doing generally. So much in the habit of sewing something I stitch up a bunch of scraps, try to see what I can make. The weather cool for the last of June, and sitting on the porch with Albert and Shug feel real pleasant. Next week be the fourth of July and us plan a big family reunion outdoors here at my house. Just hope the cool weather hold.

Could be the mailman, I say. Cept he driving a little fast.

Could be Sofia, say Shug. You know she drive like a maniac.

Could be Harpo, say Albert. But it not.

By now the car stop under the trees in the yard and all these peoples dress like old folks git out.

A big tall whitehaired man with a backward turn white collar, a little dumpty woman with her gray hair in plaits cross on top her head. A tall youngish man and two robust looking youngish women. The whitehaired man say something to the driver of the car and the car leave. They all stand down there at the edge of the drive surrounded by boxes and bags and all kinds of stuff.

By now my heart is in my mouth and I can't move.

It's Nettie, Albert say, gitting up.

All the people down by the drive look up at us. They look at the house. The yard. Shug and Albert's cars. They look round at the fields. Then they commence to walk real slow up the walk to the house.

I'm so scared I don't know what to do. Feel like my mind stuck. I try to speak, nothing come. Try to git up, almost fall. Shug reach down and give me a helping hand. Albert press me on the arm.

When Nettie's foot come down on the porch I almost die. I stand swaying, tween Albert and Shug. Nettie stand swaying tween Samuel and I reckon it must be Adam. Then us both start to moan and cry. Us totter toward one nother like us use to do when us was babies. Then us feel so weak when us touch, us knock each other down. But what us care? Us sit and lay there on the porch inside each other's arms.

After while, she say *Celie*.

I say *Nettie*.

Little bit more time pass. Us look round at a lot of peoples knees. Nettie never let go my waist. This my husband Samuel, she say, pointing up. These our children Olivia and Adam and this Adam's wife Tashi, she say.

I point up at my peoples. This Shug and Albert, I say.

Everybody say Pleased to Meetcha. Then Shug and Albert start to hug everybody one after the other.

Me and Nettie finally git up off the porch and I hug my children. And I hug Tashi. Then I hug Samuel.

Why us always have family reunion on July 4th, say Henrietta, mouth poke out, full of complaint. It so hot.

White people busy celebrating they independence from England July 4th, say Harpo, so most black folks don't have to work. Us can spend the day celebrating each other.

Ah, Harpo, say Mary Agnes, sipping some lemonade, I didn't know you knowed history. She and Sofia working together on the potato salad. Mary Agnes come back home to pick up Suzie Q. She done left Grady, move back to Memphis and live with her sister and her ma. They gon look after Suzie Q while she work. She got a lot of new songs, she say, and not too knocked out to sing 'em.

After while, being with Grady, I couldn't think, she say. Plus, he not a good influence for no child. Course, I wasn't either, she say. Smoking so much reefer.

Everybody make a lot of miration over Tashi. People look at her and Adam's scars like that's they business. Say they never suspect African ladies could look so *good*. They make a fine couple. Speak a little funny, but us gitting use to it.

What your people love best to eat over there in Africa? us ast.

She sort of blush and say *barbecue*.

Everybody laugh and stuff her with one more piece.

I feel a little peculiar round the children. For one thing, they grown. And I see they think me and Nettie and Shug and Albert and Samuel and Harpo and Sofia and Jack and Odessa real old and don't know much what going on. But I don't think us feel old at all. And us so happy. Matter of fact, I think this the youngest us ever felt.

Amen

I thank everybody in this book for coming

—A.W., author and medium

The Temple of My Familiar

To Robert,
in whom the Goddess shines

If they have lied about Me,
They have lied about everything.

—LISSIE LYLES

PART ONE

IN THE old country in South America, Carlotta's grand-mother, Zedé, had been a seamstress, but really more of a sewing magician. She was the creator of clothing, especially capes, made of feathers. These capes were worn by dancers and musicians and priests at traditional village festivals and had been worn for countless generations. When she was a young child, Carlotta's mother, also called Zedé, was sent to collect the peacock feathers used in the designs. Little Zedé had stood waiting as the fat, perspiring woman who owned the peacocks held them in ashen, scratched hands and tore out the beautiful feathers one by one. It was then that Zedé began to understand the peacock's mournful cry. It had puzzled her at first why a creature so beautiful (though admittedly with hideous feet) emitted a sound so like a soul in torment. Next she would visit the man who kept the parrots and cockatoos, and the painful plucking of feathers would be repeated. She then paid a visit to the old woman who specialized in "found feathers" and who was poorer than the others but whose face was more peaceful. This old woman thought each feather she found was a gift from the Gods, and her incomparable feathers—set in the spectacular headdresses of the priests—always added just the special flair of grace the ceremony required.

Little Zedé went to school every morning wearing a neat blue-and-white uniform, her two long braids warm against the small of her back. By high school her hair was cut short, just below her ears, and she tossed it impatiently as her mother complained of the poor quality of the modern feather. No feather, these days, she explained, was permitted to mature. Each was plucked while still relatively green. Therefore the full richness she had once been capable of expressing in her creations was now lost.

Their compound consisted of two small houses, one for sleeping, another for cooking—the cooking one was never entered by Zedé's father or brothers—and there were avocado and mango trees and coconut palms all around. From their front yard they could see the river, where the tiny prahus used by the fishermen slipped by, like floating schools of dried vanilla-bean pods, her mother always said.

Life was so peaceful that Zedé did not realize they were poor. She found this out when her father, a worker on the banana plantation they could also see from their house, became ill. At the same time, by coincidence, the traditional festivals of the village were forbidden. By whom they were forbidden, or "outlawed," as her father said, Zedé was not sure. The priests, especially, were left with nothing to do. The dancers and musicians danced, made music, and got drunk in the cantinas, but the priests wandered about the village stooped and lost, suddenly revealed as the weak-limbed old men they were.

Her father, a small, tired, brownskin man with graying black hair died while she was an earnest scholarship student at the university, far away in the noisy capital. Her mother now made her living selling her incredibly beautiful feather goods to the cold little gringa blonde who had a boutique on the bottom floor of an enormous new hotel that sprung up near their village, seemingly overnight. Sometimes her mother stayed on the street near the hotel and watched the gringas who bought her feathered earrings, pendants, and shawls—and even priestlike headdresses—and wore them as they stamped up and down the narrow dusty street. They never glanced at her; they never, she felt, even saw her. On them her work looked magnificent still, but the wearers looked very odd.

There were riots almost the whole year Zedé was finishing the university, at which she trained to be a teacher. Occasionally, on her way to class, she had to dodge stones, bricks, bottles, and all manner of raging vehicles. She hardly noticed the people involved. Some were farmers; some, students like herself. Some, police. Like her mother, she had a fabulously one-track mind. Just as Zedé the Elder never deviated from close attention to the details of her craft, no matter that the market had changed and others were turning out leaky pots and shoddy weavings for the ignorant tourist dollar, Zedé trudged along to school ignoring anything that might make her late.

She was not even aware of the threat that came, out of nowhere, she thought, to shut down the school. And yet, incredibly, one day it was shut. Not even a sign was posted. The doors were simply locked. She sat on the steps leading to her classrooms for two days. She learned that some of her classmates had been imprisoned; others, shot.

But she had almost completed the requirements to become a teacher, and when she was asked to teach a class in the hills, a class without walls and with students without uniforms, she accepted. She taught the basics—hygiene, reading, writing, and numerics—for six months before being arrested for being a Communist.

The years she spent in prison she never spoke of to Carlotta, even though that was where Carlotta was born. It was a prison that did not, anyway, look like one. It looked like the confiscated Indian village in the backwoods of the country that it was. The Indians had been "removed," and all their rich if marginal land was now planted in papaya. It was to plant, care for, and exploit these trees for an export market that the prisoners were brought to the village.

How her mother escaped with her, Carlotta did not know. Perhaps her father had been one of the guards—untutored men, fascinated, if resentful, that a young, pretty woman like Zedé could read and write. Later, when Carlotta's mother described the tiny, slivery boats that slid down the river like floating schools of dried vanilla-bean pods, she thought perhaps they'd made their escape in one. Perhaps they'd floated through the Panama Canal, mistaken by the U.S. Coast Guard for a piece of seaweed, and then floated to the coast of North America and into San Francisco Bay.

It was in San Francisco that Carlotta's own memories began. She was a dark, serious child with almond-shaped eyes and glistening black hair. In a few years she spoke English without an accent, a language her mother at first had difficulty understanding, even when Carlotta spoke it to her. Years later she would speak it quite well but with so thick an accent she sounded as if she were still speaking Spanish. Zedé could not, therefore, teach in the public schools of California. And she would have been afraid, in her shyness, to try.

They lived in a shabby, poorly lighted flat over a Thai grocery in an area of the city populated by the debris of society. Some of the people did not live indoors, although it rained so much of the time, but slept in doorways or in abandoned cars. Her mother found work in a sweatshop around the corner. There was no man in her mother's life. There were just the two of them. Her mother's responsibility was to provide food and clothing, and it was Carlotta's job to do the cooking and cleaning and, of course, to go to school.

School was a misery to her, but, like so many bad things that happened, she never told her mother. Zedé, stooped, a twitch of anxiety in her face at thirty-five, was a grim little woman, afraid of noise, other people, even of parades. When the gays paraded in costumes on Halloween, she snatched Carlotta from her perch beside the window and drew the shades. But not before Carlotta had seen one of the enormous feathered headdresses her mother made, somewhat furtively, at home, headdresses of peacock, pheasant, parrot, and cockatoo feathers, almost too resplendent for the gray, foggy city. The headdress was worn by a small, pale man, carrying a crystal scepter, who appeared to be wearing little else. He was drinking a beer.

From this glimpse of the Halloween parade Carlotta marked the beginning of her mother's new career. During the day she sewed jeans and country-and-western style shirts and ties in the sweatshop where she worked. At home they ate mainly rice and beans. With the money her mother managed to save, they bought feathers from one of the large import stores. Eventually Carlotta would work at one of these stores, called World Import, first as a sweeper in the storeroom, among the crated goods, so cheap, so colorful and pretty, from countries like her mother's (she did not think of South America as *her* continent), next as an arranger of goods on the floor, and finally as a cashier.

By then she was entering college and could work only during summers and after school. Much later in her life she heard the story of the man who worked in a factory that made farm equipment and each day passed the guards at the gates pushing a wheelbarrow. Each day the suspicious guards checked to make sure the wheelbarrow was empty. It always was. Twenty years later, when the man was rich, he told them what he'd been stealing: wheelbarrows. It was the same with Carlotta; only, she stole feathers, which she always seemed to be holding in her hand as if about to dust something. Peacock feathers mainly. Bundles and bundles of them over the years, because her mother had discovered that the rock stars of the sixties were "into" feathers and that, for one spectacular peacock cape, she could feed and clothe herself and Carlotta for a year.

During her last year in college Carlotta delivered one of these capes to a rock star so famous even she had heard of him—a slight, dark-brown man who wore a headband and looked, she thought, something like herself. It was his Indianness that she saw, not his blackness. She saw it in the way he really looked at her, really saw her. With the calm, detached concentration of a shaman. He was stoned, but even so . . . She had delivered many capes, shawls, headdresses, dresses, beaded and feathered head-bands, sandals, and jeans to rock stars and their entourages, and in the excitement of trying on what she brought, they never saw her. Never questioned how the magic of the feathered cloth-ing was done. Never wondered about her mother's pricked fin-gers and twitchy face and eyes. She did not expect them to. They were demonic to her. She hated the way they looked, so pale and raw and wet; she disliked their drugs, always so care-lessly displayed. Feathered pipes and bowls were steady sell-ers—she was not sure her mother even knew or cared what was done with them. Carlotta learned to wait silently, unob-trusively, "like an Indian," until the buyer—her mother's only word for them—stopped admiring his or her reflection and languidly fumbled for the always-hard-to-locate checkbook. They often tried to get her to lower her prices. Sometimes she spoke to them in her mother's incomprehensible Spanish and pretended she could not understand what language they spoke. At times, an especially happy buyer, going to a ball or to a pa-rade, gave her a bonus, or noticed she was pretty.

She was not "pretty." Beautiful, perhaps. Her eyes were wor-ried and watchful—she might still have been tensely afloat in the vanilla-bean-pod boat—her face drawn, her mouth hard to imagine in a smile, until she smiled. Yet she exuded an almost tropical atmosphere that was like a scent. When men looked at her they thought of TV commercials for faraway places in the Pacific, but when they actually saw her, which was rare, they thought of those dry, arid spaces closer to home. She made them think of rain.

Perhaps it was the hair on her head, so black it seemed wet. Or her eyelashes that seemed to sweep and bounce the light. Even the hair that grew beyond the hairline and into her face at temples and forehead formed wispy curls like those found in otherwise straight hair after a shower.

The rock star Arveyda saw all of this. He also saw the cape. He put it on. Resplendent within its iridescent shower of blind peacock eyes, he pranced before her watchful ones. It was he who said what no one else had even thought of.

Taking the cape off, he'd placed it about her shoulders and turned her toward the mirror.

"But of course," he said, "this is made only for you."

She looked in the mirror at the two of them. At his rich brownness; his nose like hers, eyes like hers (but playful and shrewd); his kinky, curly hair. His shapely lips. His small hands. His sensuous hips, low slung, cocked, in softly worn fitted jeans. Even his boots were feathered. And she looked at herself— almost his twin. Lighter skin, straighter hair, vanilla-bean-boat eyes—but . . .

"You mean it's made for my type," she said, sounding to herself as if she had an accent, though she did not. It was only because of how she looked.

He laughed. Hugged her.

"Our type."

For his cape he paid Zedé five thousand dollars, which Carlotta, deliriously happy, took to her. It was the most Zedé had ever been paid. With the money Carlotta knew they would buy a car.

The next cape she delivered to Arveyda, assuming it was for his sister, as he'd said, was for her. Though he sometimes wore his cape onstage—because it looked so great to break out of, and the fans went wild—the only time they could wear their capes in public together was for parades.

Within their magic capes that her mother had made they were indeed birds of a feather.

"The food you eat makes a difference," he advised her. Left to herself, she ate nothing but sweet cakes—chocolate cream puffs or Twinkies—and the inevitable rice and beans. She knew nothing of salads. She thought she hated fruit.

"You are young now," he said, "and nature is carrying your good looks along. But one day she will grow tired of your atrocious eating habits and she will stop. Then where will you be?"

Carlotta thought about her mother. How old she looked. How tired her skin was; how lusterless her hair. Her back teeth were breaking off at the gum.

Arveyda lay on his side in a bed piled high with silken pillows. The room reeked of incense and there was a faint whiff of Indian food. The room was full of smoky shadows, only one blind adjusted to let in light from the park.

"You are rich," she said. "You can eat whatever you like." Then, contradicting herself, she said, "Diet—I don't think diet has anything to do with looks. It is all in the genes. Some very poor people"—she no longer considered herself poor—"remain very beautiful even into old age."

"The poor look their best when they are old," Arveyda muttered, "because they have made it that far. A risk, anyway," he continued, stroking her face, the wispy hair that plastered itself at the front of her ear. "Oh," he said, "genes are part of it." He admired his own slim body in the mirror that ran along the wall beside the bed. He tried to imagine his father's body, the body he'd never seen. "But good food is most of the rest."

When she went to visit him, he offered her fresh juices, platters piled high with cherimoya, guava, papaya. He was a glutton for mangoes. Only those, however, from Mexico. He could not enjoy the ones from Haiti. "The misery, you know."

She grew trimmer still, eating what and how he ate. Nothing, ever, heavy in the morning. Fruit, fruit, even in the middle of the night.

He said eating cream puffs and meat turned people into murderers.

He jogged.

Jogging with him through Golden Gate Park she saw faces like hers that made her wonder if perhaps she had kinspeople, after all, in the Bay Area. She grew to recognize certain other "exotic" ethnic groups. She liked especially, for some reason, the Hmong people, who seemed particularly intense and ancient to her, as they carried their tiny babies on their backs dressed in bright multicolored clothing covered with mirrors, bells, shells, and beads. The fuzzy ball (how was it made?) atop their caps made her long to reach out and touch it. The babies and their mothers, locked in a language more foreign even than Zedé's, shopped calmly in the local stores. Pointing to this American thing or that. Murmuring in puzzlement. Holding their money trustingly out to the clerks in the stores, who were invariably patient, respectful, curious. It was the obvious culture that had gone into the making of the babies' clothes. No one in the Americas, except the Indians (called "Indians," she learned, because an Italian explorer considered them, on first take, to be *in dios*, in God), had lived long enough as a culture to create such a powerful, routine aesthetic. You looked at a Hmong baby and grieved that it should wind up in the Tenderloin on some of the city's least colorful or cultured streets. Carlotta loved, also, Samoan women. She loved their characteristic heaviness of body and their square jaws. Their seeming good nature and equanimity. Natural queens. And Balinese men; she could always recognize them because of the expression of horror in their faces as they looked about them at the glass and concrete of the city. They were not seduced, not at all.

"Exercise is to the body what thinking is to the mind," said Arveyda, gasping.

She, who never exercised but was always in motion on errands for her mother, ran easily. Breathing and running and never thinking of them as separate events. She pulled ahead of him effortlessly, her shapely legs flashing. Later they would shower at his house and lie on his bed in the sun.

H E HAD come from Terre Haute, Indiana, where his mother was one of three black women who had organized and founded their own church: the Church of Perpetual Involvement. His mother, whose name was Katherine Degos, was one of the most intrusive people he knew. She did not recognize limits, whether of body or mind. She could not stay out of other people's business; all business was her own. The church was a front for this tendency to interfere, which would otherwise have gotten her into trouble. She was a woman of such high energy she always seemed to him to be whirling, and the first time Arveyda heard the expression "whirling dervish" he thought of it as a description of his mother.

But then, in mid-whirl one day, when he was ten, after having broken up innumerable fights, delivered innumerable babies, baked and given away innumerable cakes and turkey dinners—because "doing" for others was her way of winning a place in their affairs—she simply stopped and sat down and looked out a back window of the house for three years. Her church dissolved. The women whose babies she had delivered forgot what she looked like. The hungry eyed her well-fed body with scorn. She didn't care. She began to play with her makeup, painting her face, dying her hair, doing her nails as if she were creating a work of art with her body, and with her mind she appeared to roam great empty distances.

She gave up trying to improve the world and, instead, declined to notice it. As a teenager, Arveyda had felt no strong connection to her. He was good in band, terrible in everything else. She did not seem to mind. Everyone on their block praised him for his music. He sang and played guitar and flute. She gave him no praise. She looked through him. One day the picture of his father—kept in a silver frame on the night table by his bed his whole life—disappeared.

"Nothing, No Thing, Can Replace Love." That is what she'd wanted on her headstone, but one of her sisters, his aunt Frudier, to whom she'd left this directive, thought it too risqué. His mother was instead buried under a pale gray stone that carried only her name, and not even the year she was born. But he thought of it as a kind of key to her he might use later on, when he knew more. Who was she, this woman who was his mother? He didn't know.

Lying with Carlotta on his spacious bed, the blue satin duvet cover smooth and cool beneath their legs, Arveyda told her odd bits and pieces of his life. Of the father figure he'd somehow found for his adolescent years, while his mother stared vacantly out the window. Simon Isaac. Or Uncle Isaac. Not that he would ever dare call Mr. Isaac "uncle" to his face, only in his heart; he understood he must never call anyone "uncle" except another black person.

Mr. Isaac was a greengrocer in the neighborhood where Arveyda and his mother lived. Tall and big-boned, with brooding brown eyes and a mane of wiry red hair, he sat in the doorway of his shop playing the violin.

All the children of the neighborhood crowded around, the nickels and dimes clutched in their palms for sweets temporarily forgotten. He mesmerized them with his perfectly lovely, improbable music—none of the children had seen a violin before. No one was more enchanted than Arveyda, whose fingers crept, all on their own, to rest on the box of the fiddle. "Fiddle" was the word for violin Arveyda had once heard at home. He inched ever closer, so that he could feel the sweetness of the vibrations down in the center of himself; the near orgasmic opening out in the base of his groin. It seemed natural, when he at last owned both a cheap guitar and a flute, that he would sit on a Coca-Cola crate near Mr. Isaac's straight chair and play. Natural, also, that Mr. Isaac would encourage his efforts with quick flashes of delight from his suddenly friendly eyes; and that, frequently, as they played together more and more easily, he would seem to forget Arveyda's presence and only at the end of a tune look across at him—brown, skinny, perched on the Coca-Cola crate—and, with a lopsided smile, ruffle his rough curls.

"And what happened?" asked Carlotta, imagining Isaac the Greengrocer playing his violin and never working.

"He had come from Palestine," said Arveyda. "Everyone in his village not dead or too sick to move came here, to America. He used to tell me about what it was like on the boat coming over. How packed it was. How afraid everyone was of getting sick. There had been an epidemic, some kind of plague. And the people were all herded together and actually stank, he said, from fear. And when they got to Ellis Island, on the very day they arrived, he discovered a boil in his left ear—a big fat juicy boil, like a baseball sticking out of his ear, was how he described it. Or like a spider's egg sack, when he was feeling more modest. He was sure he had 'it.' And right away the doctors 'in their white coats'—he always said that—came aboard, and they lanced the boil while looking very nervous about possible contagion. He was not permitted off the ship for two weeks, while 'those in authority' discussed whether he should be sent right back to Palestine. After that, they took him to a quarantine barrack, and there, from day to day, he 'politely rotted,' as he liked to put it. His ear began to heal but the rest of him began to feel 'not so terrific.'"

"Ellis Island?" Carlotta queried.

Arveyda explained how it was the same as Angel Island, only on the East Coast.

Angel Island, where mostly Asian immigrants were detained, sometimes for years, before being permitted into the country, was a place that, thanks to the aid of rich American friends, as Zedé once mysteriously mentioned, Carlotta and her mother had avoided.

"It was there, on Ellis Island," Arveyda continued, "that Uncle Isaac saw his first native-grown colored man. He was pushing a broom. It wasn't, he said to me once, that he'd never seen brown people; the Arabs in Palestine were brown, but their brownness seemed only skin-deep, whereas this man that he watched pushing the broom, with a little skiphop in his walk as he mumbled lyrics to songs and hummed under his breath, seemed to be colored all the way to, and past, his own bones. It was the first thing he understood about colored people—that it was probably the hopskip way the man pushed the broom, and seemed to be singing in his head, that annoyed white people, not just the color of his skin. In truth, he could not see how anyone could object to that. A more luminous, clean-brown anything was hard to imagine. 'Even if you only liked calfskin gloves,' said Uncle Isaac, 'even if you only admired a nice pair of oxblood-colored loafers! Even if you only loved Hershey bars!' And he would laugh.

"This man, as it turned out," said Arveyda, "was a musician, who worked on Ellis Island as a janitor to support himself and his family.

"Soon everyone else in the barrack had been pronounced

free of disease and left, and there were just the two of them. They talked, using their hands, eyes, strange sounds, and hops and skips, about music. The colored man's name was Ulysses, and after Isaac left Ellis Island he never saw or heard of him again. But he always remembered that on his last day in that place, just when he thought he'd go mad from the isolation and boredom, Ulysses brought the news, long before there was any official announcement to him, of his impending release, and brought him also a news magazine full of pictures of the world he was to enter, in which not a single face that looked like Ulysses' appeared. Uncle Isaac said he searched each photograph carefully, a cold dread settling in his chest; what sort of world was this, in which his very present friend did not appear? And then, from the pocket of his baggy brown coat, with its frayed holes at the elbows, Ulysses had produced and offered to him a bright red apple. This gift was Ulysses' handshake and hug. And it left Mr. Isaac hungry. For, unable to embrace a colored person — Ulysses warned him it was practically illegal to do so — what was he to offer? Nothing was yet his."

Carlotta smoothed the hair that poufed above Arveyda's ear. She kissed him on the eyes. No barrier like that for her, she thought, happily. Ever. Ever. None. None. It made her feel terribly free, and she laid herself full length against his comforting warmth, the sheen of his skin seeming to add a shimmer to her own. She nestled against all this *goodness*, which felt to her to be the very flesh of the earth. How foolish, how pitiful people were, she thought, not to know enough to try to get next to what could only do them good.

"It was a magic apple," said Arveyda, smiling into her hair. "This was before the time of poisoned, drug-filled apples. Musicians used to carry only healthful things. Really." He laughed. "There was even a time when musicians did not smoke reefer. Although probably never a time when they didn't drink wine."

Carlotta smiled with him.

"There was even a time"—Arveyda looked down mischievously into her face—"and I know you won't believe this, when music was played softly, to be heard. Only dead people need loud music, you know. I call loud rock 'Dracula music' because you look out, and there are all those dead and deaf and soulless zombies clod-hopping across the floor. Even colored people are zombies these days. It's enough to shrivel up your short hairs."

"You were talking about fruit," said Carlotta, giggling.

"So I was," said Arveyda. "So, Uncle Isaac bit into the apple and thought about his future. In Palestine he'd peddled orchard fruit and garden vegetables with his father, a hirsute, pious man. He would try the same thing in America. His basket grew into a cart, his cart into a stand, his stand into a store. He became a success. But he was not happy, even after realizing his youthful ambition to study 'in university' and to learn to play the violin. He missed the heat and the peaches and the Arabs. For Arabs had lived all around him in Palestine, just as colored people lived all around him in Terre Haute. Many of the dead he'd left behind, his friends, were Arabs.

"When he learned there would be a Jewish state, he accepted it as an excuse to go back. But he was really going back to the sun, the dates, the almonds, the oranges, the grapes, the sound of the Arab language that had filled his head as a boy, though he had spoken it only in the phrases learned on the street. He would go back to help them all build, he said. And he dosed up his shop one day and left."

It was of his mother that Arveyda thought the first time he met Zedé. That small, sad, Indian-looking woman so proud, Carlotta had told him, to be Spanish.

Zedé sat in the middle of a garishly decorated living room of sky-blue sofas with fringes on the bottom and lamps with colonial Spanish ladies endlessly promenading around their bases.

She was binding peacock feathers together to make capes, using the broken and partially ruined feathers as inset pieces in shoulder bags. She watched him suspiciously from lowered, tightly controlled, birdlike eyes. He could see he confused her. Brown skin, kinky hair, beautiful body, ready smile. She looked at him sadly, as if remembering him, and he thought she sniffled, as if she had a cold, or was about to weep.

When Arveyda was brought to meet Carlotta's mother, he had not known what to expect. Zedé had yellower skin than Carlotta, and her hair was bleached auburn, frizzed up in a style that seemed matronly. It was a surprise to him to see how young she really was. This woman who, in her lifetime, had known both magic and priests, in a country to which, for instance, television and the pickup truck—until very recently, he imagined—were unknown. A woman who had been arrested as a Communist, spent years in prison—at least three, Carlotta had thought—and then somehow made her way to North America. He bowed over her hand and would have kissed it, but Zedé shyly drew it back and put it out of sight, in the pocket of her smock.

She was dressed in an outfit of the dullest blackish-green, and from beneath the nest of her frizzy brown hair, fried lifeless, her slanting eyes glittered.

"How do you do?" she asked in the diffident style of night classes at San Francisco State.

"Just fine. How're you?" he answered in the same style. Then, because her smallness and bashfulness moved him, he added, "Not bad atall."

She and Carlotta, in their new prosperity, lived now in a roomy, light-filled flat on Clement Street, surrounded by restaurants. From one of them Zedé had gotten their dinner, which she dished out timidly, as Carlotta showed him around the flat.

Alone as he had been while growing up, and as he was now, Arveyda was wounded by the intense isolation of these two. There were schmaltzy pictures of sunsets and trees, happy white children chasing balloons, but none of relatives or of people who resembled Zedé and Carlotta at all. In Zedé's bedroom, on the night table, there was an old snapshot of her and Carlotta taken just after they arrived in San Francisco. Zedé's drawn face, seemingly frightened even of the photographer, was partly in shadow. Carlotta, her face moonlike, a string of beads around her tiny wrist, leaned out of her mother's arms, as if eager to embrace this new land. In both their faces he recognized the stress of oppression, dispossession, flight.

He would know them a very long time, he felt, sitting down to a tasty Vietnamese meal, and smiling from one to the other of them, like a man of serendipitous choice.

I T IS as if you went out," Carlotta's mother sobbed after that first meeting, "and brought your father home. Ai, ai," she cried, striking her head with her palm in a gesture of pain Carlotta had never seen before, but which she was instantly tempted to duplicate.

"He was Indio, your father, and his hair was rough."

But now Carlotta and Arveyda had been married for three years. They had two children her mother adored.

"Arveyda loves you," said Zedé. "You must believe this. But also, he and I loved each other from the start."

ARVEYDA was rich. He had more money, Carlotta sometimes thought, than the government of her mother's country. Once, to prove to her she would never again be in want, he took thousands and thousands of dollars from the bank and blew them all over her bedroom with an electric fan. Then they lay on the bills, as if on leaves in a forest, and made love.

Carlotta would have none of his money now. She had studied women's literature in college. That is what she would teach. Taking her children away from Arveyda and Zedé was the only way she could make them hurt as she was hurting. She could not know at the time how much she was hurting herself.

Letters from them as they traveled through Mexico and Central and South America she resisted opening for many months, preferring to think of them as dead. But they were her only family, after all.

Actually, only her mother wrote. Short, grieving, heavily scented letters that recalled Zedé vividly.

"Mija, mi corazón," they all began. (My daughter, my heart.) And there was the sound of Zedé weeping. But as the letters continued to arrive, Carlotta, reading through the evaporated teardrops, which had left puckered circles on the pages, sensed an animation in her mother's spirit she had never felt before. Arveyda and Zedé traveled through countries of incredible natural lushness. Zedé had never seen such rivers, such fish . . . there was a fish that mated for life, she wrote; when they caught one from the boat and prepared it for dinner, its mate swam furiously around and around the boat and actually followed it for miles . . . such trees, fruits, birds, and sky.

Carlotta imagined her mother at the railing of a ship, relaxed against Arveyda's body, the sun finding white glints in her once-again straight black hair.

"The food, every bit *is good*. Muy *delicioso!*" she wrote. And Carlotta remembered the crab sautéed in onion and peppers her mother liked and how that had been their once-a-month treat after her mother began selling the feathered things. Now she thought of her eating the food she liked all the time, growing sleek and maybe a little plump, the wrinkles around her eyes and on her forehead filling out. Her skin losing its sallowness and becoming tan and vibrant. She realized she had never known Zedé at peace. Always, she had been anxious, worried, frantic over the requirements of life for the two of them.

They'd slept together only once, Arveyda and Zedé, before Carlotta was told.

Arveyda had brought the children for Zedé to keep for the weekend, as she often did. Their brown, warm little bodies did magical things to her. She held them, squirming and wriggling or drowsy and contented, in her arms, and her cares seemed far away. That day they had been playing on Zedé's big bed, the children in the middle, she and Arveyda on the edges. It was a gray, rainy day, and her bedroom was all pink. Soft music was playing, by a man, Sidney Bechet, she liked. The children drifted off to sleep. As Arveyda lifted their limp bodies to take them into the other room, nearly asleep himself, she'd felt, as she did so often and as often tried to hide, a deep longing for him. But he is so young, she thought. El padre de mis nietos. El esposo de mi niñita. My son-in-law. Here she giggled, because she always confused the word "son" with "sun."

Arveyda looked at her, the sleeping baby in his arms, one plump arm flung wide in peace. Longing was like a note of music to him, easily read. He knew.

When he came back, he sat on the floor beside the bed. His voice shook. "We can't do anything about it, right?"

"No," she said, her voice also trembling. She tried to laugh. "I am grandmother. That's it." She meant, "That's all."

"I love you though," he said. "Not like a grandmother . . . maybe a little like a mother." He apologized with his smile, which was in his voice. His face was still turned away from her. "No," he said, "like a woman. Zedé. I love Carlotta; don't worry. I also love you."

How long had it been building between them, she wondered. Since the first day, since meeting. She'd smelled the scent in his hair as he bent toward her hand. The spiciness of it, the odor of her village flowers. She'd taken back her hand and hidden it, flaming, from him. After all, he was Carlotta's. Carlotta had found him.

"Nothing we can do, yes," she said, firmly. But with a glowing point of light, hot, growing in her heart, and between her legs she was suddenly wet.

Her hand trembled as she touched his hair, and the scent of him—the scent of safely sleeping, well-fed babies—reached her nose. His hair. There were flecks of gray. Glints of red and brown.

Kinky, firm, softly rough. Exactly the feel of raw silk. The only hair like this—*pelo negro*—in the world. Running her fingers through it, tugging. Trying for the light, resigned touch.

Trying to be *la madre*. Trying to be *friends*. Her womb contracted so sharply she nearly cried out.

She prayed Arveyda wouldn't turn and look at her. He did. His eyes inches away. His white teeth, his mustache and beard. His brown eyes that seemed so pained. His sweet breath. Like coconut. She smiled to think this about the coconut; she was such a campesina! He leaned forward to kiss the smile. She drew back.

"And you, Zedé?" he asked. "Am I just the son-in-law? I know we can never do anything . . . but I want to know."

"Ah, me," she said, attempting a little laugh that denied the hot heart and the light in her womb, the wetness nearly on her thighs. The laugh, so false, so incapable of all the deceit required of it, turned into tears. Arveyda took her face in his hands. It had become younger since he'd known her. The birdlike eyes didn't dart about so, the twitch was gone. Only the sadness of the dispossessed of love remained. He would kiss it away.

Zedé had made love only twice before in her life. Until she met Arveyda she hadn't thought about sex; she was too busy and her memories were too painful. Though she had had sex, it had been brief. Sometimes her daughter was the only proof that a man had made love to her. Now it was as if she had a new body. Arveyda was kissing all of it, the way she would have wanted someone she loved to kiss it when she was *embarazada*. Under his lips she felt the flowering of her shriveled womb and under his tongue her folded sex came alive. The hairs on her body stood like trees. In truth, the light that she felt inside her in womb and heart now seemed to cover all of her; she felt herself dissolve into the light.

Lying in bed later, exhausted from orgasms that shook her core, Zedé traced round and round the black mole on Arveyda's right breast. They were both relaxed and frantic.

"It won't happen again," she said. "It can't."

Her lips were drawn to the mole. She kissed it without knowing she did.

"No," said Arveyda. "I'm sorry. All my fault." His face was lost in her hair. He grew large again against her thigh. She grew wet.

"Mamacita. Daddy." It was the oldest child, Cedrico, calling, waking up.

For months they avoided each other. But she loved his music and played it on the stereo all the time, so she cheated. He never left her, though he was away performing in other cities and other countries. She listened to the music and sometimes she cried. Sometimes, crying, she lay back on her pink bed, her hand between her legs. There was one piece of music, especially, in his last album that moved her to her knees. She knew he had written it while thinking of her. She could come just listening to it.

Arveyda lived in the clothes she made for him, earning himself finally the nickname "Bird," or, as he loved to translate it, "Charlie Parker the Third." Wrapped in his feathered cape, his winged boots, he sent his soul flying to Zedé while holding his body, his thought, his attentions on Carlotta, whom he did not cease to love. Only, now he began to think it was Zedé he loved in Carlotta. Scrutinizing Carlotta's face he looked for traces of Zedé. When he found them he kissed them with reverence.

How do you tell someone you love that you are in love with her mother, as well? It was probably illegal, moreover. Arveyda thought and thought about the problem; his music, so mellow and rocking, became tortured and shrill. Sometimes in rehearsal and even in performance he played his guitar in a trance.

Arveyda's music was so beautiful no one minded how long he played. There he stood, his slim legs in soft jeans, his brown suede feathered boots glowing in the strobe lights, a sliver of his narrow chest revealed; his face, the face of a deeply spiritual person, intense behind guitar or flute. It was not without cause that he was rich and famous: Arveyda and his music were medicine, and, seeing or hearing him, people knew it. They flocked to him as once they might have to priests. He did not disappoint them. Each time he played, he did so with his heart and soul. Always, though he might be very tired, he played earnestly and prayerfully. Even if the music was about fucking—and because he loved fucking, a lot of it was—it was about the fucking the universe does through us as it joyfully fucks itself. Audiences felt this so much that there was a joke about how many Arveyda babies were conceived on full-moon concert nights.

He played for his dead mother and for the father he'd hardly known; the longing for both came out of the guitar as wails and sobs. There was a blue range in his music that he played when he was missing them. Carlotta was yellow. The young, hopeful immigrant color, the color of balance, the color of autumn leaves, half the planet's flowers, the color of endurance and optimism. Green was his own color, soothing green, the best color for the eyes and the heart. And Zedé—Zedé's color was peach or pink or coral. The womb colors, the woman colors. When he played for her he closed his eyes and stroked and entered her body, which he imagined translucent as a shell. He remembered making love to her and imagined himself the light within the translucent pink shell. He often wept while he played.

Carlotta could not believe the beauty of the new music, discordant as it sometimes was, and wailing. She would sit in the audience watching him play and, though she lived with him, it was as if he were a stranger, far from her, far from anyone. If she had managed to drag Zedé to a performance, she would turn to her in her excitement over a new riff. But Zedé inevitably held her head down. Carlotta could never recall later how she first became aware.

For months Arveyda and Zedé barely saw each other. This, Carlotta knew. Arveyda was traveling; often Carlotta went with him. Zedé remained in her house and cared for the children. Every night while they were away, Carlotta called to check on them. Was Cedrico eating? Was Angelita wetting the bed? Were she and Arveyda missed? Zedé answered her questions with energy and enthusiasm. Yes, Cedrico missed them, but he was "un niño muy grande." Sure, Angelita wet the bed, but there was luck in this (some superstition from the old country, Carlotta assumed, and Zedé never explained), and they were both eating like crazy. And so on. After a rundown of her own activities in whatever town they were staying, and after Zedé had mentioned any small news she had, there was an awkward silence.

"Don't you want to know about Arveyda?" Carlotta would have to ask.

"Oh, yes, very much," her mother would say. But then Carlotta had the distinct impression that her mother was not listening. She could not know that every word about Arveyda was a dagger.

Each night she reported to Arveyda about the children. He never asked a word about Zedé. "Don't you want to know about my mother?" she'd once said angrily, scorning his indifference to the sacrifice her mother made in keeping the children.

"Sure I do, sure I do," he'd mumbled absently and then looked distractedly and moodily at the door.

At first she thought it was hatred. But how could they hate each other? These two best friends of hers who, she thought, had loved each other on sight.

· · ·

When they picked up the children, after weeks of absence, Arveyda hardly bothered to thank Zedé. He barely glanced at her. Zedé, for so dark a person, looked extremely pale.

At dinner one night in a restaurant Carlotta finally spoke up. They'd sat like sticks the whole meal.

"What have I done to deserve the exquisite torture you two are inflicting on me?" she said in what she hoped was a joking tone.

"What do you mean?" her mother said quickly.

Carlotta looked at Arveyda.

"You never talk to, or even look at, each other anymore. It's hell for me. What is the matter? Come on, look at each other at least."

She thought she saw panic in her mother's eyes. But Zedé raised her head and looked at Arveyda. Arveyda, however, excused himself, got up from the table with a frown and left.

She watched them struggle until she, too, was worn out, and one day she forced the whole story out of her shockingly young-looking, vulnerable, inexperienced, terrified, and pale-as-ashes mother.

When she confronted a weary Arveyda, too listless now to think of creating new work and looking about, Carlotta suspected, for drugs, he said only: "The Greeks would know how to handle this. I don't. Zedé and I are guilty of falling in love."

"But she's my mother," she hissed.

"Tell me about it," he said.

"She's older than you!"

"*No!*" he said, mockingly.

"But she's a grandmother," Carlotta said.

"She is also an artist," said Arveyda.

"How can you love her?" she cried.

"Don't you?" he asked.

They could manage, she thought, if Arveyda and her mother had never made love. But when she asked him, he was direct.

"We made love once," he said. "We have no intention of doing it again." He paused. "To ask your understanding and forgiveness seems corniness personified."

But what of her dignity?

Zedé came to see her, wrapping her arms around Carlotta's legs, face pressed against her knees, her tears so profuse they soaked Carlotta's skirt.

"I date now. Soon, I promise, I will marry someone I love. We will go away. To Mexico, maybe. I will try to get out of your hair."

Carlotta's heart was breaking. She felt it swell with tears and then crack. What does anyone know about anything? she thought. The scene with her mother emptied her of knowledge. Once again, as when she was a small child, she felt she knew nothing. That if the chair on which she sat suddenly became a canoe that floated out the window on the river of Zedé's tears, she would not be surprised.

ACURIOUS feature of Suwelo's face was his eyebrows. They were exaggerated crescents over his bold black eyes, and they were prematurely graying, which gave him at times an owlish look. He had this look now as he sat by the window of a train on his way to Baltimore, his tall, slightly overweight body hunched to take advantage of the last of the afternoon light coming over his shoulder. He tugged absent-mindedly at his full and shapely bottom lip, while attempting to read a new novel by a former acquaintance of his:

"Forcing back Jackie's head, he rammed his . . . into her waiting . . . Half an hour later he was on top of her, making her moan with pleasure, as he galloped his horses to a heavenly finish."

Impatiently he flipped the pages, looking for more news of Jackie, some word on the development of this unappealing relationship, but there was nothing. At other points in the novel she was seen dressing, gossiping with her girlfriends, and going out to do the grocery shopping. Although she was the main love interest of the book, she was not even made love to again, probably much to her relief, Suwelo thought, as he scanned the hero's chilling seduction scene with a schoolgirl a third his age, in which drugs figured prominently.

His generation of men had failed women—and them-selves—he mused, taking off his tortoiseshell glasses and stroking the ridge of his generous and somewhat shiny nose. For all their activism and political development during the six-ties, all their understanding of the pervasiveness of oppression, for most men, the preferred place for women had remained the home; the preferred position for women, wherever they were, supine.

He threw the book aside; then picked it up again as he thought to ask himself what it was really about. It was about a robbery, the trial of the accused man, the hero, his convic-tion and execution (because all witnesses to the crime had been killed), and the realization by the town, later, that the man ex-ecuted was innocent.

But he wasn't innocent entirely, Suwelo thought. He had vi-olated Jackie, even if, as Suwelo now saw, on the last page there was a note from the hero to the grieving Jackie reminding her of all the good times they'd had and of how happy he was to have had her as "his woman."

Suwelo yawned. Then smiled wryly as he thought of his own failed attempts to make "his woman" out of either Fanny or Carlotta.

His great-uncle Rafe had already been cremated when Suwelo arrived at the house. There was a short, quiet ceremony that remembered Rafe as unobtrusive, helpful to the community, a man of peace. Looking about the small room, Suwelo was startled to see mostly women, old, bent, pale, and powdered women, a dozen or so of them, and only a couple of men, in the moss-green and snuff-colored suits peculiar to old colored men, leaning on their canes and appearing to wonder whether they were next.

His great-uncle's ashes were presented to him in a fake antique apothecary jar that looked familiar; he thought he might have seen the original in a museum. After the friends left, Suwelo remained alone in the house, which Uncle Rafe had left to him. It was a small row house, typical of old Baltimore, on a street that had been, over the past few years, ruthlessly gentrified. His uncle's place had been gentrified on the outside, presumably to placate the new yuppie neighbors, but inside, it was the same as it had been when Suwelo was a boy. Tall ceilings, dark wood, mote-filled parlors, heavy old furniture, a huge scratched dining-room table with lion-paw base. There was still a working dumbwaiter, which for years his uncle had used to haul coal up from the cellar.

As he walked through the house, spotlessly clean, its white antimacassars and starchy doilies fairly glowing under the soft light of the antique chandeliers, Suwelo realized it was not so small, after all. He began to climb, to investigate its three stories. The banister had been recently oiled; it gleamed under his hand. There were pictures everywhere, the faces so vivid he found himself stopped by them as if by the arresting faces of strangers on the street. He recognized other relatives: his grandfather, his other great-uncles, his aunts. There was his cousin Rena. Her husband, Mose. His own mother, sitting with a daunted, disillusioned look in a lawn swing, beside which his father stood. His father. His father had lost an arm in World War II. In the photograph, his sleeve pinned up, his cap at a cocky angle, he was still proud of this. But he wouldn't be for long. Suwelo sighed, deeply and wearily, as he read the inscription: "To Unk, love, Louis and Marcia." And, sighing, he passed his father's brash look, his mother's air of helpless captivity, and moved up the stairs. He could not, would not think of them; he wanted to be happy. It was strange and pleasant owning a house, even though he intended to sell it right away. The money Uncle Rafe had also left him would last about a year, long enough, with the money from the sale of the house and the time it bought, for him to sort himself out.

With all the space, which, because it was so quiet and empty of life, seemed really very large, Suwelo was amused to discover Uncle Rafe had chosen as his own bedroom the smallest room in the house. It was something between a bedroom and a closet, across the hall from the master bedroom, which was four times its size, and it was filled almost entirely by his uncle's single bed. This room, too, had been straightened up and mercilessly cleaned. Though it appeared poor and bare, there was an almost clinical neatness. The cheap wooden bed was polished until it shone. The windows sparkled and the shades were adjusted precisely. The rubber mattress pad had been washed and folded at the foot of the bed the way a nurse — or a private in the army — might have done.

He supposed it was the nurse who had cleaned things up. He wondered. Next to his uncle's bed there were several neat stacks of *National Geographic*. There were newspapers, a *Life* magazine, an *Ebony*, several copies of *Jet*, which, Suwelo recalled, his uncle had particularly loved. There was also — he stopped, picked it up, and flipped it open — a worn book, *Of Human Bondage*. This he took with him as he wandered about the rest of the house.

At last he settled in the master bedroom. As he stood at a side window looking down into the yard, he saw a black woman — youngish, trim, in her thirties, perhaps, weeding her garden. While he watched, an Asian man, very handsome and smiling, came out to embrace her. Seconds later two school-age children ran up. Something funny was apparently said, for they all laughed, and the boy, six or seven, began stacking and disposing of the debris his mother pointed out.

On the other side, a white couple was having a party, and must be somewhere in the group he saw, he supposed. There were about a dozen people, and they were talking, listening to music, and drinking heartily. They were very noisy, but there was nothing frightening about it.

On both sides of his uncle's house—he did not yet think of it as his own—the yards had a carefully restructured look, raised beds for vegetables and flowers, for instance, that went with the newly modified houses. His uncle's yard was different. There was just the yard, very plain, flat, with a thin layer of grass, neatly trimmed, and an oak tree that spread across the back of all three yards. Under this tree there was an ugly metal fake "barn" that his uncle must have used as a toolshed.

The room he was in had a high ceiling, three large windows facing the street, a fireplace, massive oak furniture that actually had presence (it was as if several massive dark people inhabited the room), and a giant bed that was the most inviting thing he'd seen on his trip. Wearily he sat down on it, marveling at its woodiness, the elegant old-fashioned carving, how high it was from the floor. A queen's or king's bed. The linens, light blanket, and comforter were spotless, ivory colored, and the spread was an extremely ancient, lacy, handmade throw that was so delicate he hesitated a moment before flinging it back. The pillow shams were edged with lace.

He had planned to stay a week, just long enough to put the house on the market, settle his uncle's affairs, and collect the money coming to him. Before he knew it, two weeks had passed. Every night he called Fanny. Every night her voice was the same: cool, distant, beyond any concern for him. He asked how she was sleeping, because he knew that for a long time she was plagued by nightmares. Something about Prince Charles grinning at her, but with Africa's teeth. He asked whether she was eating enough. To every query she merely murmured, "Fine, fine," in that absent voice of hers that so irritated him. On the nights he couldn't sleep he threw himself into a further cleanup of his uncle's house. For starters he went through all the boxes of junk in the basement. There were many boxes of old clothing; in one he found pearl buttons and a woman's wedding gown—old, mildewed, moth-eaten. There were boxes and crates of magazines and books. Hundreds of novels, but also books on learning English, on botany, on learning to sail. By the third week he'd rented a truck and made his way to the dump.

Slowly he worked his way up. In the kitchen he found little to throw out. This did not surprise him; from his first day in the house he'd been fed, as his uncle must have been before him, by the little old ladies who'd been at the postcremation ceremony. Old and slow-moving though they were, they'd lost none of their considerable culinary skills. Suwelo had never eaten so well in his life: three huge meals a day, brought to the door as punctually as sunrise. They did not pause to chatter. The doorbell would ring, he'd go to answer it, two old women leaning on and leading each other would be heading toward a car or back up the street. Sometimes they'd turn and wave. Occasionally he reached the porch fast enough to be able to say hi.

At night he sat in front of the aged television set eating his succulent dinner of smothered chicken or braised fish, and his life, for the first time since he was a child, seemed angel-protected, materially solid, spiritually secure. He was almost happy.

In Uncle Rafe's house Suwelo always seemed to himself to be in a rather idle state of mind. His life had stopped, at least the life he'd thought he was building with Fanny, and he was suspended. He sometimes felt literally as if his feet did not touch the ground. It was a relief. And at times, too, he simply thought, something that money, enough to keep you going for a while without worrying, permitted you to do. Another of the many advantages of the rich, but only if they were clever enough not to ruin this idle time by thinking about their money.

By now Suwelo had secured his. He took out his bankbook frequently, to prove its existence: $26,867.03. That's what he had to work with. Plus an old, newly valuable town house in pristine condition. A house that was slowly seducing him. It wasn't just the ceilings, so high that birds flew in through the open windows and stayed several minutes before flying out again, or the comfortable old furniture into which he sank almost out of sight. It wasn't the platters of delicious food endlessly appearing. It was actually—he'd considered it—the master bedroom. The bed.

Sprawled on its downy softness, the frilly throw about his shoulders, his back against the lacy, crunchy-sounding pillows, his eyes drowsy from the coal fire in the fireplace and the glass of Dry Sack he permitted himself in the evening, Suwelo experienced a sense of well-being that stunned him. In fact, if anyone could have seen him, his owlish eyes fixed on the fire, his mouth relaxed, his body limp, they would have said he *looked* stunned, as if someone had hit him once, sharply, over the head and he'd laid himself out to recover.

It was in his idleness that he began to notice how much his uncle Rafe had scribbled. On book jackets and in margins, on notepads and even on some of his medicine-bottle labels. Suwelo imagined him—he hadn't seen him since he himself was in college, nearly twenty years ago—a doddering, muttering old coot, a bachelor, reading about the world but slowly losing a place in it, conversing by writing his little notes.

"No good. Strained. Trite. Could do better myself." A scribbled blurb on a book by Ernest Hemingway. "Big bluster. He-Man," followed on the back flap.

"President nuts. Can't they see anything? Elect a madman. What do you get? Madness." On an old newspaper, with a front-page picture of Eisenhower, yellowed, ripped in two.

"Between rock and hard place. Colored voter. Two parties but one race running both. White one." On the cover of *Life*.

At first these little messages of his uncle's simply amused Suwelo. Though he was himself approaching middle age, he held the view common among relatively young people that old people get no closer to being real than caricature.

"Lissie called me up today. Crying. Some crackers hurt her feelings. Bus was crowded with white people coming home from a game. They made her get off and walk. She was all dressed up in her white lace. Was muddied." This was scrawled, oddly enough, on a shoe box in the master-bedroom closet. A shoe box that contained, indeed, a pair of white, out-of-fashion women's pumps. Size six. Very soiled.

"Lissie will be the death of me. Must be strong. Damn." Written, incredibly, on a used linen table napkin and stuffed in the pocket of an old black dressy pair of pants.

"Must tell Lissie not to worry about . . ." Here there was no completion, as if his uncle had been interrupted as he scrawled his note on the back of an envelope.

But who was Lissie?

He began, almost unconsciously, to scrutinize the pictures on the walls again. There were pictures of Uncle Rafe as a very young man, just after he'd come up from the Island. It must have been the very first day of his employment as a sleeping-car porter on the Baltimore Limited, the train that "tore up" the tracks between Baltimore and New York City, which Uncle Rafe had talked about as if it were a relative. He was smiling broadly and jauntily sporting his blue-and-red porter's cap. He'd loved to talk about the amount "she" was fed, what she was like when her "dander was up." How she "chased the rails." How none of the other trains could "hold a candle to her." (What did it mean, he'd wondered, to "hold a candle" to something, especially to a train. How had the expression first come into the language?) Suwelo's mind used to wander, even as Uncle Rafe grew more excited by the vividness of his memories. His rather somber dark brown eyes glowed, and once he'd said something about a minuscule tip a white millionaire miser had given him, and laughed uproariously, his temples bulging, his head thrown back, mouth open wide, revealing crooked but very white and strong teeth.

Fifty years he'd been a porter. Carrying, mainly, white people's bags. Sometimes, for his "vacation" on the job, he'd snuck up behind some pretty "brownskin" with "a shape on her hittin' ninety-nine," on her way to the sooty Jim Crow car, and insisted on carrying her bag. These were the moments that made his work bearable, and he learned to create such brief encounters, small moments of delight for himself, as the train barreled down the tracks. He got on well with small children (they almost immediately referred to him as "uncle") and their pets. Young mothers traveling alone doted on him. He was helpful, modest, quick, and definitely knew his place—they could read this easily in his demeanor—because he, like so many colored men, had perfected the art of doing the most intimate things to and for white people without once appearing to look at them. It was an invaluable skill.

At the end of his run his new "friends" pressed nickels, dimes, and sometimes quarters into his palm. There was the occasional half-dollar. He'd laughed, talking to Suwelo and the other relatives gathered around him (and around the mountains of good food always to be found in Uncle Rafe's house) about how the train's fancy food, which he had little taste for, was handed out the window to hoboes and how for one stretch during the Depression he'd developed a "paunch," in which he carried enough prosciutto and roast beef to feed the fatherless family down the street.

"Niggers steal. Yes, indeed!" he'd said, and laughed like a madman.

Suwelo imagined his uncle from his white charges' point of view. A tall, roundish, though never fat, somewhat somber presence; a being whose eyes were as expressionless as the glass eyes of a toy. (Suwelo thought his own bold but oddly unrevealing eyes resembled his uncle's.) A big brown bear of a man, bending over white people, serving them, for fifty years. The scent of their hair always in his face, their little needs and wants on the ride from Baltimore to New York the impetus for most of his activity, the words "Porter!" or "Oh, *boy*," his signal to spring into genuinely delighted or, at the least, concerned action. What a nightmare, thought Suwelo, a hellish nightmare. And how oddly moving it was that Uncle Rafe loved food and wine and dancing (he danced beautifully into old age) in his house—the spacious, uncluttered digs of a stone bachelor, or so Suwelo had thought—with family and friends, and could sit and tell of his days on the railroad and not only laugh himself, but have everybody else laughing too.

And the *depth* of the laughter! The way it seemed to go so far down inside it scraped the inside bottoms of the feet. No one laughed like that anymore. Nothing seemed funny enough. When his uncle and his guests finished laughing, they'd seemed lighter, clearer; even their activities appeared to be done more gracefully. It was as if the laughing emptied them, and sharing it placed whatever was laughable and unbearable in its proper perspective.

How he wished he could laugh like that now over the mess he'd made of his life with Fanny. And the cowardice he'd shown in his relationship to Carlotta. Fanny loved to laugh, flaunting the irresistible gap between her front teeth, as if she still lived in Africa, where it was distinctly a sign of beauty; a gap that sometimes pinched his tongue. But he could not imagine being included in the laughter, now. His would be the place of the white miser, the one who exploited; or of the children and their grateful mothers, who nonetheless never *saw*. He imagined Fanny and Carlotta laughing together—at him.

One morning an ancient gentleman, whom Suwelo recognized as one of the two who had attended his uncle Rafe's postcremation ceremony, rang the bell. He stood there in workshirt, old pants and boots, appearing to dodder. After a minimum of pleasantries—"Nice day. Warm up after a while. How you?"—he announced he'd come to "cut the yard."

Without a word Suwelo led him through the house and out the back door. Once in the yard he watched as the old fellow unlocked the shed and took out a lawn mower as old as everything else about the house. This he proceeded to push back and forth over the tiny lawn, snipping off the heads of the tender blades of grass in great stateliness and serenity. Suwelo was impressed.

"My name's Suwelo," he said when the old man had finished, put away the mower, raked up the grass, and returned the tools to the shed. Suwelo stood beside him as he ran his hands under the water from the outside faucet and used a large yellowing handkerchief to wipe the perspiration from his face.

"I know who you are," said the old man. "I knew your father and mother. I knew you as a boy, before you changed your name. 'Louis, Jr.,' we used to call you. Or 'Little Louis.'" He sighed. "You wouldn't remember me. My name's Jenkins. Harold D., for Davenport. Hal, for short." He smiled. "The children always called me 'Mr. Hal.' Pleased to meet you." He stuck out a moist hand, which Suwelo took, marveling at its smoothness and fragility—the hand of someone who worked two or three hours a month now, at most.

Suwelo offered Mr. Hal a cup of coffee, which was accepted. Mr. Hal sat comfortably at the kitchen table, as if he were used to sitting there. Indeed, when he shifted in his chair and felt the slight unevenness of its legs, he gave the kind of exasperated grunt one gives when a piece of furniture has aggravated one unceasingly for a number of years.

"Mind if I switch?" he asked, already rising from the annoying chair. "That one . . ."

"Did you know my uncle long?" asked Suwelo.

"All his life, just about. We was boys together down on the Island. Both of us come from furniture-making peoples. Went off to World War I together, the Great War. Married . . ." There he stopped. Looked at his shoe.

He was a rather small man. His head was longish; his hair, that strange shade of gray that seems to be white hair turning black again, and cut short. His mustache was a neat brush across his lip. His skin was tan and of a smoothness common to old people and babies. He had unusually large and, Suwelo thought, fine eyes. By fine, he meant there was in them a quality of patience, of having learned when and when not to speak. Like many old people's eyes, they had a bluish cast, and the dark pupils were open wide.

"I've been going through my uncle's things," said Suwelo.

"A lot of stuff to go through," said Mr. Hal. "He never could let go of nothing. The least little thing he ever got hold of he kept."

This was said matter-of-factly and in a tone of "I don't envy you."

"Oh, I'm enjoying it," said Suwelo. "I feel I'm getting to know him for the first time. I wish there were names on the pictures around here though. The faces are so expressive. They all look like they're trying to speak, but without their names I can't seem to hear them."

"Most of the women are Lissie," said Mr. Hal. "The men are different ones. Your daddy. Cousins. Uncles. Granddaddy. Maybe a aunt or somebody else female, but I don't recall anybody else."

"But there're a lot of women," said Suwelo.

"Lissie is a lot of women."

"Actually, I'm glad you brought her up," said Suwelo. "I've seen her name around here a lot."

Mr. Hal studied Suwelo. His large eyes seemed to click over

him from head to foot. Suwelo felt washed by the look, rigorously assessed.

"You've met her, haven't you?"

"No, I don't think so," Suwelo said.

"She one of the ones sometime bring your food."

"Oh," he said, disappointed. He thought of the old women leaning on each other, or turning to wave as they got into their automobile. He loved having them cook for him, and was really quite astonished that they did, but he thought they were too old to be driving a car.

"She wasn't always old," said Mr. Hal. "None of us was."

Suwelo realized with a start that in his real life, the life in California away from his uncle's cozy Baltimore row house, he was never around old people. He didn't know that one of the skills they acquired with age was the ability to read minds. For as he sat there, embarrassed, he knew Mr. Hal was reading him. Easily, casually, as he himself might read a book.

"You married?" asked Mr. Hal.

"I was," said Suwelo.

Mr. Hal waited.

"I blew it. Right now I don't know what's happening with us. I'm drifting."

"I bet she real pretty," said Mr. Hal.

This sounded false to Suwelo. And unworthy. Mr. Hal was too old to care about mere prettiness. Even *he* was. Anyhow, was Fanny pretty? "Prettiness ain't what it used to be," said Suwelo. "Probably never was."

"Don't take it so hard," said Mr. Hal, laughing.

Suwelo laughed too.

"Women," said Mr. Hal, with good humor.

"You can't live with 'em and you can't . . . you know the rest, I just *know*." They looked at each other and laughed again.

Suwelo walked Mr. Hal to a dilapidated truck. Mr. Hal leaned on the steering wheel as if resting his chest while praying for the truck to start. When it did, after much moaning and coughing, he turned to Suwelo.

"When Lissie come next time, you ask her about herself."

All these old, old people in moving vehicles, Suwelo was thinking, and wondering about their accident rate. Even now Mr. Hal was gunning the motor like a teenager hard of hearing.

"Was she a girlfriend?" Suwelo asked over the noise.

"Better than that," said Mr. Hal, rolling away. "Lissie was our wife."

Suwelo went back inside and stopped in front of the first picture he came to. A very young, barefoot, willful-looking woman wearing a long dark dress stared haughtily out at him. She was standing in front of five new, beautiful old-fashioned wooden chairs. The ground was sandy where she stood, and he noticed her dress was patched near the hem. In one of the chairs there was an unfinished basket, the bare spikes of its sides making it look like a large spider about to crawl up the back of the chair.

The chairs were exceptional-looking: tall, of a light glistening wood, with rush seats and elaborately carved backs. He'd never seen anything like them.

He continued to look at the pictures up and down the stairwell, and in the parlors. The young woman with the chairs was the only woman he didn't know. He went back several times, and could always identify his aunts and cousins, but not the young woman. And then he noticed light oval and square spots where pictures had once hung on the walls. Someone had taken them down.

"M E AND Lissie courted from the time she was in long dresses and I was in short pants," Mr. Hal said to Suwelo a few days later as they sat at the kitchen table over coffee. "It must have started, us feeling something for each other, almost from the time we was babies. You know, or maybe you young ones don't, but there was a certain kind of living in the country back then that had a lot of advantages. It wasn't all night riders and scary white people acting ugly. Course, they did that, too; I just come to believe now they can't help it, and you sort of wish they'd study the tendency. But they won't, not in this lifetime anyway. Maybe in the next. But they struck you, and if you was a child, after they struck you, and didn't kill you or run off anybody in your family, or one of your friends' families, they was gone. Hallelujah! You didn't really think about them till they caused some more grief. They are the most frightening of all people, and I'll just be fair: I am afraid of them. They will take what they want, regardless, and that's what you feel when you meet them. And so I always tried to keep the kind of life where meeting them wasn't necessary.

"But the country is a big place, and it's beautiful, and the islands 'cross the bay from Charleston are real special. And in the evenings after working in the field we sometimes would visit one another—our families would, you know—and we'd sit out on the porch. Well, the grown-ups would. Sit there chewing and smoking, and having them long conversations with them short, short words. Sometimes a hour would go by and they'd have said nearly nothing, but the world and the firmament of heaven and the battlements of hell would have been covered.

"Well, before we knowed ourselves good, as babies, me and Lissie use to play together. Her daddy and mama's place faced the beach, but we didn't think of it as 'beach' back then; it was just their yard, and you could sit on that little shackly porch and watch the sun drop into the bay. It was a beautiful sight. Sometimes all of us would be out there watching: children, grownups, the hound dogs, the cats, even the goats. Just sitting or standing around in silence watching the sunset . . . Although maybe not the cats—anyhow not up close to us—'cause I was, and am, for some reason deathly afraid of cats, and this grieved Lissie, who had a real fondness for them. And although I can't remember us as babies, I can almost remember it—Lissie remembers it perfectly, she says—and I like to think of us two fat brown babies with our asafoetida bags round our necks looking at the sunset together with the animals and slobbering all over one another's face.

"Everybody laughed to see the attraction force between us. Soon as we could walk, off we'd totter together, sticking everything in our path in our mouths and gumming each other's noses with our baby teeth. But then she became a little girl and I became a little boy, and for a number of years we went sort of separate ways. Until Miss Beaumont started up a little school back of her house for people's children, and me and Lissie fell right back together again. It wasn't even love, as such. It was more like what these young people today have when they go off to fight against nuclear war together; more like affinity. We just gravitated toward each other, 'cause that's where life felt safest and best. Lissie felt this, I felt this. It was even recognized by Miss Beaumont and everybody in that little school. Hal 'n' Lissie, Lissie 'n' Hal, they'd say.

"She was never no angel. Fact of the matter, she was mean. Always had to have her own way. But not always with me. I could usually get her to show her good side. Sometimes she took food from some of the littler kids and gave bites of it to me, and we'd stand there eating whatever it was and watching the little fellow she'd taken it from cry. Lissie got more whippings than anybody at school. She was a born ringleader. Even as a little thing she spoke right up. Other little girls had trouble with the boys bullying them. Not Lissie. She ruled over the boys, the same way she did over the girls, and she would fight at the drop of a hat. I mean fight like the very devil. She had these big white teeth, and when she got in a fight with anybody she just chopped away at them. She bit a boy's ear near about off that tried to beat up on her, and after that she was like a queen. She'd speak and the waters parted.

"I was a little afraid of Lissie, to tell the truth. She was ruthless. And she would tell lies on people just to laugh at the confusion she made. She could really be wicked. One time Mr. Beaumont almost shut down the school 'cause Lissie said, loud enough for him to hear: 'Henry Aiken'—a big hulking brute that looked like a horse seated at a desk—'look like he lost something under Miss Beaumont's desk.' It was true he always had his eyes on what he could see of Miss Beaumont's ankles, but he was harmless, and Miss Beaumont's behavior was beyond reproach. There was a big to-do in the school. Miss Beaumont and Henry were made fun of. Mr. Beaumont eventually looked like a jackass, especially because Miss Beaumont temporarily left him, left the community, and nearly lost that teaching job. Mr. Beaumont had to go to her mama's house and beg her to return. Lissie, my own little Lissie, just laughed.

"There never was enough going on to suit her, so she tended to look on people's lives as if they was plays. She was always moving people around. But she was good to me. She protected me. For one curious thing about me was that, unlike the other fellows, I couldn't fight. I just couldn't. It seemed so rude and crude. I would always rather run from a fight. And, you know, running from fights attracts 'em. I use to think there had to be some other way of settling differences. But nobody on our island seemed to have heard of it. The grown-ups sometimes talked things through, but then, come Saturday nights, they'd get to swinging at each other, too. So Lissie took up for me. She'd stand there flat-footed—barefooted, too, 'cause none of us had school shoes, just the ones we wore on Sundays to church—and she'd stick out her bony chest and bare her big white teeth and she could blow like the best and baddest of the boys, even if they was twice her size. It just didn't faze her. She never showed fear. In fact, when Lissie started to tot up all the limbs she planned to chop through and all the gashes she planned to rub sand in, her voice took on a cool disinterested quality and her eyes seemed to be looking way off in the distance just beyond her opponent's head. It was spooky. She was so little. So black. She was, like, *concentrated*, if you know what I mean. Like, anywhere you were likely to grab her would be resisting you and whipping you, too—'cause, well, her bored look said she'd dealt with your kind before and she'd really hoped for something more interesting to do than mopping up the ground with your sorry ass that afternoon. Where did it come from? This particular concentrated form of energy that was Lissie? When she told me, I was and I wasn't surprised."

THEY were exactly as Carlotta had imagined them. Standing close together at the railing of a ship. Not quite a ship; only Arveyda's olive-green sailboat, with its black-and-yellow sails, which he steered with the same meditative masterfulness with which he played his flute. On this small boat he traveled the waters of the world whenever situations on land became too intense. The quiet of the boat was soothing, and when he grew tired of sailing, he turned on the boat's motor, which droned energetically, like a large, persistent fly, or he simply permitted the boat to list as it would, in the wind.

They traveled south.

Under the open sky, the reflections of the turquoise water near her country's shoreline brightening her sad eyes, Zedé became a different woman. Gone the hesitant English that was a result of shyness, passionate excitement, or fear. Though her voice often cracked with the effort not to weep from the pain of relived experiences, she spoke with an eloquence that startled Arveyda, who held on to her as she talked, not as a lover, but as the ear that might at last reconnect her to her world.

"Of the way of my country you can have no comprehension," she said, "especially as it was when I was a child. Everything was changing, it is true, but still many of the old ways were everywhere on view. Our mothers taught us about love-making and babies when we became señoritas, of course, but all along also they taught us the history of our civilization.

"I will always remember there was a gigantic waterfall," Zedé continued, "like the one I have seen in pictures of Jamaica. This was a magic place. We went there to bathe while we had our period, whole groups of girls and their mothers. It was always on the full moon. It was warm. Even the water; but refreshing, too, on our skins and in our long hair. There was no one, in the old time, who did not have long hair. You just did! That was that! No one gave any thought to it much, either. You could wear it hanging or propped up on your head or pulled back by bits of string or flower stems, any way you could. Yes, and some of the women made these headbands of beads that were pretty and very slippery, like the hide of an iguana. Yes!

"Anyway, we would all gather by Ixtaphtaphahex, the God-dess, for that's what her name meant, and our mothers would prepare food, and the young girls went up and down the sides of the falls collecting bits of wood for a fire. After eating and bathing we drew up in a circle near the fire, and if someone was nursing a tattoo, her mother would work on it, rubbing in the dye, while someone else's mother told stories of long ago.

"That is how I first learned about the priests. The priests of our village lacked any sign of joy. They always seemed, from their sour expressions, to be hurting and as if they had given up something that now plagued them with anxiety. Of course they were feared, if not respected, and of course the fear looked like respect, I guess. Doesn't it usually? For wherever they went, the people bowed to them, and the people worked to keep them in food. The people built their houses for them. But then, people also did all these things without joy. And it was only when the priests led the parades in the ceremonies, blessing the village, the crops, and the beasts, that the people received any satisfaction from them. And the reason for this was — their costumes! Their costumes were made by women like my mother, who sometimes worked the whole year on the feathered and beaded and shell-bedecked outfits the priests wore. And every year when the priests swept by the crowd, their garments were more resplendent than the outfits made the year before. Sometimes, I tell you, they dazzled the eyes, and the heart grew immense from just the notion that such beauty could be made and could exist. You just could not believe anything so gorgeous was made by human hands, and especially not by these poor bent little women like my mother, sitting on the dirt floor of her hut.

"My mother had a special hut with mud walls and a grass roof for her work. There she would be, sometimes for days at a time. We could watch her from our main house, but we learned early not to bother her when she was doing holy work, making the costumes for the priests. I used to hide in the taraba bushes that grew beside the large mango tree in our yard and watch her as she worked. Some days she did nothing at all. My mother, you know, smoked a pipe, a little clay one with feathers along the stem, and she would sit with her back against the hut and smoke and stare out into the distance, as if she were blessing the thousands of acres of bananas. Sometimes, yes, she muttered to herself, quite loudly, and then I thought she'd discovered me hiding and watching her. But no, even if I had walked in front of her at such times, I doubt she would have seen me.

"Then eventually she would knock out her pipe — she had a set of chimes, very low, very sweet — and she would knock the pipe against these chimes, which hung beside the door, and she would listen to the sweet, light sound. And then, if she agreed with the sound, she would nod, once, and then she would begin.

"She made capes and headdresses of great beauty, and she did it truly as if by magic. There were no squinting lines around my mother's eyes, as there are around mine, because she rarely looked at what she was doing. Her fingers seemed to know just what to do, and her face remained as if she were dreaming. Only her back, from so long bending, was slightly crooked.

"Over a long stretch of work, she would sometimes lose this precious state. She would come back to our main house and cook and clean and scold like a regular mother. And we were always so glad to have her back, too, though she'd never been farther away than a few steps across the yard. My father, especially, was happy to have back his wife. And he was glad to hear if the work was going well, because then my mother smiled at him. If it was not going well, she tolerated him as a burden and an intrusion and all her words to him — and they were always few — were harsh. If he tried to speak to her when her mind was on her work, she answered him with the expression of someone who has stomach ache.

"She was someone who could not be rushed. This seems a small thing. But it is actually a very amazing quality, a very ancient one. She did everything at just the same pace as before, she could tell the time of day or night by the moisture in the atmosphere, and she went about her business as if she would live forever, and forever was very, very long. That is the kind of mujer my mama was. When you look at me you see her, but I have lost 'forever'; therefore I sometimes hurry.

"Now the story of the priests is a sad one, and I don't think the men of my village realized that the women knew it to its smallest details. Unfortunately, even in my poor village women were considered inferior and kept out of the secrets the men felt it necessary to have. But we knew! Everything! We always had secrets of our own.

"Our mothers taught us that in the old, old days, when

they were their grandmothers and their grandmothers were old—for we are our grandmothers, you understand, only with lots of new and different things added—only women had been priests. Yes! This is what they said. But really, in the beginning they were not priests to themselves; it was the men who made them so. But then the men forgot that they had made them so. Well, what happened is that in the beginning, at about the same time the toucan was created, there was also woman, and in the process of life and change she produced a being somewhat unlike herself. This frightened her. Still, she kept the little hombre with her for a long time, until he grew anxious to discover whether there existed, somewhere else, more of his own kind. Off he went and, sure enough, there were others like himself, among whom he lived. These first men were so new to each other that all they did was stare into each other's eyes—for centuries! They were so glad to be found. But this meant they had no self-consciousness about how they looked, beyond the dangling evidence of maleness, the elongated clitoris. They had no concept of dress.

"Woman was entirely used to herself, while man was still infatuated with his relative newness. Woman was already into adornment. In truth, she was already into high fashion! Yes! You can laugh, and I know this is a funny way now to put it. But! Woman did not know she was even interested in high fashion. She was more, you know, like playing with herself. Making interesting to herself and other women what she already had. So she had tits, sticking out to there! She had a soft brown belly and strong brown legs. So what, that she had hair to her ass that glistened like the wings of a bird. Woman was bored with it. And so she began to play with how she looked. She used feathers, shells, stones, flowers. She used leaves, bark, colored sand. She used mud. The toenails of birds! For days she and her sisters hung over the edge of the reflecting pools in the jungle, trying this and that. The rest of the time they spent gathering food. Occasionally they were host to a man, whom they played with, especially sexually, until they tired of him; they then abandoned him.

"But it was these abandoned men who, over time, found each other and corroborated each other's experience among the women, dressed so weirdly in their colors and feathers, and they spread the word among other men who lacked their experience. Then one of the men told of a birth among the women. That clinched it. Immediately they imagined a mujer muy grande, larger than the sky, producing, somehow, the earth. A goddess. And so, if the producer of the earth was a large woman, a goddess, then women must be her priests, and must possess great and supernatural powers.

"What the mind doesn't understand, it worships or fears. I am speaking here of man's mind. The men both worshiped and feared the women. They kept their distance from them, but spied on them when they could. The finery the women wore seemed to prove their supernaturalness. The men, lacking the centuries of clothing and adornment experience of the women, were able to make only the clumsiest imitations. The women laughed at them. Perhaps the most fatal error in the whole realm of human responses to sincere effort! So, at first, to show their worshipful intent, the men, who were better hunters than the women, but only because the women had found they could live quite well on foods other than meat, gathered those things they knew the women liked or might be encouraged to like — feathers, bones, bark for dyes, animal teeth and claws — and brought them, on their knees, to the women, who picked over them like housewives at a sale.

"It was a long time before they began demanding these gifts, just as it was a long time before the men noticed that some of the children the women were making bore a striking resemblance to themselves. Strangely, the men did not like the children; it was as if the children made them nervous, even the boy children, whom they were always given or who almost always ran off to join them and whom they, in a manner of speaking, raised. For centuries the male community revolved around the female one, and the women hardly noticed it, except to make demands about the amount and number of things they were given.

"Many grandmothers lived and died during this time. Bowed down to, feared, worshiped, spoiled. And then, one day, there was a rebellion. The men grew sick of the women they worshiped. And by now they had made an important discovery about woman's ability to produce life. That discovery was—and it had been kept well hidden by woman for a very long time—that the life that woman produced came out of a hole at her bottom! But not the hole man also had, as had been suspected (and of course many strange things had been tried with that one!), but a different one. Then it was thought that anyone with such a hole at his or her bottom could produce life through it.

"And here is where the sadness comes in. For the women, though easily bored, made a great deal of fun out of life. Dressing themselves up, they giggled. Looking into the still mirrors of the jungle pools, they laughed. There was very little pain in their lives except for the discomfort they experienced in childbirth, and they soon forgot that. They died relatively young, too, either from attacks by animals or because their natural life span was short, so there was none of the creaking pain of old age. In short, it was during this period of rebellion that the men decided they could and would be priests. That they could be the ones through whom life passed! They began to operate on themselves, cutting off and flinging away their maleness, and trying to fashion a hole through which life could come.

"They died like flies. This is why, even today, there is a certain sadness a family feels when a boy decides to become a priest. Here is the origin of celibacy, of forfeiting children of one's own. For to become a priest in the old days meant one must do without one's very genitals!

"But listen, chico mio," said Zedé, stroking Arveyda's brow, "this is how it was even when I was a child. No. Not the whole of the genitals, because they gradually learned something from the numbers of men who died—their deaths making them more and more holy!—but they cut off the balls. They forgot about the hole through which life passes. They forgot this was what they were trying to make. It hurt too much to think of this, and to do it, and it didn't work, as well. The futility nearly prostrated them. What they remembered was that they must be like women, and if they castrated themselves at a certain age—the time of puberty, when they chose or were chosen for the priesthood—they could sound like woman and speak to the universe in woman's voice.

"But, oh, the pain! The operations, which were rarely done right. The heat and the flies and the sweat! The hatred of woman, whose pain was confined to childbirth and maybe a few cramps every month. And who kept producing life and adorning herself and thinking very little of it."

L ISSIE means 'the one who remembers everything,' "
Miss Lissie said to Suwelo, her black eyes, under wrinkled eyelids, as brilliant and as steady as a hawk's, "but I am
old now and my brain cells—brain cells are like batteries, you
know—are dying, millions of them at a time. Of my earlier
lives in Egypt and Atlantis I recall nothing. I only mention
these places because everyone does, mostly people who need
to feel better about themselves in this present lifetime but cannot. To be truthful, I never remembered anything about those
places, and if it were not for the existence of pyramids and the
evidence of drowned ancient civilizations now coming to light,
I'd doubt they'd ever been. Since I know they did exist, in my
rational mind, I have to assume that those brain cells I would
need to remember them, being so many thousands of years,
and more, old, have atrophied. But on the other hand, I do not
remember with my brain itself anyway, but with my memory,
which is separate, somehow, yet contained within it. Charged, I
feel my brain is, with memory. Yes, as I said, like a battery."

Suwelo was enchanted by the hundred or so silvery white
locks of hair on Miss Lissie's finely shaped head, making an au-
reole for her dark brown face and causing it to look, even in the

shadows of Uncle Rafe's house, kissed by the sun. These locks grew out in all directions from her skull, but fell gently over her shoulders and down her very straight back, like a mantle of the brightest fleece. When he had first seen her, among the other old women in Uncle Rafe's front parlor, she, like the rest, had had her head covered. He would never have imagined, on so old a person, such wild, abundant, glorious hair. It gave her the curious look of some ancient creature, which, even at rest, is about to spring.

He had the unaccountable sensation that she was his true grandmother, and that his actual grandmother, who dyed her white hair blond in order to enhance a distant resemblance to Patricia Nixon, was an imposter. This puzzled Suwelo, who, in the abstraction of his thoughts, had been staring fixedly at Miss Lissie's reggae singer's locks since she started talking and wondering how many there were.

"Exactly one hundred and thirteen," she said, as if he'd spoken, before continuing her story.

"It is not, then, the very ancient past that I was conversant with as a child, even as a baby, but with the recent past of up to a few thousand years ago. I have always been a black woman. I say that without, I hope, any arrogance or undue pride, for I know this was just luck. And I speak of it as luck because of the struggle others have trying to discover who they are and what they should be doing and finding it difficult to know because of all the different and differing voices they are required to listen to. I have a friend in this lifetime who reminds me of myself, someone who has always been, in every lifetime, a black woman. Every word she speaks reveals this experience and is based on the ancient logic of her existence as who she is, and when she tries to manufacture the voices of others that were not there in her ancient being you hear it immediately in her voice. It becomes the voice of an almost disembodied person, though her words remain incisive, lucid, brilliantly skilled. But then, whenever she is free to speak as herself, everything has jagged edges, and listening to her is like hard walking with pebbles in your shoes. And you feel that if she judged you she would be very harsh. But underneath the armor of her voice and her skin there is this gentle person. But how many years have gone into creating the gentleness!

"I was never a gentle person. Maybe in the lifetimes I don't recall, but in all the ones I do recall I was a fighter, someone who started trouble. Someone who was easily bored by other people and was offended if they tried to present their feeble point of view. For most people, as you know, remember nothing of other lifetimes, and no matter how old they get they never remember any better. They honestly think that when they were born their brain was a clean slate. I've actually heard this said! That babies have no memories; that they are empty of knowledge and experience; that, in fact, there is no one there. This is insane. Of course, the memories that they have appear to babies as dreams indecipherable to themselves because they are no longer in those contexts, and because babies lack the ability to speak any language, not simply the languages they spoke before. Of all the periods in one's life, babyhood is the most pitiful and the most confusing. There you are, without anyone you know, surrounded by giants you may never have imagined existed. They are blowing their objectionable breath on you, oiling your skin with God knows what strange mixture, giving you food to eat that, in an earlier lifetime, might have been taboo. It is hideous! And as you lie there looking about, you summon just enough intelligence to understand this is the next classroom, these people are the next lesson you will be required to learn. Oh, the horror of it! That is the real reason babies sleep so much. Imagine where and to whom so many of them are born. They sleep to avoid the shock of the cruel thing that's been done to them and to avoid the inevitable feeling of utter helplessness.

"I did not like my parents at all. My mother was rather clumsy and obviously untutored; she seemed to speak not only in a language I'd never spoken, but in a language newly invented. She spoke of 'taters' and 'rotgut,' 'hog killin' and 'sugar tits.' She seemed to exist in a trance, and when I cried she responded with an absent-mindedness that left me breathless. I used to lie on the bed and watch her going back and forth through the house in her slovenly wrappers, her steps dragging, almost shuffling, from front porch to kitchen. She dipped snuff. Every so often she'd drag herself to the side of the porch and spit off into the weeds. I knew I'd never seen, in any of my lifetimes, a more stupid person.

"Then there was my father. Where my mother was merely clumsy—she had a habit of changing me in such a way that the old soiled diaper always came in contact with my head—my father was hopeless. He was every stereotype of the inept father of a newborn baby rolled into one. He spoke the same odd language as my mother—rather, he mumbled it—and it would take me years to master it, whereas in other lifetimes I was able to master new languages in a matter of minutes, though it was months before I could speak. For years I literally could not speak, and out of that frustration over the language I would also fight.

"The worse thing was, I'd never known these particular people before! Never. They were complete strangers to me. I didn't recognize their scent, I didn't recognize their body movements, their rhythms—of which they made so much—I didn't, as I said, recognize their speech. God knows, I didn't recognize the diet! These people lived on corn bread, lima beans, and the occasional head of boiled cabbage. That was during times of plenty. The rest of the time they lived on grease, sorghum syrup, and biscuits.

"Those first weeks and months, I slept as much as I could. And even as a big child I would fall asleep. In fact, that's one of the reasons the diet of the children on the Island was improved. I kept falling asleep in Miss Beaumont's class, and one day the visiting health nurse noticed it. They then started to test the other children, and it was discovered that none of us had sufficient vitamin C, D, or A in our diets. We never had fruit, never had raw leafy greens, never had milk. There was plenty of this on the Island, you know, but it was all sold, every scrap of it, to the mainland, and had been since slavery time. In those days, in slavery, the people were whipped for tasting the milk or stealing the greens or eating the fruit; consequently, nearly fifty years later they had to be almost forced to eat those things. And they detested fish! Many a time I heard my mother complain that fresh fruit gave her wind, milk broke her out in hives, and only the whitefolks, she reckoned, would eat 'rabbit food'—which was how she viewed raw greens. My mother and the other women on the Island had to be prodded into going back to planting little kitchen gardens. At one time they'd all had them, as well as pigs and chickens, but somehow or another they lost their animals and their seeds, maybe in one of the big floods that sometimes came as a result of coastal storms. Beautiful storms, I might add. Just deadly. Then for many years they couldn't afford to buy seeds or animals, and being on an island didn't help, because every little thing had to be brought over on one or two small flimsy boats, and it was about a ten-hour trip. The plantation overseer would pull up any vegetable growing in their yards that looked like anything planted in the field. And you could lose your house, because nobody owned their houses.

"But this little woman—she was a white woman, and she had a black woman helping her—she started to agitate on the mainland about the condition of the Island children, and pretty soon whole big boatloads of white people came to look us over. It was the first time I'd seen so many! They were in many different shapes and sizes and very healthy from having eaten *our* food all their lives. I didn't know this then, of course: how they had sound teeth because mine were rotted; how they could afford glasses to help them see, while my friend Eddie couldn't see beyond his nose and would never learn to read; how they . . . well, you get the picture. They all had a distinct quality of being apart from real life. It was like they were on one side of a glass and we were on the other, and we could have no real impact on what happened on their side, the side of the unknown, but they could have a great deal of impact on us. And I felt that was because we were where life was. For even in our frailty, we laughed. So much was so funny to us! They could not laugh freely. Their faces were like fists. When they almost touched you, they grew confused and looked about to see what others in the group did. We gathered in clumps, digging our bare toes into the sand, and looked at them as if they were a zoo. Only one man, short, fat, and disheveled, had come to be alive with or without us. He headed for the beach out in front of the school and took off most of his clothes, never looking at us. He took out a jar of liquid soap and started blowing bubbles. Pretty soon we were all out there with him chasing the bubbles and watching them float out into the bay.

"There was, at the time, a big to-do about giving us cod-liver oil, because somebody noticed that me falling asleep was the least of it. Many of the children had legs that looked like pretzels. We had people on that Island with legs so bowed they made people with straight legs look deformed. That's what we needed the cod-liver oil for, to prevent something called 'rickets.' It was funny, too, because by then, on the Island, bow legs in women were considered sexy, and you actually had people grumbling about how straight-legged women 'didn't do a thang for 'em.' Meaning sexually. My mother actually had the nerve to try to tell me I didn't have to take the stuff if I didn't want to. But I remembered sick and deformed children from hundreds of years before, and I was disgusted that this should still happen. But I did demand that the cod-liver oil be given to us in orange juice. Because, once the parents were asked if the children should take it straight or with orange juice, they got into a debate over it and tried to make it a moral issue. Their children weren't sissies, by God and his grandmother! Their children could take anything dished out to them 'like a man'! Can you believe that shit? It really made you wonder about the general thoughtfulness of the divine universal plan.

"Well, I wasn't a man. Never had been one. Unless I had orange juice, I said, I wouldn't take the cod-liver oil. If I didn't take the cod-liver oil, nobody else in the school would either. Everybody knew this to be the unvarnished truth. And besides, the cod-liver oil, taken straight, tasted like shit.

"There are few things more confusing to people than the process of regaining or attaining health. It is one of the great mysteries. And when I think of my dear mother as her mind began to clear—for she, too, was gradually induced into reinstating the kitchen garden, getting a few chickens for the eggs, and eschewing the syrupy-sweet coffee she loved—even now, long after her old head is cold, I have to laugh! She started, for the first time since she was a girl, to remember her dreams. And it was—that first morning after so many dead nights and one live one—as if she'd seen a ghost. For weeks her dreams were all she could talk about. The people and events in them, the fabulous lands she saw—she never understood they were *her* lands—the houses she visited that 'just felt so familiar,' the food she ate. In fact, she was always eating in her dreams. Milk and fruit and greens! And everything she dreamed herself eating she searched for until it was found. She enlarged her garden and her livestock and sold her surplus to the neighbors; she bought her own little boat. Off she went to the mainland with her bag of nickels and dimes. She would mentally prostrate herself before an orange. A banana drove her wild.

"Her speech remained strange, but ceased to be unintelligible as she added more of herself to it. She stopped dragging her feet. Her taste for snuff left her. I began to see her in quite a new light, with less impatience and contempt. It was from this time that we became more than mother and daughter. We became friends."

HAL, now. Hal. Thank God for Hal. He was the only person I felt I had known before. He likes to tell stories about us as babies slobbering over each other's faces and trying to get ourselves together enough to crawl away. This is the Lord's truth! When I first made contact with Hal, when my little chubby fingers got hold of a handful of his fat face, my juices (those in my mouth, of course) started to flow. Here, at last, was something, someone familiar. Now I know some folks like to tell you that the man they married, or the woman, was once their grandmother. I can't claim anything like that. I don't know who Hal was, and all these years I haven't had any success in either remembering or figuring it out. What I can tell you is that he was familiar, comfortable; and what's more, emotionally recognizable. And he felt the same way. I don't have many memories of this life that don't have Hal somewhere in the middle of them. I had to see him every day. When he had to go off anywhere—for instance, the time he went into the army—I like to have died.

"None of us ever becomes all that was in us to be. Not in the majority of our lifetimes, anyway. You take Hal, well, he was an artist. A painter. All he ever did really well was draw, on anything he could. From a baby! He'd get him a little stick and be out there in the sand digging and drawing, happy as a little clam. But his daddy hated that in him, and I've seen him take the stick away and stomp out the drawing—and Hal was a baby! Drawing was something his father wanted to do himself, something maybe he had a real talent for, but you can't draw pictures for a living, is I reckon what he thought, and maybe his own daddy had broken him early, forbidding him to try. Before that it would have been the overseer on the plantation during slavery time. But it was so cruel! Like seeing someone forced to blind himself. And also very illogical. Mr. Jenkins, Hal's daddy, became a great furniture maker, mostly chairs. He carved the most beautiful designs on them. It was from the sale of these chairs that he and his family were able to live better than the rest of us. It was beautiful, too, seeing those tall, polished, shining chairs, one to the small boat, floating out to sea! Still, he hated the tendency to art in his son. Why? Hal spent a lifetime in the dark about his father's fears.

"When he broke that commitment to art, to making beauty, to recording, to bearing witness, to saying yessiree to the life spirit, whose only request sometimes is just that you acknowledge you truly see it, he broke something in Hal. Hal could not defend himself, for instance; he didn't consider himself worthy of defense. He never learned to fight. And listen, the most amazing thing, his eyes became weak! But I always took up for him; I knew he had to be reminded that it was all right to see. And in whatever corner of privacy we could find, I forced him to draw. If I hadn't, he would have been blind as a bat within a year. His father threatened to keep him out of school if he drew. So for years I had a big reputation as an artist. It was all Hal's work—pinched and furtive, as if his father loomed over his shoulder, but still expressive, raw, and pure. And I'm proud to say I can remember almost every painting that he drew. He drew right up to the time he left for the army. After that, for quite a while, nothing. And sure enough, during that time, Hal was to tell me later, he was a regular stumblebum. But at least the army let him out finally because of his bad sight, though it kept other colored men whose disabilities were almost as pitiful. I was really glad to get him back and painting again, for a gifted artist such as Hal can paint the memory that maybe you yourself have started to doubt. He actually did that more times then I can count.

"I was talking to an African scholar one time, a man from one of these big schools. He was real skinny and black and straight, and he wore that little African-style hat that's just like an American soldier's, only in bright colors, and he was all right, I guess, but he had lifeless eyes, and I almost shivered while he was talking to me. It was like he was a well-educated, smooth-talking zombie, and he had sort of jerky movements, too. So anyway, he got to talking about how much of a cliché it was when black people here claimed their ancestors were sold into slavery by an uncle. He kinda chuckled when he said it and leaned back in his chair. I didn't say anything to him, 'cause he'd already decided that the truth, if told a number of times, can be dismissed as unbelievable, and I have lived enough times to have seen this happen a lot. Some folks actually think the truth can be worn out. But anyway, it was my uncle who sold me. It was the uncle who sold a lot of women and their children, and it's easy enough to understand why this was so. It was the African organization of family life.

"My father died of a heart attack when I was two years old. He was an old man and I was the last child by his youngest wife; even if he had lived, he would have seemed and have been someone from another century. By law my mother and her children became the responsibility of his brother, who was even older than he was, a practicing Mohametan that bathed and prayed all day. He already had more wives and children and slaves than he knew what to do with. One of his child wives egged him on to sell us, and he did. She wanted to buy some of the white man's trinkets that after the rainy season fairly flooded our part of the world. Mirrors! You've never seen so many appear out of nowhere, or as quickly disappear. Loud-colored cloth, bright tin washbasins, and things for which there was no apparent use—knickknacks; for instance, porcelain dancing ladies and their fancy gentlemen. But this happened well into the dry season, for it was very hot; it must have been something like November or December. My mother had sent me to the okra patch to get the okra that had been left on the stalks for seeds, and I was humming along, hitting at the weeds by the dusty path with a stick. I was about thirteen then. We lived in a poor little hut off by itself and out of sight of my uncle's compound. There were four huge men squatting at the edge of the okra patch, and they just looked and smelled evil, so I turned to run back home. Well, they caught me and tied me up, and one of 'em tossed me over his shoulder like a sack of grain. They then went on to the hut and grabbed my two sisters, my brother, and my mother.

"My mother was just begging and pleading and calling for mercy, because she knew about slavers, but these brutes had no ears. They were like the zombie African professor I told you about. Perhaps that is, in fact, who he was in that time. Well, they carried and dragged us up to my uncle's compound, and he came out. My mother tried to prostrate herself before him, which was the custom in our country, but she was tied up in such a way she fell over on her side. Thick dust was caked over one side of her face, and both her knees were skinned. I know now that she was someone who was never loved, because she was never really seen, except by her children, who did love her. She had four children, but she was only in her late teens. A strong-looking, somewhat plump, kind of reddish-black woman with big sullen eyes. Her specialty was weaving and, though we were poor, the little cotton our uncle let us keep from the crop we raised for him went into the cloths we wore around our waists—beautiful checks and plaids, made bright and colorful from natural dyes. She'd learned dyeing and weaving from her mother, who'd learned it from her mother and so on.

"My uncle had these cloths removed from us, for they were woven in the distinctive style of our tribe—our colors were yellow, red, and white—and gave us plain unbleached cotton ones instead. By this time I had been stood up, bound, in front of my uncle, along with my sisters and brother. We did not attempt to bow to him. We were not crying, like our mother. We hated the man. The truth is probably that we were in shock. I remember the men paid my uncle some silver money with a hole in it, and he took four of the smallest pieces and pressed them into our hands. We'd walked several miles before I was aware that I still held the one he gave me. It was Arab money, with their writing on it and everything.

"We were forced to jog for almost fifteen days without stopping, or so it felt, until we came to the big stone fort on the coast. It was then we saw the white men. They were posted all up and down the front of the fort, and we were only one small group of many converging on the fort at that time. Two white men came eventually to inspect us. They looked at our ears, our genitals—you would not believe the thoroughness, or the pitiful protestations of the women—our teeth and our eyes. They made us hop up and down to test the strength in our legs. Our feet were bleeding. My mother had sunk into a kind of walking slumber and did all she was told to do as if in a dream. We children copied her manner though we were vividly alert, so much so that the four of us managed to hide our silver pieces, before we were searched, in the thickets of our hair.

"The white men, who looked and smelled like nothing we had ever imagined, as if their sweat were vinegar, paid the men who'd brought us, and they turned right around and jogged back the way we'd come. I wanted to run after them and kill them, but the white men had called some other blacks, who seemed at home around the fort, and we were taken to the holding pen, which was like a cellar underneath the fort. It was already crowded with depressed and frightened people. When they saw my mother and her children shoved through the door, many of the men looked sad and turned their faces, in shame, to the wall. These were men sold into slavery because of their religious belief, which was not tolerated by the Mohametans. They carried on the ancient tradition of worship of the mother, and to see a mother sold into slavery—which did not turn a hair on a Mohametan's head if she was not a convert to his religion—was a great torture for them.

"It was during the hundreds of years of the slave trade in Africa that this religion was finally destroyed, although for hundreds of years previous to the slave trade it had been under attack. There were, in the earliest days, raids on the women's temples, which existed in sacred groves of trees, with the women and children dragged out by the hair and forced to marry into male-dominated tribes. The ones who were not forced to do this were either executed or sold into a tribe whose language was different. The men had decided they would be creator, and they went about dethroning woman systematically. To sell women and children for whom you no longer wished to assume responsibility or to sell those who were mentally infirm or who had in some way offended you, became a new tradition, an accepted way of life. As did the idea, later on, under the Mohametans, that a man could own many women, as he owned many cattle or hunting dogs.

"These Motherworshipers would be the hardest of the Africans to break, for they were devoted to the Goddess, and they were regular chameleons (much, very much we have learned, over time, from the lizards!); but they were broken. That is why the ultimate curse against Africa/Mother/Goddess—mother-fucker—is still in the language. It would have been unthinkable in the Old Days, and a person saying it would have been immediately asked for his tongue. Our new masters had a genius for turning us viciously—in ways that shamed and degraded even themselves, if only they'd had sense enough to know it—against anything that once we loved.

"They fed us a little millet gruel, which we dipped with our hands from a long wooden trough outside the pen twice a day. We could see the sky for the ten minutes it took us to eat. In the early morning, before daybreak, we were let out to move our bowels. Constipation was always my problem; fear and anxiety kept me locked tight. But cases of dysentery were frequent, and many people while waiting—for what, we didn't know—sickened and died. Later I was to realize that the men who bought us to sell had already calculated how many of us were liable to die and had therefore captured more of us than they were likely to need.

"After a week in the stockade, my mother fell sick. There was no room for any of us to lie down comfortably, but one of the Motherworshipers forced a little extra space by the wall, toward which my mother could turn her head for air, and when the pains wracked her, she could kneel. She was sick with vomiting and dysentery, those sicknesses it is least possible to hide. Her deeper sickness was over her shame at being filthy and exposed to strangers, in the embarrassed and helpless presence of her children. There never was a more fastidious or modest woman than my mother. She bathed at least once a day, and her cloths were spotless. I remember how sweet the oil always smelled in her hair! She could not accept so much filth on and about her person.

"On the seventh day she willed herself to die. The white men sent in a couple of brutes to drag her out by her heels—one of them held a rag to his nose as they dragged her—and place her body on a cart and carry it away. I envied her. I pitied myself. I did not know how to ask the strangers or even my sisters and brother to kill me.

"So I am very bitter about my old home, and who can claim I do not have a right to be?

"This is no hearsay. I was there.

"You do not believe I was there? I pity you.

"There was a period during the sixties when I passed myself off as a griot. I pretended I'd traveled to Africa and learned the stories of the diaspora straight from the old storytellers and record keepers there. I didn't have to go anywhere. I remembered quite enough of the story to tell, thank you. There was a little white woman professor who came to one of my lectures about the crossing of the Atlantic in a slave ship. She was one of those Afrophiles who was so protective of Africa that she claimed Idi Amin was framed. She got up and said, 'I wish you'd try not to say "I remember thus and so" about your African experiences. It is claiming more than you could possibly know, and besides that, it is confusing.' Well, I apologized for doing that. It just slipped out. I did remember everything I was talking about, though, but I knew the professional way to present my experience was as if it had merely been told to me. Some people don't understand that it is the nature of the eye to have seen forever, and the nature of the mind to recall anything that was ever known. Or that was the nature, I should say, until man started to put things on paper. The professor went on to say she couldn't even imagine what it must have been like on the slave ship. The crowdedness, the dirt, the absolute dependency on madmen to steer the ship, the absence of representation and control.

"Does this make you laugh? No?

"But anyway, there I was, in that lifetime, watching everybody's hair being cut off. A few days before we left the coast they made us kneel in the sand outside the fort and proceeded to cut great clumps of our hair out, and then to shave our heads. As you know, Africans have an abundance of hair, and there were some with locks they'd had since childhood that fell nearly to their knees. These were brutally cut off, causing much wailing and gnashing of teeth, and then came the shaving of the heads and, for the men, of whiskers with a dry, and no doubt dull, razor. The black men who did this, at the bidding of their white masters, went through the severed locks carefully. Hidden in this hair were all manner of precious small items, tokens of home: gold beads, silver pins, bits of gris-gris. In my brother's and sisters' hair and in my own the silver coins were discovered. These items were pocketed by the brutes who held us, and they grunted in satisfaction upon discovering each one. You sometimes see these same faces on the streets of our larger cities; these are the young men selling the dope, or terrorizing the young ones while they take the little money that was pinned in the smaller children's pockets for them to buy lunch. They haven't left us, those faces; they are never hard to find.

"It was while the haircutting was going on that I was surprised to see a fairly large compound, consisting of many small huts, a short distance from the fort. During the three hours it took to cut our hair, douse us with a foul-smelling liquid, and flush out our mouths with vinegar—a protection against scurvy—I had time to notice it was inhabited by variously colored women of all ages, many yellow or light brown and some almost white; the area in front of the huts was filled with similarly variegated children. This was an amazing sight to me, who'd never seen people of such different shades, and I was too young to recognize the establishment for what it was, and obviously had been for generations, the fort's brothel. I was to learn this later from one of the fair-skinned young women, who was sold onto our boat along with her young son. Her white master, recognizing himself as fat, swinish, and disagreeable to the nose and touch, had finally convinced himself of the much avoided truth that no one as lovely as this woman could possibly love him, even if she was his slave. In his cups one night he'd gambled her and his son away in a game of cards, which he assumed he was teaching his African flunkies to play.

"After the chopping down of our hair — we had worn it, some of us, in a style that made one think of trees — we were branded with pieces of hot iron shaped into configurations dreamed up by those who had, in America, purchased us sight unseen. I was branded with a C, for Croesus, which in this instance was not the name of a person but the name of an estate, a rather poor one, too, as it turned out. By these brands we were recognized, and if one of us died, her brand was checked and she was marked off the record book into which we were all entered.

"When they pressed the metal to the skin of a buttock or upper arm there was much pain. The swelling and burning continued for days afterward. Though the slavers dotted our wounds with a bit of vinegar and palm oil, nothing soothed like the milk from a nursing mother's breast, a remedy with which all Africans were familiar, and though most Africans no longer believed in the worship of the mother, this last vestige of her power was believed in firmly. Luckily there were nursing mothers among us, although without their babies. Babies were not permitted on the slave ship, nor mothers too far advanced in pregnancy. Some of the babies were simply smashed against the ground by the captors of their mothers, some were left on the trail to die, some were sold or, less usually, adopted by a tribe that did not believe in or participate in the slave trade — that is, they refused to sell or buy anyone — and to whom small children, so recently inseparable from the source of all life, were especially sacred. I was also to learn of these people on the slave ship, for one of them, on his way from marketing his commodity of salt, had been captured by a white slaver and his black henchmen, who refused to hear his protestations that saltmakers were exempted from being captured, under a separate law. To which I imagine the slaver's reply was: Under slavery, no nigger exists under a separate law.

"The breasts of the nursing mothers were a haven for the very young among us, who were permitted to drink the milk. Otherwise some of the more frightened and traumatized of the children would have died. And for the rest of us there was grace in the incredible kindness of these young mothers as they moved among us as best they could, with a drop here and a drop there on our festering wounds. When I was a child, I told Hal this story because he was the only one who wouldn't laugh at me for thinking I remembered it; the next thing I knew, he'd found crayons and painted it. He painted the face of one of the women as if he'd seen it himself. It was a sight one does not often see, but I will always remember the way it made me feel; the small, and not so small, boys and girls plastered against the sides and stomachs of our grieving young women, who nursed them standing up, crowded together in the fetid barracoon, in the white man's hell that he was permitted and sometimes even encouraged to build in our own land. And though I was big, there was a time in my despair when, in sorrow over the death of my mother and fear of the unknown journey ahead of me, I also nursed. In truth, for a period before we left the continent and for a time on board the ship I regressed to babyhood, even to the thumb-sucking stage. The first time I was raped by members of the crew on board the ship, I was in chains and sucking on my thumb. The second time I was violated, they chained me so that my arms and legs were spread out and my thumb was beyond my reach. There was nothing to solace me.

But in the hold of the ship, somewhere in the awful darkness, I knew the mothers who had suckled me also lay, and sometimes I imagined their moans of despair were songs of comfort for me and for their own lost children.

"The morning of our sailing they led us to the shore of the ocean and there, in small coffles of three, they dragged us through the salt water to cleanse our skins. Then they dragged us to the ship. At the plank that led up onto the deck, our last remaining garment, the strip of cotton around our hips, was snatched away, and we were forced onto the ship bald, branded, and naked as we came into the world. I fought to hold on to that last small badge of modesty, but a white man struck me a blow to the head almost without looking at me—and because he had blue eyes, I fancied he must be blind—and I reeled onto the ship with the rest.

"Of the style of packing slaves, you've read, and unfortunately all that you have read, and more, is true. We were packed as if we were sardines, for this two-month-long journey. Truly, sardines should not be packed so, and if it were in my power they never would be again. Our heads were in each other's laps, a long chain connecting us by the feet along one row, riveting us to the wall of the ship, and there was no movement uncontested by one's neighbors, of which one had four. In fact, an almost daily ritual was the cutting of the nails on hands and feet because there was, as you can imagine, much scratching in a quite futile effort to protect some small degree of one's space.

"Those who lived were thankful to those who died, and many, especially among the children, died almost as soon as we left the African continent. Lack of sufficient food, lack of air and exercise—never had any of us been away from air and light!—all contributed; but many of us died from anger. I was, myself, consumed with anger, and helpless even to scratch the person next to me. My heart was strained, bruised. I felt it so! And I was glad when, for reasons of their own, the slavers switched us to the other side of the hold, and I could lie on my right side, thus relieving, to a degree, the pressure and congestion about my heart.

"After a month and a half of really quite unrelatable horror—the rats, the smell of a dead head covered with sores in your lap, the screams of women and men violated for the sport of the devils that passed as crew, the painful menstrual periods of the women and the blood running over one, the miscarriages, the pleas for mercy from everyone, not simply those suffering from dysentery and claustrophobia—after an eternity, we were taken up on deck for longer than our usual half-hour-a-day run, while they swabbed out the hold, during which several women and men fairly danced over the side of the ship and into the sea. Now we were encouraged, suddenly, to remember our culture—which to the whites meant singing and dancing—and to demonstrate it. Drums appeared. An infirmary suddenly existed to look after the sick. Buckets of salt water were splashed over us. Our bald heads were darkened with boot blacking if there were signs of gray. Men and women were given such garments as could be scrounged from the ship's closets, so that you would see a tall broad-chested man wearing nothing but a much too small frilly pirate's shirt or a cloth hat, held by a string, over his privates. Or you might see a young girl wearing a handkerchief. I was given a faded piece of rag that looked as though it had been used for sailcloth, and this I thankfully put around myself as I watched the somber merriment of those suddenly set "free" upon the sun-splashed, yet chilly deck. To warm ourselves we were ordered to dance, a whip striking at our feet providing the sole source of inspiration.

"Within days we were in sight of land, the young women among us pregnant by force and too young to know it, or to know that because we were delivered to our new owners already pregnant we earned a bonus for the master of the ship, many of whose sons and daughters—for he was a violator, with the rest of his crew—entered into American slavery with us, long before they actually issued from our bodies. The slavers did not care. Color made their own seed disappear to them; the color of gold was all they saw. But not if gold was the color of a child. We were left with this bitter seed, and—unfair to the children—burdened with our hatred of the fruit.

"I was sold to one planter, my sisters and brother to others. We never saw or heard from each other again. I bore a freakish-looking, gray-eyed girl child eight months after leaving the ship. The young mistress of Croesus plantation wanted her brought up as slave companion to the child she herself was expecting. This earned us a closetlike room under the back verandah. When my baby was two years old I ran away from the house and into the woods, only to step, almost at once, into a trap that the master had, he was to claim, set for bear. It crushed the bone in my left leg. The master saved my beating—for running away, but also for stupidity: no one, he declared, could be stupid enough to step into so large and obvious a trap, although I'd never seen or heard of such a hideous thing before—until I was strong enough to bear it. He waited nearly a month; he was drunk, and his anger over being still poor in spite of his dreams of riches drove him on. The strain of losing a part of my body, namely, my leg and foot, accompanied by the loss also of my child—given to another woman to bring up—whom, against all nature, I had grown to love, was a condition a heartless beating could only exacerbate. Underneath it, my weakened body gave up the ghost—in other words, I died."

"THEY called him Jesús," whispered Zedé, clutching Arveyda's hand, though her back remained turned to him, "because they would not have been able to pronounce his real name even if he had told them what it was, which he did not, and he was a slave like the rest of us. Only, it was his own village in which we were kept. They also called him 'indio loco' because everyone else from his tribe had run away, but he could not run away. He would run a little away and hide out in the jungle, which he knew intimately, just as the animals knew it. He had always been there, you know. There was no time in life when he had not been there on that piece of the earth. So he would hide, and then he would sneak back and walk about the village in the dead of night. Nothing would be stolen, not even food, and this was very puzzling to everyone, our enslavers and ourselves alike.

"The reason he came back, a reason our enslavers never knew and would not have understood anyhow, was that he was the protector of the sacred stones of the village. These stones were three simple, ordinary-looking rocks that must always be in a certain area of the village's center. If no one ever told you they were special, believe me you'd never know it.

They blended into the earth perfectly. And yet, once Jesús had
pointed them out to me, and showed me the sacred configura-
tion — ∴ — which was the same as the nuclear-bomb-shelter
symbol, the stones leaped out at me, and I was hard-pressed
to be silent when they were kicked about or simply trod upon.
When they were kicked, as by the soldiers in their sullen idleness, or when some poor soul was beaten and blood was spilled
upon them, or when a morsel of food that someone dropped
touched them — well! This meant another definite visit from
Jesús, who would have to risk life and limb to restore the stones'
position, wash off the blood, brush off the food, and so on.
When I knew him better, I knew it would never have occurred
to him to save himself if it meant abandoning his duty to the
three small stones — about the size and color of brown pigeon
eggs. As a dog is inevitably drawn back to where a bone is buried, Jesús returned to the stones. The keeping of them was his
whole life, and it had been for thousands of years! He fully believed that if the stones were not kept, his people, the Krapoke-
chuan, or 'human beings,' would remain dispersed forever and
never again find a home. Because where the stones were was
their home, you understand. Nowhere else. It is something not
understood by norte-americanos; this I know.

"At last they captured him. How sorry we were! For though
most of us were ashamed of the Indian part of ourselves, his
presence was like that of a guardian spirit, an angel, and the
times we managed to glimpse him, as he stole through the village at odd hours of the night, convinced us he was indeed
wholly benign. He was so young! With a bush of hair to his
waist. He wore only a cloth around his loins and beautiful red
parrot feathers in his ears.

"Our captors did not understand his language, and when
they beat him he was silent. They made him work with the
rest of us, clearing the forest with a machete. The men used

machetes and pickaxes and saws to fell and uproot the trees and vines, and the women used hoes and rakes to complete the slaughter of the earth. This was our work, day in, day out, from the crow of a rooster at dawn until dark. The guards forced the women to mate with them, and before long each guard had chosen his favorite slave 'wife.' The one who chose me did not force me, but bided his time. He was someone who beat and burned and killed without emotion or remorse, yet still managed to cling to the belief that someone would want to sleep with him without the use of force. It was a matter of pride to him. I only knew I was chosen because of how he looked at me and because the other men left me alone, and I would often hear their slave women screaming or sobbing prayers into the night.

"I did not plan to love Jesús. But how unlike them he was! There is in me, deep, always somewhere, the love of the priest, but the *true* priest, the one who watches over, the one who protects. Above all, the one who is more than his fancy dress. If there is any spirit that I find wholly erotic it is that one. *Aiiee!* Jesús was such a priest I used to feel as if the trees fell before him to be blessed, because, clearly, cutting them down was for him a torture comparable to being cut down himself. They were sobbing all the while, Jesús and his trees. He had known them his whole life. And for all his lifetimes before.

"Like it was with us, querido, I did not know what was happening or what to do about it. His eyes spoke. My womb leaped. Don't laugh! Though expressed in the language of imbeciles, this is the way it was! We discovered I knew a few words of his strange language. The word for water, 'ataras,' the word for wood, 'xotmea,' the word for love, 'oooo.' The word for love, truly, *four* o's! They could not watch us every minute. During an hour they could not witness and will never own, I made love to him. He made love to me. We made love together. They had bound him by the feet so that he could not move his legs apart. I crept into his hut and without speaking caressed and kissed him for a long time before taking him into my mouth. When I placed myself on top of him he was crying, and I was crying, and he held one of my breasts in his mouth, and his damp hair was like a warm fog on my face. *Ai*, they will never own passion!

"The second, and last, time was like the first, only even more intense. I knew the instant Carlotta was conceived. The seed flew into me where I was so open, and I fell off Jesús already asleep. It was asleep together that they found us. The first thing he did, the guard that had chosen me to want to sleep with him, was to cut off Jesús' hair. He did it slowly, coldly, methodically, as if he had been thinking of doing it for a long time. He did it with a very sharp machete, and when the long, thick, rough black hair covered his dusty boots, he stamped his feet free of it as if stamping out desire.

"He never touched me himself, not even to beat me. That night the other men, the guards, one after the other came to the little hut in the forest in which they placed me. While this was happening to me, they killed Jesús. At dawn, as I lay bleeding, they brought his body and threw it in with me. Then they nailed shut the door, which was the only opening. Jesús' throat had been cut. They had also removed his genitals. He had been violated in every conceivable way. There was not even a scrap of cloth to cover him. I was naked.

"Days and nights went by. The flies came by the hundreds. The rats. The smell. I beat on the door until my hands, covered with flies also, were dripping blood. I screamed. There were only the jungle sounds outside. I had nightmares, when I could sleep, about the body of the man I had loved. He was so silent. I cursed him now for being the death of me.

"And then one night I heard a noise outside the door—soft,

almost not a noise. And then the door slowly opened, and the mournful and barbaric-looking tribesmen of Jesús filled the little hut. They wrapped his body in a large blanket before they turned to me, naked, shivering, dying on the dirt floor. Then I saw there was also a blanket for me.

"I would have stayed with them if I could. They understood, as no one else ever would, the form of my brokenness. I was broken, utterly: in that I could trust no one, that I could never again reach out to love, that it must be brought to me. But they were always on the run, and the soldiers always after them. When Carlotta was born, they made me understand I must go away in order to save her, in order to save Jesús. They took me to a house where there were Indians living the way the gringo lets Indians live; they were all busy making trinkets for the tourist dollar, of which the white man who controlled and 'protected' them from the soldiers got the largest share. They hid me and my baby. I learned to make their vivid green pottery. Since I knew Spanish, I helped the women hawk their wares on the streets of a not-too-distant town, full of the well-to-do descendants of the Spanish conquistadors and the blank-eyed americanos. I did not earn anything beyond enough for food. My friends told me of a school run by gringos where I might be able to get a job as maidslave. That was the beginning of my flight to Norte America.

"My parting from Jesús' people was one the rest of the world will never see, nor will they understand its meaning. I am not sure I understand its meaning myself. I only know that they gave me the last remaining symbols of who they were in the world—feathers from the red African parrot for my ears, this parrot that had been brought to their village so many hundreds of years ago by the men with rough hair, from a continent they called Zuma, or Sun, and they gave me, for Carlotta, the three pigeon-egg-size stones."

I T WAS at La Escuela de Jungla that I first saw that the
norte-americanos are muy dementes. There were many
acres of grass and trees at this place, and you have never in life
seen such flowers and such fruits! A little paradise, it seemed, and
I was sure I and mi cariñito would be happier there. There
was a hacienda with red tiles on the roof and long white rooms
with many ferns touching the ceiling, and sofas and chairs
never imagined, so deep, so soft. Such contours and colors. The
floor, even on the verandah, was also made of tiles, huge square
blocks, the color of muddy sunsets, that I was to know very well
because mine was the job of cleaning them every day. It was in
this hacienda, in the spacious rooms upstairs, that the gringos
stayed when they brought their children to the school. When
they left, they thought their children would remain in one of
these rooms — large, airy, full of greenery and dark old polished
furniture, a caged parrot in the window. But no. Far behind the
hacienda, in a clearing in a bamboo thicket was el barrio de los
alumnos. They lived in huts like the poorest campesinos, and
they were drugged and shut in most of the time.

"Some of them were mad and came from families so ashamed
of madness they would not even put them away in a crazy

house anywhere in Norte America. Some of them were disabled or retarded or deformed or blind. These, only the poorest of the Indian servants ever saw. But then there were those who had been politicos extremistas in Norte America. For they were all grown, these 'students'; did I tell you that? And some nearly middle-aged. There were the sick-in-the-heart radicales —a word I heard often from the gringa who helped me escape—who believed nothing their parents did was right, and sometimes, this gringa said, she herself would not come to her parents' dinner table dressed or with her hair combed, or even wearing shoes! She was very rich, you know. Such behavior grieved her parents to the heart. Nor could they find it in their hearts to ignore it.

"When I met this gringa, she was very dirty, barefoot, and wearing rags. She was sweeping out the room of one called 'The Disabled,' a hairy lump of a gringo from the Korean-American war, who smelled terrible. She was very glad to hear a word of Spanish, because she had contact mainly with los indios, and the Disabled had been fed so many drugs his tongue was lost. She was cleaning the Disabled's room because the india embarazada was sitting underneath a nearby tree having labor pains. She was muy immensa, also poor, ragged, barefoot, though not dirty, and her children's father was away in a war she did not understand.

"I asked the gringa her name, and she looked at me long before she gave it. The centers of her eyes were big in her dirty face and she seemed to turn many pages in a book mentally before she found the symbol for who she was. 'Mary Ann,' she said. 'Me llamo Zedé,' I said. She laughed. She was very high.

"I laughed with her. It was so very long since I laughed.

"I was there, let me see, two years. And it was there that Carlotta proved a great help to me. She was a wonder to everyone we met because she never cried. I don't mean she never shed tears; no, she never cried so that anyone could hear her. She cried the way one smiles. The mistress of the hacienda liked to see her crawling about the tile floor, naked except for her wrist beads, as I washed and then polished it. They did not know I could read and write and tried all the time to speak to me in what they thought was the language of the Indians or in the Spanish reserved for servants and slaves. They called me Consuelo. Connie, for short. Do this, Connie. Do that, Connie. No, I never gave them my right name, either. I told them it was Chaquita. Like the banana, the gringa said, laughing, to her husband. Like the banana! Still, when guests were there she called me Consuelo, because she liked the sound of herself saying it.

"Mary Ann had befriended los politicos extremistas in Norte America, but they were poor. No matter what she — 'the rich bitch' — did, it was, by them, ridiculed. When one of these negros radicales was sent to prison, his girlfriend tried to murder her; just walked up to her door one day with a large knife and began to chop away at her. After that attack, which scarred her neck, arms, and chest, Mary Ann left her small apartment near the black ghetto in San Francisco and retreated to Fox Hollow Farm, her parents' estate in New Jersey. There she began to talk openly of doing away with her parents, on whom she became dependent, and to take, as she herself put it, cases of drugs. With sorrow her parents watched her decline. They were not good people — they had too much money to have ever been good people — but they loved Mary Ann. Mary Ann described them as people who had personally assassinated six rivers and massacred twelve lakes, because they manufactured a deadly substance that was always swimming away from them. In their own way they were glad she refused to learn how to rob and cheat and create deadly things. Even so, she would inherit just under a billion dollars, earned from the filth they made, and they wanted her to be at least competent; not a scarred, drugged, disheveled mess, plotting assassinations and muttering into her blond locks that looked like sheep's wool. In their luck, at a party for the Republicanos that they gave at their estate, someone told them of La Escuela de Jungla. It seemed the answer to their dreams, especially because, when they asked about it among their friends, no one had heard of it, or at least they said they had not. So off they flew, right away, a bundled and bound Mary Ann between them, and in three days she shared a lovely big room with massive dark furniture and a caged red parrot. Her parents disappeared. The nice room disappeared. Even her clothing disappeared. The drugs did not disappear. They increased.

"While I was there I saw that letters from her parents gathered dust on the big desk of the gringos. I was so surprised to see in one of the letters that her father tried to stick in here and there a word or two of Spanish. At least he referred to Mary Ann as 'mi hija.' I myself wrote a letter telling them their daughter's fate. I did this partly because I grew to like Mary Ann, but also to rebel against the gringos and assert who I was. That I could read and write. That I knew reading and writing to have great power. That I was not a dumb Indian maidslave; that I was not Consuelo. I felt real pleasure seeing my own handwriting, the writing of a university-trained person, and the whiteness of the envelope gave me a feeling of dignity. Her parents flew in by helicopter in less than a month and snatched their daughter home. I was glad to see her freed. As I said, I had come to like her, though she so often failed to make sense; her brain was quite scrambled by then. She was a naturally sweet person who had no understanding of how to be rich in a world like this one, where great wealth immediately makes one think of great crimes. The gringos did not suspect me of alerting her parents, and they continued to fuss over Carlotta and to treat me as if I were a breathing piece of wood. They made much money from people like the parents of Mary Ann. And sometimes the little alumnos-prisioneros would die of the loneliness and poor food, the awful boredom and the dirt; and the letters with the checks for their care continued to arrive. This made me sad, but I never wrote another letter.

"One night I dreamed I would be rescued from the life I lived there, that I would be taken away by boat. But La Escuela was in the mountains, nowhere near the ocean, which I had heard of but never seen, and besides, the only boats I'd seen were small boats that my mother used to say looked like the dried pods of vanilla beans. But one day as I was cleaning one of the huts in the student barrio I heard someone call my name. My real name. I looked up, and it was Mary Ann! She was wearing a black shirt, attached somehow to pants, and very pretty pink lace-up boots. I had never imagined such zapatos! Two men carrying guns were with her, and she was sparkling with the life of before I knew her, ready for a fight! Her curious pale blue eyes, that made the Indians cross themselves, were full of light. She embraced me and told me to run and get Carlotta. This I did, without a moment's hesitation. On the way out we passed the bodies of the dogs, whose throats had been cut, just as the barbed wire had been. This made me sad, because I had liked the dogs. They were my only friends in that place and never barked at me. But I was happy about the barbed wire. 'It is like TV!' Mary Ann said over and over, giggling. I had never seen TV; I did not know what she meant. Now I know how right she was. Still, her action, though TV for her, made for me and mija all the difference in the world.

"In a tourist-type vehicle—muy grande, casita-like—we drove near the beach and parked underneath some trees. Just at sunset a beautiful ship, all gleaming wood, glinting brass, and white sails, a ship that seemed to be softly singing in the water, came into view. Our two gunslingers pulled a small boat from the brush, and that is how we made it to the yacht. A yacht owned by Mary Ann and called 'Recuerdo.'

"Que lástima que there was a huge storm off the coast of Norte California the day before we were to land. The mast broke in half, the boat rolled over, all our saviors were lost! The Coast Guard saw us go down and arrived in time to rescue me and Carlotta. Another yacht had been near us at the start of our difficulty, but, strangely, it had disappeared.

"On the boat I had asked Mary Ann how she had found the courage to do what she did, and she explained to me that while clearing herself of the drugs on which she'd leaned for years she had had a religious conversion of a sort. It had been based on something she vaguely remembered from Sunday school, something Christ was reported to have said. Something about 'the least of these.' She had not even bothered to look it up, she said. Her mind whispered, 'the least of these, the least of these,' until she 'spaced out' on it, she said, 'like on a mantra,' and beamed us—me and Carlotta—in! Then, too, she had begun to dream of seeing us again, happy, on a beautiful boat. She saw that her politics had not been wrong—for as a radical she had tried to stand with 'the least of these,' but she had tried to help people she did not know, with whom there was no reciprocidad; she had tried to ease the suffering of those who could not see that she, too, suffered, or even believe that she could. She loved me, she said, because I had seen this. It was true I had been able to see this, but even more true was the gratification I felt when in striking a blow for her I liberated the one called Chaquita, Connie, and Consuelo in myself.

"Alas, the suffering of the rich is seen by very few. When the parents of Mary Ann came, I could see nothing except that they held hands. They questioned me about the voyage, the nature of the storm; they asked if Mary Ann had seemed happy.

I told them she had gone down like a shooting star. They convinced la migra that Carlotta and I should be permitted to remain in Norte America. They asked to have a picture made of me and Carlotta, a copy of which was later sent to us. They disappeared. I have not heard from them since. I sometimes think of them very old, seated on a raft made out of their money, floating on a massacred river, looking for somewhere to land. But no, these personas ricas, all of them, have taken to the air. It is out *there*, in what they call 'space,' that they expect to find a home.

"I was very glad that I had spent some of my time on the boat sewing a little pouch for Jesús' feathered earrings and the stones. This I wore around my neck, and it was not lost. Gracias a Dios!"

WHEN you ask me about peace, Suwelo," said Miss
Lissie, "if I've ever in all my lifetimes experienced
peace, I am nearly perplexed. Could it be possible that after
hundreds of lifetimes I have not known peace? That seems to
be the fact. In lifetime after lifetime I have known oppression:
from parents, siblings, relatives, governments, countries, continents. As well as from my own body and mind. Some part of
every life has been spent binding up my wounds from these
forces. In the memory, I would have to say, there are only moments—at most, days—of peace, except for the times I have
been shaman or priest and have lived, for months on end, in a
kind of trance. But as you probably know, these blessed periods
are a vacation, in a sense, from life, and one screaming infant or
barking dog can force one home again.

"In the dream world of my memory, however, there is something. I do not remember this exactly, as I remember the other
things of which I have told you. But the memory, like the mind,
has the capacity to dream, and just as the memory exists at a
deeper level of consciousness than thinking, so the dream world
of the memory is at a deeper level still. I will tell you of the
dream on which my memory, as well as my mind, rests. When I
think of it I realize there was at least a peaceful foundation.

"In the dream memory we are very small people, all of us, not just the children, who are really small, and the children live with the mothers and the aunts; our fathers and uncles are nearby, and we visit and are visited by them, but we live with the women. We are in a forest that, for all we know, covers the whole earth. There is no concept of finiteness, in any sense. The trees then were like cathedrals, and each one was an apartment building at night. During the day we played under the trees as urban children today play on the streets. Our aunts and mothers foraged for food, sometimes taking us with them and sometimes leaving us in the care of the big trees. When you knew every branch, every hollow, and every crevice of a tree there was nothing safer; you could quickly hide from whatever might be pursuing you. Besides, we shared the tree with other creatures, who, in raucous or stealthy fashion—there was a python, for instance—looked out for us. Well, our aunts and mothers were often tired after a day gathering food—roots and fruits, mostly—and occasionally cross. Those were the times they could not stand us children, and so we were sent to our cousins' trees. Our cousins, like our fathers and aunts, lived in different trees from ours, and it was fun to visit them.

"Our cousins were big—as big as we were small—and black and hairy, with big teeth, flat black faces, and piercingly intelligent and gentle eyes. They seemed strange to us because they lived together as a family; that is, the fathers and uncles lived with the mothers and aunts, and all of them played with and looked after the children. They loved us, too, and would chatter with joy when we crept up on them. We crept because they were so serene, their trees so quiet that loud noises startled and frightened them. We were, by comparison, regular din makers. The only analogy I think of in this lifetime would be the experience, as small children, of being sent south to your grandparents' for the summer. Grandpa and Grandma might be old and decrepit, quiet, mellow, and unused to noise. They know a visit from the 'grands' might do them in for a while, but they let you know every day they're thrilled you are there. Same with our cousins. And I loved the little baby cousins, with their hairless pale faces, who were always clinging to somebody's back. It was a lovely feeling to hold a little cousin under one's chin, and how the parents delighted at this means of holding it! We had no hair on our bodies, you see, for the little fingers to clutch. It was from these cousins that I learned to love babies and to want to grow up and give birth.

"There was such safety around their trees. The fathers and uncles were gigantic and mean-looking when provoked, with a roar that hurt your ears. The mothers and aunts could bare their teeth viciously. They could bite through the fiercest neck. I used to practice baring my teeth and biting the way they did. My imitation tickled them very much. But they were menacing only when someone or something came into their domain uninvited. We—our mothers and aunts, fathers and uncles, too—were always welcome, and almost always, if there was anything to fear, we gathered at our cousins' trees. They had long sharp nails on their hands and feet, strong arms, and hard teeth, and they ripped rather large animals apart with one swipe. They protected us, and seemed to have great fun doing it. After they destroyed an attacker they chattered gaily and slapped each other on the back.

"They liked to feed us children, too. They did everything as if it were a game. I liked to go on the hunt with them because, unlike our fathers and mothers, who ate meat and therefore killed small game all the time, the cousins ate only plants. They would hide roots they'd already dug, just for us, who were clumsy and had hopelessly weak hands, to find.

"My mother, whose name was Guta Ru, was often angry with me; consequently, I spent a lot of time with the cousins.

The days were long and full, with food gathering and grooming taking up a good part of each day. But what adventures there were during the hunt for food; what fascinating other relatives, besides the cousins, one saw, and grooming was the most satisfyingly sensual experience I've ever had, in the dream memory or not. Because I lacked body hair—which I regretted no end!—I had a very short groom period, compared to theirs, which could last most of the day. The big cool teeth clicking over my steamy little body felt wonderful. The rough-tongued licking for lice, too. At least I had hair on my head, a ton of it. They could work on that for an hour or two, and I was, beneath their teeth and tongues, perfectly content.

"They were always trying to dress me. Leaves, skins from dead animals, moss, tree bark. It was funny. But it was from their experiments that I learned to dress and to want to be dressed; I learned to fasten a couple of pieces of leopard or panther skin fore and aft, and this pleased them, though I could tell they thought of my costume as a sort of prosthetic device. They seemed nearly unable to comprehend separateness; they lived and breathed as a family, then as a clan, then as a forest, and so on. If I hurt myself and cried, they cried with me, as if my pain was magically transposed to their bodies.

"When I reached an age to mate, I did so with one of my playmates, a boy I had known and loved all my life. After we mated and I became pregnant, he was expected, by custom, to move back with the men. This he refused to do. And I refused with him. We wanted very much to be together all the time with our babies, as we had seen happen in our cousins' trees. Well, you know adults. They haven't changed in a million years; they weren't going to have this. The women complained that he would only be in the way and possibly throw off our common monthly menstrual cycle; the men insisted they needed him for ceremonies and hunts. They punished us by isolating us from each other. We stood it as long as we could. But when the baby was born, we ran away to stay with the cousins, who in most things took a decidedly more progressive attitude than our parents. We were happy with them. They thought it natural that we would want to live together. They made a special bed out of moss for us to sleep on.

"I realize that in our smallness we were like perpetual children to them and that our babies were like the tiniest dolls. We were so small that one of their babies was too heavy for us to carry by the time it was a week old. Meanwhile, the cousins could easily carry me and my mate in one arm or with us clinging to a hairy back.

"There was no violence in them—that is to say, they did not initiate it, ever—only thoughtfulness. I used to look at them and wonder how we, so little, so naked, so easily contentious, had splintered off.

"In the dream memory there are suddenly days and nights of terror, and the faces of fathers and uncles who looked like us but were much bigger. They carried sticks with sharp points on them, and they hurled these at our cousins, striking them in the chest. To our horror, they took our cousins' skins and sometimes cooked and ate our cousins' bodies. Us, so little, they brushed off as if we were flies, and we dashed to the tops of the trees screaming and crying.

"Over time and after many attacks, our cousins and we ourselves—the little people, as we now recognized ourselves—were driven into the most remote reaches of the forest. We learned to make the sharp pointed stick and to poison its tip as well. We learned to make blowguns and slingshots. The trust that had been between us now disappeared. We were perceived as helpless and cute no longer, and, for our part, there were those among us who gloried in at last having the means to make our giant cousins fear.

"But my mate and I never forgot what we learned from the cousins. We brought up our children to be as much like them as possible; and we stayed together until death, just as the cousins did. It was this way of living that gradually took hold in all the groups of people living in the forest, at least for a very long time, until the idea of ownership—which grew out of the way the forest now began to be viewed as something cut into pieces that belonged to this tribe or that—came into human arrangements. Then it was that men, because they were stronger, at least during those periods when women were weak from childbearing, began to think of owning women and children. This very thing had happened before, and our own parents had forgotten it, but their system of separating men and women was a consequence of an earlier period when women and men had tried to live together—and it is interesting to see today that mothers and fathers are returning to the old way of only visiting each other and not wanting to live together. This is the pattern of freedom until man no longer wishes to dominate women and children or always have to prove his control. When man saw he could own one woman and her children, he became greedy and wanted as many as he could get. There is a popular African singer today who has twenty-seven. Idi Amin had so many that the ones he is rumored to have killed aren't even missed.

"My life with the cousins is the only dream memory of peace that I have. In one of the worst lifetimes, many lifetimes later, I was, by some accident, permitted to marry another man I myself actually picked and loved, and there was peace for a time, a beautiful 'rightness' about the world, but because I was apparently born without a hymen and therefore there were no bloodstains to show the villagers after, our wedding night—during which I had responded to him passionately, or, as he later claimed, shamelessly—he denounced me to the village and my parents turned me out. After that I was the lowest sort of prostitute for the men of the village, including the husband I'd loved, until I died of infection and exposure at the age of eighteen."

WHAT do human beings contribute, Suwelo was thinking morosely, as he waited one afternoon for Miss Lissie to appear. Her story about the animal cousins had moved him, and each day he found himself more conscious of his own nonhuman "relatives" in the world.

The bees contributed honey, but not really—it was taken from them. What, he now wondered, did the bees eat themselves; surely they didn't make honey for human beings. It was the flowers that contributed honey to both bees and people, the flowers that were always giving something: beauty, cheerfulness, pollen, and seeds. They did not care who saw them, whom they gave to. And on his feet, Suwelo also realized, with disgust, he was wearing moccasins made of leather. What a euphemism, "leather." A real nonword. Nowhere in it was concealed the truth of what leather was. Something's skin. And his tortoiseshell glasses. He took them off and peered nearsightedly at them, holding them at arm's length. But they were imitation tortoiseshell. Plastic, probably. But this made him even gloomier, for he knew the only reason for imitation anything was that the source of the real thing had dried up. There were probably no more tortoises to kill. And what, anyway, of plastic? It was plentiful, cheap. But even it came from somewhere. Of what was plastic made? What died? He knew it was a product of petroleum, of oil, and so he assumed plastic was made out of the very lifeblood of the planet. When all the oil was drained, he imagined the planet quaking and shrinking in on itself, like a squeezed orange that has been sucked to death.

He was glad when he heard Miss Lissie's knock. It was firm and decisive, as always. When he opened the door, he was instantly cheered by the lively, ironical eyes—that seemed to say, Well, what else, if anything, is new?—in the old, beautifully angular face. Her bright hair was covered with a woolen shawl the color of California poppies, Fanny's favorite flower. This alone made Suwelo smile. She wore a camel-hair coat, and high, lace-up black shoes. Her breath was short, from the effort of bringing a large cardboard box up the steps. Suwelo quickly reached out and took it from her.

She stepped into the foyer and took off her shawl and coat, hanging them on the coatrack and checking herself out in the dim mirror beneath the light. She was wearing a soft yellow dress that had a large embossed black paw print, or perhaps it was a flower, Suwelo thought, looking at it closely, just above her heart. In a few minutes they were seated in the front parlor, drinking tea Suwelo had prepared as he awaited her arrival, and going through the big box.

"When your uncle died," said Miss Lissie, "I didn't know for certain who would be taking over the house. I didn't want these pictures to go to just anybody. They're special, and I wanted to give them only to someone who'd understand."

Suwelo was glad Miss Lissie considered him someone who did. All over the walls of the house there were pale empty spaces where the photographs had hung. Suwelo had stopped before them many times, trying to imagine what the pictures might have been like. Miss Lissie now took each of them out, unwrapped it, and placed it face down on the oak bench next to the sofa. After she'd done this, she carefully crumpled the newspaper wrappings and put them in the box. She then took a cloth from her black leather purse and began to polish the glass of each picture. After that, she placed them in rows on the bench, sat back, and invited Suwelo to look.

Before he looked at the pictures, though, he looked carefully into the old face next to him and tried to locate the young girl standing in front of the fancy carved chairs, barefoot, clothes patched, her hair in plaits. He looked for the lovely nose, the soft mouth, the round cheeks. Perhaps she was there. It was hard to tell. Then, noting the rough and beautiful texture of the oak and pine frames, he began to look at the photographs, of which there were thirteen. Miss Lissie explained that she already had a copy of the one photograph she had left in the house, and therefore hadn't taken it when she had removed the rest.

Suwelo remembered Mr. Hal's remark: "Lissie is a lot of women," and expected to see a lot of pictures of the same woman dressed to make herself appear different; and it was true, in each picture the chair—one of those in the photograph left behind—was the same, and the outfit varied greatly. What he saw, though, were thirteen pictures of thirteen entirely different women. One seemed tall, another very short, one light-skinned, with light eyes, another dark with eyes like obsidian. One had hair to her waist, another had hardly enough to cover her skull. One appeared acrobatic, healthy, and glowing. Another seemed crippled and barely ambulatory.

He chose two pictures and held them out in front of him. In one, a short, high-yellow flapper stared boldly into the camera, lips puckered and a rakish look in what appeared to be green eyes, a spit curl of lightish hair an upside-down question mark in the middle of her forehead; in the second, a tall, dark, gangly

miss, with the sad grace of a domestic servant and former field
hand, looked out of beaten eyes at a camera and cameraman
she did not trust. She was wearing a maid's white uniform, and
her scant hair was mercilessly straightened and pulled tight under a peaked white cap. There was no similarity at all between
the two women. In fact, there was none among any of the thirteen women. Nor did they look like the elegant grandmotherly
woman at Suwelo's elbow.

"I ran off with the photographer, a colored man from
Charleston, who took that," said Miss Lissie, pointing to the
flapper one. "He was married. When I found out, I ran away
from him. I was pregnant at the time. This," she said, pointing to the one in the maid's uniform, "is how I looked when
he found me again. I was one of his models for going on thirty
years, off and on. Long after what fire there was between us
burned out. We fascinated each other. He had never, in all his
work as a photographer, photographed anyone like me, who
could never present the same self more than once, and I had
never in my life before found anyone who could recognize how
many different women I was. Oh, some people, even my mama
and papa, commented on how I didn't seem to have, as they
put it, 'no certain definite form,' but to them I looked enough
like myself from day to day so that it didn't matter. But Henry
Laytrum began to photograph me once or twice a year, and the
result is what you see; there were others, but in these the differences are most striking.

"Yes," she said, as if answering Suwelo's question, "those are
both me. All of these," she continued, with a sweep of her arm,
"all of them are me. Henry Laytrum, with his old box camera
and his break-away chair—so he could dismantle it and take it
anywhere he went—that was carved by Hal's father, was able to
photograph the women I was in many of my lifetimes before. It
was such a wonderful gift he was able to give me, although be-

cause he was so dishonest with me about his marriage—never telling me until after we'd run off together—I never told him the secret of what puzzled him so and intrigued him. And I only came to understand myself—at first it frightened me to see myself as so many different people!—after years of memory excavation and exploration, years of understanding I'm not like most other people, years of anger and confusion over this, years of fighting everyone! But finally it dawned on me that my memory and the photographs corroborated each other exactly. I had been those people, and they were still somewhere inside of me. When Henry Laytrum aimed his camera, different ones were drawn out. Over time I grew to love seeing which self would pop out. Henry Laytrum would develop the pictures, race over to see me, spread them out on the porch, and introduce us. 'Miss Lissie,' he'd say, bowing to me and the latest picture, 'say Howdy!' And I would. It was such a kick. The selves I had thought gone forever, existing only in my memory, were still there! Photographable. Sometimes it nearly thrilled me to death.

"In the wide world there was war. These white people here, trying to rule over everybody in America, and the ones in Europe, trying to rule over everybody else in the world. The Depression came. Seem like you heard of a hanging or some other monstrous thing done to colored every time you turned around. But this is what was happening to me. And because I was a colored woman, nobody would ever know about it. I was sort of glad, for I'm the kind of woman that likes to enjoy herselves in peace."

Suwelo shook his head. He did not know if he could believe this or not. And he thought about how believing in things like Halley's comet was not the same thing. Or was it?

"Remember what I told you about losing my foot and leg after being caught in a bear trap?"

"Oh," said Suwelo, his eyes going instantly to the picture of the small, sad-eyed, very black cripple. It wasn't that you could see her injury—the missing foot and leg—it was just that you looked into the ashen face, in which the spirit seemed already to have been given up, and you knew.

"Now this," said Miss Lissie, seeing in Suwelo's mournful face the heaviness of his commiseration with a self she had moved through, "is how I looked at the time when I stayed with the cousins and hung out in their trees." She handed Suwelo the happiest-looking of all the pictures, in which she appeared squat, tiny, with a waist like a wasp's, her hair in wooly ringlets, her eyes bright and laughing, her strong white teeth playfully bared in a wide smile. A pygmy.

S O THAT is why they believed Africans ate people, Suwelo mused, thinking of what Miss Lissie had told him, on the visit previous to the last, about the cousins. Someone, millennia after the time of which she spoke, had come across the gnawed skulls and bones of these ill-fated relatives. But then, obviously in Miss Lissie's estimation, her cousins *were* people, even more peoplelike than the folks from her own branch of the family. He sat looking at the picture of Miss Lissie from thousands of years ago; he imagined her mate taking the photograph and laughing with her as she made faces at him. He imagined their children crawling about under the cathedrallike trees; trees as big as Chartres, she had said. He imagined the huge black hairy cousins swinging about with their young and Miss Lissie's young, too, clinging to their backs. He thought of the big dark faces and the small paler ones.

He was still thinking of this when he heard Mr. Hal's truck and, later, his gentle, tentative knock on the door. Suwelo let him in, helped him off with his coat, and because he knew how Mr. Hal enjoyed good coffee, he hastened to make him a cup.

Suwelo had now been in Uncle Rafe's house for more than two months. He had not forgotten Fanny and California — and there was a "For Sale" sign outside on the tiny lawn—but days went by when he did not think of her. Or if he did think of her, it was to feel sad that she could not share what he was experiencing. Fanny loved old people and was conversant with them in ways he was not. He was much more likely to be embarrassed with them, as if he suspected they sensed the impatience that was frequently his frame of mind. But it wasn't simply impatience with *them* that he felt; he was impatient with the situation that young and old these days had inherited (and he forgot a lot of the time that he was getting older himself): that of being without sufficient time either to talk, really talk, to each other or to listen. Say you were at some unusual event, some kind of house party, and you found yourself next to an ancient anthropologist who just casually said: "Well, when I was in Afghanistan in the thirties . . . blah, blah, blah." What did you do? What you wanted to do was grab her by her collar and drag her home and sit her down in a big comfy chair and sit at her feet (or his feet, as the case might be) for a week, while she talked. At the party the most you were likely to get was a sly anecdote about travel by camel and the lack of roads. It was maddening.

Fanny was more likely than he to stay glued to some rare old person for an evening, completely absorbed, though both she and the old person had to strain to hear each other over the noise of the other guests.

Suwelo loved what was happening to him and was grateful for the time his uncle Rafe had provided for him to get to know his house, his friends, a life he could not have learned about any other way than by having it subsidized. He remembered the first time he had waited for Miss Lissie and her friend, Miss Rose, to bring his lunch and he had asked them to please step inside. Miss Rose had declined, hurriedly, saying she had grandchildren at home waiting for her, but Miss Lissie had come in as if she had been expecting the invitation, and had stood in the

foyer in a rather queenly way, he thought, as if waiting for him
to dispose of some earlier guest. They looked at each other for
a long moment. That day it was her dignity he noticed first; the
straightness of her posture. Next, her reserve, the way she said
"How do you do?" so formally, then nothing else, as he stood
beside her, waiting for her to take the first step into the living
room, where, he reasoned, she must have sat countless times
before. But she did not budge. He thought she looked quite
stately, for someone who wasn't very tall. And then he, too, became conscious of the guests in his living room.

"I'm sorry. Excuse me," he said hurriedly, and walking
quickly into the living room, he snapped off the TV.

"I get used to having it on for company," he said, by way of
apology. And then he thought, she probably watches the soaps
herself, so he said, "I'm getting more like my cousins and aunts
every day; they all watch the soaps."

"The whats?" asked Miss Lissie.

"You know, the stories on TV," said Suwelo, thinking the
modern shorthand for TV stories confused her. After all, she
was very old. "Which do you watch?"

"I don't watch TV," she said, sitting in a chair next to it and
at the same time drawing a blue fringed shawl that had lain on
top of the set since Suwelo arrived completely over the front
of it.

So that's its purpose, Suwelo thought, for he had looked at
the blue shawl, a large, vivid Mexican serape, and felt it made a
rather peculiar doily.

Today Mr. Hal sat in the same chair Miss Lissie usually
chose, right by the TV, and like Miss Lissie he paid more than
cursory attention to the position of the shawl. Suwelo watched
TV much less himself now that Miss Lissie and Mr. Hal talked
to him, or, as he sometimes thought of it, transmitted to him, in
much the same way the TV did. He was in the habit of cover-

ing it whenever it was off. Mr. Hal contented himself with tugging at a corner of the shawl and straightening the edge. That small ritual completed, a gesture that seemed unconsciously designed to close off completely an erroneous and trivial point of view, Mr. Hal settled back to take up his narrative where he had left off. For Suwelo's talks with him and Miss Lissie were not conversations. They were more correctly perceived as deliveries. Suwelo was grateful to receive.

"You don't know, or maybe you do," said Mr. Hal, a look of deep satisfaction with the coffee and with his thoughts on his face, "how wonderful a feeling it give you when you know somebody love you and that's just the way it is. You can be good, you can be a devil, and still that somebody love you. You can be weak, you can be strong. You can know a heap or nearly nothing. That kind of love, when you think about it, just seems like some kind of puzzle, and you can spend a lifetime trying to figure it out. If you puffed up with vanity, you can't help but think what they love is something you created yourself. Or maybe it's your money or your car. But there's something. . . . It's like how you love a certain place. You just do, that's all. And if you're lucky, while you're on this earth, you get to visit it. And the place 'knows' about your love, you feel. That was the love and still is the love between Lissie and me."

Mr. Hal settled himself more comfortably in his chair, took a large slurping sip of his coffee, just as Uncle Rafe and every old Southern gentleman Suwelo had ever met had done, and continued.

"So the white folks wanted all us boys, your uncle Rafe, too, for the army, to fight in the Great War, or so they said. The truth was, they wanted us to be servants for the white men who fought. I wasn't painting worth nothing then—did I tell you I used mostly house paint?—Lissie wasn't pushing me, for some reason, and I couldn't hardly see the road in front of me. But I

was black and able-bodied, and the white folks wanted me for
fodder in their war. The furthest I had been from the Island
was about a mile from shore. They wanted us to fight some
people none of us had heard of, and they were white folks, too.
Well, not to fight 'em, just to serve our own white masters, you
might say, while *they* fought 'em.

"So anyway, it meant leaving the Island, leaving my family, and leaving Lissie. I didn't see how I could stand it. Lissie
couldn't either, but Lissie couldn't fight the white man's army,
though I don't doubt she would've tried. She hated white
people anyway and said she didn't have one good memory from
a thousand years of dealing with them. But you know from
all the stuff Lissie's told me, she didn't have many real good
memories of anybody. She was just in a rage most of the time
about me going away. And out of that rage, she got the notion
we should be married. I was scared to say no. Besides, it was
what everybody was doing, getting married, and it's safe to say
to you today that we didn't have a clue, really and truly, about
what marriage was. Plus I loved Lissie—when hadn't I loved
Lissie?—and she loved me so much, too much, till sometimes
I was almost smothered.

"They used to speak of that time on the Island as the time
of the big rash. They meant the rash of folks getting married.
Like most of them, we got married on the front porch at Lissie's
people's house, looking out over the bay. It was a pretty spring
day, and I just itched to paint it. I never will forget we had a
woman preacher to marry us, because we had two preachers
on the Island, both of them called by the spirit, and we were
too out of the way things were done in the rest of the world to
know the spirit didn't call women. Then there was Lissie staring everybody down and saying she *remembered* that women
were called *first* and this calling was something men then took
away from them. Well, nobody was going to fight Lissie over

something nobody thought was important. We had two spirit-called people, a woman *and* a man. It seemed right. Like you have two different kinds of parents, a woman *and* a man, you know. It wasn't until I was in the army and saw how all the preachers, priests, and chaplains everywhere we went—and we got as far as France—were men that I thought about what Lissie had said, and how disgusted she looked when she said it. Of course at different times Lissie herself was a witch doctor and a sorceress and a preacher of various kinds, so she knew what she was talking about. She was so *angry*. The maddest human being I've ever seen in all my years of living. Because she saw people losing ground in the battle against ignorance and she could see how it would turn out, whatever the battle was, because she had seen it all before.

"So really, I don't know why she thought marriage was the answer for us. But I went along with her and hoped for the best. Here was a woman I loved, who loved me and let me paint—she thought nothing of spending a morning thinning enough house paint for me to use up in an hour, and she was a regular scavenger for cardboard and likely pieces of wood, since I painted on any and everything—and she encouraged it—sometimes even, what you might say, *forced* me to do it, and I couldn't give her up. For her part, I think she wanted to make the bond between us clearer to other people—we didn't need it to be clearer to ourselves—and you know how it is: trying to make a private bond a public one is like trying to turn water to wine when you prefer water to wine, and anyway you ain't Christ.

"But what did we know? There we were together in bed that night after the wedding. I was dead tired and I was leaving in the morning. Lissie was even tireder than I was, since she'd been out in the boat fishing early that morning; that's what we had to eat at our wedding, fried fish. But somehow we thought we had to have at each other, as they say. It was a pretty fumbly minute or two, and nothing much was done, or so I thought. We cried and kissed each other a few million times and whispered all our little failings and hopes and secrets to each other, and then, lying like little children in each other's arms—I suspect Lissie still sucks her thumb—we drifted off to sleep. The next morning I left.

"Well, I really couldn't see that well, not even well enough to make a decent stable boy, and pretty soon I was shipped back home. Lissie and her mother had opened up a little store on the Island in part of the front porch of their house. They sold produce out of their garden and things—kerosene, matches, bluing, baking soda—her mother brought back from the mainland in her boat. They also sold fresh fish. I remember that because, when I moved back into Lissie's little room, everything there used to smell of fish.

"Lissie was pregnant, with a passion for lemons and salt. Everytime you saw her she had half a lemon sprinkled with salt stuck in her mouth. She was healthy and strong—she did the fishing in her mother's boat—and I was soon healthy and strong with her, because fishing and crabbing became something I did, too, and did well. And with Lissie urging me on, I was also painting again, with the sun in my eyes, healing them, and the moisture from the bay. The little paintings I did, Lissie hung up in the store, and sometimes people right there on the Island just fell in love with a painting and would put it on layaway, but also white people from the mainland, who stopped by for a cold drink, bought them. I sold them for a dollar apiece, or sometimes for less than a dollar; barely enough to cover the paint. But still, it made me happy to know somebody besides me and Lissie liked what I did.

"We had both acquired a bit more knowledge by then, and our love was always strong, so we just let ourselves be free. She was already pregnant, so that wasn't something to worry about, and well, we were just all the time fucking. If you pardon the expression. I think Lissie was happy then. I know I was. I used to love looking at her as she ran about here and there. She was like a leaf leaving a tree on wind, always in motion, quick as light. And smart. Pretty soon she'd moved us out of her mother's house to a place of our own, and it was in our own house that our passion for each other reached a peak, and then sort of made itself a plateau. That kind of love, with the — what do you all call it these days? — the sex, is nothing like what you see on TV or in the picture show. It doesn't even seem like such a big thing at the time. It's just something real *good*, tasty, you know? It's something very much like food. Or sleep. We'd fuck and sleep and eat and fish, and I'd paint and she'd do her work, and the sun would shine or it would rain, and the catch would be good or the fish would all have gone to visit some other part of the bay. There was no seam. It was whole cloth. So that eating a piece of bread that really rocked the taste buds made me think of fucking Lissie. Or her fucking me; God knows she could. Drinking cool water on the boat in the sun sent us to our knees. Lissie was always laughing. At her clumsiness, her heavy breasts that I loved so much to suck, her cushy butt, her belly that loomed over my head like a melon when I made love to her little . . . kitten, let us say. Or the way we said it then, when I 'twirled her on my tongue.' I loved to have her like that in the boat. If the bay was calm, and sometimes it was like glass, we forgot about fishing, and she would stand big and naked, balanced in the boat, and spread her legs just enough. *Oh.*

"When we made love we never thought of anybody or anything else. I never did, anyway. Just as when I drank a glass of water I didn't shift my mind to some other glass of water that I tried to pretend I was also drinking. This way of loving just exactly who you're with seems totally out of reach of half the people making love in the world today. And I think it's a shame.

"But it all ended anyway, Suwelo. That part of life. It ended because our daughter, Lulu, was born. And it wasn't her fault. It wasn't anyone's fault, maybe. I try to tell myself it had to end, that time when everything was pure cool water to my thirst, good bread to my hunger. That time when, really, Lissie and I were in danger of getting lost in each other and to ourselves. Because when I was with Lissie I didn't care if neither of us was ever heard from again.

"I remember once a photographer, the first one ever seen on the Island, came over to buy a chair from my father, and seeing Lissie, asked to take a picture of her standing beside the chair. We were just fascinated by the thought of picture taking, of which we had heard, though we had never seen a live picture taker before, and he was a colored man! We tiptoed about his tripod and knocked a couple of times on the big black box that the man said made the picture, but our true feeling was, we didn't want to be bothered; that the new picture-taking science was just fine and dandy, but we had better things to do, like lay up. I'm pretty sure we were drenched in the smell of fucking. That smell some couples have, or used to have. Now it's all covered over with perfume. But Lissie used to smell loud, and I loved it. But not when other men noticed it and started to sniff around her. Like that picture taker. 'You married?' he asked her. There I was, there my daddy and mama was, there was Lissie so pregnant she could only see one foot at a time. 'You married?' asked that dog.

"Lulu was born on a night of such stillness it made us think the whole world was holding its breath. Both Lissie and I were looking forward to the birth. We had made up a little crib next to our bed and everything. Neither one of us knew that disaster was about to strike our love life, and that between the first labor pain and the disposal of the afterbirth I would be a changed man. But even if we *had* of known, what could we have done? I've asked myself that question a million times. But fate had us in its teeth.

"In those days pregnant women like Lissie didn't go to the doctor just because they were pregnant. It would have been like going to the hospital because you started to get breasts. It was a natural something that happened to women, and a good woman, meaning a sensible one, always had a granny to help her see after herself. Lissie actually had two. She had her mother, Eula—Eula Mae—and the woman Lissie was most like in the world, Dorcy—Dorcy Hogshead—her grandmother. Dorcy was a devil. The most contentious, cantankerous old witch that ever lived. However, a genius at delivering babies. Her people always claimed that Lissie took after her and that that was the reason she was so mean. They never believed in Lissie's memory, you see. I never understood how they could not believe in it myself. Lissie remembered and reported on stuff nobody'd ever heard of, stuff nobody ever could have told her. Stuff she'd never read because it wasn't in the books she had. But then that left dreaming. So her folks said she dreamed instead of remembered, and the stuff she didn't dream, she got from Granny Dorcy.

"So Granny Dorcy had been checking Lissie right along. And she remembered a lot, too, and it gave her a lot of power, just like it did Lissie, but she didn't have Lissie's kind of faith in herself, so she would content herself with the belief that she could interpret her own and other people's dreams. But really what she was doing was putting together the past in some kind of pattern so that it could be understood in the present. I think she was probably scared shitless by her gift. So many people are. She was an old woman that looked like she could have remembered seeing the warships that passed the Island on the way to firing the first rockets against Fort Sumter at the start of the Civil War, which she said she did. She looked a lot like Sojourner Truth—you know that picture you sometimes see of her with her bonnet and her long dress and her shawl and her white clay pipe. Granny smoked a pipe and sometimes, some people said, she would blow smoke on her babies to get them to sneeze and come alive. I know she used to say that, mean as people said she was, she'd never hit one of the little ones she brought into the world, and you know slapping a newborn baby was and is something that's just automatically done. Granny Dorcy thought it was barbaric.

"She lived on the other side of the Island from us, and sometimes she rode a mule over to see Lissie, and sometimes Lissie's mother went and got her and brought her back by boat. Eula was good to have around, too, while Lissie was pregnant, because she had become a food *fool* and would always double-check anything that went into Lissie's mouth. When she was pregnant herself, Eula had lived mostly on a diet of fatback, syrup, and white chalk that pregnant women dug out of a pit up in the hills, but she wouldn't let Lissie have but the occasional thimbleful because she said that craving it was a sign that Lissie needed to eat beets, which she often fixed for her, and that eaten in excess, the chalk, which was full of iron that the body couldn't absorb anyway, locked the bowels and weakened the blood vessels in the lower extremities. So both of these women seemed underfoot all the time near the end of Lissie's term.

"Then one day, about a week before they thought she was due, they took the boat out to catch some fish. I think it must have been the season for croaker; that was old Dorcy's favorite fish. Just after they left, Lissie had the first pain, and I ran down to the beach and tried to wave them back to shore. They thought I was waving good-bye, and so they waved good-bye back to me, and off into the horizon they rowed. I knew they'd be back in two or three hours at the most, so I didn't worry; Lissie didn't worry either. But what do you think happened?

"Out in the boat, Eula Mae and her mother got into an argument over which side of the boat to fish from, and as the talk got more and more heated and hearkened back to more and earlier disputes, mother and daughter almost came to blows. Dorcy's temper was a frightful thing; it lacked foresight. At some point she swung her oar at Eula, and Eula took it away from her and flung it into the bay. Then Dorcy took the other oar and threw it away too. Now how do you like that? I'm just glad me and Lissie didn't know anything about it at the time. So there they were, with no fish, no wind, mad as two hatters, sitting fuming at each other with their arms folded and their lips poked out, in a boat that went neither forward nor backward nor sideways, and wouldn't for the rest of the day.

"At the house Lissie was beginning to worry. Not so much about herself as about her mother and grandmother. After about three hours Lissie said she'd discharged her plug and that her waters had broke. That was my first understanding that if the two women didn't hurry and get back, I would have to deliver our baby. Now you can laugh if you want to, but though I could see plain as anything that Lissie was big with the baby and even beginning to sweat from the pain, and the baby was lunging about inside her, as far as I was concerned there still didn't seem any possible way she could have a baby; it just seemed farfetched. I don't know what I thought then. Nobody ever told you anything, if you were a boy, about childbirth. They just didn't. And whenever a woman was having a baby on the Island, the husband was sent out of the house. He usually hung around the potbellied stove we had in the store. After a while one of his oldest children would come get him and, with a scared and sheepish look, off he'd go back home. I think somewhere in me I still believed fairies brought babies

—I sure was praying they did—so I was beginning to wonder what I would do if that was just a rumor and fairies really didn't. Come to think about it, I didn't have the faintest notion of what fairies were supposed to be like either.

"Lissie had been walking up and down the room, but pretty soon the pains got so bad she had to lay down, and then, too, there was a trickle of something like watery mucous coming out of her. I helped her lie down on the rubber pad with a sheet over it, and I held her hand and kissed her about a thousand times every time she let out a whimper, which really just wrung my heart. Then she told me: 'You have to deliver the baby, Hal. It's a girl,—she knew this because the baby always had hung low—'and I want you to know, in case anything happens, I want to name her Lulu.'

"Lulu was the name Lissie had had when she was part of a harem in the northern part of Africa, before any of that area was desert. It wasn't called a 'harem' way back then, but some other name I can't recall. 'Weepen,' I think. But it was really the great-great-granddaddy of all the harems we hear about or read about today. She said Lulu made her think of the green hills and the green fields where they used to put up their animal-skin tents, and of how happy she was in the harem, because the master was old and sickly and had hundreds of women it tired him just to see, not to mention to try to do anything to, and Lissie (Lulu) had had two lovers. One of them was another woman in the harem, named Fadpa, and the other was one of the eunuchs, named Habisu, whose job it was to keep the women from running away. They used to all sit around and plot about how to run away together, but Habisu was afraid to leave the safety of the harem, and he liked the sweets the women shared with him and the colorful clothing he got to wear. He was from a poor family, and he thought it wasn't such a bad thing to give up his nuts for such pleasant room and board. Now I don't know whether this was really the truth or whether Lissie was committing slander on poor Habisu. She used to laugh so, and shock me, too, telling me about her life as Lulu. She would talk about Fadpa and look at me and see that I didn't quite get something, and she would just laugh and laugh. She had been a great dancer—she says she took it up out of boredom—and taught dancing to the young women who were captured or bought and brought into the harem. She had regular class hours. And she taught how to make love to a woman with just hands and tongue to all the eunuchs, who, she said, really came to love her. Of course some of them didn't care about that sort of thing with women anyhow. There were some who just sat around and talked about clothes and food and ate, ate, ate. On her birthday they would make her cakes filled with her favorite thing: dates. She and Fadpa lived, with the other women and the eunuchs, completely cut *off* from the rest of society back then, and the rest of the world in general. Over time they became devoutly religious.

"They eventually got to the place they could perform miracles. Miracles, Lissie says she learned, as Lulu, are the direct result of concentration. The greatest miracle they performed was to get their freedom from the harem at the rather ripe old ages of ninety-six and a hundred and three, which was granted them by the great-granddaughter of their old master. They had prayed and concentrated on this for eighty years. This woman had been sent off somewhere far away to school, where she passed as a man, and, upon returning home, was shocked to see these old women locked up behind her grandfather's palace. He was dead by then and had taken some of the youngest and prettiest members of his harem with him. His scowling sons had simply pitched the women into the flames on top of their father's popping and oozing body, calmly, one by one. They, of course, were screaming and scratching and clinging to the sons' ankles, but those, as the saying goes, were the breaks.

"Lulu and Fadpa had some good years left still, though their wrinkled faces looked like two raisins; so they set up shop as fortune-tellers and lived free, if not content, until they died—which they were happy enough to do, because what they noticed, once outside the security of the harem, was that in the world of men there is always war. They could not stand the noise and confusion of the battles that never ceased. They longed for the quiet and the peace of the harem, and the hours of cooking and eating and dancing or watching younger women dance. And when men came to them and asked their fortunes, they yawned. For every man, they saw war, a future of fighting. It was as clear as the sun. Their palms were bright red. But Lulu and Fadpa would say, instead, that they saw a hundred pretty women locked in a room to which the man in front of them, alone, had the key and at least half an evening of a man's favorite kind of peace. This pleased the men. If they added that they also saw stores of dates, figs, silver, and gold, the men's happiness was complete. They got used to throwing in camels, goats, and other men's wives at random. They became quite famous.

"The name Lulu was fine with me. It was more a sound than a name, but so what? When our Lulu was born, I could see that she would make anyone think of green. She was all gold and honey and amber, that made you think of pansies. She was a springtime all her own.

"Now the hardest task was before me. It was very hot. Lissie was sweating buckets. I had plenty of water boiling on the stove. This much preparation, at least, I knew you had to have. Then Lissie began to really moan. It was horrible. Timidly, and with rising fear, I managed to glance down between her legs. I expected to see the top of the baby's head. Maybe. Since something did seem to be happening down that way. And Lissie was moaning so. But no. It looked like a cheek. Either a cheek on a little face, or a cheek on a little behind. I looked again. Lissie's stomach rippled, as if the baby turned itself over. Now it looked more like a shoulder. I looked still again. It looked like a knee. Or was it a side?

"I tell you, I felt like Prissy in *Gone With the Wind.*

"Lissie was stretched so wide I didn't see why she didn't split. And, as I stood there watching, I saw she was just about to start to. At the same time, her moans were turning into screams. I couldn't bear it. My instinct was just to step outside the door and do away with myself. I couldn't stand the thought that I was causing her this pain. That making love with her caused this sad, pitiful behavior of hers. She wasn't Lissie anymore, you see? She wasn't even like an animal. She was out of her mind, out of control. She hurt so bad she couldn't even tell me what to do. The baby was obviously stuck, trying to come out sideways. Lissie had turned one of the funniest of the gray shades I had ever seen.

"Every once in a while I ran to the porch and looked out on the bay for Eula and that fool Granny Dorcy, but they were nowhere in sight. Besides, night was coming on fast. I looked up the hill for some customers coming to the store. There wasn't a soul. No one but me, Lissie, and little Lulu.

"I prayed for strength and I prayed for my wife and child. Then I washed my hands real good and greased them with Vaseline and greased Lissie with Vaseline and greased what I could get my fingers on of the baby with Vaseline. I had Lissie laughing about this one time; I said Vaseline was one big thing she and her mother had in common: her mother used it on her face, and said that's what kept her skin so young, and I used it on Lissie's behind. Anyway, I began to gently push the baby around, kind of slowly spinning her. And I started to talk to her, telling her to come on out, that everything was ready for her and we knew we were straining her but that we didn't mean her no harm. I don't know what all I said; I was dying from the pain Lissie was feeling. Hating myself and all mankind. I mean I started making some serious promises to God. Way after a while I identified the baby's arm, really the upper shoulder. Then I somehow got hold of the arm, it felt no bigger than a thumb, and I worked at it, all the time telling Lulu about how good she was going to have it out here, and I finally pulled that out. Oh, God, what next, I thought. And Lissie fainted. But then she came to, but just looked destroyed, and I could see in her eyes the hundreds of times she had suffered in giving birth, and I swore it would never happen again, and my desire for her, for sex with her or with any woman, died, and I became a eunuch myself. I just knew I would never be able to deal with making love to a woman ever again.

"And then Lissie sort of laughed and said, 'I thought somebody was supposed to tell me to push.' She hadn't, all this time, because we'd forgot—and it turned out later, according to her mother and Dorcy, *not* pushing was just the right thing to have done. I'd certainly forgot about the pushing, if I'd ever known it, and I grabbed old Lulu by the hand—it was like shaking hands with a little slippery rabbit—and stuck my other hand up in Lissie so that my fingers kind of pulled on Lulu's armpit and lower jaw and I said, 'Well go on and push then.' And she pushed like she was coming and really seemed to enjoy it in just about the same way. And that shocked the hell out of me. And then Lulu was born, snuffling and sneezing even without anybody slapping her or blowing smoke in her face, and for a minute I felt real confused and left out. I laid Lulu on Lissie's stomach, and Lissie wiped her off with a rag, and I started looking for a knife to cut the cord, and by the time I found one—it was in the boiling water on the stove and too hot to touch right away—Lissie had bitten through the cord with her teeth.

"'God, it's like rubber,' she said, making a face and spitting into the rag. And I looked at Lissie sitting up now with the naked baby next to her naked body, and I thought to myself how primitive she was.

"When the afterbirth came—a lump of bloody, liverish-looking stuff that made me feel even woozier than I was—she wrapped it in newspaper and gave it to me to bury at the corner of the house for luck, so that we could have a houseful of babies. When she wasn't looking though, I threw it into the fire. It wouldn't burn. It put the fire out."

L ISSIE had four more children," said Mr. Hal, staring into the remains of his coffee, which had long been cold, "but three of them died while they were still in babyhood. I delivered all of them, though none of them were mine. One was a little boy, the child of that picture taker I mentioned. It died before its second birthday. One was by some other lover she had, and the last two were by your great-uncle Rafe. They started out healthy enough, but only a son by Rafe made it to being grown—your uncle Cornelius, who was killed while on duty in the navy. And Lulu was always healthy as she could be from the minute she was born. Lissie never wanted anybody but me to deliver her babies, just like she didn't want anybody but me to be their daddy. I wanted to be with her, too. I got to the place I loved delivering her babies, and I loved the babies themselves. We developed what you could call an understanding. But before we reached it, we had, both of us, shed rivers of pain.

"A month after Lulu was born, Lissie was all over me. 'What's the matter?' she asked. 'Don't you love me no more?' (I guess you've noticed that both me and Lissie can talk the old way or the new when the mood strikes us.) Seem like to me I loved her more than ever. Too much to risk putting her in that kind of pain again. 'Ah, even fucking hurt sometime,' she said, when I told her how I felt, 'but if it gets real good, you soon get over it.' 'What?' I asked. Never in a million years had I thought it ever hurt her; though I have to say I did wonder sometimes why it didn't hurt women generally. Some of them are so small, and their menfolks so huge. 'Look,' she say, 'we got Lulu, we got this wonderful little baby girl that looks just like Fadpa. I thank God for every pain!' She was rubbing herself all around me, putting her hands on places she used to control. Now, nothing happened. Well, she knew a thing or two about eunuchs and what they can do, and she knew from experience that I could still love her if I had the desire—trouble was, I didn't have the desire. It was like everything between a man and a woman that had anything at all to do with creating new life just scared me limp. I didn't even want to see her naked. I didn't want to see myself. I felt ashamed. How other men could keep beating up on their wives with more and more births of babies was beyond me. It wasn't beyond Lissie. She wanted more fucking and more babies, too, and the more I said no, the hotter and madder she got.

"Finally one day she run off with the picture taker from Charleston and left me with Lulu. She came back just before their baby, Jack, was born. I never said a word to nobody. Everybody knowed it wasn't mine. I didn't call Eula and I didn't call that hellion Granny Dorcy. I heated the water and laid in the Vaseline. Jack was born fast, just slipped out of Lissie smooth as anything. By that time I had learned a thing or two from Dorcy, and so I had Lissie squat down, holding on to the bars of Lulu's crib, and I caught the baby as it came out behind her. She was sick, though, Lissie. Weak from slaving in some white woman's house, poor food, and being pregnant by a man she felt like she wanted to kill. He was married, you see. Had a bunch of children already, the dog. But Lissie was fed up with me and hot for him. Then, you see, trying to get back at me for losing feeling for her made her even sicker than she already was.

"She came back to our bed, her and Jack. 'Cause old Lulu wasn't giving up her crib. And we picked up our life as best we could—fishing, selling produce and whatnot in the store. I sometimes helped my father make furniture. He was crabby and hard to get along with, but I loved him and I knew he loved me; as long as I didn't try to paint, I was all right with him. I don't think he cared much for Lissie, but she didn't mind. She always spoke up big to people who didn't like her and she didn't like either, just to shame them. And she'd give him a mess of fish or a pie just to watch him stammer over his thanks. She was a devil with some people. While my daddy stammered, she would look at him big-eyed and innocent and laugh. Lissie tried to help out in the shop, but my daddy claimed women got in the way. So she stopped that, and instead she sewed and looked after the children, and went out fishing in the bay. They were sweet, happy children, but our house was sad. We seemed to just be going through the motions of living; and even though we loved each other with true devotion, we knew we had lost something precious. The grief we felt was almost too hard to bear. Sometimes, beaten, she'd creep into my arms, or I would creep into hers, and the two of us would just lay together, look out over the bay, and remember how it used to be and cry.

"Your uncle Rafe was my best friend. He had gone into the army, come out, and worked for the old widower, a Frenchman, who owned this house. He was able to buy the house when the old man died, and he was always telling me I ought to come stay with him. This was before he got the job on the railroad, and he was working in a slaughterhouse. It was a terrible job for someone like your uncle, so fastidious and so, you know, mild, but he was big and strong and somehow managed to tough it out for a couple of years. He wasn't about to risk losing the house—the only thing up to then he'd ever cared a whole lot about. Then, too, the Depression was coming on strong. On the Island, cash money had all but disappeared. Times were hard. There was a lot of sickness among the children, caused by a lack of quality food. We lost little Jack to a cold a healthier baby would have shaken off. I was up night after night with the little fellow. He looked just like his mother, and it was hard for us to let him go. I thought Lissie was going to die herself, she loved him so. After he died, we left our little house and left the Island—it was too sad to stay—but only for a little while, we thought; and we took Rafe up on his invitation and went to stay with him. Lissie and Lulu and me had the top floor, and I got a job as a door-to-door huckster. I peddled fish and crab and oysters. In the summers it was peaches and melons. In the rich white neighborhoods of Baltimore, where times never seemed to get very hard. In fact, for the stable rich, you know, hard times just mean cheaper prices, and so they just get great bargains on everything and do better than ever.

"Finally, and not a minute too soon, for he was sick of so much death, and he said the blood from the slaughterhouse stayed under his fingernails, and that would *not* do, Rafe got the job as sleeping-car porter. Lissie took in sewing and worked in private homes as a domestic, and with all our pay pooled together, we managed. This was a white neighborhood then, like it's becoming again now, but there were two houses on our block that had Spanish-looking people who were probably gangsters living in them. One of these houses was just across the street from us, and the other was next door. The men would speak to us as pleasantly as could be, and so we weren't too afraid of them, even though they did make a habit of sitting on their stoops in shirtsleeves, breaking down, cleaning, and reassembling their sizable collection of guns. I think it was their presence that kept the really white people from trying to run us out. They'd pitched a fit when the old Frenchman died and his niece let Rafe buy the house. She lived in France, anyway, and liked Rafe. Really liked him, if you know what I mean. What did she know or care about 'crazy American race prejudice,' as she called it, in an accent that did make it sound like the silliest thing. And then, too, Rafe was willing to pay more for the house than any white person would.

"No doubt the neighbors thought the house too fine for 'niggers.' And really we *were* there illegally. I don't think black people were allowed in that part of town back then. But we were so discreet they hardly ever saw us. We never sat or stood on the front lawn, or sat on our stoop; it just didn't exist for us as part of the house. There was an alley behind the house, and we always went in the back way. But soon another house was sold to lightbright blacks, and another. They didn't like us either—we were dark compared to them—but we said to hell with them and began to be able to relax a little bit. We kept it spotless, this house, the grass clipped and the hedges trimmed. In the early years we worked on the grass and hedges at night. It was nicer than anything we'd ever dreamed of living in.

"Lissie liked Rafe a lot, and he liked her and Lulu. I thought the world of Rafe, and I believe he felt the same about me. I remember telling him all about Lissie and me. I wasn't embarrassed or afraid he'd misunderstand. He was curious about our relationship, because in his house she and I slept in separate rooms. She slept in the back bedroom overlooking the yard and I slept in the front room that faced the street, with the baby. Lulu, I mean.

"All the passion I'd had for her mother went into my love of Lulu, and from a little teeny baby she could wrap me around her finger. I doted on that child. Lissie was a good mother, but aloof. She didn't seem to be present for the child. Always off somewhere roaming through the ages. She started seeing the photographer fellow again, not to sleep with—she hated him in that way—but to model for him. He couldn't understand how different she could look from picture to picture; he said sometimes he couldn't even believe the picture he'd taken was of Lissie, and just to punish him she never told him anything. He was the kind of ego-bound person who wouldn't have been able to hear or believe her if she had. She was excited about how each picture would turn out, and I eventually understood that God had managed, with photography, to show Lissie she was right to think she was as many women as she thought she was. It was a big load off her mind to know she wasn't crazy.

"Life is very different when you have a good friend. I've seen people without special friends, close friends. Other men, especially. For some reason men don't often make and keep friends. This is a real tragedy, I think, because in a way, without a tight male friend, you never really are able to see yourself. That is because part of shaping ourselves is done by others; and a lot of our shaping comes from that one close friend who is something like us. It was real special between Rafe and me. I was the homebody, the married husband and father, the painter. Quiet. Needing Lissie to lead me by the hand. He was even physically different from me: larger and taller, and darker, too. I admired him all my life. He was such a bachelor! No woman ever got next to Rafe for longer than a couple of weeks. He'd go at it hot and heavy for a few evenings—but always came home to wind up the night in his own bed—and then one day I'd ask when or whether he was going out and he'd say no. 'No, Bro.' And he'd laugh. I'd be glad, secretly, because it meant he'd be home with us. Lissie would make something especially nice for dinner; I would be sure we had a good fire going. And Lissie, Rafe, Lulu, and I would settle in the living room after dinner for an evening of cards and listening to records, of which your uncle always had the latest, because he was a wonderful dancer, too, along with everything else.

"Sometimes I think he would fancy himself too heartsick over his most recent ladylove to enjoy himself with us; then he would settle himself in his room—he had the big bedroom then—and read dime novels while propped up in bed. Rafe was one for dressing gowns and slippers, and I remember he had a fancy blue-and-white kimono, silk, that he said came from Japan. He was elegant! He pomaded his hair, shaped not only his mustache but his eyebrows, too, and he smoked clove cigarettes. No, he wasn't a fairy; just a man of distinction! He had a Victrola in his bedroom and pictures of several of his lady friends on the mantel, and he'd put on something highly suggestive and melancholy to listen to, and he'd smoke and read and drink the evening away. By morning he'd be cured of *that* particular lady friend, and if it was his day off, he'd be ready to play with Lulu.

"Next to her mama and me, Lulu loved her uncle Rafe. At times I thought she loved him better than us. He was shaved and dressed just so every time she saw him, for she wasn't allowed in his rooms. The three of us were extremely careful of his privacy. Often we wouldn't know whether he was home—there would be no sound whatsoever from his floor. And then Lulu would get to dragging her feet as she passed to and fro before his bedroom door, and pretty soon she would say she heard her uncle Rafe gargling.

"We could have moved, but it was pleasant and felt like family being at Rafe's. In a house where two men cared for her, Lissie recovered from the weakness that followed the loss of baby Jack. She recovered her strength and style, and began to put on a little weight. I could see she was coming into a bloom of womanhood that almost stopped your breath. *Ripeness.* Her eyes took on greater depth from her sadness; her mouth curved in a smile that still held a little hint of the timelessness of pain. Even her brow struck me as somehow humbled, and because of that I found myself touching it more often, brushing back her hair, smoothing out her eyebrows. But the most engaging thing now was the way she talked. It made you think of water, so soft and gentle, but sometimes you also heard the rapids. She laughed more, too, a knowledgeable laughter. There was in her voice and in her laughter a sound that moved me so much: the sound of acceptance of her lot, and . . . the sound of gratitude.

"Lissie had forgiven me, because she had understood. She loved me still, but she had let go. And she was grateful to be alive and yet have all she did have. She had me and Lulu and Rafe, for instance.

"She threw herself as much as she could, considering her built-in distractions, into mothering Lulu, who was a born tomboy that kept Lissie running after her. She cared for me the way she always had. She kept encouraging me to paint, and she found a place where my work could be sold to tourists in downtown Baltimore. I wasn't using house paint anymore, but watercolors and oils, and this was heaven to me. She also encouraged me to take night classes in English and botany that were offered at the new colored high school. The English made it easier for me to talk to people who didn't always understand the English we spoke on the Island, and the botany improved the way I drew plants.

"Years later there were friends of ours who guessed what might have happened. Friends who recognized the resemblance of our son Anatole—named after the old Frenchman—to Rafe. I know they pitied me. No doubt they thought Lissie and Rafe were having an affair behind my back. This was not the case.

"It had been years since I made love to Lissie, so long I

never thought about it or hardly remembered it had been possible. We still enjoyed each other's company. We might shop together or walk with Lulu to her school. We might hug or hold hands, but we'd always done that. We were back, in fact, where we started with each other as children, before Lissie really began to notice your uncle Rafe. Notice him as a man, you know.

"Looking back, I can see it was bound to happen. Both Lissie and Rafe were knockouts. When the three of us dressed up to go out to a party, even little Lulu went *oooo!* at the two of them. They had flamboyance. Both of them loved clothes, and Lissie liked to be a different woman for every ball. She loved things like sequins, baubles that sparkled, and shawls with tassels and fringe. Rafe liked his white silk shirts, shiny dress slippers, and fur-collared coat. He was the kind of Negro who, when he dressed up to go out, carried calfskin gloves *and* a silver-headed cane. He fancied himself a rogue, and to the extent that he could pull off his adventures before about two o'clock in the morning, when he just had to be home snug in his own bed, he was.

"Actually, he was a proper match for Lissie."

L AST night I dreamed I was showing you my temple," said Miss Lissie. "I don't know where it was, but it was a simple square one-room structure, very adobe or Southwestern-looking, with poles jutting out at the ceiling line and the windows set in deep. It was painted a rich dust coral and there were lots of designs—many, turquoise and deep blue, like Native American symbols for rain and storm—painted around the top. It was beautiful, though small, and I remembered going there for the ceremonies dressed in a long white cotton robe. I was tall then, and stately, with thick black hair that I wore in a bun. The other thing my temple made me think of was the pyramids in Mexico, though I'm satisfied it wasn't made of stone but of painted mud.

"Anyway, my familiar—what you might these days, unfortunately, call a 'pet'—was a small, incredibly beautiful creature that was part bird, for it was feathered, part fish, for it could swim and had a somewhat fish/bird shape, and part reptile, for it scooted about like geckoes do, and it was all over the place while I talked to you. Its movements were graceful and clever, its expression mischievous and full of humor. It was *alive!* You, by the way, Suwelo were a white man, apparently, in that life, very polite, very well-to-do, and seemingly very interested in our ways.

"My little familiar, no bigger than my hand, slithered and skidded here and there in the place outside the temple where we sat. Its predominant color was blue, but there was red and green, and flecks of gold and cerise. And purple. Yes. Its head was that of a bird. Did I say that already?

"Skittering about the way that it did was so distracting while we talked that I took it up into my hands and carried it some distance from us and placed it on the ground with a clear-glass bowl over it. As soon as I'd come back and sat down, however, I heard a noise like a muffled shot. I went over to the bowl, and, sure enough, the familiar had broken through. There was a small hole in the top. I looked about and found another bowl, a heavy white one, very slick and with very thick sides. My familiar was lying looking up at me curiously, resting up from its labor. It did not try to run as I put this white bowl on top of it. Almost before I sat down I heard another noise. When I went back, my familiar was rushing furiously about in the snow. Everything was suddenly now very cold. It was as beautiful as ever though, my familiar. How or even why I would do what I next did is beyond me, but I think it was a stupid reflex of human pride. For I understood quite well by now that all of this activity on the familiar's part was about freedom, and that by my actions I was destroying our relationship. In any event, not to be outdone—and suddenly there were dozens of your people, white people, standing about watching this contest—I next imprisoned my beautiful little familiar under a metal washtub. I paid little attention to the coldness or the snow and did not even think how cruel and torturous for it this would be. Surely it would not now be able to escape. I went back to where we were seated, you and I, and attempted to carry on with our conversation, which was about temples, and about my temple in particular. The sun was just setting, and it bathed the small, shiny coral structure in gold. It was a splendid sight. I felt such happiness that it was mine and I thought of the peace that came over me, deep, like sleep, when I entered its doors.

"Next we heard a rumbling, as if from a volcano, under our seats. As if power was being sucked along in streams from everywhere and converging at one spot under the snow. All of us, you, me, the white people dressed so strangely in high heels and fur coats, were drawn to the quaking washtub, which seemed now to be on the bottom steps of an enormous white stone building in a different city and a different century. We could not believe that a small creature, no larger than a hand, could break through metal with its fragile birdlike head. We gazed in amazement as, with a mighty whoosh, and as if from the very depths of the sea, the little familiar broke through the bottom of the tub and out into the open air. It looked at me with pity as it passed. Then, using wings it had never used before, it flew away. And I was left with only you and the rest of your people on the steps of a cold stone building, the color of cheap false teeth, in a different world from my own, in a century that I would never understand. Except by remembering the beautiful little familiar, who was so cheerful and loyal to me, and whom I so thoughtlessly, out of pride and distraction, betrayed."

"THERE were flies everywhere." That is what Arveyda told Carlotta about the place where she was born.

"And what do you think?" he asked.

She didn't know what to think. Arveyda was back, but not her mother. She tried not to think of Zedé.

"They were shooting a film there! In *Guatuzocan!*" he said.

Carlotta had never heard the name.

"It was about an ancient Indian goddess," he continued, "tall and blonde, like Bo Derek, who falls in love with a modern white anthropologist who had stumbled through a cave entrance and into the prehistoric era in which the goddess lived. It was very funny once you understood there was nothing you could do about it but laugh. Your mother found one of her old friends, a woman who looked a hundred years old, though she was no older than Zedé, and they sat under a tree watching the production of the movie most of the day. Her friend, Hidae, very dark and very wrinkled, had been hired as an extra and represented the ancient ignorant Indians from whom the smart blonde 'Indian goddess,' apparently an albino, had sprung. They were in stitches over how the goddess was dressed. In a bikini made of the pigeon feathers that are sold to the tourists. And fingernail polish and lipstick that looked like blood. On her head she was required to wear a colossal headdress, and in this headdress there were fleas. The goddess scratched her head, fanned flies, drooped from the humidity and boredom, grew sallow from the bologna sandwiches, and watched the white anthropologist steal all her people's treasures without lifting a finger, because . . . she loved him!

"But it was a job. I mean, for Zedé and her friend and for the others in the village. Because Zedé spoke English, she got a job on the production crew. She translated. The prison the place had been when you and your mother were there had indeed become a village. Or I should say had become once again a village, since it had been a village that belonged to your father's people, los indios. As in Australia, where convicts eventually became a country, the guards and slaves who had been settled in Guatuzocan to grow papaya had become a village.

"Only Hidae and six others remained of the slaves your mother had known. The rest had succumbed to the poor food, hard work, the heat and jungle diseases, plus the terrorism of the guards. Most of the women who'd borne children for their captors were dead, but their captors were not. They raped each new batch of slaves and made slave wives of the ones they preferred, ignoring the old and battered ones for whom they no longer felt lust. These women produced children. This placed the guards in the curious position of being masters over their own and each other's offspring, and where there used to be harmony in their power over so many helpless people, now there was hatred and disgust. Each captor, you see, inevitably begat a favorite son, and this son he did not want either to acknowledge or to have mistreated by any other person in authority other than himself. Then, too, there was the inevitable rape of his daughters by buddies trained not to care about her resemblance to him. Sometimes he did not recognize it himself. A hell.

"The papaya fields were yielding good crops, and the money from their sale poured in to the plantation owners from Europe and North America; the work continued hard, though it was not as horrendous as the clearing of the jungle and the planting of the trees had been. At first it puzzled us why the movie-production company was making a movie about pregringo historic Indian life in the middle of an enormous, modern, rigidly rowed papaya plantation. But when Zedé asked the movie director, he pointed out that he was making a non-stereotyped, progressive movie about the Indians, something very unusual for Americans to do; the plantation showed that the Indians had been not lazy at all, but industrious, even from earliest times. 'So there!' your mother said, when she reported this to me and the other wrinkled Indians. And we all laughed.

"The captors and the captives found themselves to be something like a family, and the children born in the village grew up in the gray area of believing themselves half-slave and half-free. They understood neither the contempt in which their fathers held their mothers nor their fathers' deep fear of these women who were so helpless; nor did they understand the bottomless hatred their mothers felt for their fathers, whose missions of rape among the women became ever more camouflaged as affection as the bastard offspring began to grow. The earliest memories of these offspring were of the muffled screams of their mothers, and the scraping of what they thought must be their mothers' backbones against the floor."

"It does not matter if you love me or not," said Arveyda. "Perhaps I don't deserve even to see you or my children. But I want to give you the gift of knowing your mother—which I don't think you would have without me, because she couldn't tell you herself; she was too ashamed—and I want to give to you exactly what I wish someone could give to me, and what, since my mother is dead, no one ever can."

Carlotta felt she hated men; their disappearances and their absences and their smugness on return. She thought of the foolish Angel Clare and saw herself as Tess. She thought of Tea Cake and saw herself as Janie. She was convinced Helga Crane was a fool. She decided the only man in all of life and literature worth her admiration was Leonard Woolf. But of course she and her class had not yet started to read his *A Village in the Jungle*. Perhaps she shouldn't hold her breath.

Arveyda had wanted to tell her about Zedé somewhere outside under trees. Outside in the open air. If you can see all of the sky, no message, not even from someone who despises you, can destroy you. But Carlotta sat in her cheaply furnished living room, arms folded, slim legs crossed. She was not hearing him. She could not make sense of what he said. It was as if they were both drunk. Besides, a funny Roadrunner cartoon was on and the children were clapping their hands and laughing.

In this atmosphere, Arveyda stopped speaking. He looked at his children lying on the floor ignoring him. He did not blame them. Who was he, this man who had deserted them, after all? Besides, it seemed important to them to see whether the Roadrunner would make it to where it was headed after so many cruel attempts on its life.

When the cartoon was finished, Arveyda, over their outraged objections, turned off the TV. He carefully closed the wooden doors of its cabinet, and taking his guitar from where he'd set it behind the front door, he seated himself in front of it, in a straight chair from the kitchen. He began to tune the guitar, as his children, glaring at him and faking yawns, huddled on the sofa with their mother. They looked at him as if at an intruder. He plucked the strings of the guitar. Its old name was Selume, in ancient African divination, the bone or rune denoting youth. He felt he must, after all his travels, think of something new.

He had an idea.

"Do you have the three little stones your mother gave you?" he asked Carlotta.

At first she did not answer. She was thinking how she hated him and then trying to remember three little stones Zedé had given her and then trying to remember where they were.

"Will you get them?" Somehow he did not doubt they would be produced.

Maybe they contain diamonds and rubies at their core, Carlotta thought, annoyed at her own docility, as she left the room.

Her dresser drawers were neat and orderly, as usual. She really had no trouble finding the three small rocks. They were always kept in a straight line at the back of the lingerie drawer. She took them up and returned to the living room.

Arveyda put out his hand, and she dropped the rocks into it.

He leaned over his guitar and put the rocks on the floor, not in a straight line, but in the shape of a pyramid.

"That is the way they belong, like the symbol for a fallout shelter," he said. "They are a gift to you from your father and his people."

This sounded pretty meaningless, actually, not to say bizarre. Carlotta's mind drifted. She wondered how it was she hadn't lost them; she'd never kept them in the bag Zedé made for them. Somehow she must have thought of the plain little rocks as her jewels and wanted them on display. She'd kept them on view on top of her dresser when she was growing up. "These are muy especial," Zedé had said, touching them with emotion at night when she came into Carlotta's room and tucked her into bed. "These stones have meaning for you." But she'd never told her what the meaning was.

Arveyda was experiencing something amazing as he sat over the stones, beginning to strum his guitar. He knew, he finally knew, why he was capable of falling in love so easily, even with his own wife's mother. It was because he was a musician, and an artist. Artists, he now understood, were simply messengers. On them fell the responsibility for uniting the world. An awesome task, but he felt up to it, in his own life. His faith must be that the pain he brought to others and to himself—so poorly concealed in the information delivered—would lead not to destruction, but to transformation.

He began to sing ever so gently, to his wife and children. A song about a country that wore green as its favorite dress; a land of rivers and of boats that from a distance made one think of the pods of dried vanilla beans. He sang of the people who came to this country long ago, from a land called Sun, how they'd discovered the river that flows through the ocean—and knew also of the one that flows through the heavens but had no means to travel it—and of how they met the people already there and how some of them ran off together to share each other's understanding of the world, and founded great civilizations almost by accident, though great civilizations never notice or boast about whether they are great; and how, over time, these fell, and the people went off in all directions and lived the simple life of small peoples everywhere. Hunting and fishing and praying and making love and having babies. He sang of the red parrot feathers in their ears—for they had brought the parrot with them; it was their familiar, symbolic of their essence—and the long rough hair that made a pillow for their heads. He sang of the coming of the enslavers and the cruel fate of the enslaved. He sang of two people who loved for a moment and of one of them who died, horribly, with nothing to leave behind but his seed that became a child, and some red parrot-feather earrings and three insignificant stones. He sang of the confusion and the terror of the mother: the scars she could never reveal to the child because they still hurt her so. The love for the child's wild father, a bitter truncheon stuck in her throat.

The children had long been asleep by the time Arveyda came to the part Carlotta most wanted to hear. Arveyda sang softly of how much the mother, far away still, loved and missed the child. How grieved she was that she had hurt her. How she prayed the child would forgive her and one day consent to see her again. He sang of how the mother missed her grandchildren. He sang of the danger the mother was in now in her old country because, working with the gringo movie-production crew as a front, she was trying to find her own mother, whom she had not seen since the soldiers came to her poor little escuela de los indios many, many years ago and dragged her away. This was the only reason she was not this moment embracing her hija, if her hija would only permit it. He sang of Zedé's courage, of her pride in not burdening her child with an unbearable history. He sang of her true humbleness. He sang until Zedé, small and tentative, was visible, a wisp, before her daughter.

Carlotta had not dreamed her numbed heart could be broken still more, or that breaking the heart opens it.

Arveyda was back. Yes. Singing as never before. Carlotta could see that now he would need neither feathers nor cloak.

Under her piercing, tear-filled gaze Arveyda closed his eyes, so as to ask nothing for himself. He knew he was singing for their lives. A true artist, the one whom God shows, he knew he dared not doubt the power of his song.

*E*CSTASY *Is Uncut Forest and the Smell of Fresh-Baked Bread.* Suwelo strained to hear the warm, lush music over the telephone, between the icy bars of Fanny's words. That is what she is still listening to, he thought, surprised. That old album of Arveyda's. She must have bought a new one after she moved out; the one they'd bought together was one long groove scratch. She'd worn it out playing it. And he remembered how she held the record album to her chest, an album on which there was nothing but a large redwood tree, with a loaf of bread beneath it, and how she swayed in rapture to every note, and how she sometimes became so filled with the sweetness of the music that she cried. And he had watched her as she tottered and danced and wept. The music carried her higher, he thought, than anything else in her life. It was all ecstasy to her.

And once, when Arveyda came to town to play a concert, he'd bought tickets for them. Finally they would see him. And at first Fanny had been very happy, and he'd laughed at her fumble-fingered excitement as she dressed. All her best things. Everything shades of lavender, deep indigo, and gentian. How beautiful she is, he'd thought.

"You might get a glimpse of him," Suwelo had teased. "He'll be onstage, and the tickets I bought should get us good seats. But he won't be able to see you except as a pinhead in the audience." She'd laughed, dousing herself with a perfume she made that smelled amazingly like fresh water.

But then, just as they were leaving the flat, just as they were entering the hallway, she stopped, and nothing he said would induce her to go further. When he took her arm, she appeared to be rooted to the spot. When he pretended to drag her, she clung to the door frame with a force that broke one of her nails.

She was afraid to see the person who created the beauty that was so much what her soul hungered for it made her weep.

Suwelo vaguely understood this, but he was also annoyed, because now he'd miss the concert—though she begged him to go ahead and take someone else. And he'd spent quite a lot of money on the tickets.

"Isn't Arveyda old?" she asked hopefully. (He wasn't.) "I'll wait until he dies, or until *I* do, and then . . . I will see him."

And what could Suwelo respond to such a love, constricted by a so much greater fatalism and fear?

"Oh, my poor baby," he'd said with exasperation and helplessness, holding her, knowing without seeing her face that tears of longing were flowing down her cheeks.

THE first time he saw Carlotta, what had he thought? Fanny had accused him of seeing only the amber skin and the long mass of black hair. The shapeliness. A woman of color, yes, but one without the kind of painful past that would threaten his sense of himself as a man or inhibit his enjoyment of her as simply a woman. But actually, he had these thoughts later on, after he had begun his affair with Carlotta. The very first time he saw her, at a faculty meeting at which she appeared restless and trapped, he'd thought she looked like a much younger, Latina Coretta King. There was a picture somewhere he had seen of Mrs. King, looking grief-stricken and betrayed, a beautiful woman, he thought, but slipping inexorably into the quagmire of Famous Widowhood. Run, run, he'd wanted to shout to her. Don't let them close you up in the tomb! But perhaps this was partly how she felt, as if part of her was entombed with her husband. But surely there was more of her own life to live? Suwelo admired only one thing about Jackie Onassis, whose fate might have been similar, except for her canny refusal to let it be: her absolute success in slipping out from under her dead husband, Jack. In the picture of Mrs. King of which he was reminded, she was standing with a large group of Native

American women, and she looked more Indian than most of them. Carlotta, as he studied her, had that same grief-stricken, betrayed look. But as he studied her more closely, ignoring the other faculty members, who were white, and whose university he understood it was, the more he saw that it was really not the look of Mrs. King. Or perhaps it was, but it moved him because he had seen it, felt the pain of it, and attempted to remove it from the weeping face of someone much closer to home: He was attracted to Carlotta because the expression on her face was identical to that on Fanny's once she knew he had betrayed her. He had spent the entire time he was with Carlotta trying to remove the reflection, on her face, of Fanny's grief. Without once daring, however, to force her to tell him its cause. Once he knew she was separated from her husband, with two children to raise on her own, once he'd seen her shabbily furnished apartment, and once he'd heard her bitter complaints about the racism of the Women's Studies Department in which she worked, he assumed he understood her grief. Now he realized he'd probably understood nothing, and it also occurred to him what a superficial, ultimately fraudulent act it was to sleep with a person you did not really know.

He began to appreciate more than ever the story Mr. Hal and Miss Lissie were relentlessly telling him.

MY FATHER was not so gay as my mother," Mr. Hal said. "She was all the time laughing; giggling really. She just couldn't help it. Everything was funny to her. Over my daddy's head, though, there was always a cloud. Now you might not want to believe this, but you do live in California, after all. I read the newspapers from time to time, so I know that a lot of the men who go with other men are dying. Every time I read about it I think of my father, because I think he would have been glad. He was not an evil person—don't get me wrong—but he just hated that kind of person and that was the only kind of person I ever heard him express any hatred of. Even about white people in general he never carried on the way he would about 'funny' men. While he was on his death-bed himself, he told me why.

"He grew up on the Island on a plantation that was owned by some white folks from the mainland and run by a black overseer. This wasn't slavery time—the slaves had been legally freed a long time ago—but it seemed a lot like it, the way things were still being run. Anyhow, on some holidays like Christmas and Easter and always during the summer, these white people came out to their place on the Island. It was cooler on the Island in summer, much more pleasant than on the mainland.

They'd sail over on their yacht—they were rich people—and bring everybody from the house on the mainland: the cook, the maids, the horse handler, even the gardeners. My father used to work for them as odd jobber and gofer, and he used to help unload the yacht, and they paid him in oranges, which we almost never had on the Island and which were the taste equivalent of gold. Anyhow, these people had a son, Heath, and he began to tag along with my father. The two boys liked each other right away, but it chafed my father that he always had to stay in his place. Heath had the run of my father's house, for instance, and during the summers would often eat there, right in the kitchen with the rest of them, but my father, whose name was David, by the way, after little David in the Bible, could never get closer to Heath's house than the back doorsteps. If you were black and you didn't work in the house, you weren't permitted. That's just the way it was.

"Heath's father and mother seemed cordial with each other rather than warm, and neither of them talked much to Heath. Still, the father seemed glad that Heath and my father were friends; the mother never appeared to notice it. She drank.

"Heath and my father were boyhood friends, seeing each other for holidays and summers, for many years. Then Heath went off to college and my father married. Eventually Heath also married, and he and his wife came to settle on the Island in the big house that Heath loved and that now belonged to him through his parents. My father was happy enough in his marriage. I don't know that he ever expected any kind of skyrockets from it. On the Island you married young, you raised a mess of kids, you and your family worked hard, you ate and slept and worshiped as well as you could. You died. That was about it. And that was plenty to most people. Excitement? The stories and rumors you heard about other people, way over there on the mainland, was your excitement.

"Having Heath around again and for good was exciting,

and as well as they could manage it, now that they were more than ever unequal in the eyes of society and the law — in other words, they were grown men — they carried on their friendship. Heath, though, had started to drink, and he really didn't like black people. He was one of those whites who, drunk, would say to a black person he had his arm around: 'You know, So-and-so, I don't like nigras, but I like you!' So you can imagine how this so-called friendship between him and my father had to walk that fine line between anger and fear. Naturally my father hated Heath's racism. Just as he feared him as a white man, even as they laughed and joked together. My father had no idea — and I don't think Heath himself knew — that Heath was drawn to him in love. I mean love of that most peculiar kind. It was an understanding that sort of crept up on them both, I imagine, as they saw how much time Heath put in at our house, and how much he and my father, in spite of everything, enjoyed it.

"I can even remember him. A heavyset, stocky, rather than fat, red-faced guy, with his high color sometimes seeming to come and go in his face. Hair that bleached almost white in the sun. Substantial teeth and a minty breath. A Teddy Roosevelt sort of guy.

"It was Heath who encouraged my father to get out of farm laboring and become a furniture maker. He'd seen and admired the things my father carved in his spare time: mostly toys and the children's beds and cradles. I don't think he could bear seeing his friend working in the fields like a slave. He didn't care about the rest of the people, you understand; he thought that working like slaves on his plantation was no more than they deserved. But not David, with his thoughtful expression and always pregnant wife and his houseful of barefoot kids. He helped my father build a shop and bought the very first pieces he made, a table and some chairs. He found a market for my father's work on the mainland, and we lived very well. Much better than we had on stoop labor, digging potatoes and picking beans.

"He wanted my father.

"Even on his deathbed this was a hard concept—no joke meant—for my father to get ahold of. It was curious, too, how no matter what words he found to tell me about the situation, they always made me laugh. Even he was finally able to laugh, a hollow cackle though it was. He wasn't laughing at Heath, but at this possibility of a way of life that just seemed totally out of the realm of nature to him. Two men together, like a man and a woman? It was just too much. What would my father have made of San Francisco?

"The long and short of it is, the friendship was soon ruined. There was nowhere for any of their best feelings about each other to go. They couldn't even sit down at a hot-dog stand somewhere to discuss the problem. They would have been arrested just for that. Heath became more drunken, nigger-hating, and sullen. He talked a lot about how his father had treated him as a boy, ridiculing and beating him for being slow to understand things said to him and slow to learn to read. He spoke of this to explain his ability to understand how 'the nigras felt,' but what it really seemed to explain was why he so often tried to make those he knew feel as bad as he'd once felt himself. Around him, my father retreated into what he called his old-time know-nothing niggerisms. Scratching his head and muttering under his breath. 'Feelin' like a damn fool.' And of course you realize he called him 'Mr. Heath' from the time they were in their teens. But my father's pretense of ignorance did not protect him. One day Heath came into the shop, and before my father knew anything he was being hugged drunkenly and, as he put it, 'cried on from behind.' My father felt pretty safe, though, because he could see my mother and some of the children playing a few yards away from the open door. Heath had been drinking heavily and fighting with his wife. It would soon blow over. It always did. My father would make coffee, lay on an ice pack, and scramble up something for Heath to eat. But this time, maybe because my father felt so safe, he really let himself feel the weeping body draped around him. Let himself feel the misery and feel the shame. Maybe he felt the love. Anyway, without ever dreaming it was possible, and looking down at himself as if someone had stuck a stick up his pants leg while he wasn't looking, he responded to Heath, who had begun to fondle him.

"It was a moment that changed his life. Without understanding how it could be possible, my father wanted to be wanted by this man holding on to him, and he wanted to want. He says he saw my mother through the door and called to her, but his voice was so weak it didn't carry. Then, a few minutes later, as if she felt something was wrong, and he was in trouble, she started briskly toward the door herself. Heath, caressing my father and feeling his response, watched my mother approach, over my father's shoulder, and said, 'Tell her not to come in.' Which my father did.

"He was never the same person after that. He was gloomy. He seldom smiled. He continued to see Heath, though, and I can still remember the sullen bitterness of the fights they had. Fights that were full of a few well-chosen cruel and cutting words, and much drinking. Because, with time, my father drank as much as Heath. Whenever my father read about a lynching of a black man by whites and that they'd cut off the man's privates and stuck them in his mouth, he said he understood the real reason why. Whether he ever did so or not, I'm sure this is something he must have wanted to shout at Mr. Heath. That he understood there was something of a sexual nature going on in any lynching.

"For the rest of his life he hated anything he thought was gay. He detested art, and the carvings by which he made his living he eventually did with disgust. He was the perfect carver for the heavy barbarous furniture that became the rage during that period before the Great War. His carved lions were snarling, his griffins were biting, his ravens were shrieking. Claws and teeth and drops of blood were everywhere. The stuff made me shudder as a child, and my mother failed to find in it anything to encourage her famous giggle, but white people bought it; pretty soon, black people did, too. It appeared even in the houses of poor people right there on the Island. Generally they liked their furniture and everything else to be straightforward and simple; God only knows what they really thought of it.

"My father hated my painting. It made him think there was something wrong with me. All my life he tried to keep me from doing it. When Heath finally died, of a heart attack, my father, the only black person permitted at the funeral, was still bitter. My mother, generally merry to the last, never acted as though she knew anything about any of this, beyond the fact that Heath was a nice if drunken white man that liked her husband, David, and sometimes ate dinner—which he always praised—at our house.

"My father wouldn't have cared if the plague killed off all the gays in the world. He hated Heath because Heath had forced him to look at the little bit of Heath there was in himself. Nobody had prepared him for that vision. Nor could he pretend he hadn't seen it. I've often thought of the battle my father must have had with himself when Heath was embracing him in the shop. What happened to him that day remained a burden on his soul. He died many unhappy years later of liver failure. There was a terrible smell, so terrible that painting over the old paint on his walls wasn't enough. After he died, we had to scrape the paint off the walls, and burn it, then paint the bare

walls many times to cover it up. This stench, I felt, must be the
rotten smell of that part of my father that he murdered and
tried to bury away from other people and from himself.

"When I told Lissie about my daddy's prejudice against
'funny' men and hatred of that part of himself, and told her
about what had happened that first time between him and
Heath, the first thing she said was that my father had been
treated like a woman; that was one of the reasons he felt so bad;
and that the way he had responded only made him feel worse.
His whole existence was compromised by what was happening,
yet he could not prevent an erotic response. She also said he
was wrong to think queers are unnatural. She said queers have
been in every century in which she found herself—and she giggled when she said it—and claimed to have seen queer behavior even among the cousins, always the epitome of moral behavior where Lissie was concerned. One of them, she claimed,
not only taught her *how* to dress, but *to* dress."

A T LAST, one day, Suwelo had a story for his friends. They sat down for tea and cookies in the living room, and he began slowly, in a soft, rusty voice.

"She was in the back, in the garden, among the roses. It was a warm April evening, bright and clear as a day in fall, and there was nothing really in the garden to see. The rosebushes had already been pruned and the branches burned. And yet, when I think of that evening I see her among blooming roses, as she'd looked the summer before, brown and healthy, eyes bright and black, skin flushed, short hair curly and crisp as the day. She was wearing a long skirt, gaily printed, and a T-shirt. On her hands were gardening gloves, and she was trying to wrap part of a climbing rose cane back on its trellis.

"'Oh, Suwelo,' she said, when she noticed me on the walk near the back door, 'you're home.'

"She seemed glad of it. But did not rush to kiss me as she once had. I felt a pang at this, but hadn't really expected anything else. After all, we had been discussing a divorce for months now. I moved closer to where she strained to place the rose, and she moved backward a bit as I reached to help her. She was small and slight and *dark*, there in the sun, and I loved the smell of her, as always, something flowery and fresh that made me long to be able to hold her as easily and as carelessly as I once had.

"I remember this evening so well because once again she brought up the subject of the divorce.

"'It isn't about not loving you,' she said. 'I will always love you. Probably.' She smiled at me. 'But I don't want to be married.'

"This was not a new statement. What she said next was. 'You will find another woman right away, or, rather, one will find you. You'll see.'

"'I don't want another woman,' I said.

"'It won't matter,' she said. 'You'll be that rarest of all quantities: black, free, gainfully employed. You'll be snapped up in no time.'

"We were having dinner by then. She was not what anyone would call a great cook, but she was certainly a good one. In an hour she'd broiled pork chops with garlic and rosemary, the way I like them, made a salad, and steamed rice. All the while, I sat at the kitchen table watching her.

"'The only problem with that,' she said, frowning at her plate and adding more salt, 'is that she'll be jealous.'

"'What?' I said. 'What *are* you talking about. *She'll* be jealous. Who'll be jealous? Of what?'

"'*She*,' she said. 'The new wife. She'll be jealous of me. You see, I don't want to end our relationship; I want to change it. I don't want to be married. Not to you, not to anybody. But I don't want to lose you either.'

"'Well,' I said, 'you can't have your cake and eat it too.'

"'But why not?' she asked, seriously. 'Say you are my cake. I want to enjoy you, to love you, to confide in you, to be your friend. Shit,' she said suddenly. 'It doesn't work. What do you suppose it means, have your cake and eat it too?'

" 'What it means for us is, you cannot have your way this time. If you love me, stay with me.'

" 'I'll stay,' she said. 'Most of the time. But unmarried. And on a separate floor.'

"I groaned. This is what I got for agreeing to buy a house with more than one floor.

" 'We were happier before we were married,' she said.

" '*Everybody's* happier before they're married.'

" 'Then why do they marry?' she asked.

" 'Because everything builds up to marriage. Don't say we haven't been happy married,' I said, almost angry. 'We've been very happy.'

" 'I don't feel free,' she said.

" 'When have you ever felt free?' I asked.

"She considered the question. 'You're right,' she said. 'I've never felt free, never in my life. And I want to.'

"At the office several of my colleagues said how sorry they were that we were breaking up. Ours was the last stable, apparently happy marriage they knew. Something in the way they offered condolences made me realize they considered the breakup Fanny's fault entirely. To a man they'd been polite to her but never liked her very much. And whenever she came to the office to see me before we went out to lunch together, she was cool, distant, never able to do much with small talk. And there was the way she dressed. The shorter the miniskirts on other men's wives, the longer her skirts. And she wore flowing scarves made of silk, and once, in conversation with one of the guys, carelessly mentioned her pipe. A pipe more for ornament than anything else, really. Bought to smoke grass in, it's true; because she could never learn to roll a cigarette; but then she smoked very little. However, certain things you don't talk about in your husband's office at a far from radical, not even liberal university, where every nonwhite instructor is already suspected of smoking dope, screwing students in the stairwells, and hiding submachine guns in his hair; and I brought this up with her.

"'Do I embarrass you?' she asked.

"'How could you embarrass me?' I said, leaning over the table to kiss her and holding her hand.

"'Freedom must mean never having (or being able) to embarrass anybody,' she said.

"And I ordered our lunch to save us from another discussion of *that* subject.

"It became harder and harder to talk with her the nearer separation approached. She begged me not to draw away.

"'It's marriage I don't want,' she insisted, 'not you.'

"But I couldn't see it. Oh, I *pretended* I could. But my heart wasn't in it. I felt abandoned, rejected, set adrift. After all, this was someone I'd known and loved for a good portion of my life. When we were married, I considered it a natural *joining*, a legal verification of what was already fact. We were one, in my opinion. And being legally married seconded that opinion.

"'Do you think your new wife will let us spend time together?' she asked, for she was convinced I would remarry.

"I hated expressions like 'spend time.' They sounded so hippie.

"'Once every few months, if more often made her upset?'

"She was sitting at the foot of the bed. I was lying down. She placed her hand on my knee.

"'I know I'll feel more sexy with you after the divorce,' she said.

"'Promises, promises,' I said bitterly. And she removed her hand."

PART TWO

Helped are those who learn that the deliberate
invocation of suffering is as much a boomerang
as the deliberate invocation of joy.

— THE GOSPEL ACCORDING TO SHUG

M Y MOTHER, Celie, was very much influenced by
color," said Olivia. She was talking to Lance, the man
she was not quite sure she would marry. They were walking
along spacious, tree-lined streets after their duties at Atlanta's
only Negro hospital, Harrison Memorial, were done. To pas-
sersby they presented an unusual couple: she, short and very
dark, he, tall and very light, with the sandy, wavy hair that
would, under certain circumstances in their rigidly segregated
city, have classified him as white.

Olivia spoke with the simplicity and earnestness that char-
acterized her, and Lance listened with the attentiveness of one
who is, by lucky chance, finally hearing the good news of life he
might otherwise have missed.

"The year I met her," continued Olivia, "in my middle thirties, she was fascinated by the color blue. Not the bright blue
of skies or the drab blue of serge Sunday suits, but a complex
royal blue with metallic glints. A combination of teal and electric blue that she one day, in her endless rummaging about in
fabric shops across the country, ecstatically found. This was a
blue that, she said, gave off energy, or, to use her own word,
power. A person wearing this blue was suddenly more confi-

dent, stronger, more present and intense than ever before. She made me a pantsuit that gave me all of these qualities when I wore it, just as she predicted, and I was sorry when my daughter, Fanny Nzingha, while helping me make tamale pie, spilled chili sauce on it, and the stain wouldn't come out, no matter how many times I took it to the cleaners. Years later I bought another blue pantsuit, but it wasn't nearly as perfect as the one my mother had made. Though it was as close to the same shade of blue as I could get, it failed to give off any particular energy. In fact, I always felt slightly enervated when I wore it. It was like wearing the shadow of my old suit.

"I do not know if she always loved color. Her childhood was an unhappy one, and most of her young adulthood was spent raising another woman's children, while her own children — my brother, Adam, and I — were brought up by our aunt Nettie, who was a missionary in Africa. We were also brought up by our adoptive mother, Corrine, until we were teenagers. She died of fever and was buried outside the village where we lived. My father, Samuel, was a missionary also, but by the time we returned to America he had long since lost his faith; not in the spiritual teachings of Jesus, the prophet and human being, but in Christianity as a religion of conquest and domination inflicted on other peoples. He and Aunt Nettie, whom he married after our adoptive mother's death, spent many long evenings with my brother and me discussing ways we might best help our people discover their own power to communicate directly with 'God.' We had all begun to see, in Africa — where people worshiped many things, including the roofleaf plant, which they used to cover their houses — that 'God' was not a monolith, and not the property of Moses, as we'd been led to think, and not separate from us, or absent from whatever world one inhabited. Once this channel was cleared, so to speak, much that our people had been taught about religion, much that diminished them and kept them in oppression, would naturally fall away. It was so hard for the Africans, in this new religion we brought, to ever feel 'God' loved them, for instance; whereas in the traditional religions they practiced they took this more or less for granted.

" 'As a minister, I am quite unnecessary to anyone else's salvation,' my father found the courage to admit. 'Surely it is one of the universe's little jokes that I must be a minister in order to make them see this.'

"The religion that one discovered on one's own was a story of the earth, the cosmos, creation itself; and whatever 'Good' one wanted could be found not down the long road of eternity, but right in one's own town, one's home, one's country. *This world.* After all, since this world is a planet spinning about in the sky, we are all of us *in heaven* already! The God discovered on one's own speaks nothing of turning the other cheek. Of rendering unto Caesar. But only of the beauty and greatness of the earth, the universe, the cosmos. Of creation. Of the possibilities for joy. You might say the white man, in his dual role of spiritual guide and religious prostitute, spoiled even the most literary form of God experience for us. By making the Bible say whatever was necessary to keep his plantations going, and using it as a tool to degrade women and enslave blacks. But the old African religions also, in which mutilation of women's bodies sometimes figured so prominently, left almost everything to be desired. Even in these, man, in his insecurity and feeling of unlovableness, made himself the sole conduit to God, if not at times the actual God *him*self. My father often commented on the way the villagers feared their holy men and prostrated themselves before them—as Catholics fear and bow before the pope—so much so that the actual assumed receiver of their petitions and prayers, God Itself, was quite often forgotten. Still, there was a small point in the colored man's favor.

" 'What is one absolute truth about the man of color on this earth?' my father would ask. 'He admits spirit,' he would answer himself. And by this he meant spirit in everything, not just in God or the Holy Ghost, who at one time was the Female in the Deity, or Jesus Christ.

"Throughout these discussions I watched my mother magically create garments in that particular shade of blue, which she eventually dubbed 'Power Blue.'

"I was fascinated by her. By the way she parted her still-black hair severely in the middle and braided it in two braids that met at the back of her head and were turned under. By the way she invariably wore pants, even to church. But pants so subtle only other women noticed they were pants. By the way she spoke little, apparently out of a childhood and young-adult habit of silence, and how, when she did speak, there was a perkiness, a plainness, that was sometimes humorous but always compelling. She was a literal speaker. What she expressed she both felt and was.

"We lived in a roomy old house in middle Georgia that she had inherited from her parents. Her father had been lynched by whites; and her mother, as a consequence of this terrorist murder, had lost her mind. My brother and I were the product of the rape of our mother by her stepfather, a man much admired by black and white in the community where he lived. It was he who gave us to our father, Samuel, who, with our adoptive mother, Corrine, and Aunt Nettie, sailed off with us to Africa when we were children.

"The Africa that we encountered had already been raped of much of its sustenance. Its people had been sold into slavery. Considering both internal and external 'markets,' this 'trade' had been going on for well over a thousand years; and had no doubt begun as the early civilizations of Africa were falling into decline, around the six-hundreds. Millions of its trees had been shipped to England and Spain and other European countries to make benches and altars in those grand European cathedrals one heard so much about; its minerals and metals mined and its land planted in rubber and cocoa and pineapples and all sorts of crops for the benefit of foreign invaders. I almost said, as foreigners do, 'investors.' And Africa itself became—was made—in the world imagination, an uninhabited region, except for its population of wild and exotic animals. On the maps of Africa of five hundred years ago, as someone has pointed out, Europeans placed elephants where there were towns.

"I left America when I was six years old. I do not remember it. But I do remember the ocean. The sheen on the endless water, the deep steady rocking of the ship, the confusion over whether so much water, by its sheer density, might not—if one stepped upon it—become a kind of glassy land. And I remember tasting the ocean spray on my face and someone mentioning at that same moment that the sea was salt. If it was salt, I wondered, why was it not white and grainy, as salt was at home. But its water tasted salty. And this puzzled me until I overheard Aunt Nettie saying sadly to my mother that, well, perhaps it was the tears and sweat of all the suffering people of the earth. She cried so much on the voyage over, and none of us, not even my mother and father, knew why.

"For several years after we arrived in Africa I was quite sickly. I had recurring bouts of malaria, as did everyone in our family. And I was plagued by rashes, sores, and other skin irritations, which were aggravated, horribly, by the heat. Aunt Nettie, whom at times we called 'Mama Nettie,' praised me for not being more complaining. As I recall it now, I was too miserable to complain. Sometimes it was so hot I could not speak. In my teen years I was much better.

"I was, in fact, happy. And why not? All day long I could be found in the company of my best friend, Tashi. We played house, we splashed in the river, we collected wild foods and firewood in the forest. A forest of magnificent fecundity, density, and mystery. There were trees in the forest thousands of years old and bigger by far than the huts in which we lived. There was nothing we did not share, and I loved her better than I would have loved my own sister; as much, or more, than I loved my brother, Adam, who, from an older boy who teased us, chased us, pulled our braids, and tattled on us to our mothers, became Tashi's confidant, then her suitor, then, many years later, her husband.

"It is in the year preceding their marriage that my own story begins. For it was in that year that Tashi became more my brother's companion than mine. This caused me much bitterness, because it caused me much loneliness; and then, too, their companionship was considered by everyone in our compound as cherished and inevitable. Even to Tashi this was so. And the days of our girlish joys together became a thing of the past. Seeing that this must be so, I steeled myself to bear it, and turned to both my brother and Tashi a face of loving willingness to serve them. But such sweetness and light takes its toll, and many dark thoughts occasionally strayed across my mind. It was my first understanding that it is possible to love people very much and to resent their happiness partly because you do love them.

"While all attention focused on Adam and Tashi, I was left to my own devices, largely ignored, or, I should say, unobserved. Corrine had long been dead. The Europeans had come and destroyed the village that had been our home. We had been moved to a barren stretch of rock that lay surrounded by a vast rubber plantation owned and run by Englishmen, whose field labor consisted entirely of our friends. This plantation system used people up in fewer than seven years, and used up the soil as well; it also effectively destroyed the native wild rubber trees, which had once grown abundantly, everywhere. Where there had once been leafy forest, there was now widespread erosion. Many of our friends were dying from various fevers, malnutrition, and overwork. Or were running away to join the Mbeles, a mythical—so we thought—group of African guerrillas who lived deep in the forest many, many miles away.

"There was one young African man who remained, finally, in the ugly, dusty, tin-roofed compound that was our common home. His Christian name was Dahvid, and since this was all he ever used, I never heard his tribal name, until years later. Dahvid stayed in the compound because of me. But I did not know this was his reason. He was a sullen, restless, sometimes impish young man without a thought in his head for anyone, I believed, least of all, girls; and at times he made my life harder than it needed to have been by his irritable, cutting remarks and rude behavior to my family and me, which my father interpreted as Dahvid's way of railing against the catastrophe that had overtaken the Olinka people and reduced them to virtual slavery. Yet why it should have been directed against us, I could not decipher, since it was not our fault that the Europeans had come.

"At other times, when he was not being abusive and calling us 'the white man's wedge,' Dahvid was capable of great charm. And I confess at those times I was drawn to him, as to Adam. I could see that the requirements for males in the world were often such that only a machine could fulfill them, or someone of no feeling and much supernatural strength. Dahvid alone could not chase out the Europeans, for instance. Could not even prevent them looking at him and at all of us as if we were born to be their own divinely ordained beasts of burden. Many of them went so far as to view the Africans themselves as having no right to be in Africa, since it was the plan of the white people to take over the continent; the Africans represented merely the burdensome responsibility of genocide.

"In the year that Adam brought Tashi back from the Mbeles, to whom she had run in her confusion over the destruction of her people and Adam's insistence that she come with him to America, I became receptive to the persistent inquiries of one of the young English engineers, who wanted to learn the Olinka language. I asked permission from my new mother, Mama Nettie, and my father before I began, in the evenings when the work was done, to try to teach him. He was a tall, sunburned, ugly man, whose earnestness and attentiveness made him attractive. And for hours we sat with our backs against the rough boards of our barrack, and I taught him the Olinka language, which I spoke as fluently as I spoke English, and which I could also write, because my father and Mama Nettie had created an Olinka alphabet. The creation of this alphabet had been Corrine's idea. She was Cherokee on her mother's side, and *her* mother's mother had been involved in the creation of the Cherokee alphabet and had also been an editor of the first Cherokee newspaper ever printed in the Cherokee language. The fact that they had a newspaper was one of the reasons the Cherokee were considered one of the five 'civilized' tribes of Indians in America. This did not, however, prevent the white man from burning them out of their homes and resettling what remained of the tribe in Oklahoma when he discovered he wanted their land.

"One day, because it was still very hot and because it simply happened and no one seemed to care what we did — all thoughts were on Adam's pursuit of Tashi — we strolled some distance from the compound and stood talking to each other in Olinka in the shade of a huge rock. And the man, whose name was Ralston Flood, leaned down his reddish, perspiring hairy face and kissed me. Out of politeness, surprise, boredom, loneliness, I returned it. That is to say, I placed both my hands on his arms while the kiss lasted. Then, when it had ended — I waited until his back was turned and he was chattering on in Olinka ahead of me—I scrubbed away the kiss with the corner of my blouse.

"This scrubbing of my mouth Dahvid did not see. Apparently he'd turned away during the kiss itself. For he was also seeking coolness that evening in the shadow of the rock.

"For days afterward he did not speak to me. The Englishman, having proved something he felt needed proving, did not attempt to kiss me again. Shortly afterward, having learned the language sufficiently to give orders to Olinka workers in the field, he ceased to arrive for his daily instruction. Nor did I miss him after the first few days, though I was alone a lot of the time. Not alone if you counted all the sick and shattered people my parents and I constantly attended, but alone because there was—with Tashi and her mother and Adam gone—no one with whom to really giggle or converse.

"I knew the Olinka had ruled it a crime to have any dealings with the Europeans, and that they were against my teaching the Englishman their language. 'Let him order us to fetch and carry in his own wretched tongue,' they said, for they enjoyed mimicking the foreigners and ridiculing them behind their backs. To the Olinka, the English language, as spoken by their captors, had a sickly, regurgitative sound and was as lacking in nuance and music as a stone. Still, when my father had asked their permission for me to teach the Englishman, they had not withheld it. This was because I was not one of them. Since I was a woman, the permission was given grudgingly and with an attitude that they washed their hands of me and of whatever might result.

"Dahvid did not go to the remaining elders with my 'crime.' The crime of having received the kiss of the Englishman. He did not have to. He took it on himself to chastise me. And, in retrospect, his chastisement took a predictable turn. Because I had not refused the Englishman, I should not refuse him. And so, one evening I kissed him. In the same shaded spot in which I'd kissed the Englishman. But, as it turned out, a kiss was not enough.

"And so it was that when I returned to America with Adam and his bride, Tashi, and my father, Samuel, and my aunt, Mama Nettie, I was, as my natural mother, Celie, immediately perceived—but said nothing—'robust' with Dahvid's child. As Tashi was 'robust' with Adam's.

"But what was I to do with a child? The general advice from my family was that I keep it; Tashi loyally offered to help me raise it along with her own. My daughter was born on the ninth of September, the birthday of Leo Tolstoi, the greatest writer, it seems to me, who has ever lived, and one of the biggest devils —in any event, a favorite of mine. One of the hottest days of the year, it was. My own mother, by now a midwife in addition to being the best seamstress around, delivered me.

"Just as my baby's head emerged, my mother shouted, 'Little Fanny!' This was even before she could tell it was a girl. She couldn't help herself. 'Fanny,' a name that apparently represented freedom to her, was a name she'd always wanted for herself. She'd hated 'Celie.' Even so, just as she was sucking in her breath to continue the naming I shouted out a very tired and weak 'Nzingha!'"

"MY EARLIEST memory is of a red bird with a suction cup on its feet and of two old ladies kissing," Fanny would later—after discovering she had one—tell her sister. "The red bird was made of cloth and feathers and rubber; the two old ladies who gave it to me were delightful-smelling flesh and blood. The little bird could be stuck on any nongreasy surface: a windowpane, the head of my crib, and when I pulled on it with all my might, it gave a satisfying plop and came off in my hand. At first I did not see the resemblance between the thing in my hand, with its brilliant yellow eyes and chartreuse tail, and the creatures flying about outside the door. The two old ladies tried hard to teach me, however, and while one scooped me up in her arms, admiring my nearly squeezed-to-death bird, the other kept saying *shush* and pointing to a creature who sat singing merrily on a nearby bush. A creature who did not resemble my red bird in any way. For instance, my bird did not sing. It lived in my fist. Its head fit in my mouth.

"Somehow, though, I must have understood the connection, because sooner or later I said 'bird!' and that was the first word I spoke. It was also my grandmother's nickname.

"The bird, any bird, it turned out, was precious to my

grandmama Celie, just as turtles and elephants were precious to her friend Miss Shug. As I crawled about the house, exploring it with my first cousin Moraga Bentu, or Benny, for short, I was constantly riding on, leaning against, drooling over some stone or metal or cloth facsimile of these treasured creatures. Compared with the rest of the house, my mother's two rooms were bare and uninteresting. There were objects on her walls—cloth and masks and here and there a string of shells or large beads—but nothing I was permitted to touch, even if I had been tall enough to reach it.

"My mother did not particularly interest me. Whereas Big Mama (as I called Grandmama Celie) and Mama Shug (as I called Miss Shug) were always good for a kiss, a laugh, a squeeze, a ride to the garden or at least to the front porch, my mother was—dare I say it?—a boring woman, who rarely laughed and always had her nose in a book.

"I used to sit on the floor at her feet, having crawled about the house until I was tired, and look up at her, hoping she would put aside her book for a moment and play with me. Occasionally she would, but there was a perfunctory quality in her caresses that irritated me. Rather than submit to her insincerity, and thereby appear to accept it, I would wriggle from her arms with a cry. Immediately one or both of my pals would arrive, and I would be hugged in all seriousness, kissed intelligently, changed if I needed to be, and fed something whether I needed it or not. I was indecently fat, as fat and round as Mama Shug. When we lay down together, it was like a small ball resting on a larger one. And how we enjoyed the contact of our fat bellies! Neither of us could imagine the other could do any wrong. And we were right.

"This period of my life was a long bliss. Very little happened that I considered threatening to me. I soon learned to pay as little attention to my mother as she paid to me, and my life was a round of fascinating events and spontaneous smiles. Visitors to our house frequently lavished their attention on Benny, it is true, because in their own homes boys were more prized. In our house, however, it paid to be a girl, and all my womanish ways were approved. I decked myself out in what finery came my way in a routine rummaging about in everybody's drawers. I peeked under dresstails and stared at the mysterious closings of men's pants. I tried to cook. I tried to cut wood as I saw Big Mama's best friend, Miss Sofia, do. I tried to build a house out of stove wood and make blinds for it out of pieces of straw. I imagined myself a car, like Mama Shug's, and drove it by the hour. I brought money home and also took everybody out.

" 'Come on, let's go, y'all,' I said to Benny and our collective toys, as we headed for a night spot miles away.

"Sometimes I imagined doing the things my mother and grandfather did. I 'read.' Or I imagined I was Papa Albert, who used to be Big Mama's husband, and stared off into space."

FINALLY one day Fanny said, "Listen, Suwelo, I love you too much to divorce you without your consent. You have been wonderful to me. Without you, how would I have grown? But I am going away for a while, with my mother. We are going back to Africa to visit the Olinka. Their country is free now, and my father wants to lay eyes on me."

From London she wrote to him: "The hotel we are staying at is dreadful. No telephones in the rooms and hostile receptionists. There was a fire on one of the upper floors some time ago and there is still a charred odor in the air. The new owners are Middle Eastern. They sit in the lobby and watch the bellboy, African; the charwoman, West Indian; the people who work in the dining room, Indian, Arab, and Greek; and the hostile receptionists, blonde English girls. One day my mother said, 'Look, it isn't even safe; I can step through this window into the street,' which she did. But we don't stay there very much. Most of our time is spent at the Africa Center, where my mother is giving lectures on her years in Africa—growing up there as a black American child and young adult.

"Mom is such a little piece of leather, as she says, but *so* well put together! She wasn't even fazed by the horrid scrutiny of the guards at the airport, who seem to think everyone who is a visitor to England and isn't white wants to settle here. What conceit! I sit and listen to her stories and I feel embarrassed that for so many years I ignored her. As I have told you, probably a really boring number of times, when I was a child, she had no real authority in our house, which was ruled by the two queens, Big Mama Celie and Mama Shug. Next to these two, and even next to Great-aunt Nettie, who raised her, my mother's flame seemed feeble. Even Uncle Adam had a certain exuberance that my mother lacked.

"What she has instead is an astonishing clarity about things, expressed in a straightforward, unassuming manner. Listening to her here makes me realize why the students in her classes at the nursing school always perform well academically, and also have some of her soul-rooted quietness. This is a quality she inherited from her adoptive mother, she says.

"Her audiences here are wonderful. African, Asian, Caribbean, and white students from all over the world. It is not too much to say that they treat her with reverence, almost as if she is a holy document. For she can actually tell them, blow by blow, the whole story of the colonization of Africa, the role of the church, and the psychic and physical toll of their work on the missionaries themselves. She always makes clear that the missionaries *are* people, the same as anyone, and that many of them have real and honorable dreams when they push off for the shores of another world. One thing she said last night really struck me, because it is just one of those small things you never think about. She said that when the missionaries first arrived in Olinka, there was no such thing as litter; the whole village was swept clean twice a day, morning and afternoon, by the women. But then, as the grip of the colonials tightened and the people were squeezed to pay taxes and also to pay for shoddy imported things, only the mission was clean. So that anyone strolling

through the village would have assumed the people were naturally slovenly and that only the foreigners cared to be clean.

"My mother still looks like a missionary, with her neatness
and unstraightened hair. And, in fact, was there ever a more
white-missionary-sounding name than hers: *Olivia*, for heav-
en's sake! It makes you think of Vanessa Redgrave teaching
the natives in the tropics! But now, here at the Center, I see
hundreds of photographs of Africans from that time, and she
looks just like them, only a shade lighter. Theirs was a definite style then, very plain, very earnest. No jewelry, or hardly
any. Their eyes—serious, dedicated, very wide open and direct—these are the jewels of that period. The students want to
know everything: Where did the water come from? The river.
Where did the people shop? No shops, until after colonization. Barter, rather. How many white people did she see while
growing up? Very few. How many wild animals? Very few. The
Olinka thought that white people presented an 'immature' ap-
pearance, as if they were fetuses, but grown. That was inevitably their comment on first seeing one of them. They then
tended to treat the white person or persons solicitously, as if
they were frail.

"'This behavior was not understood, and seriously back-
fired,' my mother said. And the students laughed.

"However, it was at the Africa Center that we learned my
father has been arrested. You would think that, never having
seen the man, I would not be in a dither. I am, though. Having
read my father's books and now, in London, having seen one of
his plays—a small student production, poorly acted and badly
staged—I can imagine why the authorities have arrested him.
My mother says what surprises her is that he wasn't arrested
before. The students were discussing this after the lecture.
They mentioned the International Alternative Peace Prize that
my father received last year, apparently just at the moment the

government was about to lock him up. As it was, they had run a bulldozer through the latest of his plays and razed the theater.

"This last play was called *The Fee*, and is about taxation. It is an antitaxes play, in other words; the kind of play no playwright in America would write and that no producer would produce, though everyone there cries about taxes. I've been trying to imagine it, and thinking how nice it would be. Anyway, some of the students at the lecture had already received copies of *The Fee* and are planning to mount a production. Apparently liberation has not lowered the people's taxes at all, nor has it increased their income. Arggh! Since they can't see their taxes at work for them—the roads are frequently ruts, the hospitals lack medicine, and the schools lack *pencils*, not to mention how *nearly everyone lacks sufficient food*—the folks are saying hell no, they ain't gonna pay the friggin' taxes! My father got the idea for the play from an actual protest—'riot,' according to the local government-controlled paper, which the students say is funded by the CIA—staged by women and children, who stormed the house of the president the day they learned how much of their money went to the U.S. and the U.S.S.R. for weapons their children are too poorly educated and weak from hunger to operate, assuming they wanted to do such a thing. But the catch is that for those who join the military, there is food, though no education. My father's position is that the reason millions of Africans are exterminating themselves in wars is that the superpowers have enormous stores of outdated weapons to be got rid of. Only the women seem to notice that everyone's children are suffering.

"But this is the concern of the African mother the world over, isn't it? The education of her children, the inevitable school fees pinched somehow out of the money earned from washing, ironing, fieldwork, minework. Any kind of work.

"The students don't call my father by his tongue-twisting

name, Abajeralasezeola, which is only a slight improvement over 'Dahvid,' to my mind, and which I can never get right either. They call him 'Ola.' Ola has this to say. Ola writes thus and so. Ola is right or wrong on such and such a question. In other words, he is theirs. They are resigned about his arrest. One of two things will happen, they say: He will be imprisoned for a long time, possibly tortured, or shot outright. 'No one in the country has the brains to try to "rehabilitate" him,' one young man said; or he will have to flee the country. 'Yes,' said a young woman exile from Kenya, who had sung for my mother a beautiful welcome song, 'he will come and join the rest of us; the African continent abroad.'

"'So many exiles,' my mother said on the way back to our wretched hotel. 'There are as many now as before liberation. How can this be?' She was tired and feeling very sad. Her eyes were full of tears. I put my arms around her shoulders and marveled at the way my head towers over hers. How is it that mothers shrink and shrink? And her *little* hands!

"At the airport outside the capital, my father came to meet us. He and my mother were cordial. They shook hands solemnly but looked warmly, if somewhat cautiously, into each other's eyes. I thought: Yes, my mother doesn't get into a car with just anybody! I was surprised that he looked so ordinary. A small dark man with prominent eyes and rather unkempt graying close-to-his-head hair. He looked exhausted, in fact, and as if he'd just tumbled out of bed. Or out of jail.

"Since he and I were strangers, there was a certain amount of awkwardness, but I felt, with his sensitivity, he would be conscious of my thoughts. Consequently I tried to censor those about his knobby knees and the way his oversize khaki shorts flapped in the wind as we walked.

"He gave me, though, just as we were about to get into his car, a swift, determined, and very shy little hug—Suwelo, I'm also taller than *he* is—and stuck a ring on my thumb. It was his ring; I'd noticed it on his finger. I understood the gesture, too. It was something I myself might have done. Overcome with confusion and emotion, he'd simply wanted to give me something tangible, immediately, to try to make up for the lost years. It was interesting, the emotion I suddenly felt; for, as you know, I've never been conscious of missing a father, and certainly not him in particular.

"He laughed when he saw my mother's wide-eyed appraisal of the car. It was not the jalopy of a jailbird. It had a flag. It had a crest.

"'Of course I have a nice car,' he said. 'I am, after all, minister of culture.'

"My mother knew this.

"'Oh, Dahvid,' she said. 'We are so very proud of you. At least it isn't a Mercedes,' she added, smiling.

"'Only because the Germans were not our masters!' said Ola. And there was only humor, I thought, not a trace of bitterness, in his voice.

"As if he read my thoughts he said, 'It does no good to be angry. I will just drive my nice little car until they take it away from me.'

"'We heard you were in jail,' my mother said.

"'And so I was!' he shouted over the noise of the killer taxis zooming by. I looked out the window at the parched African countryside. My mother says the climate has changed drastically over the years. It rains only sporadically now, and in large areas of the country there is severe drought. All up and down the road there were women walking. Some were carrying babies on their backs and basins on their heads. 'They let me out this morning. I told them I had important visitors from America.' He paused. 'A good friend and . . . my daughter.' They are not completely hardened criminals yet, these thugs in office.

I know all of them very well. They are not ready to get rid of me yet. Who will greet the literate visitor? In fact, I don't think they've hit on just what to do. They want the world to think well of them, you see.'

"He laughed, almost merrily, at the absurdity of this.

"I laughed with him. What can I tell you, Suwelo? It was like hearing my own self laugh. I knew exactly the region of the soul from which his laughter came. They were breaking my father's heart, and he saw himself small, beetlelike in his industrious work at undermining them, and there was still a little part of him that did not feel outmatched. 'As long as the people don't fear the truth, there is hope,' someone once said to me; and I thought of that while looking at the back of my father's graying head. 'For once they fear it, the one who tells it doesn't stand a chance.' And today truth is still beautiful, as Keats knew, but so frightening.

"The neighborhoods we drove through were poor, dry, dusty, and the houses were behind adobe walls. These walls were painted in the most vivid abstract designs. The women, my father explained, did this. It was a tradition that, as he put it, failed to let them go.

"'I love it!' I said.

"'I'm glad you do,' he replied. On the outskirts of one of these communities, but on an abruptly more prosperous block, was my father's compound, and it is painted in the loudest colors of all! Only in San Francisco would my father's house be appreciated. I got out of the car and immediately touched the colors, a half dozen or so of them: orange, yellow, blue, green, purple, red, and brown, white, and tan. More than a half dozen. What it looks like, really, is a design from a truly beautiful rug, but on an adobe house!

"My father's, Ola's, house is very simple. Because he is the minister of culture . . . 'Because I am the minister of culture,' he says, drawing himself up loftily, 'I have to live in a native-style house!' He laughs. It has all the conveniences, though. Two baths, four bedrooms, a large ceremonial living room, a verandah that goes completely around the inner courtyard. There are flowers, and, because he is also a farmer, a large vegetable garden. He has servants. A small, shy woman and her daughter, who cook and clean; a tall, skinny young man, who tends the gardens; and two or three other people, who just hang about, presumably as bodyguards, or—as Ola says—'presumably as spies.'

"Well. I'm sitting here on the verandah with a gin-and-tonic, as Isak Dinesen might have done, writing to you. Here's to all the children who grow up without their fathers. The world is full of us . . . and some of us have managed anyhow!"

THE night before Suwelo heard from Fanny Nzingha about her first meeting with Ola, he'd had a confusing dream about going to the market to get enough food to last him forever, only to discover when he got there that he had nothing with which to transport the mountain of food he chose—and that his pockets were abnormally small. There he stood in the Great Supermarket of Life, cartless, with pockets that wouldn't hold a penknife.

The glistening food swayed in seductive mounds well over his head as, gradually comprehending that he was in hell, he—a short babylike man in his dream—sank to the floor, his thumb and forefinger in his mouth. When Suwelo woke from this hellish dream he was crying, much to his surprise. He rarely cried. He lay in bed trying to think of his morning classes, but through every thought there rolled a glistening new shopping cart.

Then he remembered.

It was in the house they had bought in the suburbs back east; and before Fanny felt comfortable driving there. She was like that: skilled at driving, swimming, running even. But then there would be long periods when she simply couldn't seem to do any of them. Her running knees rusted, her swimming arms creaked, her driving eyes clouded over. She moved slowly, cautiously, like a tortoise, as if at any moment she expected to feel the heavens fall down about her head.

There was public transportation, luckily. Actually, it was quite reliable and was one of the reasons they chose the house. That and the little creek that meandered behind it. And the one oval window in the front of the house, with mauve-tinted beveled glass. And the large space for the garden (already composted by the departing inhabitants) in back. And they had loved, simply loved the house, although the work they'd done "restoring" it—new plumbing, new wiring, new walls, and so on—nearly did them in. There was also a supermarket five blocks away.

One day when he came home, Fanny was all smiles, and from the hall closet she cheerfully dragged a bright new shopping cart. The kind of cart old women and matrons with young babies are seen dragging behind them or bumping up over a curb. He smiled to think of Fanny Nzingha using the thing.

"You like?" she said. "From now on, no more pretzel-stick arms from carrying three bags of groceries. No more curvature of the spine. These things are wonderful!" And she trundled it back and forth over the bright rug from Guatemala a friend had given them that stretched the length of the hall.

For weeks she was content. She liked the walk to the market. It permitted her to meet her neighbors. She liked getting up early in the morning and getting the freshest food. Even if it meant the maddest dash back in order to get to work on time. This housewifely contact with the early morning was preparing her to take up once again the daily morning ritual of running. She could now see, too, wheeling the little cart, which she was learning to do expertly, how she might be able to drive around the neighborhood. And one day on the way to market, she'd passed a public pool she'd never noticed from the car. Well.

From time to time she tried to get him to do the marketing, using the little cart. He would quickly take her shopping list, throw on his coat, and dash out to the car. He'd drive the five blocks, toss the items he bought into the backseat of his car, and be back home in a matter of minutes. Fanny was slightly puzzled but, on the whole, grateful, though she reminded him what a great walk he was missing and that, as a matter of fact, a fast walk back and forth to the market, pushing the little cart, was just what might be needed to trim any incipient flab. Hint. Hint.

One day, as luck would have it, the car was at the shop for its routine checkup. He had not been able to pick it up because all that day he'd been running late. The traffic was such that he was almost glad not to have a car, temporarily, to add to it. He took a bus home.

There was Fanny, who'd also taken a bus home, in her little apron with the cat on it, busily making bread: a mound of dough was rising under a moist towel by the sink, and with flour-covered hands she was making a list.

Suwelo groaned inwardly.

"Make it a short list. A one-bag list," he said.

"But we're out of everything," said she, busily scribbling. "We should never have parties at which we serve our own food. Our friends ate all of it."

He'd forgotten the party they'd thrown the night before. Yes indeed, even the peanut butter was gone.

Suwelo went over and kissed her on the back of the neck. "One bag, okay?" he said.

She kept writing. He noticed she'd put down two dozen oranges (they both loved fresh orange juice in the morning) and a gallon of milk!

"My back won't be able to stand all that," he said.

She looked up from her list, not such a long one, after all, and gave him a quizzical look.

"But don't you remember . . . ?" she began.

And they finished in unison: "*We have the cart!*"

The time had finally come to explain himself. "Fanny," he said, "sit down."

She did. On his knee.

"I have a confession to make."

She looked ready to hear it.

"The cart," he said, "reminds me of little old ladies with funny-colored hair, net scarves, and dowager's humps." She looked puzzled. "It reminds me," he continued, "of young women who are suddenly too stout in their jeans, frowning as they push it and drag blankface kids along at the same time. It reminds me," he said, thinking of her and her enthusiasm for it, "of bright young racehorses of women who willingly put themselves in harness." She removed herself from his lap.

"It reminds you," she said, "of women."

"My mother pushed a cart. My grandmother, too," said Suwelo.

"Your *wife* pushes one," said Fanny.

"I just don't see myself pushing one," said Suwelo. "I'm sorry."

"I see," said Fanny. "I wonder if you see yourself eating?" And she lifted the mound of dough and dropped it into the blue step-on garbage can at her feet.

Oh, they had many delicious meals together after that. But it was never the same. There had been a little murder, there in their bright, homey kitchen, where, up until that time, they'd both felt light, free, almost as if they were playing their roles. The cart disappeared, and Suwelo felt terrible about the whole episode. He found a grocery-delivery service and would often call in their orders. He began to learn to cook, fish and sautéed vegetables, or lasagne. He would rush to beat her home; she was back to being afraid of driving the car in traffic and so continued taking the bus. She neither swam nor ran. He would be there cooking, with jazz on the radio and a glass of wine for her. She'd come in, sigh, kick off her shoes, drift about the kitchen. Pick up the wine, accept his kiss. There was the little murdered thing between them, though. The more he tried to revive it, the deader it got.

"I was raised to be a certain way," he began to say very often in conversations that were not about the little murder at all, but about other issues entirely, or so he thought.

And she would murmur, "Yes. *Yes, you were*"; not with the understanding he was clumsily seeking, but with a quiet astonishment.

"I DID not know anything, Fanny, when you were born," said her mother, "about the United States, or any of the Americas, for that matter. It was the strangest thing to see so many white people, first off, and to see the massive heaviness of their cities. New York was horrifying. Atlanta, though smaller, also seemed uninhabitable because so much—people and buildings—was crowded together. But then we went into some of the homes people readily opened to us—our church people—and we saw that in spite of everything one could still attain a certain graciousness of living. This was remarkable, especially among black people, because it was right at the end of World War II. Black soldiers were coming home and refusing to be segregated at restaurants and on buses, and the white men were steadily accusing them of raping white women, looking at white women—they called this 'reckless eyeballing,' and many a black man found himself in jail on this charge!—or even speaking to a white woman who was speaking to them. Needless to say, there was rarely any white woman at all involved. No American ones anyway. They knew better. The white men had simply seen red while they were fighting in Europe, in France and Italy, in particular, where the white women had not appeared to care what color American men were—their money was green. And besides, colored men do know how to have fun.

"I learned this decisively when I settled in at my mother's house. She was afraid of men in a sexual way, but she knew how to enjoy their company. There were many men who came regularly to visit 'Miss Celie and Miss Shug.' Almost always they were men with some kind of talent. There was Mr. Burgess— 'Burgie,' as he was called—who played French horn. French horn! Yancy Blake, who played guitar. Little Petey Sweetning, who played piano. Come to think of it, there must have been so many musicians because of Miss Shug, who was a great blues singer, though she rarely sang in public anymore. There were poets and funnymen, what you would now call 'comedians,' and, really, all kinds of people: magicians, jugglers, good horseshoe throwers, the occasional man who quilted or did needlepoint. 'Slavery left us with a host of skills!' one old, old optimist, who was king of the barbecue, often said. These people were remarkable in many ways, but perhaps the most remarkable thing about them, in a part of the country where there was so much oppression of black people, or of anyone that was considered 'inferior' or 'strange,' was that there was absolutely no self-pity. In fact, there was a greeting that habitues of our house used on encountering each other: 'All those at the banquet!' they'd say, and shake hands or hug. Sometimes they said this laughing, sometimes they said it in tears. But that they were still at the banquet of life was always affirmed.

"There was laughter and cold lemonade and flowers and always lots of children and older people, too, that Big Mama had helped raise. You know there had to be some folks in the community who'd have nothing to do with our house. They called Mama Celie and Mama Shug 'bull-daggers.' But I always thought the very best of the men and women were our friends, for they were usually so busy living some odd new way they'd found, and were so taken up with it, they really didn't give a damn. And then, too, Mama Shug especially had real high standards; and if you stepped on an ant in Mama Celie's presence and didn't beg forgiveness, you were just never invited to her house again. Though this sensitivity to animals was not always Mama Celie's way. It was something she learned, as she learned so many things, from Mama Shug.

"But there was really no place for me there. Not really. I was welcome and I was loved, but I was also grown. After a few years I began to feel smothered by their competence, their experience in everything, their skills that caused me to feel my own considerable attributes were not required. And they simply took over the task of raising you. By this time, too, Mama Shug had decided to found her own religion, for which she used the house, and sometimes this was very hard, because of the way she structured it. Six times during the year, for two weeks each time, she held 'church.' Ten to twenty 'seekers' would show up, and they had to sleep somewhere. Usually it was on the floor, or, when there was an overflow, in the barn or the shed. Everyone who came brought information about their own path and journey. They exchanged and shared this information. That was the substance of the church. Some of these people worshiped Isis. Some worshiped trees. Some thought the air, because it alone is everywhere, is God. ('Then God is not on the moon,' someone said.) Mama Shug felt there was only one thing anyone could say about G-O-D, and that was—it had no name.

"I don't know how they were able to talk about it, finally, if it had no name, or if everyone had a different name for it. Oh, yes, I do remember! I was telling them, Mama Celie and Miss Shug, about how the Olinka use humming instead of words sometimes and that that accounts for the musicality of their speech. The hum has meaning, but it expresses something that is fundamentally inexpressible in words. Then the listener gets to interpret the hum, out of his own experience, and to know that there is a commonality of understanding possible but that true comprehension will always be a matter of degree.

"If, for instance, you say to someone in jail who is feeling low: 'How are you?' He or she can say, 'Ummm, ugh,' and you more or less get it. Which is the way it really is. If the person replied, 'Fine' or 'Terrible,' it would hardly be the same. No work would be required on your part. They have named it.

"So that is how they resolved it. They would hum the place G-O-D would occupy. Everyone in the house talked about *ummm* a lot!

"And so, to make a long story manageably short, I left you there with these *ummm*-distracted people and went to Atlanta to enroll in the Spelman nursing school. My adoptive mother had gone there, you see, and that made it very attractive to me. She was such a lady! A word I know your generation despises, but back then it had substantial meaning. It meant someone with implacable self-respect. Besides, 'woman' meant, well, someone capable of breeding. It was strictly a biological term and, because it was associated with slavery, was considered derogatory. I had been sent to England to study nursing while we lived in Africa, so I already knew quite a lot. I'd also assisted the young African woman doctor at home, who'd trained in England; an eccentric Englishwoman writer had paid for her education. Still, I needed accreditation to work in the U.S. It wasn't easy. I was older than the other students and had a child, but they were interested in my life in Africa, and I was several times asked to speak at vespers. Come to think of it, no one ever asked me whether I was married, but they automatically called me 'Mrs.' and behaved as if they thought I was. Very respectfully. But then, everyone—I mean the students—was respectful. Too respectful, I often thought. They were so grateful to be there—one of the few places a young colored girl could go for training—they acted as if their teachers and the college administrators were gods. They acted, in fact, precisely like the colonized Africans who were educated at our mission in Olinka. Too much respect for people who are not always respectful to you is a sure sign of insecurity, and their abject gratitude rather depressed me. Well, I wasn't there to agitate. I got my accreditation in due course and applied for a job at the black hospital on Hunter Street, Harrison Memorial. I sent for you as soon as the job came through.

"It was a wonderful place! Not simply because it was there that I met your stepfather. Of course I was too dark for his family, and practically an African, a real African, to boot—but that's getting ahead of my story. By the time Lance—his parents named him Lancelot—had graduated from medical school he'd had enough of prejudice among black people; he just couldn't tolerate it. All the cadavers they'd worked on were from a certain range of shades between dark brown and black, and this had radicalized him about the amount of economic disparity that existed along intraracial lines. He started to think there were no poor, really destitute, lightskin black people, and this made him very sad. And the marks of hard knocks on the bodies he and the other students were required to work on! His heart was broken, he said, every day. There was a woman, for instance, who walked seventy miles carrying her sick child to a doctor whose existence was only a rumor to her. She died of heart failure; the baby, of dehydration caused by diarrhea. Both these bodies became the property of Lance's medical school.

"There they were cut up while some of Lance's colleagues told jokes and others talked of the food they expected to have for dinner.

"Everyone thought a doctor's life was so glamorous! I never understood it. When I went to work at the hospital and had the chance to work with him, I could see it was, very often, a depressing, soul-killing job. There were people who were sick simply because of the way they lived, and ate: a diet of fatback, biscuits, syrup, and hard fried meat. There were colon cancers, ulcers, liver and artery congestion. The ignorance of proper diet was astounding. There were people so addicted to Coca-Cola that this drink was all they consumed all day long, with salted peanuts, bought by the nickel bag. And they *boasted* of this! That this was 'good.' That this was what they liked; and by golly, this was what they would eat! Don't talk about green leafy vegetables in the same room with them, and only rabbits ate carrots, and cauliflower didn't grow in the South, to their knowledge, *so there!*

"I was not looking for a husband. I sometimes thought of Dahvid; that day you were conceived was like a dream memory. I knew that the whole country was engaged in fighting. I imagined Dahvid might be fighting, too, or he might be injured or dead. Besides, you were quite a handful and quite enough companionship, I thought, for me. During the week, you went to the Spelman day nursery school, where everyone loved you; on Saturdays we went shopping for our weekly supplies. On Sundays we went to church. A nice, orderly life.

Even when Lance started to let me know he cared for me, I hung back. I was always shy, retiring—that quality that seemed so out of place in my mother's house of laughter, horseshoe throwing, magicians sawing people into thirds, guitar players and jugglers! and with which you were so impatient. I was plain, and dark, like my mother—much darker than the other nurses—and I didn't 'play.' There was always in my mind, too, the question of how any man who came around us might behave toward you. And on that score I'd heard many frightful stories from other women, and also from my own mother. It still broke my heart to think of how she was abused by her stepfather, who never even bothered to tell her, until after she was grown, that he wasn't her father. Funny. I could never think of him as *my* father. The truth is, I never felt I had a biological father, apart from my adoptive father, Samuel, and when I learned I did have one I still couldn't grasp it. So that, to this day, I feel almost as if I am a product of an immaculate conception. Like Jesus, who didn't know who his biological father was either. I have often thought it was this lack of knowledge of his earthly father that led him to his 'heavenly' one, for there is in all of us a yearning to know our own source, and no source is likely to seem too farfetched to a lonely, fatherless child. This was considered a blasphemous thought when I ventured to express it; but the question of who impregnated Mary, that young Jewish girl, and under what possibly grim or happy circumstances—because of my mother's sad experience of abuse as a young woman—was always much on my mind. If Joseph was not the father of Jesus, and 'God in heaven' was not, and Mary, because of custom, fear, or depression could not speak up about what had actually happened to her, who was the father?

"Well, you see how to me all daily stories are in fact ancient, and ancient ones current. And it was due to the long languid days in Africa, days that seemed to go on for weeks, that I credit this sense I have that, really, *there is nothing new under the sun* and that nothing in the past is more mysterious than the behavior of the present.

"I connected instead with my mother's real father, my grandfather Simon, who was lynched when she was a baby. He was industrious, an entrepreneur. And very successful; which is why the whites killed him. They killed a lot of striving black men, for a black man's success was much more galling to them than his failure. The failures they could turn back into slaves, entertainment for themselves, and pets. Both my mother and I take after him. Her house and tailoring shop—she made and sold the kind of pants she always wore—became the light that illuminated their town, as far as black people were concerned. And I am like my grandfather, I think, in my firm determination and faith that I can take care of myself. As soon as I had you, I knew there was no work I would not do to keep you in food and shelter and clothing.

"Lance fell in love with my determination and faith. But I was afraid of his blues. It was a sad, almost listless quality that people of obvious mixed race used to have. Not for nothing was there once a stereotype of the 'tragic mulatto'! I think now that a lot of their energy was consumed by their effort to live honorably as who they were (and who *were* they?), with both sides—black and white—constantly warring against each other and despising those caught in the middle. I didn't feel I could support the heaviness; nor could I be his front in the black community or his thumbed nose to the white. Aunt Nettie used to say, 'Don't take on anybody's burdens that look heavier than yours.' And Lance's looked heavy indeed.

"But you know the rest. We courted. We married. . . . How good it was to once again have a friend and confidant! Someone, besides Tashi, to finally tell about those sad last minutes with Dahvid; those first joyous moments, my little Fanny, with you. It was Lance's idea for you to stand up with us; to decide on how you felt about the marriage and to express it that way. And he was a faithful husband and trustworthy father till the day he died. Do you remember how happy we were that day, being married on the front porch of my mother's house? No more blues for any of us, we swore. And how not only the three of us, but also the family and guests, magicians, horseshoe throwers, jugglers, French-horn players, and what have you—*all of us wore red?*"

Y OU will never guess who is in the bedroom down the
hall," Fanny wrote. "Bessie Head!"

When Suwelo read those words he strained to remember—something. But what he was trying to remember was a
consequence of an action, not the action itself. And he wasn't
sure he knew the consequence.

Balancing the letter on his knee, he took off his glasses and
closed his eyes for a moment. There rose before him a vision of
the stark, empty rooms of the house they had bought. The walls
were faded periwinkle trimmed in grayish white. They must
paint, he felt, immediately. He preferred white walls. In fact, he
could live in a totally white, buff, or eggshell interior. Strong
colors oppressed him because they demanded that you notice;
some kind of response. White all around you focused the color
attention on yourself, or on the furnishings, on the art.

Two women had owned the house, teachers like him and
Fanny, and they had left it in passable shape. Broom-swept.
The upstairs carpet had been shampooed. Downstairs in the
center of the living-room floor they'd left a bottle of champagne, and a note that wished them happiness in the house, as
they had had. In the upstairs study one of them had left a small

stack of books. He'd picked them up, one by one, looked at them. They were all by a writer named Bessie Head. There was a note saying here was someone extraordinary and not to drink the champagne and try to read her at the same time.

Ms. Head was black; there was a small snapshot of her on the back flap of the smallest book. He thought it vaguely racist that the women, both white, had left books by a black person. After a few days he thought no more about it.

Months later Fanny put one of the books, *Maru*, on the table beside him as he was completing the chore of check-writing to cover the monthly bills. He glanced at it warily. She was always trying to get him to read books that, to his way of thinking, had nothing to do with his own life. He was a teacher; he taught American history; he was good at it. He read enough. Besides, he had never read a book by a woman.

"Who is she anyway?" he asked. "Isn't she African?"

"Yes," said Fanny. "She's amazing. *Read* this."

He picked it up and flipped through the pages. Read an inscrutable line. Set it down again. "Put it on my desk," he said. "I'll try to get to it."

Eventually the whole little stack was piled on his desk. One day he got tired of them being there and shifted them to the floor.

"She has changed the way I think of Africa," Fanny said. "She's changed the way I think about a lot of things!"

"Good writers do that," he murmured, distracted.

But he did not want to change the way he thought of Africa. Besides, when he wanted insight into Africa, he'd read a man.

As if she heard what he was thinking, one day she brought him *Two Thousand Seasons*, by Ayi Kwei Armah. She had just finished reading it and was in tears.

"I can't believe a man can understand so much!" she cried.

This book, too, gathered dust on the floor by his desk.

Much later, he noticed her rereading the same book but with a different cover. She was frowning and underlining passages.

"Why are you reading that again?" he'd asked.

"They've printed a second edition," she said, furiously, "and it appears to be jumbled."

"Are you sure? Why would they do that? You don't think it was deliberate?"

"Did you ever read the first edition?" she asked.

"Well, no," he admitted.

"Then you wouldn't understand."

She slept in the guest room, her "study," that night.

But why should he try to read all the books that changed *her* life. She had the time for those kinds of books. She taught literature! He had to read the books required by his profession. The teaching of American history. This was simple enough to understand. Yet he could watch hours and hours of television, which made hash of the teachings of his profession. After the bottle of champagne the two women left, there were rivers of wine. TV, the couch, wine. If only his woman would stop reading books and changing her life, he'd sometimes think, in a wine-induced, mellow mood, and just come over and snuggle up on the sofa with him. Then Monday night NFL football, at least, would be perfect.

Did people leave you, did their spirits simply take off, because you wouldn't read a book that turned them on? He now knew the answer was yes.

"She is about our age," Fanny wrote. "And chubby. No, puffy. She says she hasn't been well in a long time. She is a peculiar brown shade because of the sallowness of her skin. In her eyes you sometimes see the most astonishing glint of green, brown-pond-water green. I wanted to ask her so many questions based on things I have read in her books. But she seemed so vulnerable and the questions loomed so intrusive! I mean, there she sat, under the umbrella on the verandah, in none too new robe and slippers—flip-flops, to be precise—her short hair drying from the shower, sipping her morning tea. 'Was your mother *really* a white South African woman?' I wanted to ask. 'Was your father *really* black? Tell me again how they met. I don't remember from your book. Was it *really* about yourself that you wrote, and about your parents? Was she really thrown into the insane asylum? And what in the world became of *him*? And was it immediately after your first book was published that they kicked you out of South Africa? Where on earth is your son's father?' You know, Suwelo, I've never before met an actual refugee.

"When my father introduced us he'd said: 'The great writer Bessie Head.'

"She'd muttered: 'The great *unheard-of* writer Bessie Head.'

"'I've read everything you've published, so far,' I said. And it was such a kick to see her response. At first she just stared at me, as if she wasn't sure what she'd heard. Then she was obviously pleased, like a little kid, but I also thought she felt somewhat foolish.

"'Yes, you see,' she said later, 'I count on not being known. I can really make people feel uninformed and guilty.' She has a deadpan sense of humor.

"'Your work is known in the States,' I said. 'I've taught some of your things. I call you the Tolstoi of Africa.'

"She stiffened. 'Have you read how he treated his wife?'

"'Well,' I said, 'I sincerely hope you don't have a wife.'

"She finally laughed outright.

"She is on her way to London for medical reasons. And, she said, to lend the shock of her impoverished presence to her publishers. Apparently she receives very little for her work, and I can certainly testify that her publishers do nothing to promote it. She showed us pictures of her life in Botswana, where she is one among thousands of South African refugees. There is just her hut, bare except for a small table on which her typewriter rests. There was no picture of her son.

"She says American writers are very strange. One came to visit her and also brought along numerous pictures of herself. In America, I told her, the women writers need pictures to remind everyone they exist.

"This she termed a typically American, childish, trivial pursuit. 'If your work exists, you exist,' she huffed. 'Ask God.'

"Last summer at the women's crafts festival in Vermont I bought two beautiful woolen tie-dyed shawls. One is red, with a yellow sun; the other, brown, with an orange-and-purple one. I gave the brown one to her, for 'chilly' London. I can just imagine her there, an ordinary colored woman from the colonies, to the people who notice her in the street. But what a writer! How else would we know all that we know about the psyche of South Africa? About the sexism of Africa? About the Bush people of the Kalahari? About Botswana? It is only because Bessie Head sits there in the desert, in her little hut, writing, that we have knowledge of a way of life that flowed for thousands of years, which would otherwise be missing from human record. This is no small thing!"

It wasn't. And yet, for just a moment, Suwelo wanted it to be. He wanted American history, the stuff he taught, to forever be the center of everyone's attention. What a few white men wanted, thought, and did. For he liked the way he could sneak in some black men's faces later on down the line. And then trace those backward until they appeared even before Columbus. It was like a backstitch in knitting, he imagined, the kind of history teaching that he did, knitting all the pieces, parts, and colors that had been omitted from the original design. But now to have to consider African women writers and Kalahari Bushmen! It seemed a bit much.

"Ola drove Ms. Head to the airport himself," Fanny continued. "As she was getting into the car I told her I had a confession to make: Though I had loved all her stories, and especially *Maru*, I had not really understood her fattest book, *A Question of Power*.

"'Oh,' she said, in her Cape Colored accent, 'I'm not surprised atall. It is the map of a soul being destroyed, and the demons that one usually only imagines behind one's eyelids have been given names and faces. They've left the skull of the sufferer and actually lounge about in her rooms. There are some people who immediately connect with the book, but that is because they've been there.' She turned to embrace my mother and say good-bye to her. Then she said: 'Those people who understand it right off don't even need to read it. They're all staring out into space quite peacefully by now.'

"Overall, I would have to say I felt she didn't quite approve of me. I felt I appeared too solid, too complacent. Too sane. Most writers, I imagine, really worship the glint of madness in other people; torture, to them, must be people who always speak and act in monochrome. She is one of the wariest people I've ever met. She actually looked over her shoulder as we talked. She has light, obviously, tons of it, but it's definitely diffused.

"When Ola came back from the airport, he told us she'd had a complete nervous breakdown some years ago. That she was simply crushed. She got her health back by taking care of an experimental community garden. In Botswana she has to report to the authorities every day.

"'What a life,' said my mother.

"'Yes,' said Ola, 'it makes the little trouble I manage to cause here seem small mangoes indeed. She is paying for who she is with her life. But, don't we all?'"

"In every book you write there's a chap called Francis," Ola was saying to a local white writer one morning as Fanny came in to breakfast. "Is this accidental or is there some sort of inscrutable meaning the reader is supposed to get?"

"Come on," said the man, "there's only one Francis, in my first book. Later on there's a Frances with an *e*, and then in my last book a Frank."

"But aren't they all the same name, more or less?" he asked.

"Good morning, Ola," Fanny said. She kissed the top of his head, and he flung an arm around her. He was in the jovial mood, as he sometimes phrased it, of the literarily inclined escaped convict.

"This is my daughter from America," he said proudly. "Fanny, meet Henry Bates, a founding member of our writers' guild, come to warn me away from harm."

Henry Bates was small and pasty-faced with light-colored hair and a beer paunch.

"I've been telling him," he said, "just because he knows or is related to everyone in the government doesn't mean they won't get tired of him."

"She doesn't know we're related to anyone," Ola said. He turned to Fanny, "We're not really related to those imbeciles in the government, because obviously we're not in progression. You know the Hindu saying that you're only related to those with whom you are in spiritual progression? But a few of your uncles are in positions of authority. And do you know, when they arrested me, after running the bulldozer through my play—a hell of a final curtain, you have to admit!—two of them came to my cell just for 'a little chat.' Politics gives them a headache, so they wanted to talk soccer. Soccer. These are men who've never read a book in their lives. Never stayed awake through a complete play. If they didn't read it or see it by form five, they don't know anything about it.

"'What are you trying to do,' one of them said, 'make us look bad in the eyes of the world?' He was serious.

"'Obenjomade, listen to me,' I said. 'Look at my mouth, and

clean out your ears, I CANNOT MAKE YOU LOOK WORSE. I am only a human being, after all.'

"'But Abajeralasezeola,' he says, patiently, 'the government is trying as hard as it can.'

"'Only the president, his wives, his mistresses, his ministers, his relatives, and the army have enough to eat. Only their children can afford to go to school. The government should try harder. You know, pave a road now and then. Build a hospital. And by the way, why is it that after curfew every night the only people one sees are in army uniform? Among other things, you would think we are an all-male country. And you know what the rest of the world would think of that. And why a curfew, come to think of it? One thing, at least, that Africans always owned before was the night. With "freedom" they seem to have lost even that.'

"'Go ahead, be funny. Everyone always laughs at your plays. But you shouldn't make fun of people who are trying hard to make something of the country now that the white man has left.'

"'Look at my mouth, Obenjomade, second son of my father's third wife; clean out your ears: THE WHITE MAN IS STILL HERE. Even when he leaves, he is not gone.'

"'But Abajeralasezeola,' he says, 'why don't you help us instead of sitting back criticizing? Why don't you write plays that show everyone at his best? You could show how the government is trying to feed and clothe and educate people, even though the whites left everything in a shambles. Why not write a play about how they blew up their own university, their own radio station, and their own hospitals and bridges rather than turn them over to us?'

"'Obenjomade, cup your endearingly large ears: EVERYONE ALL OVER THE WORLD KNOWS EVERYTHING THERE IS TO KNOW ABOUT THE WHITE MAN. That's the essential meaning of television. BUT THEY KNOW NEXT TO NOTHING ABOUT THEMSELVES.'

"'The white man?' he asked.

"'No, the people,' I said.

"'But Abajeralasezeola,' he finally said, laughing, 'you are the only one who thinks the way you do.'

"'You are wrong, Obenjemade,' I said. 'THE WOMEN THINK AS I DO.'

"'But Abajeralasezeola,' he said, shrugging, 'WHO CARES WHAT WOMEN THINK?'"

Henry Bates and Fanny were both laughing at the faces Ola made as he talked. He didn't look his sixty years. He looked boyish, even impish, as he heartily laughed himself.

In prison he had slept on the floor, he said, and he thought it had cured his neuritis. Actually, that was a line in his next play, he added.

Henry Bates threw up his hands.

Ola was suddenly sober. "Oh, Henry Bates," he said, "watch my mouth: WHERE WERE YOU AND YOUR WORRIES WHEN I WAS IMPRISONED AND TORTURED BY THE WHITES? When my people stop acting like the white man, I can write plays that show them at their best!"

H E COULD not tell the shrink that he was in love with a woman who periodically fell in love with spirits.

"But why can't you tell him?" Fanny asked him once, as he was trying to explain his sense of inadequacy, of shame, to her. "What good is a shrink who doesn't understand about spirits?"

In so many ways, in most, she was an ordinary person. Suwelo had gazed at her hopelessly as she asked this. She had her arms raised and was arranging and rearranging her long, braided hair, turning this way and that in her chair. In her feminine self-absorption and present indifference to other world views she made him think of Cleopatra.

The shrink was a middle-aged Jewish man who never said anything about himself, which made it hard to say anything to him. Week after week Suwelo waited for some sign that there was a bona-fide struggling human being across from him. Someone who had the least chance of comprehending his plight. But—nothing.

"Spirits?" he asked, moving a paperweight, like the one in *Citizen Kane*, ever so slightly on the papers that formed a neat pile on his desk.

"Yes," Suwelo said. "At the moment..." He paused. It seemed

farfetched. It seemed futile. What would Dr. Bernie Kessel-baum know?

"Yes?"

"At the moment it's a man named . . . Chief John Horse." There, he'd got that much out. He nearly wept from the effort. "But it doesn't have to be men," he said quickly. It didn't even have to be people, but he thought he'd save Fanny's attachment to trees and whales until he could see further.

Kesselbaum's face was impassive. Suwelo hated the impassivity.

"Who is Chief John Horse?"

There was a long silence.

"Guess who I discovered today!" she'd cried happily.

"Who?" he'd asked, stirring the cream of asparagus soup as she came flying through the door.

"Chief John Horse!"

He was used to these enthusiasms, yet each one managed to hurt. He always felt he wasn't enough for her and envisioned months of loneliness to come, when he would seem barely to exist.

"Oh!" he'd said, with faked interest, "and where does—who was it? Chief John Horse?—live?" But he could see that, for the time being, whoever Chief John Horse was lived in his wife.

Ramblingly she had told him of this man who was a chief, a black Indian chief, among the Seminoles of Florida, before it became a state ("Of course, before it was a state," he'd murmured, thinking how hard it was to imagine the existence of land before it was a state), of how the Seminoles refused to enslave the black people who had escaped from slavery and how they were accepted into the Seminole nation. There had been innumerable fights, she said (eyes flashing, as if she'd been present), when the white slavers pursued them. There had been a long march to Mexico. Years of working for the Mexican government, fighting Mexican bandits. Then, after slavery had ended in the United States, Chief John Horse and his people — men, women, children — returned to Texas. This was in the eighteen-seventies, she said, and Suwelo was again surprised, as he often was, that even though he was a historian he had heard nothing of this. There, because the U.S. army had never been able to beat them and saw that it never would, it hired them to help rid Texas of the same kind of bandits that John Horse and his gang had fought in Mexico.

Suwelo spun this story out for Kesselbaum to the best of his memory.

He'd said to Fanny disdainfully, "Oh, he was a buffalo soldier." By which he meant a killer of Indians. For the white man.

She'd looked at him strangely. Then said quietly, "Yes, and no. All his life he was looking for a little bit of land the whites didn't covet, a little bit of peace. He got neither. But that was the dream."

"And what became of him?" he'd asked.

She'd shrugged. "Rode off into the sunset, of course. Back to Mexico. At least in Mexico the government appreciated his skills as a soldier and offered him some land. More than this country ever did. Here, he didn't even get a pension!"

Her eyes had taken on that faraway look that said she was riding back to Mexico with John Horse; that they were busy picking up women and children and bright-faced black men who dreamed of living free along the way.

He couldn't stand it.

"And was this a real person?" asked Kesselbaum. "In history, I mean."

"Oh, yes," said Suwelo. "I feel lucky when they are real

people, for then we can talk about them somewhat. It's harder when she's possessed by a spirit but doesn't know who or what it is."

"And does this happen often?"

"Once every couple of years or so. But sometimes there'll be just a slight infatuation. We'll be going along happily enough. We'll be like two people holding hands and wading across a shallow river. Then she'll step into a deep current that seems there only for her and be swept away. While she's carried by the current, I'm left alone, holding . . . nothing. If she remembers to say good morning most days, it's a wonder. Making love is a disaster. I never know who's there. I'm certainly not, as far as she's concerned, though she claims otherwise."

For a long time Fanny had not experienced orgasm with him; she learned how it was accomplished from some of her women friends. This was at a time when every conscious woman carried a speculum and mirror in her backpack, and, it seemed to Suwelo, at the drop of a hat they were flopping down on their backs in circles together and teaching each other the most astonishing things. Still, when he asked her what she'd experienced during orgasm, she was as likely to claim she'd experienced a sunrise or a mountain or a waterfall as that she'd experienced him. Sometimes she just whispered, "Adventure," or "Resistance," or "Escape!" This was a great puzzle to him.

"Many people have passionate interests in historical figures," said the shrink.

This was true. But Fanny Nzingha found the spirit that possessed her first in herself. Then she found the historical personage who exemplified it. It gave her the strange aspect of a trinity—she, the spirit, the historical personage, all sitting across the table from you at once.

The intensity wore him out.

As he did with all her spirit lovers, he snuck behind her back and did detective work on John Horse. He was helped in this by William Loren Katz's book *Black Indians*, in which John Horse's story is told in some detail. Somewhat sheepishly, he gave the volume to Fanny for her birthday. Chief John Horse, he'd read, safely dead a hundred years. Hah! Obviously these old spirits like Horse's never died. Had had an Indian partner called "Wild Cat." Had married a pure Seminole woman. Then a Mexican one. Probably Indian as well.

"What do you love about these people," he'd asked her once.

"I dunno," she said. "They open doors inside me. It's as if they're keys. To rooms inside myself. I find a door inside and it's as if I hear a humming from behind it, and then I get inside somehow, with the key the old ones give me, and are, and as I stumble about in the darkness of the room, I begin to feel the stirring in myself, the humming of the room, and my heart starts to expand with the absolute feeling of bravery, or love, or audacity, or commitment. It becomes a light, and the light enters me, by osmosis, and a part of me that was not clear before is clarified. I radiate this expanded light. Happiness."

And *that*, Suwelo knew, was called "being in love."

O LA told us last night," Fanny wrote in her next letter, "that a play he is thinking of writing somewhere down the line — 'though admittedly,' he joked, 'my line may be quite short!' — is about Elvis Presley.

"'*The* Elvis Presley?' my mother queried. '*Our* Elvis Presley?'

"'Mr. Rocket Sockets himself?' I chimed in.

"'Precisely,' said Ola, smiling.

"'You see,' Ola said, enjoying our bemusement, 'in our country we, too, have many different tribes, just as you have in America. You know, you have Black and Indian and Anglo and Jewish tribes; Asian, Chicano, and Middle Eastern tribes. And so on. Here we have the Olinka, the Ababa, the Hama, and the white tribe, of which there are several sub or mini tribes.

"'Now all of these tribes try to maintain their own tribal identities, and that is natural to man, who perpetuates his genetic identity by controlling the woman he uses for production of his children, but it is not necessarily natural to nature, who will produce for anyone. So over time a lot of racial boundaries are crossed and new people created. What is fascinating is to see the love or hatred that is expressed for these new people, who don't, after all, have a firm tribal category in which to be imprisoned.'

"'But what has this to do with Elvis Presley?' asked my mother.

"'My play will use him only as a metaphor. He will be a kind of vehicle for what I attempt to point out.'

"'Which is?'

"'That in him white Americans found a reason to express their longing and appreciation for the repressed Native American and black parts of themselves. Those non-European qualities they have within them and all around them, constantly, but which they've been trained from birth to deny.'

"We talked on into the night about this; Ola eventually playing some of his treasured Elvis Presley and Johnny Cash records.

"'I don't listen to them as you do,' he said. 'I listen to them to hear where commercial and mainstream cultural success takes people, a part of whose lineage is hidden even from themselves, in a world—or in this case, a country—that insists on racial, cultural, and historical amnesia, if you wake up one century and find yourself "white."'

"According to Ola, Elvis Presley and Johnny Cash are both Indians. A foreigner sees this immediately, he says; Americans do not. He says this explains Elvis's clothing style. His love of buckskin and fringe, of silver. And of course culturally, he says, he was as black as all the other white people in Mississippi.

"'But didn't he have blue eyes?' asked my mother.

"'Probably the only white things he owned,' said Ola. 'Blue eyes are like money; they pay your way in.'

"So assume my father is right; what could it have meant to be as 'successful' as Elvis? Suppose that behind those blue eyes and full lips, and under that thick black Indian hair, there was another: the old, ancient Indian. Suppose he, too, or she, watched. If he was Indian, he would probably have been Choctaw, for that's the tribe that existed, and maybe still does exist, in his part of Mississippi. Suppose his ancestors hid out among the white people, as so many of the Cherokee people hid out among the blacks and whites. Trying to evade the soldiers who rounded up the Indians for the long march to Oklahoma—the Trail of Tears. Suppose that little bump-and-grind the crowds loved so was originally a movement of the circle dance. That's what it would resemble, if you watched it in slow motion. Suppose that little hiccupy singing style of his was once a war whoop. Or an Indian love call.

"On we talked into the night, listening to the crickets and appreciating the warm brilliance of the stars. People are called 'stars' not only because they shine—with the glow of self-expression and the satisfaction this brings—but because the qualities they exemplify are, as far as human lives are concerned, eternal. We are attracted to their sparkle, their warmth, their light, but they will be forever distant from us. So distant we can never quite believe our inseparability. Never quite believe that we are also composed of the light that they have. Ola says he is convinced that human beings want, above all else, to love each other freely, regardless of tribe, and that when they're finally able to do it openly—although the true essence of the person they've focused on is camouflaged by society's dictation—there is always the telltale quality of psychic recognition—that is to say, hysteria; the weeping of the womb.

"The Choctaw lad with the long black hair, full lips, and sultry eyes is the mate the pioneer maidens would have chosen, if they'd had the chance, Ola said. And for the first time I imagined Elvis as really beautiful: bronze, lithe, running lightly through the primeval forests of Mississippi, hair to his waist. Their great-great-granddaughters are still weeping over their loss. And so, to my surprise, was I!

"If Ola is exiled, he says perhaps he will come to America, and he and I together can write this play. He said this teasingly, noticing my sniffle and that he had obviously moved me very much.

"I never dreamed I would so enjoy having a father. It is like having another interesting mind, somewhat similar to your own but also strangely different, to rummage through."

I WOULDN'T mind dying if dying was all," Miss Lissie told Suwelo. "The old folks used to say that all the time down on the Island. Somebody would witness it with a heart-felt *um-huh*. And I used to think they knew more about life than they thought. For dying, I can tell you, is the least of it. Dying is even pleasant. You just recede from everything, including torture, and burn out quietly, like a candle. What's not pleasant is coming back, and whether they have sense enough to know it or not, everybody, well almost everybody, does. Don't ask me how or why. They just do. I can appreciate the idea that to come here a lot of times is no more a miracle than to come here once. That's the truth of it.

"You take the way things are going in the world today. You have your poisoned rivers and your poisoned air and your children turning into critters before your eyes. You have your leaders that look like empty cartons and the politicians who look drugged. You have a world that scares everybody to death. You can't go nowhere. You can't eat anything. You can't even hardly make love. And that's just today. There are days when the best thought you can have is that one day you'll die and leave it all behind.

"Suwelo, let me tell you, you can't leave it behind. The life in this place is your life forever. You will always be here; and the ground underneath you. And you won't die until *it* does. It *is* dying, and the people are, too—but, Suwelo, my fear is not that we people and the earth we're on will die. Everything eventually dies, maybe. But it looks like it will take a long time and death will be painful and slow. It's the difference between being blindfolded and shot dead in the first volley of bullets and being tortured to death very slowly by men paid by the hour for their work. It is not simply a struggle between life and death. That is too easy, I guess. It's between life everlasting and death everlasting, and everlasting is a very long time.

"I am tired of it. Not tired of life. But afraid of what living is going to look like and be like next time I come."

Now Suwelo was on the train going back home to California. He crossed the Rockies and he crossed the desert. He thought of his months in Uncle Rafe's house and almost crossed himself. He thought of Fanny. Of who she was, really, and of what each of *her* previous selves must have been. Though Fanny had left San Francisco, and wrote that she had no desire to see him, he wished that he could meet her all over again, from the perspective of someone who believed true love never died and that you only suffer if you struggle—and that as surely as struggle led to suffering, suffering led to a knowledge of how not to. There were, after all, lifetimes and lifetimes, and love alone was healing and balm. Love alone, mother's milk.

He had finally sold the house and would now have money on which to live while he perhaps wrote an "oral" history—one of those unofficial-looking books, full of "he said" and "she said," that he'd always despised—about Mr. Hal and Miss Lissie. Before he left Baltimore, he'd driven to Miss Lissie's address, only to find it was also the address of Mr. Hal. These two elderly friends were quietly painting in the backyard, a narrow strip of pink verbena separating their easels. They did not stop as he sat on the back steps watching them. They painted, with loving strokes, what was directly in front of them: the back of their own small, white-clapboard house, a large ivy-encircled pecan tree towering over its front, a garden along one side with flowers and fruits growing all together. There were giant dahlias and blue morning glories decorating both house and corn. The sun was warm and the day eternity itself, and Suwelo soon lay back on the porch and drifted off to sleep.

When the two old friends had sat beside him, as he was rousing himself from sleep, he felt as if he knew all about them and yet knew nothing. He knew that they had sent Anatole to Fisk University and that he became a professor of German at Tuskegee. He knew that Lulu, talented and audacious, a singer and dancer par excellence, had gone off, in high spirits, with a musical-comedy team to Paris. Paris, unfortunately, had fallen to Hitler while she was there. Lulu and many of the other black and colored performers working in Paris at the time were never heard from again. He knew that his uncle Rafe had loved Miss Lissie and loved also his best friend, and hers, her soul mate and sometime husband, Mr. Hal. He knew they had lived together more or less harmoniously for many years and had remained friends until Uncle Rafe's death. He knew that Miss Lissie was indeed an extraordinary person, whose rarity would be known and appreciated only by those people least likely to be believed, even if they spoke of it to others—and apparently Uncle Rafe and Mr. Hal and Miss Lissie herself had kept mainly mum. But they were all three of them rare people, Suwelo thought, for they had connected directly with life and not with its reflection; the mysteries they found themselves involved in, simply by being alive and knowing each other, carried them much deeper into reality than "society" often permits people to get. They had found themselves born into a fabulous, mysterious universe, filled with fabulous, mysterious others; they had never been distracted from the wonder of this gift. They had made the most of it.

"I'm leaving," said Suwelo, stretching and getting to his feet.

"And we know we go with you," said Miss Lissie, handing him, with a smile, a small flat package wrapped in brown paper and tied with a string. She stuffed a fat pink envelope into his breast pocket. A mouse came out of the house and stopped, blinked at the sun, and hurried back inside. A bird dropped, stunned, to the porch; it had flown into a windowpane, in which it no doubt saw a reflection of the sky.

When Suwelo walked back to the street, passing by Mr. Hal's ancient truck, parked neatly next to Miss Lissie's smart gray Datsun, he carried with him the image of the two old people waving him on, holding hands and smiling, it seemed, at the very word "goodbye."

And they had painted him, a part of their life, lying on their back porch, surrounded by all the things they loved. Asleep.

But what was in the package? What was their gift? Suwelo took a deep breath as he carefully pulled off the string. The brown paper crackled as he ran his fingers underneath it. He thought at first they'd given him a stack of albums, for the package was just that size, though quite light. But no, there were paintings. He lifted them out and stared at them, first one, then the other, for a long time. They were obviously self-portraits. Perhaps not obviously, though, for on one painting was written "Self-portrait, Lissie Lyles," and on the other, "Self-portrait, Harold D. Jenkins." The background of the paintings showed all the familiar things the two friends loved to paint: their trees and corn and morning glories, the pink-and-cream spider flower. It was the center of the paintings that was different from anything Suwelo had ever seen. For instead of faces, as in a portrait, there were merely the outlines of their upper bodies, a man's shape and a woman's shape, and these outlines surrounded blue, infinite space, painted with such intensity, depth, and longing that it was as luminous and as inviting as the sky. Wonderingly, Suwelo turned the paintings over, as if that infinite space might have leaked through to the other side. What he saw made him smile and hug the paintings to his heart, as the train shot through a long gray tunnel into an even blacker dark. On the back of Lissie Lyles's self-portrait were the words, in emerald lettering, "Painted by Hal Jenkins." On Hal's self-portrait, in bright red, were the words "Painted by Lissie Lyles."

SUWELO, now at home, was intrigued by the fat pink envelope, which he lifted to his nose and sniffed. It smelled like Miss Lissie—old-fashioned white roses under a hot summer sun. Turning it over, he was surprised to see, in Miss Lissie's ancient script, all sharp points and decisively rounded *o*'s: "They burned us so thoroughly we did not even leave smoke." He did not know what he expected to find on opening the letter, but the blank pages that lay in his hand, over a dozen of them, struck him as an odd missive, even from Miss Lissie.

It was days before he understood, and then, in the middle of the night, it came to him. This part of Miss Lissie's story was written in invisible ink. At the moment he realized this he also knew that all he needed to read her letter was a candle. Heaving himself out of bed, he went in search of one. Luckily he found a box of them—an earlier gift from Miss Lissie and Mr. Hal—on top of the fridge. Still in his nightshirt, hunched over the kitchen table, the candle close up behind the first sheet of paper, and the chill of the San Francisco fog seeping into his bones, he began to read . . . what at first seemed to be some kind of religious raving.

"The religion I was taught as a child, growing up on the Island," wrote Miss Lissie, "is a thing that causes people to try to eat up the earth, since we were taught 'everything is for man,' while man was never asked to be for anything in particular. Well, for 'God,' but who knew what that was?"

"Hmmm," said Suwelo, yawning, and scratching his chin.

"The first witches to die at the stake were the daughters of the Moors." *Moors?* he mused skeptically. "It was they (or, rather, we) who thought the Christian religion that flourished in Spain would let the Goddess of Africa 'pass' into the modern world as 'the Black Madonna.' After all, this was how the gods and goddesses moved from era to era before, though Islam, our official religion for quite a long time by now, would have nothing to do with this notion; instead, whole families in Africa who worshiped the Goddess were routinely killed, sold into slavery, or converted to Islam at the point of the sword.

"Yes," and here Suwelo imagined a long, hesitant breath, "I was one of those 'pagan' heretics they burned at the stake.

"They burned us first—well, we were so visible. Even after centuries of living among the Europeans. You can think of Desdemona and Othello, if you can't come at it any other way, in trying to catch even a glimpse of our presence in Europe. The Inquisition eventually traveled where they were, too, to watery Venice, a dank and still somehow beautiful place, and there were screams and firelit shadows bouncing off the walls of the Doges' Palace in St. Mark's Square for months on end.

"But did you never wonder why, in the little bit of the story the whites could not prevent Shakespeare, at least, from trying to tell (that 'mysterious' playwright about whom so very little is known), that there are only Moors (defined as men) and no Moor*esses*? I can tell you, we were there, somewhat paler than when we were in Africa, yes, but imagine Desdemona's and Othello's children. We were there, for sure, and brought up to be our fathers' daughters, our fathers who loved learning more than any other thing, and who embraced a religion that had terrorized them in Africa, and who traveled the world and married strangers and barbarians in order to learn more about their curious, alien ways. Our poor fathers, whose only crime was that they loved their Mother, but who, in seeking to protect Her and themselves, helped to change us all, finally, into another spirit and another race.

"The Inquisitors slaughtered our fathers and took their property for the church, as was done also to the Jews. Our African fathers, who, fleeing the religious dictatorship of Islam, while dressed in its cloak, had come into Spain, caught their breath, found themselves and their incredible handsomeness and learning admired, and, for the most part, settled there. Some of them pushed on into France and Germany, Poland, England, Ireland, Russia. One or two settled in Venice and inspired a famous play. Well, you get the picture. If I am not mistaken it is only in Poland that Our Black Lady, the Great Mother of All—Mother Africa, if you will—is still openly worshiped. Perhaps that is why it is said of the Poles that they are none too bright.

"But during the time of which I am speaking," the letter continued, and the smell of the tallow candle seemed suddenly to hurt Suwelo's nose, "and which I have tried to drop from memory because it is so horrible, they obliterated us. They said the mother of their white Christ (blonde, blue-eyed, even in black-headed Spain) could never have been a black woman, because both the color black and the female sex were of the devil. We were evil witches to claim otherwise. We *were* witches; our word for healers. We brought their children into the world; we cured their sick; we washed and laid out the bodies of their dead. We were far from evil. We helped Life, and they did not like this at all. Whenever they saw our power it made them feel they had none. They felt themselves the moon to our sun. And yet, as every woman knows, the moon also has great power. We are connected to all three planes—past, present, future—of life; so is man, but he will not let himself see it. He has let himself be taught that his own mother is evil and has joined religions in which her only role, after nurturing and rearing him with her blood, is to shut up."

Suwelo imagined Miss Lissie's frown.

"Can you believe it?" the letter continued. "It is as if each man forces every other man to go out into the night without a candle, to go out among the speaking without a tongue, to go out among the seeing without an eye, to go out among the standing without a leg.

" 'If you want to join the company of men,' they are told, 'you must do something about your mother.' Meekly man says, 'What must I do?' Teeth already chattering from the cold he will feel without the warmth of his best friend. Hah! 'We want you to shut her up,' he is told. 'Don't pay any attention to anything she might suggest. In return, we will help you pretend that you created yourself. Just ignore her. Don't hear her. Let her weep, let her moan, let her starve.' This is what they have done to their own mothers; it is certainly what they have done to Mother Africa.

"They burned us so thoroughly—the dark women so recently, relatively speaking, from Africa—that, unlike the Jews and homosexuals and Gypsies and artists and rebels they also burned, not to mention the rich women whose property they stole even before their ashes cooled, we did not even leave a trace of smoke. The connection between black woman and white was broken utterly; the blood sisterhood that African women shared with European women was gone as if it had never been. In France, there is nothing. Notre-Dame. Our Lady. Not our *Black* Lady. In England, nothing; unless you find it among the remnants of the Celts, their own way of life smashed to bits. In Ireland, rumors of 'the little people' and all those ignorant jokes about 'black Irish.'

"In Venice, where Othello was a nobleman, there are today endless statues of Moors, dressed in the livery of slaves. In Spain—well, there's all that 'Moorish' architecture, too exuberantly *colored* to be easily explained.

"When they burned me at the stake I cursed them; what else is a dark woman to do? I did not mind that they coveted my house and the land my father left me. I would have given it to them, to save at least the lives of my children, who were grouped around me, and whose screams burned in my ears more piercingly than the fire. But what I refused to give up was my essence; nor could I. For it was simply this: I do not share their vision of reality, but have, and cherish, my own. And when you look at the world today, it fits my curse exactly, but with one exception: Those I cursed do not suffer alone; everything and everyone does. This I would not have had. It was a long time in the learning, that lesson: You cannot curse a part without damning the whole. That is why Mother Africa, cursed by all her children, black, white, and in between, is dying today, and, after her, death will come to every other part of the globe."

Now there was an abrupt change in tone, and Suwelo noticed, with some alarm, that as he read each line, it completely disappeared; Miss Lissie had written her story not only in invisible ink, but in invisible ink that could not be read twice. He moved the page closer to the flickering candle to make sure of this observation. He lifted other sheets to the flame. They were blank. He sighed, shook his head, and read on.

"Now woman," the letter continued, "by hook and by crook, and with a strong memory of African Eden in her batteries, kept alive some feeling for the other animals, though she was reduced usually to the caring and feeding of one small house cat. Well, there she was, black, with her broom and her cat, her hair like straw. Ever wonder why witches' clothes are always black, and their hair every which way?" Suwelo knew Miss Lissie, in writing this, had laughed out loud.

"We never forgot it should be possible to communicate with anything that had big enough eyes! So there we were, the dark women, muttering familiarly to every mouse or cow or goat about the place. Their writers of fairy tales would make much of this tendency. We were shoved into the beds of men old enough to be our grandfathers, in countries where, unlike in Africa, bathing was simply not done; on estates far from human beings of any kind. The animals and our children were our world. Foolishly we thought the animals and our children, at least, would not be taken from us. But the Inquisitors, set in place to control us, declared 'consorting' with animals a crime, punishable by being burned at the stake! And our children fell into the hands of their fathers, their 'masters,' who traded them for gold, as they traded flour and land and cloth.

"The Inquisitors claimed we were fucked and suckled by bulls and goats and all manner of malformed animal creatures. For good measure, they gave their devil—the black thing that represented the people they most despised and wished to be perceived as separate from—sharp cloven hoofs and pointed horns, a tail. They made it seem not only natural but also righteous to kill, as brutally as possible, without any feeling but lustful self-justification, any animal or dark creature that one saw.

"There was something about the relationship she had with animals and with her children that deeply satisfied woman. It was of this that man was jealous.

"The animals can remember; for, like sight, memory is renewed at every birth. But our language they will never speak; not from lack of intelligence, but from the different construction of their speaking apparatus. In the world of man, someone must speak for them. And that is why, in a nutshell, Suwelo, goddesses and witches exist."

SOME months after Arveyda came back from his travels
with Zedé and told Carlotta the heartrending story of her
mother's life, she noticed that the red parrot-feather earrings
had fallen apart; there were still wispy gold threads that went
through her ears, but these had fallen free of the feathers themselves, which were bedraggled shreds that had to be smoothed
flat with an iron. Taking .. .ed, tissue-thin blots of color with
her one day, she stopped at a shop in San Francisco where anything at all, depending on size and flatness, could be encased
in plastic. Within hours a necklace had been made for her, and
so, around her neck, enclosed in clear, hard plastic, she began
to wear the feathers. In her jewel box at home she continued to
keep the stones, until one day she realized they had spent their
entire existence, in the thousands of years before they came
into her care, in the open air. She took them out and casually
placed them in their original formation—which she now saw
as a pyramid or triangle, or the women's sign for peace—beneath the arching overhang of a giant California live-oak tree
in the San Francisco arboretum. Beneath this tree she began,
quite frequently, to eat her lunch, do yoga stretches, run in
place, and meditate and pray.

It was after she began wearing the new necklace that she started, for the first time in years, to dream. In her very first dream she was a young child in a cave with her mother, only this mother was not Zedé but someone much larger and darker, and that mother was busily painting something on the walls in bright colors. Carlotta, too, was encouraged to paint, and so she painted the walls and herself. Her mother was dark bronze, with black wavy hair that bushed to her waist, but now, behind her, looming up against the very topmost reaches of the cave softly came her father, a giant of a man, bearded and fierce. But no, he was smiling. He was darker even than her mother, and his hair was dull. Then the three of them stood together in the mouth of the cave, exactly as a small San Francisco family would stand in their doorway peering out into a rainy day. Only now that they stood in the light, Carlotta saw that if they were in a cave, it was not a natural one; the sides of the entrance, where her fingers rested, were smooth as glass. Looking up, she saw that the cave entry was indeed a door, and that the lintel was made of smooth stone into which a strange beast with the head of a very ugly, big-nosed and long-lipped person was magnificently and scarily carved. But Carlotta felt no fear.

PART THREE

L IBERATING Zedé and Carlotta was the last act I did as
Mary Ann Haverstock," the playwright Mary Jane Briden,
after three decades of living in Africa, would tell her American
and African friends. "It was one of the more exciting things I'd
ever done, and I was lucid! My mind had been clouded with
drugs for such a long time that when I went back into the jungle to get them, everything, every tree, every bush, every star,
the sun, seemed to me as if just created. As we tore through the
bush, I was oohing and aahing over every little fern bank, every
little streamlet, the tiniest points of light captured in the drop-
lets of condensed dew on the leaves. I was smiling the whole
time. Admiring with each step my pretty pink boots, so bright
and flowerlike against the dark verdant tropical earth.

"It was easy to kill the dogs and steal into the compound of
the school. Easy to grab Zedé and Carlotta, easy to reach the
coast and my boat the *Recuerdo*. The voyage to San Francisco
was smooth and beautiful. Zedé, exhausted from excitement
and the escape itself, slept as if she were dead. I looked after
Carlotta, who had grown into a fat little Buddha of a girl. The
crew and I had not anticipated the storm. We'd planned a much
simpler disappearing act. We would contact the Coast Guard

and tell them the *Recuerdo* had a broken mast. By the time they
arrived, we would be long gone on my other boat, which shad-
owed our journey the whole time. But the storm did come,
and after calling the Coast Guard, we made our escape, never
dreaming the *Recuerdo*, the most seaworthy of sloops, would
capsize and fling its occupants into the sea. But I had made sure
Zedé and Carlotta always wore their life vests on deck, and so
I suppose that is what saved them.

"I read the newspapers later, with the story of my sunken
boat and the two odd boat people hauled up out of the ocean
and brought ashore. My parents, I also read, flew out to meet
them. This was in a second article, after the newspapers discovered whose daughter it was who owned the boat. And there
was an enchanting picture of Mom and Dad holding hands and
walking back to their limousine. It made me sad to see them;
they seemed so old, and so lost. The papers had spared them
nothing and raked over my 'youthfully misguided, race-mix-
ing radic-lib escapades' with typical Hearstian reacto-conser-
vative glee. Mom was still as frail as a sparrow from years of
starving herself so that she might appear a child's size next to
Dad's lumbering six feet four. I could never, once I understood
how love was made between men and women, bear to imagine
them making love, with him on top. I could feel how the breath
would be crushed out of her as her tiny rib cage supported his
heavy abdomen, chest, shoulders, and neck. Yet it wasn't likely
that she'd complain. This was all she knew. Her own father had
been huge and her mother even smaller and frailer than she
was. The family had liked to say, about my mother's mother,
that she weighed maybe a hundred pounds, soaking wet. I had
actually been pointedly reminded of this fact, growing up, as I
sat at the table refusing to eat anything but buttery mashed potatoes with a side order of chocolate milk.

"There was no reason for them to think me alive or to grieve over me excessively. For months after I became old enough to inherit my own money, I had made a quietly shocking spectacle of myself by giving it away. They looked on grimly, disapproving. But really, I had so much; and sometimes I was shaken to discover that there were weeks when, simply by letting my investments alone, I earned more, sometimes as much as three times more, than I had managed in the same period to give away. There was a dreadful feeling of creeping 'moneyism'; days when I felt for all the world like a field or forest being overtaken by kudzu. I felt I would drown in all my money, and the panic of that feeling only began to ease as I made plans to give up forever being who I was.

"How can I say this so that it doesn't seem totally awful? I was eager to give up being who I was. I had already chosen a new name, 'Rowena Rollins,' which, I was later to realize, I could only use comfortably on paper. In establishing myself in Africa, I called myself 'Mary Jane Briden,' getting rid of 'Ann,' which I'd never liked, and 'Haverstock,' which seemed just a pseudonym for cash, and adding a name that—now that I consider it—had something of the possibility of marriage in it. Prophetically, it would be in Africa that I would become, though only in name, a bride. But I simply did not know how to get about in the world without sufficient cash. This means I did not give away all my money, as my parents thought I would, saying at various times to me that when I grew old and penniless I would regret my 'foolish' behavior. I opened several foreign bank accounts under my new name and under a few long numbers and under a couple of other people's names, all deceased. I kept enough to live on, in other words, and to do whatever in the world I might modestly choose, and I left the *Recuerdo* sinking decisively into oblivion, like my old life, and went off in *The Coming Age*, the *Recuerdo*'s twin, except for a small turquoise snake embroidered on her sails. After years of barely conscious deliberation, this symbol had emerged as my personal emblem of spiritual expression. The snake, which sheds its skin but is ever itself, and, because of its knowledge of the secret places of the earth, free from the threat of extinction, apparently uneradicable; and turquoise, a color of cleansing of body and spirit, of the clarification of memories, and of powerful healing.

"I remember how I felt as the storm subsided and the fog began to clear. All that year I dressed in black jumpsuits, and as I sat in a deck chair with my steaming cup of camomile tea and my pink lace-up boots propped against the rail, I felt, for the first time that I could remember, not only mentally lucid and well defined against the landscape of my universe, but also actually *vivid*; in short, free.

"I did not really know where I was going, and so I returned to the past. But the old past, not one that I myself knew. I went to London and tramped about in the parks and museums and libraries for quite some months, listening intently, speaking when I could, until I'd developed something of a British accent. I then took the train out to Hampstead and the nursing home for the exceedingly rich and aged where *she* was. I couldn't decide, as I waited in the softly colored, restfully lighted lobby, whether I should pass myself off as a journalist or a student; surely I'd need some justification for my interest in Eleanora Burnham's life. But I had not reckoned on having been known to her in the past. The old past. The past of before I was born or even thought of.

"'Elly,' she croaked at me immediately. 'You've finally come back home! And what did you bring me?'

"She was the oldest, frailest, most ethereal-looking human being I'd ever seen, my great-aunt Eleanora. Her bright blue sunken eyes dominated her thin, wrinkled face. Her sparse white hair hung in two lusterless pigtails over her red, ethnically decorated nightdress. Daydress, too, I supposed, for she had the look and, as I bent over her, the smell of someone who, though clean, was never out of bed.

"But why should she call me 'Elly,' a diminutive of her own name?

" 'Elly Peacock!' she exclaimed happily, smiling broadly and without a tooth in her head. I sat on the edge of a chair beside the bed.

"The nurse winked at me. 'She's in and out of this world a great deal,' she said, smiling. 'Sometimes she thinks I'm her mother . . . and,' she said, looking down at her short skirt, 'dressed indecently.'

"I looked up at the blonde, plump, matronly woman. I thought she looked a bit like me—a Slav or Russian or eight-eenth-century English country version.

" 'I think Elly must be *this* person,' said the nurse, handing me an old photograph in a spotted silver frame. Two young women, with light upswept locks overflowing pins and clasps, and dressed identically in long dark dresses with lace at throat and sleeves, looked out calmly over the wheels of an old-fash-ioned bicycle built for two. 'Eleanora and Eleandra' was writ-ten in a spidery hand underneath. I immediately recognized myself in Eleandra.

" 'She's been here so long I think I know the whole family,' said the nurse. 'Or'—she smiled—'maybe I'm the one who's been here so long. Some days she can take me back as far as the eighteen hundreds, if I let her. Eleandra was her twin.'

"I looked at my great-aunt, at the neatly made bed in which her wasted frame made barely a ripple in the sheets, at the rows of old photographs on the table by the bed, and at the bottles of pebbles, all sizes, colors, degrees of roughness and smooth-ness set in among the photographs.

" 'She collected rocks,' said the nurse, raising her eyebrows for significance, 'In Africa.'

"Eleanora, however, was not to be patronized, even in her

condition; she rolled her eyes at the woman. 'Not only in Africa, you sow,' she hissed or, rather, frothed. 'All over the bloody world I traveled collecting them. You see, Elly, like you, I knew what was the real gold and silver. People used to break into places where I stayed, because I was a wealthy woman, but all they ever found were these. Once, a burglar emptied all the bottles and apparently bit every single pebble!' She chortled, but ended in a slight fit of coughing.

" 'Well,' said the nurse, '*excuse* me.' She went off to the next room, where I heard the querulous voice of her next patient greeting her at the door.

" 'You must learn to love only that which cannot be stolen,' the old woman wheezed. 'Why,' she said, 'I don't know why I should tell *you* that; after all, I learned it from you.'

" 'But how did you learn it from me?'

"She looked at me, visibly puzzled.

" 'I'm not Elly,' I said gently. 'I'm not your twin.'

"Eleanora brightened. 'Of course you're not my twin. That little twit.' She sucked her gums as toothed people suck their teeth. *Swak*, was the sound. The sound of irritation joined securely to dismissal. 'Nobody would learn anything from Elly Burnham. Elly Burnham never left home, and therefore couldn't come back. Well, she did leave home, but only to marry and then her home was just like the one she left. Oh, what a crushing bore! But Elly *Peacock*, our *aunt* Elly Burnham Peacock . . . Do you know, when she deigned to come back to England, which she did only because she needed treatment for the cancer that eventually killed her, the papers simply said, "The Lady Peacock has arrived." And for the longest time I thought my aunt was a peacock. Once, when I saw her, with my own two eyes, going by in a carriage with her dress all peacockish greens and blacks and purples and blues and her beautiful white face shaded by a tiny white parasol, I still thought perhaps she was. We were never allowed to see her up close, of course. She was a disgrace to England, and even more to the family. She had a liking for Arabs, you see. She loved Arabs, horses, and the desert, in that order. Or maybe she loved the desert, horses, and Arabs. I read all I could find about her, and I couldn't ever really tell. Then, too, she liked Africans.'

"When she stopped for breath, or wound down, as was the case — she actually seemed to have stopped breathing — I flung out my phony credentials: 'I'm a student journalist writing a paper on . . .' I stopped. What should it be on? The rich? The old and rich? The conditions in nursing homes run for the old rich? I could see that things were pretty well run here. Eleanora's bed linens were undoubtedly her own, or at least bought by someone who had a knowledge of linens. Her sheets were of that soft, rich material that made sleep delicious, her coverlet of ancient handmade lace. Her pillowcases were edged in lace also. And there was a large bouquet of spring flowers practically bursting from the Baccarat vase next to her bed. But of course she was rich enough to send fresh flowers to herself perpetually.

"'Africa!' she muttered, coming out of the snooze her long speech had induced. 'I hated Africa. The heat, the bugs, the leeches, the niggers.'

"She looked at me from under scabby white brows, her thin lips, in which the wrinkles had turned to furrows, poked out in resentment.

"Why is it, I wondered, that the racists in one's own family always come as such a surprise — and disappointment.

"'Oh, Aunt!' I said, without thinking, nonetheless claiming her as my own. But she had fallen fast asleep.

"I had a really good look at her then and thought she resembled a very old, a really, really old drooling and snoring baby girl.

"She had given her papers to a women's college in Guildford, to which the Burnhams had always been charitable, and on days when I did not go to visit her, I visited them. Not only papers, but baskets and bowls and sculptures and cloths as well. Indeed, there was, in one section of the library, 'the Eleanora Burnham Room.' It was a replica of a large bedroom and sitting room in an old colonial plantation house. There was her narrow, maidenly bed, covered with mosquito netting, a rattan easy chair and sofa, upholstered in faded blue paisley, her writing table, small and blue, beneath a fake window. The books were by her, a half dozen or so of them anyway, written while she lived in the tropics, and there were other old books: adventures, romances, studies in geography and history, and the family Bible, in which there was, among other family names, a listing of 'Eleandra Burnham, born on 29 May 1823.' My great-aunt Eleanora's twin, Eleandra, named for this adventuring aunt, was listed several decades later, and had not been like her at all, apparently. The walls of the room were lively with beautifully fierce African masks and long beaded fly whisks. There were also a couple of rat-eaten and sweat-stained 'bwana' hats.

"I was mainly interested in her diary, and to get at it I needed her permission, or, rather, the permission of her guardian. I found out who this was, a solicitor in London, and paid him a visit. Since he knew nothing of the existence of the diary—'You mean the old woman kept a diary? Whatever for, do you suppose?'—he could not find a reason to keep me from seeing it. I'd dressed carefully in a dowdy tweed suit and pulled my hair back from my face. Glasses that caused me to squint completed my outfit. This camouflage was probably not necessary, and yet I enjoyed it.

"And then, sitting in the rattan easy chair in her 'room' at the library, with the fake African sun streaming through the window and the women's college of Guildford, as far as I was concerned, on some other continent, instead of just outside the closed door (no one came, no one cared about Eleanora Burnham, no matter how much money and what quantity of 'artifacts' she'd bequeathed the college in her will, and of which the college had been informed, so naturally the administration had waited impatiently, over the years, for her to die), sitting in the easy chair, with the one volume at a time I was permitted to take, I made a startling discovery. Far from hating Africa and the bugs, leeches, and niggers, as she'd claimed, Africa had been the great love of my great-aunt's life.

> There is a little serpent here [she wrote in 1922] that is
> exactly the colour of coral. It lives only in certain trees
> and comes out of its hole, far up the tree, near dusk. It
> lives on tree spiders and bugs, and is known to sing. The
> natives tell me that it sings. They claim they have heard
> it sing millions of times, and act as if this is entirely
> ordinary. Furthermore, they ask why I have not heard
> it and why it should be so strange. Everything sings,
> they say.
>   But I do not. This, however, I cannot bear to tell them.
>   Well, today I at least saw the little creature. They
> had told me which tree at the edge of my yard I should
> keep an eye on, and, sure enough, today, just at dusk,
> down came this little coral fellow, sticking out its tongue,
> slithering primly down the tree looking for dinner and
> finding several plump *hors d'oeuvre* on the way. I watched
> it disappear into the grass, and I felt that although the
> colour was as vivid as I had been led by the natives
> to expect, I still could not believe it would sing. I felt
> perhaps they were only teasing me.

Another entry:

> I could not imagine living for a hundred years, yet the
> natives quite often live that long. They say it is because

everything they eat is alive. The grain they eat is so
alive that if they planted it instead of eating it, it would
come up. They eat fruit, grains, which they make into
porridge, and root crops. They eat a lot of boiled greens
and okra, both of which grow wild. They eat little or no
meat, and when asked to prepare thick slabs of it for me
and my English or European guests, they handle it as if
it is offensive.

BUT how had her great-aunt become interested enough in Africa to live there?

Eleanora was now a hundred years old. Mary Jane wondered if this pleased her. If it made her think of the old "natives" she had known. Such a loaded word, "natives." For people like her great-aunt, it had meant savages. It was not a word Mary Jane could imagine her great-aunt using to refer to herself, though she was a native of England.

Her great-aunt had been born in 1885, on March 23. She was an Aries, which explained her impulsive, headstrong nature. She *would* be a person who loved flying, for instance, long before anyone had any notion that flying could possibly be safe. She had flown, rapturously, in the first planes that went to Africa; Aries people were akin to birds. She would also follow her instincts regarding other worlds, other peoples. But what had been the pivotal experience of her great-aunt's life? Mary Jane sat now, several days a week, mostly watching her great-aunt sleep and thinking of that life, that grand life of the English upper class during the years before the Great (as they called it) War. Well, for one thing, they'd liked the word "great." She had gone on a tour of the "great" English country houses and been to Morley Crofts, in Warwickshire, the old house of her ancestors. She had trooped along over the checkered floors and gazed from the mullioned windows, inset with Celtic designs in stained glass, which looked oddly Egyptian. There was a profusion of coral-and-black serpents and jeweled shepherd's crooks. Morley Crofts covered many acres and resembled a medieval castle more than it did a house. Vast gardens surrounded it, and as she drifted about with the other tourists—who reminded her of rather pathetic sheep, in their polyester suits and spanking (and pinching) new tennis shoes, exclaiming with joy over each dovecote or gargoyle, each primrose path or giant dahlia—she imagined Eleanora sitting here or there among the garden statuary, reading a book or perhaps simply staring out into space, far out into the future, into Mary Jane's own time, and, with a small smirk of amusement, watching.

Mary Jane's own grandfather had left England penniless—cut off from his father's and grandfather's wealth, amassed in Ireland on the broken backs of the Irish—but with a sense of adventure and the desire to make his own fortune. He had succeeded splendidly, eventually owning copper mines in Missouri, petroleum fields in West Texas, and entire southern counties in Alabama and Georgia planted in cotton picked by illiterate blacks he probably never so much as glimpsed. His father and grandfather noted his success, so like their own—for the grandfather lived on and on. Sometimes Mary Jane thought she could almost remember him, but it was only the stories she remembered: of his fierce avarice, his contempt for weaker adversaries, his love of wealth for its own sake. The stories his children and grandchildren told about him were as pointed as morality tales and could as easily have been entitled "Lust," "Avarice," "Greed," but unlike morality tales, the message was never *against* these things. In any event, seeing this success, his antecedents heartily embraced him as the true heir of their av-

aricious genes and of course added much of their own vast re-
sources, after their deaths, to his.

By the time her own father was born, there was a need to
pull in one's fangs a bit. So Mary Jane and her brother and sister were brought up to be the kind of rich people who were as
fundamental to the country's stability as the earth but as inconspicuous as a rug. Oh, the little patent leather slippers and
simple cashmere sweaters, the plain camel's hair coats, smartly
hitting the back of the knee, the neat gray dresses, snug at the
waist, loose everywhere else, discreet hair ribbons, mostly black
and, this being the forties, sometimes plaid. And yet, when Mary
Jane and her sister walked down Fifth Avenue near the apartment her family kept there, she felt people stared at them and
knew instinctively they were rich. And laughed at their careful
squareness, and resented them.

When she left this life behind—the sleek blond hairdo that
flipped up at the ends like Doris Day's or Dina Merrill's, the
tiny white pearl earrings, the black velvet or plaid grosgrain
bow at the back of her neck—and wore paint-encrusted jeans
and funky turtleneck sweaters, and her hair had frizzed out
(with the help of a ton of chemicals) into a fiery sunburst of
resistance, well over a decade before this became de rigeur for
rich and radical white kids in the sixties, she understood why
it was that no matter how simply she and her sister dressed,
how inconspicuous they tried to make themselves, they were
always, in fact, giving themselves away. She decided that they
must have exuded a smell of quiet sufficiency, of absolute security, so lacking in the worlds they did not inhabit. This was the
smell of the upper class.

One day, in Eleanora's diary, Mary Jane saw the word
"M'Sukta," scribbled over and over in the margins of a page.
She liked the sound of it; however, flipping through the rest
of the diary she found no further evidence of the word. On

her next visit to her great-aunt she brought along some of the photographs from the Eleanora Burnham collection for her to identify. They were obviously old and rare, and not in the best condition, and this was permitted only after the library received a stern call from the London solicitor. Mary Jane's statement to the librarian that the photographs were meaningless without proper documentation—names and dates, at least—had fallen on deaf, seemingly irritated ears.

The head librarian's view was that all the photographs with white people in them *were* documented; at least, all the white people were named. Occasionally, too, a servant or hunting guide had a first name or nickname. There was a "Chumby," for instance, which hardly sounded African. But the backs of dozens of photographs of Africans without white people in them remained blank. Their faces, as thoughtful and moving as the photographs of American Indians taken by Edward Curtis in the nineteen-hundreds, deeply touched something in Mary Jane. Almost without exception the Africans were interestingly, often spectacularly, dressed, and this especially surprised and pleased her. The women's hairstyles, with their interwoven cowrie shells and feathers, were fabulous and made them look, at the same time, serene, regal, and wild. And the cloth of which their robes were made! In a museum near their apartment in New York, Mary Jane had seen Kente cloth, but she'd seen it in strips and as decoration around a sleeve or hem. In these photographs she saw an even more incredible cloth, stripped, like Kente, but glistening as if shot through with golden thread. In these photographs she saw Africans whose eyes, skin, clothes *shone*. With richness and intelligence and *health*. Finally, it was the shine of health that captivated Mary Jane, for she realized that so degraded had Africa become in the mind of the world that a healthy African, like the ones she saw in the photographs, was practically unimaginable. These were people she assumed her great-aunt had known, for without exception the eyes that looked back at the camera were kindly, acknowledging a special bond. But if they *were* people she had known, Eleanora could no longer speak of them. She gazed at the pictures Mary Jane held up to her, one by one, through a magnifying glass, and the tears spilled over her red and swollen lower lids. It was only at the last picture, not a photograph like the rest, but a painting, of the one broken face among the lot, an African woman wearing the beautiful robes of her tribe but painted against a gray stone interior of what might have been a cathedral, that Eleanora was able to utter a word. And the word she uttered, a sob really, was "M'Sukta."

The sulky head librarian, quite without knowing it, solved the problem.

"All of these pictures," she said to Mary Jane, as she was turning them in, "were taken by Lady *Eleandra* Burnham *Peacock*. I don't suppose you know anything about *her*. All her personal effects were willed to her niece, Lady *Burnham*. This explains why they are amongst Lady *Burnham's* collection." She actually sniffed when she came to the end of the second sentence. Taking the photographs with one hand, she flung down a small book with the other. "Here's something you might find interesting," she said.

When Mary Jane reached for it, however, the librarian put the carmine-colored tips of her newsprint-smudged fingers on it.

"You have to sign for it," she said, with the hateful petulance of bureaucrats everywhere.

This journal had a faded red velvet binding and a green, very faded, satin-ribbon marker. Its leaves were yellowed and water-stained, and many words, in the cramped, even script of a young woman writing by flashlight under the bedcovers, difficult to decipher. It had, however, belonged to the first—as far

as Mary Jane knew—Eleandra, and she opened it with a rapidly beating heart.

I was just out walking with my cousin T., who makes
me laugh so much I wish we were not cousins. His large
green eyes sparkle so in his ruddy face, and his lips are
as finely chiselled as a Roman statue's. I tease him all
the time about my wanting to marry him. It is a joke, of
course. I have been avoiding marriage for many years
now. T. knows I want to paint, just as I know he has no
interest in females. In all the family only we two seem
odd. The rest are adept at fitting in, of being perfectly
capable of tolerating, even condoning, and, dare I say
it, of elevating to an exalted state the condition of
boredom. How T. and I blushed with pleasure last night
at the ballet, a savage, wild thing that shocked Mother so
much Father had to pretend to be shocked as well, when
all it was was a history, in dance, of our early ancestors,
still heavily influenced by the dark peoples of these Isles
who preceded them, *alive*, as all of them no doubt were
before the Gauls and Romans descended upon them.
Where are they now, the Indians of Britain? The ballet
began with the predictable maiden with berry boughs
on her head, and, yes, she was certainly singing, but soon
her song melted her into the darker ages, or, rather,
melted the audience right to the verge of that time when
moderns and ancients faced each other squarely in the
final act of saying goodbye. There was appreciation of
the old. That is what the dance symbolized. It did not
matter that the young virgin was required to dance
herself out of existence; the modern world recognized
what it was losing. It was this dance, done by a single
young woman clad in exceedingly skimpy garb, that
mother objected to. T. and I liked it. The tilt of the

maiden's russet head, the sway of her ivory thighs, massive as beams, the rounded belly quite white and firm. I held his hand tightly in both of mine and I am sure my eyes were *beads* of light.

My mother rose from her seat, stately as ever, and swung slowly up the aisle, the moire bow at the back of her waist looking like a huge butterfly. My father followed, discreetly coughing, looking back furtively at the stage once or twice. I was horrified they were going to stop for me, and if T. had not been with me, I am sure they would have. He and I made ourselves very still and prim and proper, and hoped none of our huge enjoyment showed in our eyes or in the tension of our bodies. But oh, the excitement, to see the dancing of our history, by *Italians*, and so tumultuously and so passionately. One was tempted to the conclusion that our early folk history was probably also their own. I mean the same bonfires and dances to spring and the sprouting of grape leaves and corn!

It is thanks to T. that I go anywhere interesting. All summer long shut up at Morley Crofts! But then come the winters, and London in winter!

Yesterday I had an eerie experience of winter, unlike anything I have ever known before, and once again it was a gift—though an unsettling one, to be sure—from my cousin, my darling cousin T. It was snowing and nearly as dark within as without, and gloomy, since no one ever comes to see us, it seems, any longer. But Mother says this is not true. She says it is I who refuse to see people—especially those with expectant young marriageable males in tow—who come to visit us. Well, I have tried every way I know how to explain that I will *not* be married; if they are sick of having me about, they will simply have to think up some alternative for me.

If I were to marry I feel sure I should slit my throat, or
his, within a fortnight. But *why*, Eleandra? my parents
lament. *Why?* It is all they ask. And I do not *know* why,
except there must be more to life than opulence and
material ease, more than servants and fat horses and
fatter men ogling other men's daughters and fat wives.
I cannot—oh, but what is the point of raving? They
shall drug me and marry me off to a rich Turk, no doubt,
before it is done. No danger there, says T., confidently.
He thinks it will probably be a rich Greek, someone in
shipping, to be precise. These are the wealthy foreigners
my father knows. He has sensibly given up on finding a
husband for me among the English. Sometimes, indeed,
they do come to dinner, these Greeks, dark-haired and
dark-eyed, warmer than any men in England; that, at
least, is in their favour. Still, I would rather slip out the
door with T. . . . He will not let me call him "Theodore";
too bloody religious boring! he cries.

But I was about to write of our outing to the Museum
of Natural History. T. had come for me. We have to
make up all kinds of lies about where we are going, yet
wherever we go is entirely innocent, at least while it
is still daylight. And it was daylight today. At night, it
is true, we have been known to visit certain "houses"
of ill fame, but this is because T. and I have insisted
on seizing an education, a sexual education, wherever
it can be found. He has had clothes—trousers and
overcoat similar to his own—made for me, and I push
my worrisomely long hair under any one of several
capacious hats, and we are off. For, as T. says so well,
how am I to be a great painter if I never *see* anything?
And, with T. beside me, sometimes I feel I must have
seen it all: men and women, men and men (T.'s eyes
light up!), women and women (interesting), everyone

with animals, vegetables, and fruits. We never "buy,"
exactly. We pay to look, to study, to contemplate. I am
fascinated by the women's eyes, their bold, aggressive
stares, their businesslike appraisal. They go through
the motions professionally, rolling and tumbling like so
many slow-motion acrobats, some great beast of a man
poling them from the side, the front, or behind—and
they are apt to be looking over at the next man coming
up and calculating whether they or the next woman will
have him. No doubt the calculation involves how much
money there will be for Johnny's shoes and Susie's milk.
Sometimes the women are pregnant, hugely pregnant,
and there are grown men, sometimes grey-headed,
bearded, grandfatherly men, who pay to suck them. This
can all, for a price, be viewed. I must say it is this sucking
that the women most seem to enjoy and their enjoyment
of it in turn stirs me, and, I hazard to guess, even T.

But I was trying to get to the event of today, at the
Museum of Natural History. Well, when we got there it
was quite late, and so, nearly dark; the flickering interior
lights seemed feeble enough, in any event. T. took me
round the fossil cases and past the humanoid drawings
(as I always call them) of mankind on his wearisome
way up the evolutionary spiral. This was not my first
time at the museum, and as usual I had to be pried away
from the collection of wondrous new goods—ancient
feather cloaks, called, if I remember correctly, *moas,*
after the bird for which they are named; enormous
carved greenstones that glistened like jade; monstrously
beautiful, brilliantly painted canoes—from recently
explored, conquered, and apparently quite ravaged
New Zealand. There were pictures of lush, grinning
Polynesian women and stalwart unsmiling men. "Come
on," said T. "If you like this lot, you'll love what's next." I

followed him down halls and up stairs until we came to a
part of the museum I had never seen before. "Close your
eyes," he said as he slowly opened the door.

When I opened my eyes, I saw that T. had propelled
me into a medium-sized room (most rooms at the
museum are huge), with windows that were very high
up, and there was a strange smell. At first it looked
like a replica of part of an African village. There were
three huts, facing each other, as they always do to make
one living space (I read this in a book), but somewhat
askew, angled away from each other slightly, I suppose
one would say, *obliquely*, for privacy. Then there was
a granary and part of a wall made of mud, as was
everything else. This wall surrounded the compound
except where it was deliberately cut away to give the
viewer clearer access to the activity of the "village."
Glancing overhead, I noted that the museum, in its
intent to assure verisimilitude had even painted a blue
sky. "Come," said T., pulling me closer to the little
dwellings, for I had stopped short on entering the
room and for some reason was abnormally frightened
to hear the heavy wooden door clunk shut behind me.
It gave me gooseflesh. Suddenly I felt a little afraid of
T. Weren't buggers dangerous, after all? But he was
smiling, with an odd, strained bonhomie that seemed put
on for someone else's benefit; I had certainly never seen
such a grimace on his handsome face before. There were
colours on these huts and designs such as I had never
seen before, except in paintings from the American
West. The most abstract, totally stylized shapes and
figures in vivid yellows and oranges and tans, with black
and white jumping out to meet the eye with the vibrancy
of zebra skin. It was so completely what one was not
used to that it was hard to take it in. In the same way one
takes in a painting, say, by an English or European artist,

no matter how odd. It was as if the reference point was missing; I could not grasp either the feeling tones of the work or the meaning. It seemed natural, somehow, to begin thinking of all that was "wrong" with it. T. laughed at my expression, which was, I am sure, a vexed frown. "Just enjoy it!" he said. And I moved closer, still vaguely bothered by the smell. It was not that it was unpleasant. No, there was something almost familiar about it. I felt I had smelled it before though decidedly not in the streets or flats or great houses of London and not, for certain, at Morley Crofts. And then it seemed to me perhaps I had smelled it in a dream, for the whole room now had an aspect of dream—the bright blue sky above, as if lighted by the sun, the cosy little huts. I plopped myself down on one of the mud "porches" that extended from the wall. "Careful," said T., "the mud's dusty." Sure enough, when I got up my skirt was covered with fine dust. T. brushed me off. He was still smiling that savagely benign smile that looked so odd. My eye, though, was attracted to the gorgeous strips of woven cloth hanging on pegs by the door of one of the huts. There was a figure, its back to us, very lifelike, that one could barely make out, sitting on the floor near the doorway inside the hut, apparently spinning.

"Do you know what?" I said to T. "This is so *much* more civilized than what some other countries do. I just read an article in the *Times*—maybe you saw it too?—about the Germans—or was it the Belgians?—anyhow the people who are settling South America, and they brought back two of everything they've discovered so far: fish, leopards, birds. They even brought back a pair of Indians. People turned out in droves to see them. But the poor things shivered and shook—they were just children—the whole time, and when winter set in, *poof,* they died."

At that moment, I happened to glance up at T.,
but he was looking into the door of the hut where the
figure was spinning. But the figure was not spinning any
longer. She was standing in the doorway!

M'Sukta was little, about four feet ten, slender as
a reed, and blacker than anyone I had ever seen. She
seemed ageless—a very young child, an adolescent,
or an old woman carefully preserved. She was dressed
exquisitely in cloth made from hundreds of the strips
that decorated the pegs by the door of the hut, which
I now saw copied many of the colours, motifs, and
symbols that covered the mud walls. Her hair was in
dozens of mid-back-length plaits; on the end of each
one was a bit of seashell. Her small feet were encased
in colourfully beaded slippers of soft leather. She came
towards us holding her spindle and carrying a large
basket of cotton from which she was making thread.

She barely acknowledged us. No. She did not
acknowledge us. She just seemed to know we were there,
and that was her cue to come out, sit before us in her
splendid garb, which obviously she had made herself,
and begin a demonstration of this aspect of her village's
way of life. I looked about for other members of the
tribe to emerge, but none did.

It would not even have required a feather to knock
me down.

"The museum lets her live here," said T., still smiling
fixedly at the woman. I had never noticed before how
shallow he was, always willing to skim about on the
surface of things. The woman gave no indication that
she heard or saw or cared about our presence. But there
was an increase, barely perceptible, in the smell. It was,
I realized, the smell of *fear*. This tiny, childlike creature
was afraid of us! Of *me!* I felt myself immediately
brought into focus. Animals in zoos were afraid of me

as simply another human being come to stare at them, but this was different, somehow. If she was afraid of me, then it was definitely my whole existence that was "wrong," and not the screaming colours of her clothing or her house.

"What do you mean, they *let* her live here? Where does she *come* from?" At this question T.'s expression said: A woman so black, where *would* she come from? "But where does she *really* live?" I was frantic for an answer now, feeling my whole being, further back than I could remember, involved. My reaction was perhaps unique to me. *Was* it, I wondered. If so, this made me feel more afraid. I mean, where was this woman's *world?* That she should end up like this, on view to *us*. Black people, though not unheard of in the streets of London are nonetheless rare. There are a very few men that one glimpses from time to time and *no* women. Or maybe, I thought now, they live in a part of London, a kind of underworld, that I have never seen. Even in the brothels there are not ever any really black people, not chocolaty black and exquisite, like this woman. Only Indians and the occasional swarthy Arab, looking ashamed of himself.

T. was smiling. "She's lived here ten years," he said, through his teeth. And I noticed how straight and clean and polished they were. They glistened like pearls against his red lips. They made me think of T.'s love of food, and of him eating, eating rather than talking if any subject arose at dinner that made him uncomfortable. There were many such subjects. In another few years, I thought, T. will be quite fat. The fat of silence, the fat of silence, the fat of . . . I could not stop thinking this, even as I strained to hear what T. was saying.

"At first she was installed on the main floor, but after a year or so she had a breakdown of sorts. The young boy who was with her died. Maybe it was the cold," he said, looking up at the bright "warm" ceiling. "These old buildings are draughty and damp, really only made for ghosts. Anyway, after the boy's death, which some people ascribed to one or the other of them, she went inside herself to such a degree that everyone assumed she would be next. They watched her round the clock, just as though she were a sick elephant. But when they gave her some privacy—she and the boy had been on view in the main hall downstairs every day except Thursdays, when the museum was closed, and of course at night—she recovered."

"She has never tried to escape?" I asked T., looking at the meek creature bent over her spindle, her little black fingers, on one of which she had placed a tiny, many-coloured cotton-thread ring, fairly flying. It was a simple wooden spindle she was using, like the ones the older shepherds' wives still use in the country near Morley Crofts. There were looms of different sizes—one of them a tiny handloom on which she made the colourful inch-wide strips—propped against the wall near where she worked.

T. seemed surprised by my question. "But where would she go?" he said. "As I understand it, the tribe she comes from in Africa is no more. Intertribal warfare, slave raiding, that sort of thing. She's the last of her people." There was a hint of disgust in his voice for "that sort of thing." I welcomed it eagerly. After all, I love T. "Besides," he continued, killing this feeling entirely, "you know women like to stay at home. Here she has everything she needs, her houses, her granary—there's even grain in it—her household duties, just as she'd have back in the jungle. She's remarkably talented, as you can see. She makes her own clothes, and things to sell, too, you'll be happy to know." He looked at me and

reached for a strip of woven cloth hanging on one of
the pegs. The woman's eyes flickered when he took the
strip, but that was her only reaction. He tied it about
my hair, making a headband like American Indians wear.
He placed a shilling in a dish I had not noticed before.
I liked the strip, I kept it on. I bowed stiffly in the
woman's direction. But the thing was covered with the
smell. I would have to wash it over and over again.

Scribbled in the margin at a much later date—the ink was
darker and a different color from the rest of the writing on
the page; also, the writing was larger and written with a firmer
hand—were these words, in which Mary Jane detected a hint
of what, for all she knew, was her great-great aunt's legendary
sense of humor: "And that is how I met M'Sukta, the little
woman who carried me to Africa!"

TWICE a week now Mary Jane eagerly took the train to Guildford. She began to feel like a fixture in the Eleanora Burnham Room. The diary continued, and she read somewhat breathlessly.

M'Sukta's industry in the solitude of captivity impressed me strongly. Suddenly I felt terribly *un*accomplished. As shallow as Theodore. As superficial. As decadent. I was, after all, in my mid-twenties, almost too old for marriage, even if it were forced upon me. The middle-aged Greek merchants who came to our London house for dinner no longer stared, in feigned enchantment, at me. They rushed away after eating, with prettier and much younger young things on their minds. This was a relief. Though now the spectre of some sort of nunnery was raised. My mother reminded me frequently that in her time this would already have been tried—my tenure in a nunnery, that is.

I avoided confrontations with my parents as best I could by spending time with my old tutors. I had been educated at home always—by governesses, tutors, hired hands, who eventually became, I had thought, almost friends. I looked now at how they lived in the world. Their small flats, their meatless dinners, their threadbare cloaks. Their sense of duty, purpose, expertise. For they had *something*, these poor people who were so often viewed by my family as being a step above the family dog and a step beneath the cook. And then again, how valuable could what they had be if its sole destination was the instruction of someone like me?

I had never noticed their singular evasiveness. "How am I to live?" I queried one of them. "What has your instruction prepared me for?"

She looked at me in surprise. I read discomfiture in her face. She was pale as a potato. And as quiet.

"Why, miss," she may as well have said aloud, "we've prepared you to be a lady."

A lady.

Apparently Theodore and I alone in all the world thought every lady everywhere ought to be shot.

I do not know exactly why we felt this, and it was not by any means a constant feeling. But there was something so artificial about ladyness, something so separate from others and from the world. The ladies one saw seemed to be trapped in their long skirts. They tripped ahead on the pavement in their tight shoes, their large feathered hats floating above them. And they looked at themselves in shop windows and admired themselves. It was too much! I realized I had a hatred of women—of ladies, rather—that was almost overpowering. And I felt it especially when I had to take off the overcoat, trousers, and shirt bought by T., in which I felt so at ease, and could actually see my own feet, and put on the garb of ladies, which made me feel like a dog bound by an all-too-visible chain.

"You know history," my tutor stuttered, "you know

geography, you know science, literature, and languages. You are quite the best-educated young woman in London," she went so far as to dare say. "There's precious little you couldn't do if you put your mind to it."

I did know all those things, yet none of them worked when I visited M'Sukta, which I began to do, regularly, after that first visit with T. The history I knew was not hers, the geography I knew placed an elephant herd where her village had been, the science I knew did not teach me how to make dyes and medicines and the other things M'Sukta could do; the literature I read talked about savages and blackamoors, and that was when it was being polite. The languages I knew failed me entirely when I stood before her. ME TAO ACHE DAKEN SOMO TUK DE. This was etched in the wall of the compound as it approached the granary door. I puzzled over it each time I came. Was it Latin? Was it Greek? T. once said laughingly that, as I strained to decipher it, I looked quite pixilated. Then he showed me the brochure in which it was translated. It was an ancient saying of M'Sukta's people, a people always under siege for one reason or another: THEY CANNOT KILL US, BECAUSE WITHOUT US THEY DIE. Hardly what one would expect from the primitive philosophy of "The Savage in the Stacks," as a local paper referred to M'Sukta, assuming, ignorantly, that a museum is a library. Now I had a new quandary: What kind of people would have this thought as a life guide? The more I pondered it, the more of a riddle it became.

Now the effects on the diary of years of humidity, moths, existence in the bottoms of trunks and traveling cases in distant countries began, abruptly, to show. There were whole pages impossible to read because of faded ink; some sections were literally eaten away. Mary Jane tried to subdue her frustration by remembering that she hadn't even known there *was* a diary by Eleandra; she hadn't known Eleandra existed. She made herself thankful for the snippets of the diary she could read.

Only my painting tutor [something, something, something—this was faded] showed outright impatience with me. I had always thought him rather sullen, and an indifferent painter. I was lamenting that I had no freedom, as a woman, to paint. I could not go to Italy, for instance, as he had done, and he was poor! "Don't pity yourself, please," he said acidly.

"I can go to Italy by working every single day with people like you" (here, he bowed!), "saving all my earnings, living on rusks. I can stay two months. I can paint what I like, in two months. You are a woman, but you are rich. People may laugh but they will not harm you if you paint. You can paint all day. You can paint for months, even years, on end. Anything you like. And . . ." (he softened not at all, but appeared to look at me with an even deeper disgust) "you have some talent."

"But what good thing have I done?" I asked. I painted because I loved it, not because I had any dream of being good. He reminded me of a little thing I had done that, in truth, puzzled me even as I did it. It was a still life—all my paintings were—called "Tombstone and Fruit." A grave, a stone, fruit covering the mound like flowers. I had no idea where the image came from. I told him this.

"It came from you. From you, trying to tell yourself something." I had studied with this man, middle-aged and not unattractive, I now saw, for three years. I had never really noticed him. His jaundiced skin, his white, white hands and muscular wrists. The look in his eyes. He had worked for my family, for *me*, while his own dreams of growth and development as an artist faded.

Two months in Italy! I knew they were, in reality, his life.
This, then, was the power people like us had. The power
to enslave others and to frustrate their dreams. And I
had never even taken my painting seriously, whilst his
life—living on rusks, he said—bled slowly away.

Another tattered page:

"Those words are all that kept me going," said
M'Sukta years later, when we could, haltingly, converse.
"They were truly my ancestors' gift to me. Not even
song meant as much to me—and I used to sing all the
time just to hear my own language—or knowing how
to weave the tribal cloth, the magic of which is that as
long as it is woven, the tribe exists; as long as you know
how to weave it, so do you. These words never bored
me ('made my head heavy as rice grains in a gourd') all
the years I lived in the museum ('granary for humans').
Those words called me back when sickness and sadness
('heaviness of centre chest') threatened to carry me
away ('eat down my soul'). It is a miracle ('the end of
rainbow') that they should have been there at all, etched
in the mud wall beside the granary door; for our people
did not read or write; instead they placed their trust
('open chest, sun shining') and their history ('kisses and
kicks to the ancestors') in the memory ('head granary')
of human beings ('those alone on the earth who think of
what is just'—just, 'two hands holding equal amounts
of grain'). They believed that all that has ever happened
is stored as memories within the human mind, or in the
head granary of those who alone on earth think of what
is just. The life of my people is to remember forever;
each head granary is full. The life of your people is
to forget; your thing granaries ('museums'), and not
yourselves, are full. I can tell you truthfully ('eyes steady,

heart calm') that meeting your people was a terrible
shock ('small children running away'). Your people are
most afraid of what you have been; you have no faith
that you were as good as or better than what you are
now. This is not our way ('path'). Not only were we as
good in the beginning as we are now, but we are the
same ('two grains of sand, identical')."

When she said this, I thought of that night long
ago in London, when I sat watching the ballet with
T., the scandalous one from which Mother and
Father withdrew. I had thought I had merely been
titillated by the "savage" dissonance of the music, the
thunderous, herdlike cacophony of the dance, which
was certainly not the ballet, not the formal, precise,
unnatural movements that one was used to. I thought
I was responding to the bizarre clothing. Skimpiness
on the one hand, outrageous costumes and colours on
the other. So barbaric, so savage. But perhaps T. and I
were both responding to our first glimpse of ourselves
before we, and all Britain, all Europe, became pressed
into the forms created for us by civilization. Perhaps
the maiden dancing herself to death in her "marriage"
to the sun struck some deep chord in us. Perhaps
she was expressing a feeling for nature that English
people subsequently only expressed politely, with
restraint, in their gardens and in their insistence on
large parks.

Where had the passion of praise gone, then, among
my own people? It certainly was not in the church,
neither the Catholic nor the Church of England. The
Roman conquerors seemed to have rid us of it, and yet,
I thought, in the passionate dance of the young virginal
maiden one could glimpse part of the truth of who we
English people were. There was our passion and our
savagery before it became tamed. But it had not really

become tame, only repressed—and the worship of
nature turned into its opposite, and the end result was
wilderness ravaged and despoiled, and people in chains,
and a little black woman shut up in a museum beneath a
fake sky.

It was Sir Henley Rowanbotham who had had the
words M'Sukta lived by carved into the mud wall beside
the granary. He was a commander in the British army
sent to administer to the needs of the Royal Colonial
Exploitation Company, Ltd. The men under his charge
assured safe passage throughout Africa to those explorers
and entrepreneurs from England who boasted, if they
lived long enough—for there were such things as fevers,
quicksand, and mambas—of making quick fortunes in
Africa, buying and selling among the natives, claiming
huge tracts of land and all the minerals and diamonds
and whatnot they might contain. The slave trade had
not yet ended, though it was on its last legs, at least as
far as the West was concerned, and there was still money
to be made. Rowanbotham had been deeply influenced
by the adventures of Sir Richard Burton, another army
man, whom he accepted as his personal guide re: things
native. Like Burton, he was once thought to be deeply in
love with a native woman—African, not Persian—and
like Burton, he, in other ways, immersed himself in
native life and native affairs. He was, again like Burton,
adept at learning languages and was genuinely fascinated
by them, and whiled away the long damp tropical
evenings of the rainy season ensconced at a window
table in the Royal Colonial Club, working up a native
alphabet.

It was from his notes that I began to gather an
understanding of M'Sukta's people and their history,
besides the things I learned from her. M'Sukta's tribe,
the Balawyua, or the Ababa, colloquially, had been, since

time immemorial, a matriarchy. Rowanbotham, brought up in East London by a mother and three older sisters who adored him beyond reason, had a special affinity for matriarchies. It was he who, when all her tribe was sold into slavery or killed, rescued M'Sukta and made provision for the Museum of Natural History to shelter her; and because she alone could pass on the history of her people's ancient way of life, and because, except for her and the young boy who came with her, there was no one who understood her language, Rowanbotham had dubbed her "the African Rosetta stone."

Here there was the most maddening evidence of the work of tiny, tiny teeth. Moths had chewed away the rest of the page; indeed the rest of the diary now began to fill the air around Mary Jane's chair in the form of a cloud of dust. It made her sneeze. That was it, then. All she was likely to know of Eleandra Burnham Peacock, at least from her own pen.

But surely one mark of moral progress and spiritual maturity is the ability to be grateful for half a gift? Mary Jane kept this thought firmly in mind later that week as she stood over the empty bed of her great-aunt Eleanora. She had died while Mary Jane was sitting in "her room" at the library, going through her things.

There were only Mary Jane and the librarian, the chancellor of the college, her nurse, and the London solicitor at the funeral. There was a longish obituary, mainly about her years in Africa—her writing was dismissed in half a line—but also about her similarity to an earlier Lady Burnham, the Lady Eleandra Burnham Peacock. That name brought to the obituary writer's mind the names of two other Englishwomen, "outrageous in their day" who'd "gone native" in the grand anti–Victorian England style: Lady Hester Stanhope and the fascinating and stunningly beautiful Lady Jane Digby El-Mezrab.

The most memorably distinctive thing about the latter's life was, apparently, that not only had she left England and settled in Arabia, but she had wed an Arab.

The day after Lady Burnham's funeral, it was reported that she had left the bulk of her estate to an American great-niece, Mary Ann Haverstock, who was, unfortunately, also deceased. She was described as having been "a political radical with a fondness for blacks, and a mental psychotic with a fondness for drugs." Relieved that this misfit was no more, the obituary writer rushed on with the information that Lady Burnham's estate would go to fund an anthropological group of which she had been fond, in Africa.

Obituary writers were funnier in England than in America, Mary Jane thought. But how had Eleanora even known she existed? Perhaps during the times she was involved in scandal in the United States, her aunt had got wind of her, and found something — news of Mary Jane's blackened bare feet, her uncombed locks, her hanging out with colored lumpen — to applaud.

Back at the library for the last time, she discovered on the shelves double sets of Eleanora's five volumes, their leaves uncut. She took a set, slipped the books into her capacious shoulder bag, and smiled her way past the recently somewhat thawed librarian. Mary Jane knew she was off to Africa, and was thinking of the two Eleandras, one so eager for experience in life, one married off meekly into oblivion; seven decades had failed to dull her twin's contempt for her. She also thought of Eleanora, whose books, she hoped, would reveal her to Mary Jane, as the diary of Eleandra, "the Lady Peacock," had, in a major way, revealed Mary Jane to herself.

She stopped at an artists' supply shop on her way to the dock — her ship sailed at midnight — and bought enough brushes, turpentine, and paints to last for a year.

PART FOUR

He—for there could be no doubt of his sex, though the fashion of the time did something to disguise it—was in the act of slicing at the head of a Moor which swung from the rafters. It was the colour of an old football, and more or less the shape of one, save for the sunken cheeks and a strand or two of coarse, dry hair, like the hair on a cocoanut. Orlando's father, or perhaps his grandfather, had struck it from the shoulders of a vast Pagan who had started up under the moon in the barbarian fields of Africa; and now it swung, gently, perpetually, in the breeze which never ceased blowing through the attic rooms of the gigantic house of the lord who had slain him.

— VIRGINIA WOOLF, *Orlando*

Keep in mind always the present you are constructing.
It should be the future you want.

— OLA

C ARLOTTA had no substance," Suwelo had said to Miss Lissie's back. This was before he had sold Uncle Rafe's house and returned to San Francisco. It was a Sunday in November, and Baltimore was beginning to have an early-morning chilliness that reminded him of Northern California. He'd sat perched on a stool beside the little chopping table in the kitchen, intently cleaning a pile of boiled Maryland crabs. Mr. Hal was at a counter chopping bell peppers and onions and weeping from the onion fumes, and Miss Lissie was attentively stirring a slowly darkening roux, which sent off a buttery, burning-bread smell that Suwelo didn't know if he liked. He couldn't quite see how a base of burned flour might taste good in a stew.

"You live in San Francisco, with all that seafood, and never had gumbo?" Mr. Hal was incredulous.

Suwelo had invited them for the weekend. Deep in his heart he was probably pretending they were his parents, but he didn't mind. They'd showed up first thing that morning in Mr. Hal's truck and hauled in a half-dozen bags of stuff: tomatoes, peppers, onions, okra *and* filé, a couple of chickens, slabs of bacon and beef, a hunk of pork, long tubes of dark, savory-smelling sausage, crabs almost overrunning a basket, a colorfully stenciled croker sack of rice, and jugs of ready-made lemonade and iced tea.

As soon as they started turning about in the kitchen, opening drawers, sharpening knives, complaining that "that devilish" salt shaker had *never* worked, Suwelo knew they belonged there. Miss Lissie kicked off her shoes and padded about in bare feet, and Mr. Hal made himself comfortable by unbuttoning the front of his short-sleeved white shirt to reveal a peach-colored T-shirt, which said, across the front, "Ecstasy Is Forever." His hair was whiter and longer than when Suwelo first met him, and with his soft brown eyes, his courtly manner, even in the kitchen, he resembled a comfortable, gentle, and altogether happy George Washington Carver.

"What I mean about her having no substance is that she was all image. She was all image when I first saw her, all image when I met her, and all image . . ."

"After you went to bed with her," said Miss Lissie, completing the thought for him. "Give me the crab shells you've finished with. I need to boil them down for stock." Suwelo passed them over.

From time to time he had told them small stories from his life; though they never asked. He felt he knew them more intimately than he knew his own parents—who had been killed in a car wreck, the result of one of his father's drunken rages, when Suwelo was in college—and that not to attempt to share his life with them made him feel like a thief. Besides, he needed some help with Fanny.

"When Fanny came back from Africa that first time," said Suwelo, "we knew it wasn't going to work, us being married when she really didn't want to be. She *hated* it. She *hated* the institution of marriage. She said the ring people wore on their fingers symbolizing marriage was obviously a remnant of a chain.

She didn't hate *me*. That much, at least, I was beginning to see. For one thing, when she came back from Africa, where she'd been for six months—the only time in her life she was able to be with both her mother and her father—her love for me was unmistakable. We fell on each other in an orgy of reconciliation that lasted for weeks. And this was only possible because when I picked her up at the airport I told her straight out that I loved her and that getting a divorce was just fine with me."

"*Umm hmm . . .*" said Miss Lissie. She turned the pan so Suwelo could see the dark caramel color of the roux. Mr. Hal crossed the kitchen, his hands full of chopped onions and peppers, which he dropped into the pot. There was a searing, sizzling sound, and Miss Lissie said, "Oh, shit, the okra should have gone in first. But what the hell," she added. "The making of gumbo is like the making of the best music, an improvisational *art*." She poured herself a glass of wine and sipped as she stirred.

"We also knew," Suwelo continued, "we couldn't live on the East Coast in the suburbs of New York City. We lived, if you can believe it, in a little middle-class enclave called Forest Hills. The houses were nice, and there were trees and broad lawns, but everybody was always trying to make things look older—the houses, the trees. Sometimes I had the feeling that at night our neighbors went outdoors and beat on the walls of the houses with sticks and tugged on the bushes and trees, trying to stretch them to a more imposing height. They kept trying to pin some famous person's birth to the place but, since people moved away every few years and always had, this was hard to do. They finally found a famous baseball player who'd rented a house there once, and there was talk of putting up a plaque. Our house was actually the oldest one there. We had no trouble selling it. Once we let it be known we wanted to sell, even some of our neighbors, moving up and moving older, wanted to buy. We sold to another black family, because we knew that one of the reasons our neighbors wanted to buy our house was to keep other black people out.

"But where to go? Fanny had spent a summer in Iowa, so she knew she couldn't breathe in the Midwest. Too far from oceans, she said. And that bullshit about the prairie being oceanlike is for the birds. There's about enough prairie left to piss in.

"I had once spent five minutes in Wyoming. Another five in Montana. In fact, on the bus once, on my way to Seattle to a friend's wedding, I spent five minutes in each of those north-west states. Too isolated. Not enough colored. Not enough concrete, either.

"So Oakland really appealed to us. Not San Francisco. Because everybody knew it was full of queers and the parks were overrun with perverts, and besides, it was cold in the summer. But we knew people who lived in Oakland, and whenever they came east they always seemed real jolly at the prospect of going back to Oakland. This impressed us. We almost always dreaded coming home to New York. Pedestrians were rude. Taxi drivers were impossible. We were on edge every minute of our existence, outside our own front door.

"In Oakland, what happened? We couldn't find an apartment. Fanny didn't like the heat, and the streets, she said, made her think of L.A., which she had visited once and *loathed*. Trembling with trepidation we crossed the Bay Bridge. The fog was just rolling back off the city, as if pulled by a giant hand. The sun glanced off the white buildings so that we were practically blinded. All around us there was water. The weather was bracingly cool and the light was peculiarly bright. 'We looked at our hands and our hands looked new, we looked at our feet and they did too!'" Suwelo sang the words to this old black spiritual about deliverance, which made Miss Lissie and Mr. Hal laugh.

"We found a large flat on Broderick Street, up high, with

a view of a tiny corner of the *red* Golden Gate Bridge, and a
glimpse of the hills beyond it, which we discovered were not
in San Francisco but in Marin County. Immediately we started
thinking of things to do we'd never done before: tai chi, hiking,
learning to sail out at Lake Merced. All this time our divorce
was coming along, and we were extremely happy. Then it became final, and I became depressed.

" 'I no longer have a wife!' I cried.

" 'You have a friend,' she said. 'And your friend is moving
into her own rooms.'

" 'What?' I said.

" 'Remember how upset you were when I wanted a divorce?'
she said.

" 'Yes!' I said.

" 'Well,' she said, 'all that suffering you did was for nothing,
right?'

" 'But, but, but,' I said.

" 'But what?' She smiled.

" 'Does this mean we won't ever sleep together?'

" 'Always your first concern,' she sighed. And then she said,
'No. I hope it means that when we *do* sleep together, we won't
be sleeping apart.'

"But I was angry, I was confused. I was very, very hurt. I felt
she'd tricked me. I felt she was rejecting me.

"I tried to get her to say she wouldn't move into her 'rooms'—
she was taking the back three rooms of the house, leaving me
the sunnier, lonelier, ones in front—until I was weaned. She
laughed. I *was* trying to make it funny.

" 'Just till I'm *weaned*,' I said, creeping into her arms and putting my hands up under her blouse. I loved her tits." Suwelo
looked up at Miss Lissie, who was frowning into the gumbo
pot. "I couldn't bear to think of them moving away."

Miss Lissie took the rest of the crab shells and the crab meat.

Suwelo watched as she added them to separate pots. Mr. Hal was now dredging cubes of beef in a small mound of flour. Miss Lissie handed Suwelo a knife and a tube of the sausage. He whacked off a penis length.

"You sounding mighty innocent," said Miss Lissie.

What did she mean by that, Suwelo wondered. Did she mean this story made it sound like Fanny didn't love him? Didn't want to be with him? That he was an innocent victim? Did it make Fanny sound like a lesbian?

"Lesbians were all around us, you know," said Suwelo, in a tone of facing up to the ultimate challenge. "Beautiful, beautiful women, quite a lot of them, though some of them didn't look so hot. Just seeing them on their outings together, climbing the hills, sunning in the parks, eating noisily at the largest tables in restaurants in Berkeley, made you want to cry. They'd *left* us! Hell, these bitches were so tough, they'd left *God!* This was when they were just discovering the Goddess, and it was all the time Goddess this and Goddess that. I once asked a black woman on the street where the new bus stop was — the city was repairing the old bus stop part of the street we were on — and she just looked at me, shrugged, and said an easy 'Goddess knows.' It blew me away."

"*Hah,*" said Miss Lissie.

"So I was afraid she was going to leave me for a woman," said Suwelo. "Listen, I'm not alone. It's the cry of the times, in case you haven't noticed it. The only men who don't have this fear are living in caves and jungles somewhere with their women still tethered to the floor at night by their nose rings."

Mr. Hal laughed.

Suwelo noticed his own agitation. He sat back, took a sip of the beer Miss Lissie had poured him, and tried to control his breathing. It was hard, remembering what he'd suffered.

"*Fanny was always going out with these people,*" he said.

"With *what* people?" said Miss Lissie, sautéeing the beef

cubes in oil, into which she'd put flakes of garlic. "Surely not the people with the nose rings."

Mr. Hal guffawed.

"Naw, Lissie," he said. "The *other* people. Them that said shit on the nose-ring question."

"Oh, *them*," she said, smiling.

This was the first time, oddly enough, that Suwelo felt Miss Lissie and Mr. Hal liked him, not because he was kin to Uncle Rafe, but just because he was himself.

His story took on a somewhat more humorous aspect in his own mind.

Mr. Hal allowed as how he actually did believe — and he hoped the reality wouldn't make him out a liar — but he thought that just maybe it was possible he had some . . . reefer.

But then he couldn't find it.

"Oh, well," he said, to Suwelo, "continue the operation without anesthesia."

"But what I meant by innocent," said Miss Lissie, "was, what were you doing with yourself while Fanny was in Africa? If you're a man" — she said "man" exactly as she'd say "dog" — "you played around."

"I got into pornography," said Suwelo promptly. "I was *lonely*. I got into prostitutes. But I'm too soft-hearted. I always wanted to know all about the lives of the prostitutes — the one I liked best had *five* children — and in the end I got this terrible dose of claps." He liked saying "terrible dose of claps"; it sounded the way Mr. Hal or Miss Lissie would put it.

"*Ooo wee!*" they said simultaneously.

And Suwelo thought: When was the last time I heard anybody say "Ooo wee!" He hadn't heard this expression since he was a little boy. He felt he'd been given something precious — an old photograph, an old letter, or a scent from a time that otherwise did not exist.

"I didn't tell Fanny. Of course not. What would have been

the point? Fortunately I was able to be cured a few weeks before she came home. I gave up prostitutes. Or, rather, my member gave them up for me: it refused to function in what it feared might be contaminated territory. But I was hooked on girlie magazines, naked women in quarter-to-peek glass cages, bondage films, and 'live' sex acts on stage. When I thought of what Fanny's six months in Africa gave me, it was the enjoyment, without guilt, of pornography. My woman had left me, you see, taken my rightful stuff off to another continent, totally out of reach of my dick, and left me high and dry. Well, I knew how to get off without her. There were plenty of other women in the world. This was my attitude."

"Have another beer," Miss Lissie said curtly.

"I recovered from this depravity," Suwelo said. "Don't get too disgusted. It took a while, but . . ."

"What kills me," said Miss Lissie, "is that men think women never know."

"Fanny *didn't* know," said Suwelo. "But you'd have to know Fanny. Fanny"—Suwelo thought long and hard about how he could describe Fanny simply, so the two old people would get it—"Fanny, well, Fanny," he said, "is like a space cadet."

Miss Lissie was cutting up one of the chickens. Its yellow fat lay in a heap beside her hand. As always, naked chickens looked like naked babies to Suwelo, and he averted his eyes.

"You are a spirit that has had many bodies, and you travel through time and space that way," said Suwelo. "Fanny is a body with many spirits shooting off to different realms almost every day. If she could fall in love with a Russian poet who died fighting for the Russian Revolution of 1917, it hardly concerned her that I was going out one night a month with 'the boys.' Though there were never any 'boys,'" he added quickly. "I always went out alone, furtively, like a criminal, once she'd come back. I read all the modern women's stuff on politics and *men*. I knew what I was doing was frowned upon. Hell, I even knew it was wrong. I could feel it was. But one night I was so angry with Fanny's distractedness that I actually harassed a young woman in a glass cage. I could see she wasn't paying attention to me, even as she twisted and moaned and puckered her lips. I knew if she had really looked, I would have seemed big and black and burly, and she would have been frightened, since she was just a pubescent half-white kid, chewing gum, naked, and no doubt strung out, in the little smudged cage. I started to shake the cage and bare my teeth like King Kong. She was scared out of her wits. I think I made her swallow her gum.

"But Carlotta was a space cadet, too, in her own way," said Suwelo, taking another sip of beer. "She was so superfeminine, in the old style, that it was as if she'd never noticed there was any other way a woman could be. She wore these three-inch heels every day. I'm talking serious stiletto. She even cooked—and I saw this after she let me go home with her—in three-inch heels. Three-inch heels are designed to make a man feel like all he needs to do is push gently and a woman is on her ass. Three-inch heels say 'Fuck me.' Carlotta taught women's literature—which Fanny wondered if she ever read—in three-inch heels. She wore sweaters that followed every curve of her luscious body. Sweaters that dipped. Skirts that clung. Short skirts. Makeup. Earrings. False eyelashes sometimes. Her husband, a musician—she never told me his name—had left her, and left the country. She had no relatives, no friends. Only the two children, a boy and a girl. I took them on outings, to ballet and soccer. They grew dependent on me really quickly. Fanny was in Africa again. I knew Carlotta wanted to marry me. She knew I was already married, and Fanny and I never talked about our divorce; what was the point? It was a private matter, really. And she knew about Fanny. The college where Carlotta and I taught was a very uptight place. After ranting and raving about how uptight it was, Fanny had quit her part-time administrative job there and opened a little massage parlor right down the street. Everybody, students and teachers alike, went to her. Even Carlotta went. Fanny never knew Carlotta didn't like her. Fanny that year was into the notion that Jesus was a masseur, that *that's* what the original healing by touch that Jesus did in the Bible meant! She was into the laying on of hands. She took courses in massage at the San Francisco School of Massage. She also learned to do acupressure.

"Carlotta disliked Fanny's style. Fanny had given up so much that Carlotta still clung to. The respectable job, the dresses and skirts, the beauty parlor—Fanny cut her hair very short—the high heels, the lipstick. She dressed in T-shirts, sandals, and chi pants. Fanny was mentally in Jerusalem, at the Dead Sea, strolling in Galilee. She was, for about a year and a half, really into being Christ. Or, as she would put it, '*a* Christ,' which she said anyone could be. Everybody loved her massages because she enjoyed them so much herself. They never stopped at the appointed hour, but could go on and on, and there were some bodies she worked on that she said made her feel inspired. Soft music would be playing—you never had any idea who the musicians were; you just knew you never heard them anywhere but there—the incense would be burning, the room would be warm, Fanny's hands would be warm and slippery from the fragrant oils she used. Sweet almond was my favorite. I used to go to her myself, especially after faculty meetings. Faculty meetings always left me tight as a drum. All those white male heads of departments, pretending white people get everything on merit, and of *course* the college wasn't racist just because no one there had ever heard of George Washington Carver; how could one think so?

"Really, Fanny gave up everything for a long, long time. She even gave up books, which she loved!

"You know what she said? 'I'd rather read the trees. It's not book burning that people need to worry so much about; it's the trees that are disappearing.'

"She gave up listening to music, except when she was giving a massage. Even Mozart, whom she adored. 'I find I like silence,' she said. 'It's music to me. I like the eternal nature of silence. It's music you can have living or dead.'

"Then, when her father died, she went back to Africa. It was a terrible time for her. She'd just gotten to know him, and her sister, as well. And she liked him. He was funny and irreverent and a rebel. He made her laugh. Her mother, she said, who had been a missionary in Africa for many years, when young, had always told her Africans were rather sad people. Her father was so much like her, she felt, it tickled her just to see part of herself out there in the world in someone else. And he was her father! She hadn't even known she had one.

"Carlotta couldn't understand her leaving me alone for so long. She said she felt sorry for me. She flipped her hair from off her tinted glasses, where it always flopped, and pushed out her breasts. She fingered her fuchsia-colored cleavage. She extended her legs, her three-inch heels. I'd seen women like her, lissome, tan, with tiny flat waists and high breasts, in magazines and naked onstage. In a way, whenever I looked at her, I saw those other women. The first time I kissed her she left lipstick all over my face.

"But I got used to that. I even got to the place where I lusted after her perfume, which was as insistent as a brass door knocker. I would go to her cheap little apartment after class and watch her clack across the kitchen, making dinner in her high heels, and sometimes I'd just grab hold of her and we'd end up on the kitchen floor. I don't think she enjoyed this at all. But at the time, I thought maybe she did. She was pretty impassive; once, I thought the lipstick was painted on in the shape of a smile she used to have, but I chased the thought away and thrust deeper. I hadn't any idea how hard it was for women to relax sexually when their children were around. And hers were right down the hall. We could latch the kitchen door, which we did, and I was quick; still, it must have been a kind of torture for Carlotta. She really loved the kids and was very religious, to boot. And very religious, pious, and prudish was, for sure, how those kids saw her, because, among other things, she was always praying and lighting candles and wringing her hands and weeping. But would she talk to me about her troubles? No way, José.

" 'Tell me about your people?' I asked her once as we lay naked after sex I'd literally dragged her into bed to have.

" 'I have no people,' she said. Tears were, however, running down the sides of her nose.

" 'Aw, come on,' I said. 'Everybody's got folks!'

" 'I don't,' she said.

" 'Tell me about your father, then,' I said. In truth, it was hard to say what nationality she was. Maybe she *didn't* have 'a people.'

" 'I have no father.'

"This seemed highly improbable.

" 'Tell me about your mother. Even God,' I teased, 'is rumored to have had one of those.'

" 'I have no mother,' was her reply.

" 'Tell me about your children's father,' I coaxed.

" 'They have no father,' she said.

"She was just a body, then. It was fine with me if she stayed that way. After making love to her I always thought of Fanny anyhow. I was following her around, mentally, in Africa, trying to imagine the things she saw.

"Only if I married Carlotta would she tell me who she was, maybe. Who her people were, who her father was, and her mother. Who her husband was. I didn't even know if they were divorced. That was the bargain she had in her mind. If I married her she could trust me with her secrets. But I sort of liked being unmarried. I especially liked being unmarried to Fanny. Strange to say, I felt there was more freedom in our love. And not just because I was banging Carlotta."

"Men are *dogs*," said Miss Lissie dispassionately, stirring the black pot of gumbo with a wooden spoon. The smell was beginning to be wonderful. Mr. Hal had found his reefer and they each took a hit.

"You'd love Northern California," said Suwelo. "We grow this stuff in our yard."

Their "yard." Friends had loaned them a tiny yurt and five acres of land during the summers. They immediately put in a garden of peppers, tomatoes, onions, collard greens, and marijuana. They hauled water for the garden from the local park and manure from their neighbors' sheep. Their plants were tall, dark, and pungent. They called them "Big Women." One puff and you understood you were where you were supposed to be and so was everything else. Mellow. Suwelo and Fanny used the word a lot.

"Africa is not mellow," Fanny had written in one of her letters. "The local narcotic is a frothy home brew that leaves you stunned, and people smoke horrible American cigarettes that pollute the air, give them halitosis, and make them sick. I feel like I haven't breathed in three weeks."

"MY FATHER'S funeral, the first of three he was to have, was an impressive event," Fanny now wrote. "It was held at one of the formerly all-white churches in the capital, three blocks from the Ministry of Culture. I had no idea what to wear to such a high-level African funeral, but when I called my mother at home in Georgia—who said she wanted to come herself but the arthritis in her hip is much worse—and told her where the funeral was to take place, she said, 'Of course you wear black.' When I told her about the other two funerals, which would take place in my father's village, she said that one of them, for the men of the village, I would not be able to attend, and that to the other I should wear white, the Olinka color of mourning, and I should paint my face white, too. Also my hands, and any other part of my body that would show. For some reason, information about this last funeral, the village funeral, cheered me, though the white clothing I'd brought with me, a simple blouse and skirt, seemed too informal for something as formal as a funeral. And I had no paint with which to color myself white.

"I sat through the big national, actually international, funeral (dignitaries from many foreign countries—Cuba, Nicaragua, Angola, East Germany, Sweden, and Denmark, among others—came to pay their countries' respects) with part of my attention already on the next one, and on where to find white paint.

"My sister, Nzingha, sat beside me, her husband, Metudhi, next to her. She looked at me during one of the rather belabored eulogies and smiled. I smiled back. On the dais in front of us was Ola's casket. A creation of his own design, it was a large, minimally smoothed and polished mahogany log, the ends of which slanted up and inward, like the toes of a caliph's slippers; its oblong, oval top fit into the log as would the lid of a pot.

"In the old days, Ola's body would have been wrapped in bark cloth and left under a tree in the forest. Now it would have to be buried, but perhaps not very deep. I could not bear the thought of anything 'downpressing,' as the Rastas say, my father."

Alone in the Broderick Street apartment that he and Fanny had shared, Suwelo had looked forward to Fanny's letters, which read like serializations in a modern African adventure magazine. They were worlds apart, though at times he felt quite close to her. Sitting at his desk by the window that overlooked the busy San Francisco street, he glanced up often from her words to rest his eyes on "their" tiny corner of the Golden Gate Bridge, as the cooling fog swirled about it. Her world, at the moment, was hot and humid, he imagined, and contained all the color and drama his did not. He tried to conjure up Fanny Nzingha's face and to find a place for himself at each of Ola's funerals.

"As the eulogists droned on, I wondered if Nzingha was thinking about the day our father casually introduced us," wrote

Fanny. "She was his assistant at the Ministry of Culture, and when he took me and my mother there the first time, he told me he had a delightful surprise, someone with a remarkable resemblance to me. Who? I asked. My young assistant, he replied. As soon as we walked through the door I saw what he meant, though Nzingha was dressed, as I was to find she always was, in a voluminous, traditional robe and matching headdress. She had my eyes, and I realized for the first time, and happily, that the eyes of the newer African generations, after my father's, were clearer than the old, less yellow from the smoke of the fires in the shanties and huts, less bloodshot. She also had my nose, the Apache nose that had made my classmates, when I was in high school, call me 'Cochise.' There was also something of me in her movements and expressions. Except that she seemed to take pride, I was to notice later, in a kind of learned officiousness that struck me as unnatural. When we approached her, she was giving instructions to an underling—that's the feeling one got. That she was speaking not to her secretary or her assistant, a woman easily her equal perhaps in all but education and salary, but to some lesser being, a servant, in the old colonial style.

"After her rather long, detailed, and, I felt, extremely patronizing instructions to the woman, who heard her out with bowed head and averted eyes, Nzingha turned her face up to be kissed, which Ola did with a resounding smack, and which she endured.

" 'My two Nzinghas!' he cried, expansively, even flinging out his arms in his joy. Didn't he feel a trace of uneasiness or remorse, I wondered afterward, introducing us this way. 'At last you meet!'

"Coolly, for she was a woman used to welcoming foreign dignitaries, she extended her hand. We were exactly the same color, a rich, coffee-bean brown. I took it in my own.

"As she looked at me, and then at my mother, then at her father, beaming down on the two of us, a slight frown formed between her brows.

"'Ah,' said Ola, whose other nickname, 'the Quipper,' given him by the people, was well earned, 'the frown of recognition!'

"We were both clearly puzzled. I looked at my mother. She was smiling, composed. Obviously she had expected something like this. Yes, I thought, it would have been highly unlikely for my father not to have married, not to have had other children. He was an African. Perhaps he married many times, had many wives, many children. The thought that I might have half a dozen siblings took possession of me. How did I feel about this? I didn't know. Meanwhile, my hand clung to Nzingha's, as hers did to mine. I felt I was looking into a mirror as an African-American (in jeans and loose blouse, sandals), and the mirror was reflecting only the African.

"'You are sisters, my daughters,' said our father. 'Fanny Nzingha, meet Nzingha Anne.' This was his big surprise, and it pleased him, as all surprises, parties, unexpected verbal exchanges with people on street corners did.

"She was first to open her arms, to embrace me, which she did carefully, as if we were both breakable, and wrapped in tissue.

"A moment later, after pleasantries about our visit to the country and compliments to my mother on her stylish blue pantsuit, Nzingha excused herself and moved off regally down the hall. Later, she told me she went to the restroom, sat on the toilet, and cried.

"She had tried to be everything for her father: beautiful, a quick-minded student without discipline problems, interested in restoring the country's culture; she'd even married early in the hope of giving him grandsons. And then she discovered that she could not have been everything to him anyway, because he had my mother, an educated woman, and he had me, a beautiful and educated daughter. We had come before her and her mother; not so much in terms of affection, but in terms of time.

"I didn't get it.

"Patiently, one night over drinks in her cozy and colorful apartment, near the Ministry of Culture, where every wall was hung with weavings and paintings by the women of the villages, Nzingha explained it to me.

"We had eaten, and she had put her two boys, my young nephews, to bed. I could see that caring for them wore her out and that Metudhi was no help. He had eaten and muttered something about a meeting, as he made for the door.

" 'We are trying to bring back to people's consciousness that it takes two parents to raise a child,' she said, wearily kicking off her shoes and sinking onto the couch. 'It is only one of many beliefs the Africans have lost. In the old days what is happening now throughout the country would have been unthinkable; men are giving these women children, and that is all they give. Not a cent do they give for food or clothing or education. It is a scandal. Even men like Metudhi think it is enough to provide financial assistance; after they put down a part of their paycheck, they are out the door. Men who pay something, *anything*, are considered the *good* men. Every woman wants to get hold of one of these gems.'

"Her accent was charming. The way she said even this grim thing made me smile.

" 'Yes, it does no good to cry, I suppose,' said Nzingha, 'yet there are times when that is just the way I feel. And I feel so frus*trated*, because the men can always run on and on about the white man's destructiveness and yet they cannot look into their own families and their own children's lives and see that this is just the destruction the white man has planned. Meanwhile, the women are starting to crack from the white man's blatant success and the lack of their men's support.'

"'The same things are happening to us in the United States,' I said, 'only, there it is happening to everyone; there are many more white women and children receiving public assistance than there are black ones, for example. Though the media and the government try to make it look otherwise.'

"'Men are mangled by the system, as we are,' said Nzingha.

"'Yes,' I said. 'The difference is that they help create it. At least the part of it that oppresses women.'

"'That is true,' she said. 'And I learned this from the life of my mother.'

"Nzingha went about the room and switched off the lights. 'You haven't seen the moon until you've seen it in Africa,' she said, and, sure enough, there began to rise a giant yellow moon that soon filled the window and then the room with its cool yellow light.

"'My mother worshiped the moon,' she said, thoughtfully, sitting down again. 'She had since she was a child; and she could see in moonlight as clearly as most people can in sun. Ironically, this was to mean she would grow up to become a great guerrilla fighter, always the one who volunteered to go on missions at night. But I am getting ahead of my mother's story. Do you want some more coffee?' she asked, pouring a bit more into my cup. 'We grow this, you know,' she said, raising her cup, a booster of her country's products in all settings.

"I was enchanted by the cup, hand-thrown, a brilliant cobalt blue, with small crocodile heads decorating its sides. I turned it around and around in my hands while my sister talked.

"'My mother,' said Nzingha, 'was from the village, the bush. She was illiterate, superstitious. That is to say she did not speak anything other than her own language and she knew no other ways than those of her own people. She did not know English

or Christianity,' she added pointedly. 'When the repression became unbearable, she ran away and joined the Mbeles, the African "underground." She was a brilliant fighter—her code name
was Harriet, as in Tubman; doesn't it make you smile?—but
not a scholar or thinker or even, really, a social person. She
was very quiet, solitary, spoke more eloquently with her actions
than with her words, which were very few and uttered as if she
were weary. She saved my father's life, she saved many people's
lives, but she was lost without a gun in her hand or an explo-
sive device on her belt. After the people took back the country,
there was little for her to do, since the traditional society no
longer functioned. Or so it seemed to her. My father married
her while they were still outlaws; she became pregnant with me
between battles. With the overthrow of the white regime, my
father's stock rose very high, because he'd been partially educated in Western ways by the missionaries. He was sent off to
Sweden to further his studies. They even tried to send him to
Russia! Oh, he went to Russia but came back after two weeks.
Only Ola would have done that, come back so soon. The young
students we send today are too afraid to miss an opportunity
like that; no matter how cold it is, or how, sometimes, uncivil to
them the Russians are; they wouldn't think of coming home before getting what they've gone for. And this is good; the country needs the skills they learn there. However, too cold, Ola
said. His brain and every other part froze.' She smiled. 'The
government sent him to Sweden. He was gone several years,
studying and learning for the good of our country. My mother
took care of me, and waited. Right there in the little hut he left
her in, the hut she'd erected herself. And when he came back,
he no longer remembered how she'd saved his life or how he-
roic she was. If he did remember, it was in that way that writers
remember things, as if they happened to someone else, and you
needn't be bound by the *facts*.' She paused. 'Sometimes I try to

think what we must have looked like to him after his years in Sweden. Sweden was very cold, too, Ola said, but the women were beautiful and warmhearted.'

"Nzingha paused, placed her hands together under her chin, rubbed them as if *they* were cold, and frowned slightly. 'My mother had no education but she was extremely psychic,' she continued, 'even politically psychic, which is rare. She knew that no matter how my father studied, emulated people of other cultures, or otherwise shaped a "modern" self, he would always come into conflict with the government here, even though it was this government that sent him and other young men abroad. It was a government she had helped—through immense risk and personal sacrifice—put into power, but that, once in power, conveniently forgot she existed. This was true of all the women: they were forgotten. This was before our men had any idea there might be a different way of relating to women, other than the one they traditionally practiced. Of course, men always suspend traditional behavior during wartime. A woman was for breeding, a woman was for sex, a woman—well, in our language the word for woman is the same as for seed granary. Women like my mother were so angry, and so hurt. And my father came back from Sweden and looked at us. I remember it clearly, though I was only five or six years old. He came in a big car, with a driver. He brought presents. For my mother he brought a china tea set, bright blue and white, with a quilted cozy, and to me he brought an enormous blonde doll named Hildegarde.

"'Our hut was neat and, I thought, very pretty, for my mother had painted it the traditional way, with bold colors and geometric designs, but she had gone further, and painted giraffes all over it—small giraffes that seemed to float through the abstract spaces.

"'My father looked pained. He and my mother sat on a

bench in the yard and talked in Olinka, but every once in a while he said something in a different language—English, I later realized—which only the driver seemed to understand. It was as if he spoke it for his benefit; the driver had also been someone my father had known during the emergency. I played with the big blue-eyed, yellow-haired doll, and I could tell that my mother was also enchanted with it—she'd never had a doll—much more than with her tea set. We'd never seen anything like it. She'd seen white people, but not many, and only when she was in the process of trying to blow up their buildings or power stations; neither of us had seen anything so white and splendid as this doll.

"'I noticed they looked over at me from time to time, and that my father seemed displeased.

"'Later, I realized he was displeased because of the number of holes in my ears—three in each ear—and because I wasn't wearing a blouse. But none of the women or children wore blouses for everyday. What was the point? Everyone knew bare skin in the humid climate was more comfortable.

"'He came regularly after that. He was writing plays against imperialism. At that time the government really loved him, and, basking in their favor, he seemed quite content. He was at least confident that his work could be an instrument for change, a change his government would encourage, applaud, and, most of all, attempt to implement. He was a childless man, though, as far as his friends in government knew; at least, it was not definitely known he was married, and no doubt this was beginning to bother him. Each time he came and left, my mother was sadder and sadder. We'd always slept on the same mat, and sometimes in the night I'd wake up and she'd be crying. My mother was the kind of woman who could fight in the mountains or the caves or gorges for months, even years, alongside the men and blow up power stations, and at the same time accept, with obvious gratitude, the shelter of her five-year-old's arms in the middle of the night.

"'My father came one day and took me and Hildegarde away. My mother didn't fight to keep me with her, for which I blamed her. She told me it was for my own good—of course I couldn't see that!—and that I must study hard and learn to be of service to our country. She was a matriot, and loved our country, though she thought the men who ruled were all gesture and no effect.'

"Nzingha stopped suddenly and rubbed her eyes, which had begun to shine with unshed tears. 'We left her there in the village to rot,' she said finally. 'I missed her terribly, at first. I didn't know my father at all, and it was disconcerting to realize, once we arrived in the capital, that everyone else did. That he was famous and popular and lived in a big house to match the big car. He put me in a boarding school run by white nuns, some of the more curious of the citizens of our new country, which I now saw had, apparently, as many white people as black. But that was only in the cities. At that time my father was blind to the contradiction of putting me with the nuns, or pretended to be. He wanted to be sure I learned to speak English. The future of our country depended on the ability of its citizens to be at least bilingual, he always said. This view cut no ice with my mother. Once, on a rare visit I made to the village to see her, I said a few words in English to her, and she went into a rage, throwing things—not that there were very many things in the hut to throw—and stamping about. I thought she would attack me. She was drinking the home-brewed beer that she made to sell and smoking a cigarette. She was so unlike the mother I had left! It was really amazing. Her eyes were red, her hair matty and wild. There was a coarseness in her mannerisms and a slackness in her expression I'd never seen and never thought my gentle mother could have. Nor did I understand yet about changes in the personality wrought by grief. She was slovenly, unconcerned. The rain had eaten away a corner of the hut, and the giraffes, which she used to repaint each year at the beginning of the dry season, had faded, so they seemed to be ghost animals, shadows, floating round and round the sides of the hut.

" 'I went back only once after that, while she was still alive. I went, but I wouldn't get out of the car. She came out to see me and sat on a stool beside the car door. I handed her some things my father sent. One of them, I remember, was a book about the indigenous culture of Cameroun; there were lots of photographs of the people's houses—which were made of mud, and decorated colorfully—of their clothes and musical instruments. She was immediately interested in it, and actually looked at more than the first page before tossing it listlessly to the ground. She had that puffy, slatternly, dissipated look people get when they have no way of seeing themselves. I don't think she even owned a mirror. I didn't know *this* woman.

" 'She died, after a lingering illness, when I was sixteen. Probably from cancer. Or heart failure. Or heartbreak. The cause of death had no name, in the village. Only the reasons. She was very tired, the villagers said, very lonely. There was not enough for such a woman to do, now that there was peace, and black men ruled the country. They did not say this with the irony my mother would have.

" 'In any event, my father and I had by then become colleagues; our bond was the struggle to improve the country. He was writing skits about the proper behavior of workers in the work place and the importance of a high level of production. I would go with him to the factories where his work was performed. Because he was sincere and his work easily accessible—and, at times, very simple-minded—the workers liked him. He remained, among government officials and workers alike, very popular. And by then I was his little darling. I was very proud of him!

"'But even before my mother's death he was changing. Becoming less comfortable with being adored. He never saw her anymore, except perhaps once or twice by accident, when business took him back to the village. My father was responsible for getting a water line laid from the river to the village; the villagers, who had always carried water from the river on their heads, praised him highly for this. Yet I honestly think that in her absence, and over time, she became powerfully present to him. Perhaps this is simply the way it is with writers. It is when they don't see you that you matter. Because then you can belong to them in a way that permits them complete possession. You are determined by them. You are controlled. You are, generally speaking, exaggerated.'

"Nzingha, who had been sitting back on the couch with her legs straight out in front of her, shivered, and drew them up under her. The room was getting chilly. I drew my own legs up and draped my long skirt over them. She reached for a large, striped, earth-toned woolen shawl on a stool beside her—of the kind made in the cooperatives run by the Ministry of Culture and sold in the shops to the tourists—and spread it over our knees. The coffee had made me alert, but calmly so, and passive under the sound of her soft, familiar voice. At times I felt I was talking to myself.

"'Writers,' she mused. 'Does anybody else cause as much trouble, in the long run? But I can tell you what my father would say: Writers don't cause trouble so much as they describe it. Once it is described, trouble takes on a life visible to all, whereas until it is described, and made visible, only a few are able to see it. Still, there is something about writers . . .' Nzingha laughed. 'As the Russians are finding out, they're damned hard people to re-educate. I think it is a kind of curlicue they have in the brain. They come into the world with a certain perspective, and the drive to share it. This curlicue is totally lacking in other people; I don't know why.

" 'It was my father's play about my mother that completely dissolved the government's confidence in him and separated the people from the government. Maybe this was because "the people" contained men *and* women; the government, only men. Not that there wasn't a struggle among the people, in the cities as well as in the villages, about the issues raised in the play. There were enormous controversies, arguments, brawls. Though the play unmercifully criticized some of the people's ways, they did not take this as an attack on them, as human beings, singled out for abuse. Besides, they knew my father's work too well to take that view. They were seeing themselves, in my father's play, for the first time as they more or less were, without the patina of revolution, the slogans of imperialism, or any concern for production quotas. They responded, really, as if they had been in a fit of hysteria, and someone they knew well and liked very much hauled off and slapped them. The things that they then revealed about themselves were interesting in the extreme. For instance, it was as if they'd never before thought of women or the possibility that women were human beings in their own right at all. This was the greatest sting in the slap. My father's insights into the oppression of women, black women by black men, who should have had more understanding—having criticized the white man's ignorance in dealing with black people for so long—made many of the people uncomfortable, but they were also, eventually, stimulated to change. My father's plays were always somewhat didactic; whatever understanding he gained about life he did not hesitate to share. The people saw—as my father himself had eventually seen—my mother's struggle to be a soldier in the army against white supremacy and colonization, then her equally difficult battle to be a wife and mother, with no models for the new way of life she herself was helping to develop, followed by her complete disillusion with the government of men who took over control of the country after the triumph. My father was pitiless in depicting his own failures. There were his Swedish lovers, one of whom was left with a child, his big car, his grandiose European-style house. His cronies in power and their absorption in beer drinking, women, and soccer. His maid, a meek girl from the village, who acted like he was God, and who reminded the audience of his discarded wife. I found the scene in which the child, who was conceived in the passion of revolt, is taken away from the totally devastated mother unbearable to watch. How he could write it, as well as a scene depicting the mother's decline and death, was a mystery to me. Paradoxically, during the writing of this play, and after, as it was being performed, he became progressively joyous, calmly rebellious, one might even say radiant.

"'The play was dedicated to my mother, whom he at last publically claimed as his wife. For the first time, I began to feel it possible to imagine them together, in the same room, eating at the same table, sleeping in the same bed. I began to realize there might, indeed, have been love.

"'*Well*. It was the first of my father's plays the government banned.

"'He laughed until he cried when he was informed of this. His response to being hurt was always to laugh like a lunatic. Then he took the play to the villages and performed it one night in each village until the government caught up with him. They fined him, tossed him in jail for a week, and took away his house. It was the beginning of the end. But at least, as he used to say, it *was* a beginning.'"

"It was very late when my sister finished this story, and so she improvised a bed for me on the couch. She placed an embroidered pillow under my head and the woolen, earth-toned shawl over my legs and feet. Best of all, as she left for her bedroom, she leaned down and kissed me on the forehead. As if enchanted by her kiss, I fell almost instantly into a deep, restful sleep, interrupted only by Metudhi's return, early in the morning. After he was settled, I drifted off again, and the next thing I knew it was ten o'clock in the morning and I was alone in the apartment. The boys were at school and Nzingha and Metudhi were already at work.

"OUR father made many, many blunders, out of ignorance, mainly," said Nzingha, "but in his heart of hearts he was fearless."

They had been picnicking that day on the shores of Lake Wanza. There were low bluish hills off in the distance, and on the lake weathered fishermen's boats bobbed complacently, their ochre-colored sails flapping in the wind. It was a warm, pleasant day, with large birds wheeling overhead and with that sound of stillness that is like a hum.

Earlier, Fanny had been speaking about what it was like growing up without a father, and without even mention of one. About her two grandmothers, Big Mama Celie and Mama Shug; about the coziness of being loved by two such emotionally giving women. They laughed at Fanny's description of the way her mother told her she had been named. Mama Celie had named her Fanny, because it was the name she wished she herself had had; if she'd been named Fanny, she'd have had a sassier life, she felt, one with travel and adventure in it. She thought the sound of "Fanny" an adventure in itself. And Fanny thought that, for her, it had something mildly scandalous, rebellious, in it. That turning her "fanny" to someone, or "shaking her fanny in someone's face," was an action she'd always wished she could take, especially when she was a child, and a young woman, and suffering abuse from all around her. So she'd said, "Fanny!" as Fanny was born. And Fanny's mother, Olivia, said she was so surprised and afraid that she'd come out with some other peculiar name to follow it, like Lou or Jean, that she forgot how weak she felt from giving birth and practically yelled out "Nzingha!" To which Mama Celie and Mama Shug had said, in unison, "In *what?*" And then Olivia had told them about Anne Nzingha, the ruler of Angola, who fought the Portuguese for forty years; the woman who refused the title Queen and required that her subjects call her "King"; the woman who, like Joan of Arc, always dressed as a man and led her troops in battle. At once woman, man, king, queen, master strategist and fighter, daughter, mother, pagan and Catholic, supreme ruler and wily female. Of all news brought home about Africa, Fanny's mother had told her later, this was the most interesting to Celie, though she was never to pronounce Nzingha correctly. She called her "Zinga" when she used the word at all, and only when she was reprimanding her, which she occasionally did in the mildest possible tone. Generally she called her "Fanny." As in "Fannnneeee, darlin', come here to Big Mama. Where you been, dumplins? Give me some sugar!" This would be followed by a hug and a resounding smack on the cheek.

"I have heard this is the way some of the black people in the United States speak," said Nzingha. "Is it really true?"

Fanny assured her it was, and proceeded to carry on a monologue in Mama Celie's voice.

"I can just see her," said Nzingha, laughing. "There is so much character in how she says things. My mother was the same. When she spoke, you felt there was no greater integrity in language anywhere." She had broken out a chilled bottle of locally made palm wine, which she assured Fanny was the only intoxicant in Africa that made you feel great after drinking it, with no possibility of a nasty hangover.

Fanny chuckled at this news.

"My father had such ideas about education, you know," Nzingha continued, taking a sip of her wine and smacking her lips in loyal appreciation, "and it was hard for him to understand that being educated by people who despise you is also conquest. He understood this, to a degree, in his own life, but when it came to me—well, as he put it, he must always shift among alternatives, and the education offered here in Olinka, after secondary school, left much to be desired. I recognized this myself. *However*. You will never know what misery is until you've been an African student sent off to study in the West."

Fanny imagined her sister, small, black, alone, headed for that mythical location. Probably none of the clothing she'd carried with her was warm enough. She swallowed a large gulp of palm wine to banish the vision.

"I was sent to France," Nzingha said, "to Paris, to the Sorbonne." She made a face. "I am probably the only woman in the world who hates Paris! It was a cold place, in more ways than one. The people were so jaded, so played out spiritually. Nothing seemed to move them from the heart. They were only animated by artificial events—hopelessly abstract plays full of even more abstract ideas, for instance. Fashion excited them. Nothing whatever made them smile. I remember one day walking along the Champs-Elysées and watching each face I met to see if one would have a smile. Not one did, and I looked at hundreds of people; and it was a warm, perfectly lovely day. I couldn't stand the grayness, the heaviness of the architecture, the absence of wild trees. I couldn't abide the *pieds noirs* in the shops or the other little shivering Africans selling trinkets in the Bois. I made a few friends among the Dogon. There was a little Dogonese restaurant near the Rue des Trois-Portes not far from Notre-Dame. I used to go there whenever I could. And there they were: the smiles, the warmth, the courtesy, the edible food I'd come to Paris expecting to find. For, believe it or not, I didn't like French food! Which everyone at home, especially those who'd never tasted it and who had only heard about it from others who had been to France, spoke of as if it were food for the Gods. I detested the heavy sauces, and even the light ones. I had no physical tolerance for anything made of milk or cream. This is an African characteristic, by the way; I didn't know that, though. I just knew almost everything I ate made me ill. I felt sticky internally all the time. And I was! Ugh! And the superior attitude the waiters took when you ordered. I've sat in many a Parisian restaurant too angry to swallow a bite."

At this point, Nzingha refilled their glasses, had a sip of her wine, and smiled blissfully at its home-grown taste.

"I hated everything," she said somberly, coming out of this happy state. "I was as unappeasable as a three-year-old. I hated the Louvre! There was all the booty from other countries on display, because, really, that is what most museums are for. Instead of these looters stealing just for themselves and their own houses, they steal for their countries, their continents, their race. I couldn't stand it. And I got lost, there in the Louvre. I couldn't find my way out, and the guards were as unhelpful as any other Parisian. At last I found an open window, two stories off the ground, and I climbed out of it to a ledge and was going to jump. I couldn't stand being inside another second. But one of the tourists ambling by, an American, a man, just casually stuck his head through the window too and, as I stood there pressed against the wall looking down, he said, 'Phew, this place sure is short of fresh air.' It stank, in addition to everything else! All those dead things. All those thwarted spirits who never dreamed their physical remains would wind up in Paris under glass. The Louvre smelled like what it was: a grave. So I laughed. And he said, looking about for a way, 'How do you get out there?' And I certainly didn't want to share the ledge, or the jump, with him, and so I said, 'Let me come in first.' He was one of those tall, rangy fellows you see in American films set in Texas or Montana. But he turned out to be from Georgia, in the South, about which I knew nothing I hadn't learnt in the cinema watching *Gone With the Wind*. But that wasn't the Georgia he knew. He was poor; his family always had been. This is hard for Africans to believe, you know — that there are Southern whites who have been or are now poor. We look at them oddly when they tell us this, and mentally we are going: 'What? *Poor?* And after all that!'"

Fanny laughed. She was feeling pretty good from the wine, and slavery from this perspective had never occurred to her.

"They'd always, his family, been *decent*, he wanted me to know," said Nzingha, who was beginning to slur her words a bit, and to get that slightly argumentative tone that Africans get when they drink with someone they like but have a story to tell that they don't like. "This was the code for *decent* to colored, *your* people. He was in Paris, at the university, on scholarship. We saw each other a lot after that. I really liked Jeff. I felt the kind of affection one feels for a child or someone wandering about in the world absolutely lost while confident he or she is finding, and can show others, the way. There was so much he couldn't understand.

"When he'd left his hometown in Georgia, the whole town had turned out — though not the colored people they'd all been so decent to! — to cheer him on. And he'd been thrilled by everything since the day he arrived. The mustiness of the Louvre was the largest misfortune of his visit. He couldn't understand the torture of classes in which Africa was ignored, historically, as if it didn't or hadn't existed; and where, if a professor said something about Punt or Cyrene being African nations with whom the ancient world traded, he almost always referred to them as 'mythical' or 'mysterious'! It seemed impossible for the professors to acknowledge that ancient Cyrene was Libya, or that the ancient Egyptians were black. This seemed as hard for them to fathom as that the Sahara Desert hadn't always been a desert, or that Egypt is a part of Africa. I don't know where they thought King Tut came from, with his little black self! When they did discuss Africa, they did so in terms of its problems, its 'backwardness,' never in terms of its contributions or its centuries of oppression under whites, including the smug, self-righteous French themselves, who, even as we studied African history without a word about French colonialism, were trying to finish off the Algerian resistance by the foulest possible means. It was so degrading to sit there."

There was more anger in Nzingha's voice than Fanny had heard the whole time she had been in Olinka. She began to wonder, not for the first time, about the bottled-up, repressed anger of the African woman, silent for so long. She thought of this anger as an enormous storehouse of energy and wondered whether the women knew they owned it. Anger can also be a kind of wealth, she thought.

"I remember, though, the day I was finally fed up," continued Nzingha, now drinking in an alarmingly rapid fashion, and attempting to refill Fanny's glass so that she could keep up with her. "It was in an art history class, and the professor was discussing the *Greek* foundations of Western civilization and art. He presented a slide, at the front of the classroom, that depicted Perseus slaying Medusa. *Well.* It had been carved into a wall somewhere—I think in Melos—and looters had just chopped off the part of the wall that interested them and that they could carry." She laughed, as did Fanny, at this image. "Well, anyway, there was Perseus in his chariot, and in his hand, hanging over the side, was the severed head of Medusa, her snakelike locks of hair presented as real snakes—everywhere in Africa a symbol of fertility and wisdom—and there were even two snakes floating about the corners of her mouth. Her face was horribly contorted, as yours would be, too, if someone had just hacked off your head. The rest of her rather large, womanly body is still on its knees, and in fact she looks decidedly, if you know how to read the carving differently from Westerners, like an angel. Because she *is* an angel. She is the *mother* of Christian angels. She is Isis, mother of Horus, sister and lover of Osiris, Goddess of Egypt. The Goddess, who, long before she became Isis, was known all over Africa as simply the Great Mother, Creator of All, Protector of All, the Keeper of the Earth. *The* Goddess.

"Now, I had learned all this—" and here Nzingha burst into quite wild laughter at the absurdity of it—"from the nuns back home. And I began to understand, while I studied at the Sorbonne, why those nuns were permitted to stay in my country, when so many other white people were *encouraged* to leave." Nzingha grimaced violently as she pantomined the attempted removal of a large, heavy, obstinate object. Fanny appreciated the mental spectacle of white oppression she'd created, and the two of them laughed until tears came to their eyes.

"They were nuns who," continued Nzingha, regaining her poise as much as a rather tipsy person can do, "in the peace and solitude of Africa, far away from the indoctrination of their church's teaching in Europe, had debunked every spirit obstructionist, antifemale, white-supremacist theory they'd been taught.

"'Haven't you ever wondered where angels come from?' one of the nuns—my favorite, Sister Felicity—once asked our class sweetly. 'Well, when you study Egyptian art and life you will see where they come from. They come from the Gods and Goddesses of Africa.'

"Ah, *so!*" Fanny could only utter, in delight.

"African *angels*, of course! That's just what's been missing from everyone's life, right?" said Nzingha, a hand on her hip and her black eyes ablaze.

"I immediately visualized them," she continued, "my mother among them, not as she was in her final days, but as she was when she and I shared the same mat. Her kind face, her sweet breath and tender voice. Her psychic connectedness to events and people hundreds of miles away. I knew that Notre-Dame was built on the site of a shrine to Isis, who was later called the Black Madonna, and I hurried there as soon as I arrived in Paris, for my teachers, the nuns, had said I must. There is no trace of Isis there, of course, nor anywhere in Paris; certainly not today in the souls of its people. But at least I stood there, in Notre-Dame, where her ancient, more likely preancient, worshipers had also stood. Except, they had stood with their feet on the bare ground, under trees, and it was this feeling of being connected with the Universe directly that I missed. Notre-Dame to me was no different from the Louvre. It had been built for the same purpose. Only it had been built to colonize the spiritual remains of a goddess, as the Louvre had been built to colonize the material remains of devastated cultures.

"Dutifully I sent the nuns a postcard showing this somber edifice, and they wrote back to remind me that the Goddess is not confined in the monuments men allegedly create for her to dwell in, and which are really erected to themselves. That She—the spirit of Mothering, of Creating, of Blessing and Protecting All—lives within us, and is confined neither to shrines nor to any particular age.

"But," said Nzingha, "back to the professor. The story *he* was telling was about the ugliness of the face of the African Goddess, with her dreadlocked hair—snakes, *ugh*, right?—and its tendency to turn men to stone. And so this brave white man, Perseus the Greek, takes on the challenge of slaying her, as he would any other 'dragon,' for it is as if the only invitation the white man accepts from anything that is powerful is that he come at once to kill it. And so he cuts off her head, and in all his stories says the face is hideous, and the hair like writhing snakes, and that there is nothing redeemable about her whatsoever."

There was a look of deep sadness on Nzingha's face. "Except," she said, in a whisper, "if you are from Africa you recognize Medusa's wings as the wings of Egypt, and you recognize the head of Medusa as the head of Africa; and what you realize you are seeing is the Western world's memorialization of that period in prehistory when the white male world of Greece decapitated and destroyed the black female Goddess/Mother tradition and culture of Africa." She paused for a moment, as we considered this. "Actually," she continued thoughtfully, "the earliest known 'Athene,' though Greek, has snaky hair. Only later did they give her those flowing blond locks that the black-haired Greeks even today pretend they had." Nzingha had the last swallow of wine from the glass in her hand and shrugged, looking, for just a moment, very French. "It was hardly a challenge," she said, "to move on to my Western literature class and discover that Athena was created to be a flunky of the male order that created her. That one of her first acts, in *The Oresteia*, was to deny that there is any bond between a mother and her child, other than that of a letter to its envelope. According to her, at Orestes' trial for the murder of his mother, woman merely carries the seed, the child is totally the fruit of its father. She herself, she declares, never had, nor ever needed, a mother, having sprung full blown from the forehead of her father, the God Zeus!"

Nzingha pulled herself upright and wrapped her arms tightly around her legs. For a moment she looked remarkably like Ola. Fanny didn't think either of them had a hangover yet, but it was clear that their wine-induced euphoria, what there had been of it, was short-lived. Nzingha's story made her think of universities in the United States, and all the lies in academia that had driven her to the practice of massage.

"So what did I attempt to argue," Nzingha said wearily, sounding a bit like Ola too, "there in the Sorbonne, in one of the foremost bastions of Western civilization: that the reason Athena had sprung 'full blown' from the mind of Zeus was because she was an idea, given by Greek men to their God; and that 'idea' was the destruction of the African Goddess Isis and the metamorphosis of Isis into the Greek Goddess Athena. But since no one at the Sorbonne had been taught anything about Isis, it was impossible for them to connect her with Athena. I must have appeared to be simply another raving African.

"I left France that night. I refused to be taught that 'Black' Africa—'Negro' Africa, as they called it—was unconnected to 'Colored' Africa, that is, Egypt, or that a civilization founded on the destruction of the black woman as Goddess in her own world was superior to what I had at home, no matter how 'backward' or impoverished."

"And you were right," Fanny said emphatically, kissing her cheek.

"Father was badly disappointed," Nzingha said regretfully, putting her fingers to the spot Fanny had kissed. "He had such dreams for me! That I would know not only French and English, but also German. So he fussed quite a bit when he saw I would never go back. I learned to educate myself in the way I'm sure it must have been done in the days of old. Whenever I met someone who seemed to know a lot about a subject, and who evinced, moreover, a certain happiness in his or her being, and if I were interested in the subject, I asked to be taught what they knew. To my father I said one day: 'Show me how you write plays. Take me with you so that I can learn how they are performed. Tell me what to study in order to help develop our culture.' To the village people I said: 'Tell me about the war, tell me about the old days; show me how you made things; tell me the stories so that they will not be lost.' One thing I know," said Nzingha decisively. "Learning from one's elders does not permit pessimism. Your day is always easier than theirs. You look at them, so beautiful and so wise, and you cannot help trying to emulate them. It is courage given by osmosis, I think." She fell silent for several minutes, gazing out over the lake, which had turned maroon from the deep red rays of the setting sun.

"*You* give me courage, Nzingha," Fanny said, after a while.

Nzingha sighed, looked at her sister without any of the resentment of the long-lost sibling Fanny once or twice had glimpsed in her eyes, and smiled.

"It was the play Ola wrote about *your* mother that brought him around," she said. "He remembered how much he'd learned from the missionaries, but he also remembered how learning from them and not from his own people made him feel inferior. This had caused him to become almost mindlessly aggressive, especially against females, over whom he exerted power because of his size and because he was a man. It was when I started to work with him, first learning to write plays and then as his assistant at the Ministry of Culture, that I began, like everyone else, to call him 'Ola.'"

Nzingha gathered the food scraps and numerous empty wine bottles and put them back into the picnic hamper. Fanny rose from her mat and began to roll it up.

Isis, Athena. Egypt, Greece. There on the shores of enormous Lake Wanza it was easy to think of them, shimmering just above the horizon, Egypt itself a kind of place angel, ever beckoning on those in need of reassurance of their beauty, their worthiness, their goodness. Their place in history. And yet, as Fanny said to Nzingha, as they brushed off each other's skirts, "the fact that one felt so involved with the black and mixed-race Egyptians was not so much because of their rulers, or even their gods or their religion, but because of their artists. It is the art, above all, that is exquisite," she murmured, "and no doubt the music was beautiful also."

She should not have worried about the white paint. She dressed in the simple white informal clothes she had and rode to her father's village with Nzingha and Metudhi. When they arrived, the village women took them in hand, and within minutes Fanny's face and hands and legs had been plastered with white mud.

"In the United States," she told Nzingha, "my grandmother used to whitewash her fireplace with this stuff."

Nzingha looked puzzled, and Fanny could see she couldn't visualize it.

"Never mind," she said.

This funeral was as long on chanting and singing as the one in the capital had been on speeches. Fanny preferred it. It had been hard to sit still as one unctuous government official followed another, praising Ola for his "bold," "revolutionary" work. She felt that most of them were simply relieved he'd had the tact to die of a heart attack while at home—right in the middle of an antigovernment quip, she'd been informed—and not bloodied, on the floor, in one of their jails.

"I realize," she whispered to Nzingha, "that there is not a single government in the world I like or trust. They are all, as far as I'm concerned, unnatural bodies, male-supremacist private clubs."

Nzingha yawned. "Yes," she said, making no attempt to disguise her restlessness, "and by this time we are too bored to want to join."

WHILE the gumbo had cooled a bit, Mr. Hal had set the table with beautiful linens, crystal, and cutlery that belonged to Uncle Rafe, and that Suwelo had never seen. There was, first of all, a thick snowy-white tablecloth; over this was laid an old cream-colored square of handmade lace. There were lace-edged napkins to match. Then there were settings of bone china that resembled alabaster and that rang when hit with a spoon. Suwelo struck his teacup over and over with his spoon, with the charmed expression of a child. There were blue crystal goblets that pinged. There was richly glinting silver everywhere, picking up the flames of the candles in the heavy silver candelabra that Miss Lissie set on the table with a graceful flourish.

Suwelo had sat in what would have been Uncle Rafe's chair at such an occasion, at the head of the table. Miss Lissie and Mr. Hal were on either side of him. They raised their glasses of iced tea or lemonade to the spirit of Uncle Rafe, and set to with real appreciation and undisguised gusto. Rafe had loved himself some gumbo, Miss Lissie allowed.

The gumbo, which Mr. Hal had assured Suwelo would be even better tomorrow, and the next day and the next and the . . . was so good Suwelo could hardly believe he was tasting this dish for the first time. It had the kind of flavor that made you feel as though you were tasting all of life; there was, well, an almost sexual flavor to it. He loved the slick gumminess of it, its spicy fullness. Not one flavor that had gone into its creation was any longer distinct.

An hour later, after the dishes had been washed and they were still feelingly praising the gumbo, made even more special because the three of them had prepared it, the friends sat in the living room attempting to read different sections of the newspaper. There were the usual reports of murders, rapes, torture, wars, abandoned children, trashed apartments, and new cars. It was Miss Lissie who first threw her section to the floor.

"There's nothing I can do about any of this madness today," she said. "And just thinking about it spoils my digestion."

"You're right," said Mr. Hal, neatly folding his section and placing it beside him on the couch.

"I'd rather keep hearing about you and Fanny."

"Yes," said Mr. Hal, "if they're going to blow us up, or make us freeze to death and starve in the dark, we might as well be enjoying ourselves by hearing a good story."

Suwelo found himself in the seat next to the television set. In a gesture he now recognized as ritualistic, he turned slightly in his chair and tugged at the corners of the blue shawl, which did not really need straightening. He sat back and began.

Suwelo had thought that if he ever sat in the "hot seat" beside the television, he would never be able to talk about his life as Mr. Hal and Miss Lissie talked about theirs. His own life felt too modern, too current—who knew how his and Fanny's story would turn out?—too . . . personal. He felt a bit of the shyness he'd suffered as a small boy when asked by an adult to give an accounting of himself, and he felt exposed in a way he had not while helping to make dinner in the kitchen. Talking to them then had been indirect, somehow. They'd each been absorbed in the task before them. It seemed he was mostly talking to the crabs he was cleaning, and only incidentally had Mr. Hal and Miss Lissie heard. He cleared his throat and slid his long fingers up and down his corduroy-covered thigh. His eyes, which had lost their unreflective look, seemed both candid and full of feeling.

"The yurt that Fanny and I had," he said, in a firm, clear voice, "and our five acres, were on a ridgetop that overlooked a valley of sheep ranches and vineyards. The opening faced east, so that each morning we were awakened by the rising sun. Though we were in a small clearing, there was forest all around, and we shared the land with deer, squirrels, rabbits, raccoons, and birds of all description. There were enormous hawks playing—actually looking for food, but hovering, and appearing to play—against the wind, and the most graceful vultures, with huge wingspans, and owls—which, Fanny always said, I resembled, and so perhaps the owl was my totem—and sometimes sea gulls, for we weren't too far from the sea. If you ever come west, and I certainly hope you do, I'd love to show you this place. It really is special. We were not the first people to think so; we often found bits of chiseled flint and an occasional potsherd.

"Fanny from time to time thought she saw Indians. The only time I ever saw any was when we ran into them camping down at the state park, with everybody else. But these were not the ones she saw. At least not back up in the hills where we were. 'Just over there by the stream,' she said to me once when we'd gone down to the river to swim and she'd wandered back into the woods to find the source of a small creek that fed into the river. 'What exactly do you think you saw?' I asked. She had that intent, slightly stoned, but joyful look she too often got, for no good reason, it seemed to me. Or, I should say, for no reason I could see. She pointed downstream. 'Just over there, very quiet on the bank, two Pomo Indian boys, their spears raised, fishing for salmon.' Wrong season, I said, pedantically. It was summer and very hot and very little water was left in the river; certainly not enough for salmon, which are huge fish. She wasn't perturbed by my response. She was used to it. Generally, when I used this tone of voice, she would simply stop telling me whatever it was she had experienced. But not this time. She described them: brown skin, long black hair, very round, 'moon' faces, she said. Loincloths. *Loin*cloths? I teased. She nodded. 'As still as deer, they were,' she avowed, 'and as hard to see.'

"I didn't understand or share these flights of fancy, but when I wasn't resentful that she was the possessor of this dubious gift of—what shall I call it?—'second sight,' 'two-headedness,' whatever, I enjoyed them vicariously. They were part of what enchanted me about Fanny. And in the summers, when I had no teaching responsibilities and we were both able to 'disappear,' as she liked to say, from the world, they were a definite part of the entertainment. Truly that was—the 'disappearance'—her happiest time; when she felt she didn't exist to anyone but herself and sometimes not even to herself. I'd never known anyone who loved the thought of impermanence, invisibility, being at peace under a toadstool, more than Fanny." Suwelo laughed at this image of Fanny, which he visualized perfectly. There she sat under her little brown toadstool, happy as a toad, and being one.

"She picked up information in ways I never understood, either. She'd given up reading in any systematic way; the information she needed simply came to her. She'd visit a friend, or someone she barely knew, for example, and knock over a vase. The water from the vase would splash on a stack of books on the floor. Fanny would carefully dry off all the books, on hands and knees, apologizing profusely the whole time. Then the information, or whatever it was, she'd been looking for, vaguely, would appear on the wettest page of one of the books. She'd be drying this page in front of the fire and right there would be exactly what she'd wanted to know. Her eye would rest on the page for only a minute, as she absorbed the information, and she would be on her way. I've seen this sort of thing happen hundreds of times; and it was really, sometimes, maddening. By comparison, everything I wanted to learn, I had to work very, very hard for, spending weeks, even months, locked up in musty library stacks with decaying tomes stacked well above my head.

"Or wishes! Fanny could wish for almost anything—food, clothing, an experience, a ticket to anywhere, a phone call from a friend, anything; more otters in the river, to see a buck with really huge antlers—every September when the deer season opens, the bucks are routinely hunted down and slaughtered, yet Fanny saw not one with huge antlers, but two!—even to be taller than she was. She actually did grow taller by an inch by taking a martial-arts class twice a week. . . . And whatever she wished for would happen. It was her wish that got us the yurt, an authentic handmade yurt built by a modern Dutch witch from Amsterdam, passing through on her way to God knows where, a yurt that I'd certainly never have dreamed of one day living in. After all, the only yurts I knew anything about were those in photographs taken in Outer Mongolia that I'd seen in *National Geographic* and that were made out of yak hides. But no, the one she conjured up for us was round, yes, more or less, and made of wood. It had a tiny stove with a chimney pipe that stuck out the side, and a roof made of shingles. There were windows everywhere. She'd gone off somewhere and slept in one, after dreaming about one for months. She loved it. We have to have a yurt, she said. It wasn't a week later that our friends called with the offer of theirs. They had built a regular, square, modern house, which Fanny considered indescribably ugly, and without a soul, and had been on the verge of demolishing the yurt. We moved in. There was about enough room to curse a cat, as they say, but since we were there only during the summer, we spent most of our time outdoors. At night it was just the perfect size for cuddling close on our futon mat and looking up into the stars."

At this juncture in his story Suwelo abruptly stopped talking, got up from his chair, and went upstairs. When he returned he was carrying a small photo album. He passed it to his friends, who flipped through it quietly. They saw snapshots of Suwelo, looking as if on a lark, sitting on the ground and apparently preparing wild vegetables to eat; a funny-looking dwelling that made them think of the little crooked houses in children's fairy tales; and a shapely, sun-brown woman with a look of the most intense anticipation of good on her face. It was a face that expected everything in nature to open, unresistingly, to it. A face that said Yes not once but over and over again. It was one of those faces that people have when they've been sufficiently kissed as very young babies and small children. Though her hands were at her sides in the pictures, one had the sense that they were raised and open, offering or returning an embrace.

"Can you believe that that face is ever gloomy or defeated?" asked Suwelo, chuckling. He couldn't believe it himself, and he'd seen it so, often.

" 'I want a garden,' Fanny said. "But there was not a drop of water on the land from May to November. The water we didn't haul from the park materialized out of a long black plastic pipe connected to a well that two women on the ridge over from us, who had a vineyard, personally helped us lay down.

"Sometimes I felt swept along in a rush of experiences that felt seriously magical. I came to believe that whatever Fanny wished for would happen, and that whatever she was even remotely against, would fail. In a way this made me feel afraid in any angry confrontation with her. You know the expression 'being withered by a look'? I think Fanny could wither with a look. But, fortunately, she was not the least bit interested in withering. No, her way was to ignore, to withdraw. Suddenly she simply was not available to interact with whatever ignorance she perceived. And when she came back, there was always a definite remoteness, a feeling coming from her of 'Well, we are different, after all. I have my way, you obviously have yours. We shall simply coexist. If I can share space with bobcats, bucks, otters, and snakes, I can certainly live with you.' A week of this. Then we would talk. We'd laugh. And we'd decide my poor behavior and her stubbornness were getting in the way of celebrating the imminent rising of the full moon. We could not have that! And our lives moved right along.

"I have to laugh when I think of what I told you earlier: that Fanny didn't know about my playing around because she was a space cadet. It wasn't because she was a space cadet that she didn't know. It was because she trusted me. Trusting me, she simply didn't tune in to a lot of the signs the way she could have. And, too, there were all the other signs, from all over the place, that she was getting and trying to relate to. What did it mean, for instance, that a bird one day walked backward slowly and carefully down a big oak tree in our clearing, hopped over to Fanny, looked up at her, and climbed up and sat on her head? This made her think of Queen Nut. *Of course it did!* And of the ideogram of the vulture on *her* head. Maybe Nut was trying to tell her something? Who could know? Well, in this case, Nut *was* trying to tell her something, which she found by talking to a friend of ours who is a Goddess worshiper and an Egyptologist. Her favorite saying of Nut's, said our friend one day as we sat looking at a drawing of her on a tarot card, is: 'Whatever

I embrace, becomes.' 'That's it!' said Fanny. 'That's what?' I asked. She didn't explain. But I think now that what she meant was that we must, all of us, turn toward whatever it is that we do want, in our lives, in our loves, on the planet, and whatever we don't want, just have sense enough to leave alone. But I didn't know that then.

"I remember when I tried to get her to wear Frederick's of Hollywood–type lingerie. Fanny has a beautiful body. But you'd never know it. I knew she'd look just as good or better than the women I fantasized. But she covered herself from head to foot in the most unappealing stuff. Long gowns, long, *thick* gowns, at night. Flannel. With high necks. She wore long johns. *Long johns.* At least they were cheerful. She dyed them all kinds of colors. Red and yellow and orange. She looked cute in them, though, rather than sexy.

" 'But I get cold in that stuff you like,' she said. 'And I feel ridiculous. It's too flimsy to wear. Why do you want me to wear this?' she asked, looking at me so piercingly that I wanted to drop the whole thing.

"She reluctantly put on some red satin-and-net underwear I'd bought and came out of the yurt and showed herself to me.

" 'I feel like a neon sign,' she said.

"And I had to admit that there, in the forest, in the middle of nowhere, she looked like one.

" 'But lust loves neon,' was my feeling.

"Afterward, as they say in early twentieth-century novels, I felt okay, at least I thought I felt okay. She felt terrible. She cried and said she felt degraded. I never saw the red satin and net again.

"But this particular struggle, which I lost—the struggle to get her to wear sexy lingerie, and to enjoy it as I did—went on for a number of years. I was being influenced in my private life with Fanny by the hidden sexual life I lived elsewhere.

She would have realized this, and I'm sure it hurt her. Once, she even sat straight up in bed out of a sound sleep, or so I had thought, screaming, 'Who are all these women in this bed with us? Who are they? Who are they?' And she began to batter me with a pillow, and to weep. But we made a joke of this. For she wasn't supposed to be aware of what I was doing, and I wasn't supposed to be, as far as she was concerned, doing anything.

"Her tolerance wore thin, finally. 'Listen, Suwelo, you like that stuff, you wear it,' she said. And she actually bought me a little red bikini with a cut-out space in front, a little vee, and I pranced about in it happily. And then I did start wearing skinny, scanty, colorful underwear, because I did like it, and she got a little better when she shopped for herself, but always her choices were tasteful, understated, nunnish. I had to face the fact that to Fanny the cut of her underwear and of her gowns didn't matter very much. She wanted comfort, warmth, sturdy pieces of clothing that were well made. To be truthful, she much preferred shopping for sweaters and boots and items like that in the men's department; she said they were much better made, more generously cut, than in women's wear. Occasionally she bought something we both liked; something usually expensive, and very sexy, but it was nothing that could ever be confused with neon.

"So, yes, I think she knew. Knowing Fanny, she probably knew before I did. Maybe she stayed away in Africa for such a long time because she wanted me to have the freedom to fuck around.

"It was a freedom I'd never had. And I was brought up on *Playboy*, in which the goal of every red-blooded man is to pierce as many women as possible, and to think of their minds, their creative gifts, and their professional abilities as added sexual stimulation, nothing more. I loved that joke inspired, I'm sure, by the *Playboy* mentality: What did you do with the female scientist who discovered a cure for the common cold? You screwed her. Yuk, yuk.

"It wasn't as if she wasn't free to sleep around too. She was. And she fell in love at the drop of a hat with all kinds of people, not all of them spirits. But sleeping with them didn't seem that important to her. She tried to explain this to me, using her relationship to the planets, yes, the *planets*, as an example. 'I live on Earth,' she said. 'I love it; I see that it really needs me, whether it knows this or not.' She smiled. 'Now I know there are all those other beautiful planets out there somewhere, and they may be infinitely more exciting, but Earth is where I am, and the longer I relate to it, the more interesting and exciting it becomes. We know almost nothing about Earth. You do realize, don't you?' As it happened, at this very time Fanny confessed she had never experienced orgasm during our lovemaking, and there I was fancying myself the *compleat* lover, if only she'd dress properly for her role; though she regularly experienced what she later told me was 'a kind of ecstasy.' But no orgasms. For sure I knew almost nothing about 'Earth' and should have held off trying to get to the other 'planets.'"

"Woman is a mystery," commented Mr. Hal, encouragingly. It was, Suwelo felt, the only appropriate response.

Miss Lissie said nothing.

"And another odd thing, too," Suwelo continued, overjoyed, actually, to be talking to them, "was how many of her old lovers were still sort of 'around.' Even the one who'd been drowned in a boating accident off the coast of South Carolina when she was in high school. I don't think anyone she cared about ever left Fanny; and she was incapable of feeling sad when someone died. She felt sad about the *way* people died, or sad about their illness or whatnot, but, in a way, the living and the dead, once they *were* dead, were pretty much the same to Fanny, and present to her in about the same way.

"This was bound to give me a certain feeling of insecurity. There were times when, if *she* wasn't there, and I could see she was not, though her body was sitting quietly beside me in a chair, I wasn't sure whether *I* was. I always seemed to be chasing Fanny even when she was literally locked up tight in my arms. Carlotta didn't understand this; who could have? I used to tease Fanny that she brought a new meaning entirely to the word 'bondage.' Sometimes I felt so disillusioned, so full of self-pity and futility, so *married*—but in a way that seemed totally different from 'marriage' as it is commonly known—I was just sick. The nights I've spent rummaging about in this house"—Suwelo looked up, toward the stairs—"thinking over these things! Other men marry women and say they love them and within five years, though they still live with them, you can see they have essentially separated themselves. There is no longer a spiritual or even an authentic physical connection. Instead, they are connected by house payments, a car, children, political expediency, whatever. Over time, Fanny and I shared none of these things. The divorce was merely our first shedding of any nonintrinsic relatedness. After that, it was as if we just had to see how far we could go. Could we be two people who met anew each time, for instance? 'I couldn't stand feeling bored when I saw you coming,' she said. As for me, I couldn't bear the thought of a loss of autonomy or freedom causing her to lose her magic. Because I came to appreciate and love this aspect of her more and more.

"She moved out of the bedroom and into the back half of the house. Then she moved out altogether. Some of our friends thought surely this meant we'd separated. And they knew nothing of the divorce. But no, separate spaces increased our harmony. *Eventually.* I don't mean to make this sound easier than it was. It was often hell. We'd begun to get a glimmer of a way of life that gave us both direct sunlight, in a manner of speaking.

Neither of us wanted to overshade the other. Yet we wanted a degree of stability, a degree of coziness. We wanted to be the forest and the tree. Separate development that enhanced whatever we were creating separately and together in our . . . *journey*; that is what we were after.

"Marriage simply hadn't fit us. Fanny thought it probably didn't fit anybody. She thought it unnatural. I wasn't so sure, being a man within a patriarchal system. I could see some privileges. She thought the words 'whom God hath joined together let no man put asunder' spoken at weddings missed the point. To her, 'marriage' was a bonding of souls that was eternal, *anyway*; it was presumptuous, therefore, for anyone to think it could be put asunder. Then there was the preacher standing in front of people as they were married, pretending to represent 'God,' but in fact representing the state. She was insulted by the hypocrisy. Besides, in her view, joining with another was such a sacred affair there was almost no way it could be done with other people present, a good number of them strangers, friends of friends, relatives you didn't like, and others who couldn't possibly appreciate the significance of the moment.

"From this you can easily see how Fanny and I never lacked topics of conversation. Sometimes we were so far apart in our ideas that I became quite exasperated. She always seemed to be putting people down, their little customs, their little ways. Behind every little custom, every little way, she saw *an institution*, and one she herself would never have devised. 'Why do you even love me, if you do love me?' I'd cry. And she'd think a moment and say, 'I love you for your breath.' Typically, the least substantial thing about me! 'Also the least colonized,' she'd say sweetly. Something unseen, indeed, invisible. Not my brains, not my cock, not my heart—no, my breath. But to her, as she explained it to me, my breath represented not only my life, but also the life force itself; and what this boiled down to in day-today reality is that she could, and did, kiss me all the time. We kissed for hours. Hours. She'd hold my tongue in her mouth and, with a shiver of pleasure that unfailingly caused me to rise almost beyond the occasion, she'd draw in my breath. Her own breath, sweet, delicious, the very essence of her soul's vitality, would enter me. I'd had no idea, before being with Fanny, how steadily, increasingly seductive this kind of kissing is. We started out kissing like everyone else, a minute or two at a time, but then . . . It is a bond based on air, on *nothing;* nothing you can see, or save or take off or put on, in any event; and I found it to be the strongest bond of all. It was really funny, and we laughed about how much we both loved to kiss. The mingling of our breaths as we kissed for that second half hour, as we liked to joke, could nearly bring us to . . . ah . . . climax."

"Some of us have heard of that," said Miss Lissie wryly, and Mr. Hal laughed.

PART FIVE

The Gospel According to Shug

HELPED are those who are enemies of their own racism: they shall live in harmony with the citizens of this world, and not with those of the world of their ancestors, which has passed away, and which they shall never see again.

HELPED are those born from love: conceived in their father's tenderness and their mother's orgasm, for they shall be those—numbers of whom will be called "illegitimate"—whose spirits shall know no boundaries, even between heaven and earth, and whose eyes shall reveal the spark of the love that was their own creation. They shall know joy equal to their suffering and they will lead multitudes into dancing and Peace.

HELPED are those too busy living to respond when they are wrongfully attacked: on their walks they shall find mysteries so intriguing as to distract them from every blow.

HELPED are those who find something in Creation to admire each and every hour. Their days will overflow with beauty and the darkest dungeon will offer gifts.

HELPED are those who receive only to give; always in their house will be the circular energy of generosity; and in their hearts a beginning of a new age on Earth: when no keys will be needed to unlock the heart and no locks will be needed on the doors.

HELPED are those who love the stranger; in this they reflect the heart of the Creator and that of the Mother.

HELPED are those who are content to be themselves; they will never lack mystery in their lives and the joys of self-discovery will be constant.

HELPED are those who love the entire cosmos rather than their own tiny country, city, or farm, for to them will be shown the unbroken web of life and the meaning of infinity.

HELPED are those who live in quietness, knowing neither brand name nor fad; they shall live every day as if in eternity, and each moment shall be as full as it is long.

HELPED are those who love others unsplit off from their faults; to them will be given clarity of vision.

HELPED are those who create anything at all, for they shall relive the thrill of their own conception, and realize a partnership in the creation of the Universe that keeps them responsible and cheerful.

HELPED are those who love the Earth, their mother, and who willingly suffer that she may not die; in their grief over her pain they will weep rivers of blood, and in their joy in her lively response to love, they will converse with trees.

HELPED are those whose every act is a prayer for harmony in the Universe, for they are the restorers of balance to our planet. To them will be given the insight that every good act done anywhere in the cosmos welcomes the life of an animal or a child.

HELPED are those who risk themselves for others' sakes; to them will be given increasing opportunities for ever greater risks. Theirs will be a vision of the world in which no one's gift is despised or lost.

HELPED are those who strive to give up their anger; their reward will be that in any confrontation their first thoughts will never be of violence or of war.

HELPED are those whose every act is a prayer for peace; on them depends the future of the world.

HELPED are those who forgive; their reward shall be forgetfulness of every evil done to them. It will be in their power, therefore, to envision the new Earth.

HELPED are those who are shown the existence of the Creator's magic in the Universe; they shall experience delight and astonishment without ceasing.

HELPED are those who laugh with a pure heart; theirs will be the company of the jolly righteous.

HELPED are those who love all the colors of all the human beings, as they love all the colors of animals and plants; none of their children, nor any of their ancestors, nor any parts of themselves, shall be hidden from them.

HELPED are those who love the lesbian, the gay, and the straight, as they love the sun, the moon, and the stars. None of their children, nor any of their ancestors, nor any parts of themselves, shall be hidden from them.

HELPED are those who love the broken and the whole; none of their children, nor any of their ancestors, nor any parts of themselves shall be despised.

HELPED are those who do not join mobs; theirs shall be the understanding that to attack in anger is to murder in confusion.

HELPED are those who find the courage to do at least one small thing each day to help the existence of another—plant, animal, river, or human being. They shall be joined by a multitude of the timid.

HELPED are those who lose their fear of death; theirs is the power to envision the future in a blade of grass.

HELPED are those who love and actively support the diversity of life; they shall be secure in their differentness.

HELPED are those who *know*.

• • •

Arveyda read the pamphlet *The Gospel According to Shug* over and over again. Carlotta sat quietly by his side. She did not think she still loved him; she did not even want to consider it. She was attracted, she felt, to what he knew and to how he knew it; and to his music, always. She was visiting him at the new house he'd bought on his return from Central and South America: a spacious, low-slung acoustically perfect bungalow that jutted out of the hills over Berkeley and had been inspired by houses designed by Frank Lloyd Wright. There was a sound-proof, state-of-the-art recording studio on the bottom floor, from whose windows could be seen the Golden Gate Bridge in its misty splendor, and the sunsets from all three levels of the house were spectacular. By comparison, her own house seemed viewless, cluttered, run-down, and, for three people, absurdly small. It was also in less fashionable Oakland. He had invited her to move in with him, and also the children, but she wouldn't hear of it. She found she enjoyed living in her own, and the children's, mess.

"Who's Shug?" asked Arveyda. One foot was raised and crossed over his knee. He had a habit of jiggling the raised foot, which made him seem impatient.

Carlotta kicked off her shoes and tucked one foot under-neath her. She enjoyed these visits, which were similar, she imagined, to the visits one might make to a father or an older brother. As always, Arveyda offered luxurious surroundings and fresh, healthful food. Both children were in school from eight-thirty to three-thirty these days, and, because of spring recess, she was free from teaching for the week.

"While you were gone," she said, "I used to go to a place called Fanny's Massage Parlor. It was near the campus. Fanny gave very good massages."

She drew in her breath; but why should she hesitate or be in the least afraid? "She was the wife of the man I was interested in, the one about whose existence you once inquired, whose name is Suwelo."

"Suwelo?" said Arveyda. "Same as the rune?"

"Yes," said Carlotta. "The rune for wholeness. But I don't think it applied to Suwelo—not, anyway, when I knew him."

"Why do you say that?"

"Because he was in fragments."

Arveyda gave her a quizzical look, which Carlotta ignored. In her own time, perhaps, she would tell him all about *her* intimate experiences with another. But not now.

"Shug, as near as I could understand it, was Fanny's grandmother, or something like that. Like your mother, she founded a church." What exactly did that mean, she wondered now. She tried to picture Arveyda's mother, who had named him after a bar of soap. Was she a big, dark woman like some of the aging black women she saw on the street? No; he'd said something about her stylishness. Well, but big, dark women were often the most stylish of all. Did she have a church, a real church, with stained-glass windows and everything? Carlotta had never been to church of her own volition. Zedé had taken her to the Catholic church around the corner from their house when she was growing up. They'd understood little of the sermons and had gradually stopped going. Zedé never conceded that there were any such people as heathens. So much for Catholicism.

Arveyda was smiling at her as she thought about those days. "Well," he said, "but my mother never wrote her own beatitudes!"

"I went to Fanny because I had known her at the college. Not known her, exactly, but I saw her from time to time. She'd moved to the Bay Area from New York, along with Suwelo. They were both teachers. He taught American history, she taught women's studies. But then she got frustrated teaching and moved on to administration. Why she thought that would be easier, I can't imagine. Of course it wasn't. She walked around with a look of such unmistakable distress it was almost comical. Then next thing I knew she'd quit the college altogether and enrolled in the San Francisco School of Massage. She opened her own little parlor down the street from the college, and many of her former colleagues, laboring under the stress she'd left, became her clients.

"From the moment I learned about you and Zedé I had a migraine, and the whole of my body was one clenched knot of pain." Carlotta said this very slowly, in an almost inaudible voice. Now she speeded up, her voice firm and casual. "In the beginning I had no designs on her husband—he wasn't actually her husband any longer, but I didn't know that. They were always together. Where you saw one you almost always saw the other." Carlotta giggled. "I was attracted to their closeness. I see that now. How absurd life is! Together they represented home, a family, warmth, a place to belong. Her massage parlor was convenient," she went on soberly, "her prices were reasonable. She passed out free gift certificates to her friends and people from the college. I went. She treated me the same way she treated everyone else. After one two-hour massage that included forty-five minutes of acupressure, I was addicted.

"She was in a little cottage, the 'mother-in-law's cottage,' at the back of someone's house. You got there by following a curving flagstone path through flowering shrubs and vines—hibiscus and jasmine, I think. I remember bright colors and a lovely scent; though these two just might not bloom at the same time. I know nothing about flowers. But I liked it that she had them. Her massage table was encircled by trailing green plants that formed a living curtain and made me think of the out-of-doors, of a waterfall. There was a tiny wood-burning stove in the corner on which she occasionally laid a stick of sandalwood incense or into which she poked a braid of sweet grass. She laid a huge crystal at your head and smaller ones at your feet. I didn't know a thing about crystals at the time, and when she talked about their soothing or healing qualities the information went right past me. I was connected to nothing, you see. Not to my own body, not to the children, not, certainly, to inanimate objects. 'When you are better,' she said, putting a small amethyst crystal in my hand, 'you will be able to feel its vibration.' This kind of talk seemed the very babble of witches to me. We never became friends, or even particularly friendly. We were cordial, I guess you could say. I couldn't understand why she'd taken such a service-oriented, low-prestige job when she had such solid academic credentials. I asked her this once, politely, without the bluntness of my bewilderment. She shrugged and said, 'Oh, *academia.*' That was all.

" 'Why did you take up this particular work?' I asked her another day as she worked to loosen the cramped tendons in my legs.

"Her answer seemed impossible, given the serenity of her surroundings and her own calm expression: 'I took it up so that I would be forced to touch people, even those I might not like, in gentleness, and be forced to acknowledge both their bodily reality as people and also their pain. Otherwise,' she said, 'I am afraid I might start murdering them.'

"I'm sure my body stiffened perceptibly. Whose wouldn't have? There I was, naked in her hands. With designs on her man; not that she ever seemed to think of Suwelo that way. But who knew? Maybe she suspected that he and I were starting to have a lot of chance meetings at the water cooler.

"Regardless of this, she kept working on my legs and attempting to flex my nearly rigid toes. My bent toes were so ugly. I'd never noticed before.

" 'You should throw out those high heels, you know,' she said.

"But she'd said that before.

" 'I know,' I said, just as I'd said before.

" 'You're doing penance, huh?' she asked.

" 'I don't understand what you mean,' I said. What *could* she mean? She didn't know you, didn't know us. Didn't know Zedé. Would never have dreamed what had happened. Still, I wasn't sure. Sometimes I felt people could tell what had happened just by looking at me. I felt I'd been in a terrible accident that had scarred me; often I assured myself my scars were at least invisible. But what is invisible to a masseuse?

" 'Oh,' she said, 'women wear things that hurt them to atone for the sin of loving someone they'd rather not. Someone they may actually consider unworthy of them. It's sometimes called "seduction," ' she added grimly.

"Maybe it was true, I thought. I wore the kind of shoes you'd liked me to wear, though they hurt and you'd left me for my mother, who always wore flats." This was funny, and Carlotta laughed. "It's like an episode from *Soap*," she said. "It didn't make any sense, wearing the shoes. They were killers. But even if they destroyed my feet and crippled my legs, I knew I wasn't giving them up. I liked the way men looked at me in high heels. The look in their eyes made me forget how lonely I was. How discarded."

"And what did you see when you looked back at them?" Arveyda interjected, sadly.

"Oh, God," said Carlotta, "I wasn't going to think about *that*. . . . Fanny would massage you, and soon your body would feel yours again. And *she* would look satisfied, as if she'd achieved a sweet, if temporary, victory, and you'd wonder if you'd really heard this mild woman say anything about murdering anybody.

"Once, later, I asked Suwelo about it. He was evasive. He said she was seeing a therapist, but that essentially she was one of those victims of racism who is extremely sensitive and who grows too conscious of it. It had become like a scale or a web over her eyes. Everywhere she looked, she saw it. Racism turned her thoughts to violence. Violence made her sick. She was working on it.

"Anyway, she had this stack of pamphlets on a table by the door. Everyone who came in was encouraged to take one. I felt sorry for her, that she had apparently fallen back into the grip of her grandmother's religion. And was able to find peace doing work that was almost menial, in the smallest possible space. Yes, I pitied her; if I was doing penance by wearing high-heeled shoes, she was doing it in spades, working on my cramped legs and toes. Still, I like parts of Shug's gospel; at least she doesn't go on about blessed are the poor. And I love the next to the last line, where she talks about blessed are those who love and support diversity because, in their differentness, they shall be secure. But the last line baffles me. Blessed are those who *know*. Know *what*, I ask myself. And then I think of how I don't, in fact, *know*; and wonder if I ever will." Carlotta said this with almost childish petulance.

Arveyda looked at his wife, who had, without intending it, given the mystery of his own mother back to him; and to whom, despite the existence of their children, he felt he had never made love; and he thought, simply because of the magic she had just performed, in conjuring up an almost forgotten Katherine Degos, that she could not fail.

"You *are* beginning to *know*, Carlotta," he said, with such tenderness that both of them blushed. And then: *"How it becomes you."*

In Shug's pamphlet, illustrated back and front by several large, serenely alert elephants, the pamphlet that Carlotta had brought home ages ago from a massage parlor run by a woman whose husband had become her lover, and that she had casually

given him and he had as casually read, Arveyda recognized a
spiritual kin of his own mother. His mother. Any remembrance
of her pained him. So he never thought of her. Reading the
Gospel was the first time since his long-ago meeting with Zedé
that he'd seen anything that made him feel curious about her,
or that he missed something of her spirit in the world. Why
had his mother loved a photograph? Whose was it? "Your father," she'd always said; but now that he was a father himself
he knew how much more there was. Why had she removed it
from beside his bed? Why had she become a "whirling dervish"? Why had she never been able to affirm all that he was?
Why had she formed a church? And had it been like this, like
Shug's pamphlet, not a building or any kind of monument, but
simply a few words gleaned, like spiritual rice grains, from her
earthly passage?

THERE was a Juan Fuentes poster of Nelson Mandela in the window of a picture-framing shop near her therapist's office. It was beautiful, vibrant, with many small images of Mandela's head imposed, smiling, over a huge red ribbon. The same kind of ribbon Fanny wore, in solidarity with the South African struggle, on her denim coat. She decided she would buy the poster on her way home.

Her therapist's name was Robin Ramirez, and Fanny liked her. She was small, quiet, intense — and dark-haired, which was a relief. When a friend recommended her to Fanny, the first thought that came to mind was: Was she or wasn't she? For Fanny did not, in the compulsive fantasy that was driving her insane, slice off the heads of dark-haired people.

She'd told this to Robin on the first visit.

"Well, I guess I'm lucky to be a Chicana after all," said Robin, and asked her to say more.

"There isn't much to it," said Fanny. "Let's just say that in my fantasies blonds don't have more fun."

"Why blonds?" asked Robin, who more than once had considered bleaching her hair. Didn't people have more respect for what blond-haired people did and said? This certainly seemed to be the case among an awful lot of Chicanos she knew; her other patients, for instance.

"I think because they represent white people, really white people, to me, and therefore white oppression."

"You mean domination?"

"Yes. I mean Nazis, Klansmen, the white people and their children one has to worry about on the street."

"Did you know any blond children when you were growing up?"

It was curious, when Fanny considered the question, to realize that the only blonds she remembered seeing as a child were other children. All the white adults that she remembered had brown hair.

"There was Tanya," she said. "I don't remember much about her. She lived down the road from my grandmother's house, which is where my mother and I lived part of the time I was growing up. Sometimes we played together. She was okay." Fanny shrugged.

"Did Tanya have brothers? Parents?"

"I know she had parents. Her father was a farmer and always in the fields or, on Saturdays, in town. Her mother was always home. She baked cookies and brought them outside to us. I could play in the yard with Tanya, but I wasn't allowed to go in the house. There was a grandmother."

"How did that make you feel? Not being allowed inside Tanya's house."

"It was a dump," said Fanny, "as I recall. I don't remember thinking much about it. But I remember I wasn't permitted inside, so that means I certainly noticed."

"I'm sure you did," said Robin. "Could you imagine why you weren't allowed inside?"

Fanny thought about this. "It was funny, you know. My grandmother's house was much finer than theirs. In its own simple way, it was elegant. Well, three grown, talented, creative women—my mother and my two grandmothers—lived there; it would have to be elegant. Tanya's people were really almost what you'd call 'poor white trash.' But not quite. They aspired to better things." She laughed. "You know, I think white people in the South must have had a secret campaign of uplift among themselves to make sure every white person's house was painted—white, if possible—and every black person's house was not. I think part of the reason they paid black people barely enough to keep body and soul together was because they were afraid that if they ever had the slightest excess of funds they would paint their houses. They already knew how black people love color and how good we look in it. As it was, black people made paint out of bluing and white mud, and with this mixture they painted their fireplaces a brilliant blue. There were only two houses in the county inhabited by colored or black people that had paint. One of them belonged to my grandmother."

"Did Tanya . . . why, by the way, was she named Tanya? It's not a Southern name, is it?" Robin asked this in a tone that said, I know nothing whatsoever about that weird land, but this name sounds peculiar even to me.

"No," said Fanny, "it's as Russian as Vladimir. But only a few people ever pronounced it correctly. I always did. Most people said '*Tan*-ya,' like the color tan. She and her mother hated it when that happened, and complained. I suggested that they replace the *a* in Tan with an *o*, but they preferred to make a lifelong habit of correcting people. Whenever I thought of this later, this obstinacy, it seemed typically Southern to me. A trait as common to black as to white.

"In high school I watched the integration of the University of Georgia on television," Fanny continued. "And I was watching the night the whole campus seemed to go up in flames, and white people raged against the enrollment of two of the palest-

skinned black people anywhere. I watched the integration of
Central High in Little Rock. I saw the Freedom Riders, black
and white, beaten up in Mississippi. I still remember vividly the
face of one of them, a young white man, who died. I saw a lot of
black people and their white allies humiliated, brutally beaten,
or murdered. It seemed that the people with the most integrity
were assassinated. I grew up believing that white people, collectively speaking, cannot bear to witness wholeness and health
in others, just as they can't bear to have people different from
themselves live among them. It seemed to me that nothing, no
other people certainly, could live and be healthy in their midst.
They seemed to need to have other people look bad—poor,
ragged, dirty, illiterate. It was only then that they seemed to
think they could look good."

"And you thought this way as early as childhood?"

"No," said Fanny. "Childhood for me was pretty mellow. I
lived with grandmothers who had a lot of interesting friends. I
was the apple of their eye. I don't remember seeing any white
people, ever, at our house."

"So except for Tanya you had no experiences with them?"

"Not directly. But Mama Shug was often sick from her strug-
gles with them. She'd go into town, have a run-in—it seemed
inevitable—with some redneck and come home cursing up a
storm." Fanny chuckled. "But at the same time, she was trying, as she liked to phrase it, to keep her feet on the Goddam
Path."

"What path was this?"

"Oh," said Fanny, "my grandmothers formed their own
church; a tradition of long standing among black women. Only,
they didn't call it a 'church.' They called it a 'band.'"

"A band?"

"Sometimes a prayer band. Sometimes a band of angels,
sometimes a band of devils. 'Band' was what renegade black

women's churches were called traditionally; it means a group of people who share a common bond and purpose and whose notion of spiritual reality is radically at odds with mainstream or prevailing ones. But Mama Shug had been a great singer who'd been part of a musical band. To want to become part of a spiritual band was natural to her."

"Wasn't it unusual for both of your grandmothers to be present, in the same house, raising you?"

"One was my biological grandmother, my mother's mother. The other was her 'Special Friend.'"

Robin raised an eyebrow.

Fanny laughed. "I can't tell you how many raised eyebrows I've encountered in telling about them."

"But this was in the South . . . in the fifties? Do you mean to say they lived together as . . ."

"*Consorts*," said Fanny. "They were very happy, though they used to disagree with or stray away from each other a lot. And they had incredible fights, which made me think of storms. They liked to throw things; flashes of 'lightning' in the form of china were always brightening up the house. Temperamentally they were very different—Shug, direct; Celie, somewhat sly. They lived to be very old, then died within a year of each other. My grandmother, Celie, died first. Shug spent the remaining months of her life working on her beatitudes, which my mother helped her translate into a language somewhat more 'Biblical' than Mama Shug's own. Mama Shug's sounded more like: 'Rule number one: Don't ever mess over nobody, honey, and nobody will ever mess over you!'" Fanny laughed. "She felt that spirituality was, above all, too precious to be left to the perverted interpretations of men."

"Perhaps it's she who put the sword in your hand?"

"Perhaps," said Fanny. "And how did you know it is a sword? It really *is* a sword, with a great golden handle and shining blade. But it is in my look, not in my hand. I look at a blond head and, zip, it's in the gutter."

"And then what?" asked Robin. "Does doing this make you feel better."

"No," said Fanny. "I am always feeling better before. Besides, it's the next step that's barfingly gruesome."

"Which is?"

"That I'm down in the gutter grabbing the head and reaching for the body, which is still walking along, by the way, and furiously fastening the head back on. I won't be a racist," said Fanny grimly. "I won't be a murderer. I won't do to them what they've done to black people. I'll die first."

She would die first. (And she felt at times that this was happening.) The sword in her look would blind her first of all. Nothing could prevent the roll into the gutter of her own head. This much she knew. It was after she knew better and her fantasies changed not at all that she began to panic.

There were times when she came to Suwelo and crept into his bed and said, "Please hold me." Times when he thought they would make love. But no. She would lie in his arms shuddering and weeping.

"What's the matter?" he would coax.

It would be a long time before she could answer. Then she'd say: "I'm afraid I'll murder someone."

In the beginning he chided her. "Just because of those assholes at the college? Come on! They're not worth murdering."

"Not just those," she whispered, her tears dripping onto his neck.

"Well, who?" he'd ask. "Not me, I hope."

"Not you," she said.

One night she said: "If it is true that we commit adultery by thinking it, then is it also the same with committing murder?

What about the way it is so easy, when you watch a plane take off, to imagine it blown to bits? Does this count? Are we collectively responsible for disasters because we image them and therefore shape them into consciousness? Do all human beings nowadays automatically have murder in their eyes?"

"But why do you think of these things?" he said, holding her close, his erotic interest having died.

"Doesn't everyone? Now that they see how elusive the freedom is we've struggled so hard for in the world."

"No," he said. "I don't. Well, I do, sometimes. But I know they're just fantasies. They're meaningless."

"I don't believe fantasies are meaningless. They are as meaningful and powerful as dreams."

"You're so gentle," he said.

"I fear it's only a façade." She sighed. "Underneath, there's this raving maniac. Sometimes I see myself in the faces of the weeping, screaming, completely mad women shown every day on TV. A bomb has fallen through their roof; their children are bleeding to death; there is no ambulance for them. I hate white people," she said. "I visualize them sliding off the planet, and the planet saying, 'Ah, I can breathe again!'"

"But you can't cause that. Actually they come closer to doing that to themselves, closer to causing all of us to slide off the planet than you ever will. They, not you, should be feeling the crisis you imagine."

"Then why am *I* imagining it?"

"Obviously because we share the planet."

"They don't want to share the planet; they don't even want to share villages, towns, rivers, beaches, and bus stops," she said.

"No, they don't," said Suwelo. "But they'll have to. It's either share or destroy."

"I think they're too clever to destroy themselves intentionally," said Fanny. "But not clever enough to avoid doing it by accident."

"And we go with them," said Suwelo.

"And we go with them," echoed Fanny. "*I can't stand it!* After all we've been through"—and here she remembered Nzingha's comment on Jeff, the young white Southerner: "What? *Poor?* And after all that!"—"to die horribly because of their pharaonic arrogance. I feel so abandoned," said Fanny. "As if my very self is leaving me."

"The whole world is freaked out," said Suwelo, "not just you, not just us. Prior to this time in history, at least we thought we'd have a future, that our children would see freedom, even if we never did. Now they've made sure that none of our children will ever live the free and healthy lives so many generations of oppressed people have dreamed of for them. And fought so hard for. I very often think of violence, but any violence I could do at this point would seem, and be, so small."

"You're large," she said. "You're a man. If you feel violent toward someone, you can do something about it. You can be more direct. And you give yourself permission to feel it. Women are given no such permission."

"I approve of self-defense," said Suwelo.

"Isn't sliding them off the planet self-defense?" she asked. "I've marched so much by now and been arrested so many times, I'm really quite weary."

Suwelo laughed. "A benign and gentle wind, out of nowhere, blows. All the ungodly lose their connection to gravity and float away into the ether. Besides, you know as well as I do that not all white people are responsible for, among other things, the high cost, on the nuclear black market, of plutonium, or the way that it is slowly finding its way into the drinking water. . . . What about your friends? What about Karen and Jackson and John . . ."

"Yes, I know. Georgia O'Keeffe and Van Gogh and all of the O'Keeffes and Van Goghs to come. Pete Seeger and Dr. Charlie Clements certainly tip the scale. It's racism and greed that have to go. Not white people. But can they be separated from their racism?" Fanny sighed. "Can I? And how much time do we have?"

"But yours, Fanny, unlike theirs, is all in your head. They are not affected by your fantasies, nightmares, or dreams. Racist oppression and nuclear terrorism are two things your magic won't be enough to stop. I'm sorry, but fantasizing opening the doors of Pollsmoor prison will not bring Mandela out."

"But maybe I can stop racist oppression before it starts in myself?" And she had, next morning, made her first appointment to see Robin.

Those had been hard times for both of them. In her fear of the murderer within, Fanny withdrew, to the extent that it was possible, from human contact. She abandoned the classroom; too provocative. Heads rolled there every day. Stupid, innocent, childish heads, whose parents had taught them nothing of how not to make other people detest them in the world. She moved next to administration. Bureaucracy and racism were a deadly combination. Her silver blade was always in the air. She thought she'd never be able to scrub all the blood off her knees. Her blood pressure, like that of so many black people, reached alarming highs. Her mother, apprised of her condition by Suwelo, had suddenly called Fanny one day and encouraged her to accompany her on a quiet, restful, celebratory trip to Africa. She would meet her father, whom she had never seen, who had helped win freedom for his country through war.

I T'S an interesting question," Ola had mused, a few months after Fanny and her mother had come to visit, as they'd sat idly one day over their afternoon tea.

"What's an interesting question?" asked Fanny, who, while sipping her tea and thinking of Suwelo, had forgotten what she and her father were talking about. She'd looked at him closely after he spoke, in some alarm. He'd spent the morning "haggling" over one of his plays with an illiterate government censor; the exercise had left him drawn and gray, and as if he wouldn't be able to tolerate such foolishness long.

"Whether the better fighter against the white man is someone who has actually experienced him firsthand," said Ola. "I once knew a great fighter who'd never seen a white person in her life but who nonetheless felt their oppression in every aspect of her existence, and so, traveling on foot, she covered a thousand miles to join the fight against them. She was excellent. Quite curious about them as people, I think, for she was always asking questions, about their whiteness and their children and their ways. But she was also steady as a rock in attacking them. And ruthless."

"What do you mean, ruthless?"

Ola frowned. "It was as if she were mopping up a very foul and troublesome spill."

"And what was she like otherwise?"

"Oh, very quiet. Gentle. A wonderful person, really. Even to animals; of all the stories about revolutionaries that were told around the campfires in the mountains, gorges, and caves of our exile, the one she liked best was that one about Sandino and the monkeys. Do you know it?"

Fanny shook her head.

"Well," said Ola, "the men in his guerrilla band were capturing the little monkeys that lived in the forest where they were hiding, and eating them. Sandino made impassioned speeches in the monkeys' defense; he pointed out, among other things, that it was the monkeys' screeches that always saved the men from the surprise of enemy attack. 'They are our little brothers,' said Sandino, 'our loyal compañeros. How can you even think of eating them?'" Ola paused, thinking of the woman. "Small children adored her. *I* adored her. Her vision of the future, after the overthrow of the white regime, was very broad; it would include everyone, and everything. That is why she liked Sandino; even though he was as famished as the rest of his men, he held to the vision of the future he wanted to have, a future that would include even the monkeys."

"This woman," said Fanny, "she didn't frighten you?"

"She *did* frighten me," said Ola. "But I had to realize she *was* me. We mirrored each other almost exactly. *I* didn't want to be an assassin either. I didn't want to be ruthless. There seemed no other way, however. The whites had done terrible things to us; many of them would claim later that they'd done nothing of the kind, simply because they knew nothing about it. But beyond what they were doing to us, as adults, they were destroying our children. Who were starving to death—their bodies, their minds, their dreams—right before our eyes. We fought the white man as we fought pestilence."

"It is more honest to fight as you did, perhaps," said Fanny. "In the United States there is the maddening illusion of freedom without the substance. It's never solid, unequivocal, irrevocable. So much depends on the horrid politicians the white majority elects. Black people have the oddest feeling, I think, of forever running in place."

Ola nodded. "Of course," he said, "that could simply mean you're remaining who you are. And that's not a bad thing."

"I don't know if that's it," said Fanny. "To me, we seem to be losing who we are. We don't understand white people; that's the crux of the matter. Not that we really want to anymore; it's too frightening. We can't comprehend them at all. We pretend we do from time to time, but that's just to reassure ourselves. If we ever confront our fear at being surrounded by so many people whose ways are incomprehensible to us, I don't know what will happen. They don't do anything the way we would do it. Making those tall buildings that deaden the earth underneath them, for instance" (here she thought of the Indians who considered the weight of a teepee too heavy, and who had had chants that included the exhortation to "shift your teepee, relatives, so that Mother Earth might have sunlight!") "or digging out and claiming everything that's buried in the ground. People's bones and funerary objects, gold, diamonds, silver, and God only knows what else—uranium, plutonium. Most of what's buried in the earth, people of color would never have found, because they'd never have bothered to look for it." Fanny shrugged. "But we're savages," as Chief Seattle said, "what do we know?"

"Here's a theory of evolution you'll like," said Ola, who knew that many African-Americans hated to think of the ancient Africans as early industrialists. "The first iron, so far as is known, was smelted in Africa; so there were, at least in theory, a couple or three diggers around here, since the ingredients for iron must be dug out of the ground. The people who did this, however, were not approved of. Like the Hopi in your country, most ancient Africans thought of the earth as a body that needs all its organs and bones and blood in order to function properly. The ore miners were forced out, the theory goes. They went north."

"Yes," said Fanny, frowning, "and unfortunately in about 1492 they continued west."

She wrote to Suwelo:

"I feel like a child, asking my father what I should do. But I confess it is a great relief, having a father to ask.

"Do you know what my mother's advice is? 'Forgive them, Fanny,' she says. 'Do you think they know what they are doing, when they treat us so badly? Do you think they know what they are doing when they suck all the oil out of the earth on one side of the world and complain about earthquakes on the other? Do you think they know what they are doing when they fill the sky with space junk and rockets whose important "missions" to spy on other planets are meaningless to ninety-nine percent of the people and to absolutely all of the plants and animals on earth? Do you think they know what they are doing when they invent the things they have invented and forced on the world, especially on our worlds, things that make us sick? things that kill us? No, darling. They do not know what they are doing. But you are lucky, you live in an age when even they are finding this out.

"'When I was growing up,' she says, 'the white man's word— backed by his gun—was law. His vision, the inspiration of the world. We dared not contradict him even when he said the sole reason we were put on earth was to be his slave. He was all-powerful. In fear and dread we watched him from our compounds the world over. Some of us were greedy. We believed, as he seemed to, that he was bringing something better than what we had. This *never* happened. Always, we were left poorer, with a lowered opinion of ourselves. He blocked the view between us and our ancestors, us and our ways; not all of them good ways, but needing to be changed according to our own light. He needed to keep us terrorized and desperately poor, in order to feel powerful. No one who was secure in himself as a person would put such emphasis on the nonpersonhood and unworthiness of another. He could not make the sounds or the movements or the cloth or the food we did. The heat was unkind to him. It was the heat that his tribe had left Africa thousands of years ago to avoid.

"'The white man is our brother; we have always said this. He is also the prodigal son of Africa. Easily recognizing him for who he was when he returned to us, we prepared the fatted calf. But it has never been enough. He is so empty, so ravenous for what we have that he does not have, that the fatted calf has barely served as an appetizer. He has moved on to devour us and our children, our minds and our bones. But this is not the behavior of well people. Allowances must be made for the sick.'

"But, even as my mother is speaking, I think: And what of me? I am the first to agree that I am sick. The racism of the world has infected me; I was infected as a child, before I even knew what racism was. Now, in my fantasies, I am poised to strike. But if I do strike, if I bring my fantasies to life, will 'allowances' be made for me? More important, can I make them for myself?

"'We are too forgiving,' I say to Mom. 'I'm beginning to hate the very word.'

"'No,' she whispers (we are often in bed for these conversations), 'that isn't possible. Forgiveness is the true foundation of health and happiness, just as it is for any lasting progress. Without forgiveness there is no forgetfulness of evil; without forgetfulness there still remains the threat of violence. And violence does not solve anything; it only prolongs itself.'

"How could she have this view, which seemed not reactionary, but divorced from reality. 'The way things are going in the United States,' I said, 'there will soon be more black men in prison than on the streets. In South Africa the entire black population is incarcerated in ghettos and "homelands" they despise. Look at what was done to the Indians, and still is being done. Look at the aborigines of Australia, the Maori of New Zealand. Look at Indonesia under the Dutch. Look at the West Indies. Forgiveness isn't large enough to cover the crime.'

"'How is a person destroyed?' whispered my mother in her peculiar missionary-African accent. 'Do you know? When my three parents' (this is how she refers to her adoptive mother and father, Corrine and Samuel, and to Nettie) 'first came to Africa they taught the gospel inherited from the Jews, who were the earliest Christians, and who therefore believed in turning the other cheek, rendering unto Caesar, and so on. Over the years they saw cheeks, heads, whole bodies bloodied and destroyed, as Caesar demanded and took everything. He took the land, everything on it and under it; he took the water. He claimed the air "space" over the land. He took the people's children to work in his fields and mines. He destroyed and therefore "took" their culture, their connection to their ancestors and the universe—than which nothing is more serious. He took their future.

"'My parents saw people dying all the time.' My mother paused. 'Do you remember, by any chance, what Haydée Santamaria said to the prison guard who, having brought her the eye of her brother Abel and the testicles of her lover, next brought her the news that her beloved brother, one of the youngest and most beautiful of the young Cuban revolutionaries, had been killed? She said—this woman who, twenty years later, would kill herself—"He is not dead; for to die for one's country is to live forever."'

"'That is very beautiful,' I said. If I'd ever read it, I didn't remember it, or perhaps it was so painful I'd forgotten it.

"You and I, Suwelo, have, after all, come to maturity against the backdrop of the assassination of our leaders. By the time of Abel Santamaria's death, we'd already borne, somehow, the news that Patrice Lumumba, and so many others, were no more. Or was he killed after Abel? 'Eliminated,' as the CIA 'adventures' on television described it. Like so much waste from the common imperialist body. But while I thought of this—and I really can't bear to think of this—of all the murders, all the loss, all the pain, all the *waste*, my mother was continuing to whisper.

"'My parents attended many people as they died,' she said. 'They noticed that some people died utterly. They went, they left, they vacated their space. There was nothing left. This was not true of everyone.'

"'What are you saying?' I asked.

"'Some of the people died in a kind of rapture. These were often those to whom the worst things had been done. Some of them died with the same passion with which they'd lived, and, at the very end, appeared to see, coming to welcome them, the beloved community of souls with whom they'd kept the faith, and in whose memory they had continued to labor while on earth.

"'My dearest daughter,' said my mother, 'some of them, many of them, died *as who they were, as the best of who they were.* As whole people. There was no talk of the kind we see on TV deathbeds of who will get the silver, who will inherit the car, who is mentioned in or omitted from the will; those things are the concern of people who have no idea why they are on earth. These people, these revolutionaries, like Haydée and her brother Abel, had given their lives, but they had also kept them; for their lives were theirs right to the end, unbroken, uncorrupted. That is what they left to us.

" 'When Abel died he could not have known that years later I would be whispering about his death to my only daughter, and hoping that she will learn from it, and be inspired by it, as her mother has been. I am not a nationalist,' said my mother, 'so it is not dying for one's country that is so moving to me about Haydée Santamaria's statement. No, what is moving to me is that when people die whole, a wonderful power is released in the world; a wonderful fearlessness before death, which in turn inspires in others a more profound joyousness about life. This is what all torturers learn, and it is why, I think, torture exists. Imagine yourself eyeless, without breasts or testicles, at the mercy of those who are so broken they will have no choice when their own time comes but to die utterly, leaving not one iota of inspiration, encouragement, or joy, and you do not talk, or give information, or name other people, or lick their boots, or accept their gold, or whatever it is they are trying to get you to do. And even if you are broken by them, and you lick their boots, you understand how sick they are to need their boots licked. You think of them as they might have been as children, little children, with no one to protect them from the grown-up whose boots they were forced to lick, no one who loved them enough or was powerful enough to make them feel safe. If you tear out the tongue of another, you have a tongue in your hand the rest of your life. You are responsible, therefore, for all that person might have said. It is the torturers who come to understand this, who change. Some do, you know.'

" 'You are saying,' I asked her, 'that all evil, like racism or sexism, is a result of sickness?'

" 'Not only that,' she whispered, 'the child will always, as an adult, do to someone else whatever was done to him when he was a child. It is how we, as human beings, are made. I shudder to think what Hitler's childhood was like,' she said. 'But anyone can see that the Palestinians and their children are reliving it under the Israelis today.'

" 'But wait,' I said. 'This isn't true of everyone. I mean, some people who've had horrendous childhoods don't turn out to be vicious adults.'

" 'How do you know?' she asked.

" 'Well, we can use your mother, Big Mama Celie, as exhibit A. A more gentle, loving person it would be hard to imagine.'

"There was a long silence before Mom spoke again.

" 'One of the most disturbing things I noticed about black people in the South, when we returned home near the end of the war, was the mistreatment—casual, vicious, unfeeling—of animals. Your grandmother's behavior was no exception. She had a dog—everyone had packs of hounds—whose name was —don't laugh—Creighton. He worshiped her; he was her absolute slave. He had the most wounded, pained, saddened, completely expressive eyes I ever saw. My mother obviously never looked into them. She treated him with a detached, brutal disregard. I never saw her pet him. I never heard her mutter a kind word in his direction. Her treatment of Creighton was the only thing I remember my mother and Miss Shug coming to blows about. Miss Shug loved animals as she loved people. She could not bear it that Celie, whom she had prevented Celie's husband, Albert, from beating, beat, and beat unmercifully, the cringing dog, who, even as she swung at him with one of her husband's old belts, or somebody's old belt, tried, unsuccessfully, to lick her hand. She would kick him out of her way even when he wasn't in it.

" 'I watched this strange behavior a long time before I realized what I was watching. Before I saw it. She was my mother, and Mama Nettie had instructed me about all the pain she had endured in her life. She was wonderful to me and to Adam and Tashi and their son, Benny. She was droll, playful, creative, and fun. And so harmless. People often said of her, "Why, Miss Celie wouldn't hurt a fly!" Well, she murdered zillions of flies, as everyone does in a hot climate. But it was her mistreatment of Creighton that no one seemed to notice. Quite the opposite. In fact, because she treated Creighton so badly, other people did the same. Many nasty jokes were made at Creighton's expense; anything missing was assumed to have been stolen by him, even if it was a hairbrush or a spool of thread! Anything knocked over or spilled was his fault. He was considered stupid, lazy, clumsy, ugly, and inferior. He was a stray dog who'd simply "taken up" there, as they said. Where he came from, no one knew. I don't even know how he got the name Creighton.'

" 'What happened to him?'

" 'Miss Shug,' whispered my mother, with a smile of admiration in her voice. 'She liberated him.'

" '*No*,' I said.

" 'She *did*. She took him away with her to Memphis. She kept her own house there, always, you know.'

" 'And what did she do with him?'

" 'They were gone a whole summer. I don't know what she did. But when they came back, Creighton had been rehabilitated.'

" '*No*,' I said.

" '*Yes*,' said Mom. 'Creighton was no longer a slave; he was a dog. Not only that, Creighton knew the difference. The next time Mama Celie tried to beat him, he bit her. And Miss Shug laughed. Mama Celie never dared attempt to beat or humiliate Creighton again. It was Miss Shug's laughter, I believe, that prevented it.

" 'It was the laughter, from someone she loved with her whole being, that ripped through the callus on Mama Celie's heart. She began to feel for *everything*: ant, bat, the hoppy toad flattened on the road.' "

W HY is your name Robin?" Fanny asked.
"Because it does not sound Mexican. My mother's
name is Esperanza. When we came here and she worked for
the gringos—as she called them; a word that I, as a professional analyst must never use—they claimed they couldn't remember it or pronounce it, and anyway it meant Hope, didn't
it? So that's what they called her. Her personal name for me
was Alamo, which means poplar. And Alamo is still what I am
called at home. But enough about me," said Robin. "Have you
ever been hypnotized?"

"Yes," said Fanny. "Sort of. I was in Ohio one summer looking for work—this was when I was in college—and there
wasn't much for people like me. I saw an ad in the paper that
said the local medical school was hiring subjects to be used in
an experiment that studied the effects of hypnosis."

"Oh?" said Robin. "And what happened?"

"I was taken back to my six-year-old self. I was asked to write
as I did then. When I returned to consciousness, after having
been hypnotized, I saw my name on the piece of paper they'd
given me, and it was my six-year-old, second-year-of-public-
school scrawl."

"And did they know what questions to ask you, while they had you under their spell?"

"Of course not," Fanny said. "They were young white men who'd probably never spoken to a black woman other than the ones who cleaned their houses."

Now, there was the sensation of falling very fast inside herself; as if her interior chest and back were those coral and faded indigo walls of a desert canyon. Inside, she thought dreamily, I'm desert color. *How nice.* There was no bottom where she landed. Only space. Dark, comfortable space.

"What do you think of white people?" asked Robin's voice. But for all Fanny knew, it was the voice of God.

Her own voice seemed not to belong to her. In any case it barely escaped her lips. Was *she* speaking? "I am afraid of them," was her reply.

"When you look at them," said the voice, "how do they look to you?"

"Very fat," she said. "They are always eating, eating. Everywhere you go, they are sitting down eating. In Paris, they are eating. In London, they are eating. In Rome. They eat and eat. It makes me feel afraid."

"Why do you feel afraid?"

"When I see them eating, I feel myself to be very hungry. Skin and bones. And I feel their teeth on my leg. But when I look down, sometimes it is not their teeth on my leg, only a cold chain. I am relieved to see it is not their teeth, only a chain. I think that when they called us 'cannibals' they were projecting."

"But why are you so afraid? If it is only a chain that is on your leg, and not their teeth; it can be broken. It can be filed away."

"Sometimes I see myself joining them at the table and I am

eating, eating, eating, too. And we are all bloated and fat. We have chins down to our sternums, our eyes are clamped shut with fat. But the self that I was is still there, too. Right by the table, smelling the food. And she's as poor, as emaciated, as ever. She and her babies. Nothing but eyes and skin and bone. And I am afraid, because I love her so very much, and she is the self I have lost. And the eating goes nowhere. It is endless gluttony to no purpose whatsoever. And I am afraid because aren't those *my* teeth on her leg?"

"MAKE no mistake," Ola had said, "the people themselves must help one struggle with the truly eternal questions. That is why a resistance movement is invaluable." He and Fanny had been sitting on the verandah having breakfast: papaya juice, fruit, coffee, buttered bread, with several kinds of jam; Ola, she had thought, seemed to get his best ideas over food. "There you are in the inhospitable and, you hope, hidden caves of the countryside, having grass scones and lizard tea; your skin is welted from mosquito bites, your shoes rotted from the humidity, but you are sometimes very happy because everyone has the exact same questions about it all that *you* do. Or variations on them. Do you know what guerrilla fighters do more than they do anything else? Skirmishes and battles occupy a very small portion of their time. They *talk*." Ola stopped talking long enough to have a spoonful of fruit. "Talk," he continued, chewing rapidly and swallowing, "is the key to liberation, one's tongue the very machete of freedom. We are the only species, some say, who have created speech. But that is only because, being far less intelligent than the majority of the other animals, and more prone to disastrous blunders, in our relationships with others, speech is so necessary."

Fanny bit into a small hard roll that showered her blouse with crust flakes.

"We must have a world language," said Ola, reaching over to dust her off, and making Fanny feel like a small child, "before we can have world peace. But imagine how people will fight over which language it must be!" He laughed. "Of course it should be something elegant, but relatively simple, and you must not be able to say 'I despise your kind,' or 'I do not respect your god' in it; in short, it should be Olinka. I'm joking," said Ola.

"No, you're not," said Fanny, smiling.

"This *frustration* with the whites," Ola said, thoughtfully, and not responding to her smile, "is a natural reaction to what they have, collectively, done to you, not simply as an individual, but as a people, a culture, a race. The instinct for self-defense and self-preservation is innate, although there was a time, and very recently, too, when white scholars actually did studies that 'proved,' in their eyes, these instincts were innate in all people except us. They'd put us so far down, you see, they thought we'd never get up again, so they advanced theories that showed our innate love of being down." He sipped his coffee, added a dollop of cream to it, and frowned. "I have been responsible for the deaths of whites," said Ola. "It did not 'liberate' me psychologically, as Fanon suggested it might. It did not oppress me further, either. I was simply freeing myself from the jail that they had become for me, and making a space in the world, also, for my children."

And Fanny thought: Right. Even fifteen years ago I could not have come here. I could not walk or drive on the roads of my father's country in peace. He could not have met me at just any gate at the airport. He could not have protected me from white viciousness on the street.

"You must harmonize your own heart," said Ola. "Only you

will know how you can do that; for each of us it is different. Then harmonize, as much as this is ever possible, your surroundings." He thought for a moment, sighed. "Whatever you do," he said, "stay away from people who pity themselves. People who are always complaining have a horrifying tendency to spread their own lead into everybody's arse."

Fanny smiled at this.

"You must try not to want 'things,' too," said Ola, "for 'thingism' is the ultimate block across the path of peace. If everytime you see a tree, you want to make some *thing* out of it, soon no one on earth will even have air to breathe. Trees that are already dead are fine," he added. "Old logs dug up out of the mud are okay." He chuckled softly, as if at a private joke.

"Make peace with those you love and that love you or with those you wish to love. These are your compañeros, as the Latin Americans say. Above all, resist the temptation to think what afflicts you is peculiar to you. Have faith that what is in your consciousness can be communicated to the consciousness of all. And is, in many cases, already there."

"Even in the consciousness of those who have fallen down the drug barrel?" asked Fanny, skeptically.

"Especially those," said Ola. "The struggle with the eternal questions, the ones not definitively answered by the rebel or revolutionary in his or her late teens or early twenties, when one thinks all problems can be solved—the thoughts that so trouble you, the eternally nagging furies—these things are what probably pushed many of our people over the edge. But they can be retrieved. If they do not die from their addictions—their attempts to banish all intelligence about what is really happening to the world, while inhaling the rotten fragrance of the lotus of their 'escape'—they will have to see that they are killing themselves. Their teeth are gnawing on their own legs."

S UWELO had at last driven up from San Francisco to see Fanny. She was then living by herself in the little yurt they'd once shared during summers.

"My *father* told me, shortly before he died," said Fanny, as they warmed themselves by her small fire, in which pinecones occasionally popped, "to harmonize my relations with you." As she thought about Ola she identified with Zindzi Mandela, Nelson Mandela's daughter, whom she had recently heard on the radio, trying to keep alive the words of *her* father, imprisoned for twenty-five years. "Of course it takes two to harmonize," she said firmly, gazing into the fire. "But I am to struggle with you in the faith that harmonizing is possible. This has nothing to do with the question of whether or not we sleep together."

Suwelo sighed. What a difficult woman this was!

"And what does your *mother* say?" he asked, sardonically. Fanny seemed very small, and young, despite the threads of silver at her temples that had appeared since he last saw her.

Fanny smiled. "As you know, my mother counsels forgiveness. It is the spring castor-oil tonic of the soul."

"And why are these the messages we are given?" asked

Suwelo, feeling little hope. "Why is this what they say, and not something a wee bit more probable?"

Fanny shrugged. "Let's face it, Suwelo," she said; "it is because we are the people we are and not some other people. We are not white people, for instance. This is the message not simply from my parents, but it is the message from the beginning. We can trace this message from our earliest contact with the sun."

"No shit," he said. "The *sun?*"

"We have never considered the sun an enemy," Fanny continued gravely, "only, perhaps in the beginning, a goddess. Then later, no doubt under coercion and stretching our imagination to the limit, a god. We have never, until very recently, far less than a thousand years, known the cold. Deep in our hearts, because of our relationship to the sun, we believe we are loved simply for being here. There is no reason for us to hate ourselves. As someone has said: I can dig worshiping the sun, because it worships back. Our relationship to the sun is the bedrock of our security as black human beings. We have our melanin, we have our pads of woolly hair. We're ready for the beach. We can cope." Fanny smiled.

"But are you not," said Suwelo, "afraid of being burned? After all, even the sun is no longer what it was." What he was really asking was whether or not she had the courage to love him, changeable as he was.

"The sun hasn't changed," she said, looking into the fire. "It is exactly the same, as far as human beings are concerned, and will remain so for inconceivable lifetimes to come. It is we who have changed in relation to it. The African white man was born without melanin, or with only incredibly small amounts of it. He was born unprotected from the sun. He must have felt cursed by God. He would later project this feeling onto us and try to make us feel cursed because we are black; but black is a color the sun loves. The African white man could not blame the sun for his plight, not without seeming ridiculous, but he could eventually stop people from worshiping it. He could put a new god in its place that more closely resembled himself: cold, detached, given to violent rages and fits of jealousy. He needed to create a new god, since the one the rest of his world worshiped was so cruel to him. Burned him. How fortunate that he finally stumbled into the Mediterranean, into Europe. The coolness must have felt exquisite.

"And no," she said, "I am not afraid of loving you. At last I see you for what you are. I see the child in you that became the man and is now fast becoming the person. Your sins are no graver than my own. I indulged in my fantasies of violence for years before I tried to change; as you indulged in sterile, exploitive relationships with other women. I couldn't see why *I* should be the one asked not to seek revenge, why the buck of violence must stop with me. Besides, must I myself be the only model I had for the creature I intended to be? There is a card in tarot, the ninth card, and its message is: What you hope for, you also fear. This is how it was with me.

"I didn't feel particularly betrayed as an individual by your affairs with other women; or with Carlotta in particular. You and I are constructing our own lives; other people are bound to be important in them. I do not believe in marriage.... However, I did feel betrayed, as a woman."

"Betrayed as a woman? But I told you," said Suwelo, "Carlotta meant very little to me. She ..."

"I know," said Fanny. "What you said was, she meant nothing *whatever* to you; and, furthermore, she had no substance. It was when you said that, that I hated you. I hated you as a man."

"But why?" cried Suwelo. "I was trying not to hurt you. Trying to make you see that no woman mattered to me more than you." He paused, and continued with some bitterness, "I suppose I forgot I was talking to a womanist."

"No," said Fanny, "you forgot you were talking to Carlotta's masseuse."

"What?" he asked.

"I tried to uncramp her legs, untangle her knee joints, flatten out the knots in her back, unclench her jaw, straighten out the curve in her neck, restore free movement to her toes. Clear up a migraine that lasted for a year. She was small, but as dense and as heavy as lead. I knew the body of the woman you said had no substance. Carlotta's very substance was pain. And that you did not know this, or, if you knew it, did not care, that is what made me despise you.

"I didn't know what had happened in her life. I sometimes wondered whether you knew anything about her life at all. But each time I worked on her I was amazed to feel the pain, like waves of ice meeting my hands, the pain of a body recently and repeatedly struck. A body cringing."

Fanny had started to weep, and she swiped at her nose angrily with her sleeve. Suwelo knew how she hated to cry when she was angry.

"Men must have mercy on women, Suwelo," she said coldly. "They must feel women's bodies as a masseuse feels them; not just caress them superficially and use them as if they're calendar pinups, centerfolds, or paper dolls. What woman could trust a man who came back from another woman's arms with a story such as yours? I simply couldn't."

"I hated you for leaving me," said Suwelo, handing her his handkerchief. "Why didn't you explain?"

"I was sick of explaining everything," said Fanny, with great weariness. "In my women's studies class and in the administration office at the college I had to explain about blacks; to you and other men I had to explain about women. None of you seemed capable of using your own eyes and feelings to try to comprehend things and people for yourselves. Anyway, you wouldn't have understood."

"Right," said Suwelo, "all men are imbeciles. Of course. How do you *know* I wouldn't have understood? Are women the only half of the species that has a brain?"

"I'd tried so often before," she said, "when we still lived together. I tried with books," she said. "With records. You wouldn't read, you wouldn't listen. You seemed traumatized by the new. It seemed pointless."

"*Pointless*," he cried, and he suddenly felt as if all of himself was awake; and that his mind was not in the fog it was usually in when he argued with Fanny, "after all we've been through? Hell, we survived kidnapping together, we survived the middle passage, we survived the slave trade. For all you know," he tossed at her, "I was once your mother."

"Once my *what?*" said Fanny, shocked. "Negro, I *beg* your pardon."

"Or at least mother's milk for you. Shit," he said, thinking of Miss Lissie and Mr. Hal and all he'd learned from them that he couldn't wait for Fanny to share, "we survived living in New York. Fight with me," he said. "Scream. You have nice big teeth; *bite me.*" Fanny's lovely mouth was shaping the words, in horror, "*Bite me?*" "But don't just go off inside yourself and assume I'm too dense to follow. Who do you think I am anyway?" How he loved feeling indignant! And as if he had a right, which up to now it had seemed to him only women had, to fight back. To make his self-expression even more satisfying, he got to his feet with a bounce and paced about the small room. Something hot and passionate was opening in him, and it wasn't in his trousers; it was . . . in his chest. "I'm flesh, I'm blood," he said with decision. And for the first time truly felt he *was* flesh and blood. *Human*, the same as women. "No, I'm not some perfect old outlaw that lived a hundred years ago that you can love without being required sometimes to contradict yourself. But I'm up for the damn struggle any damn day of the week that you are."

Fanny was looking at him as if he'd lost his mind. "Why are you so angry?" she asked.

"I'm not angry," said Suwelo. "I'm mad. I'm mad about the waste that happens when people who love each other can't even bring themselves to talk.

"Talking," he said, reminding Fanny very much of Ola, "is the very *afro*-disiac of love."

She laughed and put her hand on his arm. Usually when Suwelo became angry he stuttered and muttered and made not a grain of sense. If an argument started when they were in the car and he was driving, they were likely to run off the road.

"And am I to assume by this . . . um . . . *declaration*," said Fanny, "that what we have here is an Afro who would like to come home to roost?"

"Yes," he said, joining her laughter. "Here's my hand in strugglehood. Let's shake on it."

I WAS at an exhibit of Frida Kahlo's paintings at the Mexican Museum," said Fanny. "Like so many others, I'm in love with Frida. The museum that day was thronged with women, and they each had a lot to say about every one of the paintings, but they were even more voluble in front of the photographs of Frida and Diego that were hung with the paintings. After viewing the exhibit for the first time, I sat on a bench in the middle of the floor, simply allowing the exquisiteness of Frida's paintings to wash over me.

"'Oh,' 'Ugh,' 'Blech' came the sounds from the group clustered around the picture of Frida and Diego taken on their wedding day. 'He is so huge!' said one. 'And so gross.' 'And she so tiny,' said another. 'I hate to think . . .' began still another. 'Don't!' said her partner. 'So much pain!' moaned a short, dark-haired woman, who reminded me, actually, of you, Robin."

"I'm flattered you think of me after you leave here," said Robin.

"Oh," said Fanny, "I think of you a lot."

"I saw the exhibit," said Robin. "I, too, am a Kahlo fanatic. I stood muttering and musing in front of that photograph myself. Did you know what her father called the couple? 'The elephant and the dove.'"

"How could her parents let her marry him?" said Fanny. "They knew the condition of her fractured pelvis. But no one, I suppose, not even her parents, could withstand Frida's determination to have whatever she wanted, and she wanted Diego. And just why did she want Diego? I think it is because she herself wanted to paint."

"Want to paint? Marry a painter," said Robin. "Yes, I think there's something in that. And his grossness wasn't all she saw in him, even when he wasn't painting. She was charmed by his childlike expressiveness. He was direct in his expressions, whether in a confrontation with the Mexican Communist Party, with the Rockefellers, or with his innumerable lovers. Of course, like many husbands, he wasn't capable of being direct with his wife. Women have a hard time understanding this. It hurts them deeply. Frida never recovered from having been hurt. At the same time, she thought her disability may have been the reason Diego felt a sexual necessity to stray."

"Well, anyway," said Fanny, "there I sat in the museum, letting Frida's genius wash over me. It was as if the sun were streaming in on me through so many stained-glass windows—what little I could see of it as the throngs of women, and a few men, slowly revolved around the walls. I heard a voice speaking, from in front of one of the paintings. The one in which Frida has her own face but the body of a deer, and her deer's body is shot full of arrows. I drifted over, drawn again by the painting, the horror in Frida's eyes, but also drawn by the voice. It was coming from a white woman with a Southern accent. It was a soft, good-humored voice. Incessant. She was with her mother, who'd obviously come from someplace other than San Francisco. She was dressed in one of those pastel pink polyester pantsuits and wore white sandals with stockings and carried an enormous white plastic handbag. She had graying hair, wore glasses, and was squinting at segments of the painting as if she had difficulty taking in the whole.

" 'Now I don't know what to tell you about this one,' said the daughter.

" 'Why, you don't have to tell me anything, Brenda,' the mother said. 'Look at those tears on her face. I've felt like that.'

"So I went right home," said Fanny, "and I called my mother and asked her to find out from Tanya's mother where Tanya lived. She called me back next day. She lived in Oakland."

"Really?" said Robin.

"Yes. When I called her up I said, 'Is this *Ton*ya Rucker, from Hartwell?' And she said, 'Well, this is *Tan*ya.' A total reverse.

"I was very nervous, going to her house. The woman she lives with, a Japanese-American who introduced herself as Marie, let me in. I sat on the sofa, in front of which was a table full of framed photographs. Mostly of two brownskin babies, a boy and a girl, followed from infancy through their teen years, with a smiling college-graduation picture of the two of them, grown.

"To make a long story short, Tanya looked exactly like her mother. The little child who'd been my playmate was gone. Her eyes were even different. They had become dark gray, not blue, as I remembered. Her hair was brown, and streaked with gray. She was plump and motherly, offering me tea or 'something to knosh on' every few minutes.

"I picked up a photograph and peered at it.

" 'Their father was black,' she said, as if she'd said it many times. 'They're both in grad school now. I don't know where Joe is. I think he's probably still in Atlanta.'

"I wasn't too interested in the whereabouts of Joe.

" 'I always wondered what became of you,' said Tanya. 'How you were. My mother used to ask your mother, and sometimes my mother would tell me what yours said. I knew you'd gone on to college and then become a teacher. I work in a company that makes computers,' she said. 'I get to test them at the final stage, before the customer gets them. It's hell on my eyes, but the company's gotten so many complaints from workers like me I hope they'll soon do something about it; make screens or something to put in front of the computers, or design special eyewear.'

"I was so sick of my own work I couldn't bring myself to speak of it. I told her bluntly that I was in therapy, trying to get to the roots of my anger against white people. I didn't tell her it was particularly against whites who were blond. I guess I was afraid she'd say, like so many people do: Well, everybody hates Nazis. That's what they think I mean. They think of Hitler's Aryan race as played by bleached-blond actors on TV. That image is, I know, only a small part of it.

"'You've got every right to be angry at white people,' she said. 'I'm angry at them myself. I never knew just how angry until I saw what they did to my children. Not to mention what they'd already done to Joe.'

"'Joe,' I said. 'Your parents must have had a fit.'

"'A conniption fit,' she said. 'But it was too late for them to do anything about it by the time they found out. After about five years, after I'd married Joe and moved to California and had the kids and seemed to be doing okay, my daddy just up and died, he was so frustrated. After he died, Momma came around. She loved the kids and was eventually able to be cordial to Joe. Then Joe left, and I got a divorce. And then I had to tell her I was queer.'

"Tanya paused. 'She's still out on that one.'

"'But how did all this happen?' I asked. 'You were programed to be Miss Lily White.'

"'I know it,' said Tanya. 'But you know what happened. The Civil Rights Movement happened. Selma happened. The University of Georgia happened. Dr. King happened. It just hit me one night, watching television coverage of one of the Civil

Rights marches, that the order of the world as I'd always known it, and imagined it would be forevermore, was *wrong*. I felt it was wrong down to its tiniest, white man-made construction. Anybody who couldn't honor those black people I saw on television and those pitifully few white people with them had to be fucked up.

" 'But,' said Tanya, 'I didn't dare speak up about it. Like so many young Southerners at the time, I did nothing. And then Joe came along—I met him on a trip I made out here with my mother's church group. We met at Fisherman's Wharf!' She laughed. 'And I was determined to marry him. He didn't have a chance. Our children would be my protest. Of course, he was bound to find out about this. Joe was, I mean. That marrying him was a kind of political shortcut I'd chosen to take, because as a Southerner I didn't know how to get connected up for any of the long marches. Joe's realization of my motive cast a pall over our marriage, and though I did love Joe as an individual, I wasn't crazy about his culture, which wasn't black Southern culture at all, but black urban street culture, for the most part, though Joe's parents were staunch members of the urban, really *suburban*, black middle class. They lived in the El Cerrito hills, for God's sake! The most pretentious people I ever saw. They liked Nixon. They hated hippies. They voted for Gerald Ford.

" 'I thought all black people lived more or less like the people did in your house.' Tanya laughed. 'Where there was always something lively going on. Music or parties or sun worship or something. Lots of sweet-natured people coming by from time to time. Even real interesting crazy people, so often with amazing creative skills. The best food in the world. And folks at your house were always kissing.'

" 'You used to come to our house?' I asked.

" 'Sure I did,' she said. 'Don't you remember? I'd sneak off

from home to visit your house. My folks, especially my grandmother, would have to come and drag me back. I used to hide
under Miss Shug's bed! How can you not remember that?

"'And sometimes your grandmother would lie to mine and
say, "No, us hadn't seen her." I used to love to hear her say
that. We'd both of us, you and me, be hiding under the edge
of Miss Shug's bed. It was a mammoth, silver thing that was
spoon-shaped and resembled a ship, and the lace from her bed-
spread hung down before our faces like a net. We'd be eating
teacakes.

"'First we'd hear the heavy crunch, crunch of my grandmother's step in the yard. Then we'd hear her heavy thump as
she put one foot on the bottom step. She'd never come in the
house, of course. She'd never even ascend to the porch.

"'"I've come for Tanya," she'd say.

"'And Miss Celie'd go, "Tanya? Why, us hadn't seen her."

"'And you and I would just fall over, in our hiding place, giggling.'

"'What did she look like, your grandmother?'

"'She was real fat,' said Tanya. 'And she walked with a stick.
She almost never smiled and always seemed to be remembering something she hadn't liked. My grandfather had died a long
time ago and there wasn't even a picture of him in the house.
The only nice thing about her, she had snow-white hair.

"'How can you not remember those times?' Tanya asked. 'I
could never forget them. I was never so happy in my life.'

"'I remember being at your house,' I said. 'Vaguely. Or,
rather, being in your backyard.'

"'I couldn't understand why you couldn't come in,' said
Tanya. 'And whenever I asked, one of them, my mother or father or grandmother, would say, "She wouldn't *want* to come
in, honey. Don't ask her to; it might hurt her feelings."

"'Hurting you was the last thing I wanted to do. So we played outside in the backyard—we weren't even supposed to play in the front; somebody might see us! And I never asked you inside. And you never asked, and didn't seem interested in going inside our house, which was like Tobacco Road compared to yours anyhow, so I thought my parents and grandmother were right.'

"Robin," said Fanny, frowning comically, "I didn't remember any of this. Tanya remembered it perfectly. How is this possible?"

"For some people, happiness is easier to remember than pain," said Robin. "You had to repress, 'forget' your pain in order to continue playing with Tanya. Although the 'play' had gone out of it by this time, I think."

"Yes, I think so, too," said Fanny. "What I did remember of our times together had an unreal quality, as if they existed on film, or had happened to someone else."

"You became alienated from your own body, your own self," said Robin. "You became two beings in your relationship with Tanya. The cheerfully playing little girl that others saw and the hurt child who was bewildered by her very first encounter with irrational rejection."

Fanny continued. " 'And then it ended,' Tanya said. 'Surely you remember that?'

" 'What happened?' I asked. 'Did your mother try to give me some of your old clothes?'

" 'Not hardly,' said Tanya. 'You were always dressed like a little princess. I was the one always begging to wear something of yours! But I could only wear your dresses and hair ribbons and lockets—and rhinestone socks!—at your house. Any little pretty thing you or your folks gave me promptly disappeared if I took it home.'

" 'What, then?' I asked her.

" 'Are you positive you don't remember? All these years, I've thought you were sitting somewhere remembering and cursing us.'

"Oh shit, I thought," said Fanny, leaning toward Robin. "As soon as Tanya said that I got a headache. I gritted my teeth and dug my heels into the carpet. I squinted at her in segments — at her feet, in beige house slippers, at her fat ankles, her stomach, over which her breasts flopped. Her chin. Her dark gray eyes. Her brown hair, its wide streak of gray,

"Tanya sighed. 'It was my grandmother,' she told me. 'She died eventually, by the way. In the course of things. Not because of what she did to you.'

" 'Your grandmother,' I said. 'She did something to me?' I was beginning to feel the way I feel under hypnosis. As if I were falling deep inside myself.

" 'She slapped you,' said Tanya.

" 'Did I see stars?' I asked.

" 'Yes!' said Tanya. 'You do remember!'

" 'No,' I said. 'I was being facetious.'

" 'Well, everyone kissed at your house. It was the common greeting and the common good-bye. Nobody hardly shook hands; unless they were total strangers. I loved it that everybody kissed. It certainly wasn't something any of us did at home. But when I told my folks about it, they didn't like it one little bit. They especially didn't like to hear anything about grown women kissing. I now realize they had a conference about it and made a resolution for me. Since I was into kissing — I even started in kissing them — I, as a white person, could kiss any of you. But you must never kiss me. They sent me forth with this dictum and sat back expecting me to be able to implement it. I didn't even try.

" 'But I did tell your folks about it, and they stopped on a dime. Not only did they stop kissing me, but they stopped touching me, period. I soon discovered I had my own personal glass and plate whenever I came to your house.

" 'Only you couldn't hear me the way your mother and grandmothers could. You'd always kissed and been kissed. "Give me some sugar? You want some sugar?" Those seemed to be the two main questions in your life. One day when we were playing together in my backyard, you kissed me on the cheek. My grandmother was watching from the back steps, where she tended to park herself whenever we played.'

"'Incensed, was she?' I asked.

"'Enraged,' said Tanya. 'She weighed a wet ton, and she lumbered over to us, and she slapped you so hard she knocked you down, and when you sat up you were holding your head between your hands as if you were afraid it would fall off. And you said, "I see stars."

"'And she said, "If I ever catch you putting your black mouth on Tanya again, I'll knock your little black head off." And she turned and lumbered back up the steps.

"'You cried and cried. You were very upset. I cried and cried, too. *I* was very upset. But for some reason I was afraid to try to comfort you; after all, it was you that had been hit. I stood there totally rigid, as if turned to stone. You said you were going to tell your grandmothers; and I knew if you told Miss Shug she'd kill us all. I begged you not to say anything. I was so ashamed; and I hated my grandmother so much; but more than that, I was afraid of what would happen if you told.

"'And I don't think you ever told,' said Tanya, 'but I never knew for sure because that was the last time you played with me.'"

"Well," said Robin, when Fanny finished. "How do you feel about this?"

"I still don't feel it," said Fanny.

"Do you want a tissue?" Robin asked.

And Fanny felt the tears of horror on her face.

PART SIX

REMEMBRANCE IS THE KEY TO REDEMPTION.
—Inscription on a memorial to Jews who died
in World War II concentration camps,
Land's End, San Francisco

"DEAR Suwelo," wrote Mr. Hal in a large, shaky scrawl, "I take pen in reluctant hand to write you the sad news that my beloved Lissie, companion of nearly all my years, left us on June 3rd, a week ago. You will be happy to know she wasn't sick, not in the least. In fact she painted right up until the afternoon she laid down to die. She had been complaining of a restlessness, and was all the time going around inside the house opening and closing windows. During the last month or so of her life, she didn't want to spend much time inside the house anyway. She wanted to live out-of-doors. Thank goodness, the weather was fine, for the most part (of course she would love storms, too), and we dragged her mattress out onto the porch. Her easel stood in the corner, and she would lie down and rest for a bit, then get up and paint.

"Her last paintings are incredible, and unlike anything she's done before; I mean, the subject matter itself is strange. I am enclosing some slides of them so you can see for yourself. I don't know what to make of them.

"I am also sending along these cassette tapes Lissie made for you; and also, I believe, for Fanny. Both of us took a liking to that young woman's face.

"A week ago, I didn't see how I could make it without Lissie. I thought it would be easier to do without my own breath. She died, was cremated, and her ashes were scattered within twenty-four hours, just as she had instructed, but so fast. I came in from the yard where I had just scattered her ashes and I started to call her to ask her where I should put the empty urn. But as soon as I opened my mouth to ask her, I knew it didn't matter. And that was my first inkling that grieving over Lissie's departure was a little premature.

"It's not that she's here, or that she's a ghost, Suwelo. She did die. She is gone. But she is also here, in me. And I realized Lissie was always in me, only now that I'm not distracted by her physical presence I can feel it more clearly.

"So think of me rattling around in our little house that the blue morning glories are burying and the pecan tree is sheltering from the sun. It feels big now, and for the time being I've left Lissie's mattress on the porch. I look out the window at it, and it's just a big fluffy cloud of white.

"Lissie liked you very much, Suwelo. Not just because you were Rafe's descendant. She liked you for yourself. She liked your struggle against confusion. Lissie had no patience for people whose lives weren't as convoluted as a ball of string.

"If you ever should come back to Baltimore, you must come to see me. I will make us a cup of good coffee and tell you about myself. I'm finding I'm too old to be lonely, but I miss seeing younger faces. My memories keep me company, and they are flooding back to quite a degree. I remember the years with Lissie, when we still lived on the Island. I remember her mama and that fishy-smelling little store. But that place was paradise. I remember that old witch Granny Dorcy. And baby Jack. And Lulu. We didn't know what hit us, me and Lissie and Rafe, when Lulu never came back from Europe. I try not to think about that part. Every day, every minute, for years and years, we waited for a word about our daughter. None ever came. All those hopes. All that love. Lost.

"When your daddy was called to fight in the war, we were all glad. To hell with the Germans. I think we thought he'd be able to spot Lulu. But he didn't find her; he found only terror and brutality enough to make him lose part of who he was in his soul, along with losing his arm.

"No, I don't think of those things. I think of Lulu when she was a baby. I think about dressing and feeding her. I think about teaching her to read and watching her take her first steps in a forest. She grinned and grinned to find herself so small beneath the trees, but able to stand on her own legs, like them.

"Well, they go on and on, my memories, and right now I'm going back to them. If you want Lissie's paintings, after I die, you can have them. Write me a card, and I will put it in my will. When I die, I'm convinced this house of ours will simply cave in. All that holds it up is my breath and the blue morning glories. Otherwise I'd leave it to you, too. As it is, I think our neighbors, who have a lot of children, could use the empty lot as a place for their children to play. So I will leave it to them. But do let me know about the pictures.

"Your friend.

"Harold (Hal) D. Jenkins, Esq.

"P.S. 'Being a genius means you are connected to God. And you know it.'

"Every day I think of something like this that Lissie used to say. Today this is what came to my mind. I pass it on to you, for what it's worth.

"Something else: 'Men make war to get attention.'

"Something else: 'All killing is an expression of self-hate.'

"And something she loved to say whenever people made fun of her, which was often: 'Hal, I have been laughed at by some of the *funniest* people!'"

"TO THE extent that it is possible," Ola had said one day as he and Fanny sprawled on the grass after a morning of weeding his vegetable garden, "you must live in the world today as you wish everyone to live in the world to come. That can be your contribution. Otherwise, the world you want will never be formed. Why? Because you are waiting for others to do what you are not doing; and they are waiting for you, and so on. The planet goes from bad to worse."

"Is that why you married a white woman?" Fanny asked, nibbling a blade of grass she'd broken off near her feet.

"No," said Ola, surprised. "How did you know about it?" He shrugged. "I married Mary Jane to cause trouble; that's why I married Mary Jane. And no matter how I've tried to explain it, no one is willing to listen to a different point of view."

He tugged out the large handkerchief that hung from his back pocket and thoroughly mopped his perspiring face. When he'd finished, Fanny took it, looked for and found a still-dry corner, and gingerly dabbed her own forehead.

"Mary Jane?" she said. "Not a very Swedish name, is it?"

"Mary Jane isn't Swedish," said Ola, taking back the handkerchief and tossing it to the ground. "Oh, I see it now. You've been reading my plays! Beware of assuming the playwright always writes about himself." He wagged his finger at her. "It's true I had lovers in Sweden—it's a damn cold country and I was lonely. Unbelievably lonely. And certainly there's no crime in returning the kindness of strangers. There was a woman, Margrit, whom I lived with for two years. She was pregnant once, but being as pragmatic as she was beautiful, and hefty, too, by the way, she aborted the child. I couldn't convince her to keep it; after all, I was the one who refused to wear condoms, even when she provided them. I thought it very racist of her to insist. I was the one who'd be leaving her country and coming home. I couldn't bring her with me. I wasn't Seretse Khama of Botswana, and she wasn't Ruth Williams of England. She knew what white racism was, even in Sweden, after living there with me. She couldn't bear to think of the suffering of her child. Ironically, I recently read an article that said that brown and golden children there these days are highly prized. I find this doubtful. I imagine they're considered to be . . ."

"Exotic," said Fanny. "Like Helga Crane in *Quicksand*."

"Quicksand?" queried Ola.

"Yes," said Fanny. "It's a kind of sand that you can drown in, almost as though it were water."

"Oh," said Ola.

"But I'm speaking of a novel I used when I taught women's literature; it is by Nella Larson, herself the result of a liaison between a Danish mother and a West Indian father."

She could see Ola was interested in this unheard-of writer.

"She was born in Chicago," continued Fanny, "and when she grew up she went to visit her mother's people in Denmark. Her mother had by that time married a regular American white man, and Helga/Nella, as the dark child in the family, had a very hard time of it."

"Of course," said Ola.

"When she got to Denmark she was surprised to find herself virtually 'lionized.' Everyone 'loved' her. She was painted by a famous local painter, who wanted to marry her. But she couldn't stand being the object of the Danes' expectations of what such an 'exotic'-looking woman must be. She couldn't stand the flamboyant 'African' dresses her relatives bought for her and insisted she wear. Nor did she enjoy being on display for strangers to admire. Besides, she found the country and the people very unlike the ones she'd left back home in Harlem. And she realized she preferred the ones in Harlem. This surprised the shit out of her. There's something about the old Harlem, the Harlem of the twenties, that had a tremendous hold on people's loyalties," mused Fanny. "I think it was the great music, the parties. The Emancipation Proclamation finally in action."

"I've read about Harlem," said Ola. "In Langston Hughes. And it's true, his love of the place shines in every line."

"But if you didn't marry the Swede," said Fanny, puzzled, "whom did you marry? Who is Mary Jane?"

"An American," said Ola. "And an interesting woman. You must make it your business to meet her before you go back."

"I didn't come all the way to Africa to meet American white women," said Fanny dryly.

Ola chuckled, and leaned back on an elbow. "I have to admit the first time I met Mary Jane I was also skeptical. This was at a time when whites were being urged to emigrate. Not every white person, you know, but those who had no visible means of support, other than their African serfs. There were vast numbers of parasites to be got rid of. People who'd come into the country with nothing, when it was run by the white regime, and who now had large plantations, or at the very least had nice houses and their pick of well-paying jobs. It was a custom of the country, actually one of the 'items' in the advertising that lured white people to settle here, that every white man, woman, or child was assured of having at least one African servant. Most households had two or three. Many had five. They paid these people less than one percent of their own wages, and 'made up' the rest in old clothing and leftover food.

"Some of the country's food came from America, by the way. The *natives'* food, I mean. Yes. I have myself seen stacks and stacks of American grain piled high on the wharf. 'A Gift from the American People,' stenciled on the side of each sack. You mean you never knew you were feeding us?" Ola asked Fanny. "The people in the underground used to make a joke about those sacks of grain, mainly corn; they said that America and the other white countries gave Africa a sack of vermin-infested corn for a sack of gold and diamonds, and considered it fair."

Fanny laughed.

"So we were asking whites to leave," continued Ola. "If they wanted to stay, and many of them did, they had to make a formal, legally binding commitment to assume all financial responsibilities for the health care, education, and housing of their former workers and their workers' children. They were to agree to a seven-year plan; at the end of which, the people who had served them for nothing for years and years must be certified to be in good health, to have a good education, or be well on the way to getting one, and they must be settled in decent houses that they owned. An international certification team would be put together, and it would go from house to house. Estate to estate. Plantation to plantation. And so on.

"This was an insult to most whites, of course, many of whom were astonished not only that the new 'monkey' government, as some of them called it, demanded this — which is really very reasonable, considering the unearned wealth of the whites, wealth they were now trying desperately to get out of the country; and in lieu of having their houses and property confiscated outright, which is what they'd claimed they feared for years—but that good health, education, and decent housing were things Africans wanted! Some of these people went into shock at the realization that when the African who cooked their food and nursed their children smiled at them, she or he was smiling in spite of who they were, not because of who they were.

"This was a very hectic time. There were people who took their quite large houses apart, piece by piece, and shipped them to other countries. They ripped up their own trees and gardens. They burned whole neighborhoods, exactly like the black rioters in the U.S. did during the sixties.

"There were thousands of whites who grew too depressed to function; there were suicides, especially among the young. There were people who revealed that they thought being master of black people somewhere on earth was simply their destiny, as white people. Scads of this lot emigrated to Australia and New Zealand, where the black populations are small and weak.

"But back to Mary Jane . . . One day she turned up at my office in the Department of Entertainment and Culture—the people who ran this department prior to our taking over had had a special fondness for local productions of things like *Show Boat*, *My Fair Lady*, *The Nutcracker*, and, on the risqué side, *Cabaret*. This was also before there was a Ministry of Culture. We were attached to the Ministry of Home Affairs, which was, at that time, just after our takeover, run by a man who had been out of the country while the fight for our independence was going on, and who now, upon his return, did everything he did out of guilt. He had been in America, hiding out in one of the universities there—I like to say this; it is not totally fair—and was militantly antiwhite. He especially disliked white women. Mary Jane was angry because this man had told her she'd be, *for certain,* one of the first white people 'required,' as he put it, to leave the country.

"She explained to me that she'd started and now ran an art school, the M'Sukta School. Perhaps I'd heard of it?

"Heard of it!" said Ola, suddenly sitting up and taking off his sandals. "It was not only the best art school we had in Olinka. It was the only art school. Certainly I'd heard of it. She was supporting seventy boys and girls at the school, she said. They lived there, as well. Her ambition was for the work of her artists to become part of what Olinka was known for. She even thought that somewhere down the line there might be some money for her students, and for the country, in it.

"In any case, she said, she'd staked her life on the students, the school, the country, and, being no longer young, and with no desire to go back to America or to emigrate to New Zealand or Australia, she didn't see what there was left for her to do. All her money had gone into the school, which, our department head had told her, the government would confiscate. One thing she'd done was to put the school in the names of all the people who worked there.

" 'You'll get something for it,' I assured her.

" 'Yes,' she said. 'So I hear. Enough to buy a one-way ticket "back" to England. Well, I'm not from England.'

"I went out that evening to have a look at her school, the M'Sukta School. It was located on the outskirts of town and was very modest. The girls and boys slept in separate barracks, and there was a huge communal studio that was mostly windows. Each bed was neatly made, with a locally woven woolen blanket, like the Pendleton blankets in America that are based on Indian designs, folded neatly at its foot. It was the first time I realized how similar Native American and Native African symbols and designs are. Beside each bed stood a small brightly painted wardrobe for the students' things.

"These were all disturbed children. I hadn't realized that, until I met them. A number of them had lost their parents in the rebellions against the white regime. Some of them had lost their reasoning under beatings while in detention. A good number of them had glaring physical disabilities. There were those who limped, breathed oddly, squinted, or flapped useless stumps and arms. They were the most battered and deprived of our citizens. Mary Jane had gone about collecting them pretty much off the streets. Such as they were—'streets,' that is—in 'our' part of town.

" 'Tell me,' I asked her, 'are you a nun?'

"She smoked cigarettes that were made of rolled-up eucalyptus leaves. She took a puff from the one in her hand and blew out the smoke.

" 'Why?' she said. 'Do I look like one?'

"In truth, she looked like a gangster's moll from one of those old Hollywood movies of the thirties. But only a nun would do this sort of thing. Surely.

"I was on excellent terms with the nuns who'd taught Nzingha," said Ola. "They were a radical lot, who believed with all their hearts that Jesus was a flaming revolutionary and that Mary and Martha were no better. None of them would ever fire a weapon, but when we were in hiding, we counted on them to transport weapons to us. So this was my notion of nuns.

" 'I was very rich, once,' said Mary Jane. 'Also very poor.' And that is all she said.

" 'Why is it called the M'Sukta School?' I asked her. 'M'Sukta' is not an Olinka word, but an Ababa one," Ola explained to Fanny. "The Ababa are a sister tribe. And Mary Jane proceeded to tell me the most astonishing tale about an Ababa woman who'd been taken to England and shut up for nearly fifteen years in the British Museum of Natural History. She'd spent her time there weaving. Mary Jane's great-great-aunt had sprung her—Mary Jane wasn't sure just how—and brought her back to Ababaland. Unfortunately, she was the sole survivor of her tribe. Mary Jane's great-aunt had inherited her great-great-aunt's diaries about this episode. The great-aunt, when *she* was grown, had also come out to Africa. She'd actually lived among the Olinka and done many good works: she'd educated a number of women who became doctors and social workers and agronomists and whatnot. An amazing number of these women died in the struggle against the white regime. She was living here at the time the whites destroyed our villages and forced us onto reservations. Like your Indian tribes, you know. Like our own wild animals.

"Mary Jane inherited a huge dose of gumption and the 'can do' spirit. She came to Africa and taught herself to paint. She'd dabbled before, she said, just for something useful to do, but this time she was serious. She had some money, so she bought land well away from the city—which, unfortunately, crept out, she said, to swallow her—and in complete solitude, with neither maid nor 'boy,' she painted. Sometimes as much as twelve hours a day. She had a horse, and days when she didn't paint, she'd ride. She came to know the people in the countryside, and the country itself, very well. Her paintings began to please her."

"How admiringly you speak of her," said Fanny, somewhat grudgingly. She had started to do yoga postures as she listened to Ola. Now she formed her body into the shape of a plow and gave her back a good long stretch.

"Yes," said Ola, watching her maneuvers on the grass, "wait until you meet her. She looks exactly like that actress you have in America, the one with the flat voice, blond hair, and gray eyes who is married to a man who looks like her twin. She could not be whiter-looking. I'd always thought if I ever met such an American woman, I'd be speechless. But no. Of course, by then, to help her run the school, she had a staff. I was so impressed with them. She'd sent them off, here and there — to Russia, Saudi Arabia, Berlin — to study art and psychology, and how to run a top-flight boarding school for disturbed youngsters. They were all eager-eyed, bright as pennies, affectionate toward the students and toward their headmistress. I took my cue from them and was soon chattering along a mile a minute. I immediately found an ulterior motive for trying to help her save her school. It was a fabulous place to rehearse and perform my plays!

"I'd never seen anything like it. Did I say that every inch of every wall of the buildings, outside and inside, was covered with paintings? Whenever the school ran out of paper and canvas, which was regularly, Mary Jane explained, they simply whitewashed over an old mural on one of the walls and started a new mural over it. She said the students had complained in the beginning because their barracks and the common studio had mud walls and a thatched roof. It reminded them too much of the sterile thatched huts the white regime had erected for their parents and grandparents on the reserves. But, said Mary Jane, in my great-aunt's books — she'd come to Africa to write books, you know — she'd talked about the art created by the people before their villages were bulldozed. Art they just casually did in the painting of their houses every year after the rainy season, and as casually lived in. So she'd felt the housing construction and decoration were right.

"To make a sprawling tale reasonably cogent," said Ola, "Mary Jane and I, along with her seven-member staff, the cook and the gardener, and some of the mothers of the children, and, to be fair, an older brother and a father or two, brainstormed together for many days and decided there was nothing left to do to save the school but for Mary Jane and me to marry.

"It was bound to cause trouble. There I was, one of the 'best' and most visible of the black men in Olinka, educated in the West, with a nice house and car and whatnot, and, many suspected, and a few actually knew, with a wife stuck away in the bush; there I was, an undisputed leader of our country, pointing out its needs and glories and its transgressions right and left. Occasionally pillorying the white man and his woman with well-deserved viciousness. How could I, of all people, marry a white woman? And not even one who was young, like those in the girlie magazines that were suddenly flooding the countryside and that one saw absolutely everywhere.

"For this was one of many parting ploys used by the vanquished white regime. The use of the white woman's body. The white woman's body, so long off limits, was suddenly everywhere. Her very private parts splayed out for all to see. The young boys carried the rolled-up magazines in their back pockets. This became a status symbol, like T-shirts and blue jeans. Part of their style. Their fathers and uncles kept stacks of the magazines under lock and key at home under their beds, or in the office. There was a lively black-market trade in these magazines. Our women were being encouraged to lighten their faces with bleach, to go blond. Suddenly it was understood that nudity did not denote barbarity. The very women who'd been stoned, practically, for going without their blouses were now told they must take them off in order to be modern.

"At the same time, the government, after throwing out a majority of the white man's laws, because they oppressed the native population, decided that the one law they would assuredly keep was the one forbidding interracial marriage. This proved they had as much race pride as the white man, you see. On the other hand, they had reinstated polygamy, which I was against, and which women were against. After all, polygamy is a clear forerunner of the plantation system, with the husband as 'master' and the wives as 'slaves.' Well, it wasn't a government that listened to women. Everyone knew that by then.

"If I married Mary Jane, I could harass the lawmakers twice.

"They disapproved of interracial marriage but approved of and encouraged polygamy. I would take a second wife, but she'd be white.

"The more down-to-earth reason for marrying, though, was to make Mary Jane a citizen of the country and therefore ineligible for deportation, and to keep her and her school in Olinka.

"The government was distressed by my decision. I didn't care. They needed the plays I was writing. They needed my popularity with the masses. It was only through my plays that the government could speak to the people about a way of life our country was struggling to achieve, and not frighten them to death.

"Mary Jane got to stay on in Olinka; her school grew. The people made allowances for my behavior and essentially forgave me, as they are wont to do. Besides, they came to appreciate Mary Jane's contribution to their children's and their country's future. But the government, really just the idiot head of the Ministry of Home Affairs, visited the M'Sukta School and demanded that the buildings be constructed of 'modern ingredients.' Tin and plywood. This was his perverted response to our successful maneuvers. All the children's murals were smashed, and with them the traditional character of the school. But Mary Jane and her staff were undaunted. Oh, they cried, we all cried, for weeks. But they had a vision of what the future they were working toward must be. It looked an awful lot like what they already had together every day. This was a hard spirit to smash. I was delighted to be a small part of it.

"And," said Ola finally, with a deep sigh, getting to his feet, as

Fanny, coming out of the eagle pose, stood solidly once more on hers, "there I was married to a white woman I barely knew, who rapidly became less white to me. We became staunch friends and allies, and so we remain to this day."

"And you never . . . tried anything?" asked Fanny, smiling, but with an insatiable curiosity about her father's life.

"Tried anything!" said Ola. "I wouldn't have dared. Mary Jane—wait till you meet her—she's got a glance that could chop one off at the knees."

MARY Jane Briden—Miss B to all—was a dead ringer for Joanne Woodward as she'd appeared in the last movie of hers Fanny had seen—something about a husband falling in love with a younger woman, and sharing a secret life with her, and a child, and dying, and leaving his wife with this betrayal on her hands. She had that same wide mouth, flat teeth, and level, controlled voice. Under which, though, the hearer could suspect a layer or two of hysteria. She had cool gray eyes, and her white hair was cut in a bob that looked a great deal like a wig, slightly askew, and dyed an almost gentian blue.

"I didn't go to Ola's funeral," Miss B was saying. "I couldn't bear to sit there while all the people who hated his guts went on about how much they'd valued him and how much he's going to be missed! Like hell he's going to be missed," she said, taking a drink of whiskey from the water tumbler she held in her hand. "He's going to be missed, all right. There's no one left to speak up to the government now. Nobody with any power, anyhow; the women will always rouse themselves to tell the boys what time of day it is . . . I didn't need to go to the funeral; Ola and I had already said our good-byes. He died here, at my house. You didn't know?"

"No," said Fanny, "I didn't."

"He was in the middle of rehearsals for his new play, the one about the Olinka, black and white, middle class. About how these people, with the government's blessing, are permitting the country to grow as divided along class lines as it was under the whites along color lines. It was to be the first of his outright satires, he said." She laughed. "He always claimed the middle class wasn't suitable material for drama; only comedy, or, not even comedy but satire and farce.

"That's what he was saying when he had the heart attack. A pretty innocuous comment, but I suppose it called into question his own life.

"Later, when we brought him up here to the house—rehearsals take place in the school gym—and placed him on the couch—yes, where you're sitting—he was still trying to talk, to joke. But at the very end he said a very sober thing to me, and to the actors who'd gathered around. He said that at the moment he was speaking he had a sudden realization of how endless struggle is. That it is like the layers of an onion, and smelly, too, he said, and made one cry, and that each time he sat down to write a play he was surprised, and a bit disheartened, to see he'd simply arrived at a new layer of stinking suffering that the people were enduring. They'd had such dreams, he said, when he and his friends went off to join the Mbeles. They thought that removing the whites from power would be the last of their work to insure a prosperous future for their country. Instead, it had proved only a beginning. Not, however, a small one; for that he was grateful. But still, only a start.

"Now, he saw, it was not racism alone that must be combatted, but also stupidity and greed, qualities which, unfortunately, had a much longer human history." Miss B paused.

"He'd been particularly upset," she said, and then pressed her lips together as if she'd rather not continue, but did, "in the weeks just before he died, by a rumor going around that Western Europe and the Soviet Union were clandestinely selling, for burial in Africa, millions of tons of radioactive waste to dozens of poor countries, Olinka included." She drew in a long breath, expelled it. She glanced at Fanny to see how she would take the blow.

Fanny groaned, and tears of hurt and rage leaped to her eyes. It had never occurred to her that this news might be only a rumor. As soon as she'd heard it, she knew it was true, just as Ola would have known.

"Ola was incensed that Africans could be collaborators in this long-term—forever, really—destruction of their continent and their children," Miss B said. "If true, he considered the buying and burying of this material a worse crime against Africa than even the selling of Africans by Africans during the slave trade." Miss B looked at Fanny, then looked quickly out the window toward the mountains. "And of course," she added, "the motives of the white governments involved are, as always, unspeakable."

Fanny spread her fingers over the edge of the cushion on which she sat. It was a tawny velvet sofa, like the hide of a lion. She thought of Ola, stretched out there, talking. Perhaps struggling for breath.

"In which direction was he facing?" she asked.

"Toward the window," said Miss B. "He was a frequent visitor here and had favorite views. He was my husband, legally; did you know that?"

Fanny nodded that she did.

"From the couch you can easily see the Dgoro mountains. He loved to lie here, look out at them, and think of his plays. I would make tea, and we'd sit and sip, in silence."

Fanny wiped a tear from her cheek.

"Your hair," she said, for something to say, "is the most startling shade of blue."

"I know it," said Miss B, laughing. "I assure you it isn't at all natural. Not at all. It's a color I've always loved and, as a painter, I learned to mix it myself. The one thing I liked about my old life in America was the deep blue of the delphiniums in our garden. Well, delphiniums won't grow here, but the color seems to do quite well on my head. It gives me something of the feeling of *being* a delphinium." She laughed again. "And my students, especially the little new, scared ones, who've never been anywhere but in the alleys or the bush, tend to like it. They like the strangeness of it. It's a kind of human zebra to them. I believe if there's one thing given us as human beings strictly as a play toy, it's hair," she said.

"Thank you for all that you've meant to my father," said Fanny. "I'd no idea a white person, especially a white woman, would touch upon my own life so—meaningfully."

Miss B returned Fanny's scrutinizing look with a searching look of her own. Perhaps she could see, Fanny thought, what stuntedness of perception North America had taught her in regard to other human beings, who might be white.

"We all touch upon each other's lives in ways we can't begin to imagine," Miss B said dryly.

"Yes," said Fanny, rising from the tawny sofa, preparing to go. In the back of her knees she suddenly felt the spring of her father's scrawny legs. She looked out at the mountains he'd loved, and worshiped them with his eyes.

As if she suddenly saw Ola himself standing before her, Miss B embraced her. Fanny was both startled and pleased.

"How long will you be in Africa?" she asked.

"I must leave soon," said Fanny. "There is a man back in California with whom I share a bond. But I will be back. Perhaps he will come with me. My sister, Nzingha, will want to mount productions of Ola's plays, and write her own, I suspect. She says I must come back to help her. Two Nzinghas, you see, being better than one. She swears she expects to have to fight this government for forty years, just as our namesake fought the Portuguese."

"She knows whereof she speaks," said Miss B.

"Do you think they'll harm her if she produces Ola's plays?" asked Fanny, frowning, and turning back at the door.

Miss B considered this. "Maybe not," she said, in her flat North American voice. "After all, Ola himself is dead; the plays already written will benefit, as far as the government is concerned, from his absence. To expose the authenticity of their grief over his demise, and to impress the world community that loved him, they will probably beg Nzingha to mount some of Ola's plays in his memory. Some of those *not* about taxation without representation, *not* about the oppression of women, *not* about violence by the government against the people, *not* about the smug middle class, *not* about the brutalization of the poor, *not* about the barbarity of the military, *not* about nuclear-waste dumpings . . . Umm," she said, "it'll be interesting to see what they do want produced."

Fanny laughed. She could just imagine Ola running down this list and making the same observation.

"The plays that are likely to enrage the censors—none of whom, no doubt, will ever have read a play—will probably be Nzingha's own. Or yours, if you decide to come back and write some. Nothing is harder for the men in power than to contemplate what the African woman knows. And to have *two* African women tell them!" She laughed.

"Well," said Fanny. "I guess that's that! The only question remaining is this one: If and when Nzingha and I do write the sons and daughters of our father's loathsome plays, can we perform them in your gymnasium?"

"Surely," said Miss B, smiling and waving good-bye to Fanny as she drove away in one of the government's little gray cars. She was thinking that perhaps she would also, when Nzingha and Fanny were producing their works, write a play. For her own amusement. Just for her students and herself. Just to surprise Nzingha and Fanny. She would name it something like "Recuerdo," or perhaps "The Coming Age," or perhaps "Eleandra and Eleanora," or maybe "M'Sukta," or "The Savage in the Stacks," or maybe "Zedé and Carlotta." Or perhaps — just "Carlotta."

H ELLO, son."
It was Miss Lissie's voice, yet deeper, and weaker,
older, than Suwelo remembered it. He adjusted the volume on
the cassette player and sat down on the couch in front of it. On
the left side of the sofa he'd set up his projector and filled it
with the slides of Miss Lissie's work that Mr. Hal had sent him.
After listening to her speak, he would have a look.

"By the time you get this," Miss Lissie's deep voice continued, "I will be somewhere and someone else. I have asked Hal
to send it to you only upon my death, to which I almost look
forward, knowing as I do that it is not the end, and being someone who enjoys hanging around, in spite of myselves. I regret
leaving Hal, and am anxious as to our chances of coming together again; but that is all I do regret, and I have every faith
we will meet again, and no doubt soon. For Hal and I have a
lot more stuff to work out, and though we have been at it for so
many years, and it's been hard labor, I can tell you, we've only
just begun.

"Remember that song? I've come to believe that people's
songs are their most truthful creations, when they're real
songs, not pap. Or sometimes, even when they're pap, they tell

the truth, but it isn't the truth the singers think they are telling. But before I talk about me and Hal, let me make a few observations about you.

"After you left us last summer and went back to California, I kept thinking about you, and looking at the painting of you that I'd done—Hal did one almost identical to it—that showed you surrounded by all the beauties of this life, the flowers, the corn, the ivy, the trees, the welcoming and sheltering house of your two old friends, you, asleep. Well, you *were* asleep; so there's truth, fidelity to reality in our pictures. But as I thought more about you and your time in Rafe's house and your time spent with us, I began to think about the ways in which both Hal and I feel you really are asleep.

"Terribly damaged human beings, especially if they were once beautiful and whole, are hard for people to remember by talking about. So it has been with you about your father. The war, the loss of much of his soul, the loss of his arm. The wearing down of your mother. What I'm saying, Suwelo, is that Hal and I are sorry we did not encourage you to speak to us about your parents; we regret we did not offer whatever memories we have—they are few, unfortunately—or anything that we'd heard or knew. That you did not speak of your parents, of the 'accident' that made you an orphan while you were still such a young person, seemed to us very odd, when we thought about it. I know you are caught up now in this knottedness with Fanny, and both Hal and I agree that the work with her is what has to be done. But part of your work with Fanny is the work you must do with your parents. They must be consciously called up, called *upon*, re-called. How they lived; but why and how they died, as well. Even the make and model of the car in which they died. Even the style of your father's haircut, the color of your mother's dress. The last time you stood over them.

"Hal and I felt you have "closed a door, a very important door, against memory, against the pain. That just to say their names, 'Marcia' and 'Louis,' is too heavy a key for your hand. And we urge you to open that door, to say their names. To speak of them, anything you can remember, freely and often, to Fanny. To trace what you can recognize in yourself back to them; to find the connection of spirit and heart you share with them, who are, after all, your United Front. For really, Suwelo, if our parents are not present in us, consciously present, there is much, very much about ourselves we can never know. It is as if our very flesh is blind and dumb and cannot truly feel itself. Intuition is given little validation; instinct is feared. We do not know what to trust, seeing none of ourselves in action beyond our own bodies. This is why adopted children will do anything to find their true parents. And, more important, the doors into the ancient past, the ancient self, the preancient current of life itself, remain closed. When this happens, crucial natural abilities are likely to be inaccessible to one: the ability to smile easily, to joke, to have fun, to be serious, to be thoughtful, to be limber of limb.

"Where Carlotta is concerned, the task is not difficult—or perhaps it will prove more difficult—because she is still alive. You are right to understand, as I know you now do, that it is a sin to behave as if a person whose body you use is a being without substance. 'Sin' being denial of another's reality of who and what she or he actually is. You can still go to her, as you must, for your own growth, and ask her forgiveness. Express to her something of your own trauma, which may have its origin in your mother's abandoned and suffering face, and the fear this caused you about knowing too much of women's pain, and tell her something of what you have learned.

"It is against blockage between ourselves and others—those who are alive and those who are dead—that we must work. In blocking off what hurts us, we think we are walling ourselves off from pain. But in the long run the wall, which prevents growth, hurts us more than the pain, which, if we will only bear it, soon passes over us. Washes over us and is gone. Long will we remember pain, but the pain itself, as it was at that point of intensity that made us feel as if we must die of it, eventually vanishes. Our memory of it becomes its only trace. Walls remain. They grow moss. They are difficult barriers to cross, to get to others, to get to closed-down parts of ourselves."

Miss Lissie cleared her throat.

"I am running on about this, Suwelo, because it is important, and true, but also because I am afraid to tell you how I know all this, to tell you my own news. Which is"—and here she took a long, slow breath—"that I lied when I told you I have always been a black woman, and that I can only remember as far back as a few thousand years.

"Of course I was from time to time a white woman, or as white as about half of them are. I won't bore you with tales of the centuries I spent sitting around wondering which colored woman would do my floors. Our menfolks were bringing them in all the time. You'd go to sleep one night brotherless, husbandless, fatherless, and in the morning more than likely one of them would be back. He'd be leading a string of some of the wretchedest-looking creatures you ever saw. Black, brown, red. Sometimes they looked like Mongols or Chinese. You never knew where in the world they came from. And he wouldn't tell you. 'Got you some help,' was the most he'd say, dropping his end of the chain next to where he kept the dogs tied.

"He'd stick some savagely gorgeous trinket on my neck or arm, surely made by witchcraft, I'd think, but silver or, more likely, gold, and start looking about for breakfast.

"I knew what a lady was supposed to do. I clutched the front of my wrapper shut and went to inspect the savages. I always turned up my nose and made a pukey motion toward their filthy hair. They were so beaten they could barely look at me.

"Over time, if *he* didn't pawn it, the thing on my neck or arm would start talking to me. Especially whenever one of *them* looked at it. It took me years to understand that they knew that on my careless skinny, or fat, white arm I was wearing all the history, art, and culture of their own people that they and their children would ever see."

There was a pause. "Gold," said Miss Lissie thoughtfully, "the white man worships gold because it is the sun he has lost."

There was another pause, during which Suwelo leaned forward slightly and stared into the cassette spinning noiselessly round and round. In a moment, Miss Lissie drew in a labored breath and continued.

"Let me tell you a story," she said. "It is a dream memory, too, like the one I told you about my life with the cousins; but it is more tenuous even than that one, more faded. Weak. And that has been deliberate. I have repressed it for all I am worth. Regardless, it is still with me, because, like the other memories, it *is* me."

She paused, coughed, and said, "This was very long ago, indeed."

Suwelo leaned back against the cushions of the couch, put his feet up on the coffee table in front of him, and placed his hands behind his head.

He thought he was ready.

"We lived at the edge of an immense woods," said Miss Lissie, "in the kind of houses, made of straw, that people built; insubstantial, really flimsy little things, somewhat fanciful, like an anthill or a spider's web, thrown up in a hour against the sun. My mother was queen of our group; a small group or tribe we were. Never more than a couple of hundred of us, sometimes fewer. But she was not 'queen' in the way people think of queens today. No, that way would have been incomprehensible to her, and horrid. I suppose she was what queens were originally, though: a wise woman, a healer, a woman of experience and vision, a woman superbly trained by her mother. A really good person, whose words were always heard by the clan.

"My mother kept me with her at all times, and she was always stroking me, rubbing into my skin various ointments she'd concocted from the flesh of berries and nuts that she found. As a small child I didn't notice anything wrong about spending so much time with my mother, nor was it ever unpleasant. Quite the contrary, in fact. Her familiar was an enormous and very much present lion; they went everywhere together. This lion also had a family of his own. There was a lot of visiting between us, and in the lion's little family of cubs I was always welcome.

"This perhaps sounds strange to you, Suwelo. About the lions, I mean. But it is true. This was long, long ago, before the animals had any reason to fear us and none whatever to try to eat us, which—the thought of eating us—I'm sure would have made them sick. The human body has been recognized as toxic, by the animals, for a very long time.

"In the Bible I know there's a line somewhere about a time in the future when the earth will be at peace and the lion will lie down with the lamb. Well, that has already happened, and eventually it was to the detriment of the lion.

"In these days of which I am speaking, people met other animals in much the same way people today meet each other. You were sharing the same neighborhood, after all. You used the same water, you ate the same foods, you sometimes found yourself peering out of the same cave waiting for a downpour to stop. I think my mother and her familiar had known each other since childhood; for that was the case with almost everyone. All the women, that is. For, strange to say, the women alone had familiars. In the men's group, or tribe, there was no such thing. Eventually, in imitation of the women and their familiars, companions, friends, or whatever you want to call them, the men learned to tame the barbarous forest dog and to get the occasional one of those to more or less settle down and stay by their side. I do not mean to suggest that the dogs were barbarous in the sense that we sometimes think of animals today as being 'red in tooth and claw.' No, they were barbarous because they simply lacked the sensibility of many of the other animals—of the lions, in particular; but also of the elephants and turtles, the vultures, the chimpanzees, the monkeys, orangutans, and giant apes. They were opportunistic little creatures, and basically lazy, sorely lacking in integrity and self-respect. Also, they lacked culture.

"It was an elegant sight, I can tell you, my mother and Husa walking along the river, or swimming in it. He was gigantic, and so beautiful. I am talking now about his spirit, his soul. It is a great tragedy today that no one knows anymore what a lion is. They think a lion is some curiosity in a zoo, or some wild thing that cares about tasting their foul flesh if they get out of the car in Africa.

"But this is all nonsense and grievous ignorance; as is most of what 'mankind' fancies it 'knows.' Just as my mother was queen because of her wisdom, experience, ability to soothe and to heal, because of her innate delicacy of thought and circumspection of action, and most of all because of her gentleness, so it was with Husa and his tribe. They were king of creation not because they were strong, but because they were strong and also gentle. Except to cull the sick or injured creatures from the earth, and to eat them, which was their role in creation, just as it is the role of the vulture to eat whatever has already died, they never used their awesome strength.

"We had fire by then. I say this because it was a recent in-

vention; my mother's grandmother had not had it. Husa and
his family would come of an evening to visit; they loved the
fire; and there we'd all sprawl watching the changing embers
and admiring the flames, well into the night, when we fell fast
asleep. My mother and I slept close to Husa, and in the morning's chill his great heat warmed us.

"So I was not lonely, though at times I saw that other children regarded me strangely. But then, being children, they'd
frequently play with me. I loved this. Our playing consisted
very often of finding some new thing to eat. And we would
roam for miles in search of whatever was easy to reach and ripe.
It seemed to me there was everything anyone could imagine,
and more than enough for twenty human and animal tribes
such as ours. I wish the world today could see our world as it
was then. It would see the whole tribe of creation climbing an
enormous plum tree. The little brown and black people, for I
had not yet seen myself as different; the monkeys, the birds,
and the things that today have vanished but which were bright
green and sort of a cross between a skunk and a squirrel. There
we'd be, stuffing ourselves on plums—little and sweet and
bright yellow. Husa would let us stand on his back to reach the
high inner branches. If we were eating for a long time, Husa
would lie on the ground yawning, and when we were full, the
monkeys, especially, would begin a game, which was to throw
plums into Husa's yawning mouth. It was curious to see that no
matter how rapidly we threw the plums into his mouth, Husa
never swallowed one and never choked. He could raise the back
of his tongue, you see, like a kind of trapdoor, and the plums all
bounced off it.

"What does not end, Suwelo? Only life itself, in my experience. Good times, specific to a time and place, always end. And
so it was with me. The time arrived when I was expected to
mate. In our group this was the initiation not only into adult-

hood, but into separation from the women's tribe — at least
from the day-to-day life of it that was all one had ever known.
After mating and helping his mate to conceive, a man went to
live with men. But this was not a hardship, since the men's encampment was never more than half a day's journey from our
own, and there was always, between the two tribes, the most
incessant visiting. Why didn't they, men and women, merge?
It simply wasn't thought of. People would have laughed at the
person who suggested it. There was no reason why they should
merge, since each tribe liked the arrangement they had. Besides, everyone — people and other animals — liked very much
to visit. To be honest, we loved it. That was our TV. And so it
was well to have other people and other animals *to* visit.

"Though I hated the thought of leaving my mother, I knew
I could still see her whenever I wanted to, and I also knew that
the men in the men's tribe were ready to be my father. For no
one had a particular father. That was impossible, given the way
the women chose their lovers, freely and variously. The men
found nothing strange in this, any more than the women did.
Why should they? Lovemaking was considered one of the very
best things in life, by women and men; of course it would have
to be free. See what I mean about songs?" Miss Lissie chuckled.
"Besides, when a young man arrived in the tribe of the men,
they were at long last given an opportunity — late, it's true — to
mother. Fathering *is* mothering, you know.

"There was a girl I liked, who liked me back. This was a miracle. And at the proper time, the day before the coming up of
the full moon, she and I were sent to pick plums together. I remember everything about that day: the warmth of the sun on
our naked bodies, the fine dust that covered our feet. . . . Her
own little familiar, a serpent, slid alongside us. Serpents then
were different than they are now, Suwelo. Of course almost
everything that was once free is different today. Her familiar,

whom my friend called Ba, was about the thickness of a slender person's arm and had small wheel-like extendable feet, on
which it could raise itself and whir about, like some of those
creatures you see in cartoons; or, retracting these, it could
move like snakes move today. It could also extend and retract
wings, for all serpents that we knew of at that time could fly. It
was a lovely companion for her, and she loved it dearly and was
always in conversation with it. I remember the especially convoluted and wiggly trail Ba left behind in the dust, in its happy
anticipation of eating fresh plums. . . . Later that day there was
the delicious taste of sun-warmed plums in our mouths. We
were, all three of us, chattering right along, and eating, and
feeling very happy.

"I was not to be happy long; none of us was. Eventually I
had my friend in my arms, and one of her small black nipples,
as sweet as any plum and so like my mother's, was in my mouth,
and I was inside her. It was everything I'd ever dreamed, and
much more than I'd hoped. But it was not, I think, the same for
her. When I woke up, she was wide awake, simply sitting there
quietly, stroking Ba, who was lazily twisting his full self around
and around her beautiful knees. The sun was still above the
treetops, for I remember that the light was golden, splendidly
perfect, but even as I watched, it began rapidly going down.

"And then, when I looked down at myself, I saw that while
I was sleeping she had rubbed me all over with the mixture of
dark berries and nut fat my mother always used, which I realized had been hidden beneath the plum tree. And for the first
time I could ask someone other than my mother what it was
for. My mother had said it was to make my skin strong and protect it from the sun. And so, I asked my friend. And *she* said it
was to make me look more like everyone else.

" 'You look like you don't have a skin, you know,' she said.
'But you do have one.'

"I was thrown completely by this, coming as it did after our first lovemaking. It seemed to indicate a hideous personal deficiency that I didn't need to hear about just then, on the eve of becoming a man in the tribe of men. Right away I thought: Is this how they'll see me as well?

"She took me gently by the hand and we walked to a clear reflecting pool not far away. We'd often bathed there. And she scooped up a handful of water and vigorously scrubbed my face; then we bent down over the water, and there my friend was, looking very much like my mother and her mother and the sisters and brothers and aunts of the village—all browns and blacks, with big dark eyes. And there was I—a ghost. Only, we knew nothing of ghosts, so I could not even make that comparison. I did look as though I had no skin.

"It was the first time I'd truly seen myself as different. I cried out in fear at myself. Weeping, I turned and ran. My friend came running after me. For it had not been her intention to hurt. She was taking over my mother's duty in applying the ointment, and was only trying to be truthful and help me begin to face reality.

"All I could think of was hiding myself—my kinky but pale yellow hair, the color of straw in late summer, my pebble-colored eyes, and my skin that had no color at all. I ran to a cave I knew about not far from the plum tree. And I threw myself on the floor, crying and crying.

"She came in behind me, the mess of berries and nut fat in a bamboo-joint container in her hand. She tried to talk to me, to soothe me, to spread the stuff over me. I knocked it away from me; it rolled over the earthen floor. During this movement, I suddenly caught sight of my member and saw that the color that had been there before we made love had been rubbed off during our contact. The sight shamed me. I ran outside the cave and grabbed the first tree leaves I saw and slapped them over myself.

"But then I realized it was my whole body that needed covering, not just my penis. My friend was still running around behind me, trying to comfort me. She was crying as much as I was, and beating her breasts. For we learned mourning from the giant apes, who taught us to feel grief anywhere around us, and to reflect it back to the sufferer, and to act it out. But now this behavior made me sick. I picked up a stick and chased her away. She was so shocked to see me use a stick in this way that she seemed quite happy to drop her sympathies for me and run. But as she turned to run, her familiar, seeing her fright and its cause, extended both its clawed feet and its wings and flew up at me. In my rage I struck it, a brutal blow, with my club, so hard a blow that I broke its neck, and it fell without a sound to the ground. I couldn't believe I had done this. Neither could my friend. She ran back, though she was so afraid, and scooped Ba's broken body up in her arms. The last I saw of her was her small, naked, dark brown back, with Ba's limply curling tail, which was beginning to change colors, dangling down her side.

"I never made it into the men's tribe. I never went back to my mother. The only one from my childhood I ever saw again was Husa. Perhaps he came to look for me as a courtesy to my mother. He found me holed up in a cave far, far from our encampment, my hair in kinky yellow locks, which resembled his, actually; my stone gray eyes wild with pain. He came up to me and rested a warm paw on my shoulder and breathed gently into my face. The smell made me almost faint from love and homesickness. Then he proceeded to lick me all over, thoroughly, as he would wash one of his cubs, with his warm pink tongue. I realized that night, sleeping next to Husa, that he was the only father I had ever known or was ever likely to know. And so, I felt, I had left my mother to join the men after all.

"Of course Husa could not stay forever. But he stayed long enough. Long enough to go on long walks with me, just as he did with my mother. Long enough to share fires—which I knew he loved, and so forced myself to make. Long enough to share sunrises and sunsets and to admire giant trees and sweet-smelling shrubs. For Husa greatly appreciated the tiniest particle of the kingdom in which he found himself. He taught me that there was another way of being in the world, away from one's own kind. Indeed, he reconciled me to the possibility that I had no 'own kind.' And though I missed my mother terribly, I knew I would never go back. It hurt me too much to know that everyone in our group had always noticed, since the day I was born, that I was different from anyone who had ever lived.

"One day, after a kill, Husa brought the remains, a draggle of skin, home to me. With a stone I battered it into a shape that I could drape around myself. I found a staff to support me in my walks and to represent 'my people.'

"Husa left.

"And now I gradually made a discouraging discovery. The skin that Husa gave me, which covered me so much more effectively than bark or leaves, and which I could tie on in a manner that would stay, frightened all the animals with whom I came in contact. In vain did I try to explain how I came by it, how much I needed it. That it was a gift, a leftover, from Husa the lion, who harmed no creature, ever, but was only the angel of mercy to those things in need of death. But what animal could comprehend this new thing that I was? That I, a creature with a skin of its own—for though I looked skinned, they could smell I was not—was nonetheless walking about in one of theirs? They ran from me as if from plague. And I was totally alone for many years, until, in desperation, I raided the litter of a barbarous dog, and got myself companionship in that way."

THE tape ran on and on, without Miss Lissie's voice. Suwelo rose from the couch and peered at the spinning cassette. He was about to stop it, and see if it should be turned over, when Miss Lissie's voice continued. She sounded somewhat rested, as if she'd taken a long break.

"You may wonder," she said, "why I repressed this memory. And, by the way, I don't know what else became of me, or of my dog. It is hard to believe my mother never searched for me, never found me. That I lived the rest of my days in that place without a mate. Perhaps my mate did come to me, and perhaps she brought our child, which must have been odd-looking; for she loved me, of that I had no doubt, and perhaps we began a new tribe of our own. That, anyway, is *my* fantasy." She laughed. "It is also the fantasy upon which the Old Testament rests," she said, "but without any mention of our intimacy with the other animals or of the brown and black colors of the rest of my folks.

"I will tell you why I repressed this memory. I repressed it because of Hal. But, Suwelo, there is more; for that is not the only lifetime I have given up, or, I should say, that I have deliberately taken away from myself. In each lifetime I have felt

forced to shed knowledge of other existences, other lives. The
times of today are nothing, nothing, like the times of old. The
time of writing is so different from the so much longer time of
no writing. People's very eyes are no longer the same. The time
of living separate from the earth is so much different from the
much longer time of living with it, as if being on your mother's
breast. Can you imagine a time when there was no such thing
as dirt? It is hard for people to comprehend the things that I
remember. Even Hal, the most empathetic of fellow travelers,
up to a point, could not follow some of the ancient and pre-ancient paths I knew. I swallowed past experiences all my life, as
I divulged those that I thought had a chance, not of being believed—for no one has truly, truly believed me; at least that is
my feeling, a bitter one, most of the time—but of simply being
imagined, fantasied.

"Suwelo, in addition to being a man, and white, which I was
many times after the time of which I just told you, I was also,
at least once, myself a lion. This is one of those dream memories so frayed around the edges that it is like an old, moth-
eaten shawl. But I can still sometimes feel the sun on my fur,
the ticks in my mane, the warm swollen fullness of my tongue.
I can smell the injured and dying kin who are in need of me
to bring them death. I can feel the leap in my legs, the stretch
in my belly, as I bound toward them and stun them, in great
mercy, with a blow. I can taste the sweet blood as my teeth
puncture their quivering necks, breaking them instantly, and
without pain. All of this knowledge, all of this remembrance, is
just back of my brain.

"But the experiences I best remember were sometime after
the life in which I knew Husa. It was, in fact, a terrible, cha-
otic time, though it had started out, like the eternity everyone
knew, peacefully enough. Like Husa I was friends with a
young woman and her children. We grew up together and fre-

quently shared our favorite spots in the forest, or stared by night into the same fire. But this way of life was rapidly ending, for somehow or other by the time I was fully grown, and big, as lions tend to be, the men's camp and the women's had merged. And they had both lost their freedom to each other. The men now took it on themselves to say what should and should not be done by all, which meant they lost the freedom of their long, undisturbed, contemplative days in the men's camp; and the women, in compliance with the men's bossiness, but more because they now became emotionally dependent on the individual man by whom man's law now decreed they must have all their children, lost their wildness, that quality of homey ease on the earth that they shared with the rest of the animals.

"In the merger, the men asserted themselves, alone, as the familiars of women. They moved in with their dogs, whom they ordered to chase us. This was a time of trauma for women and other animals alike. Who could understand this need of men to force us away from woman's fire? And yet, this is what they did. I remember the man and the dog who chased me away; he had a large club in one hand, and in the other, a long, sharply pointed stick. And how sad I was to leave my friend and her children, who were crying bitterly. I think I knew we were experiencing one of the great changes in the structure of earth's life, and it made me very sorrowful, but also very thoughtful. I did not know at the time that man would begin, in his rage and jealousy of us, to hunt us down, to kill and eat us, to wear our hides, our teeth, and our bones. No, not even the most cynical animal would have dreamed of that. Soon we would forget the welcome of woman's fire. Forget her language. Forget her feisty friendliness. Forget the yeasty smell of her and the warm grubbiness of her children. All of this friendship would be lost, and she, poor thing, would be left with just man, screaming for his dinner and forever murdering her friends, and with man's 'best friend,' the 'pet' familiar, the fake familiar, his dog.

"Poor woman!

"But to tell you the truth, Suwelo, I was not sorry to go. For I was a lion. To whom harmony, above everything, is sacred. I could see that, merged, man and woman were in for an eternity of strife, and I wanted no part of it. I knew that, even if man had let us remain beside woman's fire he would be throwing his weight around constantly, and woman being woman, every so often would send pots and pans flying over our heads; this would go on forever. An unbearable thought; as a lion, I could not bear loud noises, abrupt changes in behavior, voices raised in anger. *Evilness.* No lion could tolerate such things. It is our nature to be nonviolent, to be peaceful, to be calm. And ever to be fair in our dealings; and I knew this would be impossible in the present case, since the animals, except for the barbarous dogs, clearly preferred woman, and would always have been attempting to defend her. Lions felt that, no matter the circumstance, one must be dignified. In consorting with man, as he had become, woman was bound to lose her dignity, her integrity. It was a tragedy. But it was a fate lions were not prepared to share.

"In subsequent periods lions moved farther and farther away from humans, in search of peace. There were tribes with whom we kept connections, in that we taught, and they learned from us. What did they learn? They learned that rather than go to war with one's own kind it was better to pack up and remove oneself from the site of contention. That as long as there is space in which to move there is a possibility of having uncontested peace. There are tribes living today in South Africa who have never come to blows with each other for a thousand years. It is because of what they learned from the lions.

"For thousands of years our personalities were known by

all and appreciated. In a way, we were the beloved 'uncles' and 'aunts' — interesting visitors, indulgent playmates, superb listeners, and thoughtful teachers — of the human tribe, which, fortunately, could never figure out, not for a long, long time, anyhow, any reason why we should be viewed as completely different from them and separate from them. Only gradually did we fade into myth — all that was known of us previously, that is. The last people on earth who had any real comprehension of our essence are themselves faded into myth, but at least before they faded completely they erected the sphinx. . . . There are also" — Miss Lissie chuckled — "those accounts one hears of the free-roaming lions that frequently startled visitors to Haile Selassie's palace in Ethiopia. It never occurred to anyone of his ancient lineage that lions should be anything but free. Dreadlocked Rastas who made it inside the courtyard were sometimes so frightened on meeting one of these lions — their ancient totem, strolling about like they were — that their locks literally stood on end.

"I realize, too, that there are more . . . intermediate stories," continued Miss Lissie, "that is to say, between the ancient and the current ones; such as 'Androcles and the Lion' and 'Daniel in the Lion's Den,' but already in those stories you can see that no one understood what was happening from the lion's point of view. It would have been unthinkable for the lion who had the thorn removed from his paw by Androcles to hurt the friend who removed it; it would never have crossed his mind to hurt him, period, whether he removed the damn thing or not. Likewise with Daniel. Even though the Romans were into torturing lions, so brutalizing them that in their hunger and rage they attacked the hapless Christians, to the frenzied cheers of the crowds, whenever they had the least chance to reflect, to remember who they were, they did nothing that could remotely be termed violent. Even though they were all hungry, starved almost to fainting by the Romans, Daniel had a perfectly safe and comfy night's sleep, with his head resting against one of their sides. They would also have objected to the rank odor of Daniel's toxicity.

"Now," said Miss Lissie, whose voice was again becoming tired, "there were but two things on earth Hal truly feared. He feared white people, especially white men, and he feared cats. The fear of the white man was less irrational than the fear of cats, but they were both very real fears to Hal. You could make him back up twenty miles simply by asking him to hold a cat. And he arranged his life so that if he ever saw a white man, it was by accident, and also very separate from his personal life, an unheralded and unwelcome event. So how could I tell him all of who I was? By now Hal is like my son to me, and I couldn't bear it if he hated me. For such fear as Hal's *is* hatred.

"And so, I never told him. How could I say it? *Yo*, Hal, I was a white man; more than once; they're probably still in there somewhere. *Yo*, Hal, I was also, once upon a time, a very large cat."

Miss Lissie chuckled. Then laughed and laughed. Suwelo did too. Her laughter was the last sound on that side of the tape.

"But if you love someone, you want to share yourself, or, in my case," said Miss Lissie—and Suwelo imagined her wiping her eyes, still smiling—"you want to share *yourselves*. But I was afraid. When Henry Laytrum brought the pictures that showed me faded almost to a ghost, pictures that lightened my hair and washed out my eyes, I tore them up; I said he'd used defective film. When he took other pictures in which I looked feline, really like Dorothy's companion in *The Wizard of Oz*, I tore them up too. Maybe there's always a part of the self that we hide, deny, deliberately destroy.

"But oh, how we love the person who affirms even that hateful part of us. And it was for affirming these split-off parts of my memory that I loved your uncle Rafe. Rafe, unlike Hal, was afraid of no one. He thought white people the most pathetic people who ever lived. Ruling over other people, he said, automatically cuts you off from life. And to try to rule over colored people, who, anybody could see, were life itself! He was more puzzled than annoyed when otherwise intelligent-looking and acting white people called him 'boy' or 'nigger.' He was always hoping for a little better from them than he ever got. But that was because he could easily see some of himself in them, though, when looking back at him, white people apparently saw . . . But he often wondered just *what* it was that they saw. What they let themselves see. Were they blind to his very *being*, as he himself was blind to the being of a fly? To him, their constant imperative to 'civilize' us was in fact a need to blind and deaden us to their own extent.

"I told Rafe everything; and he took me north, to Canada, in the summers, to be around white people; and he took me to more zoos than I have the heart to mention. This was part and parcel of his making love to me, you see, taking me to those places of which I was, myself, most afraid. You cannot imagine the feeling I had the first time I sat down to dinner in a restaurant that was filled with white people, white people who only stared at us and whispered among themselves, but did not, as they would have done in the South, rush to throw us out of the building, or perhaps beat us up or even lynch us.

"I remember that Rafe ordered meat. Some kind of duck, I think. And when it came, he saw the look on my face. I could never eat meat among white people; of that I was sure; my stomach heaved at the thought of it. Rafe and I ate mashed potatoes and salad, and he said to me, in that deep, caressing, *sweet* Negro voice of his: 'Well, Lissie, have a *good* look.'

"And I could see how they'd closed themselves off, these descendants, there at the 'top of the heap,' and how isolated they were. They were completely without wildness, and they had forgotten how to laugh. They had also forgotten, I was to discover on our many trips, how to dance and sing. They haunted black people's dance halls and churches, trying to 'pick up' what they'd closed off in themselves. It was pitiful. One of the people I most appreciated in the sixties, by the way, was Janis Joplin. She knew Bessie Smith was her momma, and she sang her guts out trying to tear open that closed door between them.

"In a way, I preferred the zoos. Though I hated them with all my heart, naturally. But at the zoo, at least there were no illusions about who was free and who was not. The lions were always in cages too small for them. And it had never occurred to anyone that, cut off from life year upon year, as they were, with nothing whatever to do, the least that could be done was to build them a fire. It was heartbreaking—to watch them pace, to smell the sour staleness of their coats and of their cells, to hear the hysteria in their roar, to watch them devour a perfectly healthy animal that had been raised for 'meat' and killed on an assembly line by machine. It was horrible. It was a fate the most imaginative and cynical pre-ancient lion could not have imagined. And now, as a presence in the modern world, I am thankful for this.

"The most abominable thing to see was their faces. Slack, dull, unintelligent, *unthoughtful*. Stupefied from boredom, gross from the degradation of dependency. To every zoo—colored could go even to the one in Baltimore, after a long struggle; but only on maid's day off, Thursday—I carried a large mirror. Anyone else would have thought this strange, but not Rafe. He helped me carry it and hold it up outside the cages. A restless lion would amble up to the bars and have a look at himself. This was usually the first and only look at himself he'd ever had. I held my breath.

"Would there be a flicker of recognition? Even of interest?

Did the lion inside the body of the lion see itself? Though I myself had the body of a woman, I could still see my lion inside. Would they see that? Would they see the old nobility, the old impatience with inferiors? The old grace?

"One or two of them saw something. But it only made them sad. They slunk back to a corner of their cages and put their heads down between their paws. Of course I wanted to leap through the bars to comfort them. I wanted to destroy the bars.

"Rafe carried me back home, a pitiful wreck, after these excursions, and put me to bed. He and Hal and Lulu would come in to kiss me good night; and when Rafe was turning to go, I would grasp his hand—such a good, steady, clean brown hand it was. He would sit down on the bed without a word and take off his shoes.

"Your uncle Rafe was an incomparable lover, Suwelo. And I have missed him so much, I have sometimes longed to meet up with him again, which I know is not likely; there is little need for him to come back. He loved the total me. None of my selves was hidden from him, and he feared none of them. Sometimes, when I would get 'on my high horse,' as he called it, when I was ordering everybody around and complaining that nobody knew anything or could do anything right but me, he'd grin and say, 'You sure are showing your white tonight!' And I'd feel how ridiculous I was being, and laugh.

"Or, sometimes at a party, I'd realize the other people were a bunch of lowlifes, and I'd leave. Just stroll out the door. Rafe would come after me and look at me prowling along the sidewalk aching for distance, and peace, and calm; disgust at the party's members still on my face, and he'd say, 'Baby, the lion in winter's got nothing on you!'

"And of course he knew and appreciated all the other selves, and could call them by name, too.

"So, loving Rafe and being loved by Rafe was the experience of many a lifetime. And very different from being loved by Hal, even when our passion for each other was at its height, Hal loved me like a sister/mystic/warrior/woman/mother. Which was nice. But that was only part of who I was. Rafe, on the other hand, knowing me to contain everybody and everything, loved me wholeheartedly, as a goddess. Which I was."

W HEN I saw Suwelo on the back steps of Arveyda's house, I did not know who he was," Carlotta cheerfully related to Fanny one day after they had become friends. "I was coming up from the guest house, where I live, which is down the path and across a ravine from the main house. Arveyda and the children live in the main house; the studio is on the bottom floor; so I am in and out of their space constantly. However, they must ask permission to enter mine. There is a little bridge over the ravine, just before you get to my little house, and at that bridge, before you cross over a culvert that channels a rushing waterfall during the rainy season, is the first gate. It has several little bells that must be rung. If nothing happens after the ringing of these little bells—no rocks are thrown at you, or shoes—the visitor, usually Arveyda or one of my children, may proceed to the next gate. This one has chimes. It is usually locked. If it isn't, the visitor strikes the chimes and comes through the gate and up my steps. There are still more bells and chimes at my door. I will come only in response to these bells and chimes, not to calls, words of any sort, or knocks on the door itself.

"So I am coming up to work in the studio, since I am now

a musician, a bell chimist. What is a bell chimist, everyone always asks. But there is a strange man at the back of the house,
quizzically knocking. I stop just at the wall of the house where
the daphne bushes are in full bloom and the odor is so sweet,
and I notice the purple clematis is about to riot over one corner
of the carport, which is up the cliff, hanging above my head. I
stop because when I am thinking about my music I cannot bear
to be disturbed — not by Arveyda or by the children, and certainly not by a wandering insurance salesman. Which is what
this man looks like — of course, a wandering insurance salesman in Berkeley. He's casually dressed in brown corduroy jeans
and a lovely burgundy sweater. Wearing an earring and some
kind of pendant on a chain.

"Just as I'm about to duck out of sight, he looks in my direction and spots me.

"Gracious God, I think, and shrug inwardly. My little notes
of music that I have been hoarding in my soul all night and
morning disappear.

"'Hell-o,' I say, frowning. 'What can I do for you?'

"The man is startled. His eyes — nice, big, open, and friendly
eyes — open wider.

"Am I such a shock, I wonder. Is it my hair, cut nearly to my
skull and standing out like a concentration-camp victim's? Or
is it my tight black running suit and teal Reeboks? Who cares?
This is Berkeley, after all.

"But he is still staring, and his jaw is still dropped.

"Then I first really look at him. To see him. When I'm working or thinking of work, or regretting work that has just been
assassinated, I don't look at people to see them. I look at them
just enough to deal with them and get them out of my life.
But I suddenly look at this tallish, gaunt figure, with closely
cropped hair. Oh, no, I think. It can't be!

"But it is.

" 'Suwelo?' I offer, as if to a ghost.

" 'Carlotta?' he says, making a funny whirring motion over his own shorn head to indicate my missing locks.

"After this, we don't know what to do. He is even more at sea than I am.

"What the hell, I think.

" 'We're here,' I say, 'let's go in.'

" 'Is this your house?' he asks. He can't believe it, if it is. 'I went over to your old place and no one around there knew anything. Just that you'd moved.'

" 'Yes, I moved,' I say. 'The children wanted to live with their father.'

"I push open the door. The smell of baking bread hits us at once.

" 'Baby, is that you?' Arveyda's homey voice calls from the kitchen.

" 'Yeah, it's me,' I call back.

"He comes up from the kitchen to see for himself. He is wearing his Brahms apron and his Satchmo Armstrong chef's hat. He is covered with flour and seems perfectly content. He glances at Suwelo before bending down to kiss me. He kisses me always as if he's tasting something yummy.

"My mood improves with this kiss, and I actually smile.

" 'Arveyda, meet Suwelo,' I say. 'And vice versa.'

"Cedrico, seeming taller than he was the day before yesterday, darts through the room and across our path, a monster piece of freshly baked bread in his hand, a glob of it in his mouth. Why he hasn't choked to death before today is beyond me. Angelita is close behind, looking like a miniature harlot, which is how all little girls her age look these days.

" 'Here, here, wait a minute,' says Arveyda, dragged off in spite of himself, following the ominous sounds of scraping chairs and clanging utensils that instantly emerge from the kitchen.

"I glance up at Suwelo, thinking what a disgrace my no-mannered children are, and I see that his jaw has dropped even lower.

" 'Is that . . . ? Isn't that . . . ?'

" 'Yes,' I say. 'That's *that*.'

"I usher him into the living room, where he sits heavily in a chair. 'I can't believe it,' he says. 'You were married to *Arveyda*.'

" 'I'm *still* married to *Arveyda*,' I say. 'But that bond is no longer the primary basis of our relationship.'

"Suwelo looks at me quizzically. Didn't he used to have bushy eyebrows? I think. Didn't he used to wear glasses?

" 'We work together now.'

"He raises an eyebrow. A thin one.

" 'As musicians.'

" 'Oh,' he says.

" 'When I saw you at the door, I was on my way down to the studio to work.'

" 'I'm sorry if I diverted you,' he says.

" 'Want to come see?' I ask. For though I have been temporarily diverted, I still need a peek at my companions, my babies, my instruments. Just to be sure they are there. Mine. And, no matter how long it takes, waiting for me.

" 'What a lovely smell,' Suwelo comments, sniffing, as we go down the stairs.

" 'Arveyda bakes every Saturday,' I say. 'At least every Saturday we're not on the road. It relaxes him.'

" '*Umm*,' says Suwelo. 'How much bread does he bake?'

" 'There's no set amount,' I say, as we pass the nice big picture of James Baldwin, where he looks like an angel who loves fresh bread, smiling down on all who enter the hall. 'He just gets up in the morning, puts on his Miles Davis, Roberta Flack, Bob Marley, or Aretha Franklin tapes, and starts in. He can bake all morning or he can bake most of the weekend. He always bakes just enough.'

"'But,' says Suwelo, looking with skepticism at my skinniness, 'four people can't eat so much bread!'

"'More than four people live on the streets of Berkeley,' I say. 'There is never the slightest *problema.*'

"Now we are in the studio: the big room with the smaller glass room inside it that I love better than any room in the world. I love all the instruments, the lights, the booths. I especially love my own instruments, which I lead Suwelo over to see.

"He is surprised. Puzzled. He looks out at the view. He looks where I'm standing.

"'So many bells!' he exclaims, looking at them. 'So many chimes!'

"He does not think these are the instruments he's been brought down to the studio to see. He looks over at the piano, the xylophone, the twelve guitars hanging on the wall, the cello, the drums, the flutes, and even the tambourines! We do have everything, I think proudly, and sometimes Arveyda *does* play gospel music. But actually I am about to begin to consider the tambourine a bell.

"'These are my instruments,' I say, striking a wind chime with its own clapper, a wind chime that hangs in a row of several dozen. There are wind chimes of all sizes, colors, and descriptions. Some are made of sandal or balsa wood, some of bamboo, some of metal. They are all beautiful, with sweet, clear tones. Then there are my hundreds of bells—reindeer-harness bells, cowbells, school bells, every kind of bell. From all over the world. I run through a dozen bells and chimes quickly, with a hardwood stick, and the whole room vibrates with the beautiful, clear, and gentle sounds.

"'You are smiling,' says Suwelo. 'You are happy!'

"'Yes,' I say. I do not stop smiling or being happy just because he's noticed it. I run through some more chimes with another little stick I have, and the sound makes me happier still. *Oh*, I think to myself, *when he leaves!*

"But he does not leave.

"He tells me he has come to make amends. To ask my forgiveness for the way he treated me.

"I almost have no memory of the way he treated me. He was only an episode in my life. But it is true, when he dropped me—and he did drop me—I was so destroyed, I was angry enough to kill."

WHY is Miles Davis so absolutely gorgeous, even though he looks like the devil," says Arveyda. He is holding up a record album that has a picture of his idol (one of many musicians that he loves) staring out, moodily, at the world. "It really is a puzzle," he says, almost inaudibly. "Now, if he were a very large man, and you met him somewhere at night, and he glowered at you like that—" he shivers—"he'd frighten you."

Carlotta laughs. "Are you sure?" she asks.

Arveyda has finished his baking for the day, and his dirty apron and chef's hat are in a heap on the floor beside the door.

He cuts large slices of whole-wheat bread for them and pushes the butter and jam closer to Suwelo's elbow.

Suwelo is rapidly overcoming his case of being star-struck. Besides, the wonderful smell of the bread is really making the saliva flow. He glances around the kitchen, which opens out into the dining and living rooms and on out to a deck. From where he sits, he can see most of the Bay, all the way to the Golden Gate Bridge; he is appreciative of the view as he takes his first bite of the delicious bread, as good as it smells.

"I've heard . . . a bit about you," says Arveyda. He does not remember what he's heard. He connects this man somehow with massage—Carlotta has learned to give massages, and massages him frequently. It is a skill he is himself learning, and enjoying, and one that permits him to touch Carlotta intimately without always pressuring her to make love. This has relieved a lot of the tension there used to be between them, because he has discovered that when a musician is working, he or she is already making love.

Suwelo looks across at Carlotta. She is still such a shock to him. Her hair is cut so short it must feel prickly to the touch. And she is so thin; even her breasts are smaller. But she is happy. This is the biggest surprise of all. Where is that wailing he remembered? the insecurity? the wringing of hands? the prayer? the gnashing of teeth?

She is taking out her gum—she pops it a couple of times to say good-bye—and begins to butter, thinly, a minuscule slice of bread.

"We were colleagues," says Suwelo, "on a certain academic plantation. By the way," he says to Carlotta, "you don't still teach . . . or do you?"

"No," she says, chewing, "I gave it up." She frowns slightly. "I grew frustrated, *and so fat.*" She tosses her head the way she used to when she had lots of hair. Suwelo catches a glimpse of her old self. Carlotta continues. "It's too late to teach people what they need to know by the methods that are used in colleges."

This is such an unexpected response from Carlotta that Suwelo laughs. She has even found a sense of humor!

"Cómo?" asks Arveyda, looking attentively at Carlotta. Having never been to college, he thinks it is something everyone prizes. That unless you've been to college you don't really know anything. You have experience only, he thinks, but without facts. This means that at dinner with college-trained people your stomach turns over and over.

"Oh," says Carlotta, "who needs more of the kind of people colleges produce? They're all consumers, really. No matter what they study, what they're successful at is shopping."

"What about your own courses?" asks Suwelo.

"It's true," she says, "I loved them. I love teaching women's literature. But I got tired of teaching it there. I wanted to teach it—if I continued teaching it—sitting in a circle in a meadow, where cows could just casually come up and look. Even join in."

"I'm learning carpentry now, myself," says Suwelo. "Though there the question is how does the carpenter relate to the worldwide exploitation, slaughter, and waste of trees."

"What do you mean?" asks Carlotta.

"Well, wood comes from trees. Trees are alive. They have a purpose separate from becoming houseboats, firewood, and decks."

"What did you teach?" asks Arveyda.

"American history," says Suwelo. He chuckles. "But I had to be stoned or drunk to pass on such lies. It was really a no-win situation."

"But you were a guerrilla historian," says Carlotta, loyally. "The same way I was a guerrilla literaturist. It isn't impossible to teach the alternative reality, especially when it's your own."

"But exhausting," says Suwelo. "And I was always mad. Think of the history books I've read that say, in so many words, these are all the folks you need to know about to understand America; and there's no one in them who relates to what you personally know of reality in any way."

"You always lost your Indian students," muses Carlotta. "I know I did. I finally began to say, at the very first class, 'Go out and find a story or poem by Joy Harjo or Leslie Silko. This class will study these writers before we're done, I promise you.'"

Arveyda laughs, admiring Carlotta. He reaches over and

pulls her foot up in his lap; he has to walk his stool over to hers in order to do this.

"I don't know much about literature, or history," he says apologetically, and sounds enough like an old Sam Cooke song that all three burst out laughing. "I read and read but I'm such a slow reader! I will never catch up!"

He is rubbing the back of Carlotta's leg. She is as contented as a cat.

Carlotta smiles. "Don't worry about it, chico mio," she says. "What all of us are trying to learn is what you already know."

Suwelo looks at him, this humble man who gives pleasure, unasked, to so many. Of the three of them he's the only one who has gained, not lost, weight. This comfortable, rather short, almost *little* man. With his kind eyes and graying, flyaway hair. Yes, Suwelo thinks, that is true. Perhaps.

WHAT is truly regrettable is how, as a musician, you tend to lose people as you go along. They want you to keep playing music that made them feel something once, something they think your old music will help them recapture. But really, if you are at all alive as an artist, you are somewhere else, other than where you were, almost constantly."

As he talks, Arveyda flings a glob of dough on the counter with shocking gusto. Flour flies up and dusts his beard. Opposite him, Suwelo lifts his lump of dough and brings it down just as hard. He is wearing a Bugs Bunny T-shirt and a red-and-black FSLN bandanna on his head. His jeans have slipped a bit and hang just at the level of his hip bones. He is also covered with flour and has an expression of severe and earnest intent.

"Relax," says Arveyda, taking a sip of fresh grape juice. "This is serious work, it's true; but, you know, most serious work can be fun."

Suwelo thinks of making love to Fanny. How there is always a point now at which she laughs.

Arveyda is moving about the messy kitchen, tossing eggshells into the compost pot, mopping up spills, clearing a space on the counter next to the oven, greasing bread pans, and continuing to mutter, to whistle, and to talk.

He puts on a tape that is all bells and chimes and hums a bit as he resumes pounding his loaf. There is a heavy yeast smell in the air. And then, from pure whimsy, it seems to Suwelo, Arveyda reaches into a bin and pulls out raisins and walnuts and begins folding them into the dough.

Suwelo, happily conscious of being an apprentice, follows suit.

"They say, 'Oh, you have betrayed us! Why don't you play the stuff we're used to and that we expect from you? This shit you play now sounds like Elton John! What about your fucking roots?'"

Arveyda pounds his loaf and glances off down the living room. It is a foggy day and the splendid view of the Bay is simply not there. He listens for the sounds of the children, but they're off at the movies with Carlotta and Fanny. He thinks of Carlotta and Fanny and the children and imagines what Carlotta is saying to Fanny, at a moment when the children leave them some peace. "Well," he imagines her saying, "when I was seeing your husband I was really going through a period of such trauma as a woman that the only way I could deal with it was to become someone other than myself. I became a female impersonator."

Suwelo holds up his loaf. Arveyda notes the well-distributed raisins and nutmeats, and nods.

"Now check this out," he says. "If you write songs, the ones you wrote when you were nineteen are the ones they want you to write at forty-five. Because"—he laughs—"you're supposed to help a lot of forty-five-year-olds stay nineteen. And besides, you're supposed to help them justify the scummy relationships they have with women, which are just as fucked up today as they were when they heard your first song. Only they were young then, and new at the game, and couldn't see that what they had and what they were doing was fucked up."

Suwelo considers this. He thinks of how long ago it was that he and Fanny were married. Hippies at heart, they'd been married barefoot, in the spring, underneath blossoming apple trees. They had had live—and stoned—musicians. But what song had been their favorite? What song had been sung or played? Shit, he couldn't even remember. But when they got their divorce they were both in love with Ono and Lennon's *Double Fantasy* album. They played it all the time. "Give me somethin' that's not *hard*, come on, come on . . ." Fanny would mimic Yoko's insistent, knowledgeable woman's voice, and, having pushed him down onto the bed, bank of the river, beach, forest plain, or floor, she would proceed to kiss him breathless.

"There are songs that people want you to sing today," says Arveyda, thinking vaguely of the unbearably repetitive crooning of Sinatra, and placing first his loaf and then Suwelo's into the oven, "that are just inappropriate to the times. Because men and women, the ones that have any kind of life, are simply somewhere else from where they were when they were nineteen. Thank goodness." He laughs.

Suwelo looks at him questioningly.

"I suddenly remembered," says Arveyda, still smiling, "the exact moment that I knew it was time to retire even my own version of the old-fashioned 'love ballad,' in which the woman sits by the window pining while the guy strolls off into the world. One night, after a concert, a young woman fought her way up to the stage for an autograph, and as I was signing her arm—typically, she had neither record, ticket, nor even a scrap of paper from the floor—I glanced at her breasts and inadvertently read her T-shirt. It said: 'A Woman without a Man Is like a Fish without a Bicycle.' "

"I WAS a female impersonator," Carlotta says to Fanny, as she drives down a nearly perpendicular hill in San Francisco. It is so steep Cedrico and Angelita, who've been talking a mile a minute in the back seat, are quiet out of sheer terror.

"That's why it's so hard to remember anything that happened. Though I guess I thought I loved Suwelo. I know I wanted to marry him; that would have blotted out the marriage I had. But what I did was, I just dressed myself up like a tart and trundled my tits on out there. I thought every man that ever lived—except, possibly, for Leonard Woolf—was a fool, but I wanted them to look at me. 'To market, to market, to buy a fat pig,' I used to hum under my breath, but I never bothered to think why."

"You did seem pretty oblivious, actually," says Fanny, bracing for another hill. This one is so steep that, instead of sidewalks, there are steps. It isn't just the hills themselves, but the way Carlotta drives. She charges the hills. Fanny looks at her. Carlotta is dressed in a fuchsia jumpsuit and seems to enjoy the challenge of driving. She handles the jeep as if it is a pony.

"I love driving around San Francisco," she says. "The Laguna Street hill"—which they have just come down—"is such a killer thrill."

"You were on automatic pilot, I thought," says Fanny, thankful she's on more than automatic pilot now. "Sometimes I was amazed you made it to my door and didn't just wander into the cottage in the next yard." Fanny says this slowly and with gratitude that they've come at last to Union Street, which is nice and flat.

"I needed those massages," says Carlotta. "In a funny kind of way, I couldn't bear to touch my own body, myself. Not to really feel it. I just washed it, perfumed it—loudly, with tons of Joy—and dressed it. It wasn't alive to me anymore. Maybe the perfume was supposed to act as embalming fluid."

They both laugh.

Fanny thinks of the years during which her sexuality was dead to her. How, once she began to understand men's oppression of women, and to let herself feel it in her own life, she ceased to be aroused by men. By Suwelo in particular, addicted as he was to pornography. And then, the women in her consciousness-raising group had taught her how to masturbate. Suddenly she'd found herself free. Sexually free, for the first time in her life. At the same time, she was learning to meditate, and was throwing off the last clinging vestiges of organized religion. She was soon meditating and masturbating and finding herself dissolved into the cosmic All. Delicious.

But when she tried to share this new spaciousness with Suwelo, he'd almost destroyed it. "Think of me! Me! My body, my cock!" he was always crying. At least this is what she felt, even when he didn't say anything. She'd accused him of trying to colonize her orgasms.

He had laughed and pretended he didn't understand.

His own sexuality was colonized, in Fanny's opinion, by

the movies he saw and the books he read. The magazines he thumbed through on street corners.

"I don't see how you couldn't be angry with me when you found out," says Carlotta.

They are in her little guest house, which reminds Fanny of her massage parlor. It is small but has a spacious feeling. There is very little furniture: pillows and mats on the floor, a couple of round tables made of wood. Candles. Incense holders. Fresh flowers in vases attached to the walls. Each room is a different color: blue, green, olive, gold. There is a peacockish feeling somehow.

"I only found out when it was over," says Fanny. "I was informed you had been dropped, for me. I knew there had been other women, but I never knew them. Suwelo told me about you because he was afraid I'd find out from you or from one of the women in my consciousness-raising group. 'Those bitches know everything!' he used to say.

"*They did too!*" Fanny laughs. "I feel sorry for any woman who missed that phase of women's collective growth. There we all were, speculums shining, labyrises dangling from everybody's neck, colossal dykes blooming suddenly on motorcycles, whisking one away! Oh"—she smiles, remembering—"the anxiety all this used to cause poor Suwelo!"

"I was angry," says Carlotta, "to be dropped. He didn't even say good-bye. He just stopped showing up. Suddenly you were back, and everywhere I looked, there you were together. I could have murdered him; and, as Frida Kahlo might have said, 'eat it afterward.'" She pauses. "And all along he was just a figment of my imagination. A distraction from my misery. He was just 'something' to hold on to; to be seen with; to wrestle with on the kitchen floor."

"Oh, my," says Fanny, dryly. She thinks how Suwelo believes

he took advantage of Carlotta and how this is what she herself had thought. They were both wrong. There had not been a victim and an oppressor; there'd really been two victims, both of them carting around lonely, needy bodies that were essentially blind flesh.

"It's harder for me to get angry these days," says Fanny, as they walk to Arveyda's house. "I don't know why." She waits beside the bedroom door as Carlotta finishes tucking a nodding Angelita into bed. Angelita looks like a very tired, amber-colored miniature Madonna, and her chopped-off punkish hair, dyed, apparently, with black shoe polish, clashes with the frilly pastel-pink pillow on which her weary head rests.

"Maybe," she continues, "I've used it all up. I get sad, instead."

"Of course," says Carlotta. "Repressed anger leads straight to depression. Depression leads straight to suicide." She turns off Angelita's light and gently closes the door.

"No," says Fanny. "I don't feel depressed. It's a different kind of sadness. It's more like . . ." She thinks; turns the feeling over in her mind. "More like sorrow. People just seem insane to me, more than anything. Everyone seems to have been tortured by the world in which we live into a perfect state of madness. Besides, I don't consider that anger, expressed against people, as opposed to conditions, is necessarily a good thing." She thinks of white feminists she knows who are happy that they can at last express their anger. In their opinion, this is something white women have never done. They think the ability to express anger is something the white woman has to reclaim. But this seems like a delusion to Fanny. For she knows the white woman has always expressed her anger, or at least vented it, as some of her friends liked to say—and usually it was against people, often men, but primarily women, of color. And what did that get her? Well, today it made it hard for black women to talk to her, because they not only remember the white woman's ability to express anger, but they expect a replay of this anger any minute.

These same women, interestingly, thinks Fanny, always claim they fear the black woman's anger, and for that reason say they are afraid to struggle seriously with her.

"Maybe the problem is too large for anger," says Carlotta. They are standing between the dining room and the kitchen, and over Arveyda's and Suwelo's heads they can see the TV. An Israeli soldier, aided by a fat civilian, who, when he opens his mouth, reveals he is from Brooklyn, is pounding senseless, with a large stick, a young and terrified, bloody-faced Arab boy who looks like Cedrico.

"They've lost it," says Arveyda sadly, with a sigh.

FANNY finds talking to Arveyda is very easy. It is like talking to one of her women friends. He is always right there, present, emotional, sometimes barely fumbling along, mumbling and muttering his thoughts; but he does not use his mind as something to hide behind. She likes the way he often says, "I think so . . . but then again, maybe not."

For some reason, this simple uncertainty and hesitation is moving to her.

She discovers he falls in love with people dead long ago, usually musicians, just as she does; he tells her that one of these "old buddies," as he calls them, is helping him write a new song, the first line of which is "Sex is the language that leaves so much unsaid." He loves this line and hums it and shows Fanny how he thinks the lyrics will sound, when he sings them accompanied by the piano.

Fanny sits beside him on the piano bench and shares his excitement. He is so happy to have this one little line to begin a new song that he bounces up and down like a child. He tells her he is trying to still his impatience ("the assassin of art") as he waits for the rest of the song to come.

But they are both confident the rest of the song will come;

and they share this sense of connectedness with other worlds as if it is a marvelous secret between them.

Fanny tells him about the play she is writing with her sister, Nzingha. Immediately he says he will write music for her sister's name. "Nzingha," he says, "how *beautiful!*" Fanny says it is also her name. Then she must tell him all about Ola and his "wives" and the coincidence of being given the same name as her sister. "Well," she says, "it proves my parents were never very far apart, either politically or culturally."

"But the name itself has such power," says Arveyda, already familiarizing his mind with its melodic possibilities.

Arveyda wants to know about the play. Fanny shows him a page. The play is titled "Our Father's Business," and on the page she shows him, Ola, whose name has been changed to Waruma, is seen sitting on a mat on the floor of his cell and scribbling on the margins of an old newspaper.

Fanny tells Arveyda how she and Nzingha plan to present this play, which will include sections from three of the most controversial of her father's plays, at the next anniversary of his death, which is fast approaching.

Arveyda is curious about Africa. His music is well known there. He tells Fanny that if she and her sister are arrested for presenting their play, he will come to Olinka, in the spirit of Bob Marley, and chant down the walls of their cells.

"There is a good chance we will be arrested," says Fanny. "But if Africa is ever to belong to all its people, the women as well as the men . . ." She does not finish, but looks sad.

Arveyda feels very American. Too American to ever think of Africa as something that has to be rewon. Only a part of him came from there, after all.

He tells Fanny about his mother, Katherine Degos, and how little he knew her. And how this ignorance caused him to stumble blindly in the world.

"Katherine Degos wasn't even her real name!" he says, still incredulous. There is residual pain around the old wound caused by her indifference to him as a child, some emotional awkwardness. But he is healing.

"Carlotta and I went back there, to Terre Haute," he says, "and went out, with my aunt Frudier, to see my mother's grave. The stone says, big as life, 'Katherine Degos.' But my aunt says to us, with a sniff of her big nose, 'Her real name was Georgia Smith.'"

"Georgia *Smith!*"

Fanny flashes on her own mother, who isn't well these days. She is back in Big Mama Celie's old house in Georgia. She reads, watches TV, gardens, talks to Fanny on the phone. There is, Fanny believes, a gentleman caller, or callers.

"'I never liked her,' says my aunt, 'even though she was my baby sister.'" Arveyda stretches his eyes very wide to express his astonishment at this news. "'No, never could stand her phony, filthy ways.'"

"Wow," says Fanny. "No tongue biter, she."

"But wait," says Arveyda. "Carlotta says to her: 'Aunt Frudier, you didn't like Arveyda's mother? But why?' She asked this gently, as you would ask a question of someone who's ill. 'She was a fake, she was a phony,' says my aunt, 'she was never satisfied to be herself.'

"Back at my aunt's house she showed us some old photographs of my mother. Carlotta looked at them first, and I thought she grew pale. Then Aunt Frudier brought out an old silver-framed photo of my father. Carlotta grew paler still. And thoughtful. With a gentle hand on my arm, she passed the pictures to me. The one of my father had stood on a table beside my bed for a long time when I was growing up. But I'd forgotten it. Now I looked at my parents' faces, and I can't imagine how I must have looked myself. Because my mother and father looked nothing at all like Aunt Frudier—a dark brown, heavyset woman with scowling features—but looked instead like members of Carlotta's family—if, of course, she had had any, other than her mother, that is.

" 'Our family,' says old Aunt Frudier, 'was part African/Scots and part Blackfoot. Your mother got the Blackfoot part. And your father, who came through here to work on the road-construction gangs, was black Mexican mixed with Filipino and Chinese.' He was by far," says Arveyda, in wonder, "the best-looking man I'd ever seen. 'But yet and still,' says Aunt Frudier, 'your mother was just plain Georgia Smith, because that's the name our parents gave her. But would she have it? No. "The damn thang don't fit for shit," she'd say. Likewise, the colored men that were always hanging around her. She said they bored her silly. No dash, no flash, no money, either. After all, by that time she was Katherine Degos from Santa Fe, nineteen and with a wasp waist. Tan legs under dresses that never hid much . . .'

"As she talked," says Arveyda, "I could feel, after all those years since they were in their teens, the hatred Aunt Frudier still felt for my mother. It gave me chills to think of my mother growing up the object of such contempt. I felt almost sick.

"The trip back to Terre Haute had been possible for me largely because of Carlotta's support, and as we endured the envy and spite, the repressed hatred of over fifty years, that Aunt Frudier spewed over us, I was glad she was there to help prop me up. Even though I am a grown man, with children of my own, each of her words against my mother struck me as a blow; as if I myself were still a child. But, oddly enough, as she raved, I felt closer and closer to my mother.

"Aunt Frudier had married a plumber; and, strange to say, he was still alive!" Here Arveyda suddenly laughs, that pealing, gut-deep laugh of his; throwing back his head to let the sound come freely out.

"He was alive!" he almost shouts. "The old survivor, God bless his pitiful soul! After God only knows how many years of suffering under Aunt Frudier's acid tongue.

"He just stayed as close as possible to that TV, though," Arveyda says, soberly. "I think he was watching 'Soul Train' when Aunt Frudier announced dinner was ready, and she simply passed in front of him and switched it off."

Fanny feels sad at this picture of Aunt Frudier's husband.

She tells Arveyda about her grandmother Celie's former husband, Albert, and about how, all the time she knew him, his favorite activity, there being no TV, had been to stare off into space. "Maybe these old, old men just have to sit down after a while and compress life to the straight and narrow view."

"Well, but listen to this," says Arveyda. They have left the piano bench, the studio, and the house and are walking slowly up the road from Arveyda's house to Inspiration Point. "So I am feeling pretty timid by then, you know, and I'm afraid to hear anything else. But Carlotta means to hear it all, and so flings herself into the breach. 'We heard about her church,' she says, as if this is some recent gossip that just happened to come our way. We are at dinner by then, and Aunt Frudier is about to toss a wide chunk of pot roast into her spacious mouth. She drops the fork, pot roast and all. 'Humph,' she snorts, 'some church.' She looks at me with the same expression she must have looked at my mother: cold, cruel, contemptuous. 'The church the rest of us went to wasn't good enough for her. She said from what she'd heard, everybody ought to stop going to church at once and use that time instead to do for the poor. She run around for a few years after you were born "doing" for the poor. But by then your daddy had gone away on a job in the next state, and never did come back. And she soon run out of steam. Later on we heard he was killed; fell off a bridge that his gang was constructing. There was no body, nothing. We only heard about it by accident.'"

Arveyda looks so bereft, thinking about this tragic end of his beautiful father, that Fanny leans over, there in the open, on the trail—where there are sometimes rapes and even murders—and kisses him. To her, it offers the comforting, automatic reassurance of a hug. But she's been kissing a long time, and is very good at it. Her soul flies right out of her mouth, and into Arveyda's own. He feels on his tongue its warmth, like an ancient, sun-ripened plum, and is suddenly confused. But Fanny has already turned away from him and started back up the trail.

Arveyda swings along after her and soon matches her easy climbing stride. His mind is still on the kiss, but he says calmly: "Everybody loved my mother; that is what Aunt Frudier thought, anyway. That even though she was a phony and a fake and refused to be Georgia Smith or to marry a regular colored man or to go to church—and," he says, chuckling, "even though she named me after a bar of soap from India that my father gave her—'Aryuveda,' which, I think, means health—somehow she got all the good things in life anyway. Great looks, a beautiful figure, a houseful of anxious suitors . . . a fabulous-looking man, who didn't look like anybody she'd ever seen—except maybe herself—and who loved her. 'Worked himself to death for her,' my aunt said, with total incomprehension and envy. In my mother's life there was a child. *Passion.* My aunt hated her," says Arveyda, "because she exposed herself to what she wanted. What she didn't want, she made very clear. She took risks. She jumped, as that writer Carlotta used to teach in women's literature says, at the sun." Arveyda pauses; they have come to the top of the hill and can see for miles in all directions.

"These are the very things," he says, with the fullness of a grateful heart in his voice, "that I love about my mother. And . . . about my father."

Fanny and Arveyda sit on the top of the hill, just down a bit from the path. They do not touch, except in spirit. They think about these two, Arveyda's parents, in whom the African and the European and the Mexican and the Indian and the Filipino and the Chinese(!) met. Adventurers and risk takers, lovers, all of them.

Arveyda holds the knowledge of his mother's dissatisfaction with her limited reality close to his heart; he is amazingly comforted by it. And he suddenly realizes that it was Fanny's pamphlet, *The Gospel According to Shug,* and Carlotta's sharing of it with him that he has to thank.

CARLOTTA and Suwelo remain in the hot tub while Arveyda and Fanny go off to the sauna. After the sauna, Fanny has promised Arveyda the massage of his life.

Arveyda says he is thrilled at this opportunity to be touched, perhaps even healed, by the hands of the master!

Fanny looks at his high little buns bouncing along in front of her and can hardly resist cupping one of them in her palm.

It is a chilly night in the Berkeley hills, but the water in the tub is one hundred three degrees. It is a perfect temperature, and Suwelo and Carlotta sit on their benches in the water or lean into the Jacuzzi jets and look up through the overhanging foliage of the trees at the stars.

The two couples are now close friends. Though Fanny and Suwelo are constructing a house and live an hour away on an old chicken farm outside Petaluma, they find themselves visiting Arveyda and Carlotta often. They are always welcome; the house is large and comfortable; there is wonderful music, food, good vibes. Besides, they all vaguely realize they have a purpose in each other's lives. They are a collective means by which each of them will grow. They don't discuss this, but it is felt strongly by all. There is palpable trust.

Fanny and Suwelo, who are childless, are happy to be around Cedrico and Angelita, who would call them aunt and uncle if they didn't consider such titles nerdy. They are both going through the trials of what once upon a time was pre-teeny bopperism. Fanny takes them on hikes. Suwelo takes them to movies and for swims. They are both called upon from time to time to help with literature and history lessons. Tonight, though, the children are sleeping over with friends.

Suwelo thinks about the house he and Fanny are building on their homestead. It is modeled on the prehistoric ceremonial household of M'Sukta's people, the Ababa—a house designed by the ancient matriarchal mind and the first heterosexual household ever created. It has two wings, each complete with its own bedroom, bath, study, and kitchen; and in the center there is a "body"—the "ceremonial" or common space, which contains a large living room, a loft above it covered by a skylight, and a tiny kitchenette for the making of soup or hot cocoa or tea. There is a fireplace, too; and there will be couches and tables, bookcases. A stereo. Maybe even TV?

Fanny and Suwelo often read passages from the five volumes written by Eleanora Burnham and given to Fanny by Miss B. In these books they have discovered the amazing story, told to Eleanora Burnham's great-aunt by M'Sukta herself, of a peaceful, equalitarian, ancient way of life that appeals to them.

After thousands and thousands of years of women and men living apart, the Ababa had, with great trepidation, experimented with the two tribes living, a couple to a household, together. Each person must remain free, they said. That is the main thing. And so they had designed a dwelling shaped like a bird.

Suwelo's mind drifts. He enjoys the feel of the pulsating water against his genitals. It is as if hundreds of minnows from the river are nibbling at him. He enjoys the nearness of Carlotta;

though, because of the rising steam, she is only a blur on her side of the tub.

Suwelo chuckles.

"What is it?" she asks.

"When I first saw Arveyda," says Suwelo, "I was so astonished, I actually felt weak in the knees. But that was nothing compared to Fanny's response when I told her who I'd seen."

"Oh?" says Carlotta. She has no family to be impressed that she is married to a big star. Arveyda himself is like one of those great old civilizations he has sung to her about: totally unaware of being great. Only greatly conscious of being alive.

"Well I was amazed that that's who you were married to. I knew your husband was a musician. But Fanny was amazed that he wasn't dead!"

"What do you mean?" Carlotta asks, fighting the drowsiness she also loves.

"Fanny, you know, is always falling in love with spirits—with hundred-year-old souls a specialty. She's loved Arveyda's music since she was in high school, but he himself was never real to her. I think she just assumed that anybody who moved her as much as Arveyda does in his music had to be a spirit. Someone already dead." It occurs to Suwelo as he speaks that perhaps Fanny falls in love with spirits rather than living people because they are the only ones she can trust. Also, spirits can be claimed and cannot reject you, maybe, but living people can and often do.

"Come to think of it," he says, "we used to make love to Arveyda's music. It was the only music Fanny could make love to. Everybody else's music boxed her in, she said. She used to play 'Ecstasy Is the Sun' over and over again. It made our lovemaking feel like flying, she said."

Suwelo laughs.

"'Yes,' I used to say to her, 'but am I on the same plane?'

He does not say what Fanny sometimes said to him in reply. "Frankly, Suwelo?" she would ask, seriously. Then she'd say, "Actually, no."

Carlotta smiles. She thinks, Why is the language of lovemaking so hard to learn? Why is the body so often dumb flesh? Why does the mind so often choose to fly away at the moment the word waited for all one's life is about to be spoken? She sighs.

"We thought my mother was dead," she says slowly, trailing a hand in the water. The moon has come up, and Suwelo's face is very clear to her. He shaves his eyebrows, to shape them and make them smaller, he has told her. That is one reason his face is different. He also wears contact lenses. "I was tired of looking so owlish," he has said. "Tired of Fanny knocking on my head and going 'Who? Whooooo?'"

Suwelo knows nothing of Carlotta's mother, and for some reason his stomach tightens at the very mention of her. He takes a sip of water from a glass near the rim of the tub. His own mother, Marcia, flashes across his mind. It is as if she appears at a door in his memory. He slams it shut. No, he doesn't slam it; that is what he's always done before. Now he peeks at her face from behind his hands and *gently* eases the door shut.

"We thought," says Carlotta, getting out of the tub, "that she'd been killed by counterrevolutionaries in Guatuzocan, where she grew up." She goes over to the shower and splashes cold water over herself. Then she dashes inside the house. Moments later she reappears with a record album. She has put the record on the stereo inside, and soon chimes and bells, the music of flutes, the calling of birds fills the air, but quietly. It is as if they are in a dense green jungle. Suwelo is lying alongside the tub, his body steaming. Carlotta hands him the album.

"My mother, Zedé," she says.

An old blown-up photograph of a scared-looking young

woman and her child covers the front of the album, which is called *Escuchen (Listen)*. On the back, surrounding this same photograph, in a family portrait, Carlotta and Arveyda and the children are grouped. They resemble a new, small nation.

The tender music, weeping and laughing, plays.

Suwelo holds the album cover closer to the light of a flickering candle stuck in an abalone shell at his elbow. He reads the story of the return to her country of Carlotta's mother, accompanied by Arveyda. There is mention of Zedé's job with the North American movie company. There is the story of Zedé's search for her own mother. Suwelo reads about her death: She and her mother were ambushed by counterrevolutionaries in the mountains leading out of Guatuzocan.

"My mother and Arveyda were lovers," Carlotta says simply. "And from their love, I have learned many things. Things my mother could not tell me herself. Things that were, somehow or other, bound up too tightly with her shame.

"We mourned for her so long and hard," she says. "Arveyda and I. And I made him tell me over and over again every word she said to him. I even made him tell me how my mother spoke the language of love. He thought that to know these things would finish killing me; but it didn't. I just began to see Zedé as a woman, a person, a being. Sacred. And to love her more than ever."

Suwelo is touched. He feels himself slipping into an intimacy with Carlotta he's never, even with Fanny, known. He is speechless, as he plunges himself once again into the tub—only this time it feels like a baptism, and he deliberately dives to the bottom of the tub, keeping his head, for several moments, beneath the warm water.

Carlotta also returns to the tub, her slender, flat-breasted body as vulnerable, Suwelo thinks, as a flower. The damp spikes of her short hair, exquisite petals.

"You don't look like a woman anymore," he says, impulsively. Surprised to be saying such a thing. Fearful, after he's said it.

Carlotta only laughs. "Obviously," she says, "this is how a woman looks.

"Anyway," she says. "There was one part of the story that"— she laughs—"rang a bell in me. It was the story about my grandmother, Zedé the Elder, who created the capes made of feathers for the priests; the woman who taught my own mother how to make beautiful feathered things. She had been a great artist, and she had had a little chime outside the door of her hut. She would strike it, and listen closely to it, and if the sound corresponded with the vibration of her soul at the time, she would nod, once—Arveyda told me Zedé told him—and begin to create." Carlotta leans back against the side of the tub.

"That's how," she says, "I became a bell chimist."

Suwelo feels Marcia knocking timidly at the door. Knock, knock. But he is afraid his father is behind her. He pretends he doesn't hear.

"She wasn't dead," says Carlotta, triumphantly. "Neither was her mother. They escaped from the counterrevolutionaries and now live in Mexico. My mother married a shaman. My grandmother became one."

"A happy ending!" Suwelo cries, flinging his arms around her.

"MY MOTHER *is* dead," Suwelo says to Carlotta. It sounds as if he's finally admitting it to himself. He sees Marcia once again timidly approach the door. She stops, her fist upraised to knock, and listens. She is so surprised to hear he is speaking of her! 'Come in, Ma,' he says. But she stands there frozen, in shock, her fist in the air. And, just as he feared, she looks behind her.

"She was killed . . . along with my father, in something that was called a 'car wreck.' It was really," Suwelo says, "a people wreck. They were driving along—my father was driving—very fast. 'For some reason,' as so many people phrased it later, the car ran off the road, hit an embankment, at ninety miles an hour, and they were both killed instantly."

Suwelo recalls Miss Lissie's voice on the tape. "Remember the last time you stood over them," she said.

He will try.

He had taken the bus home from college, an hour away, and someone, a relative, had driven him to the funeral home. Both his parents were laid out in the same room, just as they'd been brought in. There were black and purple swellings and bruises, and deep cuts, on both their foreheads, from crashing against the windshield. His mother had crashed all the way through; his father's progress had been blocked by the steering wheel, which had crushed his chest. They were dressed for church. His mother wore a red-and-white flowered dress that Suwelo had always liked because it made her look so girlish, and lime-green T-strap slippers. His father wore his one good navy-blue suit.

"My parents' lives were so miserable," says Suwelo, "that I couldn't let myself think about it." He feels a chakra opening at the base of his spine. Something begins to unfurl, like a tiny flag, or a sleepy snake. His mother knocks on the door with more assurance. He sees that, yes indeed, the old man, whom he hates, Louis, Sr., is behind her. Suwelo stands on his side of the door and leans against it. There is no strength in his hands.

Marcia easily pushes her way in.

"They were all explaining to me how my parents died," says Suwelo. "All our neighbors and friends and the funeral-home people. The state trooper who'd gotten to the scene first said my father had been drunk, and speeding. I knew this was un-doubtedly true. I'd seen him drunk and speeding a million times, since I was a little boy. He always seemed to be trying to run away from himself. My mother would beg him, 'Slow down, Louis. You ought to slow down.' He would or he wouldn't slow down, depending on which demons he was listening to.

"It was when everybody had left and I was alone with the bodies that I realized what had happened. I went over to where they were and I looked into their faces. Daddy's face was finally peaceful. I was actually soothed by it. But *her* face. It had fro-zen in a kind of grimace, an exaggerated version of her usual look of desperation. Even her teeth were bared, as if she were struggling to give birth. It shocked me to think that's how she looked. And then I lifted the sheet, and I saw her hands. . . ."

Suwelo starts to weep. He feels Carlotta's arms around him. He feels her kisses soaking up the tears on his cheeks. He cries a long time. But Marcia is inside, standing beside him now, and there's Louis, Sr. still outside the door.

"Her nails were broken off, every one of them; her fingertips bloody," he says. "Now I understood what had happened, and why they were dead. My mother was trying to get out of the car."

He breaks down completely. He does not want his snot to fall into the tub, so he gets out, blindly, Carlotta following, and she wraps a large white towel around him and another around herself.

"I'd seen that look of desperation on my mother's face all my life. I hadn't understood what it was. My father, you know, had been a soldier in World War II and he'd lost half of one arm and all of his mind. But he was still a gung-ho army man. Even when I was leaving home for college, he was pressuring me to enlist. When I was in college and the Vietnam war was going strong, I refused the draft. I knew I'd rather rot in prison than have done to me what was done to him. He refused to understand this. I didn't think he'd ever stop cursing me for taking this stand. I couldn't understand why he would want to send me off to be maimed or killed. Did he hate me that much?" Suwelo pulls the towel closer about him, feeling his flushed body beginning to lose its heat.

"We stopped speaking. I hated my mother for staying with him. But she was trapped. Like a bird in a cage. He wasn't the man she married, but some kind of wounded, crazed patriot. More often drunk than sober. Frequently abusive. With his good arm, the one he had left," Suwelo says flatly, "he held on to my mother as she struggled to get out of the speeding car."

And now he can actually hear Marcia's voice as she says, "Just let me *and Louis, Jr.* out of the car, if you're going to drive this way." And he remembers his father reaching across her and then into the back seat, where Suwelo sits, and locking all the doors, and cursing them, and speeding up even more.

How had he repressed so much terror? Suwelo wonders about this as he relives it. There he was, all those years, all those different times, small, then not so small, and frightened. Why did he and his mother get into the car in the first place? This he still does not understand. But at least he lets himself understand his mother's determination, at last, to get out.

His father is standing at the door. He is not old and drunk, but young and handsome. He has two arms. "My name was once Suwelo, too," he says gravely, holding them out. Suwelo is suddenly too tired to keep watch over the door of his heart. It swings open on its own, and this father, whom Suwelo has never seen and whom he realizes he resembles very much, walks in.

FANNY and Arveyda are naked. After leaving the hot tub and shower, they have permitted the night air to dry them. Fanny has quickly rubbed sweet almond oil over her own body, even between her legs and between her toes, and now leans over Arveyda, who is stretched out on his stomach on the futon massage mat. They have decided to forgo the sauna, an inviting cubicle off to the side of this room they are in, which contains little besides the massage mat, a shelf full of massage oils, stacks of clean white towels, and a collection, in a corner by the door of the sauna, of straw-bottomed thong slippers.

She places her warm hands first on the center of his back; one hand is just between his shoulder blades, the other at his waist. She holds her hands there while she asks for guidance in this work she is about to do for Arveyda's healing. She asks that Arveyda's spirit guides be present, along with her own. She gently presses down and with an alternating pressure of her hands slightly rocks his body. Then she straddles his body and begins kneading his back and neck and shoulders.

Fanny is very patient, thorough, and slow. She listens to Arveyda's body as she massages it. Wherever there is the slightest ache, her fingers hover, listening, and descend. Arveyda is amazed. All the pain in his body seems to be eager to show itself to Fanny, who presses points here and there that make him cry out from the pain, but which, before she touched them, felt entirely okay. And then, after she releases the pressure on these points—pressure of which he has been unaware—he feels the energy once again flowing freely in his body. He has almost forgotten what unblocked chi feels like.

It is warm in the room, and there is only the moonlight coming through the small window across from them, and the flicker of a candle on the floor.

Arveyda sinks almost immediately to another level, a very sensual level of consciousness, assured that Fanny's touch, which never leaves his body, will hold him safe. The warmth of the room makes his mind drift to Mexico, where he and Carlotta and the children go each January to see Zedé. He recalls lying on the warm sand in the tiny village of Yelapa, where all of them, their "new age clan," gather, and how he and Angelita and Cedrico oil each other while the three women—Carlotta and the two Zedés—walk slowly, their arms loosely around each other, back and forth, up and down the crescent-shaped beach. They are always talking and listening to each other intensely, as if whole worlds hang on their words. And they are all three perfectly beautiful. Zedé the Elder, the matriarch, stooped and brown, with her long, ash-white hair tied back from her face with a scarlet ribbon; Zedé the Younger, full of vitality and joy, bright-spirited at last, kissing Carlotta over and over; and Carlotta, the most beautiful of all, with her short hair, her string bikini, and her skinny legs, which she kicks into the air from time to time in sheer exuberance, like a gamine in a Charlie Chaplin movie.

Arveyda lies on the massage mat but he is really lying on the sand. He watches these three women and he thinks of the suffering each of them has endured. He thinks of the pain he himself has felt, and caused. . . . His heart, so often full, seems to brim over with the strange mixture of all that he feels. He finds in his mind words for the beginning, the middle, or the end, of a new song: "Isn't this sadness a part of happiness?"

Fanny is stroking his body to the rhythm of one of his own guitar-and-flute melodies, from a fifteen-year-old album called *Ecstasy Suite*. In her mind, "Ecstasy Is the Sea" is playing, and she imagines her hands are the waves of the ocean that shape the ocean floor, and the dunes of the beach and the tiniest seashells.

She also thinks, with something like disbelief, that one of the spirits she's loved so long is actually right beneath her, his very neck, at this moment, under her hand. Gradually, she works her way down Arveyda's body, marveling at the beauty—smooth, glistening from the oil—of his rich brown skin. She presses points on his buns that make him squirm, then moves down his thighs and his very hairy legs. She takes her time on his feet, slipping her thumbs between his toes, working her knuckles along the arches and the balls of his feet. Arveyda groans with mingled pain and pleasure.

He has given himself up to Fanny, as if all of himself is resting in her arms. He feels there is something about her, something in her essence, that automatically heals and reconnects him with himself. He felt this even before she impulsively kissed him on the trail. He imagines making love to her, as he feels her hands sliding up his inner thighs. He thinks that if he were to join himself with her in lovemaking he would feel literally re-membered.

He utters a deep, secret sigh at this thought.

Fanny thinks of her lifelong habit of falling in love with people she'll never have to meet. Is this how people create gods, she wonders. She thinks she has always been walking just behind (oh, a hundred to a thousand years behind) the people she has found to love, and that she has been very careful that their backs were turned.

What would she do if one of them turned around?

Fanny feels a slight quiver in her stomach. She is frightened, for a moment, as if she is about to come face to face with her own self.

She takes a deep breath. It seems to her, fortunately, that this particular spirit has nodded off. She strokes him gently, just at the back of the neck. "Time to turn over," she whispers.

But Arveyda is not sleeping. Far from it. He is thinking of Fanny and of her kiss. Of the pleasure and pain of her touch, which seems easily to find the most buried knottedness in him. And if he turns over, she will see the results of his thoughts.

Fanny waits patiently, on her knees beside the mat. Will he turn over, she wonders, this spirit behind whom she finds herself? She wonders this sincerely, as if Arveyda is a real spirit who might simply disappear by sinking through the hardwood floor.

Fanny is terribly aroused, as she looks at Arveyda's smooth defenseless back, his humble neck, his beautiful hands and nimble fingers, the tips of which, touching his instruments, have already given her so much pleasure.

With a sigh of brave resignation, the "spirit" turns himself over. He is embarrassed, and is looking down. "I'm afraid," he groans, "you have lit a little candle."

Fanny, seeing its erectness and nearly comic hopefulness, readily takes Arveyda's "candle" into her warm hand.

When she has seated herself on it, and feels how snugly it fits, as if it has found its proper niche, she looks into Arveyda's face. Into his very human eyes. There are tears in them, as there are in her own. They begin to rock, turning now so that they lie, their arms around each other, equitably, on their sides. Weeping, they begin to kiss.

Fanny feels as if the glow of a candle that warms but could never burn has melted her, and she drips onto Arveyda.

Arveyda feels as if he has rushed to meet all the ancestors and they have welcomed him with joy.

It is amazing to them how quickly—like a long kiss—they both come.

She is fearful of asking him what she must. Timidly she says: "And did you also see the yellow plum tree and all the little creatures, even the fish, in its branches? And did you see and feel the ocean and the sun?"

But Arveyda says simply, "Yes. And the moon as it moves over the ocean, and the lilacs, and mountain ranges, and all the colors of valleys. But best of all," he says, kissing her, "was the plum tree and everything and everybody in it, and the warmth of your breath and the taste in my mouth of the sweet yellow plums."

They lie cuddled together in sheer astonishment.

"My . . . *spirit*," says Fanny, at last, her face against his chest.

"My . . . *flesh*," says Arveyda, his lips against her hair.

YEARS before this day, Suwelo had had a recurring dream. He did not usually remember his dreams, but this one stayed with him. It was very brief. He was sitting at the bedside of a very old man, and, though neither of them seemed to be talking, much information was being exchanged. No, not exchanged, for even in the dream Suwelo had had little to say. He was there simply to listen to the older voice of experience, for the sake of his own present pitiful life.

As he walks up the steps to the Mary McLeod Bethune Memorial Nursing Home on a tree-lined street on the outskirts of Baltimore, Suwelo remembers his dream. He says good morning to the old people gathered in rocking chairs and around Chinese checkers tables on the porch. They are black and white together, *finally*, Suwelo thinks. They are so old color seems not to matter, as they shift about for seats at the various tables, or in the rocking chairs, or simply places in the sun. Nobody seems to hear very well either. A nurse walks up and down among them, directing dim eyes and faltering feet this way and that, and giving cheerful instructions in a bright hoarse voice.

"Move on over here a little bit more, just a little bit more. You can do it, Mr. Pete!"

The old man stands rooted to the spot, appearing to wonder where the voice is coming from.

"Do you need your walker?" the nurse asks.

Mr. Pete mumbles something.

Suwelo passes through the door.

Even inside he is struck by the thorough integration, not simply of the patients but of the staff. At the front desk there are three women, two black, one white; they are jovially discussing a concert which all three attended and apparently enjoyed over the weekend.

He is distractedly given directions to a "space, way down on the end" of one of the halls that fan out from the reception area in all directions. A faint smell of cabbage permeates the place.

When he comes to Mr. Hal's and Miss Rose's "space," Suwelo knows it, without looking at the two of them. Unlike the bare walls of the rest of the nursing home, the wall behind their beds is covered with paintings. But, he quickly notices, there is also a television set, attached to the ceiling, hanging, like a threat, over Mr. Hal's bed.

Mr. Hal and Miss Rose are expecting Suwelo. They do not see him standing there at the edge of their cubicle looking at them. They are waiting for his visit with the alert expression of children in a doctor's office. There are other beds and cubicles up and down the long room, on either side of them. Old people lie in bed or sit in chairs beside the beds, sometimes talking, sometimes staring into space, sometimes simply watching TV.

The two of them are so clean they shine, and their small area, with its two twin beds, two nightstands, and two chairs, is as neat as a pin. Mr. Hal's bed is adjusted so that he is sitting up, and Miss Rose sits in a chair next to him. She is crocheting. Suwelo has seen Miss Rose only a few times before, when she came by Uncle Rafe's house to bring him food. Then, she was always with Miss Lissie.

She is old and looks something like a dumpling or a really wizened apple, with small sunken eyes and thin white hair. She finally notices Suwelo's presence and slowly pushes herself up from her chair with a soft cry. How odd it feels now to Suwelo that he has eaten so much of her food and yet knows so little about her.

He moves forward, smiling, into their space. He has brought a plant, which Miss Rose, admiring it with squinty, nearsighted eyes, places on the nightstand. Suwelo hugs her, feeling the insubstantial flesh, the soft bones, the severe curvature in her spine that makes her short and stooped. But what an energetic hug she still manages. He feels quite squeezed.

Next he turns to the bed where Mr. Hal lies smiling, with what appears to be the blissful patience of the blind. Suwelo sits on the bed and leans toward him gingerly; moving very slowly and carefully indeed, he envelops Mr. Hal in his arms.

"We had to marry!" says Miss Rose, serving Suwelo tea. "At our age!"

"But why?" asks Suwelo.

"That was the only way we could live in the home together."

"They don't want folks living here in sin," says Mr. Hal, sarcastically.

"Hal had to come here first, you know," says Miss Rose, who has pulled a chair for herself right next to Suwelo's so that they both face Mr. Hal's bed. "Among all the other things that weren't working too good, his eyes had just give out."

"That's the truth," says Mr. Hal. "I stopped painting after Lissie died. I just couldn't do it. Next thing I knew, it looked like a curtain had dropped."

"I started coming to see about him," says Miss Rose, as Suwelo sips his tea. "Brought him tasty things to snack on. We'd sit here and keep each other company. Talk about the weather; talk about the white folks and their destructiveness, black folks and their foolishness. Talked, all the time, about Lissie. We sure do miss her."

"They were friends for — what was it Rosie? — sixty years."

"No, not quite that long," says Miss Rose. "But long enough. I knew she'd want me to look after you."

"Now wait a minute," says Mr. Hal, with much of his charm still intact, "you don't want Suwelo to think that's the only thing."

Miss Rose blushes. She definitely does. Suwelo puts down his empty cup and scratches his chin. *Hummm*, he thinks. Miss Rose excuses herself and goes off to visit a friend farther down the hall. She understands that Suwelo and Mr. Hal want to talk.

"Thanks again for sending me the cassettes Miss Lissie left for me," says Suwelo. "And for the slides of the work she did before she died."

"Oh, it was all so puzzling," says Mr. Hal, "those last things she did. I couldn't make heads nor tails out of any of it. That big tree with all the black people and funny-looking critters, and snakes and everything . . . and even a white fellow in it. Then all those lions . . ."

Mr. Hal stops to catch his breath.

"Mr. Hal," says Suwelo softly, "in those last paintings, Miss Lissie painted herself."

"Sure she did," Mr. Hal says, almost laughing. "You forget how many changes I've seen Lissie go through. But I didn't see a sign of her in any of those last paintings." He pauses. "There's not even a sprig of verbena or a stalk of corn from our yard. . . ." He is almost bitter. It is as if he feels, in her very last paintings, that Miss Lissie went off without him. Left him there alone in the little morning-glory-covered house even before she died. Something she'd never done before. Mr. Hal is very mad at her.

"I couldn't recognize anything in them," he says flatly.

At that moment, Suwelo realizes one of the reasons he was born; one of his functions in assisting Creation in this life. He also realizes he will need a higher authority than his own to convince Mr. Hal of anything to do with Miss Lissie. Mr. Hal's heart is hurt, and his mind, consequently, is closed.

Out of his pocket, Suwelo takes the small cassette player that he carries with him now whenever he is likely to encounter elderly people. Miss Lissie's tape is already in it. All he has to do is place the earphones over Mr. Hal's ears and turn the machine on.

At first Mr. Hal is apprehensive and seems bothered by the wires. Suwelo adjusts everything, more than once, until Mr. Hal is comfortable. Mr. Hal also calms down when he hears Miss Lissie's voice.

They sit, the middle-aged man and the very old man, sometimes looking into each other's faces, sometimes not, as the tape spins. Suwelo is intensely conscious of the sunlight now coming through the window above the bed and the way it falls, like a blessing, on the little green plant he brought. He gets up, goes down the hall, and brings back a cup of water, which he pours over the plant. He stands and watches as the water soaks into the soil. "Say 'ahhhh,'" he whispers to the little plant. And he imagines it does so.

After half an hour, and after he's turned over the tape for Mr. Hal, Suwelo hears the *schlop, schlop* of old and hesitant feet coming down the room between the double rows of beds. A few minutes later, old Mr. Pete, whom he had seen on the front porch, is craning his hairy red neck into Mr. Hal's cubicle. "Whar's Hal?" he asks in a braying, panic-stricken voice. He is looking right at Hal, but because Mr. Hal is absorbed in listening to the tape and, furthermore, has his eyes closed, the old man can't see him. At least this is how it appears to Suwelo, who is amused.

Miss Rose comes up out of nowhere and hustles Mr. Pete away. Suwelo gets up from his chair and tiptoes down the walkway after them. Mr. Pete is one of those old tall, blue-eyed, rawboned white men who look as though they've lived long lives of perfect crime. He is leaning heavily on Miss Rose's shoulder, and she is chattering away at him. "Hal's busy right now," she says.

"What you say?" says old Pete.

"He's got company!" she shouts up at his ear.

"What's he got?" he says. "Not got a cold, is he?"

"No," she yells, "*company.*"

"What's he got?"

Miss Rose says, "Got a Co'Cola that he told me to give to you. Here"—she hands him a Coke from the machine in front of them—"have a cold drink."

Suwelo laughs and laughs. He thinks, Well, what do you know, there's life, even in nursing homes!

When he gets back to Mr. Hal's bed, after walking all over the nursing home and seeing more of its life, he finds Mr. Hal in tears.

"Oh," he moans, when Suwelo sits next to him on the bed. "She loved Rafe so much better than me!"

Suwelo takes one of his old smooth hands in his own. He is tempted to kiss it. What the hell, he thinks. What does it mean to be a man if you can't kiss when you want to? He lifts Mr. Hal's hand to his lips and kisses it, as he would kiss the mashed finger of a child.

"She loved you very much," he says. "It's you she'll be coming back to."

"Who am I kidding?" says Mr. Hal. "It's my own fault Lissie couldn't love me more. Rafe let her be everything she was. I couldn't do that."

"But how were you to know all that she was?" says Suwelo, comfortingly. "She never told you, did she?"

"People don't have to tell you every little thing," he says. "Making them tell you every little thing is brutal."

"Well," says Suwelo, pressing his hand, "she did try to tell you at the end."

"Yes," says Mr. Hal. "She did." He begins to cry afresh. "And do you know what I did?" he asks. "I ridiculed what she'd done. I laughed. I looked at the little white fellow in the tree and I said, 'Looks like you forgot to paint that one.' And Lissie just looked at me and said, 'No. That's his color.' But she looked so sad. And would I ask her what was the matter? No."

Mr. Hal blew his nose in a Kleenex from a box on the night-stand.

"And I was even worse about the lions. I told her that just the thought of a cat that big gave me the creeps."

He pauses, wondering.

"But when I said that, she just laughed. You know how Lissie could sometimes laugh. It made you feel like a perfect idiot, but because she seemed so merry you had no idea why.

"And to think . . ." Mr. Hal choked. "And here I am, out here at the home, and being out here I've had to learn so much. Why," he says, sitting up taller and straining his neck, as if he's listening for something, "my best friend is an old cracker named Pete. He ought to be shuffling over this way any minute now. We sometimes have our meals together."

Suwelo tells him Pete has been there and gone.

"He was a jerk all his life, you know," says Mr. Hal. "Only the lord and his ledger keeper know how much misery he's caused. But he's here now, and he's scared. And he's deaf, and he's old."

"He's funny, too," says Suwelo.

"The heart just goes out to the man," says Mr. Hal. "Besides, I can't see him."

"Oh," says Suwelo, "he's white, all right. You couldn't mistake it."

"I'm still afraid of cats, though." Mr. Hal sighs. "But I'm willing to work on it."

Suwelo looks at the paintings on the wall. Mr. Hal says he may take any or all of them. There are a dozen more stacked along the floor. Among those on the floor he finds Miss Lissie's last two paintings. The one of what he has come to think of as the tree of life, with everything, including "the little white fellow" in its branches, and the last one in a series of five that she did of lions.

He sits on the edge of Mr. Hal's bed and studies these two paintings. They are lush and clear and dreamlike and beautiful, and remind him of Rousseau.

"I could always see Lissie," Mr. Hal says fussily, with stubborn propriety, reaching over to take one of the paintings Suwelo holds.

Suwelo muses, guiding a painting into Mr. Hal's hand. Was it Freud who said we can't see what we don't want to see? He watches Mr. Hal strain his eyes as if they are muscles, as he tries to see the painting in his hand. It is the tree-of-life one. Groaning from frustration, he soon throws it down in despair.

Suwelo, however, begins to feel hope. And he thrusts the other painting, of the great maned lion, into Mr. Hal's hands. He does not notice he has handed it to him upside down.

"Humm . . ." says Mr. Hal, after a few minutes, "what's that reddish spot up in the corner?"

Mr. Hal is shifting the painting back and forth in front of his eyes, trying to get the reddish spot into the light that comes from the window over his head.

Suwelo sits very still, as one ought to do in the presence of miracles.

But apparently the reddish spot is all that Mr. Hal can see. This painting, too, is flung to the bed with a frown.

Suwelo takes up the painting, which he loves, turns it right side up, and looks straight into Miss Lissie's dare-to-be-every-thing lion eyes. He knows, and she knows, that Mr. Hal will be able to see all of her someday, and so she and Suwelo must simply wait, and in the meantime—if this is one of the paintings Suwelo takes home with him—she and he can while away the time contemplating the "reddish spot," which marks the return of Mr. Hal's lost vision. For on Lissie's left back paw, nearly obscured by her tawny, luxuriant tail, is a very gay, elegant, and shiny red high-heeled slipper.

Acknowledgments

For their cheerful support and independent attitudes during the writing of this novel, I thank my daughter, Rebecca Walker, and our friend Robert Allen. For editing this book with gracefulness and skill, I thank John Ferrone. For being a first reader—along with Rebecca and Robert—I thank Gloria Steinem. For their sensitive criticism of the manuscript, I thank Kim Chernin and Renate Stendhal. For the inspiring example of her personal chutzpah and her unflappable calm in pursuit of our common interests, I thank my agent, Wendy Weil. I thank Ester Hernandez for correcting my Spanish.

I thank the Universe for my participation in Existence. It is a pleasure to have always been present.